The Riverside Literature Series

TWICE-TOLD TALES

BY

NATHANIEL HAWTHORNE

EDITED FOR STUDY BY

J. HUBERT SCOTT, A.M.
Academy of Northwestern University, Illinois

WITH AN INTRODUCTORY NOTE BY
GEORGE PARSONS LATHROP

Tout bien ou rien

The Riverside Press

HOUGHTON MIFFLIN COMPANY
BOSTON · NEW YORK · CHICAGO · DALLAS
SAN FRANCISCO
The Riverside Press Cambridge

The Riverside Press

CAMBRIDGE · MASSACHUSETTS

PRINTED IN THE U.S.A.

CONTENTS.

SYNOPSIS OF HAWTHORNE'S LIFE AND WORKS.

Ancestry. (1) Major William Hathorne (– 1679) of Wigton, England, came to Boston in 1630; in 1637 settled in Salem, Mass., and became a leader against the Indians and the Quakers. (2) His son, Colonel John Hathorne (– 1717), was a noted judge in the Salem witchcraft trials. (3) John's son, Joseph (– 1762), was a farmer. (4) Joseph's son, Daniel (– 1796), was a privateersman in the Revolution. (5) Daniel's son, Nathaniel Hathorne (1775–1808), was a sea captain. Married Elisabeth Clarke Manning. (6) Their son, Nathaniel Hawthorne, was the author.

FIRST DECADE — BOYHOOD.
1804–1815.

1804 July 4, Union St., Salem, Nathaniel Hawthorne was born. (*Critic*, July, 1904, for birthplace and other views.)

1808 Nathaniel Hathorne died at Surinam, Dutch Guiana.

1809 Family moved to the Manning House, Herbert St.

1813–1815 Hawthorne confined at home by an injury to his foot; recited his lessons to Dr. J. E. Worcester.

SECOND DECADE — EDUCATION.
1815–1825.
Period of Wide Reading and Experiment in Writing.

1815–1818 Frequently visited his uncle at Raymond, Maine

1816 Began *Diary* [?]. Last entry, 1819.

1818 Family moved to Raymond, Maine.

1819 Attended school in Salem; and later at Stroudwater, Me.

1820 Prepared for college with a tutor in Salem. Wrote three numbers of a manuscript magazine, *The Spectator*. Family returned to Salem.

1821 Entered Bowdoin College, Brunswick, Maine.

1821–1825 Spent college vacations in Maine. Experiments in verse.

1825 Began to spell his name "Ha*w*thorne." Wrote, in Salem, *Seven Tales of My Native Land,* and began *Twice-Told Tales.*

THIRD DECADE — SOLITUDE.
1828–1838.
Period of Tales and Essays.

1828 Published anonymously *Fanshawe, A Tale.* Began to publish magazine articles under the pseudonyms, "Oberon," "Ashley Allen Royce," "The Rev. A. A. Royce," "Aubepine," "M. D.," "A Pedestrian." Family moved to North Salem.

1829 [?] Wrote *Provincial Tales.*

1830 Travelled in Connecticut and New York.

1831 Visited New Hampshire and Martha's Vineyard.

1832 Family returned to the old house on Herbert St.

1835 Began *American Note-Books.*

1836 Edited and contributed to *The American Magazine of Useful and Entertaining Knowledge.* Worked on *Peter Parley's Universal History* (published, 1837).

1837 Published the first edition of *Twice-Told Tales.* (*Bookman,* Sept., 1898, for title-page.) Contemplated joining an expedition to the South Seas. Visited Horatio Bridge in Maine.

1838 Wandered through western New England. Became engaged to Miss Sophia Peabody. (*Historic Towns of New Eng.,* Powell, for " Grimshawe House," house of Hawthorne's courtship.)

FOURTH DECADE — BUSINESS.
1839–1849.
Period of Literary Transition.

1839 Appointed weigher and gauger in the Boston Custom House. Finished *American Note-Books,* vol. i. Published *The Gentle Boy, A Thrice-Told Tale.*

1840 Lost Custom House position. Published *Grandfather's Chair.* (*Hawthorne and Wife*, vol. ii, for portraits.)

1841 Joined the Brook Farm Community at West Roxbury, Mass. Began *American Note-Books*, vol. ii.

1842 Published *Biographical Stories for Children.* July 9, in Boston, married Miss Peabody. Settled in the "Old Manse," Concord. Published second edition of *Twice-Told Tales* (2 vols.).

1843 Published *The Celestial Railroad.*

1844 His daughter Una born. Hawthorne a candidate for the Salem postmastership.

1845 Visited Bridge at Portsmouth, N. H. Edited *Papers of an Old Dartmoor Prisoner;* and assisted Bridge with his *Journal of an African Cruiser.*

1846 Surveyor in the Salem Custom House. Began "a year of miserable annoyances." Published *Mosses from an Old Manse.* His son Julian born. Ceased writing for a year.

1847 Began *The Scarlet Letter.*

1849 Lost position in the Custom House. Worked on *The Scarlet Letter.* His mother died. "The nadir of my father's material fortunes." — Julian Hawthorne.

FIFTH DECADE — LIFE ABROAD.
1850-1860.
Period of the Great Novels and Children's Books.

1850 Finished and published *The Scarlet Letter.* Moved with his family into the "Red House," Lenox, Mass. Entered upon the most productive period of his literary life. Began *The House of Seven Gables.* (*Bookman*, Sept., 1898, for portrait ; also *Critic*, July, 1902 ; and *Century*, Aug. 1895, for "Red House.")

1851 Published *The House of Seven Gables.* His daughter Rose born. Published *Stories from History and Biography.* Published *A Wonder Book for Girls and Boys.* Arranged *Snow Image and other Twice-Told Tales.* Began *The Blithedale Romance.* Moved to the "Horace Mann House," West Newton, Mass. (*House of Seven*

Gables, Riverside Literature Series, 91, for drawing of the House of Seven Gables from Hawthorne's description.)

1852 Bought "The Wayside," at Concord, Mass. Published *The Snow Image* and *The Blithedale Romance.* Visited the Isles of Shoals. Wrote and published the *Life of Franklin Pierce.* Wrote *Tanglewood Tales.*

1853 Appointed (by President Pierce) United States Consul at Liverpool. Published *Tanglewood Tales.* Finished *American Note-Books.* Began *English Note-Books.* Moved with his family into a small house at Rock Park (trans-Mersey). (*Century,* Nov., 1899, for portrait.)

1854 Several trips into North Wales. Published *Mosses from an Old Manse* (Revised Edition).

1855 Travelled in England.

1856 Visited London. Visited Scotland and the east coast of England. Lodged at "Brunswick Terrace," Southport (Irish Sea). Resigned consulship.

1857 Travelled in England. Planned *The Ancestral Footstep.*

1858 Went to Italy. In Rome began *French and Italian Note-Books.* In Florence began *The Marble Faun.*

1859 In Rome from January to June. Returned to England, staying at Whitby, Leamington, and Redcar. Finished *The Marble Faun.*

1860 Published, in February, *The Marble Faun.* Returned to "The Wayside." (*Bookman,* Sept. 1898, for portrait.)

SIXTH PERIOD — DECLINE.

1860–1864.

Fragmentary Writings.

1861 Much distressed by the outbreak of the Civil War. Wrote but intermittently. Began *Septimius Felton* and *Dr. Grimshawe's Secret* (cf. note for 1838).

1862 Visited Washington, D. C., and the Union Army in Virginia. With Julian made a brief trip to Maine. Published papers on the war in *The Atlantic Monthly.* Wrote *Our Old Home* for *The Atlantic Monthly.*

1863 Published *Our Old Home.* Worked on *Septimius Felton.* Depressed and unable to write. Contributed one chapter of *The Dolliver Romance* to *The Atlantic Monthly.* (See *Pansie : a fragment.*)

1864 Made a futile attempt at writing on *The Dolliver Romance.* Despaired of ever finishing the story. Visited Philadelphia with Ticknor, who suddenly died there. Very ill, returned to Concord. Met Franklin Pierce in Boston and started with him on a trip through the White Mountains. Nathaniel Hawthorne died at the "Pemigewasset House," Plymouth, N. H., and was buried in the Sleepy Hollow Cemetery, Concord, Mass. (*Harper's*, July, 1886, for portrait.)

1868 *Passages from the American Note-Books.*

1870 *Passages from the English Note-Books.*

1871 *Passages from the French and Italian Note-Books.*

1872 *Septimius Felton.*

1876 *The Dolliver Romance.*

1883 *Dr. Grimshawe's Secret.*

INTRODUCTORY NOTE.

THE TWICE–TOLD TALES.

On his return to his native town, Salem, after graduating at Bowdoin College in 1825, Hawthorne devoted himself to writing fiction. His first book was the romance of "Fanshawe," [1] which, however, made no impression on the public. He next produced a volume of stories to which he gave the title "Seven Tales of my Native Land"; but, after discouraging search for a publisher, he destroyed the manuscript. Whether any of the material composing that work was embodied in his later short stories it is impossible to determine, on the evidence now remaining. Still, it is not unlikely that he drew upon it, from memory, for the foundation of some among the "Twice-Told Tales." The sketches and stories now known collectively under this title were written mainly in a little room in the second story of a house on Herbert Street, Salem, from the windows of which Hawthorne's birthplace on the adjoining street (Union) is visible. "In this dismal chamber fame was won:" so runs a passage in the "American Note-Books." Under another date he says of it: "And here I sat a long, long time, waiting patiently for the world to know me, and sometimes wondering why it did not know me sooner, or whether it would ever know me at all."

[1] See vol. 11 of the Riverside edition of Hawthorne's works.

The Herbert Street house was habitually referred to by the members of the Hawthorne family as being on Union Street, since the family residence and the birthplace were connected by the lots of land attached respectively to each. The mansion on Union Street has since undergone considerable alteration, a large part of it having been taken down some years ago, owing to its dilapidated condition. On Dearborn Street there was another house, built for the mother of Hawthorne by her brother, Robert Manning, in which Hawthorne lived for about four years, though at what time precisely it is impossible to state. In the Dearborn Street house, also, he had a study; but the edifice has been removed to another site and altered. The Herbert Street (or, as in the Note-Books, Union Street) house was evidently the one which Hawthorne most closely associated with the production of his short stories.

The earlier pieces appeared in the " Salem Gazette " newspaper, and in the " New England Magazine " (published in Boston from 1831 to 1834). Sometimes they bore the author's real name, and sometimes a pseudonym was attached. Several among them purported to have been written by " Ashley Allen Royce," or the " Rev. A. A. Royce." Another pen-name used by the young romancer was " Oberon " ; the choice of which may be explained by the fact that, as the late Henry W. Longfellow recalled, some of the college friends of Hawthorne had nicknamed him Oberon, in allusion to his personal beauty and the imaginative tone of his conversation. But notwithstanding the variety of names under which he thus disguised himself, his writings revealed so clear an individuality that many persons recognized them as being the work of one mind. In 1836, he went to Boston to edit a magazine for S. G. Goodrich, then known as a popular compiler and publisher; and while thus engaged he wrote a large part of "Peter Parley's Universal History," which passed for Goodrich's composition and attained a wide popularity. At the same time he contributed to the Boston "Token" several of the best of his short stories, which received high praise in London. It was not until their issue in book form that they attracted similar encomiums in this country.

Hawthorne's original plan was to collect them in a series joined by an introduction and chapters of connected narrative; the whole to be called "The Story-Teller." A part of this projected framework has been preserved in the "Mosses from an Old Manse;"[1] and the Author there says: —

With each specimen will be given a sketch of the circumstances in which the story was told. Thus my air-drawn pictures will be set in a framework perhaps more valuable than the pictures themselves, since they will be embossed with groups of characteristic figures, amid the lake and mountain scenery, the villages and fertile fields, of our native land.

The plan of "The Story-Teller" was, to represent a young man of apostolical bent who set out to go from town to town, giving a sermon every morning, while a friend who accompanied him was to relate in public, every afternoon, a story illustrating the text previously discoursed upon by the preacher; the whole affair being announced in each place by posters, much in the manner of a travelling show. It might be sup-

---

[1] See "Passages from a Relinquished Work," in the second volume of the Mosses. It was intended to preface " Mr. Higginbotham's Catastrophe."

posed that the introduction of sermons in a book of fiction would offer a stumbling-block to success; but Hawthorne evaded this obvious difficulty by merely mentioning the sermons and then giving the stories in full. Mr. Goodrich gave the scheme no encouragement, but took the introductory portion describing the preacher and the *raconteur* to a magazine. It is worth recording as a curious fact in literary history that for the accompanying stories which Goodrich used in his annual he gave Hawthorne about three dollars apiece.

Finally, through the intervention of Mr. Horatio Bridge, who privately became responsible to this more than prudent publisher for the attendant expense, the first series of stories was given to the world in permanent form, as a handful of disconnected compositions, under the general heading of " Twice-Told Tales." Possibly the title was suggested by that line, given to Lewis, the Dauphin, in " King John " : —

" Life is as tedious as a twice-told tale."

About eight years after the first volume, a second one was issued; but even this did not include all the productions of the early period, some of which have since been brought to light. A few have perhaps escaped notice. The present writer discovered in a mutilated copy of the " Token," for 1835, this entry among the contents : " Alice Doane's Appeal. By the Author of ' The Gentle Boy.' " Only two pages of the story itself remained; but they sufficed to show that the contribution was one which has hitherto found no place in the collected works. A complete copy having with some difficulty been obtained, the sketch in question will be included in the 12th volume of the present edition.

" The Gentle Boy " probably did more for the

author's reputation than any other of the "Twice-Told Tales." Furthermore, as the volume containing it formed a link in his acquaintance with Miss Sophia A. Peabody, the lady whom he afterwards married, so that particular story itself was by her made the subject of a drawing, which now becomes a matter of literary interest. A special edition of "The Gentle Boy" was published in 1839: it was a thin, oblong quarto in paper covers, accompanied by an illustration engraved from Miss Peabody's outline drawing. This edition, now so rare as almost to have passed out of existence, contained a brief preface by Hawthorne, in which he said: "The tale, of which a new edition is now offered to the public, was among the earliest efforts of its author's pen; and, little noticed on its first appearance in one of the annuals, appears ultimately to have awakened the interest of a larger number of readers than any of his subsequent productions; . . . there are several among the 'Twice-Told Tales' which, on reperusal, affect him less painfully with a sense of imperfect and ill-wrought conception than 'The Gentle Boy.' But the opinion of many . . . compels him to the conclusion that nature here led him deeper into the universal heart than art has been able to follow." A letter from Hawthorne to Longfellow, referring to the first volume of the tales, contains another remark of general interest: "I have another great difficulty in the lack of materials; for I have seen so little of the world that I have nothing but thin air to concoct my stories of. . . . Sometimes, through a peep-hole, I have caught a glimpse of the real world, and the two or three articles in which I have portrayed these glimpses please me better than the others."

"The Toll-Gatherer's Day," evidently derived from minute observation of the traffic on a bridge near Salem; and "Little Annie's Ramble," which is said to have had for its heroine a child from real life, were perhaps placed by the Author in this favored category.

The paper entitled "A Sunday at Home" was based on a meeting-house, near the birthplace in Union Street, concerning which Hawthorne's surviving sister writes to the editor: "It never had a steeple, nor a clock, nor a bell, nor, of course, an organ. . . . But Hawthorne bestows all these incitements to devotion to atone for his own personal withdrawal from such influences. It was from the house on Herbert Street that he saw what he describes." But, like "The Seven Vagabonds" (founded on a trip which the Author made through part of Connecticut), such pieces as are most tinged with actuality have not interested readers so much as the pure invention of "David Swan," or the weird coloring of those half-historic records, the "Legends of the Province House."

Nevertheless, looked at closely, and with due knowledge of the accompanying facts of Hawthorne's life at the time,[1] the whole collection affords, besides the distinct imaginative pleasure to be got from it, valuable intimations as to Hawthorne's development during the first decade of his career as an author.

G. P. L.

[1] See *A Study of Hawthorne,* Chapter IV.

PREFACE.

THE Author of "Twice-Told Tales" has a claim to one distinction, which, as none of his literary brethren will care about disputing it with him, he need not be afraid to mention. He was, for a good many years, the obscurest man of letters in America.

These stories were published in magazines and annuals, extending over a period of ten or twelve years, and comprising the whole of the writer's young manhood, without making (so far as he has ever been aware) the slightest impression on the public. One or two among them, the "Rill from the Town Pump," in perhaps a greater degree than any other, had a pretty wide newspaper circulation; as for the rest, he had no grounds for supposing that, on their first appearance, they met with the good or evil fortune to be read by anybody. Throughout the time above specified, he had no incitement to literary effort in a reasonable prospect of reputation or profit, nothing but the pleasure itself of composition — an enjoyment not at all amiss in its way, and perhaps essential to the merit of the work in hand, but which, in the long run, will hardly keep the chill out of a writer's heart, or the numbness out of his fingers. To this total lack of sympathy, at the age when his mind would naturally have been most effervescent, the public owe it (and it is certainly an effect not to be regretted on either part) that the Author can show nothing for the thought and industry of that portion of his life, save the forty sketches, or thereabouts, included in these volumes.

Much more, indeed, he wrote ; and some very small part of it might yet be rummaged out (but it would not be worth the trouble) among the dingy pages of fifteen-or-twenty-year-old periodicals, or within the shabby morocco covers of faded souvenirs. The remainder of the works alluded to had a very brief existence, but, on the score of brilliancy, enjoyed a fate vastly superior to that of their brotherhood, which succeeded in getting through the press. In a word, the Author burned them without mercy or remorse, and, moreover, without any subsequent regret, and had more than one occasion to marvel that such very dull stuff, as he knew his condemned manuscripts to be, should yet have possessed inflammability enough to set the chimney on fire !

After a long while the first collected volume of the " Tales " was published. By this time, if the Author had ever been greatly tormented by literary ambition (which he does not remember or believe to have been the case), it must have perished, beyond resuscitation, in the dearth of nutriment. This was fortunate ; for the success of the volume was not such as would have gratified a craving desire for notoriety. A moderate edition was "got rid of" (to use the publisher's very significant phrase) within a reasonable time, but apparently without rendering the writer or his productions much more generally known than before. The great bulk of the reading public probably ignored the book altogether. A few persons read it, and liked it better than it deserved. At an interval of three or four years, the second volume was published, and encountered much the same sort of kindly, but calm, and very limited reception. The circulation of the two volumes was chiefly confined to New England; nor was it until long after this period, if it even yet be the case, that the Author could regard himself as addressing the American public, or, indeed, any public at all. He was merely writing to his known or unknown friends.

As he glances over these long-forgotten pages, and considers his way of life while composing them, the Author can very clearly discern why all this was so. After so many sober years, he would have reason to be ashamed if he could not criticise his own work as fairly as another man's; and, though it is little his business, and perhaps still less his interest, he can hardly resist a temptation to achieve something of the sort. If writers were allowed to do so, and would perform the task with perfect sincerity and unreserve, their opinions of their own productions would often be more valuable and instructive than the works themselves.

At all events, there can be no harm in the Author's

remarking that he rather wonders how the "Twice-Told Tales" should have gained what vogue they did than that it was so little and so gradual. They have the pale tint of flowers that blossomed in too retired a shade, — the coolness of a meditative habit, which diffuses itself through the feeling and observation of every sketch. Instead of passion there is sentiment; and, even in what purport to be pictures of actual life, we have allegory, not always so warmly dressed in its habiliments of flesh and blood as to be taken into the reader's mind without a shiver. Whether from lack of power, or an unconquerable reserve, the Author's touches have often an effect of tameness; the merriest man can hardly contrive to laugh at his broadest humor; the tenderest woman, one would suppose, will hardly shed warm tears at his deepest pathos. The book, if you would see anything in it, requires to be read in the clear, brown, twilight atmosphere in which it was written; if opened in the sunshine, it is apt to look exceedingly like a volume of blank pages.

With the foregoing characteristics, proper to the production of a person in retirement (which happened to be the Author's category at the time), the book is devoid of others that we should quite as naturally look for. The sketches are not, it is hardly necessary to say, profound; but it is rather more remarkable that they so seldom, if ever, show any design on the writer's part to make them so. They have none of the abstruseness of idea, or obscurity of ex

pression, which mark the written communications of a
solitary mind with itself. They never need translation.
It is, in fact, the style of a man of society. Every
sentence, so far as it embodies thought or sensibility,
nay be understood and felt by anybody who will
give himself the trouble to read it, and will take up
the book in a proper mood.

This statement of apparently opposite peculiarities
leads us to a perception of what the sketches truly are.
They are not the talk of a secluded man with his own
mind and heart (had it been so, they could hardly
have failed to be more deeply and permanently valua
ble), but his attempts, and very imperfectly successful
ones, to open an intercourse with the world.

The Author would regret to be understood as speaking sourly or querulously of the slight mark made by
his earlier literary efforts on the Public at large. It
is so far the contrary, that he has been moved to write
this Preface chiefly as affording him an opportunity
to express how much enjoyment he has owed to these
volumes, both before and since their publication. They
are the memorials of very tranquil and not unhappy
years. They failed, it is true, — nor could it have been
otherwise, — in winning an extensive popularity. Oc
casionally, however, when he deemed them entirely
forgotten, a paragraph or an article, from a native or
foreign critic, would gratify his instincts of authorship
with unexpected praise, — too generous praise, indeed,
and too little alloyed with censure, which, therefore,
he learned the better to inflict upon himself. And

by the by, it is a very suspicious symptom of a defi
ciency of the popular element in a book when it calls
forth no harsh criticism. This has been particularly
the fortune of the "TWICE-TOLD TALES." They
made no enemies, and were so little known and talked
about that those who read, and chanced to like them,
were apt to conceive the sort of kindness for the book
which a person naturally feels for a discovery of his
own.

This kindly feeling (in some cases, at least) extended to the Author, who, on the internal evidence of
his sketches, came to be regarded as a mild, shy, gentle, melancholic, exceedingly sensitive, and not very
forcible man, hiding his blushes under an assumed
name, the quaintness of which was supposed, somehow or other, to symbolize his personal and literary
traits. He is by no means certain that some of his
subsequent productions have not been influenced and
modified by a natural desire to fill up so amiable an
outline, and to act in consonance with the character
assigned to him; nor, even now, could he forfeit it
without a few tears of tender sensibility. To con-
clude, however : these volumes have opened the way
to most agreeable associations, and to the formation of
imperishable friendships ; and there are many golden
threads interwoven with his present happiness, which
he can follow up more or less directly, until he finds
their commencement here ; so that his pleasant pathway among realities seems to proceed out of the
Dreamland of his youth, and to be bordered with just

enough of its shadowy foliage to shelter him from the heat of the day. He is therefore satisfied with what the "TWICE-TOLD TALES" have done for him, and feels it to be far better than fame.

LENOX, *January* 11, 1851.

TWICE-TOLD TALES.

THE GRAY CHAMPION.

THERE was once a time when New England groaned under the actual pressure of heavier wrongs than those threatened ones which brought on the Revolution. James II., the bigoted successor of Charles the Voluptuous, had annulled the charters of all the colonies, and sent a harsh and unprincipled soldier to take away our liberties and endanger our religion. The administration of Sir Edmund Andros lacked scarcely a single characteristic of tyranny: a Governor and Council, holding office from the King, and wholly independent of the country; laws made and taxes levied without concurrence of the people immediate or by their representatives; the rights of private citizens violated, and the titles of all landed property declared void; the voice of complaint stifled by restrictions on the press; and, finally, disaffection overawed by the first band of mercenary troops that ever marched on our free soil. For two years our ancestors were kept in sullen submission by that filial love which had invariably secured their allegiance to the mother country, whether its head chanced to be a Parliament, Protector, or Popish Monarch. Till these evil times, however, such allegiance had been merely nominal, and the colonists had ruled themselves, enjoying far more freedom than is even yet the privilege of the native subjects of Great Britain.

At length a rumor reached our shores that the Prince of Orange had ventured on an enterprise, the success of which would be the triumph of civil and religious rights and the salvation of New England. It was but a doubtful whisper; it might be false, or the attempt might fail; and, in either case, the man that stirred against King James would lose his head. Still the intelligence produced a marked effect. The people smiled mysteriously in the streets, and threw bold glances at their oppressors; while far and wide there was a subdued and silent agitation, as if the slightest signal would rouse the whole land from its sluggish despondency. Aware of their danger, the rulers resolved to avert it by an imposing display of strength, and perhaps to confirm their despotism by yet harsher measures. One afternoon in April, 1689, Sir Edmund Andros and his favorite councillors, being warm with wine, assembled the red-coats of the Governor's Guard, and made their appearance in the streets of Boston. The sun was near setting when the march commenced.

The roll of the drum at that unquiet crisis seemed to go through the streets, less as the martial music of the soldiers, than as a muster-call to the inhabitants themselves. A multitude, by various avenues, assembled in King Street, which was destined to be the scene, nearly a century afterwards, of another encounter between the troops of Britain, and a people struggling against her tyranny. Though more than sixty years had elapsed since the pilgrims came, this crowd of their descendants still showed the strong and sombre features of their character perhaps more strik-

ingly in such a stern emergency than on happier occasions.   There were the sober garb, the general severity of mien, the gloomy but undismayed expression,
the scriptural forms of speech, and the confidence in
Heaven's blessing on a righteous cause, which would
have marked a band of the original Puritans, when
threatened by some peril of the wilderness.   Indeed,
it was not yet time for the old spirit to be extinct;
since there were men in the street that day who had
worshipped there beneath the trees, before a house
was reared to the God for whom they had become
exiles.   Old soldiers of the Parliament were here,
too, smiling grimly at the thought that their aged
arms might strike another blow against the house of
Stuart.   Here, also, were the veterans of King Philip's war, who had burned villages and slaughtered
young and old, with pious fierceness, while the godly
souls throughout the land were helping them with
prayer.   Several ministers were scattered among the
crowd, which, unlike all other mobs, regarded them
with such reverence, as if there were sanctity in their
very garments.   These holy men exerted their influence to quiet the people, but not to disperse them.
Meantime, the purpose of the Governor, in disturbing
the peace of the town at a period when the slightest
commotion might throw the country into a ferment,
was almost the universal subject of inquiry, and vari-
ously explained.

" Satan will strike his master-stroke presently,"
cried some, " because he knoweth that his time is
short.   All our godly pastors are to be dragged to
prison !   We shall see them at a Smithfield fire in
King Street ! "

Hereupon the people of each parish gathered closer

round their minister, who looked calmly upwards and assumed a more apostolic dignity, as well befitted a candidate for the highest honor of his profession, the crown of martyrdom. It was actually fancied, at that period, that New England might have a John Rogers of her own to take the place of that worthy in the Primer.

"The Pope of Rome has given orders for a new St. Bartholomew!" cried others. "We are to be massacred, man and male child!"

Neither was this rumor wholly discredited, although the wiser class believed the Governor's object somewhat less atrocious. His predecessor under the old charter, Bradstreet, a venerable companion of the first settlers, was known to be in town. There were grounds for conjecturing, that Sir Edmund Andros intended at once to strike terror by a parade of military force, and to confound the opposite faction by possessing himself of their chief.

"Stand firm for the old charter Governor!" shouted the crowd, seizing upon the idea. "The good old Governor Bradstreet!"

While this cry was at the loudest, the people were surprised by the well-known figure of Governor Bradstreet himself, a patriarch of nearly ninety, who appeared on the elevated steps of a door, and, with characteristic mildness, besought them to submit to the constituted authorities.

"My children," concluded this venerable person, "do nothing rashly. Cry not aloud, but pray for the welfare of New England, and expect patiently what the Lord will do in this matter!"

The event was soon to be decided. All this time, the roll of the drum had been approaching through

Cornhill, louder and deeper, till with reverberations from house to house, and the regular tramp of martial footsteps, it burst into the street. A double rank of soldiers made their appearance, occupying the whole breadth of the passage, with shouldered matchlocks, and matches burning, so as to present a row of fires in the dusk. Their steady march was like the prog- ress of a machine, that would roll irresistibly over everything in its way. Next, moving slowly, with a confused clatter of hoofs on the pavement, rode a party of mounted gentlemen, the central figure being Sir Edmund Andros, elderly, but erect and soldier-like. Those around him were his favorite councillors, and the bitterest foes of New England. At his right hand rode Edward Randolph, our arch-enemy, that "blasted wretch," as Cotton Mather calls him, who achieved the downfall of our ancient government, and was fol- lowed with a sensible curse, through life and to his grave. On the other side was Bullivant, scattering jests and mockery as he rode along. Dudley came behind, with a downcast look, dreading, as well he might, to meet the indignant gaze of the people, who beheld him, their only countryman by birth, among the oppressors of his native land. The captain of a frigate in the harbor, and two or three civil officers under the Crown, were also there. But the figure which most attracted the public eye, and stirred up the deepest feeling, was the Episcopal clergyman of King's Chapel, riding haughtily among the magis- trates in his priestly vestments, the fitting representa- tive of prelacy and persecution, the union of church and state, and all those abominations which had driven the Puritans to the wilderness. Another guard of soldiers, in double rank, brought up the rear.

The whole scene was a picture of the condition of New England, and its moral, the deformity of any government that does not grow out of the nature of things and the character of the people. On one side the religious multitude, with their sad visages and dark attire, and on the other, the group of despotic rulers, with the high churchman in the midst, and here and there a crucifix at their bosoms, all magnificently clad, flushed with wine, proud of unjust authority, and scoffing at the universal groan. And the mercenary soldiers, waiting but the word to deluge the street with blood, showed the only means by which obedience could be secured.

"O Lord of Hosts," cried a voice among the crowd, "provide a Champion for thy people!"

This ejaculation was loudly uttered, and served as a herald's cry, to introduce a remarkable personage. The crowd had rolled back, and were now huddled together nearly at the extremity of the street, while the soldiers had advanced no more than a third of its length. The intervening space was empty — a paved solitude, between lofty edifices, which threw almost a twilight shadow over it. Suddenly, there was seen the figure of an ancient man, who seemed to have emerged from among the people, and was walking by himself along the centre of the street, to confront the armed band. He wore the old Puritan dress, a dark cloak and a steeple-crowned hat, in the fashion of at least fifty years before, with a heavy sword upon his thigh, but a staff in his hand to assist the tremulous gait of age.

When at some distance from the multitude, the old man turned slowly round, displaying a face of antique majesty, rendered doubly venerable by the hoary beard

that descended on his breast. He made a gesture at
once of encouragement and warning, then turned
again, and resumed his way.

"Who is this gray patriarch?" asked the young
men of their sires.

"Who is this venerable brother?" asked the old
men among themselves.

But none could make reply. The fathers of the
people, those of fourscore years and upwards, were
disturbed, deeming it strange that they should forget
one of such evident authority, whom they must have
known in their early days, the associate of Winthrop,
and all the old councillors, giving laws, and making
prayers, and leading them against the savage. The
elderly men ought to have remembered him, too, with
locks as gray in their youth, as their own were now.
And the young! How could he have passed so utterly from their memories — that hoary sire, the relic
of long-departed times, whose awful benediction had
surely been bestowed on their uncovered heads, in
childhood?

"Whence did he come? What is his purpose?
Who can this old man be?" whispered the wondering
crowd.

Meanwhile, the venerable stranger, staff in hand,
was pursuing his solitary walk along the centre of the
street. As he drew near the advancing soldiers, and
as the roll of their drum came full upon his ear, the
old man raised himself to a loftier mien, while the
decrepitude of age seemed to fall from his shoulders,
leaving him in gray but unbroken dignity. Now, he
marched onward with a warrior's step, keeping time
to the military music. Thus the aged form advanced
on one side, and the whole parade of soldiers and

magistrates on the other, till, when scarcely twenty yards remained between, the old man grasped his staff by the middle, and held it before him like a leader's truncheon.

"Stand!" cried he.

The eye, the face, and attitude of command; the solemn, yet warlike peal of that voice, fit either to rule a host in the battle-field or be raised to God in prayer, were irresistible. At the old man's word and outstretched arm, the roll of the drum was hushed at once, and the advancing line stood still. A tremulous enthusiasm seized upon the multitude. That stately form, combining the leader and the saint, so gray, so dimly seen, in such an ancient garb, could only belong to some old champion of the righteous cause, whom the oppressor's drum had summoned from his grave. They raised a shout of awe and exultation, and looked for the deliverance of New England.

The Governor, and the gentlemen of his party, perceiving themselves brought to an unexpected stand, rode hastily forward, as if they would have pressed their snorting and affrighted horses right against the hoary apparition. He, however, blenched not a step, but glancing his severe eye round the group, which half encompassed him, at last bent it sternly on Sir Edmund Andros. One would have thought that the dark old man was chief ruler there, and that the Governor and Council, with soldiers at their back, representing the whole power and authority of the Crown, had no alternative but obedience.

"What does this old fellow here?" cried Edward Randolph, fiercely. "On, Sir Edmund! Bid the soldiers forward, and give the dotard the same choice that you give all his countrymen — to stand aside or be trampled on!"

"Nay, nay, let us show respect to the good grand-sire," said Bullivant, laughing. "See you not, he is some old round-headed dignitary, who hath lain asleep these thirty years, and knows nothing of the change of times? Doubtless, he thinks to put us down with a proclamation in Old Noll's name!"

"Are you mad, old man?" demanded Sir Edmund Andros, in loud and harsh tones. "How dare you stay the march of King James's Governor?"

"I have stayed the march of a King himself, ere now," replied the gray figure, with stern composure. "I am here, Sir Governor, because the cry of an oppressed people hath disturbed me in my secret place; and beseeching this favor earnestly of the Lord, it was vouchsafed me to appear once again on earth, in the good old cause of his saints. And what speak ye of James? There is no longer a Popish tyrant on the throne of England, and by to-morrow noon, his name shall be a byword in this very street, where ye would make it a word of terror. Back, thou that wast a Governor, back! With this night thy power is ended — to-morrow, the prison! — back, lest I foretell the scaffold!"

The people had been drawing nearer and nearer, and drinking in the words of their champion, who spoke in accents long disused, like one unaccustomed to converse, except with the dead of many years ago. But his voice stirred their souls. They confronted the soldiers, not wholly without arms, and ready to convert the very stones of the street into deadly weapons. Sir Edmund Andros looked at the old man; then he cast his hard and cruel eye over the multitude, and beheld them burning with that lurid wrath, so difficult to kindle or to quench; and again he fixed his gaze on the aged form, which stood obscurely in an open space, where neither friend nor foe had thrust himself. What were his thoughts, he uttered no word which might discover. But whether the oppressor were overawed by the Gray Champion's look, or perceived his peril in the threatening attitude of the people, it is certain that he gave back, and ordered his soldiers to commence a slow and guarded retreat. Before another sunset, the Governor, and all that rode so proudly with him, were prisoners, and long ere it was known that James had abdicated, King William was proclaimed throughout New England.

But where was the Gray Champion? Some reported that, when the troops had gone from King Street, and the people were thronging tumultuously in their rear, Bradstreet, the aged Governor, was seen to embrace a form more aged than his own. Others soberly affirmed, that while they marvelled at the venerable grandeur of his aspect, the old man had faded from their eyes, melting slowly into the hues of twilight, till, where he stood, there was an empty space. But all agreed that the hoary shape was gone. The men of that generation watched for his reappearance, in sunshine and in twilight, but never saw him more, nor knew when his funeral passed, nor where his gravestone was.

And who was the Gray Champion? Perhaps his name might be found in the records of that stern Court of Justice, which passed a sentence, too mighty for the age, but glorious in all after-times, for its humbling lesson to the monarch and its high example to the subject. I have heard, that whenever the descendants of the Puritans are to show the spirit of their sires, the old man appears again. When eighty years had passed, he walked once more in King Street. Five years later, in the twilight of an April morning, he stood on the green, beside the meeting-house, at Lexington, where now the obelisk of granite, with a slab of slate inlaid, commemorates the first fallen of the Revolution. And when our fathers were toiling at the breastwork on Bunker's Hill, all through that night the old warrior walked his rounds. Long, long may it be, ere he comes again! His hour is one of darkness, and adversity, and peril. But should domestic tyranny oppress us, or the invader's step pollute our soil, still may the Gray Champion come, for he is the type of New England's hereditary spirit; and his shadowy march, on the eve of danger, must ever be the pledge, that New England's sons will vindicate their ancestry.

SUNDAY AT HOME.

EVERY Sabbath morning in the summer time, I thrust back the curtain, to watch the sunrise stealing down a steeple which stands opposite my chamber window. First, the weather-cock begins to flash; then, a fainter lustre gives the spire an airy aspect; next, it encroaches on the tower, and causes the index of the dial to glisten like gold as it points to the gilded figure of the hour. Now, the loftiest window gleams, and now the lower. The carved frame-work of the portal is marked strongly out. At length, the morning glory, in its descent from heaven, comes down the stone steps, one by one; and there stands the steeple, glowing with fresh radiance, while the shades of twilight still hide themselves among the nooks of the adjacent buildings. Methinks, though the same sun brightens it every fair morning, yet the steeple has a peculiar robe of brightness for the Sabbath.

By dwelling near a church, a person soon contracts an attachment for the edifice. We naturally personify it, and conceive its massy walls, and its dim emptiness, to be instinct with a calm, and meditative, and somewhat melancholy spirit. But the steeple stands foremost, in our thoughts, as well as locally. It impresses us as a giant, with a mind comprehensive and discriminating enough to care for the great and small concerns of all the town. Hourly, while it speaks a moral to the few that think, it reminds thousands of busy individuals of their separate and most secret affairs. It is the steeple, too, that flings abroad the hurried and irregular accents of general alarm; neither have gladness and festivity found a better utterance than by its tongue; and when the dead are slowly passing to their home, the steeple has a melancholy voice to bid them welcome. Yet, in spite of this connection with human interests, what a moral loneliness, on week days, broods round about its stately height! It has no kindred with the houses above which it towers; it looks down into the narrow thoroughfare, the lonelier, because the crowd are elbowing their passage at its base. A glance at the body of the church deepens this impression. Within, by the light of distant windows, amid refracted shadows, we discern the vacant pews and empty galleries, the silent organ, the voiceless pulpit, and the clock, which tells to solitude how time is passing. Time — where man lives not — what is it but eternity? And in the church, we might suppose, are garnered up, throughout the week, all thoughts and feelings that have reference to eternity, until the holy day comes round again, to let them forth. Might not, then, its more appropriate site be in the outskirts of the town, with space for old trees to wave around it, and throw their solemn shadows over a quiet green? We will say more of this, hereafter.

But, on the Sabbath, I watch the earliest sunshine, and fancy that a holier brightness marks the day, when there shall be no buzz of voices on the exchange, nor traffic in the shops, nor crowd, nor business, anywhere but at church. Many have fancied so. For my own part, whether I see it scattered down among tangled woods, or beaming broad across the fields, or hemmed in between brick buildings, or tracing out the figure of the casement on my chamber

floor, still I recognize the Sabbath sunshine. And
ever let me recognize it! Some illusions, and this
among them, are the shadows of great truths. Doubts
may flit around me, or seem to close their evil wings,
and settle down; but, so long as I imagine that the
earth is hallowed, and the light of heaven retains its
sanctity, on the Sabbath — while that blessed sunshine
lives within me — never can my soul have lost the instinct of its faith. If it have gone astray, it will return again.

I love to spend such pleasant Sabbaths, from morning till night, behind the curtain of my open window.
Are they spent amiss? Every spot, so near the church
as to be visited by the circling shadow of the steeple,
should be deemed consecrated ground, to-day. With
stronger truth be it said, that a devout heart may consecrate a den of thieves, as an evil one may convert a
temple to the same. My heart, perhaps, has not such
holy, nor, I would fain trust, such impious potency.
It must suffice, that, though my form be absent, my
inner man goes constantly to church, while many,
whose bodily presence fills the accustomed seats, have
left their souls at home. But I am there, even before
my friend, the sexton. At length, he comes — a man
of kindly, but sombre aspect, in dark gray clothes, and
hair of the same mixture — he comes and applies his
key to the wide portal. Now, my thoughts may go in
among the dusty pews, or ascend the pulpit, without
sacrilege, but soon come forth again to enjoy the music
of the bell. How glad, yet solemn too! All the stee-
ples in town are talking together, aloft in the sunny
air, and rejoicing among themselves, while their spires
point heavenward. Meantime, here are the children
assembling to the Sabbath-school, which is kept some-

where within the church. Often, while looking at the arched portal, I have been gladdened by the sight of a score of these little girls and boys, in pink, blue, yellow, and crimson frocks, bursting suddenly forth into the sunshine, like a swarm of gay butterflies that had been shut up in the solemn gloom. Or I might compare them to cherubs, haunting that holy place.

About a quarter of an hour before the second ringing of the bell, individuals of the congregation begin to appear. The earliest is invariably an old woman in black, whose bent frame and rounded shoulders are evidently laden with some heavy affliction, which she is eager to rest upon the altar. Would that the Sabbath came twice as often, for the sake of that sorrowful old soul! There is an elderly man, also, who arrives in good season, and leans against the corner of the tower, just within the line of its shadow, looking downward with a darksome brow. I sometimes fancy that the old woman is the happier of the two. After these, others drop in singly, and by twos and threes, either disappearing through the doorway, or taking their stand in its vicinity. At last, and always with an unexpected sensation, the bell turns in the steeple overhead, and throws out an irregular clangor, jarring the tower to its foundation. As if there were magic in the sound, the sidewalks of the street, both up and down along, are immediately thronged with two long lines of people, all converging hitherward, and streaming into the church. Perhaps the far-off roar of a coach draws nearer — a deeper thunder by its contrast with the surrounding stillness — until it sets down the wealthy worshippers at the portal, among their humblest brethren. Beyond that entrance, in theory at least, there are no distinctions of earthly rank; nor, indeed, by the goodly apparel which is flaunting in the sun, would there seem to be such, on the hither side. Those pretty girls! Why will they disturb my pious meditations! Of all days in the week, they should strive to look least fascinating on the Sabbath, instead of heightening their mortal loveliness, as if to rival the blessed angels, and keep our thoughts from heaven. Were I the minister himself, I must needs look. One girl is white muslin from the waist upwards, and black silk downwards to her slippers; a second blushes from topknot to shoetie, one universal scarlet; another shines of a pervading yellow, as if she had made a garment of the sunshine. The greater part, however, have adopted a milder cheerfulness of hue. Their veils, especially when the wind raises them, give a lightness to the general effect, and make them appear like airy phantoms, as they flit up the steps, and vanish into the sombre doorway. Nearly all — though it is very strange that I should know it — wear white stockings, white as snow, and neat slippers, laced crosswise with black ribbon, pretty high above the ankles. A white stocking is infinitely more effective than a black one.

Here comes the clergyman, slow and solemn, in severe simplicity, needing no black silk gown to denote his office. His aspect claims my reverence, but cannot win my love. Were I to picture Saint Peter keeping fast the gate of heaven, and frowning, more stern than pitiful, on the wretched applicants, that face should be my study. By middle age, or sooner, the creed has generally wrought upon the heart, or been attempered by it. As the minister passes into the church the bell holds its iron tongue, and all the low murmur of the congregation dies away. The gray sexton looks up and down the street, and then at my window curtain, where, through the small peephole, I half fancy that he has caught my eye. Now every loiterer has gone in, and the street lies asleep in the quiet sun, while a feeling of loneliness comes over me, and brings also an uneasy sense of neglected privileges and duties. O, I ought to have gone to church! The bustle of the rising congregation reaches my ears. They are standing up to pray. Could I bring my heart into unison with those who are praying in yonder church, and lift it heavenward, with a fervor of supplication, but no distinct request, would not that be the safest kind of prayer? "Lord, look down upon me in mercy!" With that sentiment gushing from my soul, might I not leave all the rest to Him?

Hark! the hymn. This, at least, is a portion of the service which I can enjoy better than if I sat within the walls, where the full choir and the massive melody of the organ would fall with a weight upon me. At this distance it thrills through my frame and plays upon my heartstrings with a pleasure both of the sense and spirit. Heaven be praised, I know nothing of music as a science; and the most elaborate harmonies, if they please me, please as simply as a nurse's lullaby. The strain has ceased, but prolongs itself in my mind with fanciful echoes till I start from my reverie, and find that the sermon has commenced. It is my misfortune seldom to fructify, in a regular way, by any but printed sermons. The first strong idea which the preacher utters gives birth to a train of thought, and leads me onward, step by step, quite out of hearing of the good man's voice, unless he be indeed a son of thunder. At my open window, catching now and then a sentence of the " parson's saw,"

I am as well situated as at the foot of the pulpit
stairs. The broken and scattered fragments of this
one discourse will be the texts of many sermons,
preached by those colleague pastors — colleagues.
but often disputants — my Mind and Heart. The
former pretends to be a scholar, and perplexes me
with doctrinal points ; the latter takes me on the score
of feeling; and both, like several other preachers,
spend their strength to very little purpose. I, their
sole auditor, cannot always understand them.

Suppose that a few hours have passed, and behold
me still behind my curtain, just before the close of
the afternoon service. The hour hand on the dial has
passed beyond four o'clock. The declining sun is hidden behind the steeple, and throws its shadow straight
across the street, so that my chamber is darkened as
with a cloud. Around the church-door all is solitude,
and an impenetrable obscurity beyond the threshold. A commotion is heard. The seats are slammed
down, and the pew-doors thrown back — a multitude
of feet are trampling along the unseen aisles — and
the congregation bursts suddenly through the portal.
Foremost, scampers a rabble of boys, behind whom
moves a dense and dark phalanx of grown men, and
lastly, a crowd of females, with young children, and a
few scattered husbands. This instantaneous outbreak
of life into loneliness is one of the pleasantest scenes
of the day. Some of the good people are rubbing
their eyes, thereby intimating that they have been
wrapped, as it were, in a sort of holy trance by the
fervor of their devotion. There is a young man, a
third rate coxcomb, whose first care is always to flourish a white handkerchief, and brush the seat of a tight
pair of black silk pantaloons, which shine as if var-

nished. They must have been made of the stuff called "everlasting," or perhaps of the same piece as Christian's garments in the "Pilgrim's Progress," for he put them on two summers ago, and has not yet worn the gloss off. I have taken a great liking to those black silk pantaloons. But now, with nods and greetings among friends, each matron takes her husband's arm and paces gravely homeward, while the girls also flutter away after arranging sunset walks with their favored bachelors. The Sabbath eve is the eve of love. At length the whole congregation is dispersed. No; here, with faces as glossy as black satin, come two sable ladies and a sable gentleman, and close in their rear the minister, who softens his severe visage, and bestows a kind word on each. Poor souls! To them the most captivating picture of bliss in heaven is —— "There we shall be white!"

All is solitude again. But, hark! —— a broken warbling of voices, and now, attuning its grandeur to their sweetness, a stately peal of the organ. Who are the choristers? Let me dream that the angels, who came down from heaven, this blessed morn, to blend themselves with the worship of the truly good, are playing and singing their farewell to the earth. On the wings of that rich melody they were borne upward.

This, gentle reader, is merely a flight of poetry. A few of the singing men and singing women had lingered behind their fellows, and raised their voices fitfully, and blew a careless note upon the organ. Yet, it lifted my soul higher than all their former strains. They are gone —— the sons and daughters of music —— and the gray sexton is just closing the portal. For six days more, there will be no face of man in the pews, and aisles, and galleries, nor a voice in the

pulpit, nor music in the choir. Was it worth while
to rear this massive edifice, to be a desert in the heart
of the town, and populous only for a few hours of
each seventh day ? O, but the church is a symbol of
religion. May its site, which was consecrated on the
day when the first tree was felled, be kept holy forever, a spot of solitude and peace, amid the trouble
and vanity of our week-day world ! There is a moral,
and a religion too, even in the silent walls. And may
the steeple still point heavenward, and be decked with
the hallowed sunshine of the Sabbath morn !

THE WEDDING KNELL.

THERE is a certain church in the city of New York which I have always regarded with peculiar interest, on account of a marriage there solemnized, under very singular circumstances, in my grandmother's girlhood. That venerable lady chanced to be a spectator of the scene, and ever after made it her favorite narrative Whether the edifice now standing on the same site be the identical one to which she referred, I am not antiquarian enough to know ; nor would it be worth while to correct myself, perhaps, of an agreeable error, by reading the date of its erection on the tablet over the door. It is a stately church, surrounded by an inclosure of the loveliest green, within which appear urns, pillars, obelisks, and other forms of monumental marble, the tributes of private affection, or more splendid memorials of historic dust. With such a place, though the tumult of the city rolls beneath its tower, one would be willing to connect some legendary interest.

The marriage might be considered as the result of an early engagement, though there had been two intermediate weddings on the lady's part, and forty years of celibacy on that of the gentleman. At sixty-five, Mr. Ellenwood was a shy, but not quite a secluded man ; selfish, like all men who brood over their own hearts, yet manifesting on rare occasions a vein of generous sentiment ; a scholar throughout life, though always an indolent one, because his studies

had no definite object, either of public advantage or
personal ambition ; a gentleman, high bred and fas-
tidiously delicate, yet sometimes requiring a considerable relaxation, in his behalf, of the common rules of
society.   In truth, there were so many anomalies in
his character, and though shrinking with diseased sensibility from public notice, it had been his fatality so
often to become the topic of the day, by some wild eccentricity of conduct, that people searched his lineage
for an hereditary taint of insanity.   But there was no
need of this.   His caprices had their origin in a mind
that lacked the support of an engrossing purpose, and
in feelings that preyed upon themselves for want of
other food.   If he were mad, it was the consequence,
and not the cause, of an aimless and abortive life.

The widow was as complete a contrast to her third
bridegroom, in everything but age, as can well be conceived.   Compelled to relinquish her first engagement,
she had been united to a man of twice her own years,
to whom she became an exemplary wife, and by whose
death she was left in possession of a splendid fortune.
A southern gentleman, considerably younger than herself, succeeded to her hand, and carried her to Charleston, where, after many uncomfortable years, she found
herself again a widow.   It would have been singular,
if any uncommon delicacy of feeling had survived
through such a life as Mrs. Dabney's ; it could not
but be crushed and killed by her early disappointment,
the cold duty of her first marriage, the dislocation of
the heart's principles, consequent on a second union,
and the unkindness of her southern husband, which
had inevitably driven her to connect the idea of his
death with that of her comfort.   To be brief, she was
that wisest, but unloveliest, variety of woman, a phi-

losopher, bearing troubles of the heart with equanimity, dispensing with all that should have been her happiness, and making the best of what remained. Sage in most matters, the widow was perhaps the more amiable for the one frailty that made her ridiculous. Being childless, she could not remain beautiful by proxy, in the person of a daughter; she therefore refused to grow old and ugly, on any consideration; she struggled with Time, and held fast her roses in spite of him, till the venerable thief appeared to have relinquished the spoil, as not worth the trouble of acquiring it.

The approaching marriage of this woman of the world with such an unworldly man as Mr. Ellenwood was announced soon after Mrs. Dabney's return to her native city. Superficial observers, and deeper ones, seemed to concur in supposing that the lady must have borne no inactive part in arranging the affair; there were considerations of expediency which she would be far more likely to appreciate than Mr. Ellenwood; and there was just the specious phantom of sentiment and romance in this late union of two early lovers which sometimes makes a fool of a woman who has lost her true feelings among the accidents of life. All the wonder was, how the gentleman, with his lack of worldly wisdom and agonizing consciousness of ridicule, could have been induced to take a measure at once so prudent and so laughable. But while people talked the wedding-day arrived. The ceremony was to be solemnized according to the Episcopalian forms, and in open church, with a degree of publicity that attracted many spectators, who occupied the front seats of the galleries, and the pews near the altar and along the broad aisle. It had been arranged, or possibly it was the custom of the day, that the parties should proceed separately to church. By some accident the bridegroom was a little less punctual than the widow and her bridal attendants ; with whose arrival, after this tedious, but necessary preface, the action of our tale may be said to commence.

The clumsy wheels of several old-fashioned coaches were heard, and the gentlemen and ladies composing the bridal party came through the church door with the sudden and gladsome effect of a burst of sunshine. The whole group, except the principal figure, was made up of youth and gayety. As they streamed up the broad aisle, while the pews and pillars seemed to brighten on either side, their steps were as buoyant as if they mistook the church for a ball-room, and were ready to dance hand in hand to the altar. So brilliant was the spectacle that few took notice of a singular phenomenon that had marked its entrance. At the moment when the bride's foot touched the threshold the bell swung heavily in the tower above her, and sent forth its deepest knell. The vibrations died away and returned with prolonged solemnity, as she entered the body of the church.

"Good heavens! what an omen," whispered a young lady to her lover.

"On my honor," replied the gentleman, "I believe the bell has the good taste to toll of its own accord. What has she to do with weddings? If you, dearest Julia, were approaching the altar the bell would ring out its merriest peal. It has only a funeral knell for her."

The bride and most of her company had been too much occupied with the bustle of entrance to hear the first boding stroke of the bell, or at least to reflect on the singularity of such a welcome to the altar. They therefore continued to advance with undiminished gayety. The gorgeous dresses of the time, the crimson velvet coats, the gold-laced hats, the hoop petticoats, the silk, satin, brocade, and embroidery, the buckles, canes, and swords, all displayed to the best advantage on persons suited to such finery, made the group appear more like a bright-colored picture than anything real. But by what perversity of taste had the artist represented his principal figure as so wrinkled and decayed, while yet he had decked her out in the brightest splendor of attire, as if the loveliest maiden had suddenly withered into age, and become a moral to the beautiful around her! On they went, however, and had glittered along about a third of the aisle, when another stroke of the bell seemed to fill the church with a visible gloom, dimming and obscuring the bright pageant, till it shone forth again as from a mist.

This time the party wavered, stopped, and huddled closer together, while a slight scream was heard from some of the ladies, and a confused whispering among the gentlemen. Thus tossing to and fro, they might have been fancifully compared to a splendid bunch of flowers, suddenly shaken by a puff of wind, which threatened to scatter the leaves of an old, brown, withered rose, on the same stalk with two dewy buds, — such being the emblem of the widow between her fair young bridesmaids. But her heroism was admirable. She had started with an irrepressible shudder, as if the stroke of the bell had fallen directly on her heart; then, recovering herself, while her attendants were yet in dismay, she took the lead, and paced calmly up the aisle. The bell continued to swing, strike, and vibrate, with the same doleful regularity as when a corpse is on its way to the tomb.

"My young friends here have their nerves a little shaken," said the widow, with a smile, to the clergyman at the altar. "But so many weddings have been ushered in with the merriest peal of the bells, and yet turned out unhappily, that I shall hope for better fortune under such different auspices."

"Madam," answered the rector, in great perplexity, "this strange occurrence brings to my mind a marriage sermon of the famous Bishop Taylor, wherein he mingles so many thoughts of mortality and future woe, that, to speak somewhat after his own rich style, he seems to hang the bridal chamber in black, and cut the wedding garment out of a coffin pall. And it has been the custom of divers nations to infuse something of sadness into their marriage ceremonies, so to keep death in mind while contracting that engagement which is life's chiefest business. Thus we may draw a sad but profitable moral from this funeral knell."

But, though the clergyman might have given his moral even a keener point, he did not fail to dispatch an attendant to inquire into the mystery, and stop those sounds, so dismally appropriate to such a marriage. A brief space elapsed, during which the silence was broken only by whispers, and a few suppressed titterings, among the wedding party and the spectators, who, after the first shock, were disposed to draw an ill-natured merriment from the affair. The young have less charity for aged follies than the old for those of youth. The widow's glance was observed to wander, for an instant, towards a window of the church, as if searching for the time-worn marble that she had dedicated to her first husband; then her eyelids dropped over their faded orbs, and her thoughts were drawn irresistibly to another grave. Two buried men, with a voice at her ear, and a cry afar off, were calling her to lie down beside them. Perhaps, with momentary truth of feeling, she thought how much happier had been her fate, if, after years of bliss, the bell were now tolling for her funeral, and she were followed to the grave by the old affection of her earliest lover, long her husband. But why had she returned to him, when their cold hearts shrank from each other's embrace?

Still the death-bell tolled so mournfully, that the sunshine seemed to fade in the air. A whisper, communicated from those who stood nearest the windows, now spread through the church; a hearse, with a train of several coaches, was creeping along the street, conveying some dead man to the churchyard, while the bride awaited a living one at the altar. Immediately after, the footsteps of the bridegroom and his friends were heard at the door. The widow looked down the aisle, and clinched the arm of one of her bridemaids in her bony hand with such unconscious violence, that the fair girl trembled.

"You frighten me, my dear madam!" cried she. "For Heaven's sake, what is the matter?"

"Nothing, my dear, nothing," said the widow; then, whispering close to her ear, "There is a foolish fancy that I cannot get rid of. I am expecting my bridegroom to come into the church, with my first two husbands for groomsmen!"

"Look, look!" screamed the bridemaid. "What is here? The funeral!"

As she spoke, a dark procession paced into the

church. First came an old man and woman, like chief mourners at a funeral, attired from head to foot in the deepest black, all but their pale features and hoary hair; he leaning on a staff, and supporting her decrepit form with his nerveless arm. Behind appeared another, and another pair, as aged, as black, and mournful as the first. As they drew near, the widow recognized in every face some trait of former friends, long forgotten, but now returning, as if from their old graves, to warn her to prepare a shroud; or, with purpose almost as unwelcome, to exhibit their wrinkles and infirmity, and claim her as their companion by the tokens of her own decay. Many a merry night had she danced with them, in youth. And now, in joyless age, she felt that some withered partner should request her hand, and all unite, in a dance of death, to the music of the funeral bell.

While these aged mourners were passing up the aisle, it was observed that, from pew to pew, the spectators shuddered with irrepressible awe, as some object, hitherto concealed by the intervening figures, came full in sight. Many turned away their faces; others kept a fixed and rigid stare; and a young girl giggled hysterically, and fainted with the laughter on her lips. When the spectral procession approached the altar, each couple separated, and slowly diverged, till, in the centre, appeared a form, that had been worthily ushered in with all this gloomy pomp, the death knell, and the funeral. It was the bridegroom in his shroud!

No garb but that of the grave could have befitted such a deathlike aspect; the eyes, indeed, had the wild gleam of a sepulchral lamp; all else was fixed in the stern calmness which old men wear in the coffin.

The corpse stood motionless, but addressed the widow in accents that seemed to melt into the clang of the bell, which fell heavily on the air while he spoke.

"Come, my bride!" said those pale lips, "the hearse is ready. The sexton stands waiting for us at the door of the tomb. Let us be married; and then to our coffins!"

How shall the widow's horror be represented? It gave her the ghastliness of a dead man's bride. Her youthful friends stood apart, shuddering at the mourners, the shrouded bridegroom, and herself; the whole scene expressed, by the strongest imagery, the vain struggle of the gilded vanities of this world, when opposed to age, infirmity, sorrow, and death. The awe-struck silence was first broken by the clergyman.

"Mr. Ellenwood," said he, soothingly, yet with somewhat of authority, "you are not well. Your mind has been agitated by the unusual circumstances in which you are placed. The ceremony must be deferred. As an old friend, let me entreat you to return home."

"Home! yes, but not without my bride," answered he, in the same hollow accents. "You deem this mockery; perhaps madness. Had I bedizened my aged and broken frame with scarlet and embroidery — had I forced my withered lips to smile at my dead heart — that might have been mockery, or madness. But now, let young and old declare, which of us has come hither without a wedding garment, the bridegroom or the bride!"

He stepped forward at a ghostly pace, and stood beside the widow, contrasting the awful simplicity of his shroud with the glare and glitter in which she had arrayed herself for this unhappy scene. None, that

beheld them, could deny the terrible strength of the
moral which his disordered intellect had contrived to
draw.

"Cruel! cruel!" groaned the heart-stricken bride.

"Cruel!" repeated he; then, losing his deathlike
composure in a wild bitterness: "Heaven judge
which of us has been cruel to the other! In youth
you deprived me of my happiness, my hopes, my aims;
you took away all the substance of my life, and made
it a dream without reality enough even to grieve at —
with only a pervading gloom, through which I walked
wearily, and cared not whither. But after forty years,
when I have built my tomb, and would not give up
the thought of resting there — no, not for such a life
as we once pictured — you call me to the altar. At
your summons I am here. But other husbands have
enjoyed your youth, your beauty, your warmth of
heart, and all that could be termed your life. What
is there for me but your decay and death? And
therefore I have bidden these funeral friends, and bespoken the sexton's deepest knell, and am come, in my
shroud, to wed you, as with a burial service, that we
may join our hands at the door of the sepulchre, and
enter it together."

It was not frenzy; it was not merely the drunkenness of strong emotion, in a heart unused to it, that
now wrought upon the bride. The stern lesson of the
day had done its work; her worldliness was gone.
She seized the bridegroom's hand.

"Yes!" cried she. "Let us wed, even at the door
of the sepulchre! My life is gone in vanity and
emptiness. But at its close there is one true feeling.
It has made me what I was in youth; it makes me
worthy of you. Time is no more for both of us. Let
us wed for Eternity!"

With a long and deep regard, the bridegroom looked into her eyes, while a tear was gathering in his own. How strange that gush of human feeling from the frozen bosom of a corpse! He wiped away the tears even with his shroud.

"Beloved of my youth," said he, "I have been wild. The despair of my whole lifetime had returned at once, and maddened me. Forgive; and be forgiven. Yes; it is evening with us now; and we have realized none of our morning dreams of happiness. But let us join our hands before the altar, as lovers whom adverse circumstances have separated through life, yet who meet again as they are leaving it, and find their earthly affection changed into something holy as religion. And what is Time, to the married of Eternity?"

Amid the tears of many, and a swell of exalted sentiment, in those who felt aright, was solemnized the union of two immortal souls. The train of withered mourners, the hoary bridegroom in his shroud, the pale features of the aged bride, and the death-bell tolling through the whole, till its deep voice overpowered the marriage words, all marked the funeral of earthly hopes. But as the ceremony proceeded, the organ, as if stirred by the sympathies of this impressive scene, poured forth an anthem, first mingling with the dismal knell, then rising to a loftier strain, till the soul looked down upon its woe. And when the awful rite was finished, and with cold hand in cold hand, the Married of Eternity withdrew, the organ's peal of solemn triumph drowned the Wedding Knell

THE MINISTER'S BLACK VEIL

A PARABLE.[1]

THE sexton stood in the porch of Milford meeting
house, pulling busily at the bell-rope. The old people of the village came stooping along the street.
Children, with bright faces, tripped merrily beside
their parents, or mimicked a graver gait, in the conscious dignity of their Sunday clothes. Spruce bachelors looked sidelong at the pretty maidens, and fancied that the Sabbath sunshine made them prettier
than on week days. When the throng had mostly
streamed into the porch, the sexton began to toll the
bell, keeping his eye on the Reverend Mr. Hooper's
door. The first glimpse of the clergyman's figure was
the signal for the bell to cease its summons.

"But what has good Parson Hooper got upon his
face?" cried the sexton in astonishment.

All within hearing immediately turned about, and
beheld the semblance of Mr. Hooper, pacing slowly
his meditative way towards the meeting-house. With
one accord they started, expressing more wonder than
if some strange minister were coming to dust the
cushions of Mr. Hooper's pulpit.

[1] Another clergyman in New England, Mr. Joseph Moody, of York,
Maine, who died about eighty years since, made himself remarkable
by the same eccentricity that is here related of the Reverend Mr.
Hooper. In his case, however, the symbol had a different import.
In early life he had accidentally killed a beloved friend; and from
that day till the hour of his own death, he hid his face from men.

"Are you sure it is our parson?" inquired Good-man Gray of the sexton.

"Of a certainty it is good Mr. Hooper," replied the sexton. "He was to have exchanged pulpits with Parson Shute, of Westbury; but Parson Shute sent to excuse himself yesterday, being to preach a funeral sermon."

The cause of so much amazement may appear suffi-ciently slight. Mr. Hooper, a gentlemanly person, of about thirty, though still a bachelor, was dressed with due clerical neatness, as if a careful wife had starched his band, and brushed the weekly dust from his Sun-day's garb. There was but one thing remarkable in his appearance. Swathed about his forehead, and hanging down over his face, so low as to be shaken by his breath, Mr. Hooper had on a black veil. On a nearer view it seemed to consist of two folds of crape, which entirely concealed his features, except the mouth and chin, but probably did not intercept his sight, further than to give a darkened aspect to all living and inanimate things. With this gloomy shade before him, good Mr. Hooper walked onward, at a slow and quiet pace, stooping somewhat, and look-ing on the ground, as is customary with abstracted men, yet nodding kindly to those of his parishioners who still waited on the meeting-house steps. But so wonder-struck were they that his greeting hardly met with a return.

"I can't really feel as if good Mr. Hooper's face was behind that piece of crape," said the sexton.

"I don't like it," muttered an old woman, as she hobbled into the meeting-house. "He has changed himself into something awful, only by hiding his face."

"Our parson has gone mad!" cried Goodman Gray, following him across the threshold.

A rumor of some unaccountable phenomenon had preceded Mr. Hooper into the meeting-house, and set all the congregation astir. Few could refrain from twisting their heads towards the door; many stood upright, and turned directly about; while several little boys clambered upon the seats, and came down again with a terrible racket. There was a general bustle, a rustling of the women's gowns and shuffling of the men's feet, greatly at variance with that hushed repose which should attend the entrance of the minister. But Mr. Hooper appeared not to notice the perturbation of his people. He entered with an almost noiseless step, bent his head mildly to the pews on each side, and bowed as he passed his oldest parishioner, a white-haired great-grandsire, who occupied an arm-chair in the centre of the aisle. It was strange to observe how slowly this venerable man became conscious of something singular in the appearance of his pastor. He seemed not fully to partake of the prevailing wonder, till Mr. Hooper had ascended the stairs, and showed himself in the pulpit, face to face with his congregation, except for the black veil. That mysterious emblem was never once withdrawn. It shook with his measured breath, as he gave out the psalm; it threw its obscurity between him and the holy page, as he read the Scriptures; and while he prayed, the veil lay heavily on his uplifted countenance. Did he seek to hide it from the dread Being whom he was addressing?

Such was the effect of this simple piece of crape, that more than one woman of delicate nerves was forced to leave the meeting-house. Yet perhaps the pale-faced congregation was almost as fearful a sight to the minister, as his black veil to them.

Mr. Hooper had the reputation of a good preacher, but not an energetic one : he strove to win his people heavenward by mild, persuasive influences, rather than to drive them thither by the thunders of the Word. The sermon which he now delivered was marked by the same characteristics of style and manner as the general series of his pulpit oratory. But there was something, either in the sentiment of the discourse it-self, or in the imagination of the auditors, which made it greatly the most powerful effort that they had ever heard from their pastor's lips. It was tinged, rather more darkly than usual, with the gentle gloom of Mr. Hooper's temperament. The subject had reference to secret sin, and those sad mysteries which we hide from our nearest and dearest, and would fain conceal from our own consciousness, even forgetting that the Omnis-cient can detect them. A subtle power was breathed into his words. Each member of the congregation, the most innocent girl, and the man of hardened breast, felt as if the preacher had crept upon them, behind his awful veil, and discovered their hoarded in-iquity of deed or thought. Many spread their clasped hands on their bosoms. There was nothing terrible in what Mr. Hooper said, at least, no violence ; and yet, with every tremor of his melancholy voice, the hearers quaked. An unsought pathos came hand in hand with awe. So sensible were the audience of some unwonted attribute in their minister, that they longed for a breath of wind to blow aside the veil, al-most believing that a stranger's visage would be dis-covered, though the form, gesture, and voice were those of Mr. Hooper.

At the close of the services, the people hurried out with indecorous confusion, eager to communicate their

pent-up amazement, and conscious of lighter spirits
the moment they lost sight of the black veil. Some
gathered in little circles, huddled closely together, with
their mouths all whispering in the centre; some went
homeward alone, wrapt in silent meditation; some
talked loudly, and profaned the Sabbath day with os
tentatious laughter. A few shook their sagacious
heads, intimating that they could penetrate the mystery; while one or two affirmed that there was no
mystery at all, but only that Mr. Hooper's eyes were
so weakened by the midnight lamp, as to require a
shade. After a brief interval, forth came good Mr.
Hooper also, in the rear of his flock. Turning his
veiled face from one group to another, he paid due
reverence to the hoary heads, saluted the middle aged
with kind dignity as their friend and spiritual guide,
greeted the young with mingled authority and love,
and laid his hands on the little children's heads to
bless them. Such was always his custom on the Sabbath day. Strange and bewildered looks repaid him
for his courtesy. None, as on former occasions, as-
pired to the honor of walking by their pastor's side.
Old Squire Saunders, doubtless by an accidental lapse
of memory, neglected to invite Mr. Hooper to his table, where the good clergyman had been wont to bless
the food, almost every Sunday since his settlement.
He returned, therefore, to the parsonage, and, at the
moment of closing the door, was observed to look back
upon the people, all of whom had their eyes fixed upon
the minister. A sad smile gleamed faintly from beneath the black veil, and flickered about his mouth,
glimmering as he disappeared.

"How strange," said a lady, "that a simple black
veil, such as any woman might wear on her bonnet,

should become such a terrible thing on Mr. Hooper's face!"

"Something must surely be amiss with Mr. Hooper's intellects," observed her husband, the physician of the village. "But the strangest part of the affair is the effect of this vagary, even on a sober-minded man like myself. The black veil, though it covers only our pastor's face, throws its influence over his whole person, and makes him ghostlike from head to foot. Do you not feel it so?"

"Truly do I," replied the lady; "and I would not be alone with him for the world. I wonder he is not afraid to be alone with himself!"

"Men sometimes are so," said her husband.

The afternoon service was attended with similar circumstances. At its conclusion, the bell tolled for the funeral of a young lady. The relatives and friends were assembled in the house, and the more distant acquaintances stood about the door, speaking of the good qualities of the deceased, when their talk was interrupted by the appearance of Mr. Hooper, still covered with his black veil. It was now an appropriate emblem. The clergyman stepped into the room where the corpse was laid, and bent over the coffin, to take a last farewell of his deceased parishioner. As he stooped, the veil hung straight down from his forehead, so that, if her eyelids had not been closed for ever, the dead maiden might have seen his face. Could Mr. Hooper be fearful of her glance, that he so hastily caught back the black veil? A person who watched the interview between the dead and living, scrupled not to affirm, that, at the instant when the clergyman's features were disclosed, the corpse had slightly shuddered, rustling the shroud and muslin cap. though the countenance retained the composure of death. **A** superstitious old woman was the only witness of this prodigy. From the coffin Mr. Hooper passed into the chamber of the mourners, and thence to the head of the staircase, to make the funeral prayer. It was a tender and heart-dissolving prayer, full of sorrow, yet so imbued with celestial hopes, that the music of a heavenly harp, swept by the fingers of the dead, seemed faintly to be heard among the saddest accents of the minister. The people trembled, though they but darkly understood him when he prayed that they, and himself, and all of mortal race, might be ready, as he trusted this young maiden had been, for the dreadful hour that should snatch the veil from their faces. The bearers went heavily forth, and the mourners followed, saddening all the street, with the dead before them, and Mr. Hooper in his black veil behind.

" Why do you look back? " said one in the procession to his partner.

" I had a fancy," replied she, " that the minister and the maiden's spirit were walking hand in hand."

" And so had I, at the same moment," said the other.

That night, the handsomest couple in Milford village were to be joined in wedlock. Though reckoned a melancholy man, Mr. Hooper had a placid cheerfulness for such occasions, which often excited a sympathetic smile where livelier merriment would have been thrown away. There was no quality of his disposition which made him more beloved than this. The company at the wedding awaited his arrival with impatience, trusting that the strange awe, which had gathered over him throughout the day, would now be dispelled. But such was not the result. When Mr. Hooper came, the

first thing that their eyes rested on was the same horrible black veil, which had added deeper gloom to the
funeral, and could portend nothing but evil to the
wedding. Such was its immediate effect on the guests
that a cloud seemed to have rolled duskily from beneath the black crape, and dimmed the light of the
candles. The bridal pair stood up before the minister.
But the bride's cold fingers quivered in the tremulous
hand of the bridegroom, and her deathlike paleness
caused a whisper that the maiden who had been buried
a few hours before was come from her grave to be
married. If ever another wedding were so dismal, it
was that famous one where they tolled the wedding
knell. After performing the ceremony, Mr. Hooper
raised a glass of wine to his lips, wishing happiness to
the new-married couple in a strain of mild pleasantry
that ought to have brightened the features of the
guests, like a cheerful gleam from the hearth. At
that instant, catching a glimpse of his figure in the
looking-glass, the black veil involved his own spirit in
the horror with which it overwhelmed all others. His
frame shuddered, his lips grew white, he spilt the un-
tasted wine upon the carpet, and rushed forth into
the darkness. For the Earth, too, had on her Black
Veil.

The next day, the whole village of Milford talked
of little else than Parson Hooper's black veil. That
and the mystery concealed behind it, supplied a topic
for discussion between acquaintances meeting in the
street, and good women gossiping at their open windows. It was the first item of news that the tavern-
keeper told to his guests. The children babbled of it
on their way to school. One imitative little imp covered his face with an old black handkerchief, thereby

so affrighting his playmates that the panic seized himself, and he well-nigh lost his wits by his own waggery.

It was remarkable that of all the busybodies and
impertinent people in the parish, not one ventured to
put the plain question to Mr. Hooper, wherefore he
did this thing. Hitherto, whenever there appeared
the slightest call for such interference, he had never
lacked advisers, nor shown himself averse to be guided
by their judgment. If he erred at all, it was by so
painful a degree of self-distrust, that even the mildest
censure would lead him to consider an indifferent action as a crime. Yet, though so well acquainted with
this amiable weakness, no individual among his parishioners chose to make the black veil a subject of
friendly remonstrance. There was a feeling of dread,
neither plainly confessed nor carefully concealed, which
caused each to shift the responsibility upon another,
till at length it was found expedient to send a deputa-
tion of the church, in order to deal with Mr. Hooper
about the mystery, before it should grow into a scandal. Never did an embassy so ill discharge its duties.
The minister received them with friendly courtesy, but
became silent, after they were seated, leaving to his visitors the whole burden of introducing their important
business. The topic, it might be supposed, was obvious enough. There was the black veil swathed round
Mr. Hooper's forehead, and concealing every feature
above his placid mouth, on which, at times, they could
perceive the glimmering of a melancholy smile. But
that piece of crape, to their imagination, seemed to
hang down before his heart, the symbol of a fearful
secret between him and them. Were the veil but cast
aside, they might speak freely of it, but not till then.
Thus they sat a considerable time, speechless, confused,

and shrinking uneasily from Mr. Hooper's eye, which they felt to be fixed upon them with an invisible glance. Finally, the deputies returned abashed to their constituents, pronouncing the matter too weighty to be handled, except by a council of the churches, if, indeed, it might not require a general synod.

But there was one person in the village unappalled by the awe with which the black veil had impressed all beside herself. When the deputies returned without an explanation, or even venturing to demand one, she, with the calm energy of her character, determined to chase away the strange cloud that appeared to be settling round Mr. Hooper, every moment more darkly than before. As his plighted wife, it should be her privilege to know what the black veil concealed. At the minister's first visit, therefore, she entered upon the subject with a direct simplicity, which made the task easier both for him and her. After he had seated himself, she fixed her eyes steadfastly upon the veil, but could discern nothing of the dreadful gloom that had so overawed the multitude: it was but a double fold of crape, hanging down from his forehead to his mouth, and slightly stirring with his breath.

"No," said she aloud, and smiling, "there is nothing terrible in this piece of crape, except that it hides a face which I am always glad to look upon. Come, good sir, let the sun shine from behind the cloud. First lay aside your black veil: then tell me why you put it on."

Mr. Hooper's smile glimmered faintly.

"There is an hour to come," said he, "when all of us shall cast aside our veils. Take it not amiss, beloved friend, if I wear this piece of crape till then."

"Your words are a mystery, too," returned the

young lady. "Take away the veil from them, at least."

"Elizabeth, I will," said he, "so far as my vow may suffer me. Know, then, this veil is a type and a symbol, and I am bound to wear it ever, both in light and darkness, in solitude and before the gaze of multitudes, and as with strangers, so with my familiar friends. No mortal eye will see it withdrawn. This dismal shade must separate me from the world: even you, Elizabeth, can never come behind it!"

"What grievous affliction hath befallen you," she earnestly inquired, "that you should thus darken your eyes forever?"

"If it be a sign of mourning," replied Mr. Hooper, "I, perhaps, like most other mortals, have sorrows dark enough to be typified by a black veil."

"But what if the world will not believe that it is the type of an innocent sorrow?" urged Elizabeth. "Beloved and respected as you are, there may be whispers that you hide your face under the consciousness of secret sin. For the sake of your holy office, do away this scandal!"

The color rose into her cheeks as she intimated the nature of the rumors that were already abroad in the village. But Mr. Hooper's mildness did not forsake him. He even smiled again — that same sad smile, which always appeared like a faint glimmering of light, proceeding from the obscurity beneath the veil.

"If I hide my face for sorrow, there is cause enough," he merely replied; "and if I cover it for secret sin, what mortal might not do the same?"

And with this gentle, but unconquerable obstinacy did he resist all her entreaties. At length Elizabeth sat silent. For a few moments she appeared lost in thought, considering, probably, what new methods might be tried to withdraw her lover from so dark a fantasy, which, if it had no other meaning, was perhaps a symptom of mental disease. Though of a firmer character than his own, the tears rolled down her cheeks. But, in an instant, as it were, a new feeling took the place of sorrow: her eyes were fixed insensibly on the black veil, when, like a sudden twilight in the air, its terrors fell around her. She arose, and stood trembling before him.

"And do you feel it then, at last?" said he mournfully.

She made no reply, but covered her eyes with her hand, and turned to leave the room. He rushed forward and caught her arm.

"Have patience with me, Elizabeth!" cried he, passionately. "Do not desert me, though this veil must be between us here on earth. Be mine, and hereafter there shall be no veil over my face, no darkness between our souls! It is but a mortal veil—it is not for eternity! O! you know not how lonely I am, and how frightened, to be alone behind my black veil. Do not leave me in this miserable obscurity forever!"

"Lift the veil but once, and look me in the face," said she.

"Never! It cannot be!" replied Mr. Hooper.

"Then farewell!" said Elizabeth.

She withdrew her arm from his grasp, and slowly departed, pausing at the door, to give one long shuddering gaze, that seemed almost to penetrate the mystery of the black veil. But, even amid his grief, Mr. Hooper smiled to think that only a material emblem had separated him from happiness, though the hor rors, which it shadowed forth, must be drawn darkly between the fondest of lovers.

From that time no attempts were made to remove Mr. Hooper's black veil, or, by a direct appeal, to discover the secret which it was supposed to hide. By persons who claimed a superiority to popular prejudice, it was reckoned merely an eccentric whim, such as often mingles with the sober actions of men otherwise rational, and tinges them all with its own semblance of insanity. But with the multitude, good Mr. Hooper was irreparably a bugbear. He could not walk the street with any peace of mind, so conscious was he that the gentle and timid would turn aside to avoid him, and that others would make it a point of hardihood to throw themselves in his way. The impertinence of the latter class compelled him to give up his customary walk at sunset to the burial ground; for when he leaned pensively over the gate, there would always be faces behind the gravestones, peeping at his black veil. A fable went the rounds that the stare of the dead people drove him thence. It grieved him, to the very depth of his kind heart, to observe how the children fled from his approach, breaking up their merriest sports, while his melancholy figure was yet afar off. Their instinctive dread caused him to feel more strongly than aught else, that a preternatural horror was interwoven with the threads of the black crape. In truth, his own antipathy to the veil was known to be so great, that he never willingly passed before a mirror, nor stooped to drink at a still fountain, lest, in its peaceful bosom, he should be affrighted by himself. This was what gave plausibility to the whispers, that Mr. Hooper's conscience tortured him for some great crime too horrible to be

entirely concealed, or otherwise than so obscurely intimated. Thus, from beneath the black veil, there
rolled a cloud into the sunshine, an ambiguity of sin
or sorrow, which enveloped the poor minister, so that
love or sympathy could never reach him. It was said
that ghost and fiend consorted with him there. With
self-shudderings and outward terrors, he walked continually in its shadow, groping darkly within his own
soul, or gazing through a medium that saddened the
whole world. Even the lawless wind, it was believed,
respected his dreadful secret, and never blew aside the
veil. But still good Mr. Hooper sadly smiled at the
pale visages of the worldly throng as he passed by.

Among all its bad influences, the black veil had the
one desirable effect, of making its wearer a very efficient clergyman. By the aid of his mysterious emblem
— for there was no other apparent cause — he became
a man of awful power over souls that were in agony
for sin. His converts always regarded him with a
dread peculiar to themselves, affirming, though but
figuratively, that, before he brought them to celestial
light, they had been with him behind the black veil.
Its gloom, indeed, enabled him to sympathize with all
dark affections. Dying sinners cried aloud for Mr.
Hooper, and would not yield their breath till he appeared; though ever, as he stooped to whisper consolation, they shuddered at the veiled face so near their
own. Such were the terrors of the black veil, even
when Death had bared his visage! Strangers came
long distances to attend service at his church, with the
mere idle purpose of gazing at his figure, because it
was forbidden them to behold his face. But many
were made to quake ere they departed! Once, during
Governor Belcher's administration, Mr. Hooper was

appointed to preach the election sermon. Covered
with his black veil, he stood before the chief magistrate, the council, and the representatives, and wrought
so deep an impression, that the legislative measures
of that year were characterized by all the gloom and
piety of our earliest ancestral sway.

In this manner Mr. Hooper spent a long life, irre-
proachable in outward act, yet shrouded in dismal sus-
picions; kind and loving, though unloved, and dimly
feared; a man apart from men, shunned in their
health and joy, but ever summoned to their aid in
mortal anguish. As years wore on, shedding their
snows above his sable veil, he acquired a name
throughout the New England churches, and they called
him Father Hooper. Nearly all his parishioners, who
were of mature age when he was settled, had been
borne away by many a funeral: he had one congregation in the church, and a more crowded one in the
churchyard; and having wrought so late into the
evening, and done his work so well, it was now good
Father Hooper's turn to rest.

Several persons were visible by the shaded candle-
light, in the death chamber of the old clergyman.
Natural connections he had none. But there was the
decorously grave, though unmoved physician, seeking
only to mitigate the last pangs of the patient whom
he could not save. There were the deacons, and other
eminently pious members of his church. There, also,
was the Reverend Mr. Clark, of Westbury, a young
and zealous divine, who had ridden in haste to pray
by the bedside of the expiring minister. There was
the nurse, no hired handmaiden of death, but one
whose calm affection had endured thus long in secrecy,
in solitude, amid the chill of age, and would not per-

ish, even at the dying hour. Who, but Elizabeth!
And there lay the hoary head of good Father Hooper
upon the death pillow, with the black veil still swathed
about his brow, and reaching down over his face, so
that each more difficult gasp of his faint breath caused
it to stir. All through life that piece of crape had
hung between him and the world: it had separated
him from cheerful brotherhood and woman's love, and
kept him in that saddest of all prisons, his own heart;
and still it lay upon his face, as if to deepen the
gloom of his darksome chamber, and shade him from
the sunshine of eternity.

For some time previous, his mind had been confused, wavering doubtfully between the past and the
present, and hovering forward, as it were, at intervals,
into the indistinctness of the world to come. There
had been feverish turns, which tossed him from side
to side, and wore away what little strength he had.
But in his most convulsive struggles, and in the wildest vagaries of his intellect, when no other thought
retained its sober influence, he still showed an awful
solicitude lest the black veil should slip aside. Even
if his bewildered soul could have forgotten, there was
a faithful woman at his pillow, who, with averted eyes,
would have covered that aged face, which she had last
beheld in the comeliness of manhood. At length the
death-stricken old man lay quietly in the torpor of
mental and bodily exhaustion, with an imperceptible
pulse, and breath that grew fainter and fainter, except
when a long, deep, and irregular inspiration seemed
to prelude the flight of his spirit.

The minister of Westbury approached the bedside.

"Venerable Father Hooper," said he, "the moment
of your release is at hand. Are you ready for the lift
ing of the veil that shuts in time from eternity?"

Father Hooper at first replied merely by a feeble motion of his head; then, apprehensive, perhaps, that his meaning might be doubtful, he exerted himself to speak.

"Yea," said he, in faint accents, "my soul hath a patient weariness until that veil be lifted."

"And is it fitting," resumed the Reverend Mr. Clark, "that a man so given to prayer, of such a blameless example, holy in deed and thought, so far as mortal judgment may pronounce; is it fitting that a father in the church should leave a shadow on his memory, that may seem to blacken a life so pure? I pray you, my venerable brother, let not this thing be! Suffer us to be gladdened by your triumphant aspect as you go to your reward. Before the veil of eternity be lifted, let me cast aside this black veil from your face!"

And thus speaking, the Reverend Mr. Clark bent forward to reveal the mystery of so many years. But, exerting a sudden energy, that made all the beholders stand aghast, Father Hooper snatched both his hands from beneath the bedclothes, and pressed them strongly on the black veil, resolute to struggle, if the minister of Westbury would contend with a dying man.

"Never!" cried the veiled clergyman. "On earth, never!"

"Dark old man!" exclaimed the affrighted minister "with what horrible crime upon your soul are you now passing to the judgment?"

Father Hooper's breath heaved; it rattled in his throat; but, with a mighty effort, grasping forward with his hands, he caught hold of life, and held it back till he should speak. He even raised himself in bed; and there he sat, shivering with the arms of death around him, while the black veil hung down, awful, at that last moment, in the gathered terrors of a lifetime. And yet the faint, sad smile, so often there, now seemed to glimmer from its obscurity, and linger on Father Hooper's lips.

"Why do you tremble at me alone?" cried he, turning his veiled face round the circle of pale spectators. "Tremble also at each other! Have men avoided me, and women shown no pity, and children screamed and fled, only for my black veil? What, but the mystery which it obscurely typifies, has made this piece of crape so awful? When the friend shows his inmost heart to his friend; the lover to his best beloved; when man does not vainly shrink from the eye of his Creator, loathsomely treasuring up the secret of his sin; then deem me a monster, for the symbol beneath which I have lived, and die! I look around me, and, lo! on every visage a Black Veil!"

While his auditors shrank from one another, in mutual affright, Father Hooper fell back upon his pillow, a veiled corpse, with a faint smile lingering on the lips. Still veiled, they laid him in his coffin, and a veiled corpse they bore him to the grave. The grass of many years has sprung up and withered on that grave, the burial stone is moss-grown, and good Mr. Hooper's face is dust; but awful is still the thought that it mouldered beneath the Black Veil!

THE MAYPOLE OF MERRY MOUNT.

There is an admirable foundation for a philosophic romance in the curious history of the early settlement of Mount Wollaston, or Merry Mount. In the slight sketch here attempted, the facts, recorded on the grave pages of our New England annalists, have wrought themselves, almost spontaneously, into a sort of allegory. The masques, mummeries, and festive customs, described in the text, are in accordance with the manners of the age. Authority on these points may be found in Strutt's Book of English Sports and Pastimes.

BRIGHT were the days at Merry Mount, when the Maypole was the banner staff of that gay colony' They who reared it, should their banner be triumph ant, were to pour sunshine over New England's rugged hills, and scatter flower seeds throughout the soil. Jollity and gloom were contending for an empire. Midsummer eve had come, bringing deep verdure to the forest, and roses in her lap, of a more vivid hue than the tender buds of Spring. But May, or her mirthful spirit, dwelt all the year round at Merry Mount, sporting with the Summer months, and revelling with Autumn, and basking in the glow of Winter's fireside. Through a world of toil and care she flitted with a dreamlike smile, and came hither to find a home among the lightsome hearts of Merry Mount.

Never had the Maypole been so gayly decked as at sunset on midsummer eve. This venerated emblem was a pine-tree, which had preserved the slender grace of youth, while it equalled the loftiest height of the old wood monarchs. From its top streamed a silken banner, colored like the rainbow. Down nearly to the ground the pole was dressed with birchen boughs, and others of the liveliest green, and some with silvery leaves, fastened by ribbons that fluttered in fantastic knots of twenty different colors, but no sad ones. Garden flowers, and blossoms of the wilderness, laughed gladly forth amid the verdure, so fresh and dewy that they must have grown by magic on that happy pine-tree. Where this green and flowery splendor terminated, the shaft of the Maypole was stained with the seven brilliant hues of the banner at its top. On the lowest green bough hung an abundant wreath of roses, some that had been gathered in the sunniest spots of the forest, and others, of still richer blush, which the colonists had reared from English seed. O, people of the Golden Age, the chief of your husbandry was to raise flowers!

But what was the wild throng that stood hand in hand about the Maypole? It could not be that the fauns and nymphs, when driven from their classic groves and homes of ancient fable, had sought refuge, as all the persecuted did, in the fresh woods of the West. These were Gothic monsters, though perhaps of Grecian ancestry. On the shoulders of a comely youth uprose the head and branching antlers of a stag; a second, human in all other points, had the grim visage of a wolf; a third, still with the trunk and limbs of a mortal man, showed the beard and horns of a venerable he-goat. There was the likeness of a bear erect, brute in all but his hind legs, which were adorned with pink silk stockings. And here again, almost as wondrous, stood a real bear of the dark forest, lending each of his fore paws to the grasp of a human hand, and as ready for the dance as any in that circle. His inferior nature rose half way, to meet his companions as they stooped. Other faces wore the similitude of man or woman, but distorted or extravagant, with red noses pendulous before their mouths, which seemed of awful depth, and stretched from ear to ear in an eternal fit of laughter. Here might be seen the Salvage Man, well known in her-aldry, hairy as a baboon, and girdled with green leaves. By his side, a noble figure, but still a counterfeit, appeared an Indian hunter, with feathery crest and wampum belt. Many of this strange company wore foolscaps, and had little bells appended to their garments, tinkling with a silvery sound, responsive to the inaudible music of their gleesome spirits. Some youths and maidens were of soberer garb, yet well maintained their places in the irregular throng by the expression of wild revelry upon their features. Such were the colonists of Merry Mount, as they stood in the broad smile of sunset round their venerated Maypole.

Had a wanderer, bewildered in the melancholy forest, heard their mirth, and stolen a half-affrighted glance, he might have fancied them the crew of Comus, some already transformed to brutes, some midway between man and beast, and the others rioting in the flow of tipsy jollity that foreran the change. But a band of Puritans, who watched the scene, invisible themselves, compared the masques to those devils and ruined souls with whom their superstition peopled the black wilderness.

Within the ring of monsters appeared the two airiest forms that had ever trodden on any more solid footing than a purple and golden cloud. One was a youth in glistening apparel, with a scarf of the rainbow pattern crosswise on his breast. His right hand held a gilded staff, the ensign of high dignity among the revellers, and his left grasped the slender fingers of a fair maiden, not less gayly decorated than himself. Bright roses glowed in contrast with the dark and glossy curls of each, and were scattered round their feet, or had sprung up spontaneously there. Behind this lightsome couple, so close to the Maypole that its boughs shaded his jovial face, stood the figure of an English priest, canonically dressed, yet decked with flowers, in heathen fashion, and wearing a chaplet of the native vine leaves. By the riot of his rolling eye, and the pagan decorations of his holy garb, he seemed the wildest monster there, and the very Comus of the crew.

"Votaries of the Maypole," cried the flower-decked priest, "merrily, all day long, have the woods echoed to your mirth. But be this your merriest hour, my hearts! Lo, here stand the Lord and Lady of the May, whom I, a clerk of Oxford, and high priest of Merry Mount, am presently to join in holy matrimony. Up with your nimble spirits, ye morris-dancers, green men, and glee maidens, bears and wolves, and horned gentlemen! Come; a chorus now, rich with the old mirth of Merry England, and the wilder glee of this fresh forest; and then a dance, to show the youthful pair what life is made of, and how airily they should go through it! All ye that love the Maypole, lend your voices to the nuptial song of the Lord and Lady of the May!"

This wedlock was more serious than most affairs of Merry Mount, where jest and delusion, trick and fantasy, kept up a continual carnival. The Lord and Lady of the May, though their titles must be laid down at sunset, were really and truly to be partners for the dance of life, beginning the measure that same bright eve. The wreath of roses, that hung from the lowest green bough of the Maypole, had been twined for them, and would be thrown over both their heads, in symbol of their flowery union. When the priest had spoken, therefore, a riotous uproar burst from the rout of monstrous figures.

"Begin you the stave, reverend Sir," cried they all; "and never did the woods ring to such a merry peal as we of the Maypole shall send up!"

Immediately a prelude of pipe, cithern, and viol, touched with practised minstrelsy, began to play from a neighboring thicket, in such a mirthful cadence that the boughs of the Maypole quivered to the sound. But the May Lord, he of the gilded staff, chancing to look into his Lady's eyes, was wonder struck at the almost pensive glance that met his own.

"Edith, sweet Lady of the May," whispered he reproachfully, "is yon wreath of roses a garland to hang above our graves, that you look so sad? O, Edith, this is our golden time! Tarnish it not by any pensive shadow of the mind; for it may be that nothing of futurity will be brighter than the mere remembrance of what is now passing."

"That was the very thought that saddened me! How came it in your mind too?" said Edith, in a still lower tone than he, for it was high treason to be sad at Merry Mount. "Therefore do I sigh amid this festive music. And besides, dear Edgar, I struggle as with a dream, and fancy that these shapes of our jovial friends are visionary, and their mirth unreal, and that we are no true Lord and Lady of the May. What is the mystery in my heart?"

Just then, as if a spell had loosened them, down came a little shower of withering rose leaves from the

Maypole. Alas, for the young lovers! No sooner had their hearts glowed with real passion than they were sensible of something vague and unsubstantial in their former pleasures, and felt a dreary presentiment of inevitable change. From the moment that they truly loved, they had subjected themselves to earth's doom of care and sorrow, and troubled joy, and had no more a home at Merry Mount. That was Edith's mystery. Now leave we the priest to marry them, and the masquers to sport round the Maypole, till the last sunbeam be withdrawn from its summit, and the shadows of the forest mingle gloomily in the dance. Meanwhile, we may discover who these gay people were.

Two hundred years ago, and more, the old world and its inhabitants became mutually weary of each other. Men voyaged by thousands to the West: some to barter glass beads, and such like jewels, for the furs of the Indian hunter; some to conquer virgin empires; and one stern band to pray. But none of these motives had much weight with the colonists of Merry Mount. Their leaders were men who had sported so long with life, that when Thought and Wisdom came, even these unwelcome guests were led astray by the crowd of vanities which they should have put to flight. Erring Thought and perverted Wisdom were made to put on masques, and play the fool. The men of whom we speak, after losing the heart's fresh gayety, imagined a wild philosophy of pleasure, and came hither to act out their latest day-dream. They gathered followers from all that giddy tribe whose whole life is like the festal days of soberer men. In their train were minstrels, not unknown in London streets: wandering players, whose theatres had been the halls

of noblemen; mummers, rope-dancers, and mounte-
banks, who would long be missed at wakes, church
ales, and fairs; in a word, mirth makers of ever:
sort, such as abounded in that age, but now began to
be discountenanced by the rapid growth of Puritanism. Light had their footsteps been on land, and as
lightly they came across the sea. Many had been
maddened by their previous troubles into a gay despair; others were as madly gay in the flush of youth,
like the May Lord and his Lady; but whatever might
be the quality of their mirth, old and young were gay
at Merry Mount. The young deemed themselves
happy. The elder spirits, if they knew that mirth
was but the counterfeit of happiness, yet followed the
false shadow wilfully, because at least her garments
glittered brightest. Sworn triflers of a lifetime, they
would not venture among the sober truths of life not
even to be truly blest.

All the hereditary pastimes of Old England were
transplanted hither. The King of Christmas was duly
crowned, and the Lord of Misrule bore potent sway.
On the Eve of St. John, they felled whole acres of the
forest to make bonfires, and danced by the blaze all
night, crowned with garlands, and throwing flowers
into the flame. At harvest time, though their crop
was of the smallest, they made an image with the
sheaves of Indian corn, and wreathed it with autumna.
garlands, and bore it home triumphantly. But what
chiefly characterized the colonists of Merry Moun'
was their veneration for the Maypole. It has made
their true history a poet's tale. Spring decked the
hallowed emblem with young blossoms and fresh green
boughs; Summer brought roses of the deepest blush,
and the perfected foliage of the forest; Autumn en-

riched it with that red and yellow gorgeousness which converts each wildwood leaf into a painted flower; and Winter silvered it with sleet, and hung it round with icicles, till it flashed in the cold sunshine, itself a frozen sunbeam. Thus each alternate season did homage to the Maypole, and paid it a tribute of its own richest splendor. Its votaries danced round it, once, at least, in every month; sometimes they called it their religion, or their altar; but always, it was the banner staff of Merry Mount.

Unfortunately, there were men in the new world of a sterner faith than these Maypole worshippers. Not far from Merry Mount was a settlement of Puritans, most dismal wretches, who said their prayers before daylight, and then wrought in the forest or the cornfield till evening made it prayer time again. Their weapons were always at hand to shoot down the straggling savage. When they met in conclave, it was never to keep up the old English mirth, but to hear sermons three hours long, or to proclaim bounties on the heads of wolves and the scalps of Indians. Their festivals were fast days, and their chief pastime the singing of psalms. Woe to the youth or maiden who did but dream of a dance! The selectman nodded to the constable; and there sat the light-heeled reprobate in the stocks; or if he danced, it was round the whipping-post, which might be termed the Puritan Maypole.

A party of these grim Puritans, toiling through the difficult woods, each with a horseload of iron armor to burden his footsteps, would sometimes draw near the sunny precincts of Merry Mount. There were the silken colonists, sporting round their Maypole; perhaps teaching a bear to dance, or striving to communi-

cate their mirth to the grave Indian ; or masquerading in the skins of deer and wolves, which they had
hunted for that especial purpose. Often, the whole
colony were playing at blindman's buff, magistrates
and all, with their eyes bandaged, except a single
scapegoat, whom the blinded sinners pursued by the
tinkling of the bells at his garments. Once, it is said,
they were seen following a flower-decked corpse, with
merriment and festive music, to his grave. But did
the dead man laugh? In their quietest times, they
sang ballads and told tales, for the edification of their
pious visitors ; or perplexed them with juggling tricks ;
or grinned at them through horse collars ; and when
sport itself grew wearisome, they made game of their
own stupidity, and began a yawning match. At the
very least of these enormities, the men of iron shook
their heads and frowned so darkly that the revellers
looked up, imagining that a momentary cloud had over-
cast the sunshine, which was to be perpetual there.
On the other hand, the Puritans affirmed that, when
a psalm was pealing from their place of worship, the
echo which the forest sent them back seemed often
like the chorus of a jolly catch, closing with a roar of
laughter. Who but the fiend, and his bond slaves,
the crew of Merry Mount, had thus disturbed them?
In due time, a feud arose, stern and bitter on one side,
and as serious on the other as anything could be among
such light spirits as had sworn allegiance to the Maypole. The future complexion of New England was
involved in this important quarrel. Should the griz-
zly saints establish their jurisdiction over the gay
sinners, then would their spirits darken all the clime
and make it a land of clouded visages, of hard toil, of
sermon and psalm forever. But should the banner

staff of Merry Mount be fortunate, sunshine would break upon the hills, and flowers would beautify the forest, and late posterity do homage to the Maypole.

After these authentic passages from history, we return to the nuptials of the Lord and Lady of the May. Alas! we have delayed too long, and must darken our tale too suddenly. As we glance again at the Maypole, a solitary sunbeam is fading from the summit, and leaves only a faint, golden tinge blended with the hues of the rainbow banner. Even that dim light is now withdrawn, relinquishing the whole domain of Merry Mount to the evening gloom, which has rushed so instantaneously from the black surrounding woods. But some of these black shadows have rushed forth in human shape.

Yes, with the setting sun, the last day of mirth had passed from Merry Mount. The ring of gay masquers was disordered and broken; the stag lowered his antlers in dismay; the wolf grew weaker than a lamb; the bells of the morris-dancers tinkled with tremulous affright. The Puritans had played a characteristic part in the Maypole mummeries. Their darksome figures were intermixed with the wild shapes of their foes, and made the scene a picture of the moment, when waking thoughts start up amid the scattered fantasies of a dream. The leader of the hostile party stood in the centre of the circle, while the route of monsters cowered around him, like evil spirits in the presence of a dread magician. No fantastic foolery could look him in the face. So stern was the energy of his aspect, that the whole man, visage, frame, and soul, seemed wrought of iron, gifted with life and thought, yet all of one substance with his headpiece and breastplate. It was the Puritan of Puritans; it was Endicott himself!

"Stand off, priest of Baal!" said he, with a grim frown, and laying no reverent hand upon the surplice. "I know thee, Blackstone![1] Thou art the man who couldst not abide the rule even of thine own corrupted church, and hast come hither to preach iniquity, and to give example of it in thy life. But now shall it be seen that the Lord hath sanctified this wilderness for his peculiar people. Woe unto them that would defile it! And first, for this flower-decked abomination, the altar of thy worship!"

And with his keen sword Endicott assaulted the hallowed Maypole. Nor long did it resist his arm. It groaned with a dismal sound; it showered leaves and rosebuds upon the remorseless enthusiast; and finally, with all its green boughs and ribbons and flowers, symbolic of departed pleasures, down fell the banner staff of Merry Mount. As it sank, tradition says, the evening sky grew darker, and the woods threw forth a more sombre shadow.

"There," cried Endicott, looking triumphantly on his work, "there lies the only Maypole in New England! The thought is strong within me that, by its fall, is shadowed forth the fate of light and idle mirth makers, amongst us and our posterity. Amen, saith John Endicott."

"Amen!" echoed his followers.

But the votaries of the Maypole gave one groan for their idol. At the sound, the Puritan leader glanced at the crew of Comus, each a figure of broad mirth, yet, at this moment, strangely expressive of sorrow and dismay.

[1] Did Governor Endicott speak less positively, we should suspect a mistake here. The Rev. Mr. Blackstone, though an eccentric, is not known to have been an immoral man. We rather doubt his identity with the priest of Merry Mount.

"Valiant captain," quoth Peter Palfrey, the Ancient of the band, "what order shall be taken with the prisoners?"

"I thought not to repent me of cutting down a Maypole," replied Endicott, "yet now I could find in my heart to plant it again, and give each of these bestial pagans one other dance round their idol. It vould have served rarely for a whipping-post!"

"But there are pine-trees enow," suggested the lieu-tenant.

"True, good Ancient," said the leader. "Where-fore, bind the heathen crew, and bestow on them a small matter of stripes apiece, as earnest of our future justice. Set some of the rogues in the stocks to rest themselves, so soon as Providence shall bring us to one of our own well-ordered settlements, where such accommodations may be found. Further penalties, such as branding and cropping of ears, shall be thought of hereafter."

"How many stripes for the priest?" inquired Ancient Palfrey.

"None as yet," answered Endicott, bending his iron frown upon the culprit. "It must be for the Great and General Court to determine, whether stripes and long imprisonment, and other grievous penalty, may atone for his transgressions. Let him look to himself! For such as violate our civil order, it may be permitted us to show mercy. But woe to the wretch that troubleth our religion!"

"And this dancing bear," resumed the officer. "Must he share the stripes of his fellows?"

"Shoot him through the head!" said the energetic Puritan. "I suspect witchcraft in the beast."

"Here be a couple of shining ones," continued

Peter Palfrey, pointing his weapon at the Lord and Lady of the May. "They seem to be of high station among these misdoers. Methinks their dignity will not be fitted with less than a double share of stripes."

Endicott rested on his sword, and closely surveyed the dress and aspect of the hapless pair. There they stood, pale, downcast, and apprehensive. Yet there was an air of mutual support, and of pure affection, seeking aid and giving it, that showed them to be man and wife, with the sanction of a priest upon their love. The youth, in the peril of the moment, had dropped his gilded staff, and thrown his arm about the Lady of the May, who leaned against his breast, too lightly to burden him, but with weight enough to express that their destinies were linked together, for good or evil. They looked first at each other, and then into the grim captain's face. There they stood, in the first hour of wedlock, while the idle pleasures, of which their companions were the emblems, had given place to the sternest cares of life, personified by the dark Puritans. But never had their youthful beauty seemed so pure and high as when its glow was chastened by adversity.

"Youth," said Endicott, "ye stand in an evil case thou and thy maiden wife. Make ready presently, for I am minded that ye shall both have a token to remember your wedding day!"

"Stern man," cried the May Lord, "how can I move thee? Were the means at hand, I would resist to the death. Being powerless, I entreat! Do with me as thou wilt, but let Edith go untouched!"

"Not so," replied the immitigable zealot. "We are not wont to show an idle courtesy to that sex, which requireth the stricter discipline. What sayest thou, maid? Shall thy silken bridegroom suffer thy share of the penalty, besides his own?"

"Be it death," said Edith, "and lay it all on me!"

Truly, as Endicott had said, the poor lovers stood in a woful case. Their foes were triumphant, their friends captive and abased, their home desolate, the benighted wilderness around them, and a rigorous destiny, in the shape of the Puritan leader, their only guide. Yet the deepening twilight could not altogether conceal that the iron man was softened; he smiled at the fair spectacle of early love; he almost sighed for the inevitable blight of early hopes.

"The troubles of life have come hastily on this young couple," observed Endicott. "We will see how they comport themselves under their present trials ere we burden them with greater. If, among the spoil, there be any garments of a more decent fashion, let them be put upon this May Lord and his Lady, instead of their glistening vanities. Look to it, some of you."

"And shall not the youth's hair be cut?" asked Peter Palfrey, looking with abhorrence at the love-lock and long glossy curls of the young man.

"Crop it forthwith, and that in the true pumpkin-shell fashion," answered the captain. "Then bring them along with us, but more gently than their fellows. There be qualities in the youth, which may make him valiant to fight, and sober to toil, and pious to pray; and in the maiden, that may fit her to become a mother in our Israel, bringing up babes in better nurture than her own hath been. Nor think ye, young ones, that they are the happiest, even in our lifetime of a moment, who misspend it in dancing round a Maypole!"

And Endicott, the severest Puritan of all who laid the rock foundation of New England, lifted the wreath of roses from the ruin of the Maypole, and threw it, with his own gauntleted hand, over the heads of the Lord and Lady of the May. It was a deed of proph-ecy. As the moral gloom of the world overpowers all systematic gayety, even so was their home of wild mirth made desolate amid the sad forest. They returned to it no more. But as their flowery garland was wreathed of the brightest roses that had grown there, so, in the tie that united them, were intertwined all the purest and best of their early joys. They went heavenward, supporting each other along the difficult path which it was their lot to tread, and never wasted one regretful thought on the vanities of Merry Mount.

THE GENTLE BOY.

In the course of the year 1656, several of the people called Quakers, led, as they professed, by the inward movement of the spirit, made their appearance in New England. Their reputation, as holders of mystic and pernicious principles, having spread before them, the Puritans early endeavored to banish, and to prevent the further intrusion of the rising sect. But the measures by which it was intended to purge the land of heresy, though more than sufficiently vigorous, were entirely unsuccessful. The Quakers, esteeming persecution as a divine call to the post of danger, laid claim to a holy courage, unknown to the Puritans themselves, who had shunned the cross, by providing for the peaceable exercise of their religion in a distant wilderness. Though it was the singular fact, that every nation of the earth rejected the wandering enthusiasts who practised peace towards all men, the place of greatest uneasiness and peril, and therefore, in their eyes the most eligible, was the province of Massachusetts Bay.

The fines, imprisonments, and stripes, liberally distributed by our pious forefathers; the popular antipathy, so strong that it endured nearly a hundred years after actual persecution had ceased, were attractions as powerful for the Quakers, as peace, honor, and reward, would have been for the worldly minded. Every European vessel brought new cargoes of the sect, eager to testify against the oppression which they hoped to share; and when shipmasters were restrained by heavy fines from affording them passage, they made long and circuitous journeys through the Indian country, and appeared in the province as if conveyed by a supernatural power. Their enthusiasm, heightened almost to madness by the treatment which they received, produced actions contrary to the rules of decency, as well as of rational religion, and presented a singular contrast to the calm and staid deportment of their sectarian successors of the present day. The command of the spirit, inaudible except to the soul, and not to be controverted on grounds of human wisdom, was made a plea for most indecorous exhibitions, which, abstractedly considered, well deserved the moderate chastisement of the rod. These extravagances, and the persecution which was at once their cause and consequence, continued to increase, till, in the year 1659, the government of Massachusetts Bay indulged two members of the Quaker sect with the crown of martyrdom.

An indelible stain of blood is upon the hands of all who consented to this act, but a large share of the awful responsibility must rest upon the person then at the head of the government. He was a man of narrow mind and imperfect education, and his uncompromising bigotry was made hot and mischievous by violent and hasty passions; he exerted his influence indecorously and unjustifiably to compass the death of the enthusiasts; and his whole conduct, in respect to them, was marked by brutal cruelty. The Quakers, whose revengeful feelings were not less deep because they were inactive, remembered this man and his associates in after times. The historian of the sect affirms that, by the wrath of Heaven, a blight fell upon the land in the vicinity of the "bloody town" of Boston, so that no wheat would grow there; and he takes his stand, as it were, among the graves of the ancient persecutors, and triumphantly recounts the judgments that overtook them, in old age or at the parting hour. He tells us that they died suddenly and violently and in madness; but nothing can exceed the bitter mockery with which he records the loathsome disease, and "death by rottenness," of the fierce and cruel governor.

.   .   .   .

On the evening of the autumn day that had witnessed the martyrdom of two men of the Quaker persuasion, a Puritan settler was returning from the metropolis to the neighboring country town in which he resided. The air was cool, the sky clear, and the lingering twilight was made brighter by the rays of a young moon, which had now nearly reached the verge of the horizon. The traveller, a man of middle age, wrapped in a gray frieze cloak, quickened his pace when he had reached the outskirts of the town, for a gloomy extent of nearly four miles lay between him and his home. The low, straw-thatched houses were scattered at considerable intervals along the road, and the country having been settled but about thirty years, the tracts of original forest still bore no small proportion to the cultivated ground. The autumn wind wandered among the branches, whirling away the leaves from all except the pine-trees, and moaning as if it lamented the desolation of which it was the instrument. The road had penetrated the mass of woods that lay nearest to the town, and was just emerging into an open space, when the traveller's ears were saluted by a sound more mournful than even that of the wind. It was like the wailing of some one in distress, and it seemed to proceed from beneath a tall and lonely fir-tree, in the centre of a cleared but uninclosed and uncultivated field. The Puritan could not but remember that this was the very spot which had been made accursed a few hours before by the execution of the Quakers, whose bodies had been thrown together into one hasty grave, beneath the tree on which they suffered. He struggled, however, against the superstitious fears which belonged to the age, and compelled himself to pause and listen.

"The voice is most likely mortal, nor have I cause to tremble if it be otherwise," thought he, straining his eyes through the dim moonlight. "Methinks it is like the wailing of a child; some infant, it may be, which has strayed from its mother, and chanced upon this place of death. For the ease of mine own conscience I must search this matter out."

He therefore left the path, and walked somewhat fearfully across the field. Though now so desolate, its soil was pressed down and trampled by the thousand footsteps of those who had witnessed the spectacle of that day, all of whom had now retired, leaving the dead to their loneliness. The traveller at length reached the fir-tree, which from the middle upward was covered with living branches, although a scaffold had been erected beneath, and other preparations made for the work of death. Under this unhappy tree, which in after times was believed to drop poison with its dew, sat the one solitary mourner for innocent blood. It was a slender and light clad little boy, who leaned his face upon a hillock of fresh-turned and half-frozen earth, and wailed bitterly, yet in a suppressed tone, as if his grief might receive the punishment of crime. The Puritan, whose approach had been unperceived, laid his hand upon the child's shoulder, and addressed him compassionately.

"You have chosen a dreary lodging, my poor boy, and no wonder that you weep," said he. "But dry your eyes, and tell me where your mother dwells. I promise you, if the journey be not too far, I will leave you in her arms to-night."

The boy had hushed his wailing at once, and turned his face upward to the stranger. It was a pale, bright-eyed countenance, certainly not more than six years old, but sorrow, fear, and want had destroyed much of its infantile expression. The Puritan seeing the boy's frightened gaze, and feeling that he trembled under his hand, endeavored to reassure him.

"Nay, if I intended to do you harm, little lad, the readiest way were to leave you here. What! you do not fear to sit beneath the gallows on a new-made grave, and yet you tremble at a friend's touch. Take heart, child, and tell me what is your name and where is your home?"

"Friend," replied the little boy, in a sweet though faltering voice, "they call me Ilbrahim, and my home is here."

The pale, spiritual face, the eyes that seemed to mingle with the moonlight, the sweet, airy voice, and the outlandish name, almost made the Puritan believe that the boy was in truth a being which had sprung up out of the grave on which he sat. But perceiving that the apparition stood the test of a short mental prayer, and remembering that the arm which he had touched was lifelike, he adopted a more rational supposition. "The poor child is stricken in his intellect," thought he, "but verily his words are fearful in a

place like this." He then spoke soothingly, intend
to humor the boy's fantasy.

" Your home will scarce be comfortable, Ilbrahim,
this cold autumn night, and I fear you are ill-provided
with food. I am hastening to a warm supper and bed,
and if you will go with me you shall share them ! "

" I thank thee, friend, but though I be hungry, and
shivering with cold, thou wilt not give me food nor
lodging," replied the boy, in the quiet tone which
despair had taught him, even so young. "My father
was of the people whom all men hate. They have laid
him under this heap of earth, and here is my home."

The Puritan, who had laid hold of little Ilbrahim's
hand, relinquished it as if he were touching a loath
some reptile. But he possessed a compassionate heart,
which not even religious prejudice could harden into
stone.

" God forbid that I should leave this child to perish, though he comes of the accursed sect," said he to
himself. " Do we not all spring from an evil root?
Are we not all in darkness till the light doth shine
upon us? He shall not perish, neither in body, nor,
if prayer and instruction may avail for him, in soul."
He then spoke aloud and kindly to Ilbrahim, who had
again hid his face in the cold earth of the grave.
" Was every door in the land shut against you, my
child, that you have wandered to this unhallowed
spot ? "

" They drove me forth from the prison when they
took my father thence," said the boy, " and I stood
afar off watching the crowd of people, and when they
were gone I came hither, and found only his grave.
I knew that my father was sleeping here, and I said
this shall be my home."

"No, child, no; not while I have a roof over my head, or a morsel to share with you!" exclaimed the Puritan, whose sympathies were now fully excited. "Rise up and come with me, and fear not any harm."

The boy wept afresh, and clung to the heap of earth as if the cold heart beneath it were warmer to him than any in a living breast. The traveller, however, continued to entreat him tenderly, and seeming to acquire some degree of confidence, he at length arose. But his slender limbs tottered with weakness, his little head grew dizzy, and he leaned against the tree of death for support.

"My poor boy, are you so feeble?" said the Puritan. "When did you taste food last?"

"I ate of bread and water with my father in the prison," replied Ilbrahim, "but they brought him none neither yesterday nor to-day, saying that he had eaten enough to bear him to his journey's end. Trouble not thyself for my hunger, kind friend, for I have lacked food many times ere now."

The traveller took the child in his arms and wrapped his cloak about him, while his heart stirred with shame and anger against the gratuitous cruelty of the instruments in this persecution. In the awakened warmth of his feelings he resolved that, at whatever risk, he would not forsake the poor little defenceless being whom Heaven had confided to his care. With this determination he left the accursed field, and resumed the homeward path from which the wailing of the boy had called him. The light and motionless burden scarcely impeded his progress, and he soon beheld the fire rays from the windows of the cottage which he, a native of a distant clime, had built in the western wilderness. It was surrounded by a considerable extent of cultivated ground, and the dwelling was situated in the nook of a wood-covered hill, whither it seemed to have crept for protection.

"Look up, child," said the Puritan to Ilbrahim, whose faint head had sunk upon his shoulder, "there is our home."

At the word "home," a thrill passed through the child's frame, but he continued silent. A few moments brought them to a cottage door, at which the owner knocked ; for at that early period, when savages were wandering everywhere among the settlers, bolt and bar were indispensable to the security of a dwelling. The summons was answered by a bond-servant, a coarse-clad and dull-featured piece of humanity, who, after ascertaining that his master was the applicant, undid the door, and held a flaring pine-knot torch to light him in. Farther back in the passage-way, the red blaze discovered a matronly woman, but no little crowd of children came bounding forth to greet their father's return. As the Puritan entered, he thrust aside his cloak, and displayed Ilbrahim's face to the female.

"Dorothy, here is a little outcast, whom Providence hath put into our hands," observed he. "Be kind to him, even as if he were of those dear ones who have departed from us."

"What pale and bright-eyed little boy is this, Tobias?" she inquired. "Is he one whom the wilderness folk have ravished from some Christian mother?"

"No, Dorothy, this poor child is no captive from the wilderness," he replied. "The heathen savage would have given him to eat of his scanty morsel, and to drink of his birchen cup; but Christian men, alas! had cast him out to die."

Then he told her how he had found him beneath the gallows, upon his father's grave; and how his heart had prompted him, like the speaking of an inward voice, to take the little outcast home, and be kind unto him. He acknowledged his resolution to feed and clothe him, as if he were his own child, and to afford him the instruction which should counteract the pernicious errors hitherto instilled into his infant mind. Dorothy was gifted with even a quicker tenderness than her husband, and she approved of all his doings and intentions.

"Have you a mother, dear child?" she inquired.

The tears burst forth from his full heart, as he attempted to reply; but Dorothy at length understood that he had a mother, who, like the rest of her sect, was a persecuted wanderer. She had been taken from the prison a short time before, carried into the uninhabited wilderness, and left to perish there by hunger or wild beasts. This was no uncommon method of disposing of the Quakers, and they were accustomed to boast that the inhabitants of the desert were more hospitable to them than civilized man.

"Fear not, little boy, you shall not need a mother, and a kind one," said Dorothy, when she had gathered this information. "Dry your tears, Ilbrahim, and be my child, as I will be your mother."

The good woman prepared the little bed, from which her own children had successively been borne to another resting-place. Before Ilbrahim would consent to occupy it, he knelt down, and as Dorothy listened to his simple and affecting prayer, she marvelled how the parents that had taught it to him could have been judged worthy of death. When the boy had fallen asleep, she bent over his pale and spiritual counte-

nance, pressed a kiss upon his white brow, drew the
bedclothes up about his neck, and went away with a
pensive gladness in her heart.

Tobias Pearson was not among the earliest emi-
grants from the old country. He had remained in
England during the first years of the civil war, in
which he had borne some share as a cornet of dragoons, under Cromwell. But when the ambitious designs of his leader began to develop themselves, he
quitted the army of the Parliament, and sought a refuge from the strife, which was no longer holy, among
the people of his persuasion in the colony of Massachusetts. A more worldly consideration had perhaps
an influence in drawing him thither; for New England
offered advantages to men of unprosperous fortunes,
as well as to dissatisfied religionists, and Pearson had
hitherto found it difficult to provide for a wife and increasing family. To this supposed impurity of motive
the more bigoted Puritans were inclined to impute the
removal by death of all the children, for whose earthly
good the father had been over-thoughtful. They had
left their native country blooming like roses, and like
roses they had perished in a foreign soil. Those ex-
pounders of the ways of Providence, who had thus
judged their brother, and attributed his domestic sorrows to his sin, were not more charitable when they
saw him and Dorothy endeavoring to fill up the void
in their hearts by the adoption of an infant of the
accursed sect. Nor did they fail to communicate
their disapprobation to Tobias; but the latter, in reply, merely pointed at the little, quiet, lovely boy,
whose appearance and deportment were indeed as powerful arguments as could possibly have been adduced
in his own favor. Even his beauty, however, and his

winning manners, sometimes produced an effect ulti
mately unfavorable; for the bigots, when the outer
surfaces of their iron hearts had been softened and
again grew hard, affirmed that no merely natural
cause could have so worked upon them.

Their antipathy to the poor infant was also increased by the ill success of divers theological discus-
sions, in which it was attempted to convince him of
the errors of his sect. Ilbrahim, it is true, was not a
skilful controversialist; but the feeling of his religion
was strong as instinct in him, and he could neither be
enticed nor driven from the faith which his father had
died for. The odium of this stubbornness was shared
in a great measure by the child's protectors, insomuch
that Tobias and Dorothy very shortly began to experience a most bitter species of persecution, in the cold
regards of many a friend whom they had valued. The
common people manifested their opinions more openly.
Pearson was a man of some consideration, being a
representative to the General Court, and an approved
lieutenant in the trainbands, yet within a week after
his adoption of Ilbrahim he had been both hissed and
hooted. Once, also, when walking through a solitary
piece of woods, he heard a loud voice from some invisible speaker; and it cried, "What shall be done to
the backslider? Lo! the scourge is knotted for him,
even the whip of nine cords, and every cord three
knots!" These insults irritated Pearson's temper for
the moment; they entered also into his heart, and be
came imperceptible but powerful workers towards an
end which his most secret thought had not yet whispered.

o   .   .   .   .   .   .   o   .   .

On the second Sabbath after Ilbrahim became a

member of their family, Pearson and his wife deemed it proper that he should appear with them at public worship. They had anticipated some opposition to this measure from the boy, but he prepared himself in silence, and at the appointed hour was clad in the new mourning suit which Dorothy had wrought for him. As the parish was then, and during many subsequent years, unprovided with a bell, the signal for the commencement of religious exercises was the beat of a drum. At the first sound of that martial call to the place of holy and quiet thoughts, Tobias and Dorothy set forth, each holding a hand of little Ilbrahim, like two parents linked together by the infant of their love. On their path through the leafless woods they were overtaken by many persons of their acquaintance, all of whom avoided them, and passed by on the other side; but a severer trial awaited their constancy when they had descended the hill, and drew near the pine-built and undecorated house of prayer. Around the door, from which the drummer still sent forth his thundering summons, was drawn up a formidable phalanx, including several of the oldest members of the congregation, many of the middle aged, and nearly all the younger males. Pearson found it difficult to sustain their united and disapproving gaze, but Dorothy, whose mind was differently circumstanced, merely drew the boy closer to her, and faltered not in her approach. As they entered the door, they overheard the muttered sentiments of the assemblage, and when the reviling voices of the little children smote Ilbrahim's ear, he wept.

The interior aspect of the meeting-house was rude. The low ceiling, the unplastered walls, the naked wood work, and the undraperied pulpit, offered noth-

ing to excite the devotion, which, without such external aids, often remains latent in the heart. The floor
of the building was occupied by rows of long, cushion-
less benches, supplying the place of pews, and the
broad aisle formed a sexual division, impassable except by children beneath a certain age.

Pearson and Dorothy separated at the door of the
meeting-house, and Ilbrahim, being within the years
of infancy, was retained under the care of the latter.
The wrinkled beldams involved themselves in their
rusty cloaks as he passed by; even the mild-featured
maidens seemed to dread contamination; and many
a stern old man arose, and turned his repulsive and
unheavenly countenance upon the gentle boy, as if the
sanctuary were polluted by his presence. He was a
sweet infant of the skies that had strayed away from
his home, and all the inhabitants of this miserable
world closed up their impure hearts against him, drew
back their earth-soiled garments from his touch, and
said, "We are holier than thou."

Ilbrahim, seated by the side of his adopted mother,
and retaining fast hold of her hand, assumed a grave
and decorous demeanor, such as might befit a person
of matured taste and understanding, who should find
himself in a temple dedicated to some worship which
he did not recognize, but felt himself bound to respect.
The exercises had not yet commenced, however, when
the boy's attention was arrested by an event, apparently of trifling interest. A woman, having her face
muffled in a hood, and a cloak drawn completely about
her form, advanced slowly up the broad aisle and took
a place upon the foremost bench. Ilbrahim's faint
color varied, his nerves fluttered, he was unable to
turn his eyes from the muffled female.

When the preliminary prayer and hymn were over, the minister arose, and having turned the hour-glass which stood by the great Bible, commenced his discourse. He was now well stricken in years, a man of pale, thin countenance, and his gray hairs were closely covered by a black velvet skullcap. In his younger days he had practically learned the meaning of persecution from Archbishop Laud, and he was not now disposed to forget the lesson against which he had murmured then. Introducing the often discussed subject of the Quakers, he gave a history of that sect, and a description of their tenets, in which error predominated, and prejudice distorted the aspect of what was true. He adverted to the recent measures in the province, and cautioned his hearers of weaker parts against calling in question the just severity which God-fearing magistrates had at length been compelled to exercise. He spoke of the danger of pity, in some cases a commendable and Christian virtue, but inapplicable to this pernicious sect. He observed that such was their devilish obstinacy in error, that even the little children, the sucking babes, were hardened and desperate heretics. He affirmed that no man, without Heaven's especial warrant, should attempt their conversion, lest while he lent his hand to draw them from the slough, he should himself be precipitated into its lowest depths.

The sands of the second hour were principally in the lower half of the glass when the sermon concluded. An approving murmur followed, and the clergyman, having given out a hymn, took his seat with much self-congratulation, and endeavored to read the effect of his eloquence in the visages of the people. But while voices from all parts of the house were tuning

themselves to sing, a scene occurred, which, though
not very unusual at that period in the province, happened to be without precedent in this parish.

The muffled female, who had hitherto sat motionless
in the front rank of the audience, now arose, and with
slow, stately, and unwavering step, ascended the pulpit stairs. The quiverings of incipient harmony were
hushed, and the divine sat in speechless and almost
terrified astonishment, while she undid the door, and
stood up in the sacred desk from which his maledic-
tions had just been thundered. She then divested herself of the cloak and hood, and appeared in a most
singular array. A shapeless robe of sackcloth was
girded about her waist with a knotted cord; her raven
hair fell down upon her shoulders, and its blackness
was defiled by pale streaks of ashes, which she had
strown upon her head. Her eyebrows, dark and
strongly defined, added to the deathly whiteness of a
countenance, which, emaciated with want, and wild
with enthusiasm and strange sorrows, retained no trace
of earlier beauty. This figure stood gazing earnestly
on the audience, and there was no sound, nor any
movement, except a faint shuddering which every man
observed in his neighbor, but was scarcely conscious
of in himself. At length, when her fit of inspiration
came, she spoke, for the first few moments, in a low
voice, and not invariably distinct utterance. Her discourse gave evidence of an imagination hopelessly
entangled with her reason; it was a vague and incomprehensible rhapsody, which, however, seemed to
spread its own atmosphere round the hearer's soul,
and to move his feelings by some influence uncon-
nected with the words. As she proceeded, beautiful
but shadowy images would sometimes be seen, like

bright things moving in a turbid river; or a strong
and singularly-shaped idea leaped forth, and seized
at once on the understanding or the heart. But the
course of her unearthly eloquence soon led her to the
persecutions of her sect, and from thence the step was
short to her own peculiar sorrows. She was naturally
a woman of mighty passions, and hatred and revenge
now wrapped themselves in the garb of piety; the
character of her speech was changed, her images became distinct though wild, and her denunciations had
an almost hellish bitterness.

"The Governor and his mighty men," she said,
"have gathered together, taking counsel among themselves and saying, 'What shall we do unto this people
— even unto the people that have come into this land
to put our iniquity to the blush?' And lo! the devil
entereth into the council chamber, like a lame man of
low stature and gravely apparelled, with a dark and
twisted countenance, and a bright, downcast eye. And
he standeth up among the rulers; yea, he goeth to and
fro, whispering to each; and every man lends his ear,
for his word is 'Slay, slay!' But I say unto ye,
Woe to them that slay! Woe to them that shed the
blood of saints! Woe to them that have slain the
husband, and cast forth the child, the tender infant,
to wander homeless and hungry and cold, till he die;
and have saved the mother alive, in the cruelty of their
tender mercies! Woe to them in their lifetime! cursed
are they in the delight and pleasure of their hearts!
Woe to them in their death hour, whether it come
swiftly with blood and violence, or after long and
lingering pain! Woe, in the dark house, in the rottenness of the grave, when the children's children shall
revile the ashes of the fathers! Woe, woe, woe, at

the judgment, when all the persecuted and all the slain in this bloody land, and the father, the mother, and the child, shall await them in a day that they cannot escape! Seed of the faith, seed of the faith, ye whose hearts are moving with a power that ye know not, arise, wash your hands of this innocent blood! Lift your voices, chosen ones; cry aloud, and call down a woe and a judgment with me!"

Having thus given vent to the flood of malignity which she mistook for inspiration, the speaker was silent. Her voice was succeeded by the hysteric shrieks of several women, but the feelings of the audience generally had not been drawn onward in the current with her own. They remained stupefied, stranded as it were, in the midst of a torrent, which deafened them by its roaring, but might not move them by its violence. The clergyman, who could not hitherto have ejected the usurper of his pulpit otherwise than by bodily force, now addressed her in the tone of just indignation and legitimate authority.

"Get you down, woman, from the holy place which you profane," he said. "Is it to the Lord's house that you come to pour forth the foulness of your heart and the inspiration of the devil? Get you down, and remember that the sentence of death is on you; yea, and shall be executed, were it but for this day's work!"

"I go, friend, I go, for the voice hath had its utterance," replied she, in a depressed and even mild tone. "I have done my mission unto thee and to thy people. Reward me with stripes, imprisonment, or death, as ye shall be permitted."

The weakness of exhausted passion caused her steps to totter as she descended the pulpit stairs. The people, in the mean while, were stirring to and fro on the floor of the house, whispering among themselves, and glancing towards the intruder. Many of them now recognized her as the woman who had assaulted the Governor with frightful language as he passed by the window of her prison; they knew, also, that she was adjudged to suffer death, and had been preserved only by an involuntary banishment into the wilderness. The new outrage, by which she had provoked her fate, seemed to render further lenity impossible; and a gentleman in military dress, with a stout man of inferior rank, drew towards the door of the meeting-house, and awaited her approach.

Scarcely did her feet press the floor, however, when an unexpected scene occurred. In that moment of her peril, when every eye frowned with death, a little timid boy pressed forth, and threw his arms round his mother.

"I am here, mother; it is I, and I will go with thee to prison," he exclaimed.

She gazed at him with a doubtful and almost frightened expression, for she knew that the boy had been cast out to perish, and she had not hoped to see his face again. She feared, perhaps, that it was but one of the happy visions with which her excited fancy had often deceived her, in the solitude of the desert or in prison. But when she felt his hand warm within her own, and heard his little eloquence of childish love, she began to know that she was yet a mother.

"Blessed art thou, my son," she sobbed. "My heart was withered; yea, dead with thee and with thy father: and now it leaps as in the first moment when I pressed thee to my bosom."

She knelt down and embraced him again and again,

while the joy that could find no words expressed itself
in broken accents, like the bubbles gushing up to vanish at the surface of a deep fountain. The sorrows of
past years, and the darker peril that was nigh, cast
not a shadow on the brightness of that fleeting moment. Soon, however, the spectators saw a change
upon her face, as the consciousness of her sad estate
returned, and grief supplied the fount of tears which
joy had opened. By the words she uttered, it would
seem that the indulgence of natural love had given her
mind a momentary sense of its errors, and made her
know how far she had strayed from duty in following
the dictates of a wild fanaticism.

"In a doleful hour art thou returned to me, poor
boy," she said, "for thy mother's path has gone darkening onward, till now the end is death. Son, son, I
have borne thee in my arms when my limbs were tottering, and I have fed thee with the food that I was
fainting for; yet I have ill performed a mother's part
by thee in life, and now I leave thee no inheritance but
woe and shame. Thou wilt go seeking through the
world, and find all hearts closed against thee and their
sweet affections turned to bitterness for my sake. My
child, my child, how many a pang awaits thy gentle
spirit, and I the cause of all!"

She hid her face on Ilbrahim's head, and her long,
raven hair, discolored with the ashes of her mourning,
fell down about him like a veil. A low and interrupted moan was the voice of her heart's anguish, and
it did not fail to move the sympathies of many who
mistook their involuntary virtue for a sin. Sobs were
audible in the female section of the house, and every
man who was a father drew his hand across his eyes.
Tobias Pearson was agitated and uneasy, but a certain

feeling like the consciousness of guilt oppressed him, so that he could not go forth and offer himself as the protector of the child. Dorothy, however, had watched her husband's eye. Her mind was free from the influence that had begun to work on his, and she drew near the Quaker woman, and addressed her in the hearing of all the congregation.

" Stranger, trust this boy to me, and I will be his mother," she said, taking Ilbrahim's hand. " Providence has signally marked out my husband to protect him, and he has fed at our table and lodged under our roof now many days, till our hearts have grown very strongly unto him. Leave the tender child with us, and be at ease concerning his welfare."

The Quaker rose from the ground, but drew the boy closer to her, while she gazed earnestly in Dorothy's face. Her mild but saddened features, and neat matronly attire, harmonized together, and were like a verse of fireside poetry. Her very aspect proved that she was blameless, so far as mortal could be so, in respect to God and man; while the enthusiast, in her robe of sackcloth and girdle of knotted cord, had as evidently violated the duties of the present life and the future, by fixing her attention wholly on the latter. The two females, as they held each a hand of Ilbrahim, formed a practical allegory; it was rational piety and unbridled fanaticism contending for the empire of a young heart.

" Thou art not of our people," said the Quaker mournfully.

" No, we are not of your people," replied Dorothy, with mildness, " but we are Christians, looking upward to the same heaven with you. Doubt not that your boy shall meet you there, if there be a blessing on our tender and prayerful guidance of him. Thither, I trust, my own children have gone before me, for I also have been a mother; I am no longer so," she added, in a faltering tone, "and your son will have all my care."

"But will ye lead him in the path which his parents have trodden?" demanded the Quaker. "Can ye teach him the enlightened faith which his father has died for, and for which I, even I, am soon to become an unworthy martyr? The boy has been baptized in blood; will ye keep the mark fresh and ruddy upon his forehead?"

"I will not deceive you," answered Dorothy. "If your child become our child, we must breed him up in the instruction which Heaven has imparted to us; we must pray for him the prayers of our own faith; we must do towards him according to the dictates of our own consciences, and not of yours. Were we to act otherwise, we should abuse your trust, even in complying with your wishes."

The mother looked down upon her boy with a troubled countenance, and then turned her eyes upward to heaven. She seemed to pray internally, and the contention of her soul was evident.

"Friend," she said at length to Dorothy, "I doubt not that my son shall receive all earthly tenderness at thy hands. Nay, I will believe that even thy imperfect lights may guide him to a better world, for surely thou art on the path thither. But thou hast spoken of a husband. Doth he stand here among this multitude of people? Let him come forth, for I must know to whom I commit this most precious trust."

She turned her face upon the male auditors, and after a momentary delay, Tobias Pearson came forth frcm among them. The Quaker saw the dress which marked his military rank, and shook her head; but then she noted the hesitating air, the eyes that struggled with her own, and were vanquished; the color that went and came, and could find no resting-place. As she gazed, an unmirthful smile spread over her features, like sunshine that grows melancholy in some desolate spot. Her lips moved inaudibly, but at length she spake.

"I hear it, I hear it. The voice speaketh within me and saith, 'Leave thy child, Catharine, for his place is here, and go hence, for I have other work for thee. Break the bonds of natural affection, martyr thy love, and know that in all these things eternal wisdom hath its ends.' I go, friends; I go. Take ye my boy, my precious jewel. I go hence, trusting that all shall be well, and that even for his infant hands there is a labor in the vineyard."

She knelt down and whispered to Ilbrahim, who a first struggled and clung to his mother, with sobs and tears, but remained passive when she had kissed his cheek and arisen from the ground. Having held her hands over his head in mental prayer, she was ready to depart.

"Farewell, friends in mine extremity," she said to Pearson and his wife; "the good deed ye have done me is a treasure laid up in heaven, to be returned a thousand-fold hereafter. And farewell ye, mine enemies, to whom it is not permitted to harm so much as a hair of my head, nor to stay my footsteps even for a moment. The day is coming when ye shall call upon me to witness for ye to this one sin uncommitted, and I will rise up and answer."

She turned her steps towards the door, and the men,

who had stationed themselves to guard it, withdrew, and suffered her to pass. A general sentiment of pity overcame the virulence of religious hatred. Sanctified by her love and her affliction, she went forth, and all the people gazed after her till she had journeyed up the hill, and was lost behind its brow. She went, the apostle of her own unquiet heart, to renew the wanderings of past years. For her voice had been already heard in many lands of Christendom; and she had pined in the cells of a Catholic Inquisition before she felt the lash and lay in the dungeons of the Puritans. Her mission had extended also to the followers of the Prophet, and from them she had received the courtesy and kindness which all the contending sects of our purer religion united to deny her. Her husband and herself had resided many months in Turkey, where even the Sultan's countenance was gracious to them; in that pagan land, too, was Ilbrahim's birthplace, and his oriental name was a mark of gratitude for the good deeds of an unbeliever.

. . . .

When Pearson and his wife had thus acquired all the rights over Ilbrahim that could be delegated, their affection for him became like the memory of their native land, or their mild sorrow for the dead, a piece of the immovable furniture of their hearts. The boy, also, after a week or two of mental disquiet, began to gratify his protectors by many inadvertent proofs that he considered them as parents, and their house as home. Before the winter snows were melted, the persecuted infant, the little wanderer from a remote and heathen country, seemed native in the New England cottage, and inseparable from the warmth and security of its hearth. Under the influence of kind treatment,

and in the consciousness that he was loved, Ilbrahim's
demeanor lost a premature manliness, which had resulted from his earlier situation ; he became more
childlike, and his natural character displayed itself
with freedom. It was in many respects a beautiful
one, yet the disordered imaginations of both his father
and mother had perhaps propagated a certain un-
healthiness in the mind of the boy. In his general
state, Ilbrahim would derive enjoyment from the most
trifling events, and from every object about him; he
seemed to discover rich treasures of happiness, by a
faculty analogous to that of the witch hazel, which
points to hidden gold where all is barren to the eye.
His airy gayety, coming to him from a thousand
sources, communicated itself to the family, and Ilbrahim was like a domesticated sunbeam, brightening
moody countenances, and chasing away the gloom
from the dark corners of the cottage.

On the other hand, as the susceptibility of pleasure
is also that of pain, the exuberant cheerfulness of the
boy's prevailing temper sometimes yielded to moments
of deep depression. His sorrows could not always be
followed up to their original source, but most frequently they appeared to flow, though Ilbrahim was
young to be sad for such a cause, from wounded love
The flightiness of his mirth rendered him often guilty
of offences against the decorum of a Puritan house
hold, and on these occasions he did not invariably
escape rebuke. But the slightest word of real bitterness, which he was infallible in distinguishing from
pretended anger, seemed to sink into his heart and
poison all his enjoyments, till he became sensible that
he was entirely forgiven. Of the malice, which generally accompanies a superfluity of sensitiveness, Ilbra-

him was altogether destitute : when trodden upon, he
would not turn; when wounded, he could but die.
His mind was wanting in the stamina for self-support;
it was a plant that would twine beautifully round
something stronger than itself, but if repulsed, or torn
away, it had no choice but to wither on the ground.
Dorothy's acuteness taught her that severity would
crush the spirit of the child, and she nurtured him
with the gentle care of one who handles a butterfly.
Her husband manifested an equal affection, although
it grew daily less productive of familiar caresses.

The feelings of the neighboring people, in regard to
the Quaker infant and his protectors, had not undergone a favorable change, in spite of the momentary
triumph which the desolate mother had obtained over
their sympathies. The scorn and bitterness, of which
he was the object, were very grievous to Ilbrahim, especially when any circumstance made him sensible
that the children, his equals in age, partook of the
enmity of their parents. His tender and social nature
had already overflowed in attachments to everything
about him, and still there was a residue of unappro-
priated love, which he yearned to bestow upon the
little ones who were taught to hate him. As the warm
days of spring came on, Ilbrahim was accustomed to
remain for hours, silent and inactive, within hearing
of the children's voices at their play ; yet, with his
usual delicacy of feeling, he avoided their notice, and
would flee and hide himself from the smallest individual among them. Chance, however, at length seemed
to open a medium of communication between his heart
and theirs ; it was by means of a boy about two years
older than Ilbrahim, who was injured by a fall from
a tree in the vicinity of Pearson's habitation. As the

sufferer's own home was at some distance, Dorothy
willingly received him under her roof, and became his
tender and careful nurse.

Ilbrahim was the unconscious possessor of much
skill in physiognomy, and it would have deterred him,
in other circumstances, from attempting to make a
friend of this boy. The countenance of the latter immediately impressed a beholder disagreeably, but it
required some examination to discover that the cause
was a very slight distortion of the mouth, and the irregular, broken line, and near approach of the eyebrows. Analogous, perhaps, to these trifling deformi-
ties, was an almost imperceptible twist of every joint,
and the uneven prominence of the breast; forming a
body, regular in its general outline, but faulty in almost all its details. The disposition of the boy was
sullen and reserved, and the village schoolmaster stig-
matized him as obtuse in intellect; although, at a
later period of life, he evinced ambition and very peculiar talents. But whatever might be his personal
or moral irregularities, Ilbrahim's heart seized upon,
and clung to him, from the moment that he was
brought wounded into the cottage; the child of persecution seemed to compare his own fate with that of
the sufferer, and to feel that even different modes of
misfortune had created a sort of relationship between
them. Food, rest, and the fresh air, for which he lan-
guished, were neglected; he nestled continually by the
bedside of the little stranger, and, with a fond jealousy, endeavored to be the medium of all the cares
that were bestowed upon him. As the boy became
convalescent, Ilbrahim contrived games suitable to
his situation, or amused him by a faculty which he
had perhaps breathed in with the air of his barbaric

birthplace. It was that of reciting imaginary adventures, on the spur of the moment, and apparently in
inexhaustible succession. His tales were of course
monstrous, disjointed, and without aim ; but they were
curious on account of a vein of human tenderness
which ran through them all, and was like a sweet,
familiar face, encountered in the midst of wild and
unearthly scenery. The auditor paid much attention
to these romances, and sometimes interrupted them by
brief remarks upon the incidents, displaying shrewdness above his years, mingled with a moral obliquity
which grated very harshly against Ilbrahim's instinctive rectitude. Nothing, however, could arrest the
progress of the latter's affection, and there were many
proofs that it met with a response from the dark and
stubborn nature on which it was lavished. The boy's
parents at length removed him, to complete his cure
under their own roof.

Ilbrahim did not visit his new friend after his departure ; but he made anxious and continual inquiries
respecting him, and informed himself of the day when
he was to reappear among his playmates. On a pleasant summer afternoon, the children of the neighborhood had assembled in the little forest-crowned amphi-
theatre behind the meeting-house, and the recovering
invalid was there, leaning on a staff. The glee of a
score of untainted bosoms was heard in light and airy
voices, which danced among the trees like sunshine
become audible ; the grown men of this weary world,
as they journeyed by the spot, marvelled why life, beginning in such brightness, should proceed in gloom ;
and their hearts, or their imaginations, answered them
and said, that the bliss of childhood gushes from its
innocence. But it happened that an unexpected addi-

tion was made to the heavenly little band. It was
Ilbrahim, who came towards the children with a look
of sweet confidence on his fair and spiritual face, as
if, having manifested his love to one of them, he had
no longer to fear a repulse from their society. A
hush came over their mirth the moment they beheld
him, and they stood whispering to each other while he
drew nigh ; but, all at once, the devil of their fathers
entered into the unbreeched fanatics, and sending up
a fierce, shrill cry, they rushed upon the poor Quaker
child. In an instant, he was the centre of a brood of
baby-fiends, who lifted sticks against him, pelted him
with stones, and displayed an instinct of destruction
far more loathsome than the bloodthirstiness of manhood.

The invalid, in the meanwhile, stood apart from the
tumult, crying out with a loud voice, "Fear not, Ilbrahim, come hither and take my hand ; " and his unhappy friend endeavored to obey him. After watching the victim's struggling approach with a calm smile
and unabashed eye, the foul-hearted little villain lifted
his staff and struck Ilbrahim on the mouth, so forcibly that the blood issued in a stream. The poor child's
arms had been raised to guard his head from the storm
of blows ; but now he dropped them at once. His persecutors beat him down, trampled upon him, dragged
him by his long, fair locks, and Ilbrahim was on the
point of becoming as veritable a martyr as ever entered bleeding into heaven. The uproar, however,
attracted the notice of a few neighbors, who put themselves to the trouble of rescuing the little heretic, and
of conveying him to Pearson's door.

Ilbrahim's bodily harm was severe, but long and
careful nursing accomplished his recovery ; the injury

done to his sensitive spirit was more serious, though
not so visible. Its signs were principally of a negative
character, and to be discovered only by those who had
previously known him. His gait was thenceforth slow,
even, and unvaried by the sudden bursts of sprightlier
motion, which had once corresponded to his overflow
ing gladness; his countenance was heavier, and its
former play of expression, the dance of sunshine reflected from moving water, was destroyed by the cloud
over his existence; his notice was attracted in a far
less degree by passing events, and he appeared to find
greater difficulty in comprehending what was new to
him than at a happier period. A stranger, founding
his judgment upon these circumstances, would have
said that the dulness of the child's intellect widely
contradicted the promise of his features; but the secret
was in the direction of Ilbrahim's thoughts, which
were brooding within him when they should naturally
have been wandering abroad. An attempt of Dorothy
to revive his former sportiveness was the single occasion on which his quiet demeanor yielded to a violent
display of grief; he burst into passionate weeping, and
ran and hid himself, for his heart had become so miserably sore that even the hand of kindness tortured
it like fire. Sometimes, at night and probably in his
dreams, he was heard to cry "Mother! Mother!" as
if her place, which a stranger had supplied while Ilbrahim was happy, admitted of no substitute in his extreme affliction. Perhaps, among the many life-weary
wretches then upon the earth, there was not one who
combined innocence and misery like this poor, broken-
hearted infant, so soon the victim of his own heavenly
nature.

  While this melancholy change had taken place in

Ilbrahim, one of an earlier origin and of different
character had come to its perfection in his adopted
father. The incident with which this tale commences
found Pearson in a state of religious dulness, yet mentally disquieted, and longing for a more fervid faith
than he possessed. The first effect of his kindness to
Ilbrahim was to produce a softened feeling, and incipient love for the child's whole sect; but joined to this,
and resulting perhaps from self-suspicion, was a proud
and ostentatious contempt of all their tenets and practical extravagances. In the course of much thought,
however, for the subject struggled irresistibly into his
mind, the foolishness of the doctrine began to be less
evident, and the points which had particularly offended
his reason assumed another aspect, or vanished entirely
away. The work within him appeared to go on even
while he slept, and that which had been a doubt, when
he laid down to rest, would often hold the place of
a truth, confirmed by some forgotten demonstration,
when he recalled his thoughts in the morning. But
while he was thus becoming assimilated to the enthusiasts, his contempt, in nowise decreasing towards them,
grew very fierce against himself; he imagined, also,
that every face of his acquaintance wore a sneer, and
that every word addressed to him was a gibe. Such
was his state of mind at the period of Ilbrahim's misfortune; and the emotions consequent upon that event
completed the change, of which the child had been the
original instrument.

In the mean time, neither the fierceness of the persecutors, nor the infatuation of their victims, had de-
creased. The dungeons were never empty; the streets
of almost every village echoed daily with the lash; the
life of a woman, whose mild and Christian spirit no

cruelty could embitter, had been sacrificed; and more
innocent blood was yet to pollute the hands that were
so often raised in prayer. Early after the Restoration,
the English Quakers represented to Charles II. that
a "vein of blood was open in his dominions;" but
though the displeasure of the voluptuous king was
roused, his interference was not prompt. And now
the tale must stride forward over many months, leaving Pearson to encounter ignominy and misfortune;
his wife to a firm endurance of a thousand sorrows;
poor Ilbrahim to pine and droop like a cankered rosebud; his mother to wander on a mistaken errand, neglectful of the holiest trust which can be committed to
a woman.

. . . .

A winter evening, a night of storm, had darkened
over Pearson's habitation, and there were no cheerful
faces to drive the gloom from his broad hearth. The
fire, it is true, sent forth a glowing heat and a ruddy
light, and large logs, dripping with half-melted snow,
lay ready to be cast upon the embers. But the apartment was saddened in its aspect by the absence of
much of the homely wealth which had once adorned
it; for the exaction of repeated fines, and his own
neglect of temporal affairs, had greatly impoverished
the owner. And with the furniture of peace, the im-
plements of war had likewise disappeared; the sword
was broken, the helm and cuirass were cast away forever; the soldier had done with battles, and might not
lift so much as his naked hand to guard his head.
But the Holy Book remained, and the table on which
it rested was drawn before the fire, while two of the
persecuted sect sought comfort from its pages.

He who listened, while the other read, was the

master of the house, now emaciated in form, and altered as to the expression and healthiness of his countenance; for his mind had dwelt too long among visionary thoughts, and his body had been worn by imprisonment and stripes. The hale and weatherbeaten old man who sat beside him had sustained less injury from a far longer course of the same mode of life. In person he was tall and dignified, and, which alone would have made him hateful to the Puritans, his gray locks fell from beneath the broad-brimmed hat, and rested on his shoulders. As the old man read the sacred page the snow drifted against the windows, or eddied in at the crevices of the door, while a blast kept laughing in the chimney, and the blaze leaped fiercely up to seek it. And sometimes, when the wind struck the hill at a certain angle, and swept down by the cottage across the wintry plain, its voice was the most doleful that can be conceived; it came as if the Past were speaking, as if the Dead had contributed each a whisper, as if the Desolation of Ages were breathed in that one lamenting sound.

The Quaker at length closed the book, retaining however his hand between the pages which he had been reading, while he looked steadfastly at Pearson. The attitude and features of the latter might have indicated the endurance of bodily pain; he leaned his forehead on his hands, his teeth were firmly closed, and his frame was tremulous at intervals with a nervous agitation.

"Friend Tobias," inquired the old man, compassionately, "hast thou found no comfort in these many blessed passages of Scripture?"

"Thy voice has fallen on my ear like a sound afar off and indistinct," replied Pearson without lifting his eyes. "Yea, and when I have hearkened carefully the words seemed cold and lifeless, and intended for another and a lesser grief than mine. Remove the book," he added, in a tone of sullen bitterness. "I have no part in its consolations, and they do but fret my sorrow the more."

"Nay, feeble brother, be not as one who hath never known the light," said the elder Quaker earnestly, but with mildness. "Art thou he that wouldst be content to give all, and endure all, for conscience' sake; desiring even peculiar trials, that thy faith might be purified and thy heart weaned from worldly desires? And wilt thou sink beneath an affliction which happens alike to them that have their portion here below, and to them that lay up treasure in heaven? Faint not, for thy burden is yet light."

"It is heavy! It is heavier than I can bear!" exclaimed Pearson, with the impatience of a variable spirit. "From my youth upward I have been a man marked out for wrath; and year by year, yea, day after day, I have endured sorrows such as others know not in their lifetime. And now I speak not of the love that has been turned to hatred, the honor to ignominy, the ease and plentifulness of all things to danger, want, and nakedness. All this I could have borne, and counted myself blessed. But when my heart was desolate with many losses I fixed it upon the child of a stranger, and he became dearer to me than all my buried ones; and now he too must die as if my love were poison. Verily, I am an accursed man, and I will lay me down in the dust and lift up my head no more."

"Thou sinnest, brother, but it is not for me to rebuke thee; for I also have had my hours of darkness, wherein I have murmured against the cross," said the old Quaker. He continued, perhaps in the hope of distracting his companion's thoughts from his own sorrows. "Even of late was the light obscured within me, when the men of blood had banished me on pain of death, and the constables led me onward from village to village towards the wilderness. A strong and cruel hand was wielding the knotted cords; they sunk deep into the flesh, and thou mightst have tracked every reel and totter of my footsteps by the blood that followed. As we went on"—

"Have I not borne all this; and have I murmured?" interrupted Pearson impatiently.

"Nay, friend, but hear me," continued the other. "As we journeyed on, night darkened on our path, so that no man could see the rage of the persecutors or the constancy of my endurance, though Heaven forbid that I should glory therein. The lights began to glimmer in the cottage windows, and I could discern the inmates as they gathered in comfort and security, every man with his wife and children by their own evening hearth. At length we came to a tract of fertile land; in the dim light, the forest was not visible around it; and behold! there was a straw-thatched dwelling, which bore the very aspect of my home, far over the wild ocean, far in our own England. Then came bitter thoughts upon me; yea, remembrances that were like death to my soul. The happiness of my early days was painted to me; the disquiet of my manhood, the altered faith of my declining years. I remembered how I had been moved to go forth a wanderer when my daughter, the youngest, the dearest of my flock, lay on her dying bed, and"—

"Couldst thou obey the command at such a moment?" exclaimed Pearson, shuddering.

"Yea, yea," replied the old man hurriedly. "I was kneeling by her bedside when the voice spoke loud within me; but immediately I rose, and took my staff, and gat me gone. Oh! that it were permitted me to forget her woful look when I thus withdrew my arm, and left her journeying through the dark valley alone! for her soul was faint, and she had leaned upon my prayers. Now in that night of horror I was assailed by the thought that I had been an erring Christian and a cruel parent; yea, even my daughter, with her pale, dying features, seemed to stand by me and whisper, 'Father, you are deceived; go home and shelter your gray head.' O Thou, to whom I have looked in my farthest wanderings," continued the Quaker, raising his agitated eyes to heaven, "inflict not upon the bloodiest of our persecutors the unmitigated agony of my soul, when I believed that all I had done and suffered for Thee was at the instigation of a mocking fiend! But I yielded not; I knelt down and wrestled with the tempter, while the scourge bit more fiercely into the flesh. My prayer was heard, and I went on in peace and joy towards the wilderness."

The old man, though his fanaticism had generally all the calmness of reason, was deeply moved while reciting this tale; and his unwonted emotion seemed to rebuke and keep down that of his companion. They sat in silence, with their faces to the fire, imagining, perhaps, in its red embers new scenes of persecution yet to be encountered. The snow still drifted hard against the windows, and sometimes, as the blaze of the logs had gradually sunk, came down the spacious chimney and hissed upon the hearth. A cautious footstep might now and then be heard in a neighboring apartment, and the sound invariably drew the eyes of both Quakers to the door which led thither. When a fierce and riotous gust of wind had led his thoughts, by a natural association, to homeless travellers on such a night, Pearson resumed the conversation.

"I have well-nigh sunk under my own share of this trial," observed he, sighing heavily; "yet I would that it might be doubled to me, if so the child's mother could be spared. Her wounds have been deep and many, but this will be the sorest of all."

"Fear not for Catharine," replied the old Quaker, "for I know that valiant woman, and have seen how she can bear the cross. A mother's heart, indeed, is strong in her, and may seem to contend mightily with her faith; but soon she will stand up and give thanks that her son has been thus early an accepted sacrifice. The boy hath done his work, and she will feel that he is taken hence in kindness both to him and her. Blessed, blessed are they that with so little suffering can enter into peace!"

The fitful rush of the wind was now disturbed by a portentous sound; it was a quick and heavy knocking at the outer door. Pearson's wan countenance grew paler, for many a visit of persecution had taught him what to dread; the old man, on the other hand, stood up erect, and his glance was firm as that of the tried soldier who awaits his enemy.

"The men of blood have come to seek me," he observed with calmness. "They have heard how I was moved to return from banishment; and now am I to be led to prison, and thence to death. It is an end I have long looked for. I will open unto them, lest they say, ' Lo, he feareth!' "

"Nay, I will present myself before them," said Pearson, with recovered fortitude. " It may be that they seek me alone, and know not that thou abidest with me."

" Let us go boldly, both one and the other," rejoined his companion. " It is not fitting that thou or I should shrink."

They therefore proceeded through the entry to the door, which they opened, bidding the applicant " Come in, in God's name ! " A furious blast of wind drove the storm into their faces, and extinguished the lamp ; they had barely time to discern a figure, so white from head to foot with the drifted snow that it seemed like Winter's self, come in human shape, to seek refuge from its own desolation.

" Enter, friend, and do thy errand, be it what it may," said Pearson. "It must needs be pressing since thou comest on such a bitter night."

" Peace be with this household," said the stranger, when they stood on the floor of the inner apartment.

Pearson started, the elder Quaker stirred the slumbering embers of the fire till they sent up a clear and lofty blaze ; it was a female voice that had spoken ; it was a female form that shone out, cold and wintry, in that comfortable light.

"Catharine, blessed woman ! " exclaimed the old man, " art thou come to this darkened land again ? art thou come to bear a valiant testimony as in former years ? The scourge hath not prevailed against thee, and from the dungeon hast thou come forth triumphant ; but strengthen, strengthen now thy heart, Catharine, for Heaven will prove thee yet this once, ere thou go to thy reward."

" Rejoice, friends ! " she replied. " Thou who hast long been of our people, and thou whom a little child hath led to us, rejoice ! Lo ! I come, the messenger of glad tidings, for the day of persecution is overpast. The heart of the king, even Charles, hath been moved in gentleness towards us, and he hath sent forth his letters to stay the hands of the men of blood. A ship's company of our friends hath arrived at yonder town, and I also sailed joyfully among them."

As Catharine spoke, her eyes were roaming about the room, in search of him for whose sake security was dear to her. Pearson made a silent appeal to the old man, nor did the latter shrink from the painful task assigned him.

"Sister," he began, in a softened yet perfectly calm tone, "thou tellest us of His love, manifested in temporal good; and now must we speak to thee of that selfsame love, displayed in chastenings. Hitherto, Catharine, thou hast been as one journeying in a darksome and difficult path, and leading an infant by the hand; fain wouldst thou have looked heavenward continually, but still the cares of that little child have drawn thine eyes and thy affections to the earth. Sister! go on rejoicing, for his tottering footsteps shall impede thine own no more."

But the unhappy mother was not thus to be consoled; she shook like a leaf, she turned white as the very snow that hung drifted into her hair. The firm old man extended his hand and held her up, keeping his eye upon hers, as if to repress any outbreak of passion.

"I am a woman, I am but a woman; will He try me above my strength?" said Catharine very quickly, and almost in a whisper. "I have been wounded sore: I have suffered much; many things in the body; many in the mind; crucified in myself, and in them that were dearest to me. Surely," added she, with a

long shudder, " He hath spared me in this one thing."
She broke forth with sudden and irrepressible violence. " Tell me, man of cold heart, what has God
done to me? Hath He cast me down, never to rise
again? Hath He crushed my very heart in his hand?
And thou, to whom I committed my child, how hast
thou fulfilled thy trust? Give me back the boy, well,
sound, alive, alive; or earth and Heaven shall avenge
me!"

The agonized shriek of Catharine was answered by
the faint, the very faint, voice of a child.

On this day it had become evident to Pearson, to
his aged guest, and to Dorothy, that Ilbrahim's brief
and troubled pilgrimage drew near its close. The
two former would willingly have remained by him, to
make use of the prayers and pious discourses which
they deemed appropriate to the time, and which, if
they be impotent as to the departing traveller's reception in the world whither it goes, may at least sustain him in bidding adieu to earth. But though Ilbrahim uttered no complaint, he was disturbed by the
faces that looked upon him; so that Dorothy's entreaties, and their own conviction that the child's feet
might tread heaven's pavement and not soil it, had
induced the two Quakers to remove. Ilbrahim then
closed his eyes and grew calm, and, except for now
and then a kind and low word to his nurse, migh'
have been thought to slumber. As nightfall came
on, however, and the storm began to rise, something
seemed to trouble the repose of the boy's mind, and
to render his sense of hearing active and acute. If a
passing wind lingered to shake the casement, he strove
to turn his head towards it: if the door jarred to and
fro upon its hinges, he looked long and anxiously

thitherward ; if the heavy voice of the old man, as he
read the Scriptures, rose but a little higher, the child
almost held his dying breath to listen ; if a snow-drift
swept by the cottage, with a sound like the trailing
of a garment, Ilbrahim seemed to watch that some
visitant should enter.

But, after a little time, he relinquished whatever
secret hope had agitated him, and with one low, complaining whisper, turned his cheek upon the pillow.
He then addressed Dorothy with his usual sweetness,
and besought her to draw near him ; she did so, and
Ilbrahim took her hand in both of his, grasping it
with a gentle pressure, as if to assure himself that he
retained it.   At intervals, and without disturbing the
repose of his countenance, a very faint trembling
passed over him from head to foot, as if a mild but
somewhat cool wind had breathed upon him, and
made him shiver.   As the boy thus led her by the
hand, in his quiet progress over the borders of eternity, Dorothy almost imagined that she could discern
the near, though dim, delightfulness of the home he
was about to reach ; she would not have enticed the
little wanderer back, though she bemoaned herself
that she must leave him and return.   But just when
Ilbrahim's feet were pressing on the soil of Paradise
he heard a voice behind him, and it recalled him a few,
few paces of the weary path which he had travelled.
As Dorothy looked upon his features, she perceived
that their placid expression was again disturbed ; her
own thoughts had been so wrapped in him, that all
sounds of the storm, and of human speech, were lost
to her ; but when Catharine's shriek pierced through
the room, the boy strove to raise himself.

"Friend, she is come ! Open unto her ! " cried he

In a moment his mother was kneeling by the bedside; she drew Ilbrahim to her bosom, and he nestled
there, with no violence of joy, but contentedly, as if
he were hushing himself to sleep. He looked into her
face, and reading its agony, said, with feeble earnestness, "Mourn not, dearest mother. I am happy now."
And with these words the gentle boy was dead.

. . . .

The king's mandate to stay the New England persecutors was effectual in preventing further martyr-
doms; but the colonial authorities, trusting in the
remoteness of their situation, and perhaps in the supposed instability of the royal government, shortly renewed their severities in all other respects. Catharine's fanaticism had become wilder by the sundering
of all human ties; and wherever a scourge was lifted
there was she to receive the blow; and whenever a
dungeon was unbarred thither she came, to cast herself upon the floor. But in process of time a more
Christian spirit — a spirit of forbearance, though not
of cordiality or approbation — began to pervade the
land in regard to the persecuted sect. And then,
when the rigid old Pilgrims eyed her rather in pity
than in wrath; when the matrons fed her with the
fragments of their children's food, and offered her a
lodging on a hard and lowly bed; when no little crowd
of schoolboys left their sports to cast stones after the
roving enthusiast; then did Catharine return to Pearson's dwelling and made that her home.

As if Ilbrahim's sweetness yet lingered round his
ashes; as if his gentle spirit came down from heaven
to teach his parent a true religion, her fierce and vin-
dictive nature was softened by the same griefs which
had once irritated it. When the course of years had

made the features of the unobtrusive mourner familiar in the settlement, she became a subject of not deep, but general, interest; a being on whom the otherwise superfluous sympathies of all might be bestowed. Every one spoke of her with that degree of pity which it is pleasant to experience; every one was ready to do her the little kindnesses which are not costly, yet manifest good will; and when at last she died, a long train of her once bitter persecutors followed her, with decent sadness and tears that were not painful, to her place by Ilbrahim's green and sunken grave.

MR. HIGGINBOTHAM'S CATASTROPHE.

A YOUNG fellow, a tobacco pedlar by trade, was on his way from Morristown, where he had dealt largely with the Deacon of the Shaker settlement, to the village of Parker's Falls, on Salmon River. He had a neat little cart, painted green, with a box of cigars depicted on each side panel, and an Indian chief, holding a pipe and a golden tobacco stalk, on the rear. The pedlar drove a smart little mare, and was a young man of excellent character, keen at a bargain, but none the worse liked by the Yankees; who, as I have heard them say, would rather be shaved with a sharp razor than a dull one. Especially was he beloved by the pretty girls along the Connecticut, whose favor he used to court by presents of the best smoking tobacco in his stock; knowing well that the country lasses of New England are generally great performers on pipes. Moreover, as will be seen in the course of my story, the pedlar was inquisitive, and something of a tattler, always itching to hear the news and anxious to tell it again.

After an early breakfast at Morristown, the tobacco pedlar, whose name was Dominicus Pike, had travelled seven miles through a solitary piece of woods, without speaking a word to anybody but himself and his little gray mare. It being nearly seven o'clock, he was as eager to hold a morning gossip as a city shopkeeper to read the morning paper. An opportunity seemed at hand when, after lighting a cigar with a sun-glass, he looked up, and perceived a man coming over the brow of the hill, at the foot of which the ped-lar had stopped his green cart. Dominicus watched him as he descended, and noticed that he carried a bundle over his shoulder on the end of a stick, and travelled with a weary, yet determined pace. He did not look as if he had started in the freshness of the morning, but had footed it all night, and meant to do the same all day.

"Good morning, mister," said Dominicus, when within speaking distance. "You go a pretty good jog. What's the latest news at Parker's Falls?"

The man pulled the broad brim of a gray hat over his eyes, and answered, rather suddenly, that he did not come from Parker's Falls, which, as being the limit of his own day's journey, the pedlar had natu-rally mentioned in his inquiry.

"Well then," rejoined Dominicus Pike, "let's have the latest news where you did come from. I'm not particular about Parker's Falls. Any place will an-swer."

Being thus importuned, the traveller — who was as ill looking a fellow as one would desire to meet in a solitary piece of woods — appeared to hesitate a little, as if he was either searching his memory for news, or weighing the expediency of telling it. At last, mount-ing on the step of the cart, he whispered in the ear of Dominicus, though he might have shouted aloud and no other mortal would have heard him.

"I do remember one little trifle of news," said he. "Old Mr. Higginbotham, of Kimballton, was murdered in his orchard, at eight o'clock last night, by an Irish-man and a nigger. They strung him up to the branch of a St. Michael's pear-tree, where nobody would find him till the morning."

As soon as this horrible intelligence was communicated, the stranger betook himself to his journey again, with more speed than ever, not even turning his head when Dominicus invited him to smoke a Spanish cigar and relate all the particulars. The pedlar whistled to his mare and went up the hill, pondering on the doleful fate of Mr. Higginbotham whom he had known in the way of trade, having sold him many a bunch of long nines, and a great deal of pigtail, lady's twist, and fig tobacco. He was rather astonished at the rapidity with which the news had spread. Kimballton was nearly sixty miles distant in a straight line; the murder had been perpetrated only at eight o'clock the preceding night; yet Dominicus had heard of it at seven in the morning, when, in all probability, poor Mr. Higginbotham's own family had but just discovered his corpse, hanging on the St. Michael's peartree. The stranger on foot must have worn seven-league boots to travel at such a rate.

"Ill news flies fast, they say," thought Dominicus Pike; "but this beats railroads. The fellow ought to be hired to go express with the President's Message."

The difficulty was solved by supposing that the narrator had made a mistake of one day in the date of the occurrence; so that our friend did not hesitate to introduce the story at every tavern and country store along the road, expending a whole bunch of Spanish wrappers among at least twenty horrified audiences. He found himself invariably the first bearer of the intelligence, and was so pestered with questions that he could not avoid filling up the outline, till it became quite a respectable narrative. He met with one piece of corroborative evidence. Mr. Higginbotham was a trader; and a former clerk of his, to whom Dominicus related the facts, testified that the old gentleman was accustomed to return home through the orchard about nightfall, with the money and valuable papers of the store in his pocket. The clerk manifested but little grief at Mr. Higginbotham's catastrophe, hinting, what the pedlar had discovered in his own dealings with him, that he was a crusty old fellow, as close as a vice. His property would descend to a pretty niece who was now keeping school in Kimballton.

What with telling the news for the public good, and driving bargains for his own, Dominicus was so much delayed on the road that he chose to put up at a tavern, about five miles short of Parker's Falls. After supper, lighting one of his prime cigars, he seated himself in the bar-room, and went through the story of the murder, which had grown so fast that it took him half an hour to tell. There were as many as twenty people in the room, nineteen of whom received it all for gospel. But the twentieth was an elderly farmer, who had arrived on horseback a short time before, and was now seated in a corner smoking his pipe. When the story was concluded, he rose up very deliberately, brought his chair right in front of Dominicus, and stared him full in the face, puffing out the vilest tobacco smoke the pedlar had ever smelt.

"Will you make affidavit," demanded he, in the tone of a country justice taking an examination, "that old Squire Higginbotham of Kimballton was murdered in his orchard the night before last, and found hanging on his great pear-tree yesterday morning?"

"I tell the story as I heard it, mister," answered Dominicus, dropping his half-burnt cigar; "I don't say that I saw the thing done. So I can't take my oath that he was murdered exactly in that way."

"But I can take mine," said the farmer, "that if Squire Higginbotham was murdered night before last, I drank a glass of bitters with his ghost this morning. Being a neighbor of mine, he called me into his store, as I was riding by, and treated me, and then asked me to do a little business for him on the road. He didn't seem to know any more about his own murder than I did."

"Why, then, it can't be a fact!" exclaimed Dominicus Pike.

"I guess he'd have mentioned, if it was," said the old farmer; and he removed his chair back to the corner, leaving Dominicus quite down in the mouth.

Here was a sad resurrection of old Mr. Higginbotham! The pedlar had no heart to mingle in the conversation any more, but comforted himself with a glass of gin and water, and went to bed where, all night long, he dreamed of hanging on the St. Michael's pear-tree. To avoid the old farmer (whom he so detested that his suspension would have pleased him better than Mr. Higginbotham's), Dominicus rose in the gray of the morning, put the little mare into the green cart, and trotted swiftly away towards Parker's Falls. The fresh breeze, the dewy road, and the pleasant summer dawn, revived his spirits, and might have encouraged him to repeat the old story had there been anybody awake to hear it. But he met neither ox team, light wagon chaise, horseman, nor foot traveller, till, just as he crossed Salmon River, a man came trudging down to the bridge with a bundle over his shoulder, on the end of a stick.

"Good morning, mister," said the pedlar, reining in his mare. "If you come from Kimballton or that neighborhood, may be you can tell me the real fact about this affair of old Mr. Higginbotham. Was the old fellow actually murdered two or three nights ago, by an Irishman and a nigger ? "

Dominicus had spoken in too great a hurry to observe, at first, that the stranger himself had a deep tinge of negro blood. On hearing this sudden question, the Ethiopian appeared to change his skin, its yellow hue becoming a ghastly white, while, shaking and stammering, he thus replied : —

" No ! no ! There was no colored man ! It was an Irishman that hanged him last night, at eight o'clock. I came away at seven ! His folks can't have looked for him in the orchard yet."

Scarcely had the yellow man spoken, when he interrupted himself, and though he seemed weary enough before, continued his journey at a pace which would have kept the pedlar's mare on a smart trot. Dominicus started after him in great perplexity. If the murder had not been committed till Tuesday night, who was the prophet that had foretold it, in all its circumstances, on Tuesday morning ? If Mr. Higginbotham's corpse were not yet discovered by his own family, how came the mulatto, at above thirty miles' distance, to know that he was hanging in the orchard, especially as he had left Kimballton before the unfortunate man was hanged at all ? These ambiguous circumstances, with the stranger's surprise and terror, made Dominicus think of raising a hue and cry after him, as an accomplice in the murder ; since a murder, it seemed, had really been perpetrated.

" But let the poor devil go," thought the pedlar. " I don't want his black blood on my head ; and hanging the nigger would n't unhang Mr. Higginbotham. Unhang the old gentleman ! It 's a sin, I know ; but

I should hate to have him come to life a second time, and give me the lie ! "

With these meditations, Dominicus Pike drove into the street of Parker's Falls, which, as everybody knows, is as thriving a village as three cotton factories and a slitting mill can make it. The machinery was not in motion, and but a few of the shop doors unbarred, when he alighted in the stable yard of the tavern, and made it his first business to order the mare four quarts of oats. His second duty, of course, was to impart Mr. Higginbotham's catastrophe to the hostler. He deemed it advisable, however, not to be too positive as to the date of the direful fact, and also to be uncertain whether it were perpetrated by an Irishman and a mulatto, or by the son of Erin alone. Neither did he profess to relate it on his own authority, or that of any one person ; but mentioned it as a report generally diffused.

The story ran through the town like fire among girdled trees, and became so much the universal talk that nobody could tell whence it had originated. Mr. Higginbotham was as well known at Parker's Falls as any citizen of the place, being part owner of the slitting mill, and a considerable stockholder in the cotton factories. The inhabitants felt their own prosperity interested in his fate. Such was the excitement, that the Parker's Falls Gazette anticipated its regular day of publication, and came out with half a form of blank paper and a column of double pica emphasized with capitals, and headed HORRID MURDER OF MR. HIGGINBOTHAM ! Among other dreadful details, the printed account described the mark of the cord round the dead man's neck, and stated the number of thousand dollars of which he

had been robbed; there was much pathos also about
the affliction of his niece, who had gone from one
fainting fit to another, ever since her uncle was found
hanging on the St. Michael's pear-tree with his pockets inside out. The village poet likewise commemorated the young lady's grief in seventeen stanzas of a
ballad. The selectmen held a meeting, and, in consideration of Mr. Higginbotham's claims on the town,
determined to issue handbills, offering a reward of
five hundred dollars for the apprehension of his murderers, and the recovery of the stolen property.

Meanwhile the whole population of Parker's Falls,
consisting of shopkeepers, mistresses of boarding-
houses, factory girls, millmen, and school boys, rushed
into the street and kept up such a terrible loquacity
as more than compensated for the silence of the cotton
machines, which refrained from their usual din out of
respect to the deceased. Had Mr. Higginbotham
cared about posthumous renown, his untimely ghost
would have exulted in this tumult. Our friend Dominicus, in his vanity of heart, forgot his intended precautions, and mounting on the town pump, announced
himself as the bearer of the authentic intelligence
which had caused so wonderful a sensation. He immediately became the great man of the moment,
and had just begun a new edition of the narrative,
with a voice like a field preacher, when the mail stage
drove into the village street. It had travelled all
night, and must have shifted horses at Kimballton,
at three in the morning.

"Now we shall hear all the particulars," shouted
the crowd.

The coach rumbled up to the piazza of the tavern,
followed by a thousand people; for if any man had

been minding his own business till then, he now left it at sixes and sevens, to hear the news. The pedlar, foremost in the race, discovered two passengers, both of whom had been startled from a comfortable nap to find themselves in the centre of a mob. Every man assailing them with separate questions, all propounded at once, the couple were struck speechless, though one was a lawyer and the other a young lady.

"Mr. Higginbotham! Mr. Higginbotham! Tell us the particulars about old Mr. Higginbotham!" bawled the mob. "What is the coroner's verdict? Are the murderers apprehended? Is Mr. Higginbotham's niece come out of her fainting fits? Mr. Higginbotham! Mr. Higginbotham!!"

The coachman said not a word, except to swear awfully at the hostler for not bringing him a fresh team of horses. The lawyer inside had generally his wits about him even when asleep; the first thing he did, after learning the cause of the excitement, was to produce a large, red pocket-book. Meantime Dominicus Pike, being an extremely polite young man, and also suspecting that a female tongue would tell the story as glibly as a lawyer's, had handed the lady out of the coach. She was a fine, smart girl, now wide awake and bright as a button, and had such a sweet pretty mouth, that Dominicus would almost as lief have heard a love tale from it as a tale of murder.

"Gentlemen and ladies," said the lawyer to the shopkeepers, the millmen, and the factory girls, "I can assure you that some unaccountable mistake, or, more probably, a wilful falsehood, maliciously contrived to injure Mr. Higginbotham's credit, has excited this singular uproar. We passed through Kimballton at three o'clock this morning, and most certainly should

have been informed of the murder had any been per
petrated. But I have proof nearly as strong as Mr.
Higginbotham's own oral testimony, in the negative.
Here is a note relating to a suit of his in the Connecticut courts, which was delivered me from that
gentleman himself. I find it dated at ten o'clock last
evening."

So saying, the lawyer exhibited the date and signature of the note, which irrefragably proved, either
that this perverse Mr. Higginbotham was alive when
he wrote it, or — as some deemed the more probable
case, of two doubtful ones — that he was so absorbed
in worldly business as to continue to transact it even
after his death. But unexpected evidence was forth-
coming. The young lady, after listening to the pedlar's explanation, merely seized a moment to smooth
her gown and put her curls in order, and then appeared at the tavern door, making a modest signal to
be heard.

" Good people," said she, " I am Mr. Higginbotham's niece."

A wondering murmur passed through the crowd on
beholding her so rosy and bright ; that same unhappy
niece, whom they had supposed, on the authority of
the Parker's Falls Gazette, to be lying at death's
door in a fainting fit. But some shrewd fellows had
doubted, all along, whether a young lady would be
quite so desperate at the hanging of a rich old uncle.

"You see," continued Miss Higginbotham, with a
smile, " that this strange story is quite unfounded as
to myself ; and I believe I may affirm it to be equally
so in regard to my dear uncle Higginbotham. He
has the kindness to give me a home in his house,
though I contribute to my own support by teaching a

school. I left Kimballton this morning to spend the vacation of commencement week with a friend, about five miles from Parker's Falls. My generous uncle, when he heard me on the stairs, called me to his bed-side, and gave me two dollars and fifty cents to pay my stage fare, and another dollar for my extra expenses. He then laid his pocket-book under his pillow, shook hands with me, and advised me to take some biscuit in my bag, instead of breakfasting on the road. I feel confident, therefore, that I left my beloved relative alive, and trust that I shall find him so on my return."

The young lady courtesied at the close of her speech, which was so sensible and well worded, and delivered with such grace and propriety, that everybody thought her fit to be preceptress of the best academy in the State. But a stranger would have supposed that Mr. Higginbotham was an object of abhorrence at Parker's Falls, and that a thanksgiving had been proclaimed for his murder; so excessive was the wrath of the inhabitants on learning their mistake. The millmen resolved to bestow public honors on Dominicus Pike, only hesitating whether to tar and feather him, ride him on a rail, or refresh him with an ablution at the town pump, on the top of which he had declared himself the bearer of the news. The selectmen, by advice of the lawyer, spoke of prosecuting him for a misdemeanor, in circulating unfounded reports, to the great disturbance of the peace of the Commonwealth. Nothing saved Dominicus, either from mob law or a court of justice, but an eloquent appeal made by the young lady in his behalf. Addressing a few words of heartfelt gratitude to his benefactress, he mounted the green cart and rode out

of town, under a discharge of artillery from the school-
boys, who found plenty of ammunition in the neighboring clay-pits and mud holes. As he turned his
head to exchange a farewell glance with Mr. Higginbotham's niece, a ball, of the consistence of hasty
pudding, hit him slap in the mouth, giving him a most
grim aspect. His whole person was so bespattered
with the like filthy missiles, that he had almost a mind
to ride back, and supplicate for the threatened ablution at the town pump; for, though not meant in
kindness, it would now have been a deed of charity.

However, the sun shone bright on poor Dominicus,
and the mud, an emblem of all stains of undeserved
opprobrium, was easily brushed off when dry. Being
a funny rogue, his heart soon cheered up; nor could
he refrain from a hearty laugh at the uproar which
his story had excited. The handbills of the selectmen would cause the commitment of all the vagabonds
in the State; the paragraph in the Parker's Falls
Gazette would be reprinted from Maine to Florida,
and perhaps form an item in the London newspapers;
and many a miser would tremble for his money bags
and life, on learning the catastrophe of Mr. Higginbotham. The pedlar meditated with much fervor on
the charms of the young schoolmistress, and swore
that Daniel Webster never spoke nor looked so like
an angel as Miss Higginbotham, while defending him
from the wrathful populace at Parker's Falls.

Dominicus was now on the Kimballton turnpike,
having all along determined to visit that place, though
business had drawn him out of the most direct road
from Morristown. As he approached the scene of the
supposed murder, he continued to revolve the circumstances in his mind, and was astonished at the aspect

which the whole case assumed. Had nothing occurred to corroborate the story of the first traveller, it might now have been considered as a hoax; but the yellow man was evidently acquainted either with the report or the fact; and there was a mystery in his dismayed and guilty look on being abruptly questioned. When, to this singular combination of incidents, it was added that the rumor tallied exactly with Mr. Higginbotham's character and habits of life; and that he had an orchard, and a St. Michael's pear-tree, near which he always passed at nightfall: the circumstantial evidence appeared so strong that Dominicus doubted whether the autograph produced by the lawyer, or even the niece's direct testimony, ought to be equivalent. Making cautious inquiries along the road, the pedlar further learned that Mr. Higginbotham had in his service an Irishman of doubtful character, whom he had hired without a recommendation, on the score of economy.

"May I be hanged myself," exclaimed Dominicus Pike aloud, on reaching the top of a lonely hill, "if I 'll believe old Higginbotham is unhanged till I see him with my own eyes, and hear it from his own mouth! And as he 's a real shaver, I 'll have the minister or some other responsible man for an indorser."

It was growing dusk when he reached the toll-house on Kimballton turnpike, about a quarter of a mile from the village of this name. His little mare was fast bringing him up with a man on horseback, who trotted through the gate a few rods in advance of him, nodded to the toll-gatherer, and kept on towards the village. Dominicus was acquainted with the tollman, and, while making change, the usual remarks on the weather passed between them.

"I suppose," said the pedlar, throwing back his
whiplash, to bring it down like a feather on the mare's
flank, "you have not seen anything of old Mr. Higginbotham within a day or two?"

"Yes," answered the toll-gatherer. "He passed
the gate just before you drove up, and yonder he rides
now, if you can see him through the dusk. He's been
to Woodfield this afternoon, attending a sheriff's sale
there. The old man generally shakes hands and has
a little chat with me; but to-night, he nodded, — as
if to say, 'Charge my toll,' and jogged on; for wherever he goes, he must always be at home by eight
o'clock."

"So they tell me," said Dominicus.

"I never saw a man look so yellow and thin as the
squire does," continued the toll-gatherer. "Says I to
myself, to-night, he's more like a ghost or an old
mummy than good flesh and blood."

The pedlar strained his eyes through the twilight,
and could just discern the horseman now far ahead on
the village road. He seemed to recognize the rear of
Mr. Higginbotham; but through the evening shadows,
and amid the dust from the horse's feet, the figure appeared dim and unsubstantial; as if the shape of the
mysterious old man were faintly moulded of darkness
and gray light. Dominicus shivered.

"Mr. Higginbotham has come back from the other
world, by way of the Kimballton turnpike," thought
he.

He shook the reins and rode forward, keeping about
the same distance in the rear of the gray old shadow,
till the latter was concealed by a bend of the road.
On reaching this point, the pedlar no longer saw the
man on horseback, but found himself at the head of

the village street, not far from a number of stores and
two taverns, clustered round the meeting-house steeple.
On his left were a stone wall and a gate, the boundary
of a wood-lot, beyond which lay an orchard, farther
still, a mowing field, and last of all, a house. These
were the premises of Mr. Higginbotham, whose dwell·
ing stood beside the old highway, but had been left
in the background by the Kimballton turnpike. Dominicus knew the place; and the little mare stopped
short by instinct; for he was not conscious of tighten-
ing the reins.

"For the soul of me, I cannot get by this gate!"
said he, trembling. "I never shall be my own man
again, till I see whether Mr. Higginbotham is hanging
on the St. Michael's pear-tree!"

He leaped from the cart, gave the rein a turn round
the gate post, and ran along the green path of the
wood-lot as if Old Nick were chasing behind. Just
then the village clock tolled eight, and as each deep
stroke fell, Dominicus gave a fresh bound and flew
faster than before, till, dim in the solitary centre of
the orchard, he saw the fated pear-tree. One great
branch stretched from the old contorted trunk across
the path, and threw the darkest shadow on that one
spot. But something seemed to struggle beneath the
branch!

The pedlar had never pretended to more courage.
than befits a man of peaceable occupation, nor could
he account for his valor on this awful emergency.
Certain it is, however, that he rushed forward, prostrated a sturdy Irishman with the butt end of his
whip, and found — not indeed hanging on the St. Michael's pear-tree, but trembling beneath it, with a halter
round his neck — the old, identical Mr. Higginbotham!

"Mr. Higginbotham," said Dominicus tremulously, "you're an honest man, and I'll take your word for it. Have you been hanged or not?"

If the riddle be not already guessed, a few words will explain the simple machinery by which this "coming event" was made to "cast its shadow before." Three men had plotted the robbery and murder of Mr. Higginbotham; two of them, successively, lost courage and fled, each delaying the crime one night by their disappearance; the third was in the act of perpetration, when a champion, blindly obeying the call of fate, like the heroes of old romance, appeared in the person of Dominicus Pike.

It only remains to say, that Mr. Higginbotham took the pedlar into high favor, sanctioned his addresses to the pretty schoolmistress, and settled his whole property on their children, allowing themselves the interest. In due time, the old gentleman capped the climax of his favors, by dying a Christian death, in bed, since which melancholy event Dominicus Pike has removed from Kimballton, and established a large tobacco manufactory in my native village.

LITTLE ANNIE'S RAMBLE.

DING-DONG! Ding-dong! Ding-dong!

The town crier has rung his bell at a distant corner, and little Annie stands on her father's doorsteps, trying to hear what the man with the loud voice is talking about. Let me listen too. Oh, he is telling the people that an elephant, and a lion, and a royal tiger, and a horse with horns, and other strange beasts from foreign countries, have come to town, and will receive all visitors who choose to wait upon them. Perhaps little Annie would like to go. Yes; and I can see that the pretty child is weary of this wide and pleasant street, with the green trees flinging their shade across the quiet sunshine, and the pavements and the sidewalks all as clean as if the housemaid had just swept them with her broom. She feels that impulse to go strolling away — that longing after the mystery of the great world — which many children feel, and which I felt in my childhood. Little Annie shall take a ramble with me. See! I do but hold out my hand, and, like some bright bird in the sunny air, with her blue silk frock fluttering upwards from her white pantalets she comes bounding on tiptoe across the street.

Smooth back your brown curls, Annie; and let me tie on your bonnet, and we will set forth! What a strange couple to go on their rambles together! One walks in black attire, with a measured step, and a heavy brow, and his thoughtful eyes bent down; while the gay little girl trips lightly along, as if she were forced to keep hold of my hand, lest her feet should dance away from the earth. Yet there is sympathy between us. If I pride myself on anything, it is because I have a smile that children love; and, on the other hand, there are few grown ladies that could entice me from the side of little Annie; for I delight to let my mind go hand in hand with the mind of a sinless child. So, come, Annie; but if I moralize as we go, do not listen to me; only look about you, and be merry!

Now we turn the corner. Here are hacks with two horses, and stage-coaches with four, thundering to meet each other, and trucks and carts moving at a slower pace, being heavily laden with barrels from the wharves, and here are rattling gigs, which perhaps will be smashed to pieces before our eyes. Hitherward, also, comes a man trundling a wheelbarrow along the pavement. Is not little Annie afraid of such a tumult? No; she does not even shrink closer to my side, but passes on with fearless confidence, a happy child amidst a great throng of grown people, who pay the same reverence to her infancy that they would to extreme old age. Nobody jostles her; all turn aside to make way for little Annie; and what is most singular, she appears conscious of her claim to such respect. Now her eyes brighten with pleasure! A street musician has seated himself on the steps of yonder church, and pours forth his strains to the busy town, a melody that has gone astray among the tramp of footsteps, the buzz of voices, and the war of passing wheels. Who heeds the poor organ grinder? None but myself and little Annie, whose feet begin to move in unison with the lively tune, as if she were loath that music should be wasted without a dance. But where would Annie find a partner? Some have the gout in their toes, or the rheumatism in their joints; some are stiff with age; some feeble with disease; some are so lean that their bones would rattle, and others of such ponderous size that their agility would crack the flagstones; but many, many have leaden feet, because their hearts are far heavier than lead. It is a sad thought that I have chanced upon. What a company of dancers should we be! For I, too, am a gentleman of sober footsteps, and therefore, little Annie, let us walk sedately on.

It is a question with me, whether this giddy child or my sage self have most pleasure in looking at the shop windows. We love the silks of sunny hue, that glow within the darkened premises of the spruce dry goods' men; we are pleasantly dazzled by the burnished silver and the chased gold, the rings of wedlock and the costly love ornaments, glistening at the window of the jeweller; but Annie, more than I, seeks for a glimpse of her passing figure in the dusty looking-glasses at the hardware stores. All that is bright and gay attracts us both.

Here is a shop to which the recollections of my boyhood, as well as present partialities, give a peculiar magic. How delightful to let the fancy revel on the dainties of a confectioner: those pies, with such white and flaky paste, their contents being a mystery, whether rich mince, with whole plums intermixed, or piquant apple, delicately rose flavored; those cakes, heart-shaped or round, piled in a lofty pyramid; those sweet little circlets, sweetly named kisses; those dark majestic masses, fit to be bridal loaves at the wedding of an heiress, mountains in size, their summits deeply snow-covered with sugar! Then the mighty treasures of sugar-plums, white and crimson and yellow, in large glass vases; and candy of all varieties; and those little cockles, or whatever they are called, much prized by children for their sweetness, and more for the mottoes which they inclose, by love-sick maids and bachelors! Oh, my mouth waters, little Annie, and so doth yours; but we will not be tempted, except to an imaginary feast; so let us hasten onward, devouring the vision of a plum cake.

Here are pleasures, as some people would say, of a more exalted kind, in the window of a bookseller. Is Annie a literary lady? Yes; she is deeply read in Peter Parley's tomes, and has an increasing love for fairy tales, though seldom met with nowadays, and she will subscribe, next year, to the Juvenile Miscellany. But, truth to tell, she is apt to turn away from the printed page, and keep gazing at the pretty pictures, such as the gay-colored ones which make this shop window the continual loitering-place of children. What would Annie think if, in the book which I mean to send her on New Year's Day, she should find her sweet little self, bound up in silk or morocco with gilt edges, there to remain till she become a woman grown, with children of her own to read about their mother's childhood! That would be very queer.

Little Annie is weary of pictures, and pulls me onward by the hand, till suddenly we pause at the most wondrous shop in all the town. Oh, my stars! Is this a toyshop, or is it fairyland? For here are gilded chariots, in which the king and queen of the fairies might ride side by side, while their courtiers, on these small horses, should gallop in triumphal procession before and behind the royal pair. Here, too, are dishes of china ware, fit to be the dining set of those same princely personages, when they make a regal banquet in the stateliest hall of their palace, full five feet high, and behold their nobles feasting adown the long perspective of the table. Betwixt the king and queen should sit my little Annie, the prettiest fairy of them all. Here stands a turbaned turk, threatening us with his sabre, like an ugly heathen as he is. And next a Chinese mandarin, who nods his head at Annie and myself. Here we may review a whole army of horse and foot, in red and blue uniforms, with drums, fifes, trumpets, and all kinds of noiseless music; they have halted on the shelf of this window, after their weary march from Liliput. But what cares Annie for soldiers? No conquering queen is she, neither a Semiramis nor a Catharine; her whole heart is set upon that doll, who gazes at us with such a fashionable stare. This is the little girl's true plaything. Though made of wood, a doll is a visionary and ethereal personage, endowed by childish fancy with a peculiar life; the mimic lady is a heroine of romance, an actor and a sufferer in a thousand shadowy scenes, the chief inhabitant of that wild world with which children ape the real one. Little Annie does not understand what I am saying, but looks wishfully at the proud lady in the window. We wilt invite her home with us as we return. Meantime, good-by, Dame Doll! A toy yourself, you look forth from your window upon many ladies that are also toys, though they walk and speak, and upon a crowd in pursuit of toys, though they wear grave visages. Oh, with your never closing eyes, had you but an intellect to moralize on all that flits before them, what a wise doll would you be! Come, little Annie, we shall find toys enough, go where we may.

Now we elbow our way among the throng again

It is curious, in the most crowded part of a town, to meet with living creatures that had their birthplace in some far solitude, but have acquired a second nature in the wilderness of men. Look up, Annie, at that canary bird, hanging out of the window in his cage. Poor little fellow! His golden feathers are all tarnished in this smoky sunshine; he would have glistened twice as brightly among the summer islands; but still he has become a citizen in all his tastes and habits, and would not sing half so well without the uproar that drowns his music. What a pity that he does not know how miserable he is! There is a parrot, too, calling out, "Pretty Poll! Pretty Poll!" as we pass by. Foolish bird, to be talking about her prettiness to strangers, especially as she is not a pretty Poll, though gaudily dressed in green and yellow. If she had said "Pretty Annie," there would have been some sense in it. See that gray squirrel, at the door of the fruit shop, whirling round and round so merrily within his wire wheel! Being condemned to the treadmill, he makes it an amusement. Admirable philosophy!

Here comes a big, rough dog, a countryman's dog, in search of his master; smelling at everybody's heels, and touching little Annie's hand with his cold nose, but hurrying away, though she would fain have patted him. Success to your search, Fidelity! And there sits a great yellow cat upon a window sill, a very corpulent and comfortable cat, gazing at this transitory world, with owl's eyes, and making pithy comments, doubtless, or what appear such, to the silly beast. O, sage puss, make room for me beside you, and we will be a pair of philosophers!

Here we see something to remind us of the town

crier, and his ding-dong bell! Look! look at that
great cloth spread out in the air, pictured all over
with wild beasts, as if they had met together to choose
a king, according to their custom in the days of Æsop.
But they are choosing neither a king nor a president,
else we should hear a most horrible snarling! They
have come from the deep woods, and the wild mountains, and the desert sands, and the polar snows, only
to do homage to my little Annie. As we enter among
them, the great elephant makes us a bow, in the best
style of elephantine courtesy, bending lowly down his
mountain bulk, with trunk abased, and leg thrust out
behind. Annie returns the salute, much to the gratifi-
cation of the elephant, who is certainly the best-bred
monster in the caravan. The lion and the lioness are
busy with two beef bones. The royal tiger, the beautiful, the untamable, keeps pacing his narrow cage with
a haughty step, unmindful of the spectators, or recall-
ing the fierce deeds of his former life, when he was
wont to leap forth upon such inferior animals from
the jungles of Bengal.

Here we see the very same wolf — do not go near
him, Annie! — the selfsame wolf that devoured little
Red Riding Hood and her grandmother. In the next
cage, a hyena from Egypt, who has doubtless howled
around the pyramids, and a black bear from our own
forests, are fellow-prisoners, and most excellent friends.
Are there any two living creatures who have so few
sympathies that they cannot possibly be friends?
Here sits a great white bear, whom common observers
would call a very stupid beast, though I perceive him
to be only absorbed in contemplation; he is thinking
of his voyages on an iceberg, and of his comfortable
home in the vicinity of the north pole, and of the lit-

tle cubs whom he left rolling in the eternal snows.
In fact, he is a bear of sentiment. But, oh, those un-
sentimental monkeys! the ugly, grinning, aping, chat-
tering, ill-natured, mischievous, and queer little brutes.
Annie does not love the monkeys. Their ugliness
shocks her pure, instinctive delicacy of taste, and
makes her mind unquiet, because it bears a wild and
dark resemblance to humanity. But here is a little
pony, just big enough for Annie to ride, and round
and round he gallops in a circle, keeping time with
his trampling hoofs to a band of music. And here —
with a laced coat and a cocked hat, and a riding whip
in his hand — here comes a little gentleman, small
enough to be king of the fairies, and ugly enough to
be king of the gnomes, and takes a flying leap into the
saddle. Merrily, merrily plays the music, and merrily gallops the pony, and merrily rides the little old
gentleman. Come, Annie, into the street again; perchance we may see monkeys on horseback there!

Mercy on us, what a noisy world we quiet people
live in! Did Annie ever read the Cries of London
City? With what lusty lungs doth yonder man proclaim that his wheelbarrow is full of lobsters! Here
comes another mounted on a cart, and blowing a
hoarse and dreadful blast from a tin horn, as much as
to say "Fresh fish!" And hark! a voice on high,
like that of a muezzin from the summit of a mosque,
announcing that some chimney sweeper has emerged
from smoke and soot, and darksome caverns, into the
upper air. What cares the world for that? But,
welladay, we hear a shrill voice of affliction, the
scream of a little child, rising louder with every repetition of that smart, sharp, slapping sound, produced
by an open hand on tender flesh. Annie sympathizes,

though without experience of such direful woe. Lo!
the town crier again, with some new secret for the
public ear. Will he tell us of an auction, or of a lost
pocket-book, or a show of beautiful wax figures, or of
some monstrous beast more horrible than any in the
caravan? I guess the latter. See how he uplifts the
bell in his right hand, and shakes it slowly at first,
then with a hurried motion, till the clapper seems to
strike both sides at once, and the sounds are scattered
forth in quick succession, far and near.

Ding-dong! Ding-dong! Ding-dong!

Now he raises his clear, loud voice, above all the
din of the town; it drowns the buzzing talk of many
tongues, and draws each man's mind from his own
business; it rolls up and down the echoing street,
and ascends to the hushed chamber of the sick, and
penetrates downward to the cellar kitchen, where the
hot cook turns from the fire to listen. Who, of all
that address the public ear, whether in church, or
court-house, or hall of state, has such an attentive
audience as the town crier? What said the people's
orator?

"Strayed from her home, a LITTLE GIRL, of five
years old, in a blue silk frock and white pantalets,
with brown curling hair and hazel eyes. Whoever
will bring her back to her afflicted mother" —

Stop, stop, town crier! The lost is found. O, my
pretty Annie, we forgot to tell your mother of our
ramble, and she is in despair, and has sent the town
crier to bellow up and down the streets, affrighting
old and young, for the loss of a little girl who has not
once let go my hand? Well, let us hasten homeward;
and as we go, forget not to thank Heaven, my Annie,
that, after wandering a little way into the world, you

may return at the first summons, with an untainted and unwearied heart, and be a happy child again. But I have gone too far astray for the town crier to call me back.

Sweet has been the charm of childhood on my spirit, throughout my ramble with little Annie! Say not that it has been a waste of precious moments, an idle matter, a babble of childish talk, and a reverie of childish imaginations, about topics unworthy of a grown man's notice. Has it been merely this? Not so; not so. They are not truly wise who would affirm it. As the pure breath of children revives the life of aged men, so is our moral nature revived by their free and simple thoughts, their native feeling, their airy mirth, for little cause or none, their grief, soon roused and soon allayed. Their influence on us is at least reciprocal with ours on them. When our infancy is almost forgotten, and our boyhood long departed, though it seems but as yesterday; when life settles darkly down upon us, and we doubt whether to call ourselves young any more, then it is good to steal away from the society of bearded men, and even of gentler woman, and spend an hour or two with children. After drinking from those fountains of still fresh existence, we shall return into the crowd, as I do now, to struggle onward and do our part in life, perhaps as fervently as ever, but, for a time, with a kinder and purer heart, and a spirit more lightly wise. All this by thy sweet magic, dear little Annie!

WAKEFIELD.

In some old magazine or newspaper I recollect a story, told as truth, of a man — let us call him Wakefield — who absented himself for a long time from his wife. The fact, thus abstractedly stated, is not very uncommon, nor — without a proper distinction of circumstances — to be condemned either as naughty or nonsensical. Howbeit, this, though far from the most aggravated, is perhaps the strangest, instance on record, of marital delinquency; and, moreover, as remarkable a freak as may be found in the whole list of human oddities. The wedded couple lived in London. The man, under pretence of going a journey, took lodgings in the next street to his own house, and there, unheard of by his wife or friends, and without the shadow of a reason for such self-banishment, dwelt upwards of twenty years. During that period, he beheld his home every day, and frequently the forlorn Mrs. Wakefield. And after so great a gap in his matrimonial felicity — when his death was reckoned certain, his estate settled, his name dismissed from memory, and his wife, long, long ago, resigned to her autumnal widowhood — he entered the door one evening, quietly, as from a day's absence, and became a loving spouse till death.

This outline is all that I remember. But the incident, though of the purest originality, unexampled, and probably never to be repeated, is one, I think, which appeals to the generous sympathies of mankind.

We know, each for himself, that none of us would perpetrate such a folly, yet feel as if some other might. To my own contemplations, at least, it has often recurred, always exciting wonder, but with a sense that the story must be true, and a conception of its hero's character. Whenever any subject so forcibly affects the mind, time is well spent in thinking of it. If the reader choose, let him do his own meditation; or if he prefer to ramble with me through the twenty years of Wakefield's vagary, I bid him welcome; trusting that there will be a pervading spirit and a moral, even should we fail to find them, done up neatly, and condensed into the final sentence. Thought has always its efficacy, and every striking incident its moral.

What sort of a man was Wakefield? We are free to shape out our own idea, and call it by his name. He was now in the meridian of life; his matrimonial affections, never violent, were sobered into a calm, habitual sentiment; of all husbands, he was likely to be the most constant, because a certain sluggishness would keep his heart at rest, wherever it might be placed. He was intellectual, but not actively so; his mind occupied itself in long and lazy musings, that ended to no purpose, or had not vigor to attain it; his thoughts were seldom so energetic as to seize hold of words. Imagination, in the proper meaning of the term, made no part of Wakefield's gifts. With a cold but not depraved nor wandering heart, and a mind never feverish with riotous thoughts, nor perplexed with originality, who could have anticipated that our friend would entitle himself to a foremost place among the doers of eccentric deeds? Had his acquaintances been asked, who was the man in London the surest to perform nothing to-day which should be remembered on the morrow, they would have thought of Wakefield. Only the wife of his bosom might have hesitated. She, without having analyzed his character, was partly aware of a quiet selfishness, that had rusted into his inactive mind ; of a peculiar sort of vanity, the most uneasy attribute about him ; of a disposition to craft, which had seldom produced more positive effects than the keeping of petty secrets, hardly worth revealing ; and, lastly, of what she called a little strangeness, sometimes, in the good man. This latter quality is indefinable, and perhaps non-existent.

Let us now imagine Wakefield bidding adieu to his wife. It is the dusk of an October evening. His equipment is a drab great-coat, a hat covered with an oilcloth, top-boots, an umbrella in one hand and a small portmanteau in the other. He has informed Mrs. Wakefield that he is to take the night coach into the country. She would fain inquire the length of his journey, its object, and the probable time of his return; but, indulgent to his harmless love of mystery, interrogates him only by a look. He tells her not to expect him positively by the return coach, nor to be alarmed should he tarry three or four days ; but, at all events, to look for him at supper on Friday evening. Wakefield himself, be it considered, has no suspicion of what is before him. He holds out his hand, she gives her own, and meets his parting kiss in the matter-of-course way of a ten years' matrimony ; and forth goes the middle-aged Mr. Wakefield, almost resolved to perplex his good lady by a whole week's absence. After the door has closed behind him, she perceives it thrust partly open, and a vision of her husband's face, through the aperture, smiling on her,

and gone in a moment. For the time, this little incident is dismissed without a thought. But, long afterwards, when she has been more years a widow than a
wife, that smile recurs, and flickers across all her reminiscences of Wakefield's visage. In her many musings, she surrounds the original smile with a multitude of fantasies, which make it strange and awful :
as, for instance, if she imagines him in a coffin, that
parting look is frozen on his pale features ; or, if she
dreams of him in heaven, still his blessed spirit wears
a quiet and crafty smile. Yet, for its sake, when all
others have given him up for dead, she sometimes
doubts whether she is a widow.

But our business is with the husband. We must
hurry after him along the street, ere he lose his individuality, and melt into the great mass of London
life. It would be vain searching for him there. Let
us follow close at his heels, therefore, until, after several superfluous turns and doublings, we find him comfortably established by the fireside of a small apartment, previously bespoken. He is in the next street
to his own, and at his journey's end. He can scarcely
trust his good fortune, in having got thither unperceived — recollecting that, at one time, he was delayed
by the throng, in the very focus of a lighted lantern ;
and, again, there were footsteps that seemed to tread
behind his own, distinct from the multitudinous tramp
around him ; and, anon, he heard a voice shouting
afar, and fancied that it called his name. Doubtless,
a dozen busybodies had been watching him, and told
his wife the whole affair. Poor Wakefield ! Little
knowest thou thine own insignificance in this great
world ! No mortal eye but mine has traced thee.
Go quietly to thy bed, foolish man ; and, on the mor

row, if thou wilt be wise, get thee home to good Mrs. Wakefield, and tell her the truth. Remove not thy-self, even for a little week, from thy place in her chaste bosom. Were she, for a single moment, to deem thee dead, or lost, or lastingly divided from her, thou wouldst be wofully conscious of a change in thy true wife forever after. It is perilous to make a chasm in human affections; not that they gape so long and wide — but so quickly close again!

Almost repenting of his frolic, or whatever it may be termed, Wakefield lies down betimes, and starting from his first nap, spreads forth his arms into the wide and solitary waste of the unaccustomed bed. "No," — thinks he, gathering the bedclothes about him, — "I will not sleep alone another night."

In the morning he rises earlier than usual, and sets himself to consider what he really means to do. Such are his loose and rambling modes of thought that he has taken this very singular step with the conscious-ness of a purpose, indeed, but without being able to define it sufficiently for his own contemplation. The vagueness of the project, and the convulsive effort with which he plunges into the execution of it, are equally characteristic of a feeble-minded man. Wakefield sifts his ideas, however, as minutely as he may, and finds himself curious to know the progress of matters at home — how his exemplary wife will endure her widow-hood of a week; and, briefly, how the little sphere of creatures and circumstances, in which he was a central object, will be affected by his removal. A morbid vanity, therefore, lies nearest the bottom of the affair. But, how is he to attain his ends? Not, certainly, by keeping close in this comfortable lodging, where, though he slept and awoke in the next street to his home, he is as effectually abroad as if the stage-coach had been whirling him away all night. Yet, should he reappear, the whole project is knocked in the head. His poor brains being hopelessly puzzled with this dilemma, he at length ventures out, partly resolving to cross the head of the street, and send one hasty glance towards his forsaken domicile. Habit—for he is a man of habits—takes him by the hand, and guides him, wholly unaware, to his own door, where, just at the critical moment, he is aroused by the scraping of his foot upon the step. Wakefield! whither are you going?

At that instant his fate was turning on the pivot. Little dreaming of the doom to which his first backward step devotes him, he hurries away, breathless with agitation hitherto unfelt, and hardly dares turn his head at the distant corner. Can it be that nobody caught sight of him? Will not the whole household — the decent Mrs. Wakefield, the smart maid servant, and the dirty little footboy — raise a hue and cry, through London streets, in pursuit of their. fugitive lord and master? Wonderful escape! He gathers courage to pause and look homeward, but is perplexed with a sense of change about the familiar edifice, such as affects us all, when, after a separation of months or years, we again see some hill or lake, or work of art, with which we were friends of old. In ordinary cases, this indescribable impression is caused by the comparison and contrast between our imperfect reminiscences and the reality. In Wakefield, the magic of a single night has wrought a similar transformation, because, in that brief period, a great moral change has been effected. But this is a secret from himself. Before leaving the spot, he catches a far and momentary glimpse of his wife, passing athwart the front window, with her face turned towards the head of the street. The crafty nincompoop takes to his heels, scared with the idea that, among a thousand such atoms of mortality, her eye must have detected him. Right glad is his heart, though his brain be somewhat dizzy, when he finds himself by the coal fire of his lodgings.

So much for the commencement of this long whim-wham. After the initial conception, and the stirring up of the man's sluggish temperament to put it in practice, the whole matter evolves itself in a natural train. We may suppose him, as the result of deep deliberation, buying a new wig, of reddish hair, and selecting sundry garments, in a fashion unlike his customary suit of brown, from a Jew's old-clothes bag. It is accomplished. Wakefield is another man. The new system being now established, a retrograde movement to the old would be almost as difficult as the step that placed him in his unparalleled position. Furthermore, he is rendered obstinate by a sulkiness occasionally incident to his temper, and brought on at present by the inadequate sensation which he conceives to have been produced in the bosom of Mrs. Wakefield. He will not go back until she be frightened half to death. Well; twice or thrice has she passed before his sight, each time with a heavier step, a paler cheek, and more anxious brow; and in the third week of his non-appearance he detects a portent of evil entering the house, in the guise of an apothecary. Next day the knocker is muffled. Towards nightfall comes the chariot of a physician, and deposits its big-wigged and solemn burden at Wakefield's door, whence, after a quarter of an hour's visit, he emerges, perchance the herald of a funeral. Dear woman! Will she die?

By this time, Wakefield is excited to something like
energy of feeling, but still lingers away from his wife's
bedside, pleading with his conscience that she must
not be disturbed at such a juncture. If aught else re-
strains him, he does not know it. In the course of a
few weeks she gradually recovers; the crisis is over;
her heart is sad, perhaps, but quiet; and, let him return soon or late, it will never be feverish for him
again. Such ideas glimmer through the mist of Wakefield's mind, and render him indistinctly conscious
that an almost impassable gulf divides his hired apartment from his former home. "It is but in the next
street!" he sometimes says. Fool! it is in another
world. Hitherto, he has put off his return from one
particular day to another; henceforward, he leaves the
precise time undetermined. Not to-morrow — probably next week — pretty soon. Poor man! The dead
have nearly as much chance of revisiting their earthly
homes as the self-banished Wakefield.

Would that I had a folio to write, instead of an
article of a dozen pages! Then might I exemplify
how an influence beyond our control lays its strong
hand on every deed which we do, and weaves its consequences into an iron tissue of necessity. Wakefield
is spell-bound. We must leave him, for ten years or
so, to haunt around his house, without once crossing
the threshold, and to be faithful to his wife, with all
the affection of which his heart is capable. while he is
slowly fading out of hers. Long since, it must be remarked, he had lost the perception of singularity in
his conduct.

Now for a scene! Amid the throng of a London
street we distinguish a man. now waxing elderly. with
few characteristics to attract careless observers, yet

bearing, in his whole aspect, the handwriting of no common fate, for such as have the skill to read it. He is meagre; his low and narrow forehead is deeply wrinkled; his eyes, small and lustreless, sometimes wander apprehensively about him, but oftener seem to look inward. He bends his head, and moves with an indescribable obliquity of gait, as if unwilling to display his full front to the world. Watch him long enough to see what we have described, and you will allow that circumstances—which often produce remarkable men from nature's ordinary handiwork—have produced one such here. Next, leaving him to sidle along the footwalk, cast your eyes in the opposite direction, where a portly female, considerably in the wane of life, with a prayer-book in her hand, is proceeding to yonder church. She has the placid mien of settled widowhood. Her regrets have either died away, or have become so essential to her heart, that they would be poorly exchanged for joy. Just as the lean man and well-conditioned woman are passing, a slight obstruction occurs, and brings these two figures directly in contact. Their hands touch; the pressure of the crowd forces her bosom against his shoulder; they stand, face to face, staring into each other's eyes. After a ten years' separation, thus Wakefield meets his wife!

The throng eddies away, and carries them asunder. The sober widow, resuming her former pace, proceeds to church, but pauses in the portal, and throws a perplexed glance along the street. She passes in, however, opening her prayer-book as she goes. And the man! with so wild a face that busy and selfish London stands to gaze after him, he hurries to his lodgings, bolts the door, and throws himself upon the bed. The latent feelings of years break out; his feeble mind ao quires a brief energy from their strength; all the miserable strangeness of his life is revealed to him at a glance: and he cries out, passionately, "Wakefield! Wakefield! You are mad!"

Perhaps he was so. The singularity of his situation must have so moulded him to himself, that, considered in regard to his fellow-creatures and the business of life, he could not be said to possess his right mind. He had contrived, or rather he had happened, to dissever himself from the world — to vanish — to give up his place and privileges with living men, without being admitted among the dead. The life of a hermit is nowise parallel to his. He was in the bustle of the city, as of old; but the crowd swept by and saw him not; he was, we may figuratively say, always beside his wife and at his hearth, yet must never feel the warmth of the one nor the affection of the other. It was Wakefield's unprecedented fate to retain his original share of human sympathies, and to be still involved in human interests, while he had lost his reciprocal influence on them. It would be a most curious speculation to trace out the effect of such circumstances on his heart and intellect, separately, and in unison. Yet, changed as he was, he would seldom be conscious of it. but deem himself the same man as ever; glimpses of the truth, indeed, would come, but only for the moment; and still he would keep saying, "I shall soon go back!" — nor reflect that he had been saying so for twenty years.

I conceive, also, that these twenty years would appear, in the retrospect, scarcely longer than the week to which Wakefield had at first limited his absence. He would look on the affair as no more than an interlude in the main business of his life. When, after a little while more, he should deem it time to reënter his parlor, his wife would clap her hands for joy, on beholding the middle-aged Mr. Wakefield. Alas, what a mistake! Would Time but await the close of our favorite follies, we should be young men, all of us, and till Doomsday.

One evening, in the twentieth year since he vanished, Wakefield is taking his customary walk towards the dwelling which he still calls his own. It is a gusty night of autumn, with frequent showers that patter down upon the pavement, and are gone before a man can put up his umbrella. Pausing near the house, Wakefield discerns, through the parlor windows of the second floor, the red glow and the glimmer and fitful flash of a comfortable fire. On the ceiling appears a grotesque shadow of good Mrs. Wakefield. The cap, the nose and chin, and the broad waist, form an admirable caricature, which dances, moreover, with the up-flickering and down-sinking blaze, almost too merrily for the shade of an elderly widow. At this instant a shower chances to fall, and is driven, by the unmannerly gust, full into Wakefield's face and bosom. He is quite penetrated with its autumnal chill. Shall he stand, wet and shivering here, when his own hearth has a good fire to warm him, and his own wife will run to fetch the gray coat and small-clothes, which, doubtless, she has kept carefully in the closet of their bed chamber? No! Wakefield is no such fool. He ascends the steps — heavily! — for twenty years have stiffened his legs since he came down — but he knows it not. Stay, Wakefield! Would you go to the sole home that is left you? Then step into your grave! The door opens. As he passes in, we have a parting glimpse of his visage, and recognize the crafty smile, which was the precursor of the little joke that he has ever since been playing off at his wife's expense. How unmercifully has he quizzed the poor woman! Well, a good night's rest to Wakefield!

This happy event — supposing it to be such — could only have occurred at an unpremeditated moment. We will not follow our friend across the threshold. He has left us much food for thought, a portion of which shall lend its wisdom to a moral, and be shaped into a figure. Amid the seeming confusion of our mysterious world, individuals are so nicely adjusted to a system, and systems to one another and to a whole, that, by stepping aside for a moment, a man exposes himself to a fearful risk of losing his place forever. Like Wakefield, he may become, as it were, the Outcast of the Universe.

A RILL FROM THE TOWN PUMP.

(SCENE — *the corner of two principal streets.*[1] *The* TOWN PUMP
talking through its nose.)

NOON, by the North clock! Noon, by the east!
High noon, too, by these hot sunbeams which fall,
scarcely aslope, upon my head, and almost make the
water bubble and smoke in the trough under my nose.
Truly, we public characters have a tough time of it!
And, among all the town officers, chosen at March
meeting, where is he that sustains, for a single year,
the burden of such manifold duties as are imposed,
in perpetuity, upon the Town Pump? The title of
"town treasurer" is rightfully mine, as guardian of
the best treasure that the town has. The overseers of
the poor ought to make me their chairman, since I
provide bountifully for the pauper, without expense to
him that pays taxes. I am at the head of the fire department, and one of the physicians to the board of
health. As a keeper of the peace, all water drinkers
will confess me equal to the constable. I perform
some of the duties of the town clerk, by promulgating
public notices, when they are posted on my front. To
speak within bounds, I am the chief person of the
municipality, and exhibit, moreover, an admirable pattern to my brother officers, by the cool, steady, upright, downright, and impartial discharge of my business, and the constancy with which I stand to my post.
Summer or winter, nobody seeks me in vain; for, all

[1] Essex and Washington Streets, Salem.

day long, I am seen at the busiest corner, just above
the market, stretching out my arms to rich and poor
alike ; and at night, I hold a lantern over my head,
both to show where I am, and keep people out of the
gutters.

At this sultry noontide, I am cupbearer to the
parched populace, for whose benefit an iron goblet is
chained to my waist.   Like a dram seller on the mall,
at muster day, I cry aloud to all and sundry, in my
plainest accents, and at the very tiptop of my voice:
Here it is, gentlemen!   Here is the good liquor!
Walk up, walk up, gentlemen, walk up, walk up!
Here is the superior stuff!   Here is the unadulterated
ale of father Adam — better than Cognac, Hollands,
Jamaica, strong beer, or wine of any price ; here it is,
by the hogshead or the single glass, and not a cent to
pay!   Walk up, gentlemen, walk up, and help yourselves!

It were a pity if all this outcry should draw no
customers.   Here they come.   A hot day, gentlemen!
Quaff, and away again, so as to keep yourselves in a
nice cool sweat.   You, my friend, will need another
cupful, to wash the dust out of your throat, if it be as
thick there as it is on your cowhide shoes.   I see that
you have trudged half a score of miles to-day; and,
like a wise man, have passed by the taverns, and
stopped at the running brooks and well curbs.   Otherwise, betwixt heat without and fire within, you would
have been burned to a cinder, or melted down to nothing at all, in the fashion of a jelly-fish.   Drink, and
make room for that other fellow, who seeks my aid to
quench the fiery fever of last night's potations, which
he drained from no cup of mine.   Welcome, most
rubicund sir!   You and I have been great strangers,

hitherto; nor, to confess the truth, will my nose be anxious for a closer intimacy, till the fumes of your breath be a little less potent. Mercy on you, man! the water absolutely hisses down your red-hot gullet, and is converted quite to steam in the miniature tophet which you mistake for a stomach. Fill again, and tell me, on the word of an honest toper, did you ever, in cellar, tavern, or any kind of a dram shop, spend the price of your children's food for a swig half so delicious? Now, for the first time these ten years, you know the flavor of cold water. Good-by; and, whenever you are thirsty, remember that I keep a constant supply at the old stand. Who next? O, my little friend, you are let loose from school, and come hither to scrub your blooming face, and drown the memory of certain taps of the ferule, and other school-boy troubles, in a draught from the Town Pump. Take it, pure as the current of your young life. Take it, and may your heart and tongue never be scorched with a fiercer thirst than now! There, my dear child, put down the cup, and yield your place to this elderly gentleman, who treads so tenderly over the paving-stones, that I suspect he is afraid of breaking them. What! he limps by, without so much as thanking me, as if my hospitable offers were meant only for people who have no wine cellars. Well, well, sir — no harm done, I hope! Go draw the cork, tip the decanter; but, when your great toe shall set you a-roaring, it will be no affair of mine. If gentlemen love the pleasant titillation of the gout, it is all one to the Town Pump. This thirsty dog, with his red tongue lolling out, does not scorn my hospitality, but stands on his hind legs, and laps eagerly out of the trough. See how lightly he capers away again! Jowler, did your worship ever have the gout?

Are you all satisfied? Then wipe your mouths, my good friends; and, while my spout has a moment's leisure, I will delight the town with a few historical reminiscences. In far antiquity, beneath a darksome shadow of venerable boughs, a spring bubbled out of the leaf-strewn earth, in the very spot where you now behold me, on the sunny pavement. The water was as bright and clear, and deemed as precious, as liquid diamonds. The Indian sagamores drank of it from time immemorial, till the fatal deluge of the fire water burst upon the red men, and swept their whole race away from the cold fountains. Endicott and his followers came next, and often knelt down to drink, dipping their long beards in the spring. ' The richest goblet, then, was of birch bark. Governor Winthrop, after a journey afoot from Boston, drank here, out of the hollow of his hand. The elder Higginson here wet his palm, and laid it on the brow of the first town-born child. For many years it was the watering-place, and, as it were, the washbowl of the vicinity — whither all decent folks resorted, to purify their visages and gaze at them afterwards — at least the pretty maidens did — in the mirror which it made. On Sabbath days, whenever a babe was to be baptized, the sexton filled his basin here, and placed it on the communion table of the humble meeting-house, which partly covered the site of yonder stately brick one. Thus, one generation after another was consecrated to Heaven by its waters, and cast their waxing and waning shadows into its glassy bosom, and vanished from the earth, as if mortal life were but a flitting image in a fountain. Finally, the fountain vanished also. Cellars were dug on all sides, and cartloads of gravel flung upon its source, whence oozed a turbid stream, forming a mud puddle.

at the corner of two streets. In the hot months, when its refreshment was most needed, the dust flew in clouds over the forgotten birthplace of the waters, now their grave. But, in the course of time, a Town Pump was sunk into the source of the ancient spring; and when the first decayed, another took its place — and then another, and still another — till here stand I, gentlemen and ladies, to serve you with my iron goblet. Drink, and be refreshed! The water is as pure and cold as that which slaked the thirst of the red sagamore beneath the aged boughs, though now the gem of the wilderness is treasured under these hot stones, where no shadow falls but from the brick buildings. And be it the moral of my story, that, as this wasted and long-lost fountain is now known and prized again, so shall the virtues of cold water, too little valued since your fathers' days, be recognized by all.

Your pardon, good people! I must interrupt my stream of eloquence, and spout forth a stream of water, to replenish the trough for this teamster and his two yoke of oxen, who have come from Topsfield, or somewhere along that way. No part of my business is pleasanter than the watering of cattle. Look! how rapidly they lower the watermark on the sides of the trough, till their capacious stomachs are moistened with a gallon or two apiece, and they can afford time to breathe it in, with sighs of calm enjoyment. Now they roll their quiet eyes around the brim of their monstrous drinking vessel. An ox is your true toper.

But I perceive, my dear auditors, that you are impatient for the remainder of my discourse. Impute it, I beseech you, to no defect of modesty, if I insist a little longer on so fruitful a topic as my own multifarious merits. It is altogether for your good. The

better you think of me, the better men and women
will you find yourselves. I shall say nothing of my
all-important aid on washing days ; though, on that
account alone, I might call myself the household god
of a hundred families. Far be it from me also to hint,
my respectable friends, at the show of dirty faces
which you would present, without my pains to keep
you clean. Nor will I remind you how often, when
the midnight bells make you tremble for your combus-
tible town, you have fled to the Town Pump, and
found me always at my post, firm amid the confusion,
and ready to drain my vital current in your behalf.
Neither is it worth while to lay much stress on my
claims to a medical diploma, as the physician whose
simple rule of practice is preferable to all the nauseous
lore which has found men sick or left them so, since
the days of Hippocrates. Let us take a broader view
of my beneficial influence on mankind.

No; these are trifles compared with the merits
which wise men concede to me — if not in my single
self, yet as the representative of a class — of being the
grand reformer of the age. From my spout, and such
spouts as mine, must flow the stream that shall cleanse
our earth of the vast portion of its crime and anguish,
which has gushed from the fiery fountains of the still.
In this mighty enterprise, the cow shall be my great
confederate. Milk and water! The Town Pump and
the Cow! Such is the glorious copartnership that
shall tear down the distilleries and brewhouses, uproot
the vineyards, shatter the cider presses, ruin the tea
and coffee trade, and, finally, monopolize the whole
business of quenching thirst. Blessed consummation!
Then, Poverty shall pass away from the land, finding
no hovel so wretched where her squalid form may

shelter itself. Then Disease, for lack of other victims, shall gnaw its own heart, and die. Then Sin, if she do not die, shall lose half her strength. Until now, the frenzy of hereditary fever has raged in the human blood, transmitted from sire to son, and rekindled, in every generation, by fresh draughts of liquid flame. When that inward fire shall be extinguished, the heat of passion cannot but grow cool, and war — the drunkenness of nations — perhaps will cease. At least, there will be no war of households. The husband and wife, drinking deep of peaceful joy, — a calm bliss of temperate affections, — shall pass hand in hand through life, and lie down, not reluctantly, at its protracted close. To them, the past will be no turmoil of mad dreams, nor the future an eternity of such moments as follow the delirium of the drunkard. Their dead faces shall express what their spirits were, and are to be, by a lingering smile of memory and hope.

Ahem! Dry work, this speechifying; especially to an unpractised orator. I never conceived, till now, what toil the temperance lecturers undergo for my sake. Hereafter, they shall have the business to themselves. Do, some kind Christian, pump a stroke or two, just to wet my whistle. Thank you, sir! My dear hearers, when the world shall have been regenerated by my instrumentality, you will collect your useless vats and liquor casks into one great pile, and make a bonfire in honor of the Town Pump. And, when I shall have decayed, like my predecessors, then, if you revere my memory, let a marble fountain, richly sculptured, take my place upon this spot. Such monuments should be erected everywhere, and inscribed with the names of the distinguished champions of my cause. Now listen, for something very important is to come next.

There are two or three honest friends of mine — and true friends, I know, they are — who nevertheless, by their fiery pugnacity in my behalf, do put me in fearful hazard of a broken nose or even a total overthrow upon the pavement, and the loss of the treasure which I guard. I pray you, gentlemen, let this fault be amended. Is it decent, think you, to get tipsy with zeal for temperance, and take up the honorable cause of the Town Pump in the style of a toper fighting for his brandy bottle? Or, can the excellent qualities of cold water be not otherwise exemplified than by plunging, slapdash, into hot water, and wofully scalding yourselves and other people? Trust me, they may. In the moral warfare which you are to wage — and, indeed, in the whole conduct of your lives — you cannot choose a better example than myself, who have never permitted the dust and sultry atmosphere, the turbulence and manifold disquietudes of the world around me, to reach that deep, calm well of purity, which may be called my soul. And whenever I pour out that soul, it is to cool earth's fever or cleanse its stains.

One o'clock! Nay, then, if the dinner bell begins to speak, I may as well hold my peace. Here comes a pretty young girl of my acquaintance, with a large stone pitcher for me to fill. May she draw a husband while drawing her water, as Rachel did of old. Hold out your vessel, my dear! There it is, full to the brim; so now run home, peeping at your sweet image in the pitcher as you go; and forget not, in a glass of my own liquor, to drink — " SUCCESS TO THE TOWN PUMP!"

THE GREAT CARBUNCLE.[1]

A MYSTERY OF THE WHITE MOUNTAINS.

At nightfall, once in the olden time, on the rugged side of one of the Crystal Hills, a party of adventurers were refreshing themselves, after a toilsome and fruitless quest for the Great Carbuncle. They had come thither, not as friends nor partners in the enterprise, but each, save one youthful pair, impelled by his own selfish and solitary longing for this wondrous gem. Their feeling of brotherhood, however, was strong enough to induce them to contribute a mutual aid in building a rude hut of branches, and kindling a great fire of shattered pines, that had drifted down the headlong current of the Amonoosuck, on the lower bank of which they were to pass the night. There was but one of their number, perhaps, who had become so estranged from natural sympathies, by the absorbing spell of the pursuit, as to acknowledge no satisfaction at the sight of human faces, in the remote and solitary region whither they had ascended. A vast extent of wilderness lay between them and the nearest settlement, while a scant mile above their heads was that black verge where the hills throw off their shaggy mantle of forest trees, and either robe themselves in clouds

[1] The Indian tradition, on which this somewhat extravagant tale is founded, is both too wild and too beautiful to be adequately wrought up in prose. Sullivan, in his History of Maine, written since the Revolution, remarks, that even then the existence of the Great Carbuncle was not entirely discredited.

or tower naked into the sky. The roar of the Amonoosuck would have been too awful for endurance if
only a solitary man had listened, while the mountain
stream talked with the wind.

The adventurers, therefore, exchanged hospitable
greetings, and welcomed one another to the hut, where
each man was the host, and all were the guests of the
whole company. They spread their individual sup-
plies of food on the flat surface of a rock, and partook
of a general repast; at the close of which, a sentiment
of good fellowship was perceptible among the party,
though repressed by the idea, that the renewed search
for the Great Carbuncle must make them strangers
again in the morning. Seven men and one young
woman, they warmed themselves together at the fire,
which extended its bright wall along the whole front
of their wigwam. As they observed the various and
contrasted figures that made up the assemblage, each
man looking like a caricature of himself, in the unsteady light that flickered over him, they came mutually to the conclusion, that an odder society had never
met, in city or wilderness, on mountain or plain.

The eldest of the group, a tall, lean, weather-beaten
man, some sixty years of age, was clad in the skins of
wild animals, whose fashion of dress he did well to
imitate, since the deer, the wolf, and the bear, had
long been his most intimate companions. He was one
of those ill-fated mortals, such as the Indians told of,
whom, in their early youth, the Great Carbuncle smote
with a peculiar madness, and became the passionate
dream of their existence. All who visited that region
knew him as the Seeker, and by no other name. As
none could remember when he first took up the search,
there went a fable in the valley of the Saco, that for

his inordinate lust after the Great Carbuncle, he had been condemned to wander among the mountains till the end of time, still with the same feverish hopes at sunrise — the same despair at eve. Near this miserable Seeker sat a little elderly personage, wearing a high-crowned hat, shaped somewhat like a crucible. He was from beyond the sea, a Doctor Cacaphodel, who had wilted and dried himself into a mummy by continually stooping over charcoal furnaces, and inhaling unwholesome fumes during his researches in chemistry and alchemy. It was told of him, whether truly or not, that, at the commencement of his studies, he had drained his body of all its richest blood, and wasted it, with other inestimable ingredients, in an unsuccessful experiment — and had never been a well man since. Another of the adventurers was Master Ichabod Pigsnort, a weighty merchant and selectman of Boston, and an elder of the famous Mr. Norton's church. His enemies had a ridiculous story that Master Pigsnort was accustomed to spend a whole hour after prayer time, every morning and evening, in wallowing naked among an immense quantity of pine-tree shillings, which were the earliest silver coinage of Massachusetts. The fourth whom we shall notice had no name that his companions knew of, and was chiefly distinguished by a sneer that always contorted his thin visage, and by a prodigious pair of spectacles, which were supposed to deform and discolor the whole face of nature, to this gentleman's perception. The fifth adventurer likewise lacked a name, which was the greater pity, as he appeared to be a poet. He was a bright-eyed man, but wofully pined away, which was no more than natural, if, as some people affirmed, his ordinary diet was fog, morning mist, and a slice of the densest cloud within his reach, sauced with moonshine, whenever he could get it. Certain it is, that the poetry which flowed from him had a smack of all these dainties. The sixth of the party was a young man of haughty mien, and sat somewhat apart from the rest, wearing his plumed hat loftily among his elders, while the fire glittered on the rich embroidery of his dress, and gleamed intensely on the jewelled pommel of his sword. This was the Lord de Vere, who, when at home, was said to spend much of his time in the burial vault of his dead progenitors, rummaging their mouldy coffins in search of all the earthly pride and vainglory that was hidden among bones and dust; so that, besides his own share, he had the collected haughtiness of his whole line of ancestry.

Lastly, there was a handsome youth in rustic garb, and by his side a blooming little person, in whom a delicate shade of maiden reserve was just melting into the rich glow of a young wife's affection. Her name was Hannah, and her husband's Matthew; two homely names, yet well enough adapted to the simple pair, who seemed strangely out of place among the whimsical fraternity whose wits had been set agog by the Great Carbuncle.

Beneath the shelter of one hut, in the bright blaze of the same fire, sat this varied group of adventurers, all so intent upon a single object, that, of whatever else they began to speak, their closing words were sure to be illuminated with the Great Carbuncle. Several related the circumstances that brought then. thither. One had listened to a traveller's tale of this marvellous stone in his own distant country, and had immediately been seized with such a thirst for beholding it as could only be quenched in its intensest

lustre. Another, so long ago as when the famous
Captain Smith visited these coasts, had seen it blazing
far at sea, and had felt no rest in all the intervening
years till now that he took up the search. A third,
being encamped on a hunting expedition full forty
miles south of the White Mountains, awoke at mid
night, and beheld the Great Carbuncle gleaming like
a meteor, so that the shadows of the trees fell backward from it. They spoke of the innumerable attempts which had been made to reach the spot, and of
the singular fatality which had hitherto withheld success from all adventurers, though it might seem so
easy to follow to its source a light that overpowered
the moon, and almost matched the sun. It was ob-
servable that each smiled scornfully at the madness of
every other in anticipating better fortune than the
past, yet nourished a scarcely hidden conviction that
he would himself be the favored one. As if to allay
their too sanguine hopes, they recurred to the Indian
traditions that a spirit kept watch about the gem, and
bewildered those who sought it either by removing it
from peak to peak of the higher hills, or by calling up
a mist from the enchanted lake over which it hung.
But these tales were deemed unworthy of credit, all
professing to believe that the search had been baffled
by want of sagacity or perseverance in the adventurers, or such other causes as might naturally obstruct
the passage to any given point among the intricacies
of forest, valley, and mountain.

In a pause of the conversation the wearer of the
prodigious spectacles looked round upon the party,
making each individual, in turn, the object of the
sneer which invariably dwelt upon his countenance.

"So, fellow-pilgrims," said he, "here we are, seven

wise men, and one fair damsel — who, doubtless, is as wise as any graybeard of the company: here we are, I say, all bound on the same goodly enterprise. Methinks, now, it were not amiss that each of us declare what he proposes to do with the Great Carbuncle, provided he have the good hap to clutch it. What says our friend in the bear skin? How mean you, good sir, to enjoy the prize which you have been seeking, the Lord knows how long, among the Crystal Hills?"

"How enjoy it!" exclaimed the aged Seeker, bitterly. "I hope for no enjoyment from it; that folly has passed long ago! I keep up the search for this accursed stone because the vain ambition of my youth has become a fate upon me in old age. The pursuit alone is my strength, — the energy of my soul, — the warmth of my blood, — and the pith and marrow of my bones! Were I to turn my back upon it I should fall down dead on the hither side of the Notch, which is the gateway of this mountain region. Yet not to have my wasted lifetime back again would I give up my hopes of the Great Carbuncle! Having found it, I shall bear it to a certain cavern that I wot of, and there, grasping it in my arms, lie down and die, and keep it buried with me forever."

"O wretch, regardless of the interests of science!" cried Doctor Cacaphodel, with philosophic indignation. "Thou art not worthy to behold, even from afar off, the lustre of this most precious gem that ever was concocted in the laboratory of Nature. Mine is the sole purpose for which a wise man may desire the possession of the Great Carbuncle. Immediately on obtaining it — for I have a presentiment, good people, that the prize is reserved to crown my scientific repu

tation — I shall return to Europe, and employ my remaining years in reducing it to its first elements. A
portion of the stone will I grind to impalpable powder; other parts shall be dissolved in acids, or what
ever solvents will act upon so admirable a composi
tion; and the remainder I design to melt in the crucible, or set on fire with the blow-pipe. By these various
methods I shall gain an accurate analysis, and finally
bestow the result of my labors upon the world in a
folio volume."

"Excellent!" quoth the man with the spectacles.
"Nor need you hesitate, learned sir, on account of the
necessary destruction of the gem; since the perusal
of your folio may teach every mother's son of us to
concoct a Great Carbuncle of his own."

"But, verily," said Master Ichabod Pigsnort, "for
mine own part I object to the making of these coun-
terfeits, as being calculated to reduce the marketable
value of the true gem. I tell ye frankly, sirs, I have
an interest in keeping up the price. Here have I
quitted my regular traffic, leaving my warehouse in
the care of my clerks, and putting my credit to great
hazard, and, furthermore, have put myself in peril of
death or captivity by the accursed heathen savages --
and all this without daring to ask the prayers of the
congregation, because the quest for the Great Carbuncle is deemed little better than a traffic with the
Evil One. Now think ye that I would have done this
grievous wrong to my soul, body, reputation, and estate, without a reasonable chance of profit?"

"Not I, pious Master Pigsnort," said the man with
the spectacles. "I never laid such a great folly to
thy charge."

"Truly, I hope not," said the merchant. "Now,

as touching this Great Carbuncle, I am free to own that I have never had a glimpse of it; but be it only the hundredth part so bright as people tell, it will surely outvalue the Great Mogul's best diamond, which he holds at an incalculable sum. Wherefore, I am minded to put the Great Carbuncle on shipboard, and voyage with it to England, France, Spain, Italy, or into Heathendom, if Providence should send me thither, and, in a word, dispose of the gem to the best bidder among the potentates of the earth, that he may place it among his crown jewels. If any of ye have a wiser plan, let him expound it."

"That have I, thou sordid man!" exclaimed the poet. "Dost thou desire nothing brighter than gold that thou wouldst transmute all this ethereal lustre into such dross as thou wallowest in already? For myself, hiding the jewel under my cloak, I shall hie me back to my attic chamber, in one of the darksome alleys of London. There, night and day, will I gaze upon it; my soul shall drink its radiance; it shall be diffused throughout my intellectual powers, and gleam brightly in every line of poesy that I indite. Thus, long ages after I am gone, the splendor of the Great Carbuncle will blaze around my name!"

"Well said, Master Poet!" cried he of the spectacles. "Hide it under thy cloak, sayest thou? Why, it will gleam through the holes, and make thee look like a jack-o'-lantern!"

"To think!" ejaculated the Lord de Vere, rather to himself than his companions, the best of whom he held utterly unworthy of his intercourse — "to think that a fellow in a tattered cloak should talk of conveying the Great Carbuncle to a garret in Grub Street! Have not I resolved within myself that the whole

earth contains no fitter ornament for the great hall of
my ancestral castle? There shall it flame for ages,
making a noonday of midnight, glittering on the suits
of armor, the banners, and escutcheons, that hang
around the wall, and keeping bright the memory of
heroes. Wherefore have all other adventurers sought
the prize in vain but that I might win it, and make it
a symbol of the glories of our lofty line? And never,
on the diadem of the White Mountains, did the Great
Carbuncle hold a place half so honored as is reserved
for it in the hall of the De Veres!"

"It is a noble thought," said the Cynic, with an ob-
sequious sneer. "Yet, might I presume to say so, the
gem would make a rare sepulchral lamp, and would
display the glories of your lordship's progenitors more
truly in the ancestral vault than in the castle hall."

"Nay, forsooth," observed Matthew, the young rustic, who sat hand in hand with his bride, "the gentleman has bethought himself of a profitable use for this
bright stone. Hannah here and I are seeking it for a
like purpose."

"How, fellow!" exclaimed his lordship, in surprise.
"What castle hall hast thou to hang it in?"

"No castle," replied Matthew, "but as neat a cottage as any within sight of the Crystal Hills. Ye
must know, friends, that Hannah and I, being wedded
the last week, have taken up the search of the Great
Carbuncle, because we shall need its light in the long
winter evenings ; and it will be such a pretty thing to
show the neighbors when they visit us. It will shine
through the house so that we may pick up a pin in
any corner, and will set all the windows aglowing as
if there were a great fire of pine knots in the chimney.
And then how pleasant, when we awake in the night,
to be able to see one another's faces!"

There was a general smile among the adventurers
at the simplicity of the young couple's project in regard to this wondrous and invaluable stone, with which
the greatest monarch on earth might have been proud
to adorn his palace. Especially the man with spectacles, who had sneered at all the company in turn, now
twisted his visage into such an expression of ill-natured mirth, that Matthew asked him, rather peevishly,
what he himself meant to do with the Great Carbuncle.

"The Great Carbuncle!" answered the Cynic, with
ineffable scorn. "Why, you blockhead, there is no
such thing in *rerum natura*. I have come three thousand miles, and am resolved to set my foot on every
peak of these mountains, and poke my head into every
chasm, for the sole purpose of demonstrating to the
satisfaction of any man one whit less an ass than thy-
self that the Great Carbuncle is all a humbug!"

Vain and foolish were the motives that had brought
most of the adventurers to the Crystal Hills; but
none so vain, so foolish, and so impious too, as that of
the scoffer with the prodigious spectacles. He was
one of those wretched and evil men whose yearnings
are downward to the darkness, instead of heavenward, and who, could they but extinguish the lights
which God hath kindled for us, would count the midnight gloom their chiefest glory. As the Cynic spoke,
several of the party were startled by a gleam of red
splendor, that showed the huge shapes of the surrounding mountains and the rock-bestrewn bed of the
turbulent river with an illumination unlike that of
their fire on the trunks and black boughs of the
forest trees. They listened for the roll of thunder,
but heard nothing, and were glad that the tempest

came not near them. The stars, those dial-points of heaven, now warned the adventurers to close their eyes on the blazing logs, and open them, in dreams, to the glow of the Great Carbuncle.

The young married couple had taken their lodgings in the farthest corner of the wigwam, and were separated from the rest of the party by a curtain of curiously-woven twigs, such as might have hung, in deep festoons, around the bridal-bower of Eve. The modest little wife had wrought this piece of tapestry while the other guests were talking. She and her husband fell asleep with hands tenderly clasped, and awoke from visions of unearthly radiance to meet the more blessed light of one another's eyes. They awoke at the same instant, and with one happy smile beaming over their two faces, which grew brighter with their consciousness of the reality of life and love. But no sooner did she recollect where they were, than the bride peeped through the interstices of the leafy curtain, and saw that the outer room of the hut was deserted.

"Up, dear Matthew!" cried she, in haste. "The strange folk are all gone! Up, this very minute, or we shall lose the Great Carbuncle!"

In truth, so little did these poor young people deserve the mighty prize which had lured them thither, that they had slept peacefully all night, and till the summits of the hills were glittering with sunshine; while the other adventurers had tossed their limbs in feverish wakefulness, or dreamed of climbing precipices, and set off to realize their dreams with the earliest peep of dawn. But Matthew and Hannah, after their calm rest, were as light as two young deer, and merely stopped to say their prayers and wash themselves in a cold pool of the Amonoosuck, and then to taste a morsel of food, ere they turned their faces to the mountain-side. It was a sweet emblem of conjugal affection, as they toiled up the difficult ascent, gathering strength from the mutual aid which they afforded. After several little accidents, such as a torn robe, a lost shoe, and the entanglement of Hannah's hair in a bough, they reached the upper verge of the forest, and were now to pursue a more adventurous course. The innumerable trunks and heavy foliage of the trees had hitherto shut in their thoughts, which now shrank affrighted from the region of wind and cloud and naked rocks and desolate sunshine, that rose immeasurably above them. They gazed back at the obscure wilderness which they had traversed, and longed to be buried again in its depths rather than trust themselves to so vast and visible a solitude.

"Shall we go on?" said Matthew, throwing his arm round Hannah's waist, both to protect her and to comfort his heart by drawing her close to it.

But the little bride, simple as she was, had a woman's love of jewels, and could not forego the hope of possessing the very brightest in the world, in spite of the perils with which it must be won.

"Let us climb a little higher," whispered she, yet tremulously, as she turned her face upward to the lonely sky.

"Come, then," said Matthew, mustering his manly courage and drawing her along with him, for she became timid again the moment that he grew bold.

And upward, accordingly, went the pilgrims of the Great Carbuncle, now treading upon the tops and thickly-interwoven branches of dwarf pines, which, by the growth of centuries, though mossy with age had

barely reached three feet in altitude. Next, they
came to masses and fragments of naked rock heaped
confusedly together, like a cairn reared by giants in
memory of a giant chief. In this bleak realm of
upper air nothing breathed, nothing grew; there was
no life but what was concentrated in their two hearts;
they had climbed so high that Nature herself seemed
no longer to keep them company. She lingered beneath them, within the verge of the forest trees, and
sent a farewell glance after her children as they
strayed where her own green footprints had never
been. But soon they were to be hidden from her eye.
Densely and dark the mists began to gather below,
casting black spots of shadow on the vast landscape,
and sailing heavily to one centre, as if the loftiest
mountain peak had summoned a council of its kindred
clouds. Finally, the vapors welded themselves, as it
were, into a mass, presenting the appearance of a
pavement over which the wanderers might have
trodden, but where they would vainly have sought an
avenue to the blessed earth which they had lost. And
the lovers yearned to behold that green earth again,
more intensely, alas! than, beneath a clouded sky,
they had ever desired a glimpse of heaven. They
even felt it a relief to their desolation when the
mists, creeping gradually up the mountain, concealed
its lonely peak, and thus annihilated, at least for
them, the whole region of visible space. But they
drew closer together, with a fond and melancholy
gaze, dreading lest the universal cloud should snatch
them from each other's sight.

Still, perhaps, they would have been resolute to
climb as far and as high, between earth and heaven,
as they could find foothold, if Hannah's strength had

not begun to fail, and with that, her courage also. Her breath grew short. She refused to burden her husband with her weight, but often tottered against his side, and recovered herself each time by a feebler effort. At last, she sank down on one of the rocky steps of the acclivity.

"We are lost, dear Matthew," said she, mournfully. "We shall never find our way to the earth again. And oh how happy we might have been in our cottage!"

"Dear heart! — we will yet be happy there," answered Matthew. "Look! In this direction, the sunshine penetrates the dismal mist. By its aid, I can direct our course to the passage of the Notch. Let us go back, love, and dream no more of the Great Carbuncle!"

"The sun cannot be yonder," said Hannah, with despondence. "By this time it must be noon. If there could ever be any sunshine here, it would come from above our heads."

"But look!" repeated Matthew, in a somewhat altered tone. "It is brightening every moment. If not sunshine, what can it be?"

Nor could the young bride any longer deny that a radiance was breaking through the mist, and changing its dim hue to a dusky red, which continually grew more vivid, as if brilliant particles were interfused with the gloom. Now, also, the cloud began to roll away from the mountain, while, as it heavily withdrew, one object after another started out of its impenetrable obscurity into sight, with precisely the effect of a new creation, before the indistinctness of the old chaos had been completely swallowed up. As the process went on, they saw the gleaming of water close at their feet, and found themselves on the very border of a mountain lake, deep, bright, clear, and calmly beautiful, spreading from brim to brim of a basin that had been scooped out of the solid rock. A ray of glory flashed across its surface. The pilgrims looked whence it should proceed, but closed their eyes with a thrill of awful admiration, to exclude the fervid splendor that glowed from the brow of a cliff impending over the enchanted lake. For the simple pair had reached that lake of mystery, and found the long-sought shrine of the Great Carbuncle!

They threw their arms around each other, and trembled at their own success; for, as the legends of this wondrous gem rushed thick upon their memory, they felt themselves marked out by fate — and the consciousness was fearful. Often, from childhood upward, they had seen it shining like a distant star. And now that star was throwing its intensest lustre on their hearts. They seemed changed to one another's eyes, in the red brilliancy that flamed upon their cheeks, while it lent the same fire to the lake, the rocks, and sky, and to the mists which had rolled back before its power. But, with their next glance, they beheld an object that drew their attention even from the mighty stone. At the base of the cliff, directly beneath the Great Carbuncle, appeared the figure of a man, with his arms extended in the act of climbing, and his face turned upward, as if to drink the full gush of splendor. But he stirred not, no more than if changed to marble.

"It is the Seeker," whispered Hannah, convulsively grasping her husband's arm. "Matthew, he is dead."

"The joy of success has killed him," replied Matthew, trembling violently. "Or, perhaps, the very light of the Great Carbuncle was death!"

"The Great Carbuncle," cried a peevish voice behind them. "The Great Humbug! If you have found it, prithee point it out to me."

They turned their heads, and there was the Cynic, with his prodigious spectacles set carefully on his nose, staring now at the lake, now at the rocks, now at the distant masses of vapor, now right at the Great Carbuncle itself, yet seemingly as unconscious of its light as if all the scattered clouds were condensed about his person. Though its radiance actually threw the shadow of the unbeliever at his own feet, as he turned his back upon the glorious jewel, he would not be convinced that there was the least glimmer there.

"Where is your Great Humbug?" he repeated. "I challenge you to make me see it!"

"There," said Matthew, incensed at such perverse blindness, and turning the Cynic round towards the illuminated cliff. "Take off those abominable spectacles, and you cannot help seeing it!"

Now these colored spectacles probably darkened the Cynic's sight, in at least as great a degree as the smoked glasses through which people gaze at an eclipse. With resolute bravado, however, he snatched them from his nose, and fixed a bold stare full upon the ruddy blaze of the Great Carbuncle. But scarcely had he encountered it, when, with a deep, shuddering groan, he dropped his head, and pressed both hands across his miserable eyes. Thenceforth there was, in very truth, no light of the Great Carbuncle, nor any other light on earth, nor light of heaven itself, for the poor Cynic. So long accustomed to view all objects through a medium that deprived them of every glimpse of brightness, a single flash of so glorious a phenomenon, striking upon his naked vision, had blinded him forever.

"Matthew," said Hannah, clinging to him, "let us go hence!"

Matthew saw that she was faint, and kneeling down, supported her in his arms, while he threw some of the thrillingly cold water of the enchanted lake upon her face and bosom. It revived her, but could not renovate her courage.

"Yes, dearest!" cried Matthew, pressing her tremulous form to his breast, — "we will go hence, and return to our humble cottage. The blessed sunshine and the quiet moonlight shall come through our window. We will kindle the cheerful glow of our hearth, at eventide, and be happy in its light. But never again will we desire more light than all the world may share with us."

"No," said his bride, "for how could we live by day, or sleep by night, in this awful blaze of the Great Carbuncle!"

Out of the hollow of their hands, they drank each a draught from the lake, which presented them its waters uncontaminated by an earthly lip. Then, lending their guidance to the blinded Cynic, who uttered not a word, and even stifled his groans in his own most wretched heart, they began to descend the mountain. Yet, as they left the shore, till then untrodden, of the spirit's lake, they threw a farewell glance towards the cliff, and beheld the vapors gathering in dense volumes, through which the gem burned duskily.

As touching the other pilgrims of the Great Carbuncle, the legend goes on to tell, that the worshipful Master Ichabod Pigsnort soon gave up the quest as a desperate speculation, and wisely resolved to betake himself again to his warehouse, near the town dock, in Boston. But, as he passed through the Notch of the

mountains, a war party of Indians captured our unlucky merchant, and carried him to Montreal, there
holding him in bondage, till, by the payment of a
heavy ransom, he had wofully subtracted from his
hoard of pine-tree shillings. By his long absence,
moreover, his affairs had become so disordered that,
for the rest of his life, instead of wallowing in silver,
he had seldom a sixpence worth of copper. Doctor
Cacaphodel, the alchemist, returned to his laboratory
with a prodigious fragment of granite, which he ground
to powder, dissolved in acids, melted in the crucible,
and burned with the blow-pipe, and published the result of his experiments in one of the heaviest folios of
the day. And, for all these purposes, the gem itself
could not have answered better than the granite. The
poet, by a somewhat similar mistake, made prize of a
great piece of ice, which he found in a sunless chasm
of the mountains, and swore that it corresponded, in
all points, with his idea of the Great Carbuncle. The
critics say, that, if his poetry lacked the splendor of
the gem, it retained all the coldness of the ice. The
Lord de Vere went back to his ancestral hall, where
he contented himself with a wax-lighted chandelier,
and filled, in due course of time, another coffin in the
ancestral vault. As the funeral torches gleamed within
that dark receptacle, there was no need of the Great
Carbuncle to show the vanity of earthly pomp.

The Cynic, having cast aside his spectacles, wandered about the world, a miserable object, and was
punished with an agonizing desire of light, for the wilful blindness of his former life. The whole night long,
he would lift his splendor-blasted orbs to the moon
and stars; he turned his face eastward, at sunrise, as
duly as a Persian idolater; he made a pilgrimage to

Rome, to witness the magnificent illumination of St. Peter's Church; and finally perished in the great fire of London, into the midst of which he had thrust himself, with the desperate idea of catching one feeble ray from the blaze that was kindling earth and heaven.

Matthew and his bride spent many peaceful years, and were fond of telling the legend of the Great Carbuncle. The tale, however, towards the close of their lengthened lives, did not meet with the full credence that had been accorded to it by those who remembered the ancient lustre of the gem. For it is affirmed that, from the hour when two mortals had shown themselves so simply wise as to reject a jewel which would have dimmed all earthly things, its splendor waned. When other pilgrims reached the cliff, they found only an opaque stone, with particles of mica glittering on its surface. There is also a tradition that, as the youthful pair departed, the gem was loosened from the forehead of the cliff, and fell into the enchanted lake, and that, at noontide, the Seeker's form may still be seen to bend over its quenchless gleam.

Some few believe that this inestimable stone is blazing as of old, and say that they have caught its radiance, like a flash of summer lightning, far down the valley of the Saco. And be it owned that, many a mile from the Crystal Hills, I saw a wondrous light around their summits, and was lured, by the faith of poesy, to be the latest pilgrim of the GREAT CARBUNCLE.

THE PROPHETIC PICTURES.[1]

"But this painter!" cried Walter Ludlow, with animation. "He not only excels in his peculiar art, but possesses vast acquirements in all other learning and science. He talks Hebrew with Dr. Mather, and gives lectures in anatomy to Dr. Boylston. In a word, he will meet the best instructed man among us on his own ground. Moreover, he is a polished gentleman — a citizen of the world — yes, a true cosmopolite; for he will speak like a native of each clime and country of the globe except our own forests, whither he is now going. Nor is all this what I most admire in him."

"Indeed!" said Elinor, who had listened with a woman's interest to the description of such a man. "Yet this is admirable enough."

"Surely it is," replied her lover, "but far less so than his natural gift of adapting himself to every variety of character, insomuch that all men — and all women too, Elinor — shall find a mirror of themselves in this wonderful painter. But the greatest wonder is yet to be told."

"Nay, if he have more wonderful attributes than these," said Elinor, laughing, "Boston is a perilous abode for the poor gentleman. Are you telling me of a painter or a wizard?"

[1] This story was suggested by an anecdote of Stuart, related in Dunlap's *History of the Arts of Design*, — a most entertaining book to the general reader, and a deeply interesting one, we should think, to the artist.

"In truth," answered he, "that question might be asked much more seriously than you suppose. They say that he paints not merely a man's features, but his mind and heart. He catches the secret sentiments and passions, and throws them upon the canvas, like sunshine — or perhaps, in the portraits of dark-souled men, like a gleam of infernal fire. It is an awful gift," added Walter, lowering his voice from its tone of enthusiasm. "I shall be almost afraid to sit to him."

"Walter, are you in earnest?" exclaimed Elinor.

"For Heaven's sake, dearest Elinor, do not let him paint the look which you now wear," said her lover, smiling, though rather perplexed. "There: it is passing away now, but when you spoke you seemed frightened to death, and very sad besides. What were you thinking of?"

"Nothing, nothing," answered Elinor hastily. "You paint my face with your own fantasies. Well, come for me to-morrow, and we will visit this wonderful artist."

But when the young man had departed, it cannot be denied that a remarkable expression was again visible on the fair and youthful face of his mistress. It was a sad and anxious look, little in accordance with what should have been the feelings of a maiden on the eve of wedlock. Yet Walter Ludlow was the chosen of her heart.

"A look!" said Elinor to herself. "No wonder that it startled him, if it expressed what I sometimes feel. I know, by my own experience, how frightful a look may be. But it was all fancy. I thought nothing of it at the time — I have seen nothing of it since — I did but dream it."

And she busied herself about the embroidery of a

ruff, in which she meant that her portrait should be taken.

The painter, of whom they had been speaking, was not one of those native artists who, at a later period than this, borrowed their colors from the Indians, and manufactured their pencils of the furs of wild beasts. Perhaps, if he could have revoked his life and prearranged his destiny, he might have chosen to belong to that school without a master, in the hope of being at least original, since there were no works of art to imitate nor rules to follow. But he had been born and educated in Europe. People said that he had studied the grandeur or beauty of conception, and every touch of the master hand, in all the most famous pictures, in cabinets and galleries, and on the walls of churches, till there was nothing more for his powerful mind to learn. Art could add nothing to its lessons, but Nature might. He had therefore visited a world whither none of his professional brethren had preceded him, to feast his eyes on visible images that were noble and picturesque, yet had never been transferred to canvas. America was too poor to afford other temptations to an artist of eminence, though many of the colonial gentry, on the painter's arrival, had expressed a wish to transmit their lineaments to posterity by means of his skill. Whenever such proposals were made, he fixed his piercing eyes on the applicant, and seemed to look him through and through. If he beheld only a sleek and comfortable visage, though there were a gold-laced coat to adorn the picture and golden guineas to pay for it, he civilly rejected the task and the reward. But if the face were the index of any thing uncommon, in thought, sentiment, or experience; or if he met a beggar in the street, with a white beard and a furrowed brow; or if sometimes a child hap-pened to look up and smile, he would exhaust all the art on them that he denied to wealth.

Pictorial skill being so rare in the colonies, the painter became an object of general curiosity. If few or none could appreciate the technical merit of his productions, yet there were points, in regard to which the opinion of the crowd was as valuable as the refined judgment of the amateur. He watched the effect that each picture produced on such untutored beholders, and derived profit from their remarks, while they would as soon have thought of instructing Nature herself as him who seemed to rival her. Their admiration, it must be owned, was tinctured with the prejudices of the age and country. Some deemed it an offence against the Mosaic law, and even a presumptuous mockery of the Creator, to bring into existence such lively images of his creatures. Others, frightened at the art which could raise phantoms at will, and keep the form of the dead among the living, were inclined to consider the painter as a magician, or perhaps the famous Black Man, of old witch times, plotting mis-chief in a new guise. These foolish fancies were more than half believed among the mob. Even in superior circles his character was invested with a vague awe, partly rising like smoke wreaths from the popular superstitions, but chiefly caused by the varied knowl-edge and talents which he made subservient to his profession.

Being on the eve of marriage, Walter Ludlow and Elinor were eager to obtain their portraits, as the first of what, they doubtless hoped, would be a long series of family pictures. The day after the conversation above recorded they visited the painter's rooms. A

servant ushered them into an apartment, where, though
the artist himself was not visible, there were personages whom they could hardly forbear greeting with
reverence. They knew, indeed, that the whole assembly were but pictures, yet felt it impossible to separate
the idea of life and intellect from such striking coun-
terfeits. Several of the portraits were known to them,
either as distinguished characters of the day or their
private acquaintances. There was Governor Burnet,
looking as if he had just received an undutiful communication from the House of Representatives, and
were inditing a most sharp response. Mr. Cooke hung
beside the ruler whom he opposed, sturdy, and somewhat puritanical, as befitted a popular leader. The
ancient lady of Sir William Phipps eyed them from
the wall, in ruff and farthingale, — an imperious old
dame, not unsuspected of witchcraft. John Winslow,
then a very young man, wore the expression of war-
like enterprise, which long afterwards made him a distinguished general. Their personal friends were recognized at a glance. In most of the pictures, the
whole mind and character were brought out on the
countenance, and concentrated into a single look, so
that, to speak paradoxically, the originals hardly resembled themselves so strikingly as the portraits did.

Among these modern worthies there were two old
bearded Saints, who had almost vanished into the darkening canvas. There was also a pale, but unfaded
Madonna, who had perhaps been worshipped in Rome,
and now regarded the lovers with such a mild and
holy look that they longed to worship too.

"How singular a thought," observed Walter Ludlow, "that this beautiful face has been beautiful for
above two hundred years! Oh, if all beauty would endure so well! Do you not envy her, Elinor?"

"If earth were heaven, I might," she replied. "But where all things fade, how miserable to be the one that could not fade!"

"This dark old St. Peter has a fierce and ugly scowl, saint though he be," continued Walter. "He troubles me. But the Virgin looks kindly at us."

"Yes; but very sorrowfully, methinks," said Elinor.

The easel stood beneath these three old pictures, sustaining one that had been recently commenced. After a little inspection, they began to recognize the features of their own minister, the Rev. Dr. Colman, growing into shape and life, as it were, out of a cloud.

"Kind old man!" exclaimed Elinor. "He gazes at me as if he were about to utter a word of paternal advice."

"And at me," said Walter, "as if he were about to shake his head and rebuke me for some suspected iniquity. But so does the original. I shall never feel quite comfortable under his eye till we stand before him to be married."

They now heard a footstep on the floor, and turning, beheld the painter, who had been some moments in the room, and had listened to a few of their remarks. He was a middle-aged man, with a countenance well worthy of his own pencil. Indeed, by the picturesque, though careless arrangement of his rich dress, and, perhaps, because his soul dwelt always among painted shapes, he looked somewhat like a portrait himself. His visitors were sensible of a kindred between the artist and his works, and felt as if one of the pictures had stepped from the canvas to salute them.

Walter Ludlow, who was slightly known to the painter, explained the object of their visit. While he spoke, a sunbeam was falling athwart his figure and

Elinor's, with so happy an effect that they also seemed
living pictures of youth and beauty, gladdened by
bright fortune.   The artist was evidently struck.

"My easel is occupied for several ensuing days, and
my stay in Boston must be brief," said he, thought
fully; then, after an observant glance, he added.
"but your wishes shall be gratified, though I disap-
point the Chief Justice and Madam Oliver.   I must
not lose this opportunity, for the sake of painting a
few ells of broadcloth and brocade."

The painter expressed a desire to introduce both
their portraits into one picture, and represent them
engaged in some appropriate action.   This plan would
have delighted the lovers, but was necessarily rejected,
because so large a space of canvas would have been
unfit for the room which it was intended to decorate.
Two half-length portraits were therefore fixed upon.
After they had taken leave, Walter Ludlow asked
Elinor, with a smile, whether she knew what an influence over their fates the painter was about to acquire.

"The old women of Boston affirm," continued he,
"that after he has once got possession of a person's
face and figure, he may paint him in any act or situation whatever — and the picture will be prophetic. Do
you believe it?"

"Not quite," said Elinor, smiling.   "Yet if he has
such magic, there is something so gentle in his mar-
ner that I am sure he will use it well."

It was the painter's choice to proceed with both the
portraits at the same time, assigning as a reason, in
the mystical language which he sometimes used, that
the faces threw light upon each other.   Accordingly
he gave now a touch to Walter, and now to Elinor,
and the features of one and the other began to start

forth so vividly that it appeared as if his triumphant
art would actually disengage them from the canvas.
Amid the rich light and deep shade, they beheld their
phantom selves. But, though the likeness promised
to be perfect, they were not quite satisfied with the
expression ; it seemed more vague than in most of the
painter's works. He, however, was satisfied with the
prospect of success, and being much interested in the
lovers, employed his leisure moments, unknown to
them, in making a crayon sketch of their two figures.
During their sittings, he engaged them in conversation,
and kindled up their faces with characteristic traits,
which, though continually varying, it was his purpose
to combine and fix. At length he announced that at
their next visit both the portraits would be ready for
delivery.

"If my pencil will but be true to my conception, in
the few last touches which I meditate," observed he,
" these two pictures will be my very best performances.
Seldom, indeed, has an artist such subjects."

While speaking, he still bent his penetrative eye
upon them, nor withdrew it till they had reached the
bottom of the stairs.

Nothing, in the whole circle of human vanities, takes
stronger hold of the imagination than this affair of
having a portrait painted. Yet why should it be so?
The looking-glass, the polished globes of the andirons,
the mirror-like water, and all other reflecting surfaces
continually present us with portraits, or rather ghosts
of ourselves, which we glance at, and straightway forget them. But we forget them only because they
vanish. It is the idea of duration — of earthly immortality — that gives such a mysterious interest to
our own portraits. Walter and Elinor were not in-

sensible to this feeling, and hastened to the painter's room, punctually at the appointed hour, to meet those pictured shapes which were to be their representatives with posterity. The sunshine flashed after them into the apartment, but left it somewhat gloomy as they closed the door.

Their eyes were immediately attracted to their portraits, which rested against the farthest wall of the room. At the first glance, through the dim light and the distance, seeing themselves in precisely their natural attitudes, and with all the air that they recognized so well, they uttered a simultaneous exclamation of delight.

"There we stand," cried Walter, enthusiastically, "fixed in sunshine forever! No dark passions can gather on our faces!"

"No," said Elinor, more calmly; "no dreary change can sadden us."

This was said while they were approaching, and had yet gained only an imperfect view of the pictures. The painter, after saluting them, busied himself at a table in completing a crayon sketch, leaving his visitors to form their own judgment as to his perfected labors. At intervals, he sent a glance from beneath his deep eyebrows, watching their countenances in profile, with his pencil suspended over the sketch. They had now stood some moments, each in front of the other's picture, contemplating it with entranced attention, but without uttering a word. At length, Walter stepped forward — then back — viewing Elinor's portrait in various lights, and finally spoke.

"Is there not a change?" said he, in a doubtful and meditative tone. "Yes; the perception of it grows more vivid the longer I look. It is certainly the same picture that I saw yesterday; the dress — the features — all are the same; and yet something is altered."

"Is then the picture less like than it was yesterday?" inquired the painter, now drawing near, with irrepressible interest.

"The features are perfect, Elinor," answered Walter, "and, at the first glance, the expression seemed also hers. But, I could fancy that the portrait has changed countenance, while I have been looking at it. The eyes are fixed on mine with a strangely sad and anxious expression. Nay, it is grief and terror! Is this like Elinor?"

"Compare the living face with the pictured one," said the painter.

Walter glanced sidelong at his mistress, and started. Motionless and absorbed — fascinated, as it were — in contemplation of Walter's portrait, Elinor's face had assumed precisely the expression of which he had just been complaining. Had she practised for whole hours before a mirror, she could not have caught the look so successfully. Had the picture itself been a mirror, it could not have thrown back her present aspect with stronger and more melancholy truth. She appeared quite unconscious of the dialogue between the artist and her lover.

"Elinor," exclaimed Walter, in amazement, "what change has come over you?"

She did not hear him, nor desist from her fixed gaze, till he seized her hand, and thus attracted her notice; then, with a sudden tremor, she looked from the picture to the face of the original.

"Do you see no change in your portrait?" asked

"In mine? — None!" replied Walter, examining it. "But let me see! Yes; there is a slight change — an improvement, I think, in the picture, though none in the likeness. It has a livelier expression than yesterday, as if some bright thought were flashing from the eyes, and about to be uttered from the lips. Now that I have caught the look, it becomes very decided.'

While he was intent on these observations, Elinor turned to the painter. She regarded him with grief and awe, and felt that he repaid her with sympathy and commiseration, though wherefore, she could but vaguely guess.

"That look!" whispered she, and shuddered. "How came it there?"

"Madam," said the painter, sadly, taking her hand, and leading her apart, "in both these pictures, I have painted what I saw. The artist — the true artist — must look beneath the exterior. It is his gift — his proudest, but often a melancholy one — to see the inmost soul, and, by a power indefinable even to himself, to make it glow or darken upon the canvas, in glances that express the thought and sentiment of years. Would that I might convince myself of error in the present instance!"

They had now approached the table, on which were heads in chalk, hands almost as expressive as ordinary faces, ivied church towers, thatched cottages, old thunder-stricken trees, Oriental and antique costume, and all such picturesque vagaries of an artist's idle moments. Turning them over, with seeming carelessness, a crayon sketch of two figures was disclosed.

"If I have failed," continued he — "if your heart does not see itself reflected in your own portrait — if you have no secret cause to trust my delineation of the other — it is not yet too late to alter them. I might change the action of these figures too. But would it influence the event?"

He directed her notice to the sketch. A thrill ran through Elinor's frame; a shriek was upon her lips, but she stifled it, with the self-command that becomes habitual to all who hide thoughts of fear and anguish within their bosoms. Turning from the table, she perceived that Walter had advanced near enough to have seen the sketch, though she could not determine whether it had caught his eye.

" We will not have the pictures altered," said she, hastily. " If mine is sad, I shall but look the gayer for the contrast."

" Be it so," answered the painter, bowing. " May your griefs be such fanciful ones that only your picture may mourn for them! For your joys — may they be true and deep, and paint themselves upon this lovely face till it quite belie my art!"

After the marriage of Walter and Elinor, the pictures formed the two most splendid ornaments of their abode. They hung side by side, separated by a narrow panel, appearing to eye each other constantly, yet always returning the gaze of the spectator. Travelled gentlemen, who professed a knowledge of such subjects, reckoned these among the most admirable specimens of modern portraiture; while common observers compared them with the originals, feature by feature, and were rapturous in praise of the likeness. But it was on a third class — neither travelled connoisseurs nor common observers, but people of natural sensibility — that the pictures wrought their strongest effect. Such persons might gaze carelessly at first, but, becoming interested, would return day after day,

and study these painted faces like the pages of a mystic volume.   Walter Ludlow's portrait attracted their
earliest notice.   In the absence of himself and his
bride, they sometimes disputed as to the expression
which the painter had intended to throw upon the
features ; all agreeing that there was a look of earnest
import, though no two explained it alike.   There was
less diversity of opinion in regard to Elinor's picture.
They differed, indeed, in their attempts to estimate
the nature and depth of the gloom that dwelt upon
her face, but agreed that it was gloom, and alien from
the natural temperament of their youthful friend.   A
certain fanciful person announced, as the result of
much scrutiny, that both these pictures were parts of
one design, and that the melancholy strength of feeling, in Elinor's countenance, bore reference to the
more vivid emotion, or, as he termed it, the wild passion, in that of Walter.   Though unskilled in the art,
he even began a sketch, in which the action of the two
figures was to correspond with their mutual expression.

It was whispered among friends that, day by day,
Elinor's face was assuming a deeper shade of pensiveness, which threatened soon to render her too true a
counterpart of her melancholy picture.   Walter, on the
other hand, instead of acquiring the vivid look which
the painter had given him on the canvas, became
reserved and downcast, with no outward flashes of
emotion, however it might be smouldering within.   In
course of time, Elinor hung a gorgeous curtain of purple silk, wrought with flowers and fringed with heavy
golden tassels, before the pictures, under pretence that
the dust would tarnish their hues, or the light dim
them.   It was enough.   Her visitors felt, that the

massive folds of the silk must never be withdrawn, nor the portraits mentioned in her presence.

Time wore on; and the painter came again. He had been far enough to the north to see the silver cascade of the Crystal Hills, and to look over the vast round of cloud and forest from the summit of New England's loftiest mountain. But he did not profane that scene by the mockery of his art. He had also lain in a canoe on the bosom of Lake George, making his soul the mirror of its loveliness and grandeur, till not a picture in the Vatican was more vivid than his recollection. He had gone with the Indian hunters to Niagara, and there, again, had flung his hopeless pencil down the precipice, feeling that he could as soon paint the roar, as aught else that goes to make up the wondrous cataract. In truth, it was seldom his impulse to copy natural scenery, except as a framework for the delineations of the human form and face, instinct with thought, passion, or suffering. With store of such his adventurous ramble had enriched him: the stern dignity of Indian chiefs; the dusky loveliness of Indian girls; the domestic life of wigwams; the stealthy march; the battle beneath gloomy pine-trees; the frontier fortress with its garrison; the anomaly of the old French partisan, bred in courts, but grown gray in shaggy deserts; such were the scenes and portraits that he had sketched. The glow of perilous moments; flashes of wild feeling; struggles of fierce power, — love, hate, grief, frenzy; in a word, all the worn-out heart of the old earth had been revealed to him under a new form. His portfolio was filled with graphic illustrations of the volume of his memory, which genius would transmute into its own substance, and imbue with immortality. He felt that the deep wisdom in his art, which he had sought so far, was found.

But amid stern or lovely nature, in the perils of the forest or its overwhelming peacefulness, still there had been two phantoms, the companions of his way. Like all other men around whom an engrossing purpose wreathes itself, he was insulated from the mass of human kind. He had no aim — no pleasure — no ympathies — but what were ultimately connected with his art. Though gentle in manner and upright in intent and action, he did not possess kindly feelings ; his heart was cold ; no living creature could be brought near enough to keep him warm. For these two beings, however, he had felt, in its greatest intensity, the sort of interest which always allied him to the subjects of his pencil. He had pried into their souls with his keenest insight, and pictured the result upon their features with his utmost skill, so as barely to fall short of that standard which no genius ever reached, his own severe conception. He had caught from the duskiness of the future — at least, so he fancied — a fearful secret, and had obscurely revealed it on the portraits. So much of himself — of his imagination and all other powers — had been lavished on the study of Walter and Elinor, that he almost regarded them as creations of his own, like the thousands with which he had peopled the realms of Picture. Therefore did they flit through the twilight of the woods, hover on the mist of waterfalls, look forth from the mirror of the lake, nor melt away in the noontide sun. They haunted his pictorial fancy, not as mockeries of life, nor pale goblins of the dead, but in the guise of portraits, each with the unalterable expression which his magic had evoked from the caverns of the soul. He could not recross the Atlantic till he had again beheld the originals of those airy pictures.

"O glorious Art!" thus mused the enthusiastic painter as he trod the street, "thou art the image of the Creator's own. The innumerable forms, that wander in nothingness, start into being at thy beck. The dead live again. Thou recallest them to their old scenes, and givest their gray shadows the lustre of a bet-ter life, at once earthly and immortal. Thou snatchest back the fleeting moments of History. With thee there is no Past, for, at thy touch, all that is great becomes forever present; and illustrious men live through long ages, in the visible performance of the very deeds which made them what they are. O potent Art! as thou bringest the faintly revealed Past to stand in that narrow strip of sunlight, which we call Now, canst thou summon the shrouded Future to meet her there? Have I not achieved it? Am I not thy Prophet?"

Thus, with a proud, yet melancholy fervor, did he almost cry aloud, as he passed through the toilsome street, among people that knew not of his reveries, nor could understand nor care for them. It is not good for man to cherish a solitary ambition. Unless there be those around him by whose example he may regulate himself, his thoughts, desires, and hopes will become extravagant, and he the semblance, perhaps the real-ity, of a madman. Reading other bosoms with an acuteness almost preternatural, the painter failed to see the disorder of his own.

"And this should be the house," said he, looking up and down the front, before he knocked. "Heaven help my brains! That picture! Methinks it will never vanish. Whether I look at the windows or the door, there it is framed within them, painted strongly, and glowing in the richest tints — the faces of the portraits — the figures and action of the sketch!"

He knocked.

"The Portraits! Are they within?" inquired he of the domestic; then recollecting himself — "your master and mistress! Are they at home?"

"They are, sir," said the servant, adding, as he noticed that picturesque aspect of which the painter could never divest himself, "and the Portraits too!"

The guest was admitted into a parlor, communicating by a central door with an interior room of the same size. As the first apartment was empty, he passed to the entrance of the second, within which his eyes were greeted by those living personages, as well as their pictured representatives, who had long been the objects of so singular an interest. He involuntarily paused on the threshold.

They had not perceived his approach. Walter and Elinor were standing before the portraits, whence the former had just flung back the rich and voluminous folds of the silken curtain, holding its golden tassel with one hand, while the other grasped that of his bride. The pictures, concealed for months, gleamed forth again in undiminished splendor, appearing to throw a sombre light across the room, rather than to be disclosed by a borrowed radiance. That of Elinor had been almost prophetic. A pensiveness, and next a gentle sorrow, had successively dwelt upon her countenance, deepening, with the lapse of time, into a quiet anguish. A mixture of affright would now have made it the very expression of the portrait. Walter's face was moody and dull, or animated only by fitful flashes, which left a heavier darkness for their momentary illumination. He looked from Elinor to her portrait, and thence to his own, in the contemplation of which he finally stood absorbed.

The painter seemed to hear the step of Destiny approaching behind him, on its progress towards its victims. A strange thought darted into his mind. Was not his own the form in which that destiny had embodied itself, and he a chief agent of the coming evil which he had foreshadowed?

Still, Walter remained silent before the picture, communing with it as with his own heart, and abandoning himself to the spell of evil influence that the painter had cast upon the features. Gradually his eyes kindled; while as Elinor watched the increasing wildness of his face, her own assumed a look of terror; and when at last he turned upon her, the resemblance of both to their portraits was complete.

"Our fate is upon us!" howled Walter. "Die!"

Drawing a knife, he sustained her, as she was sinking to the ground, and aimed it at her bosom. In the action, and in the look and attitude of each, the painter beheld the figures of his sketch. The picture, with all its tremendous coloring, was finished.

"Hold, madman!" cried he, sternly.

He had advanced from the door, and interposed himself between the wretched beings, with the same sense of power to regulate their destiny as to alter a scene upon the canvas. He stood like a magician, controlling the phantoms which he had evoked.

"What!" muttered Walter Ludlow, as he relapsed from fierce excitement into silent gloom. "Does Fate impede its own decree?"

"Wretched lady!" said the painter, "did I not warn you?"

"You did," replied Elinor, calmly, as her terror gave place to the quiet grief which it had disturbed. "But — I loved him!"

Is there not a deep moral in the tale? Could the result of one, or all our deeds, be shadowed forth and set before us, some would call it Fate, and hurry onward, others be swept along by their passionate desires, and none be turned aside by the PROPHETIC PICTURES.

DAVID SWAN.

A FANTASY.

WE can be but partially acquainted even with the events which actually influence our course through life, and our final destiny. There are innumerable other events — if such they may be called — which come close upon us, yet pass away without actual results, or even betraying their near approach, by the reflection of any light or shadow across our minds. Could we know all the vicissitudes of our fortunes, life would be too full of hope and fear, exultation or disappointment, to afford us a single hour of true serenity. This idea may be illustrated by a page from the secret history of David Swan.

We have nothing to do with David until we find him, at the age of twenty, on the high road from his native place to the city of Boston, where his uncle, a small dealer in the grocery line, was to take him behind the counter. Be it enough to say that he was a native of New Hampshire, born of respectable parents, and had received an ordinary school education, with a classic finish by a year at Gilmanton Academy. After journeying on foot from sunrise till nearly noon of a summer's day, his weariness and the increasing heat determined him to sit down in the first convenient shade, and await the coming up of the stage-coach. As if planted on purpose for him, there soon appeared a little tuft of maples, with a delightful recess in the midst, and such a fresh bubbling spring that it seemed never to have sparkled for any wayfarer but David Swan. Virgin or not, he kissed it with his thirsty lips, and then flung himself along the brink, pillowing his head upon some shirts and a pair of pantaloons, tied up in a striped cotton handkerchief. The sunbeams could not reach him ; the dust did not yet rise from the road after the heavy rain of yesterday ; and his grassy lair suited the young man better than a bed of down. The spring murmured drowsily beside him ; the branches waved dreamily across the blue sky overhead ; and a deep sleep, perchance hiding dreams within its depths, fell upon David Swan. But we are to relate events which he did not dream of.

While he lay sound asleep in the shade, other people were wide awake, and passed to and fro, afoot, on horseback, and in all sorts of vehicles, along the sunny road by his bedchamber. Some looked neither to the right hand nor the left, and knew not that he was there ; some merely glanced that way, without admitting the slumberer among their busy thoughts ; some laughed to see how soundly he slept ; and several, whose hearts were brimming full of scorn, ejected their venomous superfluity on David Swan. A middle-aged widow, when nobody else was near, thrust her head a little way into the recess, and vowed that the young fellow looked charming in his sleep. A temperance lecturer saw him, and wrought poor David into the texture of his evening's discourse, as an awful instance of dead drunkenness by the roadside. But censure, praise, merriment, scorn, and indifference were all one, or rather all nothing, to David Swan.

He had slept only a few moments when a brown carriage, drawn by a handsome pair of horses, bowled easily along, and was brought to a stand-still nearly in front of David's resting-place. A linchpin had fallen out, and permitted one of the wheels to slide off. The damage was slight, and occasioned merely a momentary alarm to an elderly merchant and his wife, who were returning to Boston in the carriage. While the coachman and a servant were replacing the wheel, the lady and gentleman sheltered themselves beneath the maple-trees, and there espied the bubbling fountain, and David Swan asleep beside it. Impressed with the awe which the humblest sleeper usually sheds around him, the merchant trod as lightly as the gout would allow; and his spouse took good heed not to rustle her silk gown, lest David should start up all of a sudden.

"How soundly he sleeps!" whispered the old gentleman. "From what a depth he draws that easy breath! Such sleep as that, brought on without an opiate, would be worth more to me than half my income; for it would suppose health and an untroubled mind."

"And youth, besides," said the lady. "Healthy and quiet age does not sleep thus. Our slumber is no more like his than our wakefulness."

The longer they looked the more did this elderly couple feel interested in the unknown youth, to whom the wayside and the maple shade were as a secret chamber, with the rich gloom of damask curtains brooding over him. Perceiving that a stray sunbeam glimmered down upon his face, the lady contrived to twist a branch aside, so as to intercept it. And having done this little act of kindness, she began to feel like a mother to him.

"Providence seems to have laid him here," whis-

pered she to her husband, "and to have brought us
hither to find him, after our disappointment in our
cousin's son. Methinks I can see a likeness to our
departed Henry. Shall we waken him?"

"To what purpose?" said the merchant, hesitating.
"We know nothing of the youth's character."

"That open countenance!" replied his wife, in the
same hushed voice, yet earnestly. "This innocent
sleep!"

While these whispers were passing, the sleeper's
heart did not throb, nor his breath become agitated,
nor his features betray the least token of interest.
Yet Fortune was bending over him, just ready to let
fall a burden of gold. The old merchant had lost his
only son, and had no heir to his wealth except a distant relative, with whose conduct he was dissatisfied.
In such cases, people sometimes do stranger things
than to act the magician, and awaken a young man to
splendor who fell asleep in poverty.

"Shall we not waken him?" repeated the lady,
persuasively.

"The coach is ready, sir," said the servant, behind.

The old couple started, reddened, and hurried
away, mutually wondering that they should ever have
dreamed of doing anything so very ridiculous. The
merchant threw himself back in the carriage, and occupied his mind with the plan of a magnificent asylum
for unfortunate men of business. Meanwhile, David
Swan enjoyed his nap.

The carriage could not have gone above a mile or
two, when a pretty young girl came along, with a
tripping pace, which showed precisely how her little
heart was dancing in her bosom. Perhaps it was this
merry kind of motion that caused—is there any harm

in saying it? — her garter to slip its knot. Conscious
that the silken girth — if silk it were — was relaxing
its hold, she turned aside into the shelter of the maple-
trees, and there found a young man asleep by the
spring! Blushing as red as any rose that she should
have intruded into a gentleman's bedchamber, and for
such a purpose, too, she was about to make her escape
on tiptoe. But there was peril near the sleeper. A
monster of a bee had been wandering overhead —
buzz, buzz, buzz — now among the leaves, now flashing
through the strips of sunshine, and now lost in the
dark shade, till finally he appeared to be settling on
the eyelid of David Swan. The sting of a bee is sometimes deadly. As free hearted as she was innocent,
the girl attacked the intruder with her handkerchief,
brushed him soundly, and drove him from beneath the
maple shade. How sweet a picture! This good deed
accomplished, with quickened breath, and a deeper
blush, she stole a glance at the youthful stranger for
whom she had been battling with a dragon in the
air.

"He is handsome!" thought she, and blushed redder
yet.

How could it be that no dream of bliss grew so
strong within him, that, shattered by its very strength,
it should part asunder, and allow him to perceive the
girl among its phantoms? Why, at least, did no smile
of welcome brighten upon his face? She was come,
the maid whose soul, according to the old and beautiful idea, had been severed from his own, and whom,
in all his vague but passionate desires, he yearned to
meet. Her, only, could he love with a perfect love;
him, only, could she receive into the depths of her
heart; and now her image was faintly blushing in the

fountain, by his side ; should it pass away, its happy lustre would never gleam upon his life again.

" How sound he sleeps ! " murmured the girl.

She departed, but did not trip along the road so lightly as when she came.

Now, this girl's father was a thriving country merchant in the neighborhood, and happened, at that identical time, to be looking out for just such a young man as David Swan. Had David formed a wayside acquaintance with the daughter, he would have become the father's clerk, and all else in natural succession. So here, again, had good fortune — the best of fortunes — stolen so near that her garments brushed against him ; and he knew nothing of the matter.

The girl was hardly out of sight when two men turned aside beneath the maple shade. Both had dark faces, set off by cloth caps, which were drawn down aslant over their brows. Their dresses were shabby, yet had a certain smartness. These were a couple of rascals who got their living by whatever the devil sent them, and now, in the interim of other business, had staked the joint profits of their next piece of villany on a game of cards, which was to have been decided here under the trees. But, finding David asleep by the spring, one of the rogues whispered to his fellow, —

" Hist ! — Do you see that bundle under his head ? "

The other villain nodded, winked, and leered.

" I 'll bet you a horn of brandy," said the first, " that the chap has either a pocket-book, or a snug little hoard of small change, stowed away amongst his shirts. And if not there, we shall find it in his pantaloons pocket."

" But how if he wakes ? " said the other.

His companion thrust aside his waistcoat, pointed to the handle of a dirk, and nodded.

"So be it!" muttered the second villain.

They approached the unconscious David, and, while one pointed the dagger towards his heart, the other began to search the bundle beneath his head. Their two faces, grim, wrinkled, and ghastly with guilt and fear, bent over their victim, looking horrible enough to be mistaken for fiends, should he suddenly awake. Nay, had the villains glanced aside into the spring, even they would hardly have known themselves as reflected there. But David Swan had never worn a more tranquil aspect, even when asleep on his mother's breast.

"I must take away the bundle," whispered one.

"If he stirs, I'll strike," muttered the other.

But, at this moment, a dog, scenting along the ground, came in beneath the maple-trees, and gazed alternately at each of these wicked men, and then at the quiet sleeper. He then lapped out of the fountain.

"Pshaw!" said one villain. "We can do nothing now. The dog's master must be close behind."

"Let's take a drink and be off," said the other.

The man with the dagger thrust back the weapon into his bosom, and drew forth a pocket pistol, but not of that kind which kills by a single discharge. It was a flask of liquor, with a block-tin tumbler screwed upon the mouth. Each drank a comfortable dram, and left the spot, with so many jests, and such laughter at their unaccomplished wickedness, that they might be said to have gone on their way rejoicing. In a few hours they had forgotten the whole affair, nor once imagined that the recording angel had written down the crime of murder against their souls, in letters as durable as eternity. As for David Swan, he still slept quietly, neither conscious of the shadow of death when it hung over him, nor of the glow of renewed life when that shadow was withdrawn.

He slept, but no longer so quietly as at first. An hour's repose had snatched, from his elastic frame, the weariness with which many hours of toil had burdened it. Now he stirred — now, moved his lips, without a sound — now, talked, in an inward tone, to the noonday spectres of his dream. But a noise of wheels came rattling louder and louder along the road, until it dashed through the dispersing mist of David's slumber — and there was the stage-coach. He started up with all his ideas about him.

"Halloo, driver! — Take a passenger?" shouted he.

"Room on top!" answered the driver.

Up mounted David, and bowled away merrily towards Boston, without so much as a parting glance at that fountain of dreamlike vicissitude. He knew not that a phantom of Wealth had thrown a golden hue upon its waters — nor that one of Love had sighed softly to their murmur — nor that one of Death had threatened to crimson them with his blood — all, in the brief hour since he lay down to sleep. Sleeping or waking, we hear not the airy footsteps of the strange things that almost happen. Does it not argue a superintending Providence that, while viewless and unexpected events thrust themselves continually athwart our path, there should still be regularity enough in mortal life to render foresight even partially available?

SIGHTS FROM A STEEPLE.

So! I have climbed high, and my reward is small.
Here I stand, with wearied knees, earth, indeed, at a
dizzy depth below, but heaven far, far beyond me
still. Oh that I could soar up into the very zenith,
where man never breathed, nor eagle ever flew, and
where the ethereal azure melts away from the eye,
and appears only a deepened shade of nothingness!
And yet I shiver at that cold and solitary thought.
What clouds are gathering in the golden west, with
direful intent against the brightness and the warmth
of this summer afternoon! They are ponderous air
ships, black as death, and freighted with the tempest;
and at intervals their thunder, the signal guns of that
unearthly squadron, rolls distant along the deep of
heaven. These nearer heaps of fleecy vapor — methinks I could roll and toss upon them the whole day
long! — seem scattered here and there for the repose
of tired pilgrims through the sky. Perhaps — for
who can tell? — beautiful spirits are disporting themselves there, and will bless my mortal eye with the
brief appearance of their curly locks of golden light
and laughing faces, fair and faint as the people of a
rosy dream. Or, where the floating mass so imperfectly obstructs the color of the firmament, a slender
foot and fairy limb, resting too heavily upon the frail
support, may be thrust through, and suddenly withdrawn, while longing fancy follows them in vain.
Yonder again is an airy archipelago, where the sun

beams love to linger in their journeyings through space. Every one of those little clouds has been dipped and steeped in radiance, which the slightest pressure might disengage in silvery profusion, like water wrung from a sea-maid's hair. Bright they are as a young man's visions, and, like them, would be realized in chillness, obscurity, and tears. I will look on them no more.

In three parts of the visible circle, whose centre is this spire, I discern cultivated fields, villages, white country seats, the waving lines of rivulets, little placid lakes, and here and there a rising ground, that would fain be termed a hill. On the fourth side is the sea, stretching away towards a viewless boundary, blue and calm, except where the passing anger of a shadow flits across its surface, and is gone. Hitherward, a broad inlet penetrates far into the land; on the verge of the harbor, formed by its extremity, is a town; and over it am I, a watchman, all-heeding and unheeded. Oh that the multitude of chimneys could speak, like those of Madrid, and betray, in smoky whispers, the secrets of all who, since their first foundation, have assembled at the hearths within! Oh that the Limping Devil of Le Sage would perch beside me here, extend his wand over this contiguity of roofs, uncover every chamber, and make me familiar with their inhabitants! The most desirable mode of existence might be that of a spiritualized Paul Pry, hovering invisible round man and woman, witnessing their deeds, searching into their hearts, borrowing brightness from their felicity and shade from their sorrow, and retaining no emotion peculiar to himself. But none of these things are possible; and if I would know the interior of brick walls, or the mystery of human bosoms, I can but guess.

Yonder is a fair street, extending north and south. The stately mansions are placed each on its carpet of verdant grass, and a long flight of steps descends from every door to the pavement. Ornamental trees — the broad-leafed horse-chestnut, the elm so lofty and bending, the graceful but infrequent willow, and others whereof I know not the names — grow thrivingly among brick and stone. The oblique rays of the sun are intercepted by these green citizens, and by the houses, so that one side of the street is a shaded and pleasant walk. On its whole extent there is now but a single passenger, advancing from the upper end; and he, unless distance and the medium of a pocket spy-glass do him more than justice, is a fine young man of twenty. He saunters slowly forward, slapping his left hand with his folded gloves, bending his eyes upon the pavement, and sometimes raising them to throw a glance before him. Certainly, he has a pensive air. Is he in doubt, or in debt? Is he, if the question be allowable, in love? Does he strive to be melancholy and gentleman-like? Or, is he merely overcome by the heat? But I bid him farewell for the present. The door of one of the houses — an aristocratic edifice, with curtains of purple and gold waving from the windows, is now opened, and down the steps come two ladies, swinging their parasols, and lightly arrayed for a summer ramble. Both are young, both are pretty, but methinks the left-hand lass is the fairer of the twain; and, though she be so serious at this moment, I could swear that there is a treasure of gentle fun within her. They stand talking a little while upon the steps, and finally proceed up the street. Meantime, as their faces are now turned from me, I may look elsewhere.

Upon that wharf, and down the corresponding street, is a busy contrast to the quiet scene which I have just noticed. Business evidently has its centre there, and many a man is wasting the summer afternoon in labor and anxiety, in losing riches or in gaining them, when he would be wiser to flee away to some pleasant country village, or shaded lake in the forest, or wild and cool sea-beach. I see vessels unlading at the wharf, and precious merchandise strewn upon the ground, abundantly as at the bottom of the sea, that market whence no goods return, and where there is no captain nor supercargo to render an account of sales. Here, the clerks are diligent with their paper and pencils, and sailors ply the block and tackle that hang over the hold, accompanying their toil with cries, long drawn and roughly melodious, till the bales and puncheons ascend to upper air. At a little distance a group of gentlemen are assembled round the door of a warehouse. Grave seniors be they, and I would wager — if it were safe in these times to be responsible for any one — that the least eminent among them might vie with old Vicentio, that incomparable trafficker of Pisa. I can even select the wealthiest of the company. It is the elderly personage, in somewhat rusty black, with powdered hair, the superfluous whiteness of which is visible upon the cape of his coat. His twenty ships are wafted on some of their many courses by every breeze that blows, and his name — I will venture to say, though I know it not — is a familiar sound among the far separated merchants of Europe and the Indies.

But I bestow too much of my attention in this quarter. On looking again to the long and shady walk, I perceive that the two fair girls have encountered the young man. After a sort of shyness in the recognition, he turns back with them. Moreover, he has sanctioned my taste in regard to his companions by placing him-self on the inner side of the pavement, nearest the Venus to whom I — enacting, on a steeple top, the part of Paris on the top of Ida — adjudged the golder apple.

In two streets, converging at right angles towards my watchtower, I distinguish three different proces-sions. One is a proud array of voluntary soldiers, in bright uniform, resembling, from the height whence I look down, the painted veterans that garrison the win-dows of a toyshop. And yet, it stirs my heart; their regular advance, their nodding plumes, the sunflash on their bayonets and musket barrels, the roll of their drums ascending past me, and the fife ever and anon piercing through — these things have wakened a war-like fire, peaceful though I be. Close to their rear marches a battalion of school-boys, ranged in crooked and irregular platoons, shouldering sticks, thumping a harsh and unripe clatter from an instrument of tin, and ridiculously aping the intricate manoeuvres of the foremost band. Nevertheless, as slight differences are scarcely perceptible from a church spire, one might be tempted to ask, " Which are the boys ? " — or rather, " Which the men ? " But, leaving these, let us turn to the third procession, which, though sadder in out ward show, may excite identical reflections in the thoughtful mind. It is a funeral. A hearse, drawn by a black and bony steed, and covered by a dusty pall ; two or three coaches rumbling over the stones, their drivers half asleep ; a dozen couple of careless mourners in their every-day attire ; such was not the fashion of our fathers, when they carried a friend to his grave. There is now no doleful clang of the bell to proclaim sorrow to the town. Was the King of Terrors more awful in those days than in our own, that wisdom and philosophy have been able to produce this change? Not so. Here is a proof that he retains his proper majesty. The military men and the military boys are wheeling round the corner, and meet the funeral full in the face. Immediately the drum is silent, all but the tap that regulates each simultaneous footfall. The soldiers yield the path to the dusty hearse and unpretending train, and the children quit their ranks, and cluster on the sidewalks, with timorous and instinctive curiosity. The mourners enter the churchyard at the base of the steeple, and pause by an open grave among the burial stones; the lightning glimmers on them as they lower down the coffin, and the thunder rattles heavily while they throw the earth upon its lid. Verily, the shower is near, and I tremble for the young man and the girls, who have now disappeared from the long and shady street.

How various are the situations of the people covered by the roofs beneath me, and how diversified are the events at this moment befalling them! The new born, the aged, the dying, the strong in life, and the recent dead, are in the chambers of these many mansions. The full of hope, the happy, the miserable, and the desperate, dwell together within the circle of my glance. In some of the houses over which my eyes roam so coldly, guilt is entering into hearts that are still tenanted by a debased and trodden virtue,— guilt is on the very edge of commission, and the impending deed might be averted; guilt is done, and the criminal wonders if it be irrevocable. There are broad thoughts struggling in my mind, and, were I able to give them distinctness, they would make their way in eloquence. Lo! the raindrops are descending.

The clouds, within a little time, have gathered over all the sky, hanging heavily, as if about to drop in one unbroken mass upon the earth. At intervals, the lightning flashes from their brooding hearts, quivers disappears. and then comes the thunder, travelling slowly after its twin-born flame. A strong wind has sprung up, howls through the darkened streets, and raises the dust in dense bodies, to rebel against the approaching storm. The disbanded soldiers fly, the funeral has already vanished like its dead, and all people hurry homeward — all that have a home; while a few lounge by the corners, or trudge on desperately, at their leisure. In a narrow lane, which communicates with the shady street, I discern the rich old merchant, putting himself to the top of his speed, lest the rain should convert his hair powder to a paste. Unhappy gentleman! By the slow vehemence and painful moderation wherewith he journeys, it is but too evident that Podagra has left its thrilling tenderness in his great toe. But yonder, at a far more rapid pace, come three other of my acquaintance, the two pretty girls and the young man, unseasonably interrupted in their walk. Their footsteps are supported by the risen dust, — the wind lends them its velocity, — they fly like three sea-birds driven landward by the tempestuous breeze. The ladies would not thus rival Atalanta if they but knew that any one were at leisure to observe them. Ah! as they hasten onward, laughing in the angry face of nature, a sudden catastrophe has chanced. At the corner where the narrow lane enters into the street, they come plump against the old merchant, whose tortoise motion has just brought him to that point. He likes not the sweet encounter; the darkness of the whole air gathers speedily upon his visage, and there is a pause on both sides. Finally, he thrusts aside the youth with little courtesy, seizes an arm of each of the two girls, and plods onward, like a magician with a prize of captive fairies. All this is easy to be understood. How disconsolate the poor lover stands! regardless of the rain that threatens an exceeding damage to his well-fashioned habiliments, till he catches a backward glance of mirth from a bright eye, and turns away with whatever comfort it conveys.

The old man and his daughters are safely housed, and now the storm lets loose its fury. In every dwelling I perceive the faces of the chambermaids as they shut down the windows, excluding the impetuous shower, and shrinking away from the quick fiery glare. The large drops descend with force upon the slated roofs, and rise again in smoke. There is a rush and roar, as of a river through the air, and muddy streams bubble majestically along the pavement, whirl their dusky foam into the kennel, and disappear beneath iron grates. Thus did Arethusa sink. I love not my station here aloft, in the midst of the tumult which I am powerless to direct or quell, with the blue lightning wrinkling on my brow, and the thunder muttering its first awful syllables in my ear I will descend. Yet let me give another glance to the sea, where the foam breaks out in long white lines upon a broad expanse of blackness, or boils up in far distant points, like snowy mountain tops in the eddies of a flood ; and let me look once more at the green plain, and little hills of the country, over which the giant of the storm is striding in robes of mist, and at the town, whose obscured and desolate streets might beseem a city of the dead ; and turning a single moment to the sky, now gloomy as an author's prospects, I prepare to resume my station on lower earth. But stay ! A little speck of azure has widened in the western heavens ; the sunbeams find a passage, and go rejoicing through the tempest ; and on yonder larkest cloud, born, like hallowed hopes, of the glory of another world and the trouble and tears of this, brightens forth the Rainbow !

THE HOLLOW OF THE THREE HILLS.

IN those strange old times, when fantastic dreams and madmen's reveries were realized among the actual circumstances of life, two persons met together at an appointed hour and place. One was a lady, graceful in form and fair of feature, though pale and troubled, and smitten with an untimely blight in what should have been the fullest bloom of her years; the other was an ancient and meanly-dressed woman, of ill-favored aspect, and so withered, shrunken, and decrepit, that even the space since she began to decay must have exceeded the ordinary term of human existence. In the spot where they encountered, no mortal could observe them. Three little hills stood near each other, and down in the midst of them sunk a hollow basin, almost mathematically circular, two or three hundred feet in breadth, and of such depth that a stately cedar might but just be visible above the sides. Dwarf pines were numerous upon the hills, and partly fringed the outer verge of the intermediate hollow, within which there was nothing but the brown grass of October, and here and there a tree trunk that had fallen long ago, and lay mouldering with no green successor from its roots. One of these masses of decaying wood, formerly a majestic oak, rested close beside a pool of green and sluggish water at the bottom of the basin. Such scenes as this (so gray tradition tells) were once the resort of the Power of Evil and his plighted subjects; and here, at midnight

or on the dim verge of evening, they were said to
stand round the mantling pool, disturbing its putrid
waters in the performance of an impious baptismal
rite. The chill beauty of an autumnal sunset was
now gilding the three hill-tops, whence a paler tint
stole down their sides into the hollow.

"Here is our pleasant meeting come to pass," said
the aged crone, "according as thou hast desired. Say
quickly what thou wouldst have of me, for there is but
a short hour that we may tarry here."

As the old withered woman spoke, a smile glimmered on her countenance, like lamplight on the wall
of a sepulchre. The lady trembled, and cast her eyes
upward to the verge of the basin, as if meditating to
return with her purpose unaccomplished. But it was
not so ordained.

"I am a stranger in this land, as you know," said
she at length. "Whence I come it matters not; but
I have left those behind me with whom my fate was
intimately bound, and from whom I am cut off forever. There is a weight in my bosom that I cannot
away with, and I have come hither to inquire of their
welfare."

"And who is there by this green pool that can
bring thee news from the ends of the earth?" cried
the old woman, peering into the lady's face. "Not
from my lips mayst thou hear these tidings; yet, be
thou bold, and the daylight shall not pass away from
yonder hill-top before thy wish be granted."

"I will do your bidding though I die," replied the
lady desperately.

The old woman seated herself on the trunk of the
fallen tree, threw aside the hood that shrouded her
gray locks, and beckoned her companion to draw near.

"Kneel down," she said, "and lay your forehead on my knees."

She hesitated a moment, but the anxiety that had long been kindling burned fiercely up within her. As she knelt down, the border of her garment was dipped into the pool; she laid her forehead on the old woman's knees, and the latter drew a cloak about the lady's face, so that she was in darkness. Then she heard the muttered words of prayer, in the midst of which she started, and would have arisen.

"Let me flee, — let me flee and hide myself, that they may not look upon me!" she cried. But, with returning recollection, she hushed herself, and was still as death.

For it seemed as if other voices — familiar in infancy, and unforgotten through many wanderings, and in all the vicissitudes of her heart and fortune — were mingling with the accents of the prayer. At first the words were faint and indistinct, not rendered so by distance, but rather resembling the dim pages of a book which we strive to read by an imperfect and gradually brightening light. In such a manner, as the prayer proceeded, did those voices strengthen upon the ear; till at length the petition ended, and the conversation of an aged man, and of a woman broken and decayed like himself, became distinctly audible to the lady as she knelt. But those strangers appeared not to stand in the hollow depth between the three hills. Their voices were encompassed and reëchoed by the walls of a chamber, the windows of which were rattling in the breeze; the regular vibration of a clock, the crackling of a fire, and the tinkling of the embers as they fell among the ashes, rendered the scene almost as vivid as if painted to the eye. By a melan-

choly hearth sat these two old people, the man calmly
despondent, the woman querulous and tearful, and
their words were all of sorrow. They spoke of a
daughter, a wanderer they knew not where, bearing
dishonor along with her, and leaving shame and affliction to bring their gray heads to the grave. They
alluded also to other and more recent woe, but in the
midst of their talk their voices seemed to melt into the
sound of the wind sweeping mournfully among the autumn leaves ; and when the lady lifted her eyes, there
was she kneeling in the hollow between three hills.

" A weary and lonesome time yonder old couple
have of it," remarked the old woman, smiling in the
lady's face.

" And did you also hear them ? " exclaimed she, a
sense of intolerable humiliation triumphing over her
agony and fear.

" Yea ; and we have yet more to hear," replied the
old woman. " Wherefore, cover thy face quickly."

Again the withered hag poured forth the monoto-
nous words of a prayer that was not meant to be acceptable in heaven ; and soon, in the pauses of her
breath, strange murmurings began to thicken, gradually increasing so as to drown and overpower the
charm by which they grew. Shrieks pierced through
the obscurity of sound, and were succeeded by the
singing of sweet female voices, which, in their turn,
gave way to a wild roar of laughter, broken suddenly
by groanings and sobs, forming altogether a ghastly
confusion of terror and mourning and mirth. Chains
were rattling, fierce and stern voices uttered threats,
and the scourge resounded at their command. All
these noises deepened and became substantial to the
listener's ear, till she could distinguish every soft and

dreamy accent of the love songs that died causelessly into funeral hymns. She shuddered at the unprovoked wrath which blazed up like the spontaneous kindling of flame, and she grew faint at the fearful merriment raging miserably around her. In the midst of this wild scene, where unbound passions jostled each other in a drunken career, there was one solemn voice of a man, and a manly and melodious voice it might once have been. He went to and fro continually, and his feet sounded upon the floor. In each member of that frenzied company, whose own burning thoughts had become their exclusive world, he sought an auditor for the story of his individual wrong, and interpreted their laughter and tears as his reward of scorn or pity. He spoke of woman's perfidy, of a wife who had broken her holiest vows, of a home and heart made desolate. Even as he went on, the shout, the laugh, the shriek, the sob, rose up in unison, till they changed into the hollow, fitful, and uneven sound of the wind, as it fought among the pine-trees on those three lonely hills. The lady looked up, and there was the withered woman smiling in her face.

" Couldst thou have thought there were such merry times in a mad-house ?" inquired the latter.

"True, true," said the lady to herself; "there is mirth within its walls, but misery, misery without."

" Wouldst thou hear more?" demanded the old woman.

" There is one other voice I would fain listen to again," replied the lady, faintly.

" Then, lay down thy head speedily upon my knees, that thou mayst get thee hence before the hour be past."

The golden skirts of day were yet lingering upon

the hills, but deep shades obscured the hollow and the pool, as if sombre night were rising thence to over-spread the world. Again that evil woman began to weave her spell. Long did it proceed unanswered, till the knolling of a bell stole in among the intervals of her words, like a clang that had travelled far over valley and rising ground, and was just ready to die in the air. The lady shook upon her companion's knees as she heard that boding sound. Stronger it grew and sadder, and deepened into the tone of a death bell, knolling dolefully from some ivy-mantled tower, and bearing tidings of mortality and woe to the cot-tage, to the hall, and to the solitary wayfarer, that all might weep for the doom appointed in turn to them. Then came a measured tread, passing slowly, slowly on, as of mourners with a coffin, their garments trail-ing on the ground, so that the ear could measure the length of their melancholy array. Before them went the priest, reading the burial service, while the leaves of his book were rustling in the breeze. And though no voice but his was heard to speak aloud, still there were revilings and anathemas, whispered but distinct, from women and from men, breathed against the daughter who had wrung the aged hearts of her par-ents, — the wife who had betrayed the trusting fond-ness of her husband, — the mother who had sinned against natural affection, and left her child to die. The sweeping sound of the funeral train faded away like a thin vapor, and the wind, that just before had seemed to shake the coffin pall, moaned sadly round the verge of the Hollow between three Hills. But when the old woman stirred the kneeling lady, she lifted not her head.

"Here has been a sweet hour's sport!" said the withered crone, chuckling to herself.

THE TOLL-GATHERER'S DAY.

A SKETCH OF TRANSITORY LIFE.

METHINKS, for a person whose instinct bids him rather to pore over the current of life than to plunge into its tumultuous waves, no undesirable retreat were a toll-house beside some thronged thoroughfare of the land. In youth, perhaps, it is good for the observer to run about the earth — to leave the track of his footsteps far and wide — to mingle himself with the action of numberless vicissitudes; and, finally, in some calm solitude, to feed a musing spirit on all that he has seen and felt. But there are natures too indolent, or too sensitive, to endure the dust, the sunshine, or the rain, the turmoil of moral and physical elements, to which all the wayfarers of the world expose themselves. For such a man, how pleasant a miracle, could life be made to roll its variegated length by the threshold of his own hermitage, and the great globe, as it were, perform its revolutions and shift its thousand scenes before his eyes without whirling him onward in its course. If any mortal be favored with a lot analogous to this, it is the toll-gatherer. So, at least, have I often fancied, while lounging on a bench at the door of a small square edifice, which stands between shore and shore in the midst of a long bridge. Beneath the timbers ebbs and flows an arm of the sea; while above, like the life-blood through a great artery, the travel of the north and east is continually throbbing. Sitting on the aforesaid bench I amuse myself with a conception, illustrated by numerous pencil sketches in the air, of the toll-gatherer's day.

In the morning — dim, gray, dewy summer's morn — the distant roll of ponderous wheels begins to mingle with my old friend's slumbers, creaking more and more harshly through the midst of his dream, and gradually replacing it with realities. Hardly conscious of the change from sleep to wakefulness, he finds himself partly clad and throwing wide the toll-gates for the passage of a fragrant load of hay. The timbers groan beneath the slow-revolving wheels; one sturdy yeoman stalks beside the oxen, and, peering from the summit of the hay, by the glimmer of the half-extinguished lantern over the toll-house, is seen the drowsy visage of his comrade, who has enjoyed a nap some ten miles long. The toll is paid — creak, creak, again go the wheels, and the huge haymow vanishes into the morning mist. As yet, nature is but half awake, and familiar objects appear visionary. But yonder, dashing from the shore with a rattling thunder of the wheels and a confused clatter of hoofs, comes the never-tiring mail, which has hurried onward at the same headlong, restless rate, all through the quiet night. The bridge resounds in one continued peal as the coach rolls on without a pause, merely affording the toll-gatherer a glimpse at the sleepy passengers, who now bestir their torpid limbs and snuff a cordial in the briny air. The morn breathes upon them and blushes, and they forget how wearily the darkness toiled away. And behold now the fervid day, in his bright chariot, glittering aslant over the waves, nor scorning to throw a tribute of his golden beams on the toll-gatherer's little hermitage. The old man looks eastward, and (for he is a moralizer) frames a simile of the stage-coach and the sun.

While the world is rousing itself, we may glance slightly at the scene of our sketch. It sits above the bosom of the broad flood, a spot not of earth, but in the midst of waters, which rush with a murmuring sound among the massive beams beneath. Over the door is a weather-beaten board, inscribed with the rates of toll, in letters so nearly effaced that the gilding of the sunshine can hardly make them legible. Beneath the window is a wooden bench, on which a long succession of weary wayfarers have reposed themselves. Peeping within doors, we perceive the whitewashed walls bedecked with sundry lithographic prints and advertisements of various import, and the immense showbill of a wandering caravan. And there sits our good old toll-gatherer, glorified by the early sunbeams. He is a man, as his aspect may announce, of quiet soul, and thoughtful, shrewd, yet simple mind, who, of the wisdom which the passing world scatters along the wayside, has gathered a reasonable store.

Now the sun smiles upon the landscape, and earth smiles back again upon the sky. Frequent, now, are the travellers. The toll-gatherer's practised ear can distinguish the weight of every vehicle, the number of its wheels, and how many horses beat the resounding timbers with their iron tramp. Here, in a substantial family chaise, setting forth betimes to take advantage of the dewy road, come a gentleman and his wife, with their rosy-cheeked little girl sitting gladsomely between them. The bottom of the chaise is heaped with multifarious band-boxes, and carpet-bags, and beneath the axle swings a leathern trunk, dusty with yesterday's journey. Next appears a four-wheeled

carryall, peopled with a round half dozen of pretty
girls, all drawn by a single horse, and driven by a
single gentleman. Luckless wight, doomed, through
a whole summer day, to be the butt of mirth and mischief among the frolicsome maidens! Bolt upright
in a sulky rides a thin, sour-visaged man, who, as he
pays his toll, hands the toll-gatherer a printed card
to stick upon the wall. The vinegar-faced traveller
proves to be a manufacturer of pickles. Now paces
slowly from timber to timber a horseman clad in
black, with a meditative brow, as of one who, whith-
ersoever his steed might bear him, would still journey
through a mist of brooding thought. He is a country
preacher, going to labor at a protracted meeting. The
next object passing townward is a butcher's cart, canopied with its arch of snow-white cotton. Behind
comes a " sauceman," driving a wagon full of new po
tatoes, green ears of corn, beets, carrots, turnips, and
summer squashes; and next, two wrinkled, withered,
witch-looking old gossips, in an antediluvian chaise,
drawn by a horse of former generations, and going to
peddle out a lot of huckleberries. See there, a man
trundling a wheelbarrow load of lobsters. And now
a milk cart rattles briskly onward, covered with green
canvas, and conveying the contributions of a whole
herd of cows in large tin canisters. But let all these
pay their toll and pass. Here comes a spectacle that
causes the old toll-gatherer to smile benignantly, as if
the travellers brought sunshine with them and lavished its gladsome influence all along the road.

It is a barouche of the newest style, the varnished
panels of which reflect the whole moving panorama
of the landscape, and show a picture, likewise, of our
friend, with his visage broadened, so that his medita-

tive smile is transformed to grotesque merriment. Within, sits a youth, fresh as the summer morn, and beside him a young lady in white, with white gloves upon her slender hands, and a white veil flowing down over her face. But methinks her blushing cheek burns through the snowy veil. Another white-robed virgin sits in front. And who are these, on whom, and on all that appertains to them, the dust of earth seems never to have settled? Two lovers, whom the priest has blessed this blessed morn, and sent them forth, with one of the bridemaids, on the matrimonial tour. Take my blessing, too, ye happy ones! May the sky not frown upon you, nor clouds bedew you with their chill and sullen rain! May the hot sun kindle no fever in your hearts! May your whole life's pilgrimage be as blissful as this first day's journey, and its close be gladdened with even brighter anticipations than those which hallow your bridal night!

They pass; and ere the reflection of their joy has faded from his face, another spectacle throws a melancholy shadow over the spirit of the observing man. In a close carriage sits a fragile figure, muffled carefully, and shrinking even from the mild breath of summer. She leans against a manly form, and his arm enfolds her, as if to guard his treasure from some enemy. Let but a few weeks pass, and when he shall strive to embrace that loved one, he will press only desolation to his heart.

And now has morning gathered up her dewy pearls and fled away. The sun rolls blazing through the sky, and cannot find a cloud to cool his face with. The horses toil sluggishly along the bridge, and heave their glistening sides in short quick pantings, when the reins are tightened at the toll-house. Glisten, too, the faces of the travellers. Their garments are thickly bestrewn with dust; their whiskers and hair look hoary; their throats are choked with the dusty atmosphere which they have left behind them. No air is stirring on the road. Nature dares draw no breath, lest she should inhale a stifling cloud of dust. "A hot and dusty day!" cry the poor pilgrims, as they wipe their begrimed foreheads, and woo the doubtful breeze which the river bears along with it. "Awful hot! Dreadful dusty!" answers the sympathetic toll-gatherer. They start again to pass through the fiery furnace, while he reënters his cool hermitage, and besprinkles it with a pail of briny water from the stream beneath. He thinks within himself that the sun is not so fierce here as elsewhere, and that the gentle air does not forget him in these sultry days. Yes, old friend; and a quiet heart will make a dog-day temperate. He hears a weary footstep, and perceives a traveller with pack and staff, who sits down upon the hospitable bench, and removes the hat from his wet brow. The toll-gatherer administers a cup of cold water, and discovering his guest to be a man of homely sense, he engages him in profitable talk, uttering the maxims of a philosophy which he has found in his own soul, but knows not how it came there. And as the wayfarer makes ready to resume his journey, he tells him a sovereign remedy for blistered feet.

Now comes the noontide hour — of all the hours nearest akin to midnight; for each has its own calmness and repose. Soon, however, the world begins to turn again upon its axis, and it seems the busiest epoch of the day; when an accident impedes the march of sublunary things. The draw being lifted to permit the passage of a schooner, laden with wood from the

eastern forests, she sticks immovably, right athwart
the bridge! Meanwhile, on both sides of the chasm,
a throng of impatient travellers fret and fume. Here
are two sailors in a gig, with the top thrown back, both
puffing cigars, and swearing all sorts of forecastle
oaths; there, in a smart chaise, a dashingly dressed
gentleman and lady, he from a tailor's shopboard and
she from a milliner's back room — the aristocrats of
a summer afternoon. And what are the haughtiest of
us but the ephemeral aristocrats of a summer's day?
Here is a tin pedlar, whose glittering ware bedazzles
all beholders, like a travelling meteor or opposition
sun; and on the other side a seller of spruce beer,
which brisk liquor is confined in several dozen of stone
bottles. Here comes a party of ladies on horseback,
in green riding habits, and gentlemen attendant; and
there a flock of sheep for the market, pattering over
the bridge with a multitudinous clatter of their little
hoofs. Here a Frenchman, with a hand organ on his
shoulder; and there an itinerant Swiss jeweller. On
this side, heralded by a blast of clarions and bugles,
appears a train of wagons, conveying all the wild beasts
of a caravan; and on that, a company of summer soldiers, marching from village to village on a festival
campaign, attended by the "Brass band." Now look
at the scene, and it presents an emblem of the myste
rious confusion, the apparently insolvable riddle, in
which individuals, or the great world itself, seem often
to be involved. What miracle shall set all things
right again?

But see! the schooner has thrust her bulky carcass
through the chasm; the draw descends; horse and
foot pass onward, and leave the bridge vacant from
end to end. "And thus," muses the toll-gatherer,

" have I found it with all stoppages, even though the universe seemed to be at a stand." The sage old man!

Far westward now the reddening sun throws a broad sheet of splendor across the flood, and to the eyes of distant boatmen gleams brightly among the timbers of the bridge. Strollers come from the town to quaff the freshening breeze. One or two let down long lines and haul up flapping flounders, or cunners, or small cod, or perhaps an eel. Others, and fair girls among them, with the flush of the hot day still on their cheeks, bend over the railing and watch the heaps of seaweed floating upward with the flowing tide. The horses now tramp heavily along the bridge, and wistfully bethink them of their stables. Rest, rest, thou weary world! for to-morrow's round of toil and pleasure will be as wearisome as to-day's has been; yet both shall bear thee onward a day's march of eternity. Now the old toll-gatherer looks seaward, and discerns the light-house kindling on a far island, and the stars, too, kindling in the sky, as if but a little way beyond; and mingling reveries of heaven with remembrances of earth, the whole procession of mortal travellers, all the dusty pilgrimage which he has witnessed, seems like a flitting show of phantoms for his thoughtful soul to muse upon.

THE VISION OF THE FOUNTAIN.

AT fifteen I became a resident in a country village, more than a hundred miles from home. The morning after my arrival—a September morning, but warm and bright as any in July—I rambled into a wood of oaks, with a few walnut-trees intermixed, forming the closest shade above my head. The ground was rocky, uneven, overgrown with bushes and clumps of young saplings, and traversed only by cattle paths. The track which I chanced to follow led me to a crystal spring, with a border of grass as freshly green as on May morning, and overshadowed by the limb of a great oak. One solitary sunbeam found its way down, and played like a goldfish in the water.

From my childhood I have loved to gaze into a spring. The water filled a circular basin, small but deep, and set round with stones, some of which were covered with slimy moss, the others naked, and of variegated hue, reddish, white, and brown. The bottom was covered with coarse sand, which sparkled in the lonely sunbeam, and seemed to illuminate the spring with an unborrowed light. In one spot the gush of the water violently agitated the sand, but without obscuring the fountain, or breaking the glassiness of its surface. It appeared as if some living creature were about to emerge—the Naiad of the spring, perhaps—in the shape of a beautiful young woman, with a gown of filmy water moss, a belt of rainbow drops, and a cold, pure, passionless countenance. How would the beholder shiver, pleasantly yet fearfully, to see her sitting on one of the stones, paddling her white feet in the ripples, and throwing up water to sparkle in the sun! Wherever she laid her hands on grass and flowers, they would immediately be moist as with morning dew. Then would she set about her labors, like a careful housewife. to clear the fountain of withered leaves, and bits of slimy wood, and old acorns from the oaks above, and grains of corn left by cattle in drinking, till the bright sand, in the bright water, was like a treasury of diamonds. But, should the intruder approach too near, he would find only the drops of a summer shower glistening about the spot where he had seen her.

Reclining on the border of grass, where the dewy goddess should have been, I bent forward, and a pair of eyes met mine within the watery mirror. They were the reflection of my own. I looked again, and lo! another face, deeper in the fountain than my own image, more distinct in all the features, yet faint as thought. The vision had the aspect of a fair young girl, with locks of paly gold. A mirthful expression laughed in the eyes and dimpled over the whole shadowy countenance, till it seemed just what a fountain would be, if, while dancing merrily into the sunshine, it should assume the shape of woman. Through the dim rosiness of the cheeks I could see the brown leaves, the slimy twigs, the acorns, and the sparkling sand. The solitary sunbeam was diffused among the golden hair, which melted into its faint brightness, and became a glory round that head so beautiful!

My description can give no idea how suddenly the fountain was thus tenanted, and how soon it was left desolate. I breathed, and there was the face! I held my breath, and it was gone! Had it passed away, or faded into nothing? I doubted whether it had ever been.

My sweet readers, what a dreamy and delicious hour did I spend, where that vision found and left me! For a long time I sat perfectly still, waiting ill it should reappear, and fearful that the slightest motion, or even the flutter of my breath, might frighten it away. Thus have I often started from a pleasant dream, and then kept quiet in hopes to while it back. Deep were my musings, as to the race and attributes of that ethereal being. Had I created her? Was she the daughter of my fancy, akin to those strange shapes which peep under the lids of children's eyes? And did her beauty gladden me, for that one moment, and then die? Or was she a water nymph within the fountain, or fairy, or woodland goddess, peeping over my shoulder, or the ghost of some forsaken maid who had drowned herself for love? Or, in good truth, had a lovely girl, with a warm heart and lips that would bear pressure, stolen softly behind me, and thrown her image into the spring?

I watched and waited, but no vision came again. I departed, but with a spell upon me which drew me back, that same afternoon, to the haunted spring. There was the water gushing, the sand sparkling, and the sunbeam glimmering. There the vision was not, but only a great frog, the hermit of that solitude, who immediately withdrew his speckled snout and made himself invisible, all except a pair of long legs, beneath a stone. Methought he had a devilish look! I could have slain him as an enchanter who kept the mysterious beauty imprisoned in the fountain.

Sad and heavy, I was returning to the village. Between me and the church spire rose a little hill, and on its summit a group of trees, insulated from all the rest of the wood, with their own share of radiance hovering on them from the west, and their own solitary shadow falling to the east. The afternoon being far declined, the sunshine was almost pensive, and the shade almost cheerful; glory and gloom were mingled in the placid light; as if the spirits of the Day and Evening had met in friendship under those trees, and found themselves akin. I was admiring the picture, when the shape of a young girl emerged from behind the clump of oaks. My heart knew her; it was the Vision; but so distant and ethereal did she seem, so unmixed with earth, so imbued with the pensive glory of the spot where she was standing, that my spirit sunk within me, sadder than before. How could I ever reach her?

While I gazed, a sudden shower came pattering down upon the leaves. In a moment the air was full of brightness, each raindrop catching a portion of sunlight as it fell, and the whole gentle shower appearing like a mist, just substantial enough to bear the burden of radiance. A rainbow, vivid as Niagara's, was painted in the air. Its southern limb came down before the group of trees, and enveloped the fair Vision, as if the hues of heaven were the only garment for her beauty. When the rainbow vanished, she, who had seemed a part of it, was no longer there. Was her existence absorbed in nature's loveliest phenomenon, and did her pure frame dissolve away in the varied light? Yet, I would not despair of her return; for, robed in the rainbow, she was the emblem of Hope.

Thus did the vision leave me ; and many a doleful day succeeded to the parting moment. By the spring, and in the wood, and on the hill, and through the village ; at dewy sunrise, burning noon, and at that magic hour of sunset when she had vanished from my sight, I sought her, but in vain. Weeks came and went, months rolled away, and she appeared not in them. I imparted my mystery to none, but wandered to and fro, or sat in solitude, like one that had caught a glimpse of heaven, and could take no more joy on earth. I withdrew into an inner world, where my thoughts lived and breathed, and the Vision in the midst of them. Without intending it, I became at once the author and hero of a romance, conjuring up rivals, imagining events, the actions of others and my own, and experiencing every change of passion, till jealousy and despair had their end in bliss. Oh, had I the burning fancy of my early youth, with manhood's colder gift, the power of expression, your hearts, sweet ladies, should flutter at my tale !

In the middle of January I was summoned home. The day before my departure, visiting the spots which had been hallowed by the Vision, I found that the spring had a frozen bosom, and nothing but the snow and a glare of winter sunshine on the hill of the rainbow. " Let me hope," thought I, " or my heart will be as icy as the fountain, and the whole world as desolate as this snowy hill." Most of the day was spent in preparing for the journey, which was to commence at four o'clock the next morning. About an hour after supper, when all was in readiness, I descended from my chamber to the sitting-room, to take leave of the old clergyman and his family with whom I had been an inmate. A gust of wind blew out my lamp as I passed through the entry.

According to their invariable custom, so pleasant a one when the fire blazes cheerfully, the family were sitting in the parlor, with no other light than what came from the hearth. As the good clergyman's scanty stipend compelled him to use all sorts of economy, the foundation of his fires was always a large heap of tan, or ground bark, which would smoulder away, from morning till night, with a dull warmth and no flame. This evening the heap of tan was newly put on, and surmounted with three sticks of red oak, full of moisture, and a few pieces of dry pine, that had not yet kindled. There was no light, except the little that came sullenly from two half-burned brands, without even glimmering on the andirons. But I knew the position of the old minister's arm-chair, and also where his wife sat, with her knitting-work, and how to avoid his two daughters, one a stout country lass, and the other a consumptive girl. Groping through the gloom, I found my own place next to that of the son, a learned collegian, who had come home to keep school in the village during the winter vacation. I noticed that there was less room than usual, to-night, between the collegian's chair and mine.

As people are always taciturn in the dark, not a word was said for some time after my entrance. Nothing broke the stillness but the regular click of the matron's knitting-needles. At times, the fire threw out a brief and dusky gleam, which twinkled on the old man's glasses, and hovered doubtfully round our circle, but was far too faint to portray the individuals who composed it. Were we not like ghosts? Dreamy as the scene was, might it not be a type of the mode in which departed people, who had known and loved

each other here, would hold communion in eternity?
We were aware of each other's presence, not by sight,
nor sound, nor touch, but by an inward consciousness.
Would it not be so among the dead?

The silence was interrupted by the consumptive
daughter, addressing a remark to some one in the
circle whom she called Rachel. Her tremulous and
decayed accents were answered by a single word, but
in a voice that made me start, and bend towards the
spot whence it had proceeded. Had I ever heard that
sweet, low tone? If not, why did it rouse up so many
old recollections, or mockeries of such, the shadows of
things familiar, yet unknown, and fill my mind with
confused images of her features who had spoken,
though buried in the gloom of the parlor? Whom
had my heart recognized, that it throbbed so? I
listened to catch her gentle breathing, and strove, by
the intensity of my gaze, to picture forth a shape
where none was visible.

Suddenly the dry pine caught; the fire blazed up
with a ruddy glow; and where the darkness had been,
there was she — the Vision of the Fountain! A spirit
of radiance only, she had vanished with the rainbow,
and appeared again in the firelight, perhaps to flicker
with the blaze, and be gone. Yet, her cheek was rosy
and life-like, and her features, in the bright warmth of
the room, were even sweeter and tenderer than my
recollection of them. She knew me! The mirthful
expression that had laughed in her eyes and dimpled
over her countenance, when I beheld her faint beauty
in the fountain, was laughing and dimpling there now.
One moment our glance mingled — the next, down
rolled the heap of tan upon the kindled wood — and
darkness snatched away the Daughter of the Light,
and gave her back to me no more!

Fair ladies, there is nothing more to tell. Must the simple mystery be revealed, then, that Rachel was the daughter of the village squire, and had left home for a boarding-school, the morning after I arrived and returned the day before my departure? If I transformed her to an angel, it is what every youthful lover does for his mistress. Therein consists the essence of my story. But slight the change, sweet maids, to make angels of yourselves!

FANCY'S SHOW BOX.

A MORALITY.

WHAT is Guilt? A stain upon the soul. And it is a point of vast interest whether the soul may contract such stains, in all their depth and flagrancy, from deeds which may have been plotted and resolved upon, but which, physically, have never had existence. Must the fleshly hand and visible frame of man set its seal to the evil designs of the soul, in order to give them their entire validity against the sinner? Or, while none but crimes perpetrated are cognizable before an earthly tribunal, will guilty thoughts — of which guilty deeds are no more than shadows — will these draw down the full weight of a condemning sentence, in the supreme court of eternity? In the solitude of a midnight chamber or in a desert, afar from men or in a church, while the body is kneeling, the soul may pollute itself even with those crimes which we are accustomed to deem altogether carnal If this be true, it is a fearful truth.

Let us illustrate the subject by an imaginary exam ple. A venerable gentleman, one Mr. Smith, who had long been regarded as a pattern of moral excellence, was warming his aged blood with a glass or two of generous wine. His children being gone forth about their worldly business, and his grandchildren at school, he sat alone, in a deep, luxurious arm-chair, with his feet beneath a richly-carved mahogany table. Some

old people have a dread of solitude, and when better
company may not be had, rejoice even to hear the
quiet breathing of a babe, asleep upon the carpet.
But Mr. Smith, whose silver hair was the bright symbol of a life unstained, except by such spots as are
inseparable from human nature, had no need of a
babe to protect him by its purity, nor of a grown per
son to stand between him and his own soul. Nevertheless, either Manhood must converse with Age, or
Womanhood must soothe him with gentle cares, or
Infancy must sport around his chair, or his thoughts
will stray into the misty region of the past, and the
old man be chill and sad. Wine will not always cheer
him. Such might have been the case with Mr. Smith,
when, through the brilliant medium of his glass of old
Madeira, he beheld three figures entering the room.
These were Fancy, who had assumed the garb and aspect of an itinerant showman, with a box of pictures
on her back; and Memory, in the likeness of a clerk,
with a pen behind her ear, an inkhorn at her button-
hole, and a huge manuscript volume beneath her arm;
and lastly, behind the other two, a person shrouded in
a dusky mantle, which concealed both face and form.
But Mr. Smith had a shrewd idea that it was Conscience.

How kind of Fancy, Memory, and Conscience to
visit the old gentleman, just as he was beginning to
imagine that the wine had neither so bright a sparkle
nor so excellent a flavor as when himself and the
liquor were less aged! Through the dim length of the
apartment, where crimson curtains muffled the glare
of sunshine and created a rich obscurity, the three
guests drew near the silver-haired old man. Memory,
with a finger between the leaves of her huge volume,

placed herself at his right hand. Conscience, with her face still hidden in the dusky mantle, took her station on the left, so as to be next his heart; while Fancy set down her picture box upon the table, with the magnifying glass convenient to his eye. We can sketch merely the outlines of two or three out of the many pictures which, at the pulling of a string, successively peopled the box with the semblances of living scenes.

One was a moonlight picture: in the background, a lowly dwelling; and in front, partly shadowed by a tree, yet besprinkled with flakes of radiance, two youthful figures, male and female. The young man stood with folded arms, a haughty smile upon his lip, and a gleam of triumph in his eye, as he glanced downward at the kneeling girl. She was almost prostrate at his feet, evidently sinking under a weight of shame and anguish, which hardly allowed her to lift her clasped hands in supplication. Her eyes she could not lift. But neither her agony, nor the lovely features on which it was depicted, nor the slender grace of the form which it convulsed, appeared to soften the obduracy of the young man. He was the personification of triumphant scorn. Now, strange to say, as old Mr. Smith peeped through the magnifying glass, which made the objects start out from the canvas with magical deception, he began to recognize the farm-house, the tree, and both the figures of the picture. The young man, in times long past, had often met his gaze within the looking-glass; the girl was the very image of his first love — his cottage love — his Martha Burroughs! Mr. Smith was scandalized. "O vile and slanderous picture!" he exclaims. "When have I triumphed over ruined innocence? Was not Martha wedded, in her teens, to David Tomkins, who won her girlish love, and long enjoyed her affection as a wife? And ever since his death she has lived a reputable widow!" Meantime, Memory was turning over the leaves of her volume, rustling them to and fro with uncertain fingers, until, among the earlier pages, she found one which had reference to this picture. She reads it, close to the old gentleman's ear; it is a record merely of sinful thought, which never was embodied in an act; but while Memory is reading, Conscience unveils her face, and strikes a dagger to the heart of Mr. Smith. Though not a death-blow, the torture was extreme.

The exhibition proceeded. One after another, Fancy displayed her pictures, all of which appeared to have been painted by some malicious artist on purpose to vex Mr. Smith. Not a shadow of proof could have been adduced, in any earthly court, that he was guilty of the slightest of those sins which were thus made to stare him in the face. In one scene there was a table set out, with several bottles, and glasses half filled with wine, which threw back the dull ray of an expiring lamp. There had been mirth and revelry, until the hand of the clock stood just at midnight, when murder stepped between the boon companions. A young man had fallen on the floor, and lay stone dead, with a ghastly wound crushed into his temple, while over him, with a delirium of mingled rage and horror in his countenance, stood the youthful likeness of Mr. Smith. The murdered youth wore the features of Edward Spencer! "What does this rascal of a painter mean?" cries Mr. Smith, provoked beyond all patience. "Edward Spencer was my earliest and dearest friend, true to me as I to him, through more than half a century. Neither I, nor any other, ever murdered him. Was he not alive within

five years, and did he not, in token of our long friendship, bequeath me his gold-headed cane and a mourning ring?" Again had Memory been turning over
her volume, and fixed at length upon so confused a
page that she surely must have scribbled it when she
was tipsy. The purport was, however, that while Mr.
Smith and Edward Spencer were heating their young
blood with wine, a quarrel had flashed up between
them, and Mr. Smith, in deadly wrath, had flung a
bottle at Spencer's head. True, it missed its aim,
and merely smashed a looking-glass; and the next
morning, when the incident was imperfectly remembered, they had shaken hands with a hearty laugh.
Yet, again, while Memory was reading, Conscience
unveiled her face, struck a dagger to the heart of Mr.
Smith, and quelled his remonstrance with her iron
frown. The pain was quite excruciating.

Some of the pictures had been painted with so
doubtful a touch, and in colors so faint and pale, that
the subjects could barely be conjectured. A dull,
semi-transparent mist had been thrown over the surface of the canvas, into which the figures seemed to
vanish, while the eye sought most earnestly to fix
them. But in every scene, however dubiously portrayed, Mr. Smith was invariably haunted by his own
lineaments, at various ages, as in a dusty mirror. After poring several minutes over one of these blurred
and almost indistinguishable pictures, he began to see
that the painter had intended to represent him, now
in the decline of life, as stripping the clothes from the
backs of three half-starved children. " Really, this
puzzles me!" quoth Mr. Smith, with the irony of
conscious rectitude. " Asking pardon of the painter,
I pronounce him a fool, as well as a scandalous knave.

A man of my standing in the world to be robbing little children of their clothes! Ridiculous!" But while he spoke, Memory had searched her fatal volume, and found a page, which, with her sad, calm voice, she poured into his ear. It was not altogether inapplicable to the misty scene. It told how Mr. Smith had been grievously tempted by many devilish sophistries, on the ground of a legal quibble, to commence a lawsuit against three orphan children, joint heirs to a considerable estate. Fortunately, before he was quite decided, his claims had turned out nearly as devoid of law as justice. As Memory ceased to read, Conscience again thrust aside her mantle, and would have struck her victim with the envenomed dagger, only that he struggled and clasped his hands before his heart. Even then, however, he sustained an ugly gash.

Why should we follow Fancy through the whole series of those awful pictures? Painted by an artist of wondrous power, and terrible acquaintance with the secret soul, they embodied the ghosts of all the never perpetrated sins that had glided through the lifetime of Mr. Smith. And could such beings of cloudy fantasy, so near akin to nothingness, give valid evidence against him at the day of judgment? Be that the case or not, there is reason to believe that one truly penitential tear would have washed away each hateful picture, and left the canvas white as snow. But Mr. Smith, at a prick of Conscience too keen to be endured, bellowed aloud, with impatient agony, and suddenly discovered that his three guests were gone. There he sat alone, a silver-haired and highly-venerated old man, in the rich gloom of the crimson-curtained room, with no box of pictures on

the table, but only a decanter of most excellent Madeira. Yet his heart still seemed to fester with the
venom of the dagger.

Nevertheless, the unfortunate old gentleman might
have argued the matter with Conscience, and alleged
many reasons wherefore she should not smite him so
pitilessly. Were we to take up his cause, it should
be somewhat in the following fashion : A scheme of
guilt, till it be put in execution, greatly resembles a
train of incidents in a projected tale. The latter, in
order to produce a sense of reality in the reader's
mind, must be conceived with such proportionate
strength by the author as to seem, in the glow of
fancy, more like truth, past, present, or to come, than
purely fiction. The prospective sinner, on the other
hand, weaves his plot of crime, but seldom or never
feels a perfect certainty that it will be executed.
There is a dreaminess diffused about his thoughts ;
in a dream, as it were, he strikes the death-blow
into his victim's heart, and starts to find an indelible
blood-stain on his hand. Thus a novel writer or a
dramatist, in creating a villain of romance and fitting
him with evil deeds, and the villain of actual life, in
projecting crimes that will be perpetrated, may almost
meet each other half-way between reality and fancy.
It is not until the crime is accomplished that guilt
clinches its gripe upon the guilty heart, and claims it
for its own. Then, and not before, sin is actually felt
and acknowledged, and, if unaccompanied by repentance, grows a thousand-fold more virulent by its self-
consciousness. Be it considered, also, that men often
over-estimate their capacity for evil. At a distance,
while its attendant circumstances do not press upon
their notice, and its results are dimly seen, they can

bear to contemplate it. They may take the steps which lead to crime, impelled by the same sort of mental action as in working out a mathematical problem, yet be powerless with compunction at the final moment. They knew not what deed it was that they deemed themselves resolved to do. In truth, there is no such thing in man's nature as a settled and full resolve, either for good or evil, except at the very moment of execution. Let us hope, therefore, that all the dreadful consequences of sin will not be incurred, unless the act have set its seal upon the thought.

Yet, with the slight fancy work which we have framed, some sad and awful truths are interwoven. Man must not disclaim his brotherhood, even with the guiltiest, since, though his hand be clean, his heart has surely been polluted by the flitting phantoms of iniquity. He must feel that, when he shall knock at the gate of heaven, no semblance of an unspotted life can entitle him to entrance there. Penitence must kneel, and Mercy come from the footstool of the throne, or that golden gate will never open!

DR. HEIDEGGER'S EXPERIMENT.

THAT very singular man, old Dr. Heidegger, once invited four venerable friends to meet him in his study. There were three white-bearded gentlemen, Mr. Medbourne, Colonel Killigrew, and Mr. Gascoigne, and a withered gentlewoman, whose name was the Widow Wycherly. They were all melancholy old creatures, who had been unfortunate in life, and whose greatest misfortune it was that they were not long ago in their graves. Mr. Medbourne, in the vigor of his age, had been a prosperous merchant, but had lost his all by a frantic speculation, and was now little better than a mendicant. Colonel Killigrew had wasted his best years, and his health and substance, in the pursuit of sinful pleasures, which had given birth to a brood of pains, such as the gout, and divers other torments of soul and body. Mr. Gascoigne was a ruined politician, a man of evil fame, or at least had been so till time had buried him from the knowledge of the present generation, and made him obscure instead of infamous. As for the Widow Wycherly, tradition tells us that she was a great beauty in her day ; but, for a long while past, she had lived in deep seclusion, on account of certain scandalous stories which had prejudiced the gentry of the town against her. It is a circumstance worth mentioning that each of these three old gentlemen, Mr. Medbourne, Colonel Killigrew, and Mr. Gascoigne, were early lovers of the Widow Wycherly, and had once been on the point of cutting each other's throats for her sake. And, before proceeding further, I will merely hint that Dr. Heidegger and all his four guests were sometimes thought to be a little beside themselves, — as is not unfrequently the case with old people, when worried either by present troubles or woful recollections.

"My dear old friends," said Dr. Heidegger, motioning them to be seated, "I am desirous of your assistance in one of those little experiments with which I amuse myself here in my study."

If all stories were true, Dr. Heidegger's study must have been a very curious place. It was a dim, old-fashioned chamber, festooned with cobwebs, and besprinkled with antique dust. Around the walls stood several oaken bookcases, the lower shelves of which were filled with rows of gigantic folios and black-letter quartos, and the upper with little parchment-covered duodecimos. Over the central bookcase was a bronze bust of Hippocrates, with which, according to some authorities, Dr. Heidegger was accustomed to hold consultations in all difficult cases of his practice. In the obscurest corner of the room stood a tall and narrow oaken closet, with its door ajar, within which doubtfully appeared a skeleton. Between two of the bookcases hung a looking-glass, presenting its high and dusty plate within a tarnished gilt frame. Among many wonderful stories related of this mirror, it was fabled that the spirits of all the doctor's deceased patients dwelt within its verge, and would stare him in the face whenever he looked thitherward. The opposite side of the chamber was ornamented with the full-length portrait of a young lady, arrayed in the faded magnificence of silk, satin, and brocade, and with a visage as faded as her dress. Above half a century ago, Dr. Heidegger had been on the point of marriage with this young lady; but, being affected with some slight disorder, she had swallowed one of her lover's prescriptions, and died on the bridal evening. The greatest curiosity of the study remains to be mentioned; it was a ponderous folio volume, bound in black leather, with massive silver clasps. There were no letters on the back, and nobody could tell the title of the book. But it was well known to be a book of magic; and once, when a chambermaid had lifted it, merely to brush away the dust, the skeleton had rattled in its closet, the picture of the young lady had stepped one foot upon the floor, and several ghastly faces had peeped forth from the mirror; while the brazen head of Hippocrates frowned, and said, — "Forbear!"

Such was Dr. Heidegger's study. On the summer afternoon of our tale a small round table, as black as ebony, stood in the centre of the room, sustaining a cut-glass vase of beautiful form and elaborate workmanship. The sunshine came through the window, between the heavy festoons of two faded damask curtains, and fell directly across this vase; so that a mild splendor was reflected from it on the ashen visages of the five old people who sat around. Four champagne glasses were also on the table.

"My dear old friends," repeated Dr. Heidegger, "may I reckon on your aid in performing an exceedingly curious experiment?"

Now Dr. Heidegger was a very strange old gentleman, whose eccentricity had become the nucleus for a thousand fantastic stories. Some of these fables, to my shame be it spoken, might possibly be traced back to my own veracious self; and if any passages of the present tale should startle the reader's faith, I must be content to bear the stigma of a fiction monger.

When the doctor's four guests heard him talk of his proposed experiment, they anticipated nothing more wonderful than the murder of a mouse in an air pump, or the examination of a cobweb by the microscope, or some similar nonsense, with which he was constantly in the habit of pestering his intimates. But without waiting for a reply, Dr. Heidegger hobbled across the chamber, and returned with the same ponderous folio, bound in black leather, which common report affirmed to be a book of magic. Undoing the silver clasps, he opened the volume, and took from among its black-letter pages a rose, or what was once a rose, though now the green leaves and crimson petals had assumed one brownish hue, and the ancient flower seemed ready to crumble to dust in the doctor's hands.

"This rose," said Dr. Heidegger, with a sigh, "this same withered and crumbling flower, blossomed five and fifty years ago. It was given me by Sylvia Ward, whose portrait hangs yonder; and I meant to wear it in my bosom at our wedding. Five and fifty years it has been treasured between the leaves of this old volume. Now, would you deem it possible that this rose of half a century could ever bloom again?"

"Nonsense!" said the Widow Wycherly, with a peevish toss of her head. "You might as well ask whether an old woman's wrinkled face could ever bloom again."

"See!" answered Dr. Heidegger.

He uncovered the vase, and threw the faded rose into the water which it contained. At first, it lay lightly on the surface of the fluid, appearing to imbibe none of its moisture. Soon, however, a singular

change began to be visible. The crushed and dried
petals stirred, and assumed a deepening tinge of crimson, as if the flower were reviving from a deathlike
slumber; the slender stalk and twigs of foliage became green; and there was the rose of half a century,
looking as fresh as when Sylvia Ward had first given.
it to her lover. It was scarcely full blown; for some
of its delicate red leaves curled modestly around its
moist bosom, within which two or three dewdrops
were sparkling.

"That is certainly a very pretty deception," said
the doctor's friends; carelessly, however, for they had
witnessed greater miracles at a conjurer's show; "pray
how was it effected?"

"Did you never hear of the 'Fountain of Youth?'"
asked Dr. Heidegger, "which Ponce De Leon, the
Spanish adventurer, went in search of two or three
centuries ago?"

"But did Ponce De Leon ever find it?" said the
Widow Wycherly.

"No," answered Dr. Heidegger, "for he never
sought it in the right place. The famous Fountain of
Youth, if I am rightly informed, is situated in the
southern part of the Floridian peninsula, not far from
Lake Macaco. Its source is overshadowed by several
gigantic magnolias, which, though numberless centuries old, have been kept as fresh as violets by the virtues of this wonderful water. An acquaintance of
mine, knowing my curiosity in such matters, has sent
me what you see in the vase."

"Ahem!" said Colonel Killigrew, who believed not
a word of the doctor's story; "and what may be the
effect of this fluid on the human frame?"

"You shall judge for yourself, my dear colonel,"

replied Dr. Heidegger; "and all of you, my respected friends, are welcome to so much of this admirable fluid as may restore to you the bloom of youth. For my own part, having had much trouble in growing old, I am in no hurry to grow young again. With your permission, therefore, I will merely watch the progress of the experiment."

While he spoke, Dr. Heidegger had been filling the four champagne glasses with the water of the Fountain of Youth. It was apparently impregnated with an effervescent gas, for little bubbles were continually ascending from the depths of the glasses, and bursting in silvery spray at the surface. As the liquor diffused a pleasant perfume, the old people doubted not that it possessed cordial and comfortable properties; and though utter sceptics as to its rejuvenescent power, they were inclined to swallow it at once. But Dr. Heidegger besought them to stay a moment.

"Before you drink, my respectable old friends," said he, "it would be well that, with the experience of a lifetime to direct you, you should draw up a few general rules for your guidance, in passing a second time through the perils of youth. Think what a sin and shame it would be, if, with your peculiar advantages, you should not become patterns of virtue and wisdom to all the young people of the age!"

The doctor's four venerable friends made him no answer, except by a feeble and tremulous laugh; so very ridiculous was the idea that, knowing how closely repentance treads behind the steps of error, they should ever go astray again.

"Drink, then," said the doctor, bowing: "I rejoice that I have so well selected the subjects of my experiment."

With palsied hands, they raised the glasses to their lips. The liquor, if it really possessed such virtues as Dr. Heidegger imputed to it, could not have been bestowed on four human beings who needed it more wofully. They looked as if they had never known what youth or pleasure was, but had been the offspring of Nature's dotage, and always the gray, decrepit, sapless, miserable creatures, who now sat stooping round the doctor's table, without life enough in their souls or bodies to be animated even by the prospect of growing young again. They drank off the water, and replaced their glasses on the table.

Assuredly there was an almost immediate improvement in the aspect of the party, not unlike what might have been produced by a glass of generous wine, together with a sudden glow of cheerful sunshine brightening over all their visages at once. There was a healthful suffusion on their cheeks, instead of the ashen hue that had made them look so corpse-like. They gazed at one another, and fancied that some magic power had really begun to smooth away the deep and sad inscriptions which Father Time had been so long engraving on their brows. The Widow Wycherly adjusted her cap, for she felt almost like a woman again.

"Give us more of this wondrous water!" cried they, eagerly. "We are younger — but we are still too old! Quick — give us more!"

"Patience, patience!" quoth Dr. Heidegger, who sat watching the experiment with philosophic coolness. "You have been a long time growing old. Surely, you might be content to grow young in half an hour! But the water is at your service."

Again he filled their glasses with the liquor of

youth, enough of which still remained in the vase to turn half the old people in the city to the age of their own grandchildren. While the bubbles were yet sparkling on the brim, the doctor's four guests snatched their glasses from the table, and swallowed the contents at a single gulp. Was it delusion? even while the draught was passing down their throats, it seemed to have wrought a change on their whole systems. Their eyes grew clear and bright; a dark shade deepened among their silvery locks, they sat around the table, three gentlemen of middle age, and a woman, hardly beyond her buxom prime.

"My dear widow, you are charming!" cried Colonel Killigrew, whose eyes had been fixed upon her face, while the shadows of age were flitting from it like darkness from the crimson daybreak.

The fair widow knew, of old, that Colonel Killigrew's compliments were not always measured by sober truth; so she started up and ran to the mirror, still dreading that the ugly visage of an old woman would meet her gaze. Meanwhile, the three gentlemen behaved in such a manner as proved that the water of the Fountain of Youth possessed some intoxicating qualities; unless, indeed, their exhilaration of spirits were merely a lightsome dizziness caused by the sudden removal of the weight of years. Mr. Gascoigne's mind seemed to run on political topics, but whether relating to the past, present, or future, could not easily be determined, since the same ideas and phrases have been in vogue these fifty years. Now he rattled forth full-throated sentences about patriotism, national glory, and the people's right; now he muttered some perilous stuff or other, in a sly and doubtful whisper, so cautiously that even his own conscience could scarcely catch the secret; and now, again, he spoke in measured accents, and a deeply deferential tone, as if a royal ear were listening to his well-turned periods. Colonel Killigrew all this time had been trolling forth a jolly bottle song, and ringing his glass in symphony with the chorus, while his eyes wandered toward the buxom figure of the Widow Wycherly. On the other side of the table, Mr. Medbourne was involved in a calculation of dollars and cents, with which was strangely intermingled a project for supplying the East Indies with ice, by harnessing a team of whales to the polar icebergs.

As for the Widow Wycherly, she stood before the mirror courtesying and simpering to her own image, and greeting it as the friend whom she loved better than all the world beside. She thrust her face close to the glass, to see whether some long-remembered wrinkle or crow's foot had indeed vanished. She examined whether the snow had so entirely melted from her hair that the venerable cap could be safely thrown aside. At last, turning briskly away, she came with a sort of dancing step to the table.

"My dear old doctor," cried she, "pray favor me with another glass!"

"Certainly, my dear madam, certainly!" replied the complaisant doctor; "see! I have already filled the glasses."

There, in fact, stood the four glasses, brimful of this wonderful water, the delicate spray of which, as it effervesced from the surface, resembled the tremulous glitter of diamonds. It was now so nearly sunset that the chamber had grown duskier than ever; but a mild and moonlike splendor gleamed from within the vase, and rested alike on the four guests and on the doctor's venerable figure. He sat in a high-backed, elaborately-carved, oaken arm-chair, with a gray dignity of aspect that might have well befitted that very Father Time, whose power had never been disputed, save by this fortunate company. Even while quaffing the third draught of the Fountain of Youth, they were almost awed by the expression of his mysterious visage.

But, the next moment, the exhilarating gush of young life shot through their veins. They were now in the happy prime of youth. Age, with its miserable train of cares and sorrows and diseases, was remembered only as the trouble of a dream, from which they had joyously awoke. The fresh gloss of the soul, so early lost, and without which the world's successive scenes had been but a gallery of faded pictures, again threw its enchantment over all their prospects. They felt like new-created beings in a new-created universe.

"We are young! We are young!" they cried exultingly.

Youth, like the extremity of age, had effaced the strongly-marked characteristics of middle life, and mutually assimilated them all. They were a group of merry youngsters, almost maddened with the exuberant frolicsomeness of their years. The most singular effect of their gayety was an impulse to mock the infirmity and decrepitude of which they had so lately been the victims. They laughed loudly at their old-fashioned attire, the wide-skirted coats and flapped waistcoats of the young men, and the ancient cap and gown of the blooming girl. One limped across the floor like a gouty grandfather; one set a pair of spectacles astride of his nose, and pretended to pore over

the black-letter pages of the book of magic; a third
seated himself in an arm-chair, and strove to imitate
the venerable dignity of Dr. Heidegger. Then all
shouted mirthfully, and leaped about the room. The
Widow Wycherly — if so fresh a damsel could be
called a widow — tripped up to the docter's chair,
with a mischievous merriment in her rosy face.

"Doctor, you dear old soul," cried she, "get up and
dance with me!" And then the four young people
laughed louder than ever, to think what a queer figure
the poor old doctor would cut.

"Pray excuse me," answered the doctor quietly.
"I am old and rheumatic, and my dancing days
were over long ago. But either of these gay
young gentlemen will be glad of so pretty a partner."

"Dance with me, Clara!" cried Colonel Killigrew.

"No, no, I will be her partner!" shouted Mr.
Gascoigne.

"She promised me her hand, fifty years ago!"
exclaimed Mr. Medbourne.

They all gathered round her. One caught both
her hands in his passionate grasp — another threw
his arm about her waist — the third buried his hand
among the glossy curls that clustered beneath the
widow's cap. Blushing, panting, struggling, chiding,
laughing, her warm breath fanning each of their
faces by turns, she strove to disengage herself, yet
still remained in their triple embrace. Never was
there a livelier picture of youthful rivalship, with
bewitching beauty for the prize. Yet, by a strange
deception, owing to the duskiness of the chamber,
and the antique dresses which they still wore, the
tall mirror is said to have reflected the figures of

the three old, gray, withered grandsires, ridiculously contending for the skinny ugliness of a shrivelled grandam.

But they were young: their burning passions proved them so. Inflamed to madness by the co- quetry of the girl-widow, who neither granted nor quite withheld her favors, the three rivals began to interchange threatening glances. Still keeping hold of the fair prize, they grappled fiercely at one an- other's throats. As they struggled to and fro, the table was overturned, and the vase dashed into a thou- sand fragments. The precious Water of Youth flowed in a bright stream across the floor, moistening the wings of a butterfly, which, grown old in the decline of summer, had alighted there to die. The insect flut- tered lightly through the chamber, and settled on the snowy head of Dr. Heidegger.

"Come, come, gentlemen! — come, Madam Wych- erly," exclaimed the doctor, "I really must protest against this riot."

They stood still and shivered; for it seemed as if gray Time were calling them back from their sunny youth, far down into the chill and darksome vale of years. They looked at old Dr. Heidegger, who sat in his carved arm-chair, holding the rose of half a cent- ury, which he had rescued from among the fragments of the shattered vase. At the motion of his hand, the four rioters resumed their seats; the more readily, be- cause their violent exertions had wearied them, youth- ful though they were.

"My poor Sylvia's rose!" ejaculated Dr. Heideg- ger, holding it in the light of the sunset clouds; "it appears to be fading again."

And so it was. Even while the party were looking

at it, the flower continued to shrivel up, till it became as dry and fragile as when the doctor had first thrown it into the vase. He shook off the few drops of moisture which clung to its petals.

"I love it as well thus as in its dewy freshness," observed he, pressing the withered rose to his withered lips. While he spoke, the butterfly fluttered down from the doctor's snowy head, and fell upon the floor.

His guests shivered again. A strange chillness, whether of the body or spirit they could not tell, was creeping gradually over them all. They gazed at one another, and fancied that each fleeting moment snatched away a charm, and left a deepening furrow where none had been before. Was it an illusion? Had the changes of a lifetime been crowded into so brief a space, and were they now four aged people, sitting with their old friend, Dr. Heidegger?

"Are we grown old again, so soon?" cried they, dolefully.

In truth they had. The Water of Youth possessed merely a virtue more transient than that of wine. The delirium which it created had effervesced away. Yes! they were old again. With a shuddering impulse, that showed her a woman still, the widow clasped her skinny hands before her face, and wished that the coffin lid were over it, since it could be no longer beautiful.

"Yes, friends, ye are old again," said Dr. Heidegger, "and lo! the Water of Youth is all lavished on the ground. Well—I bemoan it not; for if the fountain gushed at my very doorstep, I would not stoop to bathe my lips in it — no, though its delirium were for years instead of moments. Such is the lesson ye have taught me!"

But the doctor's four friends had taught no such lesson to themselves. They resolved forthwith to make a pilgrimage to Florida, and quaff at morning, noon, and night, from the Fountain of Youth.

Note. — In an English review, not long since, I have been accused of plagiarizing the idea of this story from a chapter in one of the novels of Alexandre Dumas. There has undoubtedly been a plagiarism on one side or the other; but as my story was written a good deal more than twenty years ago, and as the novel is of considerably more recent date, I take pleasure in thinking that M. Dumas has done me the honor to appropriate one of the fanciful conceptions of my earlier days. He is heartily welcome to it; nor is it the only instance, by many, in which the great French romancer has exercised the privilege of commanding genius by confiscating the intellectual property of less famous people to his own use and behoof.

September, 1860.

LEGENDS OF THE PROVINCE HOUSE.

I.

HOWE'S MASQUERADE.

ONE afternoon, last summer, while walking along Washington Street, my eye was attracted by a sign-board protruding over a narrow archway, nearly opposite the Old South Church. The sign represented the front of a stately edifice, which was designated as the "OLD PROVINCE HOUSE, kept by Thomas Waite." I was glad to be thus reminded of a purpose, long entertained, of visiting and rambling over the mansion of the old royal governors of Massachusetts; and entering the arched passage, which penetrated through the middle of a brick row of shops, a few steps transported me from the busy heart of modern Boston into a small and secluded court-yard. One side of this space was occupied by the square front of the Province House, three stories high, and surmounted by a cupola, on the top of which a gilded Indian was discernible, with his bow bent and his arrow on the string, as if aiming at the weathercock on the spire of the Old South. The figure has kept this attitude for seventy years or more, ever since good Deacon Drowne, a cunning carver of wood, first stationed him on his long sentinel's watch over the city.

The Province House is constructed of brick, which seems recently to have been overlaid with a coat of light-colored paint. A flight of red freestone steps,

fenced in by a balustrade of curiously wrought iron,
ascends from the court-yard to the spacious porch,
over which is a balcony, with an iron balustrade of
similar pattern and workmanship to that beneath.
These letters and figures — 16 P. S. 79 — are wrought
into the iron work of the balcony, and probably express the date of the edifice, with the initials of its
founder's name. A wide door with double leaves admitted me into the hall or entry, on the right of which
is the entrance to the bar-room.

It was in this apartment, I presume, that the ancient governors held their levees, with vice-regal pomp,
surrounded by the military men, the councillors, the
judges, and other officers of the crown, while all the
loyalty of the province thronged to do them honor.
But the room, in its present condition, cannot boast
even of faded magnificence. The panelled wainscot
is covered with dingy paint, and acquires a duskier
hue from the deep shadow into which the Province
House is thrown by the brick block that shuts it in
from Washington Street. A ray of sunshine never
visits this apartment any more than the glare of the
festal torches, which have been extinguished from the
era of the Revolution. The most venerable and ornamental object is a chimney-piece set round with Dutch
tiles of blue-figured China, representing scenes from
Scripture; and, for aught I know, the lady of Pownall
or Bernard may have sat beside this fire-place, and
told her children the story of each blue tile. A bar
in modern style, well replenished with decanters, bottles, cigar boxes, and net-work bags of lemons, and
provided with a beer pump and a soda fount, extends
along one side of the room. At my entrance, an elderly person was smacking his lips with a zest which

satisfied me that the cellars of the Province House still hold good liquor, though doubtless of other vintages than were quaffed by the old governors. After sipping a glass of port sangaree, prepared by the skilful hands of Mr. Thomas Waite, I besought that worthy successor and representative of so many historic personages to conduct me over their time honored mansion.

He readily complied; but, to confess the truth, I was forced to draw strenuously upon my imagination, in order to find aught that was interesting in a house which, without its historic associations, would have seemed merely such a tavern as is usually favored by the custom of decent city boarders, and old-fashioned country gentlemen. The chambers, which were probably spacious in former times, are now cut up by partitions, and subdivided into little nooks, each affording scanty room for the narrow bed and chair and dressing-table of a single lodger. The great staircase, however, may be termed, without much hyperbole, a feature of grandeur and magnificence. It winds through the midst of the house by flights of broad steps, each flight terminating in a square landing-place, whence the ascent is continued towards the cupola. A carved balustrade, freshly painted in the lower stories, but growing dingier as we ascend, borders the staircase with its quaintly twisted and inter twined pillars, from top to bottom. Up these stairs the military boots, or perchance the gouty shoes, of many a governor have trodden, as the wearers mounted to the cupola, which afforded them so wide a view over their metropolis and the surrounding country. The cupola is an octagon, with several windows, and a door opening upon the roof. From this station, as I pleased myself with imagining, Gage may have beheld his disastrous victory on Bunker Hill (unless one of the trimountains intervened), and Howe have marked the approaches of Washington's besieging army; although the buildings since erected in the vicinity have shut out almost every object, save the steeple of the Old South, which seems almost within arm's length. Descending from the cupola, I paused in the garret to observe the ponderous white-oak framework, so much more massive than the frames of modern houses, and thereby resembling an antique skeleton. The brick walls, the materials of which were imported from Holland, and the timbers of the mansion, are still as sound as ever ; but the floors and other interior parts being greatly decayed, it is contemplated to gut the whole, and build a new house within the ancient frame and brick work. Among other inconveniences of the present edifice, mine host mentioned that any jar or motion was apt to shake down the dust of ages out of the ceiling of one chamber upon the floor of that beneath it.

We stepped forth from the great front window into the balcony, where, in old times, it was doubtless the custom of the king's representative to show himself to a loyal populace, requiting their huzzas and tossed-up hats with stately bendings of his dignified person. In those days the front of the Province House looked upon the street ; and the whole site now occupied by the brick range of stores, as well as the present courtyard, was laid out in grass plats, overshadowed by trees and bordered by a wrought-iron fence. Now, the old aristocratic edifice hides its time-worn visage behind an upstart modern building ; at one of the back windows I observed some pretty tailoresses, sewing and chatting and laughing, with now and then a careless glance towards the balcony. Descending thence, we again entered the bar-room, where the elderly gentleman above mentioned, the smack of whose lips had spoken so favorably for Mr. Waite's good liquor, was still lounging in his chair. He seemed to be, if not a lodger, at least a familiar visitor of the house, who might be supposed to have his regular score at the bar, his summer seat at the open window, and his prescriptive corner at the winter's fireside. Being of a sociable aspect, I ventured to address him with a remark calculated to draw forth his historical reminiscences, if any such were in his mind; and it gratified me to discover, that, between memory and tradition, the old gentleman was really possessed of some very pleasant gossip about the Province House. The portion of his talk which chiefly interested me was the outline of the following legend. He professed to have received it at one or two removes from an eye-witness; but this derivation, together with the lapse of time, must have afforded opportunities for many variations of the narrative; so that despairing of literal and absolute truth, I have not scrupled to make such further changes as seemed conducive to the reader's profit and delight.

———

At one of the entertainments given at the Province House, during the latter part of the siege of Boston, there passed a scene which has never yet been satisfactorily explained. The officers of the British army, and the loyal gentry of the province, most of whom were collected within the beleaguered town, had been invited to a masked ball; for it was the policy of Sir William Howe to hide the distress and danger of the

period, and the desperate aspect of the siege, undei
an ostentation of festivity. The spectacle of this evening, if the oldest members of the provincial court circle might be believed, was the most gay and gorgeous
affair that had occurred in the annals of the government. The brilliantly-lighted apartments were
thronged with figures that seemed to have stepped
from the dark canvas of historic portraits, or to have
flitted forth from the magic pages of romance, or at
least to have flown hither from one of the London
theatres, without a change of garments. Steeled
knights of the Conquest, bearded statesmen of Queen
Elizabeth, and high-ruffled ladies of her court, were
mingled with characters of comedy, such as a party-
colored Merry Andrew, jingling his cap and bells; a
Falstaff, almost as provocative of laughter as his pro-
totype; and a Don Quixote, with a bean pole for a
lance, and a pot lid for a shield.

But the broadest merriment was excited by a group
of figures ridiculously dressed in old regimentals,
which seemed to have been purchased at a military
rag fair, or pilfered from some receptacle of the cast-
off clothes of both the French and British armies.
Portions of their attire had probably been worn at the
siege of Louisburg, and the coats of most recent cut
might have been rent and tattered by sword, ball, or
bayonet, as long ago as Wolfe's victory. One of
these worthies — a tall, lank figure, brandishing a
rusty sword of immense longitude — purported to be
no less a personage than General George Washington; and the other principal officers of the American
army, such as Gates, Lee, Putnam, Schuyler, Ward
and Heath, were represented by similar scarecrows.
An interview in the mock heroic style, between the

rebel warriors and the British commander-in-chief, was received with immense applause, which came loudest of all from the loyalists of the colony. There was one of the guests, however, who stood apart, eyeing these antics sternly and scornfully, at once with a frown and a bitter smile.

It was an old man, formerly of high station and great repute in the province, and who had been a very famous soldier in his day. Some surprise had been expressed that a person of Colonel Joliffe's known whig principles, though now too old to take an active part in the contest, should have remained in Boston during the siege, and especially that he should consent to show himself in the mansion of Sir William Howe. But thither he had come, with a fair granddaughter under his arm; and there, amid all the mirth and buffoonery, stood this stern old figure, the best sustained character in the masquerade, because so well representing the antique spirit of his native land. The other guests affirmed that Colonel Joliffe's black puritanical scowl threw a shadow round about him; although in spite of his sombre influence their gayety continued to blaze higher, like — (an ominous comparison) — the flickering brilliancy of a lamp which has but a little while to burn. Eleven strokes, full half an hour ago, had pealed from the clock of the Old South, when a rumor was circulated among the company that some new spectacle or pageant was about to be exhibited, which should put a fitting close to the splendid festivities of the night.

"What new jest has your Excellency in hand?" asked the Rev. Mather Byles, whose Presbyterian scruples had not kept him from the entertainment. "Trust me, sir, I have already laughed more than

beseems my cloth at your Homeric confabulation with
yonder ragamuffin General of the rebels. One other
such fit of merriment, and I must throw off my clerical wig and band."

"Not so, good Doctor Byles," answered Sir William Howe; "if mirth were a crime, you had never
gained your doctorate in divinity. As to this new
foolery, I know no more about it than yourself; perhaps not so much. Honestly now, Doctor, have you
not stirred up the sober brains of some of your countrymen to enact a scene in our masquerade?"

"Perhaps," slyly remarked the granddaughter of
Colonel Joliffe, whose high spirit had been stung by
many taunts against New England, — "perhaps we
are to have a mask of allegorical figures. Victory,
with trophies from Lexington and Bunker Hill —
Plenty, with her overflowing horn, to typify the present abundance in this good town — and Glory, with a
wreath for his Excellency's brow."

Sir William Howe smiled at words which he would
have answered with one of his darkest frowns had
they been uttered by lips that wore a beard. He was
spared the necessity of a retort, by a singular inter-
ruption. A sound of music was heard without the
house, as if proceeding from a full band of military
instruments stationed in the street, playing not such a
festal strain as was suited to the occasion, but a slow
funeral march. The drums appeared to be muffled,
and the trumpets poured forth a wailing breath, which
at once hushed the merriment of the auditors, filling
all with wonder, and some with apprehension. The
idea occurred to many that either the funeral procession of some great personage had halted in front of
the Province House, or that a corpse, in a velvet-

covered and gorgeously-decorated coffin, was about to be borne from the portal. After listening a moment, Sir William Howe called, in a stern voice, to the leader of the musicians, who had hitherto enlivened the entertainment with gay and lightsome melodies. The man was drum-major to one of the British regiments.

"Dighton," demanded the general, "what means this foolery? Bid your band silence that dead march — or, by my word, they shall have sufficient cause for their lugubrious strains! Silence it, sirrah!"

"Please your honor," answered the drum-major, whose rubicund visage had lost all its color, "the fault is none of mine. I and my band are all here together, and I question whether there be a man of us that could play that march without book. I never heard it but once before, and that was at the funeral of his late Majesty, King George the Second."

"Well, well!" said Sir William Howe, recovering his composure — "it is the prelude to some masquerading antic. Let it pass."

A figure now presented itself, but among the many fantastic masks that were dispersed through the apartments none could tell precisely from whence it came. It was a man in an old-fashioned dress of black serge, and having the aspect of a steward or principal domestic in the household of a nobleman or great English landholder. This figure advanced to the outer door of the mansion, and throwing both its leaves wide open, withdrew a little to one side and looked back towards the grand staircase as if expecting some person to descend. At the same time the music in the street sounded a loud and doleful summons. The eyes of Sir William Howe and his guests being di-

rected to the staircase, there appeared, on the uppermost landing-place that was discernible from the bottom, several personages descending towards the door.
The foremost was a man of stern visage, wearing a
steeple-crowned hat and a skull-cap beneath it; a dark
cloak, and huge wrinkled boots that came half-way up
his legs. Under his arm was a rolled-up banner,
which seemed to be the banner of England, but
strangely rent and torn; he had a sword in his right
hand, and grasped a Bible in his left. The next figure
was of milder aspect, yet full of dignity, wearing a
broad ruff, over which descended a beard, a gown of
wrought velvet, and a doublet and hose of black satin.
He carried a roll of manuscript in his hand. Close
behind these two came a young man of very striking
countenance and demeanor, with deep thought and
contemplation on his brow, and perhaps a flash of enthusiasm in his eye. His garb, like that of his predecessors, was of an antique fashion, and there was a
stain of blood upon his ruff. In the same group with
those were three or four others, all men of dignity and
evident command, and bearing themselves like personages who were accustomed to the gaze of the multitude.
It was the idea of the beholders that these figures
went to join the mysterious funeral that had halted in
front of the Province House; yet that supposition
seemed to be contradicted by the air of triumph with
which they waved their hands, as they crossed the
threshold and vanished through the portal.

"In the devil's name what is this?" muttered Sir
William Howe to a gentleman beside him; "a procession of the regicide judges of King Charles the
martyr?"

"These," said Colonel Joliffe, breaking silence al-

most for the first time that evening, — " these, if I in-
terpret them aright, are the Puritan governors — the
rulers of the old original Democracy of Massachusetts.
Endicott, with the banner from which he had torn the
symbol of subjection, and Winthrop, and Sir Henry
Vane, and Dudley, Haynes, Bellingham, and Leverett."

" Why had that young man a stain of blood upon
his ruff ? " asked Miss Joliffe.

" Because, in after years," answered her grandfather, " he laid down the wisest head in England
upon the block for the principles of liberty."

" Will not your Excellency order out the guard?"
whispered Lord Percy, who, with other British officers,
had now assembled round the General. " There may
be a plot under this mummery."

" Tush ! we have nothing to fear," carelessly replied
Sir William Howe. " There can be no worse treason
in the matter than a jest, and that somewhat of the
dullest. Even were it a sharp and bitter one, our best
policy would be to laugh it off. See — here come
more of these gentry."

Another group of characters had now partly descended the staircase. The first was a venerable and
white-bearded patriarch, who cautiously felt his way
downward with a staff. Treading hastily behind him,
and stretching forth his gauntleted hand as if to gras
the old man's shoulder, came a tall, soldier-like figure,
equipped with a plumed cap of steel, a bright breastplate, and a long sword, which rattled against the
stairs. Next was seen a stout man, dressed in rich
and courtly attire, but not of courtly demeanor ; his
gait had the swinging motion of a seaman's walk;
and chancing to stumble on the staircase, he suddenly

grew wrathful, and was heard to mutter an oath. He was followed by a noble-looking personage in a curled wig, such as are represented in the portraits of Queen Anne's time and earlier; and the breast of his coat was decorated with an embroidered star. While advancing to the door, he bowed to the right hand and to the left, in a very gracious and insinuating style; but as he crossed the threshold, unlike the early Puritan governors, he seemed to wring his hands with sorrow.

"Prithee, play the part of a chorus, good Doctor Byles," said Sir William Howe. "What worthies are these?"

"If it please your Excellency they lived somewhat before my day," answered the doctor; "but doubtless our friend, the Colonel, has been hand and glove with them."

"Their living faces I never looked upon," said Colonel Joliffe, gravely; "although I have spoken face to face with many rulers of this land, and shall greet yet another with an old man's blessing ere I die. But we talk of these figures. I take the venerable patriarch to be Bradstreet, the last of the Puritans, who was governor at ninety, or thereabouts. The next is Sir Edmund Andros, a tyrant, as any New England school-boy will tell you; and therefore the people cast him down from his high seat into a dungeon. Then comes Sir William Phipps, shepherd, cooper, sea-captain, and governor — may many of his countrymen rise as high from as low an origin! Lastly, you saw the gracious Earl of Bellamont, who ruled us under King William."

"But what is the meaning of it all?" asked Lord Percy.

"Now, were I a rebel," said Miss Joliffe, half aloud, "I might fancy that the ghosts of these ancient governors had been summoned to form the funeral procession of royal authority in New England."

Several other figures were now seen at the turn of the staircase. The one in advance had a thoughtful, anxious, and somewhat crafty expression of face, and in spite of his loftiness of manner, which was evidently the result both of an ambitious spirit and of long continuance in high stations, he seemed not incapable of cringing to a greater than himself. A few steps behind came an officer in a scarlet and embroidered uniform, cut in a fashion old enough to have been worn by the Duke of Marlborough. His nose had a rubicund tinge, which, together with the twinkle of his eye, might have marked him as a lover of the wine cup and good fellowship; notwithstanding which tokens he appeared ill at ease, and often glanced around him as if apprehensive of some secret mischief. Next came a portly gentleman, wearing a coat of shaggy cloth, lined with silken velvet; he had sense, shrewdness, and humor in his face, and a folio volume under his arm; but his aspect was that of a man vexed and tormented beyond all patience, and harassed almost to death. He went hastily down, and was followed by a dignified person, dressed in a purple velvet suit, with very rich embroidery; his demeanor would have possessed much stateliness, only that a grievous fit of the gout compelled him to hobble from stair to stair, with contortions of face and body. When Dr. Byles beheld this figure on the staircase, he shivered as with an ague, but continued to watch him steadfastly, until the gouty gentleman had reached the threshold, made a gesture of anguish and despair, and vanished into the outer gloom, whither the funeral music summoned him.

"Governor Belcher! — my old patron! — in his very shape and dress!" gasped Doctor Byles. "This is an awful mockery!"

"A tedious foolery, rather," said Sir William Howe, with an air of indifference. "But who were the three that preceded him?"

"Governor Dudley, a cunning politician — yet his craft once brought him to a prison," replied Colonel Joliffe. "Governor Shute, formerly a Colonel under Marlborough, and whom the people frightened out of the province; and learned Governor Burnet, whom the legislature tormented into a mortal fever."

"Methinks they were miserable men, these royal governors of Massachusetts," observed Miss Joliffe. "Heavens, how dim the light grows!"

It was certainly a fact that the large lamp which illuminated the staircase now burned dim and duskily: so that several figures, which passed hastily down the stairs and went forth from the porch, appeared rather like shadows than persons of fleshly substance. Sir William Howe and his guests stood at the doors of the contiguous apartments, watching the progress of this singular pageant, with various emotions of anger, contempt, or half-acknowledged fear, but still with an anxious curiosity. The shapes which now seemed hastening to join the mysterious procession were recognized rather by striking peculiarities of dress, or broad characteristics of manner, than by any perceptible resemblance of features to their proto-types. Their faces, indeed, were invariably kept in deep shadow. But Doctor Byles, and other gentle-men who had long been familiar with the successive rulers of the province, were heard to whisper the names of Shirley, of Pownall, of Sir Francis Bernard, and of the well-remembered Hutchinson; thereby confessing that the actors, whoever they might be, in this spectral march of governors, had succeeded in putting on some distant portraiture of the real personages. As they vanished from the door, still did these shadows toss their arms into the gloom of night, with a dread expression of woe. Following the mimic representative of Hutchinson came a military figure, holding before his face the cocked hat which he had taken from his powdered head; but his epaulettes and other insignia of rank were those of a general officer, and something in his mien reminded the beholders of one who had recently been master of the Province House, and chief of all the land.

"The shape of Gage, as true as in a looking-glass," exclaimed Lord Percy, turning pale.

"No, surely," cried Miss Joliffe, laughing hysterically; "it could not be Gage, or Sir William would have greeted his old comrade in arms! Perhaps he will not suffer the next to pass unchallenged."

"Of that be assured, young lady," answered Sir William Howe, fixing his eyes, with a very marked expression, upon the immovable visage of her grandfather. "I have long enough delayed to pay the ceremonies of a host to these departing guests. The next that takes his leave shall receive due courtesy."

A wild and dreary burst of music came through the open door. It seemed as if the procession, which had been gradually filling up its ranks, were now about to move, and that this loud peal of the wailing trumpets, and roll of the muffled drums, were a call to some loiterer to make haste. Many eyes, by an irresistible

Impulse, were turned upon Sir William Howe, as if
it were he whom the dreary music summoned to the
funeral of departed power.

"See! — here comes the last!" whispered Miss
Joliffe, pointing her tremulous finger to the staircase

A figure had come into view as if descending the
stairs; although so dusky was the region whence it
emerged, some of the spectators fancied that they had
seen this human shape suddenly moulding itself amid
the gloom. Downward the figure came, with a stately
and martial tread, and reaching the lowest stair was
observed to be a tall man, booted and wrapped in a
military cloak, which was drawn up around the face
so as to meet the flapped brim of a laced hat. The
features, therefore, were completely hidden. But the
British officers deemed that they had seen that military cloak before, and even recognized the frayed embroidery on the collar, as well as the gilded scabbard
of a sword which protruded from the folds of the
cloak, and glittered in a vivid gleam of light. Apart
from these trifling particulars, there were characteristics of gait and bearing which impelled the wondering
guests to glance from the shrouded figure to Sir William Howe, as if to satisfy themselves that their host
had not suddenly vanished from the midst of them.

With a dark flush of wrath upon his brow they saw
the General draw his sword and advance to meet the
figure in the cloak before the latter had stepped one
pace upon the floor.

"Villain, unmuffle yourself!" cried he. "You pass
no farther!"

The figure, without blenching a hair's breadth from
the sword which was pointed at his breast, made a
solemn pause and lowered the cape of the cloak from

about his face, yet not sufficiently for the spectators
to catch a glimpse of it.   But Sir William Howe had
evidently seen enough.   The sternness of his countenance gave place to a look of wild amazement, if not
horror, while he recoiled several steps from the figure,
and let fall his sword upon the floor.   The martial
shape again drew the cloak about his features and
passed on; but reaching the threshold, with his back
towards the spectators, he was seen to stamp his foot
and shake his clinched hands in the air.   It was afterwards affirmed that Sir William Howe had repeated
that selfsame gesture of rage and sorrow, when, for
the last time, and as the last royal governor, he passed
through the portal of the Province House.

" Hark ! — the procession moves," said Miss Joliffe.
The music was dying away along the street, and its
dismal strains were mingled with the knell of midnight from the steeple of the Old South, and with the
roar of artillery, which announced that the beleaguer-
ing army of Washington had intrenched itself upon
a nearer height than before.   As the deep boom of the
cannon smote upon his ear, Colonel Joliffe raised himself to the full height of his aged form, and smiled
sternly on the British General.

" Would your Excellency inquire further into the
mystery of the pageant ? " said he.

" Take care of your gray head ! " cried Sir William
Howe, fiercely, though with a quivering lip.   " It has
stood too long on a traitor's shoulders ! "

" You must make haste to chop it off, then," calmly
replied the Colonel ; " for a few hours longer, and not
all the power of Sir William Howe, nor of his master,
shall cause one of these gray hairs to fall.   The em
pire of Britain in this ancient province is at its last

gasp to-night; — almost while I speak it is a dead corpse; — and methinks the shadows of the old governors are fit mourners at its funeral!"

With these words Colonel Joliffe threw on his cloak, and drawing his granddaughter's arm within his own, retired from the last festival that a British ruler ever held in the old province of Massachusetts Bay. It was supposed that the Colonel and the young lady possessed some secret intelligence in regard to the mysterious pageant of that night. However this might be, such knowledge has never become general. The actors in the scene have vanished into deeper obscurity than even that wild Indian band who scattered the cargoes of the tea ships on the waves, and gained a place in history, yet left no names. But superstition, among other legends of this mansion, repeats the wondrous tale, that on the anniversary night of Britain's discomfiture the ghosts of the ancient governors of Massachusetts still glide through the portal of the Province House. And, last of all, comes a figure shrouded in a military cloak, tossing his clinched hands into the air, and stamping his iron-shod boots upon the broad freestone steps, with a semblance of feverish despair, but without the sound of a foot-tramp.

When the truth-telling accents of the elderly gentleman were hushed, I drew a long breath and looked round the room, striving, with the best energy of my imagination, to throw a tinge of romance and historic grandeur over the realities of the scene. But my nostrils snuffed up a scent of cigar smoke, clouds of which the narrator had emitted by way of visible emblem, I suppose, of the nebulous obscurity of his tale.

Moreover, my gorgeous fantasies were wofully disturbed by the rattling of the spoon in a tumbler of whiskey punch, which Mr. Thomas Waite was mingling for a customer. Nor did it add to the picturesque appearance of the panelled walls that the slate of the Brookline stage was suspended against them, instead of the armorial escutcheon of some far-descended governor. A stage-driver sat at one of the windows, reading a penny paper of the day — the Boston Times — and presenting a figure which could nowise be brought into any picture of " Times in Boston " seventy or a hundred years ago. On the window seat lay a bundle, neatly done up in brown paper, the direction of which I had the idle curiosity to read. " Miss Susan Huggins, at the Province House." A pretty chambermaid, no doubt. In truth, it is desperately hard work, when we attempt to throw the spell of hoar antiquity over localities with which the living world, and the day that is passing over us, have aught to do. Yet, as I glanced at the stately staircase down which the procession of the old governors had descended, and as I emerged through the venerable portal whence their figures had preceded me, it gladdened me to be conscious of a thrill of awe. Then, diving through the narrow archway, a few strides transported me into the densest throng of Washington Street.

LEGENDS OF THE PROVINCE HOUSE.

II.

EDWARD RANDOLPH'S PORTRAIT.

THE old legendary guest of the Province House abode in my remembrance from midsummer till January. One idle evening last winter, confident that he would be found in the snuggest corner of the barroom, I resolved to pay him another visit, hoping to deserve well of my country by snatching from oblivion some else unheard-of fact of history. The night was chill and raw, and rendered boisterous by almost a gale of wind, which whistled along Washington Street, causing the gas-lights to flare and flicker within the lamps. As I hurried onward, my fancy was busy with a comparison between the present aspect of the street and that which it probably wore when the British governors inhabited the mansion whither I was now going. Brick edifices in those times were few, till a succession of destructive fires had swept, and swept again, the wooden dwellings and warehouses from the most populous quarters of the town. The buildings stood insulated and independent, not, as now, merging their separate existences into connected ranges, with a front of tiresome identity, — but each possessing features of its own, as if the owner's individual taste had shaped it, — and the whole presenting a picturesque irregularity, the absence of which is hardly compensated by any beauties of our modern architecture. Such a scene, dimly vanishing from the eye by the ray of here and there a tallow candle, glimmering through the small panes of scattered windows, would form a sombre contrast to the street as I beheld it, with the gas-lights blazing from corner to corner, flaming within the shops, and throwing a noonday brightness through the huge plates of glass.

But the black, lowering sky, as I turned my eyes upward, wore, doubtless, the same visage as when it frowned upon the ante-revolutionary New Englanders. The wintry blast had the same shriek that was familiar to their ears. The Old South Church, too, still pointed its antique spire into the darkness, and was lost between earth and heaven; and as I passed, its clock, which had warned so many generations how transitory was their lifetime, spoke heavily and slow the same unregarded moral to myself. "Only seven o'clock," thought I. "My old friend's legends will scarcely kill the hours 'twixt this and bedtime."

Passing through the narrow arch, I crossed the court-yard, the confined precincts of which were made visible by a lantern over the portal of the Province House. On entering the bar-room, I found, as I expected, the old tradition monger seated by a special good fire of anthracite, compelling clouds of smoke from a corpulent cigar. He recognized me with evident pleasure; for my rare properties as a patient listener invariably make me a favorite with elderly gentlemen and ladies of narrative propensities. Drawing a chair to the fire, I desired mine host to favor us with a glass apiece of whiskey punch, which was speedily prepared, steaming hot, with a slice of lemon at the bottom, a dark-red stratum of port wine upon the surface, and a sprinkling of nutmeg strewn over all. As we touched our

glasses together, my legendary friend made himself
kno·vn to me as Mr. Bela Tiffany; and I rejoiced at
the oddity of the name, because it gave his image and
character a sort of individuality in my conception.
The old gentleman's draught acted as a solvent upon
his memory, so that it overflowed with tales, traditions,
anecdotes of famous dead people, and traits of ancient
manners, some of which were childish as a nurse's lullaby, while others might have been worth the notice of
the grave historian. Nothing impressed me more than
a story of a black mysterious picture, which used to
hang in one of the chambers of the Province House,
directly above the room where we were now sitting.
The following is as correct a v·rsion of the fact as the
reader would be likely to obtain from any other source,
although, assuredly, it has a tinge of romance approaching to the marvellous.

In one of the apartments of the Province House
there was long preserved an ancient picture, the frame
of which was as black as ebony, and the canvas itself
so dark with age, damp, and smoke, that not a touch
of the painter's art could be discerned. Time had
thrown an impenetrable veil over it, and left to tradition and fable and conjecture to say what had once
been there portrayed. During the rule of many successive governors, it had hung, by prescriptive and
undisputed right, over the mantel-piece of the same
chamber; and it still kept its place when Lieutenant-
Governor Hutchinson assumed the administration of
the province, on the departure of Sir Francis Bernard.
The Lieutenant-Governor sat, one afternoon, resting
his head against the carved back of his stately arm-

chair, and gazing up thoughtfully at the void blackness of the picture. It was scarcely a time for such inactive musing, when affairs of the deepest moment required the ruler's decision; for, within that very hour Hutchinson had received intelligence of the arrival of a British fleet, bringing three regiments from Halifax to overawe the insubordination of the people. These troops awaited his permission to occupy the fortress of Castle William, and the town itself. Yet, instead of affixing his signature to an official order, there sat the Lieutenant-Governor, so carefully scrutinizing the black waste of canvas that his demeanor attracted the notice of two young persons who attended him. One, wearing a military dress of buff, was his kinsman, Francis Lincoln, the Provincial Captain of Castle William; the other, who sat on a low stool beside his chair, was Alice Vane, his favorite niece.

She was clad entirely in white, a pale, ethereal creature, who, though a native of New England, had been educated abroad, and seemed not merely a stranger from another clime, but almost a being from another world. For several years, until left an orphan, she had dwelt with her father in sunny Italy, and there had acquired a taste and enthusiasm for sculpture and painting which she found few opportunities of gratifying in the undecorated dwellings of the colonial gentry. It was said that the early productions of her own pencil exhibited no inferior genius, though, perhaps, the rude atmosphere of New England had cramped her hand, and dimmed the glowing colors of her fancy. But observing her uncle's steadfast gaze, which appeared to search through the mist of years to discover the subject of the picture, her curiosity was excited

" Is it known, my dear uncle," inquired she, " what

this old picture once represented? Possibly, could it be made visible, it might prove a masterpiece of some great artist — else, why has it so long held such a conspicuous place?"

As her uncle, contrary to his usual custom (for he was as attentive to all the humors and caprices of Alice as if she had been his own best-beloved child), did not immediately reply, the young Captain of Castle William took that office upon himself.

"This dark old square of canvas, my fair cousin," said he, "has been an heirloom in the Province House from time immemorial. As to the painter, I can tell you nothing; but, if half the stories told of it be true, not one of the great Italian masters has ever produced so marvellous a piece of work as that before you."

Captain Lincoln proceeded to relate some of the strange fables and fantasies which, as it was impossible to refute them by ocular demonstration, had grown to be articles of popular belief, in reference to this old picture. One of the wildest, and at the same time the best accredited, accounts, stated it to be an original and authentic portrait of the Evil One, taken at a witch meeting near Salem; and that its strong and terrible resemblance had been confirmed by several of the confessing wizards and witches, at their trial, in open court. It was likewise affirmed that a familiar spirit or demon abode behind the blackness of the picture, and had shown himself, at seasons of public calamity, to more than one of the royal governors. Shirley, for instance, had beheld this ominous apparition, on the eve of General Abercrombie's shameful and bloody defeat under the walls of Ticonderoga. Many of the servants of the Province House had caught glimpses of a visage frowning down upon them.

at morning or evening twilight, — or in the depths of night, while raking up the fire that glimmered on the hearth beneath; although, if any were bold enough to hold a torch before the picture, it would appear as black and undistinguishable as ever. The oldest inhabitant of Boston recollected that his father, in whose days the portrait had not wholly faded out of sight, had once looked upon it, but would never suffer himself to be questioned as to the face which was there represented. In connection with such stories, it was remarkable that over the top of the frame there were some ragged remnants of black silk, indicating that a veil had formerly hung down before the picture, until the duskiness of time had so effectually concealed it. But, after all, it was the most singular part of the affair that so many of the pompous governors of Massachusetts had allowed the obliterated picture to remain in the state chamber of the Province House.

"Some of these fables are really awful," observed Alice Vane, who had occasionally shuddered, as well as smiled, while her cousin spoke. "It would be almost worth while to wipe away the black surface of the canvas, since the original picture can hardly be so formidable as those which fancy paints instead of it."

"But would it be possible," inquired her cousin, "to restore this dark picture to its pristine hues?"

"Such arts are known in Italy," said Alice.

The Lieutenant-Governor had roused himself from his abstracted mood, and listened with a smile to the conversation of his young relatives. Yet his voice had something peculiar in its tones when he undertook the explanation of the mystery.

"I am sorry, Alice, to destroy your faith in the legends of which you are so fond," remarked he; "but my antiquarian researches have long since made me acquainted with the subject of this picture — if picture it can be called — which is no more visible, nor ever will be, than the face of the long buried man whom it once represented. It was the portrait of Edward Randolph, the founder of this house, a person famous in the history of New England."

"Of that Edward Randolph," exclaimed Captain Lincoln, "who obtained the repeal of the first provincial charter, under which our forefathers had enjoyed almost democratic privileges! He that was styled the arch-enemy of New England, and whose memory is still held in detestation as the destroyer of our liberties!"

"It was the same Randolph," answered Hutchinson, moving uneasily in his chair. "It was his lot to taste the bitterness of popular odium."

"Our annals tell us," continued the Captain of Castle William, "that the curse of the people followed this Randolph where he went, and wrought evil in all the subsequent events of his life, and that its effect was seen likewise in the manner of his death. They say, too, that the inward misery of that curse worked itself outward, and was visible on the wretched man's countenance, making it too horrible to be looked upon. If so, and if this picture truly represented his aspect, it was in mercy that the cloud of blackness has gathered over it."

"These traditions are folly to one who has proved, as I have, how little of historic truth lies at the bottom," said the Lieutenant-Governor. "As regards the life and character of Edward Randolph, too implicit credence has been given to Dr. Cotton Mather, who — I must say it, though some of his blood runs in my veins — has filled our early history with old women's tales, as fanciful and extravagant as those of Greece or Rome."

"And yet," whispered Alice Vane, "may not such fables have a moral? And, methinks, if the visage of this portrait be so dreadful, it is not without a cause that it has hung so long in a chamber of the Province House. When the rulers feel themselves irresponsible, it were well that they should be reminded of the awful weight of a people's curse."

The Lieutenant-Governor started, and gazed for a moment at his niece, as if her girlish fantasies had struck upon some feeling in his own breast, which all his policy or principles could not entirely subdue. He knew, indeed, that Alice, in spite of her foreign education, retained the native sympathies of a New England girl.

"Peace, silly child," cried he, at last, more harshly than he had ever before addressed the gentle Alice. "The rebuke of a king is more to be dreaded than the clamor of a wild, misguided multitude. Captain Lincoln, it is decided. The fortress of Castle William must be occupied by the royal troops. The two remaining regiments shall be billeted in the town, or encamped upon the Common. It is time, after years of tumult, and almost rebellion, that his majesty's government should have a wall of strength about it."

"Trust, sir — trust yet awhile to the loyalty of the people," said Captain Lincoln; "nor teach them that they can ever be on other terms with British soldiers than those of brotherhood, as when they fought side by side through the French War. Do not convert the streets of your native town into a camp. Think twice before you give up old Castle William, the key of

the province, into other keeping than that of true-born
New Englanders."

"Young man, it is decided," repeated Hutchinson,
rising from his chair. "A British officer will be in
attendance this evening, to receive the necessary in-
structions for the disposal of the troops. Your presence also will be required. Till then, farewell."

With these words the Lieutenant-Governor hastily
left the room, while Alice and her cousin more slowly
followed, whispering together, and once pausing to
glance back at the mysterious picture. The Captain
of Castle William fancied that the girl's air and mien
were such as might have belonged to one of those
spirits of fable — fairies, or creatures of a more antique
mythology — who sometimes mingled their agency
with mortal affairs, half in caprice, yet with a sensibility to human weal or woe. As he held the door for
her to pass, Alice beckoned to the picture and smiled.

"Come forth, dark and evil Shape!" cried she.
"It is thine hour!"

In the evening, Lieutenant-Governor Hutchinson
sat in the same chamber where the foregoing scene
had occurred, surrounded by several persons whose
various interests had summoned them together. There
were the Selectmen of Boston, plain, patriarchal fathers of the people, excellent representatives of the
old puritanical founders, whose sombre strength had
stamped so deep an impress upon the New England
character. Contrasting with these were one or two
members of Council, richly dressed in the white wigs,
the embroidered waistcoats and other magnificence of
the time, and making a somewhat ostentatious display
of courtier-like ceremonial. In attendance, likewise,
was a major of the British army, awaiting the Lieu-

tenant-Governor's orders for the landing of the troops, which still remained on board the transports. The Captain of Castle William stood beside Hutchinson's chair with folded arms, glancing rather haughtily at the British officer, by whom he was soon to be super seded in his command. On a table, in the centre of the chamber, stood a branched silver candlestick, throwing down the glow of half a dozen wax-lights upon a paper apparently ready for the Lieutenant-Governor's signature.

Partly shrouded in the voluminous folds of one of the window curtains, which fell from the ceiling to the floor, was seen the white drapery of a lady's robe. It may appear strange that Alice Vane should have been there at such a time; but there was something so childlike, so wayward, in her singular character, so apart from ordinary rules, that her presence did not surprise the few who noticed it. Meantime, the chairman of the Selectmen was addressing to the Lieutenant-Governor a long and solemn protest against the reception of the British troops into the town.

"And if your Honor," concluded this excellent but somewhat prosy old gentleman, "shall see fit to per sist in bringing these mercenary sworders and mus-keteers into our quiet streets, not on our heads be the responsibility. Think, sir, while there is yet time, that if one drop of blood be shed, that blood shall be an eternal stain upon your Honor's memory. You sir, have written with an able pen the deeds of our forefathers. The more to be desired is it, therefore, that yourself should deserve honorable mention, as a true patriot and upright ruler, when your own doings shall be written down in history."

"I am not insensible, my good sir, to the natural

desire to stand well in the annals of my country,"
replied Hutchinson, controlling his impatience into
courtesy, "nor know I any better method of attaining
that end than by withstanding the merely temporary
spirit of mischief, which, with your pardon, seems to
have infected elder men than myself. Would you
have me wait till the mob shall sack the Province
House, as they did my private mansion? Trust me,
sir, the time may come when you will be glad to flee
for protection to the king's banner, the raising of
which is now so distasteful to you."

"Yes," said the British major, who was impatiently
expecting the Lieutenant-Governor's orders. "The
demagogues of this Province have raised the devil
and cannot lay him again. We will exorcise him,
in God's name and the king's."

"If you meddle with the devil, take care of his
claws!" answered the Captain of Castle William,
stirred by the taunt against his countrymen.

"Craving your pardon, young sir," said the venerable Selectman, "let not an evil spirit enter into
your words. We will strive against the oppressor
with prayer and fasting, as our forefathers would have
done. Like them, moreover, we will submit to whatever lot a wise Providence may send us, — always, after our own best exertions to amend it."

"And there peep forth the devil's claws!" muttered
Hutchinson, who well understood the nature of Puri
tan submission. "This matter shall be expedited
forthwith. When there shall be a sentinel at every
corner, and a court of guard before the town house, a
loyal gentleman may venture to walk abroad. What
to me is the outcry of a mob, in this remote province
of the realm? The king is my master, and England

is my country! Upheld by their armed strength, I set my foot upon the rabble, and defy them!"

He snatched a pen, and was about to affix his signature to the paper that lay on the table, when the Captain of Castle William placed his hand upon his shoulder. The freedom of the action, so contrary to the ceremonious respect which was then considered due to rank and dignity, awakened general surprise. and in none more than in the Lieutenant-Governor himself. Looking angrily up, he perceived that his young relative was pointing his finger to the opposite wall. Hutchinson's eye followed the signal; and he saw, what had hitherto been unobserved, that a black silk curtain was suspended before the mysterious picture, so as completely to conceal it. His thoughts immediately recurred to the scene of the preceding afternoon; and, in his surprise, confused by indistinct emotions, yet sensible that his niece must have had an agency in this phenomenon, he called loudly upon her.

"Alice! — come hither, Alice!"

No sooner had he spoken than Alice Vane glided from her station, and pressing one hand across her eyes, with the other snatched away the sable curtain that concealed the portrait. An exclamation of surprise burst from every beholder; but the Lieutenant-Governor's voice had a tone of horror.

"By Heaven!" said he, in a low, inward murmur, speaking rather to himself than to those around him, "if the spirit of Edward Randolph were to appear among us from the place of torment, he could not wear more of the terrors of hell upon his face!"

"For some wise end," said the aged Selectman, solemnly, "hath Providence scattered away the mist of years that had so long hid this dreadful effigy. Until this hour no living man hath seen what we behold!"

Within the antique frame, which so recently had inclosed a sable waste of canvas, now appeared a visible picture, still dark, indeed, in its hues and shadings, but thrown forward in strong relief. It was a half-length figure of a gentleman in a rich but very old-fashioned dress of embroidered velvet, with a broad ruff and a beard, and wearing a hat, the brim of which overshadowed his forehead. Beneath this cloud the eyes had a peculiar glare, which was almost lifelike. The whole portrait started so distinctly out of the background, that it had the effect of a person looking down from the wall at the astonished and awe-stricken spectators. The expression of the face, if any words can convey an idea of it, was that of a wretch detected in some hideous guilt, and exposed to the bitter hatred and laughter and withering scorn of a vast surrounding multitude. There was the struggle of defiance, beaten down and overwhelmed by the crushing weight of ignominy. The torture of the soul had come forth upon the countenance. It seemed as if the picture, while hidden behind the cloud of immemorial years, had been all the time acquiring an intenser depth and darkness of expression, till now it gloomed forth again, and threw its evil omen over the present hour. Such, if the wild legend may be credited, was the portrait of Edward Randolph, as he appeared when a people's curse had wrought its influence upon his nature.

"'T would drive me mad — that awful face!" said Hutchinson, who seemed fascinated by the contemplation of it.

"Be warned, then!" whispered Alice. "He trampled on a people's rights. Behold his punishment — and avoid a crime like his!"

The Lieutenant-Governor actually trembled for an instant; but, exerting his energy — which was not, however, his most characteristic feature — he strove to shake off the spell of Randolph's countenance.

"Girl!" cried he, laughing bitterly as he turned to Alice, "have you brought hither your painter's art — your Italian spirit of intrigue — your tricks of stage effect — and think to influence the councils of rulers and the affairs of nations by such shallow contrivances? See here!"

"Stay yet a while," said the Selectman, as Hutchinson again snatched the pen; "for if ever mortal man received a warning from a tormented soul, your Honor is that man!"

"Away!" answered Hutchinson fiercely. "Though yonder senseless picture cried 'Forbear!' — it should not move me!"

Casting a scowl of defiance at the pictured face (which seemed at that moment to intensify the horror of its miserable and wicked look), he scrawled on the paper, in characters that betokened it a deed of desperation, the name of Thomas Hutchinson. Then, it is said, he shuddered, as if that signature had granted away his salvation.

"It is done," said he; and placed his hand upon his brow.

"May Heaven forgive the deed," said the soft, sad accents of Alice Vane, like the voice of a good spirit flitting away.

When morning came there was a stifled whisper through the household, and spreading thence about the town, that the dark, mysterious picture had started from the wall, and spoken face to face with Lieutenant-Governor Hutchinson. If such a miracle had been wrought, however, no traces of it remained behind, for within the antique frame nothing could be discerned save the impenetrable cloud, which had covered the canvas since the memory of man. If the figure had, indeed, stepped forth, it had fled back, spirit-like, at the daydawn, and hidden itself behind a century's obscurity. The truth probably was, that Alice Vane's secret for restoring the hues of the picture had merely effected a temporary renovation. But those who, in that brief interval, had beheld the awful visage of Edward Randolph, desired no second glance, and ever afterwards trembled at the recollection of the scene, as if an evil spirit had appeared visibly among them. And as for Hutchinson, when, far over the ocean, his dying hour drew on, he gasped for breath, and complained that he was choking with the blood of the Boston Massacre; and Francis Lincoln, the former Captain of Castle William, who was standing at his bedside, perceived a likeness in his frenzied look to that of Edward Randolph. Did his broken spirit feel, at that dread hour, the tremendous burden of a People's curse?

At the conclusion of this miraculous legend, I inquired of mine host whether the picture still remained in the chamber over our heads; but Mr. Tiffany informed me that it had long since been removed, and was supposed to be hidden in some out-of-the-way corner of the New England Museum. Perchance some curious antiquary may light upon it there, and, with the assistance of Mr. Howorth, the picture cleaner, may supply a not unnecessary proof of the authenticity of the facts here set down. During the progress of the story a storm had been gathering abroad, and raging and rattling so loudly in the upper regions of the Province House, that it seemed as if all the old governors and great men were running riot above stairs while Mr. Bela Tiffany babbled of them below. In the course of generations, when many people have lived and died in an ancient house, the whistling of the wind through its crannies, and the creaking of its beams and rafters, become strangely like the tones of the human voice, or thundering laughter, or heavy footsteps treading the deserted chambers. It is as if the echoes of half a century were revived. Such were the ghostly sounds that roared and murmured in our ears when I took leave of the circle round the fireside of the Province House, and plunging down the door steps, fought my way homeward against a drifting snow-storm.

III.

LADY ELEANORE'S MANTLE.

MINE excellent friend, the landlord of the Province House, was pleased, the other evening, to invite Mr. Tiffany and myself to an oyster supper. This slight mark of respect and gratitude, as he handsomely observed, was far less than the ingenious tale-teller, and I, the humble note-taker of his narratives, had fairly earned, by the public notice which our joint lucubrations had attracted to his establishment. Many a cigar had been smoked within his premises — many a glass of wine, or more potent aqua vitæ, had been quaffed — many a dinner had been eaten by curious strangers, who, save for the fortunate conjunction of Mr. Tiffany and me, would never have ventured through that darksome avenue which gives access to the historic precincts of the Province House. In short, if any credit be due to the courteous assurances of Mr. Thomas Waite, we had brought his forgotten mansion almost as effectually into public view as if we had thrown down the vulgar range of shoe shops and dry goods stores, which hides its aristocratic front from Washington Street. It may be unadvisable, however, to speak too loudly of the increased custom of the house, lest Mr. Waite should find it difficult to renew the lease on so favorable terms as heretofore.

Being thus welcomed as benefactors, neither Mr

Tiffany nor myself felt any scruple in doing full justice to the good things that were set before us. If the
feast were less magnificent than those same panelled
walls had witnessed in a by-gone century, — if mine
host presided with somewhat less of state than might
have befitted a successor of the royal Governors, — if
the guests made a less imposing show than the be-
wigged and powdered and embroided dignitaries, who
erst banqueted at the gubernatorial table, and now
sleep, within their armorial tombs on Copp's Hill, or
round King's Chapel, — yet never, I may boldly say,
did a more comfortable little party assemble in the
Province House, from Queen Anne's days to the
Revolution. The occasion was rendered more interesting by the presence of a venerable personage, whose
own actual reminiscences went back to the epoch of
Gage and Howe, and even supplied him with a doubtful anecdote or two of Hutchinson. He was one of
that small, and now all but extinguished, class, whose
attachment to royalty, and to the colonial institutions
and customs that were connected with it, had never
yielded to the democratic heresies of after times. The
young queen of Britain has not a more loyal subject
in her realm — perhaps not one who would kneel before her throne with such reverential love — as this
old grandsire, whose head has whitened beneath the
mild sway of the Republic, which still, in his mel-
lower moments, he terms a usurpation. Yet prejudices so obstinate have not made him an ungentle
or impracticable companion. If the truth must be
told, the life of the aged loyalist has been of such a
scrambling and unsettled character, — he has had so
little choice of friends and been so often destitute of
any, — that I doubt whether he would refuse a cup of

kindness with either Oliver Cromwell or John Hancock, — to say nothing of any democrat now upon the
stage. In another paper of this series I may perhaps
give the reader a closer glimpse of his portrait.

Our host, in due season, uncorked a bottle of Ma
deira, of such exquisite perfume and admirable flavor
that he surely must have discovered it in an ancient
bin, down deep beneath the deepest cellar, where some
jolly old butler stored away the Governor's choicest
wine, and forgot to reveal the secret on his death-bed.
Peace to his red-nosed ghost, and a libation to his
memory! This precious liquor was imbibed by Mr.
Tiffany with peculiar zest; and after sipping the third
glass, it was his pleasure to give us one of the oddest
legends which he had yet raked from the storehouse
where he keeps such matters. With some suitable
adornments from my own fancy, it ran pretty much as
follows.

Not long after Colonel Shute had assumed the government of Massachusetts Bay, now nearly a hundred
and twenty years ago, a young lady of rank and fortune arrived from England, to claim his protection as
her guardian. He was her distant relative, but the
nearest who had survived the gradual extinction of her
family; so that no more eligible shelter could be found
for the rich and high-born Lady Eleanore Rochcliffe
than within the Province House of a transatlantic
colony. The consort of Governor Shute, moreover,
had been as a mother to her childhood, and was now
anxious to receive her, in the hope that a beautiful
young woman would be exposed to infinitely less peril
from the primitive society of New England than amid

the artifices and corruptions of a court. If either the Governor or his lady had especially consulted their own comfort, they would probably have sought to devolve the responsibility on other hands ; since, with some noble and splendid traits of character, Lady Eleanore was remarkable for a harsh, unyielding pride, a haughty consciousness of her hereditary and personal advantages, which made her almost incapable of control. Judging from many traditionary anecdotes, this peculiar temper was hardly less than a monomania ; or, if the acts which it inspired were those of a sane person, it seemed due from Providence that pride so sinful should be followed by as severe a retribution. That tinge of the marvellous, which is thrown over so many of these half-forgotten legends, has probably imparted an additional wildness to the strange story of Lady Eleanore Rochcliffe.

The ship in which she came passenger had arrived at Newport, whence Lady Eleanore was conveyed to Boston in the Governor's coach, attended by a small escort of gentlemen on horseback. The ponderous equipage, with its four black horses, attracted much notice as it rumbled through Cornhill, surrounded by the prancing steeds of half a dozen cavaliers, with swords dangling to their stirrups and pistols at their holsters. Through the large glass windows of the coach, as it rolled along, the people could discern the figure of Lady Eleanore, strangely combining an almost queenly stateliness with the grace and beauty of a maiden in her teens. A singular tale had gone abroad among the ladies of the province, that their fair rival was indebted for much of the irresistible charm of her appearance to a certain article of dress — an embroidered mantle — which had been wrought by the most skilful artist in London, and possessed even magical properties of adornment. On the present occasion, however, she owed nothing to the witchery of dress, being clad in a riding habit of velvet, which would have appeared stiff and ungraceful on any other form.

The coachman reined in his four black steeds, and the whole cavalcade came to a pause in front of the contorted iron balustrade that fenced the Province House from the public street. It was an awkward coincidence that the bell of the Old South was just then tolling for a funeral; so that, instead of a gladsome peal with which it was customary to announce the arrival of distinguished strangers, Lady Eleanore Rochcliffe was ushered by a doleful clang, as if calamity had come embodied in her beautiful person.

"A very great disrespect!" exclaimed Captain Langford, an English officer, who had recently brought dispatches to Governor Shute. "The funeral should have been deferred, lest Lady Eleanore's spirits be affected by such a dismal welcome."

"With your pardon, sir," replied Doctor Clarke, a physician, and a famous champion of the popular party, "whatever the heralds may pretend, a dead beggar must have precedence of a living queen. King Death confers high privileges."

These remarks were interchanged while the speakers waited a passage through the crowd, which had gathered on each side of the gateway, leaving an open avenue to the portal of the Province House. A black slave in livery now leaped from behind the coach, and threw open the door; while at the same moment Governor Shute descended the flight of steps from his mansion, to assist Lady Eleanore in alighting. But the Governor's stately approach was anticipated in a

manner that excited general astonishment. A pale
young man, with his black hair all in disorder, rushed
from the throng, and prostrated himself beside the
coach, thus offering his person as a footstool for Lady
Eleanore Rochcliffe to tread upon. She held back an
instant, yet with an expression as if doubting whether
the young man were worthy to bear the weight of her
footstep, rather than dissatisfied to receive such awful
reverence from a fellow-mortal.

"Up, sir," said the Governor, sternly, at the same
time lifting his cane over the intruder. "What means
the Bedlamite by this freak?"

"Nay," answered lady Eleanore playfully, but with
more scorn than pity in her tone, "your Excellency
shall not strike him. When men seek only to be
trampled upon, it were a pity to deny them a favor so
easily granted — and so well deserved!"

Then, though as lightly as a sunbeam on a cloud,
she placed her foot upon the cowering form, and extended her hand to meet that of the Governor. There
was a brief interval, during which Lady Eleanore
retained this attitude; and never, surely, was there an
apter emblem of aristocracy and hereditary pride
trampling on human sympathies and the kindred of
nature, than these two figures presented at that moment. Yet the spectators were so smitten with her
beauty, and so essential did pride seem to the existence of such a creature, that they gave a simultaneous
acclamation of applause.

"Who is this insolent young fellow?" inquired
Captain Langford, who still remained beside Doctor
Clarke. "If he be in his senses, his impertinence
demands the bastinado. If mad, Lady Eleanore
should be secured from further inconvenience, by his
confinement."

"His name is Jervase Helwyse," answered the Doctor; "a youth of no birth or fortune, or other advantages, save the mind and soul that nature gave him; and being secretary to our colonial agent in London, it was his misfortune to meet this Lady Eleanore Rochcliffe. He loved her — and her scorn has driven him mad."

"He was mad so to aspire," observed the English officer.

"It may be so," said Doctor Clarke, frowning as he spoke. "But I tell you, sir, I could well-nigh doubt the justice of the Heaven above us if no signal humiliation overtake this lady, who now treads so haughtily into yonder mansion. She seeks to place herself above the sympathies of our common nature, which envelops all human souls. See, if that nature do not assert its claim over her in some mode that shall bring her level with the lowest!"

"Never!" cried Captain Langford indignantly — "neither in life, nor when they lay her with her ancestors."

Not many days afterwards the Governor gave a ball in honor of Lady Eleanore Rochcliffe. The principal gentry of the colony received invitations, which were distributed to their residences, far and near, by messengers on horseback, bearing missives sealed with all the formality of official dispatches. In obedience to the summons, there was a general gathering of rank, wealth, and beauty; and the wide door of the Province House had seldom given admittance to more numerous and honorable guests than on the evening of Lady Eleanore's ball. Without much extravagance of eulogy, the spectacle might even be termed splendid; for, according to the fashion of the times, the ladies

shone in rich silks and satins, outspread over wide-
projecting hoops ; and the gentlemen glittered in gold
embroidery, laid unsparingly upon the purple, or scar
let, or sky-blue velvet, which was the material of their
coats and waistcoats. The latter article of dress was
of great importance, since it enveloped the wearer's
body nearly to the knees, and was perhaps bedizened
with the amount of his whole year's income, in golden
flowers and foliage. The altered taste of the present
day — a taste symbolic of a deep change in the whole
system of society — would look upon almost any of
those gorgeous figures as ridiculous ; although that
evening the guests sought their reflections in the pier-
glasses, and rejoiced to catch their own glitter amid
the glittering crowd. What a pity that one of the
stately mirrors has not preserved a picture of the
scene, which, by the very traits that were so transitory, might have taught us much that would be worth
knowing and remembering!

Would, at least, that either painter or mirror could
convey to us some faint idea of a garment, already
noticed in this legend, — the Lady Eleanore's embroidered mantle, — which the gossips whispered was invested with magic properties, so as to lend a new and
untried grace to her figure each time that she put it
on ! Idle fancy as it is, this mysterious mantle has
thrown an awe around my image of her, partly from
its fabled virtues, and partly because it was the handi
work of a dying woman, and, perchance, owed the fantastic grace of its conception to the delirium of approaching death.

After the ceremonial greetings had been paid, Lady
Eleanore Rochcliffe stood apart from the mob of
guests, insulating herself within a small and distin-

guished circle, to whom she accorded a more cordial
favor than to the general throng. The waxen torches
threw their radiance vividly over the scene, bringing
out its brilliant points in strong relief; but she gazed
carelessly, and with now and then an expression of
weariness or scorn, tempered with such feminine grace
that her auditors scarcely perceived the moral deformity of which it was the utterance. She beheld the
spectacle not with vulgar ridicule, as disdaining to be
pleased with the provincial mockery of a court festival,
but with the deeper scorn of one whose spirit held itself too high to participate in the enjoyment of other
human souls. Whether or no the recollections of
those who saw her that evening were influenced by
the strange events with which she was subsequently
connected, so it was that her figure ever after recurred
to them as marked by something wild and unnatural, –
although, at the time, the general whisper was of her
exceeding beauty, and of the indescribable charm
which her mantle threw around her. Some close observers, indeed, detected a feverish flush and alternate
paleness of countenance, with a corresponding flow and
revulsion of spirits, and once or twice a painful and
helpless betrayal of lassitude, as if she were on the
point of sinking to the ground. Then, with a nervous
shudder, she seemed to arouse her energies and threw
some bright and playful yet half-wicked sarcasm into
the conversation. There was so strange a characteristic in her manners and sentiments that it astonished
every right-minded listener; till looking in her face, a
lurking and incomprehensible glance and smile perplexed them with doubts both as to her seriousness
and sanity. Gradually, Lady Eleanore Rochcliffe's
circle grew smaller, till only four gentlemen remained

in it. These were Captain Langford, the English officer before mentioned; a Virginian planter, who had come to Massachusetts on some political errand; a young Episcopal clergyman, the grandson of a British earl; and, lastly, the private secretary of Governor Shute, whose obsequiousness had won a sort of tolerance from Lady Eleanore.

At different periods of the evening the liveried servants of the Province House passed among the guests, bearing huge trays of refreshments and French and Spanish wines. Lady Eleanore Rochcliffe, who refused to wet her beautiful lips even with a bubble of Champagne, had sunk back into a large damask chair, apparently overwearied either with the excitement of the scene or its tedium, and while, for an instant, she was unconscious of voices, laughter and music, a young man stole forward, and knelt down at her feet. He bore a salver in his hand, on which was a chased silver goblet, filled to the brim with wine, which he offered as reverentially as to a crowned queen, or rather with the awful devotion of a priest doing sacrifice to his idol. Conscious that some one touched her robe, Lady Eleanore started, and unclosed her eyes upon the pale, wild features and dishevelled hair of Jervase Helwyse.

"Why do you haunt me thus?" said she, in a languid tone, but with a kindlier feeling than she ordinarily permitted herself to express. "They tell me that I have done you harm."

"Heaven knows if that be so," replied the young man solemnly. "But, Lady Eleanore, in requital of that harm, if such there be, and for your own earthly and heavenly welfare, I pray you to take one sip of this holy wine, and then to pass the goblet round among the guests. And this shall be a symbol that you have not sought to withdraw yourself from the chain of human sympathies — which whoso would shake off must keep company with fallen angels."

" Where has this mad fellow stolen that sacramental vessel ? " exclaimed the Episcopal clergyman.

This question drew the notice of the guests to the silver cup, which was recognized as appertaining to the communion plate of the Old South Church; and, for aught that could be known, it was brimming over with the consecrated wine.

"Perhaps it is poisoned," half whispered the Governor's secretary.

" Pour it down the villain's throat ! " cried the Virginian fiercely.

"Turn him out of the house ! " cried Captain Langford, seizing Jervase Helwyse so roughly by the shoulder that the sacramental cup was overturned, and its contents sprinkled upon Lady Eleanore's mantle. "Whether knave, fool, or Bedlamite, it is intolerable that the fellow should go at large."

" Pray, gentlemen, do my poor admirer no harm," said Lady Eleanore, with a faint and weary smile. "Take him out of my sight, if such be your pleasure; for I can find in my heart to do nothing but laugh at him; whereas, in all decency and conscience, it would become me to weep for the mischief I have wrought ! "

But while the by-standers were attempting to lead away the unfortunate young man, he broke from them, and with a wild, impassioned earnestness, offered a new and equally strange petition to Lady Eleanore. It was no other than that she should throw off the mantle, which, while he pressed the silver cup of wine upon her, she had drawn more closely around her form, so as almost to shroud herself within it.

"Cast it from you!" exclaimed Jervase Helwyse, clasping his hands in an agony of entreaty. "It may not yet be too late! Give the accursed garment to the flames!"

But Lady Eleanore, with a laugh of scorn, drew the rich folds of the embroidered mantle over her head, in such a fashion as to give a completely new aspect to her beautiful face, which — half hidden, half revealed — seemed to belong to some being of mysterious character and purposes.

'Farewell, Jervase Helwyse!" said she. "Keep my image in your remembrance, as you behold it now."

"Alas, lady!" he replied, in a tone no longer wild, but sad as a funeral bell. "We must meet shortly, when your face may wear another aspect — and that shall be the image that must abide within me."

He made no more resistance to the violent efforts of the gentlemen and servants, who almost dragged him out of the apartment, and dismissed him roughly from the iron gate of the Province House. Captain Langford, who had been very active in this affair, was returning to the presence of Lady Eleanore Rochcliffe, when he encountered the physician, Doctor Clarke, with whom he had held some casual talk on the day of her arrival. The Doctor stood apart, separated from Lady Eleanore by the width of the room, but eying her with such keen sagacity that Captain Langford involuntarily gave him credit for the discovery of some deep secret.

"You appear to be smitten, after all, with the charms of this queenly maiden," said he, hoping thus to draw forth the physician's hidden knowledge.

"God forbid!" answered Doctor Clarke, with a grave

smile; "and if you be wise you will put up the same prayer for yourself. Woe to those who shall be smitten by this beautiful Lady Eleanore! But yonder stands the Governor — and I have a word or two for his private ear. Good night!"

He accordingly advanced to Governor Shute, and addressed him in so low a tone that none of the by-standers could catch a word of what he said, although the sudden change of his Excellency's hitherto cheerful visage betokened that the communication could be of no agreeable import. A very few moments afterwards it was announced to the guests that an unforeseen circumstance rendered it necessary to put a premature close to the festival.

The ball at the Province House supplied a topic of conversation for the colonial metropolis for some days after its occurrence, and might still longer have been the general theme, only that a subject of all-engrossing interest thrust it, for a time, from the public recollection. This was the appearance of a dreadful epidemic, which, in that age and long before and afterwards, was wont to slay its hundreds and thousands on both sides of the Atlantic. On the occasion of which we speak, it was distinguished by a peculiar virulence, insomuch that it has left its traces — its pit-marks, to use an appropriate figure — on the history of the country, the affairs of which were thrown into confusion by its ravages. At first, unlike its ordinary course, the disease seemed to confine itself to the higher circles of society, selecting its victims from among the proud, the well-born, and the wealthy, entering unabashed into stately chambers, and lying down with the slumberers in silken beds. Some of the most distinguished guests of the Province House — even those whom the haughty

Lady Eleanore Rochcliffe had deemed not unworthy of her favor — were stricken by this fatal scourge. It was noticed, with an ungenerous bitterness of feeling, that the four gentlemen — the Virginian, the British officer, the young clergyman, and the Governor's secretary — who had been her most devoted attendants on the evening of the ball, were the foremost on whom the plague stroke fell. But the disease, pursuing its onward progress, soon ceased to be exclusively a prerogative of aristocracy. Its red brand was no longer conferred like a noble's star, or an order of knighthood. It threaded its way through the narrow and crooked streets, and entered the low, mean, darksome dwellings, and laid its hand of death upon the artisans and laboring classes of the town. It compelled rich and poor to feel themselves brethren then; and stalking to and fro across the Three Hills, with a fierceness which made it almost a new pestilence, there was that mighty conqueror — that scourge and horror of our forefathers — the Small-Pox!

We cannot estimate the affright which this plague inspired of yore, by contemplating it as the fangless monster of the present day. We must remember, rather, with what awe we watched the gigantic footsteps of the Asiatic cholera, striding from shore to shore of the Atlantic, and marching like destiny upon cities far remote which flight had already half depopulated. There is no other fear so horrible and unhumanizing as that which makes man dread to breathe heaven's vital air lest it be poison, or to grasp the hand of a brother or friend lest the gripe of the pestilence should clutch him. Such was the dismay that now followed in the track of the disease, or ran before it throughout the town. Graves were hastily dug, and

the pestilential relics as hastily covered, because the
dead were enemies of the living, and strove to draw
them headlong, as it were, into their own dismal pit.
The public councils were suspended, as if mortal wisdom might relinquish its devices, now that an unearthly usurper had found his way into the ruler's
mansion. Had an enemy's fleet been hovering on the
coast, or his armies trampling on our soil, the people
would probably have committed their defence to that
same direful conqueror who had wrought their own
calamity, and would permit no interference with his
sway. This conqueror had a symbol of his triumphs.
It was a blood-red flag, that fluttered in the tainted
air, over the door of every dwelling into which the
Small-Pox had entered.

Such a banner was long since waving over the
portal of the Province House; for thence, as was
proved by tracking its footsteps back, had all this
dreadful mischief issued. It had been traced back to
a lady's luxurious chamber — to the proudest of the
proud — to her that was so delicate, and hardly owned
herself of earthly mould — to the haughty one, who
took her stand above human sympathies — to Lady
Eleanore! There remained no room for doubt that
the contagion had lurked in that gorgeous mantle,
which threw so strange a grace around her at the
festival. Its fantastic splendor had been conceived in
the delirious brain of a woman on her death-bed, and
was the last toil of her stiffening fingers, which had
interwoven fate and misery with its golden threads
This dark tale, whispered at first, was now bruited
far and wide. The people raved against the Lady
Eleanore, and cried out that her pride and scorn had
evoked a fiend, and that, between them both, this

monstrous evil had been born. At times, their rage
and despair took the semblance of grinning mirth;
and whenever the red flag of the pestilence was hoisted
over another and yet another door, they clapped their
hands and shouted through the streets, in bitter mockery: " Behold a new triumph for the Lady Eleanore! "

One day, in the midst of these dismal times, a wild
figure approached the portal of the Province House,
and folding his arms, stood contemplating the scarlet
banner which a passing breeze shook fitfully, as if to
fling abroad the contagion that it typified. At length,
climbing one of the pillars by means of the iron balustrade, he took down the flag and entered the mansion, waving it above his head. At the foot of the
staircase he met the Governor, booted and spurred,
with his cloak drawn around him, evidently on the
point of setting forth upon a journey.

" Wretched lunatic, what do you seek here? " exclaimed Shute, extending his cane to guard himself
from contact. " There is nothing here but Death.
Back — or you will meet him! "

" Death will not touch me, the banner-bearer of the
pestilence! " cried Jervase Helwyse, shaking the red
flag aloft. " Death, and the Pestilence, who wears
the aspect of the Lady Eleanore, will walk through
the streets to-night, and I must march before them
with this banner! "

" Why do I waste words on the fellow? " muttered
the Governor, drawing his cloak across his mouth.
" What matters his miserable life, when none of us
are sure of twelve hours' breath? On, fool, to your
own destruction! "

He made way for Jervase Helwyse, who immediately ascended the staircase, but, on the first landing

place, was arrested by the firm grasp of a hand upon his shoulder. Looking fiercely up, with a madman's impulse to struggle with and rend asunder his opponent, he found himself powerless beneath a calm, stern eye, which possessed the mysterious property of quelling frenzy at its height. The person whom he had now encountered was the physician, Doctor Clarke, the duties of whose sad profession had led him to the Province House, where he was an infrequent guest in more prosperous times.

"Young man, what is your purpose?" demanded he.

"I seek the Lady Eleanore," answered Jervase Helwyse, submissively.

"All have fled from her," said the physician. "Why do you seek her now? I tell you, youth, her nurse fell death-stricken on the threshold of that fatal chamber. Know ye not, that never came such a curse to our shores as this lovely Lady Eleanore? — that her breath has filled the air with poison? — that she has shaken pestilence and death upon the land, from the folds of her accursed mantle?"

"Let me look upon her!" rejoined the mad youth, more wildly. "Let me behold her, in her awful beauty, clad in the regal garments of the pestilence! She and Death sit on a throne together. Let me kneel down before them!"

"Poor youth!" said Doctor Clarke; and, moved by a deep sense of human weakness, a smile of caustic humor curled his lip even then. "Wilt thou still worship the destroyer and surround her image with fantasies the more magnificent, the more evil she has wrought? Thus man doth ever to his tyrants. Approach, then! Madness, as I have noted, has that good efficacy, that it will guard you from contagion — and perchance its own cure may be found in yonder chamber."

Ascending another flight of stairs, he threw open a door and signed to Jervase Helwyse that he should enter. The poor lunatic, it seems probable, had cherished a delusion that his haughty mistress sat in state, unharmed herself by the pestilential influence, which, as by enchantment, she scattered round about her. He dreamed, no doubt, that her beauty was not dimmed, but brightened into superhuman splendor. With such anticipations, he stole reverentially to the door at which the physician stood, but paused upon the threshold, gazing fearfully into the gloom of the darkened chamber.

" Where is the Lady Eleanore?" whispered he.

" Call her," replied the physician.

" Lady Eleanore! — Princess! — Queen of Death!" cried Jervase Helwyse, advancing three steps into the chamber. " She is not here! There, on yonder table, I behold the sparkle of a diamond which once she wore upon her bosom. There " — and he shuddered — " there hangs her mantle, on which a dead woman embroidered a spell of dreadful potency. But where is the Lady Eleanore?"

Something stirred within the silken curtains of a canopied bed; and a low moan was uttered, which, listening intently, Jervase Helwyse began to distinguish as a woman's voice, complaining dolefully of thirst. He fancied, even, that he recognized its tones.

" My throat! — my throat is scorched," murmured the voice. " A drop of water!"

" What thing art thou?" said the brain-stricken youth, drawing near the bed and tearing asunder its curtains. "Whose voice hast thou stolen for thy murmurs and miserable petitions, as if Lady Eleanore could be conscious of mortal infirmity? Fie! Heap of diseased mortality, why lurkest thou in my lady's chamber?"

"O Jervase Helwyse," said the voice — and as it spoke the figure contorted itself, struggling to hide its blasted face — "look not now on the woman you once loved! The curse of Heaven hath stricken me, because I would not call man my brother, nor woman sister. I wrapped myself in PRIDE as in a MANTLE, and scorned the sympathies of nature; and therefore has nature made this wretched body the medium of a dreadful sympathy. You are avenged — they are all avenged — Nature is avenged — for I am Eleanore Rochcliffe!"

The malice of his mental disease. the bitterness lurking at the bottom of his heart, mad as he was, for a blighted and ruined life, and love that had been paid with cruel scorn, awoke within the breast of Jervase Helwyse. He shook his finger at the wretched girl, and the chamber echoed, the curtains of the bed were shaken, with his outburst of insane merriment.

"Another triumph for the Lady Eleanore!" he cried. "All have been her victims! Who so worthy to be the final victim as herself?"

Impelled by some new fantasy of his crazed intellect, he snatched the fatal mantle and rushed from the chamber and the house. That night a procession passed, by torchlight, through the streets, bearing in the midst the figure of a woman, enveloped with a richly embroidered mantle; while in advance stalked Jervase Helwyse, waving the red flag of the pestilence. Arriving opposite the Province House, the mob burned

the effigy, and a strong wind came and swept away
the ashes.   It was said that, from that very hour, the
pestilence abated, as if its sway had some mysterious
connection, from the first plague stroke to the last,
with Lady Eleanore's Mantle.   A remarkable uncer-
tainty broods over that unhappy lady's fate.   There is
a belief, however, that in a certain chamber of this
mansion a female form may sometimes be duskily discerned, shrinking into the darkest corner and muffling her face within an embroidered mantle.   Supposing the legend true, can this be other than the once
proud Lady Eleanore ?

Mine host and the old loyalist and I bestowed no
little warmth of applause upon this narrative, in which
we had all been deeply interested ; for the reader can
scarcely conceive how unspeakably the effect of such
a tale is heightened when, as in the present case, we
may repose perfect confidence in the veracity of him
who tells it.   For my own part, knowing how scrupu-
lous is Mr. Tiffany to settle the foundation of his facts,
I could not have believed him one whit the more faith-
fully had he professed himself an eye-witness of the
doings and sufferings of poor Lady Eleanore.   Some
sceptics, it is true, might demand documentary evidence, or even require him to produce the embroidered
mantle, forgetting that — Heaven be praised — it was
consumed to ashes.   But now the old loyalist, whose
blood was warmed by the good cheer, began to talk, in
his turn, about the traditions of the Province House,
and hinted that he, if it were agreeable, might add a
few reminiscences to our legendary stock.   Mr. Tiffany,
having no cause to dread a rival, immediately besought

him to favor us with a specimen; my own entreaties, of course, were urged to the same effect; and our venerable guest, well pleased to find willing auditors, awaited only the return of Mr. Thomas Waite, who had been summoned forth to provide accommodations for several new arrivals. Perchance the public — but be this as its own caprice and ours shall settle the matter — may read the result in another Tale of the Province House.

LEGENDS OF THE PROVINCE HOUSE.

IV.

OLD ESTHER DUDLEY.

OUR host having resumed the chair, he, as well as Mr. Tiffany and myself, expressed much eagerness to be made acquainted with the story to which the loyalist had alluded. That venerable man first of all saw fit to moisten his throat with another glass of wine, and then, turning his face towards our coal fire, looked steadfastly for a few moments into the depths of its cheerful glow. Finally, he poured forth a great fluency of speech. The generous liquid that he had imbibed, while it warmed his age-chilled blood, likewise took off the chill from his heart and mind, and gave him an energy to think and feel, which we could hardly have expected to find beneath the snows of fourscore winters. His feelings, indeed, appeared to me more excitable than those of a younger man; or at least, the same degree of feeling manifested itself by more visible effects than if his judgment and will had possessed the potency of meridian life. At the pathetic passages of his narrative he readily melted into tears. When a breath of indignation swept across his spirit the blood flushed his withered visage even to the roots of his white hair; and he shook his clinched fist at the trio of peaceful auditors, seeming to fancy enemies in those who felt very kindly towards the desolate old soul. But ever and anon, sometimes in the midst of his most earnest talk, this ancient person's intellect would wander vaguely, losing its hold of the matter in hand, and groping for it amid misty shadows. Then would he cackle forth a feeble laugh, and express a doubt whether his wits — for by that phrase it pleased our ancient friend to signify his mental powers — were not getting a little the worse for wear.

Under these disadvantages, the old loyalist's story required more revision to render it fit for the public eye than those of the series which have preceded it; nor should it be concealed that the sentiment and tone of the affair may have undergone some slight, or perchance more than slight, metamorphosis, in its transmission to the reader through the medium of a thorough-going democrat. The tale itself is a mere sketch, with no involution of plot, nor any great interest of events, yet possessing, if I have rehearsed it aright, that pensive influence over the mind which the shadow of the old Province House flings upon the loiterer in its court-yard.

The hour had come — the hour of defeat and humiliation — when Sir William Howe was to pass over the threshold of the Province House, and embark, with no such triumphal ceremonies as he once promised himself, on board the British fleet. He bade his servants and military attendants go before him, and lingered a moment in the loneliness of the mansion, to quell the fierce emotions that struggled in his bosom as with a death throb. Preferable, then, would he have deemed his fate, had a warrior's death left him a claim to the narrow territory of a grave within the soil which the King had given him to defend. With

an ominous perception that, as his departing footsteps
echoed adown the staircase, the sway of Britain was
passing forever from New England, he smote his
clinched hand on his brow, and cursed the destiny
that had flung the shame of a dismembered empire
upon him.

"Would to God," cried he, hardly repressing his
ears of rage, "that the rebels were even now at the
doorstep ! A blood-stain upon the floor should then
bear testimony that the last British ruler was faithful
to his trust."

The tremulous voice of a woman replied to his exclamation.

"Heaven's cause and the King's are one," it said.
"Go forth, Sir William Howe, and trust in Heaven
to bring back a Royal Governor in triumph."

Subduing, at once, the passion to which he had
yielded only in the faith that it was unwitnessed, Sir
William Howe became conscious that an aged woman,
leaning on a gold-headed staff, was standing betwixt
him and the door. It was old Esther Dudley, who
had dwelt almost immemorial years in this mansion,
until her presence seemed as inseparable from it as
the recollections of its history. She was the daughter
of an ancient and once eminent family, which had
fallen into poverty and decay, and left its last descendant no resource save the bounty of the King, nor
any shelter except within the walls of the Province
House. An office in the household, with merely nominal duties, had been assigned to her as a pretext for
the payment of a small pension, the greater part of
which she expended in adorning herself with an antique magnificence of attire. The claims of Esther
Dudley's gentle blood were acknowledged by all the

successive Governors; and they treated her with the
punctilious courtesy which it was her foible to demand,
not always with success, from a neglectful world. The
only actual share which she assumed in the business
of the mansion was to glide through its passages and
public chambers, late at night, to see that the servants
had dropped no fire from their flaring torches, nor
left embers crackling and blazing on the hearths.
Perhaps it was this invariable custom of walking her
rounds in the hush of midnight that caused the superstition of the times to invest the old woman with attributes of awe and mystery: fabling that she had entered the portal of the Province House, none knew
whence, in the train of the first Royal Governor, and
that it was her fate to dwell there till the last should
have departed. But Sir William Howe, if he ever
heard this legend, had forgotten it.

"Mistress Dudley, why are you loitering here?"
asked he, with some severity of tone. "It is my
pleasure to be the last in this mansion of the King."

"Not so, if it please your Excellency," answered
the time-stricken woman. "This roof has sheltered
me long. I will not pass from it until they bear me
to the tomb of my forefathers. What other shelter is
there for old Esther Dudley, save the Province House
or the grave?"

"Now Heaven forgive me!" said Sir William
Howe to himself. "I was about to leave this wretched
old creature to starve or beg. Take this, good Mistress Dudley," he added, putting a purse into her
hands. "King George's head on these golden guineas
is sterling yet, and will continue so, I warrant you,
even should the rebels crown John Hancock their
king. That purse will buy a better shelter than the
Province House can now afford."

" While the burden of life remains upon me, I will have no other shelter than this roof," persisted Esther Dudley, striking her staff upon the floor with a gesture that expressed immovable resolve. " And when your Excellency returns in triumph, I will totter into the porch to welcome you."

" My poor old friend ! " answered the British General, — and all his manly and martial pride could no longer restrain a gush of bitter tears. " This is an evil hour for you and me. The Province which the King intrusted to my charge is lost. I go hence in misfortune — perchance in disgrace — to return no more. And you, whose present being is incorporated with the past — who have seen Governor after Governor, in stately pageantry, ascend these steps — whose whole life has been an observance of majestic ceremonies, and a worship of the King — how will you endure the change ? Come with us ! Bid farewell to a land that has shaken off its allegiance, and live still under a royal government, at Halifax."

" Never, never ! " said the pertinacious old dame. " Here will I abide ; and King George shall still have one true subject in his disloyal Province."

" Beshrew the old fool ! " muttered Sir William Howe, growing impatient of her obstinacy, and ashamed of the emotion into which he had been betrayed. " She is the very moral of old-fashioned prejudice, and could exist nowhere but in this musty edifice. Well, then, Mistress Dudley, since you will needs tarry, I give the Province House in charge to you. Take this key, and keep it safe until myself, or some other Royal Governor, shall demand it of you."

Smiling bitterly at himself and her, he took the heavy key of the Province House, and delivering it

into the old lady's hands, drew his cloak around him
for departure. As the General glanced back at Esther Dudley's antique figure, he deemed her well fitted
for such a charge, as being so perfect a representative
of the decayed past — of an age gone by, with its
manners, opinions, faith and feelings, all fallen into
oblivion or scorn — of what had once been a reality,
but was now merely a vision of faded magnificence.
Then Sir William Howe strode forth, smiting his
clinched hands together, in the fierce anguish of his
spirit; and old Esther Dudley was left to keep watch
in the lonely Province House, dwelling there with
memory; and if Hope ever seemed to flit around her,
still was it Memory in disguise.

The total change of affairs that ensued on the departure of the British troops did not drive the venerable lady from her stronghold. There was not, for
many years afterwards, a Governor of Massachusetts;
and the magistrates, who had charge of such matters,
saw no objection to Esther Dudley's residence in the
Province House, especially as they must otherwise
have paid a hireling for taking care of the premises,
which with her was a labor of love. And so they left
her the undisturbed mistress of the old historic edifice.
Many and strange were the fables which the gossips
whispered about her, in all the chimney corners of the
town. Among the time-worn articles of furniture that
had been left in the mansion there was a tall, antique
mirror, which was well worthy of a tale by itself, and
perhaps may hereafter be the theme of one. The gold
of its heavily-wrought frame was tarnished, and its
surface so blurred, that the old woman's figure, whenever she paused before it, looked indistinct and ghost-
like. But it was the general belief that Esther could

cause the Governors of the overthrown dynasty, with
the beautiful ladies who had once adorned their festivals, the Indian chiefs who had come up to the Province House to hold council or swear allegiance, the
grim Provincial warriors, the severe clergymen — in
short, all the pageantry of gone days — all the figures
that ever swept across the broad plate of glass in
former times — she could cause the whole to reappear,
and people the inner world of the mirror with shadows
of old life. Such legends as these, together with the
singularity of her isolated existence, her age, and the
infirmity that each added winter flung upon her, made
Mistress Dudley the object both of fear and pity; and
it was partly the result of either sentiment that, amid
all the angry license of the times, neither wrong nor
insult ever fell upon her unprotected head. Indeed,
there was so much haughtiness in her demeanor towards intruders, among whom she reckoned all persons acting under the new authorities, that it was
really an affair of no small nerve to look her in the
face. And to do the people justice, stern republicans
as they had now become, they were well content that
the old gentlewoman, in her hoop petticoat and faded
embroidery, should still haunt the palace of ruined
pride and overthrown power, the symbol of a departed
system, embodying a history in her person. So Esther
Dudley dwelt year after year in the Province House,
still reverencing all that others had flung aside, still
faithful to her King, who, so long as the venerable
dame yet held her post, might be said to retain one
true subject in New England, and one spot of the empire that had been wrested from him.

And did she dwell there in utter loneliness? Rumor
said, not so. Whenever her chill and withered heart

desired warmth, she was wont to summon a black slave
of Governor Shirley's from the blurred mirror, and
send him in search of guests who had long ago been
familiar in those deserted chambers. Forth went the
sable messenger, with the starlight or the moonshine
gleaming through him, and did his errand in the burial
ground, knocking at the iron doors of tombs, or upon
the marble slabs that covered them, and whispering to
those within: "My mistress, old Esther Dudley, bids
you to the Province House at midnight." And punctually as the clock of the Old South told twelve came
the shadows of the Olivers, the Hutchinsons, the Dud-
leys, all the grandees of a by-gone generation, gliding
beneath the portal into the well-known mansion, where
Esther mingled with them as if she likewise were a
shade. Without vouching for the truth of such traditions, it is certain that Mistress Dudley sometimes assembled a few of the stanch, though crestfallen, old
tories, who had lingered in the rebel town during those
days of wrath and tribulation. Out of a cobwebbed
bottle, containing liquor that a royal Governor might
have smacked his lips over, they quaffed healths to
the King, and babbled treason to the Republic, feeling as if the protecting shadow of the throne were still
flung around them. But, draining the last drops of
their liquor, they stole timorously homeward, and answered not again if the rude mob reviled them in the
street.

Yet Esther Dudley's most frequent and favored
guests were the children of the town. Towards them
she was never stern. A kindly and loving nature,
hindered elsewhere from its free course by a thousand
rocky prejudices, lavished itself upon these little ones.
By bribes of gingerbread of her own making, stamped

with a royal crown, she tempted their sunny sportive
ness beneath the gloomy portal of the Province House,
and would often beguile them to spend a whole play-
day there, sitting in a circle round the verge of her
hoop petticoat, greedily attentive to her stories of a
dead world. And when these little boys and girls
stole forth again from the dark, mysterious mansion,
they went bewildered, full of old feelings that graver
people had long ago forgotten, rubbing their eyes at
the world around them as if they had gone astray into
ancient times, and become children of the past. At
home, when their parents asked where they had loi-
tered such a weary while, and with whom they had
been at play, the children would talk of all the departed worthies of the Province, as far back as Governor Belcher and the haughty dame of Sir William
Phipps. It would seem as though they had been sitting on the knees of these famous personages, whom
the grave had hidden for half a century, and had toyed
with the embroidery of their rich waistcoats, or rogu-
ishly pulled the long curls of their flowing wigs.
"But Governor Belcher has been dead this many a
year," would the mother say to her little boy. "And
did you really see him at the Province House?" "Oh
yes, dear mother! yes!" the half-dreaming child would
answer. "But when old Esther had done speaking
about him he faded away out of his chair." Thus,
without affrighting her little guests, she led them by
the hand into the chambers of her own desolate heart,
and made childhood's fancy discern the ghosts that
haunted there.

Living so continually in her own circle of ideas, and
never regulating her mind by a proper reference to
present things, Esther Dudley appears to have grown

partially crazed. It was found that she had no right
sense of the progress and true state of the Revolutionary War, but held a constant faith that the armies of
Britain were victorious on every field, and destined
to be ultimately triumphant. Whenever the town rejoiced for a battle won by Washington, or Gates, or
Morgan, or Greene, the news, in passing through the
door of the Province House, as through the ivory gate
of dreams, became metamorphosed into a strange tale
of the prowess of Howe, Clinton, or Cornwallis.
Sooner or later it was her invincible belief the colonies would be prostrate at the footstool of the King.
Sometimes she seemed to take for granted that such
was already the case. On one occasion, she startled
the towns-people by a brilliant illumination of the
Province House, with candles at every pane of glass,
and a transparency of the King's initials and a crown
of light in the great balcony window. The figure of
the aged woman in the most gorgeous of her mildewed
velvets and brocades was seen passing from casement
to casement, until she paused before the balcony, and
flourished a huge key above her head. Her wrinkled
visage actually gleamed with triumph, as if the soul
within her were a festal lamp.

"What means this blaze of light? What does old
Esther's joy portend?" whispered a spectator. "It
is frightful to see her gliding about the chambers, and
rejoicing there without a soul to bear her company."

"It is as if she were making merry in a tomb,"
said another.

"Pshaw! It is no such mystery," observed an old
man, after some brief exercise of memory. "Mistress Dudley is keeping jubilee for the King of Eng
land's birthday."

Then the people laughed aloud, and would have thrown mud against the blazing transparency of the King's crown and initials, only that they pitied the poor old dame, who was so dismally triumphant amid the wreck and ruin of the system to which she appertained.

Oftentimes it was her custom to climb the weary staircase that wound upward to the cupola, and thence strain her dimmed eyesight seaward and countryward, watching for a British fleet, or for the march of a grand procession, with the King's banner floating over it. The passengers in the street below would discern her anxious visage, and send up a shout, "When the golden Indian on the Province House shall shoot his arrow, and when the cock on the Old South spire shall crow, then look for a Royal Governor again!" — for this had grown a byword through the town. And at last, after long, long years, old Esther Dudley knew, or perchance she only dreamed, that a Royal Governor was on the eve of returning to the Province House, to receive the heavy key which Sir William Howe had committed to her charge. Now it was the fact that intelligence bearing some faint analogy to Esther's version of it was current among the townspeople. She set the mansion in the best order that her means allowed, and, arraying herself in silks and tarnished gold, stood long before the blurred mirror to admire her own magnificence. As she gazed, the gray and withered lady moved her ashen lips, murmuring half aloud, talking to shapes that she saw within the mirror, to shadows of her own fantasies, to the household friends of memory, and bidding them rejoice with her and come forth to meet the Governor. And while absorbed in this communion, Mistress Dudley heard the tramp of many footsteps in the street, and, looking out at the window, beheld what she construed as the Royal Governor's arrival.

"O happy day! O blessed, blessed hour!" she exclaimed. "Let me but bid him welcome within the portal, and my task in the Province House, and on earth, is done!"

Then with tottering feet, which age and tremulous joy caused to tread amiss, she hurried down the grand staircase, her silks sweeping and rustling as she went, so that the sound was as if a train of spectral courtiers were thronging from the dim mirror. And Esther Dudley fancied that as soon as the wide door should be flung open, all the pomp and splendor of by-gone times would pace majestically into the Province House, and the gilded tapestry of the past would be brightened by the sunshine of the present. She turned the key — withdrew it from the lock — unclosed the door — and stepped across the threshold. Advancing up the court-yard appeared a person of most dignified mien, with tokens, as Esther interpreted them, of gentle blood, high rank, and long-accustomed authority, even in his walk and every gesture. He was richly dressed, but wore a gouty shoe, which, however, did not lessen the stateliness of his gait. Around and behind him were people in plain civic dresses, and two or three war-worn veterans, evidently officers of rank, arrayed in a uniform of blue and buff. But Esther Dudley, firm in the belief that had fastened its roots about her heart, beheld only the principal personage, and never doubted that this was the long-looked-for Governor, to whom she was to surrender up her charge. As he approached, she involuntary sank down on her knees and tremblingly held forth the heavy key.

"Receive my trust! take it quickly!" cried she; "for methinks Death is striving to snatch away my triumph. But he comes too late. Thank Heaven for this blessed hour! God save King George!"

"That, Madam, is a strange prayer to be offered up at such a moment," replied the unknown guest of the Province House, and courteously removing his hat, he offered his arm to raise the aged woman. "Yet, in reverence for your gray hairs and long-kept faith, Heaven forbid that any here should say you nay. Over the realms which still acknowledge his sceptre, God save King George!"

Esther Dudley started to her feet, and hastily clutching back the key, gazed with fearful earnestness at the stranger; and dimly and doubtfully, as if suddenly awakened from a dream, her bewildered eyes half recognized his face. Years ago she had known him among the gentry of the province. But the ban of the King had fallen upon him! How, then, came the doomed victim here? Proscribed, excluded from mercy, the monarch's most dreaded and hated foe, this New England merchant had stood triumphantly against a kingdom's strength; and his foot now trod upon humbled Royalty, as he ascended the steps of the Province House, the people's chosen Governor of Massachusetts.

"Wretch, wretch that I am!" muttered the old woman, with such a heart-broken expression that the tears gushed from the stranger's eyes. "Have I bidden a traitor welcome? Come, Death! come quickly!"

"Alas, venerable lady!" said Governor Hancock, lending her his support with all the reverence that a courtier would have shown to a queen. "Your life has been prolonged until the world has changed around you. You have treasured up all that time has rendered worthless — the principles, feelings, manners, modes of being and acting, which another generation has flung aside — and you are a symbol of the past. And I, and these around me — we represent a new race of men — living no longer in the past, scarcely in the present — but projecting our lives forward into the future. Ceasing to model ourselves on ancestral superstitions, it is our faith and principle to press onward, onward! Yet," continued he, turning to his attendants, "let us reverence, for the last time, the stately and gorgeous prejudices of the tottering Past!"

While the Republican Governor spoke, he had continued to support the helpless form of Esther Dudley; her weight grew heavier against his arm; but at last, with a sudden effort to free herself, the ancient woman sank down beside one of the pillars of the portal. The key of the Province House fell from her grasp, and clanked against the stone.

"I have been faithful unto death," murmured she. "God save the King!"

"She hath done her office!" said Hancock solemnly. "We will follow her reverently to the tomb of her ancestors; and then, my fellow-citizens, onward — onward! We are no longer children of the Past!"

As the old loyalist concluded his narrative, the enthusiasm which had been fitfully flashing within his sunken eyes, and quivering across his wrinkled visage, faded away, as if all the lingering fire of his soul were extinguished. Just then, too, a lamp upon the mantel-piece threw out a dying gleam, which vanished as speedily as it shot upward, compelling our eyes to grope for one another's features by the dim glow of the hearth. With such a lingering fire, methought, with such a dying gleam, had the glory of the ancient system vanished from the Province House, when the spirit of old Esther Dudley took its flight. And now, again, the clock of the Old South threw its voice of ages on the breeze, knolling the hourly knell of the Past, crying out far and wide through the multitudinous city, and filling our ears, as we sat in the dusky chamber, with its reverberating depth of tone. In that same mansion — in that very chamber — what a volume of history had been told off into hours, by the same voice that was now trembling in the air. Many a Governor had heard those midnight accents, and longed to exchange his stately cares for slumber. And as for mine host and Mr. Bela Tiffany and the old loyalist and me, we had babbled about dreams of the past, until we almost fancied that the clock was still striking in a bygone century. Neither of us would have wondered, had a hoop-petticoated phantom of Esther Dudley tottered into the chamber, walking her rounds in the hush of midnight, as of yore, and motioned us to quench the fading embers of the fire, and leave the historic precincts to herself and her kindred shades. But as no such vision was vouchsafed, I retired unbidden, and would advise Mr. Tiffany to lay hold of another auditor, being resolved not to show my face in the Province House for a good while hence — if ever.

THE HAUNTED MIND.

WHAT a singular moment is the first one, when you have hardly begun to recollect yourself, after starting from midnight slumber? By unclosing your eyes so suddenly, you seem to have surprised the personages of your dream in full convocation round your bed, and catch one broad glance at them before they can flit into obscurity. Or, to vary the metaphor, you find yourself, for a single instant, wide awake in that realm of illusions, whither sleep has been the passport, and behold its ghostly inhabitants and wondrous scenery, with a perception of their strangeness such as you never attain while the dream is undisturbed. The distant sound of a church clock is borne faintly on the wind. You question with yourself, half seriously, whether it has stolen to your waking ear from some gray tower that stood within the precincts of your dream. While yet in suspense, another clock flings its heavy clang over the slumbering town, with so full and distinct a sound, and such a long murmur in the neighboring air, that you are certain it must proceed from the steeple at the nearest corner. You count the strokes — one — two, and there they cease, with a booming sound, like the gathering of a third stroke within the bell.

If you could choose an hour of wakefulness out of the whole night, it would be this. Since your sober bedtime, at eleven, you have had rest enough to take off the pressure of yesterday's fatigue ; while before

you, till the sun comes from " far Cathay " to brighten
your window, there is almost the space of a summer
night; one hour to be spent in thought, with the
mind's eye half shut, and two in pleasant dreams,
and two in that strangest of enjoyments, the forget-
fulness alike of joy and woe. The moment of rising
belongs to another period of time, and appears so distant that the plunge out of a warm bed into the frosty
air cannot yet be anticipated with dismay. Yesterday
has already vanished among the shadows of the past;
to-morrow has not yet emerged from the future. You
have found an intermediate space, where the business
of life does not intrude; where the passing moment
lingers, and becomes truly the present; a spot where
Father Time, when he thinks nobody is watching him,
sits down by the wayside to take breath. Oh, that
he would fall asleep, and let mortals live on without
growing older!

Hitherto you have lain perfectly still, because the
slightest motion would dissipate the fragments of your
slumber. Now, being irrevocably awake, you peep
through the half-drawn window curtain, and observe
that the glass is ornamented with fanciful devices in
frostwork, and that each pane presents something like
a frozen dream. There will be time enough to trace
out the analogy while waiting the summons to breakfast. Seen through the clear portion of the glass,
where the silvery mountain peaks of the frost scenery
do not ascend, the most conspicuous object is the steeple; the white spire of which directs you to the wintry
lustre of the firmament. You may almost distinguish
the figures on the clock that has just told the hour.
Such a frosty sky, and the snow-covered roofs, and the
long vista of the frozen street, all white, and the dis-

tant water hardened into rock, might make you shiver, even under four blankets and a woollen comforter. Yet look at that one glorious star! Its beams are distinguishable from all the rest, and actually cast the shadow of the casement on the bed, with a radiance of deeper hue than moonlight, though not so accurate an outline.

You sink down and muffle your head in the clothes, shivering all the while, but less from bodily chill than the bare idea of a polar atmosphere. It is too cold even for the thoughts to venture abroad. You speculate on the luxury of wearing out a whole existence in bed, like an oyster in its shell, content with the sluggish ecstasy of inaction, and drowsily conscious of nothing but delicious warmth, such as you now feel again. Ah! that idea has brought a hideous one in its train. You think how the dead are lying in their cold shrouds and narrow coffins, through the drear winter of the grave, and cannot persuade your fancy that they neither shrink nor shiver, when the snow is drifting over their little hillocks, and the bitter blast howls against the door of the tomb. That gloomy thought will collect a gloomy multitude, and throw its complexion over your wakeful hour.

In the depths of every heart there is a tomb and a dungeon, though the lights, the music, and revelry above may cause us to forget their existence, and the buried ones, or prisoners, whom they hide. But some-times, and oftenest at midnight, these dark receptacles are flung wide open. In an hour like this, when the mind has a passive sensibility, but no active strength; when the imagination is a mirror, imparting vividness to all ideas, without the power of selecting or control-ling them; then pray that your griefs may slumber,

and the brotherhood of remorse not break their chain.
It is too late! A funeral train comes gliding by your
bed, in which Passion and Feeling assume bodily
shape, and things of the mind become dim spectres to
the eye. There is your earliest Sorrow, a pale young
mourner, wearing a sister's likeness to first love, sadly
beautiful, with a hallowed sweetness in her melancholy features, and grace in the flow of her sable robe。
Next appears a shade of ruined loveliness, with dust
among her golden hair, and her bright garments all
faded and defaced, stealing from your glance with
drooping head, as fearful of reproach; she was your
fondest Hope, but a delusive one; so call her Disappointment now. A sterner form succeeds, with a brow
of wrinkles, a look and gesture of iron authority;
there is no name for him unless it be Fatality, an emblem of the evil influence that rules your fortunes; a
demon to whom you subjected yourself by some error
at the outset of life, and were bound his slave forever,
by once obeying him. See! those fiendish lineaments
graven on the darkness, the writhed lip of scorn, the
mockery of that living eye, the pointed finger, touching the sore place in your heart! Do you remember
any act of enormous folly at which you would blush,
even in the remotest cavern of the earth? Then recognize your Shame.

Pass, wretched band! Well for the wakeful one, if,
riotously miserable, a fiercer tribe do not surround
him, the devils of a guilty heart, that holds its hell
within itself. What if Remorse should assume the
features of an injured friend? What if the fiend
should come in woman's garments, with a pale beauty
amid sin and desolation, and lie down by your side?
What if he should stand at your bed's foot, in the

likeness of a corpse, with a bloody stain upon the shroud? Sufficient, without such guilt, is this nightmare of the soul; this heavy, heavy sinking of the spirits; this wintry gloom about the heart; this indistinct horror of the mind, blending itself with the darkness of the chamber.

By a desperate effort you start upright, breaking from a sort of conscious sleep, and gazing wildly round the bed, as if the fiends were anywhere but in your haunted mind. At the same moment, the slumbering embers on the hearth send forth a gleam which palely illuminates the whole outer room, and flickers through the door of the bed-chamber, but cannot quite dispel its obscurity. Your eye searches for whatever may remind you of the living world. With eager minuteness you take note of the table near the fireplace, the book with an ivory knife between its leaves, the unfolded letter, the hat, and the fallen glove. Soon the flame vanishes, and with it the whole scene is gone, though its image remains an instant in your mind's eye, when darkness has swallowed the reality. Throughout the chamber there is the same obscurity as before, but not the same gloom within your breast. As your head falls back upon the pillow, you think — in a whisper be it spoken — how pleasant, in these night solitudes, would be the rise and fall of a softer breathing than your own, the slight pressure of a tenderer bosom, the quiet throb of a purer heart, imparting its peacefulness to your troubled one, as if the fond sleeper were involving you in her dream.

Her influence is over you, though she have no existence but in that momentary image. You sink down in a flowery spot, on the borders of sleep and wakefulness, while your thoughts rise before you in pictures, all disconnected, yet all assimilated by a pervading gladsomeness and beauty. The wheeling of gorgeous squadrons that glitter in the sun is succeeded by the merriment of children round the door of a school-house, beneath the glimmering shadow of old trees, at the corner of a rustic lane. You stand in the sunny rain of a summer shower, and wander among the sunny trees of an autumnal wood, and look upward at the brightest of all rainbows, overarching the unbroken sheet of snow, on the American side of Niagara. Your mind struggles pleasantly between the dancing radiance round the hearth of a young man and his recent bride, and the twittering flight of birds in spring about their new-made nest. You feel the merry bounding of a ship before the breeze, and watch the tuneful feet of rosy girls as they twine their last and merriest dance in a splendid ball-room, and find yourself in the brilliant circle of a crowded theatre as the curtain falls over a light and airy scene.

With an involuntary start you seize hold on consciousness, and prove yourself but half awake, by running a doubtful parallel between human life and the hour which has now elapsed. In both you emerge from mystery, pass through a vicissitude that you can but imperfectly control, and are borne onward to another mystery. Now comes the peal of the distant clock, with fainter and fainter strokes as you plunge farther into the wilderness of sleep. It is the knell of a temporary death. Your spirit has departed, and strays, like a free citizen, among the people of a shadowy world, beholding strange sights, yet without wonder or dismay. So calm, perhaps, will be the final change; so undisturbed, as if among familiar things the entrance of the soul to its Eternal home!

THE VILLAGE UNCLE.

AN IMAGINARY RETROSPECT.

COME! another log upon the hearth. True, our little parlor is comfortable, especially here, where the old man sits in his old arm-chair; but on Thanksgiving night the blaze should dance higher up the chimney, and send a shower of sparks into the outer darkness. Toss on an armful of those dry oak chips, the last relics of the Mermaid's knee timbers, the bones of your namesake, Susan. Higher yet, and clearer be the blaze, till our cottage windows glow the ruddiest in the village, and the light of our household mirth flash far across the bay to Nahant. And now, come, Susan, come, my children, draw your chairs round me, all of you. There is a dimness over your figures! You sit quivering indistinctly with each motion of the blaze, which eddies about you like a flood, so that you all have the look of visions, or people that dwell only in the firelight, and will vanish from existence as completely as your own shadows when the flame shall sink among the embers. Hark! let me listen for the swell of the surf; it should be audible a mile inland on a night like this. Yes; there I catch the sound, but only an uncertain murmur, as if a good way down over the beach; though, by the almanac, it is high tide at eight o'clock, and the billows must now be dashing within thirty yards of our door. Ah! the old man's ears are failing him — and so is his eyesight, and perhaps his mind; else you would not all be so shadowy in the blaze of his Thanksgiving fire.

How strangely the past is peeping over the shoulders of the present! To judge by my recollections, it is but a few moments since I sat in another room; yonder model of a vessel was not there, nor the old chest of drawers, nor Susan's profile and mine, in that gilt frame; nothing, in short, except this same fire, which glimmered on books, papers, and a picture, and half discovered my solitary figure in a looking-glass. But it was paler than my rugged old self, and younger, too, by almost half a century. Speak to me, Susan; speak, my beloved ones; for the scene is glimmering on my sight again, and as it brightens you fade away. Oh, I should be loath to lose my treasure of past happiness, and become once more what I was then; a hermit in the depths of my own mind; sometimes yawning over drowsy volumes, and anon a scribbler of wearier trash than what I read; a man who had wandered out of the real world and got into its shadow, where his troubles, joys, and vicissitudes were of such slight stuff that he hardly knew whether he lived, or only dreamed of living. Thank Heaven, I am an old man now, and have done with all such vanities.

Still this dimness of mine eyes! Come nearer, Susan, and stand before the fullest blaze of the hearth. Now I behold you illuminated from head to foot, in your clean cap and decent gown, with the dear lock of gray hair across your forehead, and a quiet smile about your mouth, while the eyes alone are concealed by the red gleam of the fire upon your spectacles. There, you made me tremble again! When the flame quivered, my sweet Susan, you quivered with it, and grew indistinct, as if melting into the warm light, that my last glimpse of you might be as visionary as the first was, full many a year since. Do you remember it? You stood on the little bridge over the brook that runs across King's Beach into the sea. It was twilight; the waves rolling in, the wind sweeping by, the crimson clouds fading in the west, and the silver moon brightening above the hill; and on the bridge were you, fluttering in the breeze like a sea-bird that might skim away at your pleasure. You seemed a daughter of the viewless wind, a creature of the ocean foam and the crimson light, whose merry life was spent in dancing on the crests of the billows, that threw up their spray to support your footsteps. As I drew nearer I fancied you akin to the race of mermaids, and thought how pleasant it would be to dwell with you among the quiet coves, in the shadow of the cliffs, and to roam along secluded beaches of the purest sand; and when our northern shores grew bleak, to haunt the islands, green and lonely, far amid summer seas. And yet it gladdened me, after all this nonsense, to find you nothing but a pretty young girl, sadly perplexed with the rude behavior of the wind about your petticoats.

Thus I did with Susan as with most other things in my earlier days, dipping her image into my mind and coloring it of a thousand fantastic hues, before I could see her as she really was. Now, Susan, for a sober picture of our village! It was a small collection of dwellings that seemed to have been cast up by the sea, with the rockweed and marine plants that it vomits after a storm, or to have come ashore among the pipe staves and other lumber which had been washed from the deck of an eastern schooner. There was just space for the narrow and sandy street, between the beach in front and a precipitous hill that lifted its

rocky forehead in the rear, among a waste of juniper
bushes and the wild growth of a broken pasture. The
village was picturesque in the variety of its edifices,
though all were rude. Here stood a little old hovel,
built perhaps of driftwood; there a row of boat-houses;
and beyond them a two-story dwelling, of dark and
weather-beaten aspect, the whole intermixed with one
or two snug cottages, painted white, a sufficiency of
pigsties, and a shoemaker's shop. Two grocery stores
stood opposite each other, in the centre of the village.
These were the places of resort, at their idle hours, of
a hardy throng of fishermen, in red baize shirts, oilcloth trousers, and boots of brown leather covering the
whole leg ; true seven-league boots, but fitter to wade
the ocean than walk the earth. The wearers seemed
amphibious, as if they did but creep out of salt water
to sun themselves ; nor would it have been wonderful
to see their lower limbs covered with clusters of little
shell-fish, such as cling to rocks and old ship timber
over which the tide ebbs and flows. When their fleet
of boats was weather-bound, the butchers raised their
price, and the spit was busier than the frying-pan :
for this was a place of fish, and known as such, to all
the country round about ; the very air was fishy, being
perfumed with dead sculpins, hardheads, and dogfish
strewn plentifully on the beach. You see, children,
the village is but little changed since your mother
and I were young.

How like a dream it was, when I bent over a pool
of water one pleasant morning, and saw that the ocean
had dashed its spray over me and made me a fisherman ! There were the tarpauling, the baize shirt, the
oil cloth trousers and seven-league boots, and there my
own features, but so reddened with sunburn and sea-

breezes, that methought I had another face, and on
other shoulders too. The sea-gulls and the loons and
I had now all one trade; we skimmed the crested
waves and sought our prey beneath them, the man
with as keen enjoyment as the birds. Always, when
the east grew purple, I launched my dory, my little
flat-bottomed skiff, and rowed cross-handed to Point
Ledge, the Middle Ledge, or, perhaps beyond Egg
Rock; often, too, did I anchor off Dread Ledge, a spot
of peril to ships unpiloted; and sometimes spread an
adventurous sail and tracked across the bay to South
Shore, casting my lines in sight of Scituate. Ere
nightfall, I hauled my skiff high and dry on the beach,
laden with red rock cod, or the white-bellied ones of
deep water; haddock, bearing the black marks of Saint
Peter's fingers near the gills; the long-bearded hake,
whose liver holds oil enough for a midnight lamp; and
now and then a mighty halibut, with a back broad as
my boat. In the autumn, I tolled and caught those
lovely fish, the mackerel. When the wind was high,
— when the whale-boats, anchored off the Point,
nodded their slender masts at each other, and the dories pitched and tossed in the surf, — when Nahant
Beach was thundering three miles off, and the spray
broke a hundred feet in air round the distant base of
Egg Rock, — when the brimful and boisterous sea
threatened to tumble over the street of our village, —
then I made a holiday on shore.

Many such a day did I sit snugly in Mr. Bartlett's
store, attentive to the yarns of Uncle Parker; uncle to
the whole village by right of seniority, but of southern
blood, with no kindred in New England. His figure
is before me now, enthroned upon a mackerel barrel:
a lean old man, of great height, but bent with years,

and twisted into an uncouth shape by seven broken
limbs ; furrowed also, and weather-worn, as if every
gale, for the better part of a century, had caught him
somewhere on the sea. He looked like a harbinger
of tempest ; a shipmate of the Flying Dutchman.
After innumerable voyages aboard men-of-war and
merchant-men, fishing schooners and chebacco boats,
the old salt had become master of a handcart, which
he daily trundled about the vicinity, and sometimes
blew his fish-horn through the streets of Salem. One
of Uncle Parker's eyes had been blown out with gun-
powder, and the other did but glimmer in its socket.
Turning it upward as he spoke, it was his delight to
tell of cruises against the French, and battles with his
own shipmates, when he and an antagonist used to be
seated astride of a sailor's chest, each fastened down
by a spike nail through his trousers, and there to
fight it out. Sometimes he expatiated on the delicious
flavor of the hagden, a greasy and goose-like fowl,
which the sailors catch with hook and line on the
Grand Banks. He dwelt with rapture on an interminable winter at the Isle of Sables, where he had
gladdened himself, amid polar snows, with the rum
and sugar saved from the wreck of a West India
schooner. And wrathfully did he shake his fist, as
he related how a party of Cape Cod men had robbed
him and his companions of their lawful spoil, and
sailed away with every keg of old Jamaica, leaving
him not a drop to drown his sorrow. Villains they
were, and of that wicked brotherhood who are said to
tie lanterns to horses' tails, to mislead the mariner
along the dangerous shores of the Cape.

Even now, I seem to see the group of fishermen,
with that old salt in the midst. One fellow sits on

the counter, a second bestrides an oil barrel, a third lolls at his length on a parcel of new cod lines, and another has planted the tarry seat of his trousers on a heap of salt, which will shortly be sprinkled over a lot of fish. They are a likely set of men. Some have voyaged to the East Indies or the Pacific, and most of them have sailed in Marblehead schooners to New-foundland; a few have been no farther than the Mid-dle Banks, and one or two have always fished along the shore; but, as Uncle Parker used to say, they have all been christened in salt water, and know more than men ever learn in the bushes. A curious figure, by way of contrast, is a fish dealer from far-up country, listening with eyes wide open to narratives that might startle Sinbad the Sailor. Be it well with you, my brethren! Ye are all gone, some to your graves ashore, and others to the depths of ocean; but my faith is strong that ye are happy; for whenever I behold your forms, whether in dream or vision, each departed friend is puffing his long nine, and a mug of the right black strap goes round from lip to lip.

But where was the mermaid in those delightful times? At a certain window near the centre of the village appeared a pretty display of gingerbread men and horses, picture-books and ballads, small fish-hooks, pins, needles, sugar-plums, and brass thimbles, articles on which the young fishermen used to expend their money from pure gallantry. What a picture was Susan behind the counter! A slender maiden, though the child of rugged parents, she had the slimmest of all waists, brown hair curling on her neck, and a com-plexion rather pale, except when the sea-breeze flushed it. A few freckles became beauty-spots beneath her eyelids. How was it, Susan, that you talked and acted so carelessly, yet always for the best, doing whatever was right in your own eyes, and never once doing wrong in mine, nor shocked a taste that had been morbidly sensitive till now? And whence had you that happiest gift of brightening every topic with an unsought gayety, quiet but irresistible, so that even gloomy spirits felt your sunshine, and did not shrink from it? Nature wrought the charm. She made you a frank, simple, kind-hearted, sensible, and mirthful girl. Obeying nature, you did free things without indelicacy, displayed a maiden's thoughts to every eye, and proved yourself as innocent as naked Eve.

It was beautiful to observe how her simple and happy nature mingled itself with mine. She kindled a domestic fire within my heart, and took up her dwelling there, even in that chill and lonesome cavern, hung round with glittering icicles of fancy. She gave me warmth of feeling, while the influence of my mind made her contemplative. I taught her to love the moonlight hour, when the expanse of the encircled bay was smooth as a great mirror and slept in a transparent shadow; while beyond Nahant the wind rippled the dim ocean into a dreamy brightness, which grew faint afar off without becoming gloomier. I held her hand and pointed to the long surf wave, as it rolled calmly on the beach, in an unbroken line of silver; we were silent together till its deep and peaceful murmur had swept by us. When the Sabbath sun shone down into the recesses of the cliffs, I led the mermaid thither, and told her that those huge, gray, shattered rocks, and her native sea, that raged forever like a storm against them, and her own slender beauty in so stern a scene, were all combined into a strain of poetry. But on the Sabbath eve, when her mother had gone early to bed, and her gentle sister had smiled and left us, as we sat alone by the quiet hearth, with household things around, it was her turn to make me feel that here was a deeper poetry, and that this was the dearest hour of all. Thus went on our wooing till I had shot wild fowl enough to feather our bridal bed, and the Daughter of the Sea was mine.

I built a cottage for Susan and myself, and made a gateway in the form of a Gothic arch, by setting up a whale's jaw-bones. We bought a heifer with her first calf, and had a little garden on the hill-side, to supply us with potatoes and green sauce for our fish. Our parlor, small and neat, was ornamented with our two profiles in one gilt frame, and with shells and pretty pebbles on the mantel-piece, selected from the sea's treasury of such things, on Nahant Beach. On the desk, beneath the looking-glass, lay the Bible, which I had begun to read aloud at the book of Genesis, and the singing-book that Susan used for her evening psalm. Except the almanac, we had no other literature. All that I heard of books was when an Indian history, or tale of shipwreck, was sold by a pedlar or wandering subscription man, to some one in the village, and read through its owner's nose to a slumberous auditory. Like my brother fishermen, I grew into the belief that all human erudition was collected in our pedagogue, whose green spectacles and solemn phiz, as he passed to his little school-house amid a waste of sand, might have gained him a diploma from any college in New England. In truth I dreaded him. When our children were old enough to claim his care, you remember, Susan, how I frowned, though you were pleased, at this learned man's encomiums on their proficiency. I feared to trust them even with the alphabet; it was the key to a fatal treasure.

But I loved to lead them by their little hands along the beach, and point to nature in the vast and the minute, the sky, the sea, the green earth, the pebbles, and the shells. Then did I discourse of the mighty works and coextensive goodness of the Deity, with the simple wisdom of a man whose mind had profited by lonely days upon the deep, and his heart by the strong and pure affections of his evening home. Sometimes my voice lost itself in a tremulous depth; for I felt His eye upon me as I spoke. Once, while my wife and all of us were gazing at ourselves, in the mirror left by the tide in a hollow of the sand, I pointed to the pictured heaven below, and bade her observe how religion was strewn everywhere in our path; since even a casual pool of water recalled the idea of that home whither we were travelling, to rest forever with our children. Suddenly, your image, Susan, and all the little faces made up of yours and mine, seemed to fade away and vanish around me, leaving a pale visage like my own of former days within the frame of a large looking-glass. Strange illusion!

My life glided on, the past appearing to mingle with the present and absorb the future, till the whole lies before me at a glance. My manhood has long been waning with a stanch decay; my earlier contemporaries, after lives of unbroken health, are all at rest, without having known the weariness of later age; and now, with a wrinkled forehead and thin white hair as badges of my dignity, I have become the patriarch, the Uncle of the village. I love that name; it widens the circle of my sympathies; it joins all the youthful to my household in the kindred of affection.

Like Uncle Parker, whose rheumatic bones were dashed against Egg Rock, full forty years ago, I am a spinner of long yarns. Seated on the gunwale of a dory, or on the sunny side of a boat-house, where the warmth is grateful to my limbs, or by my own hearth, when a friend or two are there, I overflow with talk, and yet am never tedious. With a broken voice I give utterance to much wisdom. Such, Heaven be praised! is the vigor of my faculties, that many a forgotten usage, and traditions ancient in my youth, and early adventures of myself or others, hitherto effaced by things more recent, acquire new distinctness in my memory. I remember the happy days when the haddock were more numerous on all the fishing grounds than sculpins in the surf; when the deep-water cod swam close in shore, and the dogfish, with his poisonous horn, had not learned to take the hook. I can number every equinoctial storm in which the sea has overwhelmed the street, flooded the cellars of the village, and hissed upon our kitchen hearth. I give the history of the great whale that was landed on Whale Beach, and whose jaws, being now my gateway, will last for ages after my coffin shall have passed beneath them. Thence it is an easy digression to the halibut, scarcely smaller than the whale, which ran out six cod lines, and hauled my dory to the mouth of Boston Harbor, before I could touch him with the gaff.

If melancholy accidents be the theme of conversation, I tell how a friend of mine was taken out of his boat by an enormous shark; and the sad, true tale of a young man on the eve of marriage, who had been nine days missing, when his drowned body floated into the very pathway, on Marblehead Neck, that had often led him to the dwelling of his bride, — as if the dripping corpse would have come where the mourner was. With such awful fidelity did that lover return to fulfil his vows! Another favorite story is of a crazy maiden who conversed with angels and had the gift of prophecy, and whom all the village loved and pitied, though she went from door to door accusing us of sin, exhorting to repentance, and foretelling our destruction by flood or earthquake. If the young men boast their knowledge of the ledges and sunken rocks, I speak of pilots who knew the wind by its scent and the wave by its taste, and could have steered blindfold to any port between Boston and Mount Desert, guided only by the rote of the shore, — the peculiar sound of the surf on each island, beach, and line of rocks, along the coast. Thus do I talk, and all my auditors grow wise while they deem it pastime.

I recollect no happier portion of my life than this, my calm old age. It is like the sunny and sheltered slope of a valley, where, late in the autumn, the grass is greener than in August, and intermixed with golden dandelions that have not been seen till now, since the first warmth of the year. But with me the verdure and the flowers are not frost-bitten in the midst of winter. A playfulness has revisited my mind ; a sympathy with the young and gay ; an unpainful interest in the business of others ; a light and wandering curiosity ; arising, perhaps, from the sense that my toil on earth is ended, and the brief hour till bedtime may be spent in play. Still I have fancied that there is a depth of feeling and reflection under this superficial levity peculiar to one who has lived long and is soon to die.

Show me anything that would make an infant smile, and you shall behold a gleam of mirth over the hoary ruin of my visage. I can spend a pleasant hour in the sun, watching the sports of the village children on the edge of the surf: now they chase the retreating wave far down over the wet sand ; now it steals softly up to kiss their naked feet; now it comes onward with threatening front, and roars after the laughing crew, as they scamper beyond its reach. Why should not an old man be merry too, when the great sea is at play with those little children? I delight, also, to follow in the wake of a pleasure party of young men and girls, strolling along the beach after an early supper at the Point. Here, with handkerchiefs at nose, they bend over a heap of eel-grass, entangled in which is a dead skate, so oddly accoutred with two legs and a long tail that they mistake him for a drowned animal. A few steps farther the ladies scream, and the gentlemen make ready to protect them against a young shark of the dogfish kind, rolling with a lifelike motion in the tide that has thrown him up. Next, they are smit with wonder at the black shells of a wagon load of live lobsters, packed in rockweed for the country market. And when they reach the fleet of dories, just hauled ashore after the day's fishing, how do I laugh in my sleeve, and sometimes roar outright, at the simplicity of these young folks and the sly humor of the fishermen! In winter, when our village is thrown into a bustle by the arrival of perhaps a score of country dealers, bargaining for frozen fish, to be transported hundreds of miles, and eaten fresh in Vermont or Canada, I am a pleased but idle spectator in the throng. For I launch my boat no more.

When the shore was solitary I have found a pleasure that seemed even to exalt my mind, in observing the sports or contentions of two gulls, as they wheeled and hovered about each other, with hoarse screams, one moment flapping on the foam of the wave, and then soaring aloft, till their white bosoms melted into the upper sunshine. In the calm of the summer sunset I drag my aged limbs, with a little ostentation of activity, because I am so old, up to the rocky brow of the hill. There I see the white sails of many a vessel, outward bound or homeward from afar, and the black trail of a vapor behind the eastern steamboat; there, too, is the sun going down, but not in gloom, and there the illimitable ocean mingling with the sky, to remind me of Eternity.

But sweetest of all is the hour of cheerful musing and pleasant talk, that comes between the dusk and the lighted candle, by my glowing fireside. And never, even on the first Thanksgiving night, when Susan and I sat alone with our hopes, nor the second, when a stranger had been sent to gladden us, and be the visible image of our affection, did I feel such joy as now. All that belong to me are here; Death has taken none, nor Disease kept them away, nor Strife divided them from their parents or each other; with neither poverty nor riches to disturb them, nor the misery of desires beyond their lot, they have kept New England's festival round the patriarch's board. For I am a patriarch! Here I sit among my descendants, in my old arm-chair and immemorial corner, while the firelight throws an appropriate glory round my venerable frame. Susan! My children! Something whispers me that this happiest hour must be the final one, and that nothing remains but to bless you all, and depart with a treasure of recollected joys to heaven. Will you meet me there? Alas! your figures grow indistinct, fading into pictures on the air, and now to fainter outlines, while the fire is glimmering on the walls of a familiar room, and shows the book that I flung down, and the sheet that I left half written, some fifty years ago. I lift my eyes to the looking-glass and perceive myself alone, unless those be the mermaid's features retiring into the depths of the mirror with a tender and melancholy smile.

Ah! one feels a chillness, not bodily, but about the heart, and, moreover, a foolish dread of looking behind him, after these pastimes. I can imagine precisely how a magician would sit down in gloom and terror, after dismissing the shadows that had personated dead or distant people, and stripping his cavern of the unreal splendor which had changed it to a palace. And now for a moral to my reverie. Shall it be that, since fancy can create so bright a dream of happiness, it were better to dream on from youth to age, than to awake and strive doubtfully for something real. Oh, the slight tissue of a dream can no more preserve us from the stern reality of misfortune than a robe of cobweb could repel the wintry blast. Be this the moral then. In chaste and warm affections, humble wishes, and honest toil for some useful end, there is health for the mind, and quiet for the heart, the prospect of a happy life, and the fairest hope of heaven.

THE AMBITIOUS GUEST.

ONE September night a family had gathered round
their hearth, and piled it high with the driftwood of
mountain streams, the dry cones of the pine, and the
splintered ruins of great trees that had come crashing
down the precipice. Up the chimney roared the fire,
and brightened the room with its broad blaze. The
faces of the father and mother had a sober gladness;
the children laughed; the eldest daughter was the
image of Happiness at seventeen; and the aged grandmother, who sat knitting in the warmest place, was the
image of Happiness grown old. They had found the
" herb, heart's-ease," in the bleakest spot of all New
England. This family were situated in the Notch of
the White Hills, where the wind was sharp throughout
the year, and pitilessly cold in the winter, — giving
their cottage all its fresh inclemency before it descended on the valley of the Saco. They dwelt in a
cold spot and a dangerous one; for a mountain tow-
ered above their heads, so steep, that the stones would
often rumble down its sides and startle them at midnight.

The daughter had just uttered some simple jest that
filled them all with mirth, when the wind came through
the Notch and seemed to pause before their cottage —
rattling the door, with a sound of wailing and lamentation, before it passed into the valley. For a moment
it saddened them, though there was nothing unusual in
the tones. But the family were glad again when they

perceived that the latch was lifted by some traveller, whose footsteps had been unheard amid the dreary blast which heralded his approach, and wailed as he was entering, and went moaning away from the door.

Though they dwelt in such a solitude, these people held daily converse with the world. The romantic pass of the Notch is a great artery, through which the life-blood of internal commerce is continually throbbing between Maine, on one side, and the Green Mountains and the shores of the St. Lawrence, on the other. The stage-coach always drew up before the door of the cottage. The wayfarer, with no companion but his staff, paused here to exchange a word, that the sense of loneliness might not utterly overcome him ere he could pass through the cleft of the mountain, or reach the first house in the valley. And here the teamster, on his way to Portland market, would put up for the night; and, if a bachelor, might sit an hour beyond the usual bedtime, and steal a kiss from the mountain maid at parting. It was one of those primitive taverns where the traveller pays only for food and lodging, but meets with a homely kindness beyond all price. When the footsteps were heard, therefore, between the outer door and the inner one, the whole family rose up, grandmother, children, and all, as if about to welcome some one who belonged to them, and whose fate was linked with theirs.

The door was opened by a young man. His face at first wore the melancholy expression, almost despondency, of one who travels a wild and bleak road, at nightfall and alone, but soon brightened up when he saw the kindly warmth of his reception. He felt his heart spring forward to meet them all, from the old woman, who wiped a chair with her apron, to the little child that held out its arms to him. One glance and smile placed the stranger on a footing of innocent familiarity with the eldest daughter.

"Ah, this fire is the right thing!" cried he, "especially when there is such a pleasant circle round it. I am quite benumbed; for the Notch is just like the pipe of a great pair of bellows; it has blown a terrible blast in my face all the way from Bartlett."

"Then you are going towards Vermont?" said the master of the house, as he helped to take a light knapsack off the young man's shoulders.

"Yes; to Burlington, and far enough beyond," replied he. "I meant to have been at Ethan Crawford's to-night; but a pedestrian lingers along such a road as this. It is no matter; for, when I saw this good fire, and all your cheerful faces, I felt as if you had kindled it on purpose for me, and were waiting my arrival. So I shall sit down among you, and make myself at home."

The frank-hearted stranger had just drawn his chair to the fire when something like a heavy footstep was heard without, rushing down the steep side of the mountain, as with long and rapid strides, and taking such a leap in passing the cottage as to strike the opposite precipice. The family held their breath, because they knew the sound, and their guest held his by instinct.

"The old mountain has thrown a stone at us, for fear we should forget him," said the landlord, recovering himself. "He sometimes nods his head and threatens to come down; but we are old neighbors, and agree together pretty well upon the whole. Besides we have a sure place of refuge hard by if he should be coming in good earnest."

Let us now suppose the stranger to have finished his supper of bear's meat; and, by his natural felicity of manner, to have placed himself on a footing of kindness with the whole family, so that they talked as freely together as if he belonged to their mountain brood. He was of a proud, yet gentle spirit — haughty and reserved among the rich and great; but ever ready to stoop his head to the lowly cottage door, and be like a brother or a son at the poor man's fireside. In the household of the Notch he found warmth and simplicity of feeling, the pervading intelligence of New England, and a poetry of native growth, which they had gathered when they little thought of it from the mountain peaks and chasms, and at the very threshold of their romantic and dangerous abode. He had travelled far and alone; his whole life, indeed, had been a solitary path; for, with the lofty caution of his nature, he had kept himself apart from those who might otherwise have been his companions. The family, too, though so kind and hospitable, had that consciousness of unity among themselves, and separation from the world at large, which, in every domestic circle, should still keep a holy place where no stranger may intrude. But this evening a prophetic sympathy impelled the refined and educated youth to pour out his heart before the simple mountaineers, and constrained them to answer him with the same free confidence. And thus it should have been. Is not the kindred of a common fate a closer tie than that of birth?

The secret of the young man's character was a high and abstracted ambition. He could have borne to live an undistinguished life, but not to be forgotten in the grave. Yearning desire had been transformed to hope; and hope, long cherished, had become like certainty,

that, obscurely as he journeyed now, a glory was to
beam on all his pathway, — though not, perhaps, while
he was treading it. But when posterity should gaze
back into the gloom of what was now the present, they
would trace the brightness of his footsteps, brightening
as meaner glories faded, and confess that a gifted one
had passed from his cradle to his tomb with none to
recognize him.

"As yet," cried the stranger — his cheek glowing
and his eye flashing with enthusiasm — "as yet, I
have done nothing. Were I to vanish from the earth
to-morrow, none would know so much of me as you :
that a nameless youth came up at nightfall from the
valley of the Saco, and opened his heart to you in the
evening, and passed through the Notch by sunrise,
and was seen no more. Not a soul would ask, ' Who
was he ? Whither did the wanderer go ? ' But I
cannot die till I have achieved my destiny. Then, let
Death come ! I shall have built my monument ! "

There was a continual flow of natural emotion, gushing forth amid abstracted reverie, which enabled the
family to understand this young man's sentiments,
though so foreign from their own. With quick sensibility of the ludicrous, he blushed at the ardor into
which he had been betrayed.

"You laugh at me," said he, taking the eldest
daughter's hand, and laughing himself. "You think
my ambition as nonsensical as if I were to freeze myself to death on the top of Mount Washington, only
that people might spy at me from the country round
about. And, truly, that would be a noble pedestal for
a man's statue ! "

"It is better to sit here by this fire," answered the
girl, blushing, "and be comfortable and contented,
though nobody thinks about us."

" I suppose," said her father, after a fit of musing, " there is something natural in what the young man says ; and if my mind had been turned that way, I might have felt just the same. It is strange, wife, how his talk has set my head running on things that are pretty certain never to come to pass."

"Perhaps they may," observed the wife. "Is the man thinking what he will do when he is a widower?"

"No, no!" cried he, repelling the idea with reproachful kindness. "When I think of your death, Esther, I think of mine, too. But I was wishing we had a good farm in Bartlett, or Bethlehem, or Littleton, or some other township round the White Mountains ; but not where they could tumble on our heads. I should want to stand well with my neighbors and be called Squire, and sent to General Court for a term or two ; for a plain, honest man may do as much good there as a lawyer. And when I should be grown quite an old man, and you an old woman, so as not to be long apart, I might die happy enough in my bed, and leave you all crying around me. A slate gravestone would suit me as well as a marble one — with just my name and age, and a verse of a hymn, and something to let people know that I lived an honest man and died a Christian."

" There now ! " exclaimed the stranger ; " it is our nature to desire a monument, be it slate or marble, or a pillar of granite, or a glorious memory in the universal heart of man."

" We 're in a strange way, to-night," said the wife, with tears in her eyes. " They say it 's a sign of something, when folks' minds go a wandering so. Hark to the children ! "

They listened accordingly. The younger children

had been put to bed in another room, but with an open door between, so that they could be heard talking busily among themselves. One and all seemed to have caught the infection from the fireside circle, and were outvying each other in wild wishes, and childish projects of what they would do when they came to be men and women. At length a little boy, instead of addressing his brothers and sisters, called out to his mother.

"I'll tell you what I wish, mother," cried he. "I want you and father and grandma'm, and all of us, and the stranger too, to start right away, and go and take a drink out of the basin of the Flume!"

Nobody could help laughing at the child's notion of leaving a warm bed, and dragging them from a cheerful fire, to visit the basin of the Flume, — a brook, which tumbles over the precipice, deep within the Notch. The boy had hardly spoken when a wagon rattled along the road, and stopped a moment before the door. It appeared to contain two or three men, who were cheering their hearts with the rough chorus of a song, which resounded, in broken notes, between the cliffs, while the singers hesitated whether to continue their journey or put up here for the night."

"Father," said the girl, "they are calling you by name."

But the good man doubted whether they had really called him, and was unwilling to show himself too solicitous of gain by inviting people to patronize his house. He therefore did not hurry to the door; and the lash being soon applied, the travellers plunged into the Notch, still singing and laughing, though their music and mirth came back drearily from the heart of the mountain.

" There, mother ! " cried the boy, again. " They 'd have given us a ride to the Flume."

Again they laughed at the child's pertinacious fancy for a night ramble. But it happened that a light cloud passed over the daughter's spirit ; she looked gravely into the fire, and drew a breath that was almost a sigh. It forced its way, in spite of a little struggle to repress it. Then starting and blushing, she looked quickly round the circle, as if they had caught a glimpse into her bosom. The stranger asked what she had been thinking of.

" Nothing," answered she, with a downcast smile. " Only I felt lonesome just then."

" Oh, I have always had a gift of feeling what is in other people's hearts," said he, half seriously. " Shall I tell the secrets of yours? For I know what to think when a young girl shivers by a warm hearth, and complains of lonesomeness at her mother's side. Shall I put these feelings into words? "

" They would not be a girl's feelings any longer if they could be put into words," replied the mountain nymph, laughing, but avoiding his eye.

All this was said apart. Perhaps a germ of love was springing in their hearts, so pure that it might blossom in Paradise, since it could not be matured on earth ; for women worship such gentle dignity as his ; and the proud, contemplative, yet kindly soul is oftenest captivated by simplicity like hers. But while they spoke softly, and he was watching the happy sadness, the lightsome shadows, the shy yearnings of a maiden's nature, the wind through the Notch took a deeper and drearier sound. It seemed, as the fanciful stranger said, like the choral strain of the spirits of the blast, who in old Indian times had their dwelling among these mountains, and made their heights and recesses a sacred region. There was a wail along the road, as if a funeral were passing. To chase away the gloom, the family threw pine branches on their fire, till the dry leaves crackled and the flame arose, discovering once again a scene of peace and humble happiness. The light hovered about them fondly, and caressed them all. There were the little faces of the children, peeping from their bed apart, and here the father's frame of strength, the mother's subdued and careful mien, the high-browed youth, the budding girl, and the good old grandam, still knitting in the warmest place. The aged woman looked up from her task, and, with fingers ever busy, was the next to speak.

" Old folks have their notions," said she, " as well as young ones. You 've been wishing and planning; and letting your heads run on one thing and another, till you 've set my mind a wandering too. Now what should an old woman wish for, when she can go but a step or two before she comes to her grave? Children, it will haunt me night and day till I tell you."

" What is it, mother? " cried the husband and wife at once.

Then the old woman, with an air of mystery which drew the circle closer round the fire, informed them that she had provided her grave-clothes some years before, — a nice linen shroud, a cap with a muslin ruff, and everything of a finer sort than she had worn since her wedding day. But this evening an old superstition had strangely recurred to her. It used to be said, in her younger days, that if anything were amiss with a corpse, if only the ruff were not smooth, or the cap did not set right, the corpse in the coffin and beneath the clods would strive to put up its cold hands and arrange it. The bare thought made her nervous.

"Don't talk so, grandmother!" said the girl, shud-dering.

"Now," — continued the old woman, with singular earnestness, yet smiling strangely at her own folly, — "I want one of you, my children — when your mother is dressed and in the coffin — I want one of you to hold a looking-glass over my face. Who knows but I may take a glimpse at myself, and see whether all's right?"

"Cld and young, we dream of graves and monu-ments," murmured the stranger youth. "I wonder how mariners feel when the ship is sinking, and they, unknown and undistinguished, are to be buried to-gether in the ocean — that wide and nameless sep-ulchre?"

For a moment, the old woman's ghastly conception so engrossed the minds of her hearers that a sound abroad in the night, rising like the roar of a blast, had grown broad, deep, and terrible, before the fated group were conscious of it. The house and all within it trembled; the foundations of the earth seemed to be shaken, as if this awful sound were the peal of the last trump. Young and old exchanged one wild glance, and remained an instant, pale, affrighted, with-out utterance, or power to move. Then the same shriek burst simultaneously from all their lips.

"The Slide! The Slide!"

The simplest words must intimate, but not portray, the unutterable horror of the catastrophe. The vic-tims rushed from their cottage, and sought refuge in what they deemed a safer spot — where, in contempla-tion of such an emergency, a sort of barrier had been reared. Alas! they had quitted their security, and fled right into the pathway of destruction. Down came the whole side of the mountain, in a cataract of ruin. Just before it reached the house, the stream broke into two branches — shivered not a window there, but overwhelmed the whole vicinity, blocked up the road, and annihilated everything in its dreadful course. Long ere the thunder of the great Slide had ceased to roar among the mountains, the mortal agony had been endured, and the victims were at peace. Their bodies were never found.

The next morning, the light smoke was seen stealing from the cottage chimney up the mountain side. Within, the fire was yet smouldering on the hearth, and the chairs in a circle round it, as if the inhabitants had but gone forth to view the devastation of the Slide, and would shortly return, to thank Heaven for their miraculous escape. All had left separate tokens, by which those who had known the family were made to shed a tear for each. Who has not heard their name? The story has been told far and wide, and will forever be a legend of these mountains. Poets have sung their fate.

There were circumstances which led some to suppose that a stranger had been received into the cottage on this awful night, and had shared the catastrophe of all its inmates. Others denied that there were sufficient grounds for such a conjecture. Woe for the high-souled youth, with his dream of Earthly Immortality! His name and person utterly unknown; his history, his way of life, his plans, a mystery never to be solved, his death and his existence equally a doubt! Whose was the agony of that death moment?

THE SISTER YEARS.

LAST night, between eleven and twelve o'clock, when the Old Year was leaving her final footprints on the borders of Time's empire, she found herself in possession of a few spare moments, and sat down — of all places in the world — on the steps of our new City Hall. The wintry moonlight showed that she looked weary of body and sad of heart, like many another wayfarer of earth. Her garments, having been exposed to much foul weather and rough usage, were in very ill condition; and as the hurry of her journey had never before allowed her to take an instant's rest, her shoes were so worn as to be scarcely worth the mending. But, after trudging only a little distance farther, this poor Old Year was destined to enjoy a long, long sleep. I forgot to mention that, when she seated herself on the steps, she deposited by her side a very capacious bandbox, in which, as is the custom among travellers of her sex, she carried a great deal of valuable property. Besides this luggage, there was a folio book under her arm, very much resembling the annual volume of a newspaper. Placing this volume across her knees, and resting her elbows upon it, with her forehead in her hands, the weary, bedraggled, world-worn Old Year heaved a heavy sigh, and appeared to be taking no very pleasant retrospect of her past existence.

While she thus awaited the midnight knell that was to summon her to the innumerable sisterhood of departed Years, there came a young maiden treading lightsomely on tiptoe along the street, from the direction of the Railroad Depot. She was evidently a stranger, and perhaps had come to town by the evening train of cars. There was a smiling cheerfulness in this fair maiden's face, which bespoke her fully confident of a kind reception from the multitude of people with whom she was soon to form acquaintance. Her dress was rather too airy for the season, and was bedizened with fluttering ribbons and other vanities, which were likely soon to be rent away by the fierce storms or to fade in the hot sunshine, amid which she was to pursue her changeful course. But still she was a wonderfully pleasant looking figure, and had so much promise and such an indescribable hopefulness in her aspect, that hardly anybody could meet her without anticipating some very desirable thing — the consummation of some long-sought good — from her kind offices. A few dismal characters there may be, here and there about the world, who have so often been trifled with by young maidens as promising as she, that they have now ceased to pin any faith upon the skirts of the New Year. But, for my own part, I have great faith in her; and should I live to see fifty more such, still, from each of these successive sisters, I shall reckon upon receiving something that will be worth living for.

The New Year — for this young maiden was no less a personage — carried all her goods and chattels in a basket of no great size or weight, which hung upon her arm. She greeted the disconsolate Old Year with great affection, and sat down beside her on the steps of the City Hall, waiting for the signal to begin her rambles through the world. The two were own sisters, being both granddaughters of Time: and though one looked so much older than the other, it was rather owing to hardships and trouble than to age, since there was but a twelvemonth's difference between them.

"Well, my dear sister," said the New Year, after the first salutations, "you look almost tired to death. What have you been about during your sojourn in this part of Infinite Space?"

"Oh, I have it all recorded here in my Book of Chronicles," answered the Old Year, in a heavy tone. "There is nothing that would amuse you; and you will soon get sufficient knowledge of such matters from your own personal experience. It is but tiresome reading."

Nevertheless, she turned over the leaves of the folio, and glanced at them by the light of the moon, feeling an irresistible spell of interest in her own biography, although its incidents were remembered without pleasure. The volume, though she termed it her Book of Chronicles, seemed to be neither more nor less than the " Salem Gazette " for 1838; in the accuracy of which journal this sagacious Old Year had so much confidence that she deemed it needless to record her history with her own pen.

" What have you been doing in the political way? " asked the New Year.

" Why, my course here in the United States," said the Old Year, — " though perhaps I ought to blush at the confession, — my political course, I must acknowledge, has been rather vacillatory, sometimes inclining towards the Whigs — then causing the Administration party to shout for triumph — and now again uplifting what seemed the almost prostrate banner of the Opposition ; so that historians will hardly know what to make of me in this respect. But the Loco Focos " —

" I do not like these party nicknames," interrupted her sister, who seemed remarkably touchy about some points. " Perhaps we shall part in better humor if we avoid any political discussion."

" With all my heart," replied the Old Year, who had already been tormented half to death with squabbles of this kind. " I care not if the names of Whig or Tory, with their interminable brawls about Banks and the Sub-Treasury, Abolition, Texas, the Florida War, and a million of other topics — which you will learn soon enough for your own comfort — I care not, I say, if no whisper of these matters ever reaches my ears again. Yet they have occupied so large a share of my attention that I scarcely know what else to tell you. There has indeed been a curious sort of war on the Canada border, where blood has streamed in the names of Liberty and Patriotism ; but it must remain for some future, perhaps far distant Year, to tell whether or no those holy names have been rightfully invoked. Nothing so much depresses me, in my view of mortal affairs, as to see high energies wasted, and human life and happiness thrown away, for ends that appear oftentimes unwise, and still oftener remain unaccomplished. But the wisest people and the best keep a steadfast faith that the progress of Mankind is onward and upward, and that the toil and anguish of the path serve to wear away the imperfections of the Immortal Pilgrim, and will be felt no more when they have done their office."

" Perhaps," cried the hopeful New Year, — " perhaps I shall see that happy day ! "

" I doubt whether it be so close at hand," answered

the Old Year, gravely smiling. "You will soon grow weary of looking for that blessed consummation, and will turn for amusement (as has frequently been my own practice) to the affairs of some sober little city, like this of Salem. Here we sit on the steps of the new City Hall, which has been completed under my administration; and it would make you laugh to see how the game of politics, of which the Capitol at Washington is the great chess-board, is here played in miniature. Burning Ambition finds its fuel here; here Patriotism speaks boldly in the people's behalf, and virtuous Economy demands retrenchment in the emoluments of a lamplighter; here the Aldermen range their senatorial dignity around the Mayor's chair of state, and the Common Council feel that they have liberty in charge. In short, human weakness and strength, passion and policy, Man's tendencies, his aims and modes of pursuing them, his individual character and his character in the mass, may be studied almost as well here as on the theatre of nations: and with this great advantage, that, be the lesson ever so disastrous, its Liliputian scope still makes the beholder smile."

"Have you done much for the improvement of the City?" asked the New Year. "Judging from what little I have seen, it appears to be ancient and time-worn."

"I have opened the Railroad," said the elder Year, "and half a dozen times a day you will hear the bell (which once summoned the Monks of a Spanish Convent to their devotions) announcing the arrival or departure of the cars. Old Salem now wears a much livelier expression than when I first beheld her. Strangers rumble down from Boston by hundreds at a time. New faces throng in Essex Street. Railroad hacks and omnibuses rattle over the pavements. There is a perceptible increase of oyster shops, and other establishments for the accommodation of a transitory diurnal multitude. But a more important change awaits the venerable town. An immense accumulation of musty prejudices will be carried off by the free circulation of society. A peculiarity of character, of which the inhabitants themselves are hardly sensible, will be rubbed down and worn away by the attrition of foreign substances. Much of the result will be good ; there will likewise be a few things not so good. Whether for better or worse, there will be a probable diminution of the moral influence of wealth, and the sway of an aristocratic class, which, from an era far beyond my memory, has held firmer dominion here than in any other New England town."

The Old Year having talked away nearly all of her little remaining breath, now closed her Book of Chronicles, and was about to take her departure. But her sister detained her a while longer, by inquiring the contents of the huge bandbox which she was so painfully lugging along with her.

"These are merely a few trifles," replied the Old Year, "which I have picked up in my rambles, and am going to deposit in the receptacle of things past and forgotten. We sisterhood of Years never carry anything really valuable out of the world with us. Here are patterns of most of the fashions which I brought into vogue, and which have already lived out their allotted term. You will supply their place with others equally ephemeral. Here, put up in little China pots, like rouge, is a considerable lot of beautiful women's bloom, which the disconsolate fair ones

owe me a bitter grudge for stealing. I have likewise
a quantity of men's dark hair, instead of which, I have
left gray locks, or none at all. The tears of widows
and other afflicted mortals, who have received comfort during the last twelve months, are preserved in
some dozens of essence bottles, well corked and sealed.
I have several bundles of love-letters, eloquently
breathing an eternity of burning passion, which grew
cold and perished almost before the ink was dry.
Moreover, here is an assortment of many thousand
broken promises, and other broken ware, all very light
and packed into little space. The heaviest articles
in my possession are a large parcel of disappointed
hopes, which a little while ago were buoyant enough
to have inflated Mr. Lauriat's balloon."

"I have a fine lot of hopes here in my basket,"
remarked the New Year. "They are a sweet-smelling
flower — a species of rose."

"They soon lose their perfume," replied the sombre
Old Year. "What else have you brought to insure a
welcome from the discontented race of mortals?"

"Why, to say the truth, little or nothing else," said
her sister, with a smile, — "save a few new Annuals
and Almanacs, and some New Year's gifts for the
children. But I heartily wish well to poor mortals,
and mean to do all I can for their improvement and
happiness."

"It is a good resolution," rejoined the Old Year;
"and, by the way, I have a plentiful assortment of
good resolutions, which have now grown so stale and
musty that I am ashamed to carry them any farther.
Only for fear that the City authorities would send Constable Mansfield with a warrant after me, I should toss
them into the street at once. Many other matters go

to make up the contents of my bandbox, but the whole lot would not fetch a single bid, even at an auction of worn-out furniture; and as they are worth nothing either to you or anybody else. I need not trouble you with a longer catalogue."

"And must I also pick up such worthless luggage in my travels?" asked the New Year.

"Most certainly — and well, if you have no heavier load to bear," replied the other. "And now, my dear sister, I must bid you farewell, earnestly advising and exhorting you to expect no gratitude nor good-will from this peevish, unreasonable, inconsiderate, ill-intending, and worse-behaving world. However warmly its inhabitants may seem to welcome you, yet, do what you may, and lavish on them what means of happiness you please, they will still be complaining, still craving what it is not in your power to give, still looking forward to some other Year for the accomplishment of projects which ought never to have been formed, and which, if successful, would only provide new occasions of discontent. If these ridiculous people ever see anything tolerable in you, it will be after you are gone forever."

"But I," cried the fresh-hearted New Year, "I shall try to leave men wiser than I find them. I will offer them freely whatever good gifts Providence permits me to distribute, and will tell them to be thankful for what they have, and humbly hopeful for more; and surely, if they are not absolute fools, they will condescend to be happy, and will allow me to be a happy Year. For my happiness must depend on them."

"Alas for you, then, my poor sister!" said the Old Year, sighing, as she uplifted her burden. "We, grandchildren of Time, are born to trouble. Happi-

ness, they say, dwells in the mansions of Eternity;
but we can only lead mortals thither, step by step, with
reluctant murmurings, and ourselves must perish on
the threshold. But hark! my task is done."

The clock in the tall steeple of Dr. Emerson's
church struck twelve; there was a response from Dr.
Flint's, in the opposite quarter of the city; and while
the strokes were yet dropping into the air, the Old
Year either flitted or faded away, — and not the wisdom and might of Angels, to say nothing of the re-
morseful yearnings of the millions who had used her
ill, could have prevailed with that departed Year to
return one step. But she, in the company of Time
and all her kindred, must hereafter hold a reckoning
with Mankind. So shall it be, likewise, with the maid-
enly New Year, who, as the clock ceased to strike, arose
from the steps of the City Hall, and set out rather
timorously on her earthly course.

"A happy New Year!" cried a watchman, eying
her figure very questionably, but without the least
suspicion that he was addressing the New Year in
person.

"Thank you kindly! said the New Year; and she
gave the watchman one of the roses of hope from her
basket. "May this flower keep a sweet smell, long
after I have bidden you good-by."

Then she stepped on more briskly through the silent
streets; and such as were awake at the moment heard
her footfall, and said, — "The New Year is come!"
Wherever there was a knot of midnight roisterers they
quaffed her health. She sighed, however, to perceive
that the air was tainted — as the atmosphere of this
world must continually be — with the dying breaths of
mortals who had lingered just long enough for her to

bury them. But there were millions left alive to
rejoice at her coming; and so she pursued her way
with confidence, strewing emblematic flowers on the
doorstep of almost every dwelling, which some persons
will gather up and wear in their bosoms, and others
will trample under foot. The Carrier Boy can only
say further that, early this morning, she filled his basket with New Year's Addresses, assuring him that the
whole City, with our new Mayor, and the Aldermen
and Common Council at its head, would make a general
rush to secure copies. Kind Patrons, will not you re-
deem the pledge of the NEW YEAR?

SNOW-FLAKES.

THERE is snow in yonder cold gray sky of the morning! — and, through the partially frosted window panes, I love to watch the gradual beginning of the storm. A few feathery flakes are scattered widely through the air, and hover downward with uncertain flight, now almost alighting on the earth, now whirled again aloft into remote regions of the atmosphere. These are not the big flakes, heavy with moisture, which melt as they touch the ground, and are portentous of a soaking rain. It is to be, in good earnest, a wintry storm. The two or three people visible on the sidewalks have an aspect of endurance, a blue-nosed, frosty fortitude, which is evidently assumed in anticipation of a comfortless and blustering day. By nightfall, or at least before the sun sheds another glimmering smile upon us, the street and our little garden will be heaped with mountain snow-drifts. The soil, already frozen for weeks past, is prepared to sustain whatever burden may be laid upon it; and, to a northern eye, the landscape will lose its melancholy bleakness and acquire a beauty of its own, when Mother Earth, like her children, shall have put on the fleecy garb of her winter's wear. The cloud spirits are slowly weaving her white mantle. As yet, indeed, there is barely a rime like hoarfrost over the brown surface of the street; the withered grass of the grass-plat is still discernible; and the slated roofs of the houses do but begin to look gray instead of black.

All the snow that has yet fallen within the circumfer‑ ence of my view, were it heaped up together, would hardly equal the hillock of a grave. Thus gradually, by silent and stealthy influences, are great changes wrought. These little snow particles, which the storm spirit flings by handfuls through the air, will bury the great earth under their accumulated mass, nor permit her to behold her sister sky again for dreary months. We, likewise, shall lose sight of our mother's familiar visage, and must content ourselves with looking heaven‑ ward the oftener.

Now, leaving the storm to do his appointed office, let us sit down, pen in hand, by our fireside. Gloomy as it may seem, there is an influence productive of cheerfulness, and favorable to imaginative thought, in the atmosphere of a snowy day. The native of a southern clime may woo the muse beneath the heavy shade of summer foliage, reclining on banks of turf, while the sound of singing birds and warbling rivulets chimes in with the music of his soul. In our brief summer, I do not think, but only exist in the vague enjoyment of a dream. My hour of inspiration — if that hour ever comes — is when the green log hisses upon the hearth, and the bright flame, brighter for the gloom of the chamber, rustles high up the chimney, and the coals drop tinkling down among the glowing heaps of ashes. When the casement rattles in the gust, and the snow-flakes or the sleety raindrops pelt hard against the window panes, then I spread out my sheet of paper, with the certainty that thoughts and fancies will gleam forth upon it like stars at twilight, or like violets in May, — perhaps to fade as soon. However transitory their glow, they at least shine amid the darksome shadow which the clouds of the

outward sky fling through the room. Blessed, therefore, and reverently welcomed by me, her true-born
son, be New England's winter, which makes us, one
and all, the nurslings of the storm, and sings a familiar lullaby even in the wildest shriek of the December
blast. Now look we forth again, and see how much of
his task the storm spirit has done.

Slow and sure! He has the day, perchance the
week, before him, and may take his own time to accomplish Nature's burial in snow. A smooth mantle
is scarcely yet thrown over the withered grass-plat,
and the dry stocks of annuals still thrust themselves
through the white surface in all parts of the garden.
The leafless rose-bushes stand shivering in a shallow
snow-drift, looking, poor things! as disconsolate as if
they possessed a human consciousness of the dreary
scene. This is a sad time for the shrubs that do not
perish with the summer; they neither live nor die;
what they retain of life seems but the chilling sense of
death. Very sad are the flower shrubs in midwinter!
The roofs of the houses are now all white, save where
the eddying wind has kept them bare at the bleak corners. To discern the real intensity of the storm, we
must fix upon some distant object, — as yonder spire,
— and observe how the riotous gust fights with the
descending snow throughout the intervening space.
Sometimes the entire prospect is obscured; then,
again, we have a distinct, but transient, glimpse of
the tall steeple, like a giant's ghost; and now the
dense wreaths sweep between, as if demons were flinging snow-drifts at each other in mid-air. Look next
into the street, where we have an amusing parallel to
the combat of those fancied demons in the upper regions. It is a snow battle of school-boys. What a

pretty satire on war and military glory might be written, in the form of a child's story, by describing the snow-ball fights of two rival schools, the alternate defeats and victories of each, and the final triumph of one party, or perhaps of neither! What pitched battles, worthy to be chanted in Homeric strains! What storming of fortresses, built all of massive snow blocks! What feats of individual prowess, and embodied onsets of martial enthusiasm! And when some well-contested and decisive victory had put a period to the war, both armies should unite to build a lofty monument of snow upon the battle-field and crown it with the victor's statue, hewn of the same frozen marble. In a few days or weeks thereafter the passer-by would observe a shapeless mound upon the level common; and, unmindful of the famous victory, would ask, — " How came it there? Who reared it? And what means it?" The shattered pedestal of many a battle monument has provoked these questions when none could answer.

Turn we again to the fireside, and sit musing there, lending our ears to the wind, till perhaps it shall seem like an articulate voice, and dictate wild and airy matter for the pen. Would it might inspire me to sketch out the personification of a New England winter! And that idea, if I can seize the snow-wreathed figures that flit before my fancy, shall be the theme of the next page.

How does Winter herald his approach? By the shrieking blast of latter autumn, which is Nature's cry of lamentation, as the destroyer rushes among the shivering groves where she has lingered, and scatters the sear leaves upon the tempest. When that cry is heard, the people wrap themselves in cloaks, and shake their heads disconsolately, saying,—·"Winter is at hand!" Then the axe of the woodcutter echoes sharp and diligently in the forest; then the coal merchants rejoice, because each shriek of Nature in her agony adds something to the price of coal per ton then the peat smoke spreads its aromatic fragrance through the atmosphere. A few days more; and at eventide the children look out of the window, and dimly perceive the flaunting of a snowy mantle in the air. It is stern Winter's vesture. They crowd around the hearth, and cling to their mother's gown, or press between their father's knees, affrighted by the hollow roaring voice that bellows adown the wide flue of the chimney. It is the voice of Winter; and when parents and children hear it, they shudder and exclaim, — "Winter is come! Cold Winter has begun his reign already!" Now, throughout New England, each hearth becomes an altar, sending up the smoke of a continued sacrifice to the immitigable deity who tyrannizes over forest, country side, and town. Wrapped in his white mantle, his staff a huge icicle, his beard and hair a wind-tossed snow-drift, he travels over the land, in the midst of the northern blast; and woe to the homeless wanderer whom he finds upon his path! There he lies stark and stiff, a human shape of ice, on the spot where Winter overtook him. On strides the tyrant over the rushing rivers and broad lakes, which turn to rock beneath his footsteps. His dreary empire is established; all around stretches the desolation of the Pole. Yet not ungrateful be his New England children—for Winter is our sire, though a stern and rough one—not ungrateful even for the severities which have nourished our unyielding strength of character. And let us thank him, too, for the

sleigh-rides, cheered by the music of merry bells —
for the crackling and rustling hearth, when the ruddy
firelight gleams on hardy Manhood and the blooming
cheek of Woman — for all the home enjoyments, and
the kindred virtues, which flourish in a frozen soil.
Not that we grieve, when, after some seven months of
storm and bitter frost, Spring, in the guise of a flower-
crowned virgin, is seen driving away the hoary despot,
pelting him with violets by the handful, and strewing
green grass on the path behind him. Often, ere he
will give up his empire, old Winter rushes fiercely
back, and hurls a snow-drift at the shrinking form of
Spring; yet, step by step, he is compelled to retreat
northward, and spends the summer months within the
Arctic circle.

Such fantasies, intermixed among graver toils of
mind, have made the winter's day pass pleasantly.
Meanwhile, the storm has raged without abatement,
and now, as the brief afternoon declines, is tossing
denser volumes to and fro about the atmosphere. On
the window-sill there is a layer of snow reaching
half way up the lowest pane of glass. The garden is
one unbroken bed. Along the street are two or three
spots of uncovered earth, where the gust has whirled
away the snow, heaping it elsewhere to the fence tops,
or piling huge banks against the doors of houses. A
solitary passenger is seen, now striding mid-leg deep
across a drift, now scudding over the bare ground,
while his cloak is swollen with the wind. And now
the jingling of bells, a sluggish sound, responsive to
the horse's toilsome progress through the unbroken
drifts, announces the passage of a sleigh, with a boy
clinging behind, and ducking his head to escape detec-
tion by the driver. Next comes a sledge, laden with

wood for some unthrifty housekeeper, whom winter has surprised at a cold hearth. But what dismal equipage now struggles along the uneven street? A sable hearse, bestrewn with snow, is bearing a dead man through the storm to his frozen bed. Oh, how dreary is a burial in winter, when the bosom of Mother Earth has no warmth for her poor child!

Evening — the early eve of December — begins to spread its deepening veil over the comfortless scene, the firelight gradually brightens, and throws my flickering shadow upon the walls and ceiling of the chamber; but still the storm rages and rattles against the windows. Alas! I shiver, and think it time to be disconsolate. But, taking a farewell glance at dead nature in her shroud, I perceive a flock of snow-birds skimming lightsomely through the tempest, and flitting from drift to drift, as sportively as swallows in the delightful prime of summer. Whence come they? Where do they build their nests and seek their food? Why, having airy wings, do they not follow summer around the earth, instead of making themselves the playmates of the storm, and fluttering on the dreary verge of the winter's eve? I know not whence they come, nor why; yet my spirit has been cheered by that wandering flock of snow-birds.

THE SEVEN VAGABONDS.

RAMBLING on foot in the spring of my life and the summer of the year, I came one afternoon to a point which gave me the choice of three directions. Straight before me the main road extended its dusty length to Boston ; on the left a branch went towards the sea, and would have lengthened my journey a trifle of twenty or thirty miles ; while, by the right-hand path I might have gone over hills and lakes to Canada, visiting in my way the celebrated town of Stamford. On a level spot of grass, at the foot of the guide-post, appeared an object which, though locomotive on a different principle, reminded me of Gulliver's portable mansion among the Brobdignags. It was a huge covered wagon, or, more properly, a small house on wheels, with a door on one side and a window shaded by green blinds on the other. Two horses, munching provender out of the baskets which muzzled them, were fastened near the vehicle : a delectable sound of music proceeded from the interior ; and I immediately conjectured that this was some itinerant show halting at the confluence of the roads to intercept such idle travellers as myself. A shower had long been climbing up the western sky, and now hung so blackly over my onward path that it was a point of wisdom to seek shelter here.

"Halloo ! Who stands guard here ? Is the door-keeper asleep ?" cried I, approaching a ladder of two or three steps which was let down from the wagon.

The music ceased at my summons, and there appeared at the door, not the sort of figure that I had mentally assigned to the wandering showman, but a most respectable old personage, whom I was sorry to have addressed in so free a style. He wore a snuff-colored coat and smallclothes, with white top-boots, and exhibited the mild dignity of aspect and manner which may often be noticed in aged schoolmasters, and sometimes in deacons, selectmen, or other potentates of that kind. A small piece of silver was my passport within his premises, where I found only one other person, hereafter to be described.

" This is a dull day for business," said the old gentleman, as he ushered me in ; " but I merely tarry here to refresh the cattle, being bound for the camp-meeting at Stamford."

Perhaps the movable scene of this narrative is still peregrinating New England, and may enable the reader to test the accuracy of my description. The spectacle — for I will not use the unworthy term of puppet show — consisted of a multitude of little people assembled on a miniature stage. Among them were artisans of every kind, in the attitudes of their toil, and a group of fair ladies and gay gentlemen standing ready for the dance ; a company of foot-soldiers formed a line across the stage, looking stern, grim, and terrible enough, to make it a pleasant consideration that they were but three inches high ; and conspicuous above the whole was seen a Merry Andrew, in the pointed cap and motley coat of his profession. All the inhabitants of this mimic world were motionless, like the figures in a picture, or like that people who one moment were alive in the midst of their business and delights, and the next were trans formed to statues, preserving an eternal semblance of labor that was ended, and pleasure that could be felt no more. Anon, however, the old gentleman turned the handle of a barrel organ, the first note of which produced a most enlivening effect upon the figures, and awoke them all to their proper occupations and amusements. By the self-same impulse the tailor plied his needle, the blacksmith's hammer descended upon the anvil, and the dancers whirled away on feathery tiptoes ; the company of soldiers broke into platoons, retreated from the stage, and were succeeded by a troop of horse, who came prancing onward with such a sound of trumpets and trampling of hoofs as might have startled Don Quixote himself ; while an old toper, of inveterate ill habits, uplifted his black bottle and took off a hearty swig. Meantime the Merry Andrew began to caper and turn somersets, shaking his sides, nodding his head, and winking his eyes in as life-like a manner as if he were ridiculing the non- sense of all human affairs, and making fun of the whole multitude beneath him. At length the old magician (for I compared the showman to Prospero entertaining his guests with a mask of shadows) paused that I might give utterance to my wonder.

"What an admirable piece of work is this!" exclaimed I, lifting up my hands in astonishment.

Indeed I liked the spectacle, and was tickled with the old man's gravity as he presided at it, for I had none of that foolish wisdom which reproves every occupation that is not useful in this world of vanities. If there be a faculty which I possess more perfectly than most men, it is that of throwing myself mentally into situations foreign to my own, and detecting, with a cheerful eye, the desirable circumstances of each.

I could have envied the life of this gray-headed showman, spent as it had been in a course of safe and
pleasurable adventure, in driving his huge vehicle
sometimes through the sands of Cape Cod, and sometimes over the rough forest roads of the north and
east, and halting now on the green before a village
meeting-house, and now in a paved square of the metropolis. How often must his heart have been gladdened by the delight of children as they viewed these
animated figures! or his pride indulged by harangu-
ing learnedly to grown men on the mechanical powers
which produced such wonderful effects, or his gallantry brought into play (for this is an attribute
which such grave men do not lack) by the visits of
pretty maidens! And then with how fresh a feeling
must he return, at intervals, to his own peculiar home!

"I would I were assured of as happy a life as his,"
thought I.

Though the showman's wagon might have accom-
modated fifteen or twenty spectators, it now contained
only himself and me, and a third person at whom I
threw a glance on entering. He was a neat and thin
young man of two or three and twenty; his drab hat,
and green frock coat with velvet collar, were smart,
though no longer new; while a pair of green spectacles that seemed needless to his brisk little eyes gave
him something of a scholar-like and literary air.
After allowing me a sufficient time to inspect the
puppets, he advanced with a bow, and drew my attention to some books in a corner of the wagon. These
he forthwith began to extol with an amazing volubil-
ity of well-sounding words, and an ingenuity of praise
that won him my heart, as being myself one of the
most merciful of critics. Indeed his stock required

some considerable powers of commendation in the salesman ; there were several ancient friends of mine, the novels of those happy days when my affections wavered between the Scottish Chiefs and Thomas Thumb ; besides a few of later date, whose merits had not been acknowledged by the public. I was glad to find that dear little venerable volume, the New England Primer, looking as antique as ever, though in its thousandth new edition; a bundle of superannuated gilt picture-books made such a child of me, that partly for the glittering covers, and partly for the fairy tales within, I bought the whole ; and an assortment of ballads and popular theatrical songs drew largely on my purse. To balance these expenditures, I meddled neither with sermons, nor science, nor morality, though volumes of each were there; nor with a Life of Franklin in the coarsest of paper, but so showily bound that it was emblematical of the Doctor himself, in the court-dress which he refused to wear at Paris ; nor with Webster's Spelling-Book, nor some of Byron's minor poems, nor half a dozen little Testaments at twenty-five cents each.

Thus far the collection might have been swept from some great bookstore, or picked up at an evening auction room ; but there was one small blue-covered pamphlet, which the pedlar handed me with so peculiar an air, that I purchased it immediately at his own price; and then, for the first time, the thought struck me, that I had spoken face to face with the veritable author of a printed book. The literary man now evinced a great kindness for me, and I ventured to inquire which way he was travelling.

"Oh," said he, "I keep company with this old gentleman here, and we are moving now towards the camp-meeting at Stamford."

He then explained to me that for the present season he had rented a corner of the wagon as a bookstore, which, as he wittily observed, was a true Circulating Library, since there were few parts of the country where it had not gone its rounds. I approved of the plan exceedingly, and began to sum up within my mind the many uncommon felicities in the life of a book pedlar, especially when his character resembled that of the individual before me. At a high rate was to be reckoned the daily and hourly enjoyment of such interviews as the present, in which he seized upon the admiration of a passing stranger, and made him aware that a man of literary taste, and even of literary achievement, was travelling the country in a show-man's wagon. A more valuable, yet not infrequent, triumph, might be won in his conversations with some elderly clergyman, long vegetating in a rocky, woody, watery back settlement of New England, who, as he recruited his library from the pedlar's stock of ser-mons, would exhort him to seek a college education and become the first scholar in his class. Sweeter and prouder yet would be his sensations when, talking po-etry while he sold spelling-books, he should charm the mind, and haply touch the heart, of a fair country schoolmistress, herself an unhonored poetess, a wearer of blue stockings which none but himself took pains to look at. But the scene of his completest glory would be when the wagon had halted for the night, and his stock of books was transferred to some crowded bar-room. Then would he recommend to the multi-farious company, whether traveller from the city, or teamster from the hills, or neighboring squire, or the landlord himself, or his loutish hostler, works suited to each particular taste and capacity ; proving, all the

while, by acute criticism and profound remark, that
the lore in his books was even exceeded by that in his
brain.

Thus happily would he traverse the land; sometimes a herald before the march of Mind; sometimes
walking arm in arm with awful Literature; and reap-
ing everywhere a harvest of real and sensible popularity, which the secluded bookworms, by whose toil he
lived, could never hope for.

"If ever I meddle with literature," thought I, fixing myself in adamantine resolution, "it shall be as a
travelling bookseller."

Though it was still mid afternoon, the air had now
grown dark about us, and a few drops of rain came
down upon the roof of our vehicle, pattering like the
feet of birds that had flown thither to rest. A sound
of pleasant voices made us listen, and there soon appeared half-way up the ladder the pretty person of a
young damsel, whose rosy face was so cheerful that
even amid the gloomy light it seemed as if the sunbeams were peeping under her bonnet. We next saw
the dark and handsome features of a young man, who,
with easier gallantry than might have been expected
in the heart of Yankee land, was assisting her into
the wagon. It became immediately evident to us,
when the two strangers stood within the door, that
they were of a profession kindred to those of my companions; and I was delighted with the more than hospitable, the even paternal, kindness of the old showman's manner, as he welcomed them ; while the man
of literature hastened to lead the merry-eyed girl to a
seat on the long bench.

"You are housed but just in time, my young
friends," said the master of the wagon. " The sky
would have been down upon you within five minutes."

The young man's reply marked him as a foreigner, not by any variation from the idiom and accent of good English, but because he spoke with more caution and accuracy than if perfectly familiar with the language.

"We knew that a shower was hanging over us," said he, "and consulted whether it were best to enter the house on the top of yonder hill, but seeing your wagon in the road" —

"We agreed to come hither," interrupted the girl, with a smile, "because we should be more at home in a wandering house like this."

I meanwhile, with many a wild and undetermined fantasy, was narrowly inspecting these two doves that had flown into our ark. The young man, tall, agile, and athletic, wore a mass of black shining curls clustering round a dark and vivacious countenance, which, if it had not greater expression, was at least more active, and attracted readier notice, than the quiet faces of our countrymen. At his first appearance he had been laden with a neat mahogany box, of about two feet square, but very light in proportion to its size, which he had immediately unstrapped from his shoulders and deposited on the floor of the wagon.

The girl had nearly as fair a complexion as our own beauties, and a brighter one than most of them; the lightness of her figure, which seemed calculated to traverse the whole world without weariness, suited well with the glowing cheerfulness of her face; and her gay attire, combining the rainbow hues of crimson, green, and a deep orange, was as proper to her lightsome aspect as if she had been born in it. This gay stranger was appropriately burdened with that mirth-inspiring instrument, the fiddle, which her com-

panion took from her hands, and shortly began the
process of tuning. Neither of us — the previous com
pany of the wagon — needed to inquire their trade;
for this could be no mystery to frequenters of brigade
musters, ordinations, cattle-shows, commencements, and
other festal meetings in our sober land; and there
is a dear friend of mine who will smile when this
page recalls to his memory a chivalrous deed per
formed by us, in rescuing the showbox of such a
couple from a mob of great double-fisted countrymen.

"Come," said I to the damsel of gay attire, "shall
we visit all the wonders of the world together?"

She understood the metaphor at once; though indeed it would not much have troubled me if she had
assented to the literal meaning of my words. The
mahogany box was placed in a proper position, and I
peeped in through its small round magnifying window, while the girl sat by my side, and gave short
descriptive sketches, as one after another the pictures
were unfolded to my view. We visited together, at
least our imaginations did, full many a famous city,
in the streets of which I had long yearned to tread;
once, I remember, we were in the harbor of Barce-
lona gazing townwards; next, she bore me through
the air to Sicily, and bade me look up at blazing
Ætna; then we took wing to Venice, and sat in a
gondola beneath the arch of the Rialto; and anon she
sat me down among the thronged spectators at the
coronation of Napoleon. But there was one scene, its
locality she could not tell, which charmed my attention
longer than all those gorgeous palaces and churches,
because the fancy haunted me that I myself, the preceding summer, had beheld just such a humble meeting-house, in just such a pine-surrounded nook, among

our own green mountains. All these pictures were tolerably executed, though far inferior to the girl's touches of description; nor was it easy to comprehend how, in so few sentences, and these, as I supposed, in a language foreign to her, she contrived to present an airy copy of each varied scene. When we had travelled through the vast extent of the mahogany box I looked into my guide's face.

"Where are you going, my pretty maid?" inquired I, in the words of an old song.

"Ah," said the gay damsel, "you might as well ask where the summer wind is going. We are wanderers here, and there, and everywhere. Wherever there is mirth, our merry hearts are drawn to it. To-day, indeed, the people have told us of a great frolic and festival in these parts; so perhaps we may be needed at what you call the camp-meeting at Stamford."

Then in my happy youth, and while her pleasant voice yet sounded in my ears, I sighed; for none but myself, I thought, should have been her companion in a life which seemed to realize my own wild fancies, cherished all through visionary boyhood to that hour. To these two strangers the world was in its golden age, not that indeed it was less dark and sad than ever, but because its weariness and sorrow had no community with their ethereal nature. Wherever they might appear in their pilgrimage of bliss, Youth would echo back their gladness, care-stricken Maturity would rest a moment from its toil, and Age, tottering among the graves, would smile in withered joy for their sakes. The lonely cot, the narrow and gloomy street, the sombre shade, would catch a passing gleam like that now shining on ourselves, as these bright spirits wandered by. Blessed pair, whose happy home was throughout all the earth! I looked at my shoulders, and thought them broad enough to sustain those pictured towns and mountains; mine, too, was an elastic foot, as tireless as the wing of the bird of paradise; mine was then an untroubled heart, that would have gone singing on its delightful way.

"O maiden!" said I aloud, "why did you not come hither alone?"

While the merry girl and myself were busy with the showbox, the unceasing rain had driven another wayfarer into the wagon. He seemed pretty nearly of the old showman's age, but much smaller, leaner, and more withered than he, and less respectably clad in a patched suit of gray; withal, he had a thin, shrewd countenance, and a pair of diminutive gray eyes, which peeped rather too keenly out of their puckered sockets. This old fellow had been joking with the showman, in a manner which intimated previous acquaintance; but perceiving that the damsel and I had terminated our affairs, he drew forth a folded document, and presented it to me. As I had anticipated, it proved to be a circular, written in a very fair and legible hand, and signed by several distinguished gentlemen whom I had never heard of, stating that the bearer had encountered every variety of misfortune, and recommending him to the notice of all charitable people. Previous disbursements had left me no more than a five-dollar bill, out of which, however, I offered to make the beggar a donation, provided he would give me change for it. The object of my beneficence looked keenly in my face, and discerned that I had none of that abominable spirit, characteristic though it be, of a full-blooded Yankee, which takes pleasure in detecting every little harmless piece of knavery.

" Why, perhaps," said the ragged old mendicant, " if the bank is in good standing, I can't say but I may have enough about me to change your bill."

" It is a bill of the Suffolk Bank," said I, " and better than the specie."

As the beggar had nothing to object, he now produced a small buff-leather bag, tied up carefully with a shoestring. When this was opened, there appeared a very comfortable treasure of silver coins, of all sorts and sizes ; and I even fancied that I saw, gleaming among them, the golden plumage of that rare bird in our currency, the American Eagle. In this precious heap was my bank-note deposited, the rate of exchange being considerably against me. His wants being thus relieved, the destitute man pulled out of his pocket an old pack of greasy cards, which had probably contributed to fill the buff-leather bag in more ways than one.

" Come," said he, " I spy a rare fortune in your face, and for twenty-five cents more, I 'll tell you what it is."

I never refuse to take a glimpse into futurity; so, after shuffling the cards, and when the fair damsel had cut them, I dealt a portion to the prophetic beggar. Like others of his profession, before predicting the shadowy events that were moving on to meet me, he gave proof of his preternatural science by describing scenes through which I had already passed. Here let me have credit for a sober fact. When the old man had read a page in his book of fate, he bent his keen gray eyes on mine, and proceeded to relate, in all its minute particulars, what was then the most

singular event of my life. It was one which I had
no purpose to disclose till the general unfolding of all
secrets ; nor would it be a much stranger instance of
inscrutable knowledge, or fortune conjecture, if the
beggar were to meet me in the street to-day, and repeat, word for word, the page which I have here written. The fortune-teller, after predicting a destiny
which Time seems loath to make good, put up his
cards, secreted his treasure bag, and began to converse with the other occupants of the wagon.

" Well, old friend," said the showman, " you have
not yet told us which way your face is turned this
afternoon."

"I am taking a trip northward, this warm weather,"
replied the conjurer, " across the Connecticut first,
and then up through Vermont, and may be into Canada before the fall. But I must stop and see the
breaking up of the camp-meeting at Stamford."

I began to think that all the vagrants in New England were converging to the camp-meeting, and had
made this wagon their rendezvous by the way. The
showman now proposed that, when the shower was
over, they should pursue the road to Stamford together, it being sometimes the policy of these people
to form a sort of league and confederacy.

"And the young lady too," observed the gallant
bibliopolist, bowing to her profoundly, "and this foreign gentleman, as I understand, are on a jaunt of
pleasure to the same spot. It would add incalculably
to my own enjoyment, and I presume to that of my
colleague and his friend, if they could be prevailed
upon to join our party."

This arrangement met with approbation on all
hands, nor were any of those concerned more sensi-

ble of its advantages than myself, who had no title to be included in it. Having already satisfied myself as to the several modes in which the four others attained felicity, I next set my mind at work to discover what enjoyments were peculiar to the old "Straggler," as the people of the country would have termed the wandering mendicant and prophet. As he pretended to familiarity with the Devil, so I fancied that he was fitted to pursue and take delight in his way of life, by possessing some of the mental and moral characteristics, the lighter and more comic ones, of the Devil in popular stories. Among them might be reckoned a love of deception for its own sake, a shrewd eye and keen relish for human weakness and ridiculous infirmity, and the talent of petty fraud. Thus to this old man there would be pleasure even in the consciousness so insupportable to some minds, that his whole life was a cheat upon the world, and that, so far as he was concerned with the public, his little cunning had the upper hand of its united wisdom. Every day would furnish him with a succession of minute and pungent triumphs: as when, for instance, his importunity wrung a pittance out of the heart of a miser; or when my silly good nature transferred a part of my slender purse to his plump leather bag; or when some ostentatious gentleman should throw a coin to the ragged beggar who was richer than himself; or when, though he would not always be so decidedly diabolical, his pretended wants should make him a sharer in the scanty living of real indigence. And then what an inexhaustible field of enjoyment, both as enabling him to discern so much folly and achieve such quantities of minor mischief, was opened to his sneering spirit by his pretensions to prophetic knowledge.

All this was a sort of happiness which I could conceive of, though I had little sympathy with it. Perhaps, had I been then inclined to admit it, I might have found that the roving life was more proper to him than to either of his companions; for Satan, to whom I had compared the poor man, has delighted, ever since the time of Job, in "wandering up and down upon the earth;" and indeed a crafty disposition which operates not in deep-laid plans, but in disconnected tricks, could not have an adequate scope, unless naturally impelled to a continual change of scene and society. My reflections were here interrupted.

"Another visitor!" exclaimed the old showman.

The door of the wagon had been closed against the tempest, which was roaring and blustering with prodigious fury and commotion, and beating violently against our shelter, as if it claimed all those homeless people for its lawful prey, while we, caring little for the displeasure of the elements, sat comfortably talking. There was now an attempt to open the door, succeeded by a voice uttering some strange, unintelligible gibberish, which my companions mistook for Greek, and I suspected to be thieves' Latin. However, the showman stepped forward, and gave admittance to a figure which made me imagine, either that our wagon had rolled back two hundred years into past ages, or that the forest and its old inhabitants had sprung up around us by enchantment.

It was a red Indian, armed with his bow and arrow. His dress was a sort of cap, adorned with a single feather of some wild bird, and a frock of blue cotton girded tight about him; on his breast, like orders of knighthood, hung a crescent and a circle, and other ornaments of silver; while a small crucifix betokened that our Father the Pope had interposed between the Indian and the Great Spirit, whom he had worshipped in his simplicity. This son of the wilderness and pilgrim of the storm took his place silently in the midst of us. When the first surprise was over, I rightly conjectured him to be one of the Penobscot tribe, parties of which I had often seen, in their summer excursions down our Eastern rivers. There they paddle their birch canoes among the coasting schooners, and build their wigwam beside some roaring mill-dam, and drive a little trade in basket work where their fathers hunted deer. Our new visitor was probably wandering through the country towards Boston, subsisting on the careless charity of the people, while he turned his archery to profitable account by shooting at cents, which were to be the prize of his successful aim.

The Indian had not long been seated ere our merry damsel sought to draw him into conversation. She, indeed, seemed all made up of sunshine in the month of May; for there was nothing so dark and dismal that her pleasant mind could not cast a glow over it; and the wild man, like a fir-tree in his native forest, soon began to brighten into a sort of sombre cheerfulness. At length, she inquired whether his journey had any particular end or purpose.

"I go shoot at the camp-meeting at Stamford," replied the Indian.

"And here are five more," said the girl, "all aiming at the camp-meeting too. You shall be one of us, for we travel with light hearts; and as for me, I sing merry songs, and tell merry tales, and am full of merry thoughts, and I dance merrily along the road,

so that there is never any sadness among them that
keep me company. But, oh, you would find it very
dull indeed to go all the way to Stamford alone!"

My ideas of the aboriginal character led me to fear
that the Indian would prefer his own solitary musings
to the gay society thus offered him; on the contrary,
the girl's proposal met with immediate acceptance, and
seemed to animate him with a misty expectation of enjoyment. I now gave myself up to a course of thought
which, whether it flowed naturally from this combination of events, or was drawn forth by a wayward
fancy, caused my mind to thrill as if I were listening
to deep music. I saw mankind, in this weary old age
of the world, either enduring a sluggish existence amid
the smoke and dust of cities, or, if they breathed a
purer air, still lying down at night with no hope but
to wear out to-morrow, and all the to-morrows which
make up life, among the same dull scenes and in the
same wretched toil that had darkened the sunshine of
to-day. But there were some, full of the primeval instinct, who preserved the freshness of youth to their
latest years by the continual excitement of new objects, new pursuits, and new associates; and cared
little, though their birthplace might have been here
in New England, if the grave should close over them
in Central Asia. Fate was summoning a parliament
of these free spirits; unconscious of the impulse which
directed them to a common centre, they had come
hither from far and near, and last of all appeared
the representative of those mighty vagrants who had
chased the deer during thousands of years, and were
chasing it now in the Spirit Land. Wandering down
through the waste of ages, the woods had vanished
around his path; his arm had lost somewhat of its

strength, his foot of its fleetness, his mien of its wild
regality, his heart and mind of their savage virtue and
uncultured force; but here, untamable to the routine
of artificial life, roving now along the dusty road as
of old over the forest leaves, here was the Indian still.

"Well," said the old showman, in the midst of my
meditations, "here is an honest company of us — one,
two, three, four, five, six — all going to the camp-
meeting at Stamford. Now, hoping no offence, I
should like to know where this young gentleman may
be going?"

I started. How came I among these wanderers?
The free mind, that preferred its own folly to another's wisdom; the open spirit, that found companions everywhere; above all, the restless impulse, that
had so often made me wretched in the midst of enjoyments; these were my claims to be of their society.

"My friends!" cried I, stepping into the centre of
the wagon, "I am going with you to the camp-meeting at Stamford."

"But in what capacity?" asked the old showman,
after a moment's silence. "All of us here can get our
bread in some creditable way. Every honest man
should have his livelihood. You, sir, as I take it, are
a mere strolling gentleman."

I proceeded to inform the company that, when Nature gave me a propensity to their way of life, she had
not left me altogether destitute of qualifications for it;
though I could not deny that my talent was less respectable, and might be less profitable, than the mean-
est of theirs. My design, in short, was to imitate the
story-tellers of whom Oriental travellers have told us,
and become an itinerant novelist, reciting my own ex-
temporaneous fictions to such audiences as I could collect.

"Either this," said I, "is my vocation, or I have been born in vain."

The fortune-teller, with a sly wink to the company, proposed to take me as an apprentice to one or other of his professions, either of which, undoubtedly, would have given full scope to whatever inventive talent I might possess. The bibliopolist spoke a few words in opposition to my plan, influenced partly, I suspect, by the jealousy of authorship, and partly by an apprehension that the *viva voce* practice would become general among novelists, to the infinite detriment of the book trade. Dreading a rejection, I solicited the interest of the merry damsel.

"Mirth," cried I, most aptly appropriating the words of L'Allegro, "to thee I sue! Mirth, admit me of thy crew!"

"Let us indulge the poor youth," said Mirth, with a kindness which made me love her dearly, though I was no such coxcomb as to misinterpret her motives. "I have espied much promise in him. True, a shadow sometimes flits across his brow, but the sunshine is sure to follow in a moment. He is never guilty of a sad thought, but a merry one is twin born with it. We will take him with us; and you shall see that he will set us all a-laughing before we reach the camp-meeting at Stamford."

Her voice silenced the scruples of the rest, and gained me admittance into the league; according to the terms of which, without a community of goods or profits, we were to lend each other all the aid, and avert all the harm, that might be in our power. This affair settled, a marvellous jollity entered into the whole tribe of us, manifesting itself characteristically in each individual. The old showman, sitting down

to his barrel organ, stirred up the souls of the pygmy
people with one of the quickest tunes in the music
book; tailors, blacksmiths, gentlemen and ladies, all
seemed to share in the spirit of the occasion; and the
Merry Andrew played his part more facetiously than
ever, nodding and winking particularly at me. The
young foreigner flourished his fiddle bow with a master's hand, and gave an inspiring echo to the showman's melody. The bookish man and the merry damsel started up simultaneously to dance; the former
enacting the double shuffle in a style which everybody must have witnessed ere Election week was
blotted out of time; while the girl, setting her arms
akimbo with both hands at her slim waist, displayed
such light rapidity of foot, and harmony of varying
attitude and motion, that I could not conceive how she
ever was to stop; imagining, at the moment, that Nature had made her, as the old showman had made his
puppets, for no earthly purpose but to dance jigs.
The Indian bellowed forth a succession of most hideous outcries, somewhat affrighting us till we interpreted them as the war-song, with which, in imitation
of his ancestors, he was prefacing the assault on Stamford. The conjurer, meanwhile, sat demurely in a corner, extracting a sly enjoyment from the whole scene,
and, like the facetious Merry Andrew, directing his
queer glance particularly at me.

As for myself, with great exhilaration of fancy, I
began to arrange and color the incidents of a tale,
wherewith I proposed to amuse an audience that very
evening; for I saw that my associates were a little
ashamed of me, and that no time was to be lost in obtaining a public acknowledgment of my abilities.

" Come, fellow-laborers," at last said the old showman, whom we had elected President; "the shower is over, and we must be doing our duty by these poor souls at Stamford."

"We'll come among them in procession with music and dancing," cried the merry damsel.

Accordingly — for it must be understood that our pilgrimage was to be performed on foot — we sallied joyously out of the wagon, each of us, even the old gentleman in his white top-boots, giving a great skip as we came down the ladder. Above our heads there was such a glory of sunshine and splendor of clouds, and such brightness of verdure below, that, as I modestly remarked at the time, Nature seemed to have washed her face, and put on the best of her jewelry and a fresh green gown, in honor of our confederation. Casting our eyes northward, we beheld a horseman approaching leisurely, and splashing through the little puddles on the Stamford road. Onward he came, sticking up in his saddle with rigid perpendicularity, a tall, thin figure in rusty black, whom the showman and the conjurer shortly recognized to be, what his aspect sufficiently indicated, a travelling preacher of great fame among the Methodists. What puzzled us was the fact that his face appeared turned from, instead of to, the camp-meeting at Stamford. However, as this new votary of the wandering life drew near the little green space where the guide-post and our wagon were situated, my six fellow-vagabonds and myself rushed forward and surrounded him, crying out with united voices, —

"What news, what news from the camp-meeting at Stamford?"

The missionary looked down in surprise at as singular a knot of people as could have been selected from all his heterogeneous auditors. Indeed, considering that we might all be classified under the general head of Vagabond, there was great diversity of character among the grave old showman, the sly, prophetic beggar, the fiddling foreigner and his merry damsel, the smart bibliopolist, the sombre Indian, and myself, the itinerant novelist, a slender youth of eighteen. I even fancied that a smile was endeavoring to disturb the iron gravity of the preacher's mouth.

"Good people," answered he, "the camp-meeting is broke up."

So saying, the Methodist minister switched his steed and rode westward. Our union being thus nullified by the removal of its object, we were sundered at once to the four winds of heaven. The fortune-teller giving a nod to all, and a peculiar wink to me, departed on his northern tour, chuckling within himself as he took the Stamford road. The old showman and his literary coadjutor were already tackling their horses to the wagon, with a design to peregrinate southwest along the sea-coast. The foreigner and the merry damsel took their laughing leave, and pursued the eastern road, which I had that day trodden; as they passed away, the young man played a lively strain and the girl's happy spirit broke into a dance: and thus, dissolving, as it were, into sunbeams and gay music, that pleasant pair departed from my view. Finally, with a pensive shadow thrown across my mind, yet envious of the light philosophy of my late companions, I joined myself to the Penobscot Indian and set forth towards the distant city.

THE WHITE OLD MAID.

THE moonbeams came through two deep and narrow windows, and showed a spacious chamber richly furnished in an antique fashion. From one lattice the shadow of the diamond panes was thrown upon the floor; the ghostly light, through the other, slept upon a bed, falling between the heavy silken curtains, and illuminating the face of a young man. But, how quietly the slumberer lay! how pale his features! and how like a shroud the sheet was wound about his frame! Yes; it was a corpse, in its burial clothes.

Suddenly, the fixed features seemed to move with dark emotion. Strange fantasy! It was but the shadow of the fringed curtain waving betwixt the dead face and the moonlight, as the door of the chamber opened and a girl stole softly to the bedside. Was there delusion in the moonbeams, or did her gesture and her eye betray a gleam of triumph, as she bent over the pale corpse — pale as itself — and pressed her living lips to the cold ones of the dead? As she drew back from that long kiss, her features writhed as if a proud heart were fighting with its anguish. Again it seemed that the features of the corpse had moved responsive to her own. Still an illusion! The silken curtain had waved, a second time, betwixt the dead face and the moonlight, as another fair young girl unclosed the door, and glided, ghost-like, to the bedside. There the two maidens stood, both beautiful, with the pale beauty of the dead between them. But she who had first entered was proud and stately, and the other a soft and fragile thing.

"Away!" cried the lofty one. "Thou hadst him living! The dead is mine!"

"Thine!" returned the other, shuddering. "Well hast thou spoken! The dead is thine!"

The proud girl started, and stared into her face with a ghastly look. But a wild and mournful expression passed across the features of the gentle one; and weak and helpless, she sank down on the bed, her head pillowed beside that of the corpse, and her hair mingling with his dark locks. A creature of hope and joy, the first draught of sorrow had bewildered her.

"Edith!" cried her rival.

Edith groaned, as with a sudden compression of the heart; and removing her cheek from the dead youth's pillow, she stood upright, fearfully encountering the eyes of the lofty girl.

"Wilt thou betray me?" said the latter, calmly.

"Till the dead bid me speak, I will be silent," answered Edith. "Leave us alone together! Go, and live many years, and then return, and tell me of thy life. He, too, will be here! Then, if thou tellest of sufferings more than death, we will both forgive thee."

"And what shall be the token?" asked the proud girl, as if her heart acknowledged a meaning in these wild words.

"This lock of hair," said Edith, lifting one of the dark, clustering curls that lay heavily on the dead man's brow.

The two maidens joined their hands over the bosom of the corpse, and appointed a day and hour, far, far in time to come, for their next meeting in that chamber. The statelier girl gave one deep look at the mo-

tionless countenance, and departed — yet turned again
and trembled ere she closed the door, almost believing
that her dead lover frowned upon her. And Edith,
too! Was not her white form fading into the moonlight? Scorning her own weakness she went forth,
and perceived that a negro slave was waiting in the
passage with a wax-light, which he held between her
face and his own, and regarded her, as she thought,
with an ugly expression of merriment. Lifting his
torch on high, the slave lighted her down the staircase, and undid the portal of the mansion. The young
clergyman of the town had just ascended the steps,
and bowing to the lady, passed in without a word.

Years, many years, rolled on; the world seemed
new again, so much older was it grown since the night
when those pale girls had clasped their hands across
the bosom of the corpse. In the interval, a lonely
woman had passed from youth to extreme age, and
was known by all the town as the "Old Maid in the
Winding Sheet." A taint of insanity had affected
her whole life, but so quiet, sad, and gentle, so utterly
free from violence, that she was suffered to pursue
her harmless fantasies, unmolested by the world, with
whose business or pleasures she had nought to do.
She dwelt alone, and never came into the daylight,
except to follow funerals. Whenever a corpse was
borne along the street in sunshine, rain, or snow;
whether a pompous train of the rich and proud
thronged after it, or few and humble were the mourners, behind them came the lonely woman in a long
white garment which the people called her shroud.
She took no place among the kindred or the friends,
but stood at the door to hear the funeral prayer, and
walked in the rear of the procession, as one whose

earthly charge it was to haunt the house of mourning, and be the shadow of affliction, and see that the dead were duly buried. So long had this been her custom that the inhabitants of the town deemed her a part of every funeral, as much as the coffin pall, or the very corpse itself, and augured ill of the sinner's destiny unless the "Old Maid in the Winding Sheet" came gliding, like a ghost, behind. Once, it is said, she affrighted a bridal party with her pale presence, appearing suddenly in the illuminated hall, just as the priest was uniting a false maid to a wealthy man, before her lover had been dead a year. Evil was the omen to that marriage! Sometimes she stole forth by moonlight and visited the graves of venerable Integrity, and wedded Love, and virgin Innocence, and every spot where the ashes of a kind and faithful heart were mouldering. Over the hillocks of those favored dead would she stretch out her arms, with a gesture, as if she were scattering seeds; and many believed that she brought them from the garden of Paradise; for the graves which she had visited were green beneath the snow, and covered with sweet flowers from April to November. Her blessing was better than a holy verse upon the tombstone. Thus wore away her long, sad, peaceful, and fantastic life, till few were so old as she, and the people of later generations wondered how the dead had ever been buried, or mourners had endured their grief, without the "Old Maid in the Winding Sheet."

Still years went on, and still she followed funerals, and was not yet summoned to her own festival of death. One afternoon the great street of the town was all alive with business and bustle, though the sun now gilded only the upper half of the church spire,

having left the housetops and loftiest trees in shadow.
The scene was cheerful and animated, in spite of the
sombre shade between the high brick buildings. Here
were pompous merchants, in white wigs and laced
velvet ; the bronzed faces of sea-captains ; the foreign
garb and air of Spanish creoles ; and the disdainful
port of natives of Old England ; all contrasted with
the rough aspect of one or two back settlers, negoti-
ating sales of timber from forests where axe had never
sounded. Sometimes a lady passed, swelling roundly
forth in an embroidered petticoat, balancing her steps
in high-heeled shoes, and courtesying with lofty grace
to the punctilious obeisances of the gentlemen. The
life of the town seemed to have its very centre not
far from an old mansion that stood somewhat back
from the pavement, surrounded by neglected grass,
with a strange air of loneliness, rather deepened than
dispelled by the throng so near it. Its site would
have been suitably occupied by a magnificent Exchange or a brick block, lettered all over with various
signs ; or the large house itself might have made a
noble tavern, with the " King's Arms " swinging before it, and guests in every chamber, instead of the
present solitude. But owing to some dispute about
the right of inheritance, the mansion had been long
without a tenant, decaying from year to year, and
throwing the stately gloom of its shadow over the
busiest part of the town. Such was the scene, and
such the time, when a figure unlike any that have
been described was observed at a distance down the
street.

" I espy a strange sail, yonder," remarked a Liverpool captain ; " that woman in the long white garment ! "

The sailor seemed much struck by the object, as were several others who, at the same moment, caught a glimpse of the figure that had attracted his notice. Almost immediately the various topics of conversation gave place to speculations, in an undertone, on this unwonted occurrence.

" Can there be a funeral so late this afternoon ? " inquired some.

They looked for the signs of death at every door — the sexton, the hearse, the assemblage of black-clad relatives — all that makes up the woful pomp of funerals. They raised their eyes, also, to the sun-gilt spire of the church, and wondered that no clang proceeded from its bell, which had always tolled till now when this figure appeared in the light of day. But none had heard that a corpse was to be borne to its home that afternoon, nor was there any token of a funeral, except the apparition of the " Old Maid in the Winding Sheet."

" What may this portend ? " asked each man of his neighbor.

All smiled as they put the question, yet with a certain trouble in their eyes, as if pestilence or some other wide calamity were prognosticated by the untimely intrusion among the living of one whose presence had always been associated with death and woe. What a comet is to the earth was that sad woman to the town. Still she moved on, while the hum of surprise was hushed at her approach, and the proud and the humble stood aside, that her white garment might not wave against them. It was a long, loose robe, of spotless purity. Its wearer appeared very old, pale, emaciated, and feeble, yet glided onward without the unsteady pace of extreme age. At one point of her course a little rosy boy burst forth from a door, and ran, with open arms, towards the ghostly woman, seeming to expect a kiss from her bloodless lips. She made a slight pause, fixing her eye upon him with an expression of no earthly sweetness, so that the child shivered and stood awe-struck, rather than affrighted, while the Old Maid passed on. Perhaps her garment might have been polluted even by an infant's touch; perhaps her kiss would have been death to the sweet boy within a year.

"She is but a shadow," whispered the superstitious. "The child put forth his arms and could not grasp her robe!"

The wonder was increased when the Old Maid passed beneath the porch of the deserted mansion, ascended the moss-covered steps, lifted the iron knocker, and gave three raps. The people could only conjecture that some old remembrance, troubling her bewildered brain, had impelled the poor woman hither to visit the friends of her youth; all gone from their home long since and forever, unless their ghosts still haunted it — fit company for the "Old Maid in the Winding Sheet." An elderly man approached the steps, and, reverently uncovering his gray locks, essayed to explain the matter.

"None, Madam," said he, "have dwelt in thi house these fifteen years agone — no, not since the death of old Colonel Fenwicke, whose funeral you may remember to have followed. His heirs, being ill agreed among themselves, have let the mansion-house go to ruin."

The Old Maid looked slowly round with a slight gesture of one hand, and a finger of the other upon her lip, appearing more shadow-like than ever in the obscurity of the porch. But again she lifted the hammer, and gave, this time, a single rap. Could it be that a footstep was now heard coming down the staircase of the old mansion, which all conceived to have been so long untenanted? Slowly, feebly, yet heavily, like the pace of an aged and infirm person, the step approached, more distinct on every downward stair, till it reached the portal. The bar fell on the inside; the door was opened. One upward glance towards the church spire, whence the sunshine had just faded, was the last that the people saw of the " Old Maid in the Winding Sheet."

" Who undid the door?" asked many.

This question, owing to the depth of shadow beneath the porch, no one could satisfactorily answer. Two or three aged men, while protesting against an inference which might be drawn, affirmed that the person within was a negro, and bore a singular resemblance to old Cæsar, formerly a slave in the house, but freed by death some thirty years before.

" Her summons has waked up a servant of the old family," said one, half seriously.

" Let us wait here," replied another. " More guests will knock at the door, anon. But the gate of the graveyard should be thrown open ! "

Twilight had overspread the town before the crowd began to separate, or the comments on this incident were exhausted. One after another was wending his way homeward, when a coach — no common spectacle in those days — drove slowly into the street. It was an old-fashioned equipage, hanging close to the ground, with arms on the panels, a footman behind, and a grave, corpulent coachman seated high in front — the whole giving an idea of solemn state and dignity.

There was something awful in the heavy rumbling of the wheels. The coach rolled down the street, till, coming to the gateway of the deserted mansion, it drew up, and the footman sprang to the ground.

"Whose grand coach is this?" asked a very inquisitive body.

The footman made no reply, but ascended the steps of the old house, gave three raps with the iron hammer, and returned to open the coach door. An old man, possessed of the heraldic lore so common in that day, examined the shield of arms on the panel.

"Azure, a lion's head erased, between three flower-de-luces," said he; then whispered the name of the family to whom these bearings belonged. The last inheritor of his honors was recently dead, after a long residence amid the splendor of the British court, where his birth and wealth had given him no mean station. "He left no child," continued the herald, "and these arms, being in a lozenge, betoken that the coach appertains to his widow."

Further disclosures, perhaps, might have been made, had not the speaker suddenly been struck dumb by the stern eye of an ancient lady who thrust forth her head from the coach, preparing to descend. As she emerged, the people saw that her dress was magnificent, and her figure dignified, in spite of age and infirmity — a stately ruin but with a look, at once, of pride and wretchedness. Her strong and rigid features had an awe about them, unlike that of the white Old Maid, but as of something evil. She passed up the steps, leaning on a gold-headed cane; the door swung open as she ascended — and the light of a torch glittered on the embroidery of her dress, and gleamed on the pillars of the porch. After a momen-

tary pause — a glance backwards — and then a desperate effort — she went in. The decipherer of the
coat of arms had ventured up the lowest step, and
shrinking back immediately, pale and tremulous, affirmed that the torch was held by the very image of
old Cæsar.

"But such a hideous grin," added he, "was never
seen on the face of mortal man, black or white! It
will haunt me till my dying day."

Meantime, the coach had wheeled round, with a
prodigious clatter on the pavement, and rumbled up
the street, disappearing in the twilight, while the ear
still tracked its course. Scarcely was it gone, when
the people began to question whether the coach and
attendants, the ancient lady, the spectre of old Cæsar,
and the Old Maid herself, were not all a strangely
combined delusion, with some dark purport in its mystery. The whole town was astir, so that, instead of
dispersing, the crowd continually increased, and stood
gazing up at the windows of the mansion, now silvered
by the brightening moon. The elders, glad to indulge
the narrative propensity of age, told of the long-faded
splendor of the family, the entertainments they had
given, and the guests, the greatest of the land, and
even titled and noble ones from abroad, who had
passed beneath that portal. These graphic reminiscences seemed to call up the ghosts of those to whom
they referred. So strong was the impression on some
of the more imaginative hearers, that two or three
were seized with trembling fits, at one and the same
moment, protesting that they had distinctly heard
three other raps of the iron knocker.

"Impossible!" exclaimed others. "See! The
moon shines beneath the porch, and shows every part

of it, except in the narrow shade of that pillar. There is no one there!"

"Did not the door open?" whispered one of these fanciful persons.

"Didst thou see it, too?" said his companion, in a startled tone.

But the general sentiment was opposed to the idea that a third visitant had made application at the door of the deserted house. A few, however, adhered to this new marvel, and even declared that a red gleam like that of a torch had shone through the great front window, as if the negro were lighting a guest up the staircase. This, too, was pronounced a mere fantasy. But at once the whole multitude started, and each man beheld his own terror painted in the faces of all the rest.

"What an awful thing is this!" cried they.

A shriek too fearfully distinct for doubt had been heard within the mansion, breaking forth suddenly, and succeeded by a deep stillness, as if a heart had burst in giving it utterance. The people knew not whether to fly from the very sight of the house, or to rush trembling in, and search out the strange mystery. Amid their confusion and affright, they are somewhat reassured by the appearance of their clergyman, a venerable patriarch, and equally a saint, who had taught them and their fathers the way to heaven for more than the space of an ordinary lifetime. He was a reverend figure, with long, white hair upon his shoulders, a white beard upon his breast, and a back so bent over his staff that he seemed to be looking downward continually, as if to choose a proper grave for his weary frame. It was some time before the good old man, being deaf and of impaired intellect, could be made to comprehend such portions of the affair as were comprehensible at all. But, when possessed of the facts, his energies assumed unexpected vigor.

"Verily," said the old gentleman, "it will be fitting that I enter the mansion-house of the worthy Colonel Fenwicke, lest any harm should have befallen that true Christian woman whom ye call the 'Old Maid in the Winding Sheet.'"

Behold, then, the venerable clergyman ascending the steps of the mansion, with a torch-bearer behind him. It was the elderly man who had spoken to the Old Maid, and the same who had afterwards explained the shield of arms and recognized the features of the negro. Like their predecessors, they gave three raps with the iron hammer.

"Old Cæsar cometh not," observed the priest. "Well I wot he no longer doth service in this mansion."

"Assuredly, then, it was something worse, in old Cæsar's likeness!" said the other adventurer.

"Be it as God wills," answered the clergyman. "See! my strength, though it be much decayed, hath sufficed to open this heavy door. Let us enter and pass up the staircase."

Here occurred a singular exemplification of the dreamy state of a very old man's mind. As they ascended the wide flight of stairs, the aged clergyman appeared to move with caution, occasionally standing aside, and oftener bending his head, as it were in salutation, thus practising all the gestures of one who makes his way through a throng. Reaching the head of the staircase, he looked around with sad and solemn benignity, laid aside his staff, bared his

hoary locks, and was evidently on the point of com-
mencing a prayer.

"Reverend Sir," said his attendant, who conceived
this a very suitable prelude to their further search,
"would it not be well that the people join with us in
prayer?"

"Welladay!" cried the old clergyman, staring
strangely around him. "Art thou here with me,
and none other? Verily, past times were present
to me, and I deemed that I was to make a funeral
prayer, as many a time heretofore, from the head of
this staircase. Of a truth, I saw the shades of many
that are gone. Yea, I have prayed at their burials,
one after another, and the 'Old Maid in the Winding
Sheet' hath seen them to their graves!"

Being now more thoroughly awake to their present
purpose, he took his staff and struck forcibly on the
floor, till there came an echo from each deserted chamber, but no menial to answer their summons. They
therefore walked along the passage, and again paused,
opposite to the great front window through which was
seen the crowd, in the shadow and partial moonlight of
the street beneath. On their right hand was the open
door of a chamber, and a closed one on their left. The
clergyman pointed his cane to the carved oak panel of
the latter.

"Within that chamber," observed he, "a whole
life-time since, did I sit by the death-bed of a goodly
young man, who, being now at the last gasp" —

Apparently there was some powerful excitement in
the ideas which had now flashed across his mind. He
snatched the torch from his companion's hand, and
threw open the door with such sudden violence that
the flame was extinguished, leaving them no other

light than the moonbeams, which fell through two windows into the spacious chamber. It was sufficient to discover all that could be known. In a high-backed oaken arm-chair, upright, with her hands clasped across her breast, and her head thrown back, sat the " Old Maid in the Winding Sheet." The stately dame had fallen on her knees, with her forehead on the holy knees of the Old Maid, one hand upon the floor and the other pressed convulsively against her heart. It clutched a lock of hair, once sable, now discolored with a greenish mould. As the priest and layman advanced into the chamber, the Old Maid's features assumed such a semblance of shifting expression that they trusted to hear the whole mystery explained by a single word. But it was only the shadow of a tattered curtain waving betwixt the dead face and the moonlight.

"Both dead!" said the venerable man. "Then who shall divulge the secret? Methinks it glimmers to and fro in my mind, like the light and shadow across the Old Maid's face. And now 't is gone!"

PETER GOLDTHWAITE'S TREASURE.

"And so, Peter, you won't even consider of the business?" said Mr. John Brown, buttoning his surtout over the snug rotundity of his person, and drawing on his gloves. "You positively refuse to let me have this crazy old house, and the land under and adjoining, at the price named?"

"Neither at that, nor treble the sum," responded the gaunt, grizzled, and threadbare Peter Goldthwaite. "The fact is, Mr. Brown, you must find another site for your brick block, and be content to leave my estate with the present owner. Next summer, I intend to put a splendid new mansion over the cellar of the old house."

"Pho, Peter!" cried Mr. Brown, as he opened the kitchen door; "content yourself with building castles in the air, where house-lots are cheaper than on earth, to say nothing of the cost of bricks and mortar. Such foundations are solid enough for your edifices, while this underneath us is just the thing for mine; and so we may both be suited. What say you again?"

"Precisely what I said before, Mr. Brown," answered Peter Goldthwaite. "And as for castles in the air, mine may not be as magnificent as that sort of architecture, but perhaps as substantial, Mr. Brown, as the very respectable brick block with dry goods stores, tailors' shops, and banking rooms on the lower floor, and lawyers' offices in the second story, which you are so anxious to substitute."

" And the cost, Peter, eh?" said Mr. Brown, as he withdrew, in something of a pet. "That, I suppose, will be provided for, off-hand, by drawing a check on Bubble Bank! "

John Brown and Peter Goldthwaite had been jointly known to the commercial world between twenty and thirty years before, under the firm of Goldthwaite & Brown; which copartnership, however, was speedily dissolved by the natural incongruity of its constituent parts. Since that event, John Brown, with exactly the qualities of a thousand other John Browns, and by just such plodding methods as they used, had prospered wonderfully, and become one of the wealthiest John Browns on earth. Peter Goldthwaite, on the contrary, after innumerable schemes, which ought to have collected all the coin and paper currency of the country into his coffers, was as needy a gentleman as ever wore a patch upon his elbow. The contrast between him and his former partner may be briefly marked; for Brown never reckoned upon luck, yet always had it; while Peter made luck the main condition of his projects, and always missed it. While the means held out, his speculations had been magnificent, but were chiefly confined, of late years, to such small business as adventures in the lottery. Once he had gone on a gold-gathering expedition somewhere to the South, and ingeniously contrived to empty his pockets more thoroughly than ever; while others, doubtless, were filling theirs with native bullion by the handful. More recently he had expended a legacy of a thousand or two of dollars in purchasing Mexican scrip, and thereby became the proprietor of a province; which, however, so far as Peter could find out, was situated where he might have had an empire for the same money, — in the clouds. From a search after this valuable real estate Peter returned so gaunt and threadbare that, on reaching New England, the scarecrows in the cornfields beckoned to him, as he passed by. "They did but flutter in the wind," quoth Peter Goldthwaite. No, Peter, they beckoned, for the scarecrows knew their brother!

At the period of our story his whole visible income would not have paid the tax of the old mansion in which we find him. It was one of those rusty, moss-grown, many-peaked wooden houses, which are scattered about the streets of our elder towns, with a beetle-browed second story projecting over the foundation, as if it frowned at the novelty around it. This old paternal edifice, needy as he was, and though, being centrally situated on the principal street of the town, it would have brought him a handsome sum, the sagacious Peter had his own reasons for never parting with, either by auction or private sale. There seemed, indeed, to be a fatality that connected him with his birthplace; for, often as he had stood on the verge of ruin, and standing there even now, he had not yet taken the step beyond it which would have compelled him to surrender the house to his creditors. So here he dwelt with bad luck till good should come.

Here then in his kitchen, the only room where a spark of fire took off the chill of a November evening, poor Peter Goldthwaite had just been visited by his rich old partner. At the close of their interview, Peter, with rather a mortified look, glanced downwards at his dress, parts of which appeared as ancient as the days of Goldthwaite & Brown. His upper garment was a mixed surtout, wofully faded, and patched with newer stuff on each elbow; beneath this he wore a threadbare black coat, some of the silk buttons of which had been replaced with others of a different pattern; and lastly, though he lacked not a pair of gray pantaloons, they were very shabby ones, and had been partially turned brown by the frequent toasting of Peter's shins before a scanty fire. Peter's person was in keeping with his goodly apparel. Gray-headed, hollow-eyed, pale-cheeked, and lean-bodied, he was the perfect picture of a man who had fed on windy schemes and empty hopes, till he could neither live on such unwholesome trash, nor stomach more substantial food. But, withal, this Peter Goldthwaite, crack-brained simpleton as, perhaps, he was, might have cut a very brilliant figure in the world, had he employed his imagination in the airy business of poetry, instead of making it a demon of mischief in mercantile pursuits. After all, he was no bad fellow, but as harmless as a child, and as honest and honorable, and as much of the gentleman which nature meant him for, as an irregular life and depressed circumstances will permit any man to be.

As Peter stood on the uneven bricks of his hearth, looking round at the disconsolate old kitchen, his eyes began to kindle with the illumination of an enthusiasm that never long deserted him. He raised his hand, clinched it, and smote it energetically against the smoky panel over the fireplace.

"The time is come!" said he. "With such a treasure at command, it were folly to be a poor man any longer. To-morrow morning I will begin with the garret, nor desist till I have torn the house down!"

Deep in the chimney-corner, like a witch in a dark cavern, sat a little old woman, mending one of the two pairs of stockings wherewith Peter Goldthwaite kept his toes from being frostbitten. As the feet were ragged past all darning, she had cut pieces out of a cast-off flannel petticoat, to make new soles. Tabitha Porter was an old maid, upwards of sixty years of age, fifty-five of which she had sat in that same chimney-corner, such being the length of time since Peter's grandfather had taken her from the almshouse. She had no friend but Peter, nor Peter any friend but Tabitha; so long as Peter might have a shelter for his own head, Tabitha would know where to shelter hers; or, being homeless elsewhere, she would take her master by the hand and bring him to her native home, the almshouse. Should it ever be necessary, she loved him well enough to feed him with her last morsel, and clothe him with her under petticoat. But Tabitha was a queer old woman, and, though never infected with Peter's flightiness, had become so accustomed to his freaks and follies that she viewed them all as matters of course. Hearing him threaten to tear the house down, she looked quietly up from her work.

"Best leave the kitchen till the last, Mr. Peter," said she.

"The sooner we have it all down the better," said Peter Goldthwaite. "I am tired to death of living in this cold, dark, windy, smoky, creaking, groaning, dismal old house. I shall feel like a younger man when we get into my splendid brick mansion, as, please Heaven, we shall by this time next autumn. You shall have a room on the sunny side, old Tabby, finished and furnished as best may suit your own notions."

"I should like it pretty much such a room as this kitchen," answered Tabitha. "It will never be like home to me till the chimney-corner gets as black with smoke as this ; and that won't be these hundred years. How much do you mean to lay out on the house, Mr. Peter ? "

" What is that to the purpose ? " exclaimed Peter, oftily. " Did not my great-granduncle, Peter Gold, chwaite, who died seventy years ago, and whose name. sake I am, leave treasure enough to build twenty such ? "

" I can't say but he did, Mr. Peter," said Tabitha, threading her needle.

Tabitha well understood that Peter had reference to an immense hoard of the precious metals, which was said to exist somewhere in the cellar or walls, or under the floors, or in some concealed closet, or other out-of-the-way nook of the house. This wealth, accord- ing to tradition, had been accumulated by a former Peter Goldthwaite, whose character seems to have borne a remarkable similitude to that of the Peter of our story. Like him he was a wild projector, seeking to heap up gold by the bushel and the cartload, in- stead of scraping it together, coin by coin. Like Peter the second, too, his projects had almost invaria- bly failed, and, but for the magnificent success of the final one, would have left him with hardly a coat and pair of breeches to his gaunt and grizzled person. Reports were various as to the nature of his fortunate speculation : one intimating that the ancient Peter had made the gold by alchemy; another, that he had con- jured it out of people's pockets by the black art ; and a third, still more unaccountable, that the devil had given him free access to the old provincial treasury. It was affirmed, however, that some secret impediment had debarred him from the enjoyment of his riches, and that he had a motive for concealing them from his heir, or at any rate had died without disclosing the place of deposit. The present Peter's father had faith enough in the story to cause the cellar to be dug over. Peter himself chose to consider the legend as an indisputable truth, and, amid his many troubles, had this one consolation that, should all other resources fail, he might build up his fortunes by tearing his house down. Yet, unless he felt a lurking distrust of the golden tale, it is difficult to account for his permitting the paternal roof to stand so long, since he had never yet seen the moment when his predecessor's treasure would not have found plenty of room in his own strong box. But now was the crisis. Should he delay the search a little longer, the house would pass from the lineal heir, and with it the vast heap of gold, to remain in its burial-place, till the ruin of the aged walls should discover it to strangers of a future generation.

"Yes!" cried Peter Goldthwaite, again, "to-morrow I will set about it."

The deeper he looked at the matter the more certain of success grew Peter. His spirits were naturally so elastic that even now, in the blasted autumn of his age, he could often compete with the spring-time gayety of other people. Enlivened by his brightening prospects, he began to caper about the kitchen like a hobgoblin, with the queerest antics of his lean limbs, and gesticulations of his starved features. Nay, in the exuberance of his feelings, he seized both of Tabitha's hands, and danced the old lady across the floor, till the oddity of her rheumatic motions set him into a roar of laughter, which was echoed back from the rooms and chambers, as if Peter Goldthwaite were laughing in every one. Finally he bounded upward almost out of sight, into the smoke that clouded the roof of the kitchen, and, alighting safely on the floor again, endeavored to resume his customary gravity.

"To-morrow, at sunrise," he repeated, taking his lamp to retire to bed, "I 'll see whether this treasure be hid in the wall of the garret."

"And as we 're out of wood, Mr. Peter," said Tabitha, puffing and panting with her late gymnastics, "as fast as you tear the house down, I 'll make a fire with the pieces."

Gorgeous that night were the dreams of Peter Goldthwaite! At one time he was turning a ponderous key in an iron door not unlike the door of a sepulchre, but which, being opened, disclosed a vault heaped up with gold coin, as plentifully as golden corn in a granary. There were chased goblets, also, and tureens, salvers, dinner dishes, and dish covers of gold, or silver gilt, besides chains and other jewels, incalculably rich, though tarnished with the damps of the vault; for, of all the wealth that was irrevocably lost to man, whether buried in the earth or sunken in the sea, Peter Goldthwaite had found it in this one treasure-place. Anon, he had returned to the old house as poor as ever, and was received at the door by the gaunt and grizzled figure of a man whom he might have mistaken for himself, only that his garments were of a much elder fashion. But the house, without losing its former aspect, had been changed into a palace of the precious metals. The floors, walls, and ceiling were of burnished silver; the doors, the window frames, the cornices, the balustrades, and the steps of the staircase, of pure gold; and silver, with gold bottoms, were the chairs, and gold, standing on silver legs, the high chests of drawers, and silver the bedsteads, with blankets of woven gold, and sheets of silver tissue. The house had evidently been transmuted by a single touch; for it retained all the marks that Peter remembered, but in gold or silver instead of wood; and the initials of his name, which, when a boy, he had cut in the wooden door-post, remained as deep in the pillar of gold. A happy man would have been Peter Goldthwaite except for a certain ocular deception, which, whenever he glanced backwards, caused the house to darken from its glittering magnificence into the sordid gloom of yesterday.

Up, betimes, rose Peter, seized an axe, hammer, and saw, which he had placed by his bedside, and hied him to the garret. It was but scantily lighted up, as yet, by the frosty fragments of a sunbeam, which began to glimmer through the almost opaque bull's-eyes of the window. A moralizer might find abundant themes for his speculative and impracticable wisdom in a garret. There is the limbo of departed fashions, aged trifles of a day, and whatever was valuable only to one generation of men, and which passed to the garret when that generation passed to the grave, not for safe keeping, but to be out of the way. Peter saw piles of yellow and musty account-books, in parchment covers, wherein creditors, long dead and buried, had written the names of dead and buried debtors in ink now so faded that their moss-grown tombstones were more legible. He found old moth-eaten garments all in rags and tatters, or Peter would have put them on. Here was a naked and rusty sword, not a sword of service, but a gentleman's small French rapier, which had never left its scabbard till it lost it. Here were canes of twenty different sorts, but no gold-headed ones, and shoe-buckles of various pattern

and material, but not silver nor set with precious
stones. Here was a large box full of shoes, with high
heels and peaked toes. Here, on a shelf, were a multitude of phials, half-filled with old apothecaries' stuff
which, when the other half had done its business on
Peter's ancestors, had been brought hither from the
death chamber. Here — not to give a longer inven-
tory of articles that will never be put up at auction —
was the fragment of a full-length looking-glass, which,
by the dust and dimness of its surface, made the picture of these old things look older than the reality.
When Peter, not knowing that there was a mirror
there, caught the faint traces of his own figure, he
partly imagined that the former Peter Goldthwaite
had come back, either to assist or impede his search
for the hidden wealth. And at that moment a strange
notion glimmered through his brain that he was the
identical Peter who had concealed the gold, and ought
to know whereabout it lay. This, however, he had
unacountably forgotten.

"Well, Mr. Peter!" cried Tabitha, on the garret
stairs. "Have you torn the house down enough to
heat the teakettle?"

"Not yet, old Tabby," answered Peter; "but that's
soon done — as you shall see."

With the word in his mouth, he uplifted the axe
and laid about him so vigorously that the dust flew,
the boards crashed, and, in a twinkling, the old woman
had an apron full of broken rubbish.

"We shall get our winter's wood cheap," quoth
Tabitha.

The good work being thus commenced, Peter beat
down all before him, smiting and hewing at the joists
and timbers, unclinching spike-nails, ripping and tear-

ing away boards, with a tremendous racket, from morning till night. He took care, however, to leave the outside shell of the house untouched, so that the neighbors might not suspect what was going on.

Never, in any of his vagaries, though each had ,made him happy while it lasted, had Peter been happier than now. Perhaps, after all, there was something in Peter Goldthwaite's turn of mind, which brought him an inward recompense for all the external evil that it caused. If he were poor, ill-clad, even hungry, and exposed, as it were, to be utterly annihilated by a precipice of impending ruin, yet only his body remained in these miserable circumstances, while his aspiring soul enjoyed the sunshine of a bright futurity. It was his nature to be always young, and the tendency of his mode of life to keep him so. Gray hairs were nothing, no, nor wrinkles, nor infirmity; he might look old, indeed, and be somewhat disagreeably connected with a gaunt old figure, much the worse for wear; but the true, the essential Peter was a young man of high hopes, just entering on the world. At the kindling of each new fire, his burnt-out youth rose afresh from the old embers and ashes. It rose exulting now. Having lived thus long — not too long, but just to the right age — a susceptible bachelor, with warm and tender dreams, he resolved, so soon as the hidden gold should flash to light, to go a-wooing, and win the love of the fairest maid in town. What heart could resist him? Happy Peter Goldthwaite!

Every evening — as Peter had long absented himself from his former lounging-places, at insurance offices, news-rooms, and bookstores, and as the honor of his company was seldom requested in private circles — he and Tabitha used to sit down sociably by the kitchen hearth. This was always heaped plentifully with the rubbish of his day's labor. As the foundation of the fire, there would be a goodly-sized backlog of red oak, which, after being sheltered from rain or damp above a century, still hissed with the heat, and distilled streams of water from each end, as if the tree had been cut down within a week or two. Next these were large sticks, sound, black, and heavy, which had lost the principle of decay, and were indestructible except by fire, wherein they glowed like red-hot bars of iron. On this solid basis, Tabitha would rear a lighter structure, composed of the splinters of door panels, ornamented mouldings, and such quick combustibles, which caught like straw, and threw a brilliant blaze high up the spacious flue, making its sooty sides visible almost to the chimney-top. Meantime, the gleam of the old kitchen would be chased out of the cobwebbed corners, and away from the dusky cross-beams overhead, and driven nobody could tell whither, while Peter smiled like a gladsome man, and Tabitha seemed a picture of comfortable age. All this, of course, was but an emblem of the bright fortune which the destruction of the house would shed upon its occupants.

While the dry pine was flaming and crackling, like an irregular discharge of fairy musketry, Peter sat looking and listening, in a pleasant state of excitement. But, when the brief blaze and uproar were succeeded by the dark-red glow, the substantial heat, and the deep singing sound, which were to last throughout the evening, his humor became talkative. One night, the hundredth time, he teased Tabitha to tell him something new about his great-granduncle.

" You have been sitting in that chimney-corner fifty-five years, old Tabby, and must have heard many a tradition about him," said Peter. "Did not you tell me that, when you first came to the house, there was an old woman sitting where you sit now, who had been housekeeper to the famous Peter Goldthwaite?"

"So there was, Mr. Peter," answered Tabitha, "and she was near about a hundred years old. She used to say that she and old Peter Goldthwaite had often spent a sociable evening by the kitchen fire — pretty much as you and I are doing now, Mr. Peter."

"The old fellow must have resembled me in more points than one," said Peter, complacently, "or he never would have grown so rich. But, methinks, he might have invested the money better than he did — no interest! — nothing but good security! — and the house to be torn down to come at it! What made him hide it so snug, Tabby?"

"Because he could not spend it," said Tabitha; "for as often as he went to unlock the chest, the Old Scratch came behind and caught his arm. The money, they say, was paid Peter out of his purse; and he wanted Peter to give him a deed of this house and land, which Peter swore he would not do."

"Just as I swore to John Brown, my old partner," remarked Peter. "But this is all nonsense, Tabby! I don't believe the story."

"Well, it may not be just the truth," said Tabitha; "for some folks say that Peter did make over the house to the Old Scratch, and that's the reason it has always been so unlucky to them that lived in it. And as soon as Peter had given him the deed, the chest flew open, and Peter caught up a handful of the gold. But, lo and behold! — there was nothing in his fist but a parcel of old rags."

"Hold your tongue, you silly old Tabby!" cried

Peter in great wrath. "They were as good golden
guineas as ever bore the effigies of the king of England. It seems as if I could recollect the whole circumstance, and how I, or old Peter, or whoever it was,
thrust in my hand, or his hand, and drew it out all of
a blaze with gold. Old rags, indeed!"

But it was not an old woman's legend that would
discourage Peter Goldthwaite. All night long he
slept among pleasant dreams, and awoke at daylight
with a joyous throb of the heart, which few are fortunate enough to feel beyond their boyhood. Day
after day he labored hard without wasting a moment,
except at meal times, when Tabitha summoned him to
the pork and cabbage, or such other sustenance as she
had picked up, or Providence had sent them. Being a
truly pious man, Peter never failed to ask a blessing;
if the food were none of the best, then so much the
more earnestly, as it was more needed; — nor to return thanks, if the dinner had been scanty, yet for the
good appetite, which was better than a sick stomach
at a feast. Then did he hurry back to his toil, and, in
a moment, was lost to sight in a cloud of dust from
the old walls, though sufficiently perceptible to the ear
by the clatter which he raised in the midst of it. How
enviable is the consciousness of being usefully employed! Nothing troubled Peter; or nothing but
those phantoms of the mind which seem like vague
recollections, yet have also the aspect of presentiments.
He often paused, with his axe uplifted in the air, and
said to himself, — "Peter Goldthwaite, did you never
strike this blow before?" — or, "Peter, what need of
tearing the whole house down? Think a little while,
and you will remember where the gold is hidden."
Days and weeks passed on, however, without any re-

markable discovery. Sometimes, indeed, a lean, gray
rat peeped forth at the lean, gray man, wondering
what devil had got into the old house, which had always been so peaceable till now. And, occasionally,
Peter sympathized with the sorrows of a female mouse,
who had brought five or six pretty, little, soft and
delicate young ones into the world just in time to
see them crushed by its ruin. But, as yet, no treasure!

By this time, Peter, being as determined as Fate
and as diligent as Time, had made an end with the
uppermost regions, and got down to the second story,
where he was busy in one of the front chambers. It
had formerly been the state bed-chamber, and was
honored by tradition as the sleeping apartment of
Governor Dudley, and many other eminent guests.
The furniture was gone. There were remnants of
faded and tattered paper-hangings, but larger spaces
of bare wall ornamented with charcoal sketches, chiefly
of people's heads in profile. These being specimens of
Peter's youthful genius, it went more to his heart to
obliterate them than if they had been pictures on a
church wall by Michael Angelo. One sketch, however, and that the best one, affected him differently.
It represented a ragged man, partly supporting himself on a spade, and bending his lean body over a hole
in the earth, with one hand extended to grasp something that he had found. But close behind him, with
a fiendish laugh on his features, appeared a figure with
horns, a tufted tail, and a cloven hoof.

"Avaunt, Satan!" cried Peter. "The man shall
have his gold!"

Uplifting his axe, he hit the horned gentleman such
a blow on the head as not only demolished him, but

the treasure-seeker also, and caused the whole scene to vanish like magic. Moreover, his axe broke quite through the plaster and laths, and discovered a cavity.

"Mercy on us, Mr. Peter, are you quarrelling with the Old Scratch?" said Tabitha, who was seeking some fuel to put under the pot.

Without answering the old woman, Peter broke down a further space of the wall, and laid open a small closet or cupboard, on one side of the fireplace, about breast high from the ground. It contained nothing but a brass lamp, covered with verdigris, and a dusty piece of parchment. While Peter inspected the latter, Tabitha seized the lamp, and began to rub it with her apron.

"There is no use in rubbing it, Tabitha," said Peter. "It is not Aladdin's lamp, though I take it to be a token of as much luck. Look here, Tabby!"

Tabitha took the parchment and held it close to her nose, which was saddled with a pair of iron-bound spectacles. But no sooner had she began to puzzle over it than she burst into a chuckling laugh, holding both her hands against her sides.

"You can't make a fool of the old woman!" cried she. "This is your own handwriting, Mr. Peter! the same as in the letter you sent me from Mexico."

"There is certainly a considerable resemblance," said Peter, again examining the parchment. "But you know yourself, Tabby, that this closet must have been plastered up before you came to the house, or I came into the world. No, this is old Peter Goldthwaite's writing; these columns of pounds, shillings and pence are his figures, denoting the amount of the treasure; and this at the bottom is, doubtless, a reference to the place of concealment. But the ink has either faded or peeled off, so that it is absolutely illegible. What a pity!"

"Well, this lamp is as good as new. That's some comfort," said Tabitha.

"A lamp!" thought Peter. "That indicates light on my researches."

For the present, Peter felt more inclined to ponder on this discovery than to resume his labors. After Tabitha had gone down stairs, he stood poring over the parchment, at one of the front windows, which was so obscured with dust that the sun could barely throw an uncertain shadow of the casement across the floor. Peter forced it open, and looked out upon the great street of the town, while the sun looked in at his old house. The air, though mild, and even warm, thrilled Peter as with a dash of water.

It was the first day of the January thaw. The snow lay deep upon the house-tops, but was rapidly dissolving into millions of water-drops, which sparkled downwards through the sunshine, with the noise of a summer shower beneath the eaves. Along the street, the trodden snow was as hard and solid as a pavement of white marble, and had not yet grown moist in the spring-like temperature. But when Peter thrust forth his head, he saw that the inhabitants, if not the town, were already thawed out by this warm day, after two or three weeks of winter weather. It gladdened him — a gladness with a sigh breathing through it — to see the stream of ladies, gliding along the slippery sidewalks, with their red cheeks set off by quilted hoods, boas, and sable capes, like roses amidst a new kind of foliage. The sleigh-bells jingled to and fro continually: sometimes announcing the arrival of a sleigh from Vermont, laden with the frozen bodies of

porkers, or sheep, and perhaps a deer or two ; sometimes of a regular market-man, with chickens, geese,
and turkeys, comprising the whole colony of a barn
yard ; and sometimes of a farmer and his dame, who
had come to town partly for the ride, partly to go
a-shopping, and partly for the sale of some eggs and
butter. This couple rode in an old-fashioned square
sleigh, which had served them twenty winters, and
stood twenty summers in the sun beside their door.
Now, a gentleman and lady skimmed the snow in an
elegant car, shaped somewhat like a cockle-shell.
Now, a stage-sleigh, with its cloth curtains thrust aside
to admit the sun, dashed rapidly down the street,
whirling in and out among the vehicles that obstructed
its passage. Now came, round a corner, the similitude
of Noah's ark on runners, being an immense open
sleigh with seats for fifty people, and drawn by a
dozen horses. This spacious receptacle was populous
with merry maids and merry bachelors, merry girls
and boys, and merry old folks, all alive with fun, and
grinning to the full width of their mouths. They kept
up a buzz of babbling voices and low laughter, and
sometimes burst into a deep, joyous shout, which the
spectators answered with three cheers, while a gang
of roguish boys let drive their snowballs right among
the pleasure party. The sleigh passed on, and, when
concealed by a bend of the street, was still audible by
a distant cry of merriment.

Never had Peter beheld a livelier scene than was
constituted by all these accessories : the bright sun,
the flashing water-drops, the gleaming snow, the cheerful multitude, the variety of rapid vehicles, and the
jingle jangle of merry bells which made the heart
dance to their music. Nothing dismal was to be seen,

except that peaked piece of antiquity, Peter Goldthwaite's house, which might well look sad externally, since such a terrible consumption was preying on its insides. And Peter's gaunt figure, half visible in the projecting second story, was worthy of his house.

"Peter! How goes it, friend Peter?" cried a voice across the street, as Peter was drawing in his head. "Look out here, Peter!"

Peter looked, and saw his old partner, Mr. John Brown, on the opposite sidewalk, portly and comfortable, with his furred cloak thrown open, disclosing a handsome surtout beneath. His voice had directed the attention of the whole town to Peter Goldthwaite's window, and to the dusty scarecrow which appeared at it.

"I say, Peter," cried Mr. Brown again, "what the devil are you about there, that I hear such a racket whenever I pass by? You are repairing the old house, I suppose, — making a new one of it, — eh?"

"Too late for that, I am afraid, Mr. Brown," replied Peter. "If I make it new, it will be new inside and out, from the cellar upwards."

"Had not you better let me take the job?" said Mr. Brown, significantly.

"Not yet!" answered Peter, hastily shutting the window; for, ever since he had been in search of the treasure, he hated to have people stare at him.

As he drew back, ashamed of his outward poverty, yet proud of the secret wealth within his grasp, a haughty smile shone out on Peter's visage, with precisely the effect of the dim sunbeams in the squalid chamber. He endeavored to assume such a mien as his ancestor had probably worn, when he gloried in the building of a strong house for a home to many

generations of his posterity. But the chamber was
very dark to his snow-dazzled eyes, and very dismal
too, in contrast with the living scene that he had just
looked upon. His brief glimpse into the street had
given him a forcible impression of the manner in
which the world kept itself cheerful and prosperous,
by social pleasures and an intercourse of business,
while he, in seclusion, was pursuing an object that
might possibly be a phantasm, by a method which
most people would call madness. It is one great advantage of a gregarious mode of life that each person
rectifies his mind by other minds, and squares his conduct to that of his neighbors, so as seldom to be lost
in eccentricity. Peter Goldthwaite had exposed himself to this influence by merely looking out of the
window. For a while, he doubted whether there were
any hidden chest of gold, and, in that case, whether
he was so exceedingly wise to tear the house down,
only to be convinced of its non-existence.

But this was momentary. Peter, the Destroyer,
resumed the task which fate had assigned him, nor
faltered again till it was accomplished. In the course
of his search, he met with many things that are usually
found in the ruins of an old house, and also with some
that are not. What seemed most to the purpose was
a rusty key, which had been thrust into a chink of the
wall, with a wooden label appended to the handle
bearing the initials, P. G. Another singular discovery
was that of a bottle of wine, walled up in an old oven.
A tradition ran in the family, that Peter's grandfather, a jovial officer in the old French War, had set
aside many dozens of the precious liquor for the benefit of topers then unborn. Peter needed no cordial to
sustain his hopes, and therefore kept the wine to glad-

den his success. Many halfpence did he pick up, that had been lost through the cracks of the floor, and some few Spanish coins, and the half of a broken sixpence, which had doubtless been a love token. There was likewise a silver coronation medal of George the Third. But old Peter Goldthwaite's strong box fled from one dark corner to another, or otherwise eluded the second Peter's clutches, till, should he seek much farther, he must burrow into the earth.

We will not follow him in his triumphant progress, step by step. Suffice it that Peter worked like a steam-engine, and finished, in that one winter, the job which all the former inhabitants of the house, with time and the elements to aid them, had only half done in a century. Except the kitchen, every room and chamber was now gutted. The house was nothing but a shell, — the apparition of a house, — as unreal as the painted edifices of a theatre. It was like the perfect rind of a great cheese, in which a mouse had dwelt and nibbled till it was a cheese no more. And Peter was the mouse.

What Peter had torn down, Tabitha had burned up; for she wisely considered that, without a house, they should need no wood to warm it; and therefore economy was nonsense. Thus the whole house might be said to have dissolved in smoke, and flown up among the clouds, through the great black flue of the kitchen chimney. It was an admirable parallel to the feat of the man who jumped down his own throat.

On the night between the last day of winter and the first of spring, every chink and cranny had been ransacked, except within the precincts of the kitchen. This fated evening was an ugly one. A snow-storm had set in some hours before, and was still driven and tossed about the atmosphere by a real hurricane, which fought against the house as if the prince of the air, in person, were putting the final stroke to Peter's labors. The framework being so much weakened, and the inward props removed, it would have been no marvel if, in some stronger wrestle of the blast, the rotten walls of the edifice, and all the peaked roofs, had come crushing down upon the owner's head. He, however, was careless of the peril, but as wild and restless as the night itself, or as the flame that quivered up the chimney at each roar of the tempestuous wind.

"The wine, Tabitha!" he cried. "My grandfather's rich old wine! We will drink it now!"

Tabitha arose from her smoke-blackened bench in the chimney-corner, and placed the bottle before Peter, close beside the old brass lamp, which had likewise been the prize of his researches. Peter held it before his eyes, and, looking through the liquid medium, beheld the kitchen illuminated with a golden glory, which also enveloped Tabitha and gilded her silver hair, and converted her mean garments into robes of queenly splendor. It reminded him of his golden dream.

"Mr. Peter," remarked Tabitha, "must the wine be drunk before the money is found?"

"The money *is* found!" exclaimed Peter, with a sort of fierceness. "The chest is within my reach. I will not sleep, till I have turned this key in the rusty lock. But, first of all, let us drink!"

There being no corkscrew in the house, he smote the neck of the bottle with old Peter Goldthwaite's rusty key, and decapitated the sealed cork at a single blow. He then filled two little china teacups, which Tabitha had brought from the cupboard. So clear

and brilliant was this aged wine that it shone within
the cups, and rendered the sprig of scarlet flowers, at
the bottom of each, more distinctly visible than when
there had been no wine there.   Its rich and delicate
perfume wasted itself round the kitchen.

"Drink, Tabitha!" cried Peter.   "Blessings on the
honest old fellow who set aside this good liquor for
you and me!   And here's to Peter Goldthwaite's
memory!"

"And good cause have we to remember him," quoth
Tabitha, as she drank.

How many years, and through what changes of
fortune and various calamity, had that bottle hoarded
up its effervescent joy, to be quaffed at last by two
such boon companions!   A portion of the happiness
of the former age had been kept for them, and was
now set free, in a crowd of rejoicing visions, to sport
amid the storm and desolation of the present time.
Until they have finished the bottle, we must turn our
eyes elsewhere.

It so chanced that, on this stormy night, Mr. John
Brown found himself ill at ease in his wire-cushioned
arm-chair, by the glowing grate of anthracite which
heated his handsome parlor.   He was naturally a good
sort of a man, and kind and pitiful whenever the misfortunes of others happened to reach his heart through
the padded vest of his own prosperity.   This evening
he had thought much about his old partner, Peter
Goldthwaite, his strange vagaries, and continual ill
luck, the poverty of his dwelling, at Mr. Brown's last
visit, and Peter's crazed and haggard aspect when he
had talked with him at the window.

"Poor fellow!" thought Mr. John Brown.   "Poor,
crackbrained Peter Goldthwaite!   For old acquaint-

ance' sake, I ought to have taken care that he was comfortable this rough winter."

These feelings grew so powerful that, in spite of the inclement weather, he resolved to visit Peter Goldthwaite immediately. The strength of the impulse was really singular. Every shriek of the blast seemed a summons, or would have seemed so, had Mr. Brown been accustomed to hear the echoes of his own fancy in the wind. Much amazed at such active benevolence, he huddled himself in his cloak, muffled his throat and ears in comforters and handkerchiefs, and, thus fortified, bade defiance to the tempest. But the powers of the air had rather the best of the battle. Mr. Brown was just weathering the corner, by Peter Goldthwaite's house, when the hurricane caught him off his feet, tossed him face downward into a snow bank, and proceeded to bury his protuberant part beneath fresh drifts. There seemed little hope of his reappearance earlier than the next thaw. At the same moment his hat was snatched away, and whirled aloft into some far distant region, whence no tidings have as yet returned.

Nevertheless Mr. Brown contrived to burrow a passage through the snow-drift, and, with his bare head bent against the storm, floundered onward to Peter's door. There was such a creaking and groaning and rattling, and such an ominous shaking throughout the crazy edifice, that the loudest rap would have been inaudible to those within. He therefore entered, without ceremony, and groped his way to the kitchen.

His intrusion, even there, was unnoticed. Peter and Tabitha stood with their backs to the door, stooping over a large chest, which, apparently, they had just dragged from a cavity, or concealed closet, on the left side of the chimney. By the lamp in the old woman's hand, Mr. Brown saw that the chest was barred and clamped with iron, strengthened with iron plates and studded with iron nails, so as to be a fit receptacle in which the wealth of one century might be hoarded up for the wants of another. Peter Goldthwaite was inserting a key into the lock.

"O Tabitha!" cried he, with tremulous rapture, "how shall I endure the effulgence? The gold!— the bright, bright gold! Methinks I can remember my last glance at it, just as the iron-plated lid fell down. And ever since, being seventy years, it has been blazing in secret, and gathering its splendor against this glorious moment! It will flash upon us like the noonday sun!"

"Then shade your eyes, Mr. Peter!" said Tabitha, with somewhat less patience than usual. "But, for mercy's sake, do turn the key!"

And, with a strong effort of both hands, Peter did force the rusty key through the intricacies of the rusty lock. Mr. Brown, in the mean time, had drawn near, and thrust his eager visage between those of the other two, at the instant that Peter threw up the lid. No sudden blaze illuminated the kitchen.

"What's here?" exclaimed Tabitha, adjusting her spectacles, and holding the lamp over the open chest. "Old Peter Goldthwaite's hoard of old rags."

"Pretty much so, Tabby," said Mr. Brown, lifting a handful of the treasure.

Oh, what a ghost of dead and buried wealth had Peter Goldthwaite raised, to scare himself out of his scanty wits withal! Here was the semblance of an incalculable sum, enough to purchase the whole town, and build every street anew, but which, vast as it was, no sane man would have given a solid sixpence for. What then, in sober earnest, were the delusive treasures of the chest? Why, here were old provincial bills of credit, and treasury notes, and bills of land, banks, and all other bubbles of the sort, from the first issue, above a century and a half ago, down nearly to the Revolution. Bills of a thousand pounds were intermixed with parchment pennies, and worth no more than they.

"And this, then, is old Peter Goldthwaite's treasure!" said John Brown. "Your namesake, Peter, was something like yourself; and, when the provincial currency had depreciated fifty or seventy-five per cent., he bought it up in expectation of a rise. I have heard my grandfather say that old Peter gave his father a mortgage of this very house and land, to raise cash for his silly project. But the currency kept sinking, till nobody would take it as a gift; and there was old Peter Goldthwaite, like Peter the second, with thousands in his strong box and hardly a coat to his back. He went mad upon the strength of it. But, never mind, Peter! It is just the sort of capital for building castles in the air."

"The house will be down about our ears!" cried Tabitha, as the wind shook it with increasing violence.

"Let it fall!" said Peter, folding his arms, as he seated himself upon the chest.

"No, no, my old friend Peter," said John Brown. "I have house room for you and Tabby, and a safe vault for the chest of treasure. To-morrow we will try to come to an agreement about the sale of this old house. Real estate is well up, and I could afford you a pretty handsome price."

"And I," observed Peter Goldthwaite, with reviving spirits, "have a plan for laying out the cash to great advantage."

"Why, as to that," muttered John Brown to him self, "we must apply to the next court for a guardian to take care of the solid cash; and if Peter insists upon speculating, he may do it, to his heart's content, with old PETER GOLDTHWAITE'S TREASURE."

CHIPPINGS WITH A CHISEL.

PASSING a summer, several years since, at Edgar-town, on the island of Martha's Vineyard, I became acquainted with a certain carver of tombstones, who had travelled and voyaged thither from the interior of Massachusetts, in search of professional employment. The speculation had turned out so successful that my friend expected to transmute slate and marble into silver and gold, to the amount of at least a thousand dollars, during the few months of his sojourn at Nantucket and the Vineyard. The secluded life, and the simple and primitive spirit which still characterizes the inhabitants of those islands, especially of Martha's Vineyard, insure their dead friends a longer and dearer remembrance than the daily novelty and revolving bustle of the world can elsewhere afford to beings of the past. Yet while every family is anxious to erect a memorial to its departed members, the untainted breath of ocean bestows such health and length of days upon the people of the isles, as would cause a melancholy dearth of business to a resident artist in that line. His own monument, recording his death by starvation, would probably be an early specimen of his skill. Gravestones, therefore, have generally been an article of imported merchandise.

In my walks through the burial-ground of Edgar-town — where the dead have lain so long that the soil, once enriched by their decay, has returned to its original barrenness — in that ancient burial-ground I noticed much variety of monumental sculpture. The elder stones, dated a century back or more, have borders elaborately carved with flowers, and are adorned with a multiplicity of death's heads, cross-bones, scythes, hour-glasses, and other lugubrious emblems of mortality, with here and there a winged cherub to direct the mourner's spirit upward. These productions of Gothic taste must have been quite beyond the colonial skill of the day, and were probably carved in London, and brought across the ocean to commemorate the defunct worthies of this lonely isle. The more recent monuments are mere slabs of slate, in the ordinary style, without any superfluous flourishes to set off the bald inscriptions. But others — and those far the most impressive both to my taste and feelings — were roughly hewn from the gray rocks of the island, evidently by the unskilled hands of surviving friends and relatives. On some there were merely the initials of a name; some were inscribed with misspelt prose or rhyme, in deep letters, which the moss and wintry rain of many years had not been able to obliterate. These, these were graves where loved ones slept! It is an old theme of satire, the falsehood and vanity of monumental eulogies; but when affection and sorrow grave the letters with their own painful labor, then we may be sure that they copy from the record on their hearts.

My acquaintance, the sculptor, — he may share that title with Greenough, since the dauber of signs is a painter as well as Raphael, — had found a ready market for all his blank slabs of marble, and full occupation in lettering and ornamenting them. He was an elderly man, a descendant of the old Puritan family of Wigglesworth, with a certain simplicity and single-ness both of heart and mind, which, methinks, is more

rarely found among us Yankees than in any other community of people. In spite of his gray head and wrinkled brow, he was quite like a child in all matters save what had some reference to his own business; he seemed, unless my fancy misled me, to view mankind in no other relation than as people in want of tomb-stones; and his literary attainments evidently comprehended very little, either of prose or poetry, which had not, at one time or other, been inscribed on slate or marble. His sole task and office among the immortal pilgrims of the tomb — the duty for which Providence had sent the old man into the world as it were with a chisel in his hand — was to label the dead bodies, lest their names should be forgotten at the resurrection. Yet he had not failed, within a narrow scope, to gather a few sprigs of earthly, and more than earthly, wisdom, — the harvest of many a grave.

And lugubrious as his calling might appear, he was as cheerful an old soul as health and integrity and lack of care could make him, and used to set to work upon one sorrowful inscription or another with that sort of spirit which impels a man to sing at his labor. On the whole I found Mr. Wigglesworth an entertaining, and often instructive, if not an interesting, character; and partly for the charm of his society, and still more because his work has an invariable attraction for "man that is born of woman," I was accustomed to spend some hours a day at his workshop. The quaintness of his remarks, and their not infrequent truth — a truth condensed and pointed by the limited sphere of his view — gave a raciness to his talk, which mere worldliness and general cultivation would at once have destroyed.

Sometimes we would discuss the respective merits

of the various qualities of marble, numerous slabs of
which were resting against the walls of the shop; or
sometimes an hour or two would pass quietly, without
a word on either side, while I watched how neatly his
chisel struck out letter after letter of the names of the
Nortons, the Mayhews, the Luces, the Daggets, and
other immemorial families of the Vineyard. Often,
with an artist's pride, the good old sculptor would
speak of favorite productions of his skill which were
scattered throughout the village graveyards of New
England. But my chief and most instructive amusement was to witness his interviews with his customers,
who held interminable consultations about the form
and fashion of the desired monuments, the buried excellence to be commemorated, the anguish to be expressed, and finally, the lowest price in dollars and
cents for which a marble transcript of their feelings
might be obtained. Really, my mind received many
fresh ideas which, perhaps, may remain in it even
longer than Mr. Wigglesworth's hardest marble will
retain the deepest strokes of his chisel.

An elderly lady came to bespeak a monument for
her first love who had been killed by a whale in the
Pacific Ocean no less than forty years before. It was
singular that so strong an impression of early feeling
should have survived through the changes of her subsequent life, in the course of which she had been a
wife and a mother, and, so far as I could judge, a comfortable and happy woman. Reflecting within myself,
it appeared to me that this lifelong sorrow — as, in all
good faith, she deemed it — was one of the most fortunate circumstances of her history. It had given an
ideality to her mind; it had kept her purer and less
earthly than she would otherwise have been, by draw-

ing a portion of her sympathies apart from earth. Amid the throng of enjoyments and the pressure of worldly care, and all the warm materialism of this life, she had communed with a vision, and had been the better for such intercourse. Faithful to the husband of her maturity, and loving him with a far more real affection than she ever could have felt for this dream of her girlhood, there had still been an imaginative faith to the ocean-buried, so that an ordinary character had thus been elevated and refined. Her sighs had been the breath of heaven to her soul. The good lady earnestly desired that the proposed monument should be ornamented with a carved border of marine plants, intertwined with twisted sea-shells, such as were probably waving over her lover's skeleton, or strewn around it in the far depths of the Pacific. But Mr. Wigglesworth's chisel being inadequate to the task, she was forced to content herself with a rose hanging its head from a broken stem. After her departure, I remarked that the symbol was none of the most apt.

"And yet," said my friend the sculptor, embodying in this image the thoughts that had been passing through my own mind, "that broken rose has shed its sweet smell through forty years of the good woman's life."

It was seldom that I could find such pleasant food for contemplation as in the above instance. None of the applicants, I think, affected me more disagreeably than an old man who came, with his fourth wife hanging on his arm, to bespeak gravestones for the three former occupants of his marriage-bed. I watched with some anxiety to see whether his remembrance of either were more affectionate than of the other two, but could discover no symptom of the kind. The three monuments were all to be of the same material and form, and each decorated, in bass-relief, with two weeping willows, one of these sympathetic trees bending over its fellow, which was to be broken in the midst and rest upon a sepulchral urn. This, indeed, was Mr. Wigglesworth's standing emblem of conjugal bereavement. 1 shuddered at the gray polygamist who had so utterly lost the holy sense of individuality in wedlock, that methought he was fain to reckon upon his fingers how many women, who had once slept by his side, were now sleeping in their graves. There was even — if I wrong him it is no great matter — a glance sidelong at his living spouse, as if he were inclined to drive a thriftier bargain by bespeaking four gravestones in a lot. I was better pleased with a rough old whaling captain, who gave directions for a broad marble slab, divided into two compartments, one of which was to contain an epitaph on his deceased wife, and the other to be left vacant, till death should engrave his own name there. As is frequently the case among the whalers of Martha's Vineyard, so much of this storm-beaten widower's life had been tossed away on distant seas, that out of twenty years of matrimony he had spent scarce three, and those at scattered intervals, beneath his own roof. Thus the wife of his youth, though she died in his and her declining age, retained the bridal dew-drops fresh around her memory.

My observations gave me the idea, and Mr. Wigglesworth confirmed it, that husbands were more faithful in setting up memorials to their dead wives than widows to their dead husbands. I was not ill-natured enough to fancy that women, less than men, feel so sure of their constancy as to be willing to give a

pledge of it in marble. It is more probably the fact
that while men are able to reflect upon their lost
companions as remembrances apart from themselves,
women, on the other hand, are conscious that a portion of their being has gone with the departed whith-
ersoever he has gone. Soul clings to soul; the living
dust has a sympathy with the dust of the grave; and,
by the very strength of that sympathy, the wife of the
dead shrinks the more sensitively from reminding the
world of its existence. The link is already strong
enough; it needs no visible symbol. And though a
shadow walks ever by her side, and the touch of a chill
hand is on her bosom, yet life, and perchance its natural yearnings, may still be warm within her, and inspire her with new hopes of happiness. Then would
she mark out the grave, the scent of which would be
perceptible on the pillow of the second bridal? No —
but rather level its green mound with the surrounding
earth, as if, when she dug up again her buried heart,
the spot had ceased to be a grave. Yet, in spite of
these sentimentalities, I was prodigiously amused by
an incident, of which I had not the good fortune to be
a witness, but which Mr. Wigglesworth related with
considerable humor. A gentlewoman of the town,
receiving news of her husband's loss at sea, had bespoken a handsome slab of marble, and came daily to
watch the progress of my friend's chisel. One afternoon, when the good lady and the sculptor were in the
very midst of the epitaph, which the departed spirit
might have been greatly comforted to read, who
should walk into the workshop but the deceased himself, in substance as well as spirit! He had been
picked up at sea, and stood in no present need of
tombstone or epitaph.

"And how," inquired I, "did his wife bear the shock of joyful surprise?"

"Why," said the old man, deepening the grin of a death's-head, on which his chisel was just then employed, "I really felt for the poor woman; it was one of my best pieces of marble — and to be thrown away on a living man!"

A comely woman, with a pretty rosebud of a daughter, came to select a gravestone for a twin daughter, who had died a month before. I was impressed with the different nature of their feelings for the dead; the mother was calm and wofully resigned, fully conscious of her loss, as of a treasure which she had not always possessed, and, therefore, had been aware that it might be taken from her; but the daughter evidently had no real knowledge of what death's doings were. Her thoughts knew, but not her heart. It seemed to me, that by the print and pressure which the dead sister had left upon the survivor's spirit, her feelings were almost the same as if she still stood side by side and arm in arm with the departed, looking at the slabs of marble; and once or twice she glanced around with a sunny smile, which, as its sister smile had faded forever, soon grew confusedly overshadowed. Perchance her consciousness was truer than her reflection — perchance her dead sister was a closer companion than in life. The mother and daughter talked a long while with Mr. Wigglesworth about a suitable epitaph, and finally chose an ordinary verse of ill-matched rhymes, which had already been inscribed upon innumerable tombstones. But when we ridicule the triteness of monumental verses, we forget that Sorrow reads far deeper in them than we can, and finds a profound and individual purport in what seems so vague and inexpressive, unless interpreted by her. She makes the epitaph anew, though the selfsame words may have served for a thousand graves.

"And yet," said I afterwards to Mr. Wigglesworth, "they might have made a better choice than this. While you were discussing the subject, I was struck by at least a dozen simple and natural expressions from the lips of both mother and daughter. One of these would have formed an inscription equally original and appropriate."

"No, no," replied the sculptor, shaking his head ; "there is a good deal of comfort to be gathered from these little old scraps of poetry ; and so I always recommend them in preference to any new-fangled ones. And somehow, they seem to stretch to suit a great grief, and shrink to fit a small one."

It was not seldom that ludicrous images were excited by what took place between Mr. Wigglesworth and his customers. A shrewd gentlewoman, who kept a tavern in the town, was anxious to obtain two or three gravestones for the deceased members of her family, and to pay for these solemn commodities by taking the sculptor to board. Hereupon a fantasy arose in my mind of good Mr. Wigglesworth sitting down to dinner at a broad, flat tombstone, carving one of his own plump little marble cherubs, gnawing a pair of cross-bones, and drinking out of a hollow death's-head, or perhaps a lachrymatory vase, or sepulchral urn, while his hostess's dead children waited on him at the ghastly banquet. On communicating this nonsensical picture to the old man he laughed heartily, and pronounced my humor to be of the right sort.

"I have lived at such a table all my days," said he, "and eaten no small quantity of slate and marble."

"Hard fare!" rejoined I, smiling; "but you seemed to have found it excellent of digestion, too."

A man of fifty, or thereabouts, with a harsh, unpleasant countenance, ordered a stone for the grave of his bittter enemy, with whom he had waged warfare half a lifetime, to their mutual misery and ruin. The secret of this phenomenon was, that hatred had become the sustenance and enjoyment of the poor wretch's soul; it had supplied the place of all kindly affections; it had been really a bond of sympathy between himself and the man who shared the passion; and when its object died the unappeasable foe was the only mourner for the dead. He expressed a purpose of being buried side by side with his enemy.

"I doubt whether their dust will mingle," remarked the old sculptor to me; for often there was an earthliness in his conceptions.

"Oh yes," replied I, who had mused long upon the incident; "and when they rise again, these bitter foes may find themselves dear friends. Methinks what they mistook for hatred was but love under a mask."

A gentleman of antiquarian propensities provided a memorial for an Indian of Chabbiquidick, one of the few of untainted blood remaining in that region, and said to be an hereditary chieftain, descended from the sachem who welcomed Governor Mayhew to the Vineyard. Mr. Wigglesworth exerted his best skill to carve a broken bow and scattered sheaf of arrows, in memory of the hunters and warriors whose race was ended here; but he likewise sculptured a cherub, to denote that the poor Indian had shared the Christian's hope of immortality.

"Why," observed I, taking a perverse view of the winged boy and the bow and arrows, "it looks more like Cupid's tomb than an Indian chief's!"

" You talk nonsense," said the sculptor, with the offended pride of art; he then added with his usual good nature, " How can Cupid die when there are such pretty maidens in the Vineyard ? "

" Very true," answered I — and for the rest of the day I thought of other matters than tombstones.

At our next meeting I found him chiselling an open book upon a marble headstone, and concluded that it was meant to express the erudition of some black-letter clergyman of the Cotton Mather school. It turned out, however, to be emblematical of the script-ural knowledge of an old woman who had never read anything but her Bible : and the monument was a trib-ute to her piety and good works from the Orthodox church, of which she had been a member. In strange contrast with this Christian woman's memorial was that of an infidel, whose gravestone, by his own di-rection, bore an avowal of his belief that the spirit within him would be extinguished like a flame, and that the nothingness whence he sprang would receive him again. Mr. Wigglesworth consulted me as to the propriety of enabling a dead man's dust to utter this dreadful creed.

" If I thought," said he, " that a single mortal would read the inscription without a shudder, my chisel should never cut a letter of it. But when the grave speaks such falsehoods, the soul of man will know the truth by its own horror."

" So it will," said I, struck by the idea ; " the poor infidel may strive to preach blasphemies from his grave ; but it will be only another method of impress-ing the soul with a consciousness of immortality."

There was an old man by the name of Norton, acted throughout the island for his greath wealth.

which he had accumulated by the exercise of strong
and shrewd faculties, combined with a most penurious
disposition. This wretched miser, conscious that he
had not a friend to be mindful of him in his grave, had
himself taken the needful precautions for posthumous
remembrance, by bespeaking an immense slab of
white marble, with a long epitaph in raised letters,
the whole to be as magnificent as Mr. Wigglesworth's
skill could make it. There was something very characteristic in this contrivance to have his money's
worth even from his own tombstone, which, indeed,
afforded him more enjoyment in the few months that
he lived thereafter, than it probably will in a whole
century, now that it is laid over his bones. This inci
dent reminds me of a young girl, — a pale, slender, feeble creature, most unlike the other rosy and healthful
damsels of the Vineyard, amid whose brightness she
was fading away. Day after day did the poor maiden
come to the sculptor's shop, and pass from one piece
of marble to another, till at last she pencilled her
name upon a slender slab, which, I think, was of a
more spotless white than all the rest. I saw her no
more, but soon afterwards found Mr. Wigglesworth
cutting her virgin name into the stone which she had
chosen.

"She is dead — poor girl," said he, interrupting the
tune which he was whistling, "and she chose a good
piece of stuff for her headstone. Now which of these
slabs would you like best to see your own name
upon?"

"Why, to tell you the truth, my good Mr. Wigglesworth," replied I, after a moment's pause, — for the
abruptness of the question had somewhat startled me,
—"to be quite sincere with you, I care little or noth-

ing about a stone for my own grave, and am somewhat inclined to scepticism as to the propriety of erecting monuments at all over the dust that once was human. The weight of these heavy marbles, though unfelt by the dead corpse of the enfranchised soul, presses drearily upon the spirit of the survivor, and causes him to connect the idea of death with the dungeon-like imprisonment of the tomb, instead of with the freedom of the skies. Every gravestone that you ever made is the visible symbol of a mistaken system. Our thoughts should soar upward with the butterfly — not linger with the exuviæ that confined him. In truth and reason, neither those whom we call the living, and still less the departed, have anything to do with the grave."

"I never heard anything so heathenish!" said Mr. Wigglesworth, perplexed and displeased at sentiments which controverted all his notions and feelings, and implied the utter waste, and worse, of his whole life's labor; "would you forget your dead friends, the moment they are under the sod?"

"They are not under the sod," I rejoined; "then why should I mark the spot where there is no treasure hidden! Forget them? No! But to remember them aright, I would forget what they have cast off. And to gain the truer conception of DEATH, I would forget the GRAVE!"

But still the good old sculptor murmured, and stumbled, as it were, over the gravestones amid which he had walked through life. Whether he were right or wrong, I had grown the wiser from our companionship, and from my observations of nature and character as displayed by those who came, with their old griefs or their new ones, to get them recorded upon his slabs of marble. And yet, with my gain of wisdom, I had likewise gained perplexity; for there was a strange doubt in my mind, whether the dark shadowing of this life, the sorrows and regrets, have not as much real comfort in them — leaving religious influences out of the question — as what we term life's joys.

THE SHAKER BRIDAL.

ONE day, in the sick chamber of Father Ephraim, who had been forty years the presiding elder over the Shaker settlement at Goshen, there was an assemblage of several of the chief men of the sect. Individuals had come from the rich establishment at Lebanon, from Canterbury, Harvard, and Alfred, and from all the other localities where this strange people have fertilized the rugged hills of New England by their systematic industry. An elder was likewise there, who had made a pilgrimage of a thousand miles from a village of the faithful in Kentucky, to visit his spiritual kindred, the children of the sainted mother Ann. He had partaken of the homely abundance of their tables, had quaffed the far-famed Shaker cider, and had joined in the sacred dance, every step of which is believed to alienate the enthusiast from earth, and bear him onward to heavenly purity and bliss. His brethren of the north had now courteously invited him to be present on an occasion, when the concurrence of every eminent member of their community was peculiarly desirable.

The venerable Father Ephraim sat in his easy chair, not only hoary headed and infirm with age, but worn down by a lingering disease, which, it was evident, would very soon transfer his patriarchal staff to other hands. At his footstool stood a man and woman, both clad in the Shaker garb.

"My brethren," said Father Ephraim to the surrounding elders, feebly exerting himself to utter these few words, " here are the son and daughter to whom I would commit the trust of which Providence is about to lighten my weary shoulders. Read their faces, I pray you, and say whether the inward movement of the spirit hath guided my choice aright."

Accordingly, each elder looked at the two candidates with a most scrutinizing gaze. The man, whose name was Adam Colburn, had a face sunburnt with labor in the fields, yet intelligent, thoughtful, and traced with cares enough for a whole lifetime, though he had barely reached middle age. There was something severe in his aspect, and a rigidity throughout his person, characteristics that caused him generally to be taken for a school-master; which vocation, in fact, he had formerly exercised for several years. The woman, Martha Pierson, was somewhat above thirty, thin and pale, as a Shaker sister almost invariably is, and not entirely free from that corpse-like appearance which the garb of the sisterhood is so well calculated to impart.

" This pair are still in the summer of their years," observed the elder from Harvard, a shrewd old man. " I would like better to see the hoar-frost of autumn on their heads. Methinks, also, they will be exposed to peculiar temptations, on account of the carnal desires which have heretofore subsisted between them."

" Nay, brother," said the elder from Canterbury, " the hoar-frost and the black-frost hath done its work on Brother Adam and Sister Martha, even as we sometimes discern its traces in our cornfields, while they are yet green. And why should we question the wisdom of our venerable Father's purpose although this pair, in their early youth, have loved one another

as the world's people love? Are there not many
brethren and sisters among us, who have lived long
together in wedlock, yet, adopting our faith, find their
hearts purified from all but spiritual affection?"

Whether or no the early loves of Adam and Martha
had rendered it inexpedient that they should now pre-
side together over a Shaker village, it was certainly
most singular that such should be the final result of
many warm and tender hopes. Children of neighboring families, their affection was older even than their
school-days ; it seemed an innate principle, interfused
among all their sentiments and feelings, and not so
much a distinct remembrance, as connected with their
whole volume of remembrances. But, just as they
reached a proper age for their union, misfortunes had
fallen heavily on both, and made it necessary that they
should resort to personal labor for a bare subsistence.
Even under these circumstances, Martha Pierson
would probably have consented to unite her fate with
Adam Colburn's, and, secure of the bliss of mutual
love, would patiently have awaited the less important
gifts of fortune. But Adam, being of a calm and
cautious character, was loath to relinquish the advantages which a single man possesses for raising himself
in the world. Year after year, therefore, their marriage had been deferred. Adam Colburn had followed
many vocations, had travelled far, and seen much of
the world and of life. Martha had earned her bread
sometimes as a seamstress, sometimes as help to a
farmer's wife, sometimes as school-mistress of the village children, sometimes as a nurse or watcher of the
sick, thus acquiring a varied experience, the ultimate
use of which she little anticipated. But nothing had
gone prosperously with either of the lovers ; at no

subsequent moment would matrimony have been so prudent a measure as when they had first parted, in the opening bloom of life, to seek a better fortune. Still they had held fast their mutual faith. Martha might have been the wife of a man who sat among the senators of his native state, and Adam could have won the hand, as he had unintentionally won the heart, of a rich and comely widow. But neither of them desired good fortune save to share it with the other.

At length that calm despair which occurs only in a strong and somewhat stubborn character, and yields to no second spring of hope, settled down on the spirit of Adam Colburn. He sought an interview with Martha, and proposed that they should join the Society of Shakers. The converts of this sect are oftener driven within its hospitable gates by worldly misfortune than drawn thither by fanaticism, and are received without inquisition as to their motives. Martha, faithful still, had placed her hand in that of her lover, and accompanied him to the Shaker village. Here the natural capacity of each, cultivated and strengthened by the difficulties of their previous lives, had soon gained them an important rank in the Society, whose members are generally below the ordinary standard of intelligence. Their faith and feelings had, in some degree, become assimilated to those of their fellow-worshippers. Adam Colburn gradually acquired reputation, not only in the management of the temporal affairs of the Society, but as a clear and efficient preacher of their doctrines. Martha was not less distinguished in the duties proper to her sex. Finally, when the infirmities of Father Ephraim had admonished him to seek a successor in his patriarchal office, he thought of Adam and Martha, and proposed to renew, in their persons, the primitive form of Shaker government, as established by Mother Ann. They were to be the Father and Mother of the village. The simple ceremony, which would constitute them such, was now to be performed.

"Son Adam, and daughter Martha," said the venerable Father Ephraim, fixing his aged eyes piercingly upon them, "if ye can conscientiously undertake this charge, speak, that the brethren may not doubt of your fitness."

"Father," replied Adam, speaking with the calmness of his character, "I came to your village a disappointed man, weary of the world, worn out with continual trouble, seeking only a security against evil fortune, as I had no hope of good. Even my wishes of worldly success were almost dead within me. I came hither as a man might come to a tomb, willing to lie down in its gloom and coldness, for the sake of its peace and quiet. There was but one earthly affection in my breast, and it had grown calmer since my youth; so that I was satisfied to bring Martha to be my sister, in our new abode. We are brother and sister; nor would I have it otherwise. And in this peaceful village I have found all that I hoped for, — all that I desire. I will strive, with my best strength, for the spiritual and temporal good of our community. My conscience is not doubtful in this matter. I am ready to receive the trust."

"Thou hast spoken well, son Adam," said the Father. "God will bless thee in the office which I am about to resign."

"But our sister!" observed the elder from Harvard, "hath she not likewise a gift to declare her sentiments?"

Martha started, and moved her lips, as if she would

have made a formal reply to this appeal. But, had she attempted it, perhaps the old recollections, the long-repressed feelings of childhood, youth, and womanhood, might have gushed from her heart, in words that it would have been profanation to utter there.

"Adam has spoken," said she hurriedly; "his sentiments are likewise mine."

But while speaking these few words, Martha grew so pale that she looked fitter to be laid in her coffin than to stand in the presence of Father Ephraim and the elders; she shuddered, also, as if there were something awful or horrible in her situation and destiny. It required, indeed, a more than feminine strength of nerve, to sustain the fixed observance of men so exalted and famous throughout the sect as these were. They had overcome their natural sympathy with human frailties and affections. One, when he joined the Society, had brought with him his wife and children, but never, from that hour, had spoken a fond word to the former, or taken his best-loved child upon his knee. Another, whose family refused to follow him, had been enabled — such was his gift of holy fortitude — to leave them to the mercy of the world. The youngest of the elders, a man of about fifty, had been bred from infancy in a Shaker village, and was said never to have clasped a woman's hand in his own, and to have no conception of a closer tie than the cold fraternal one of the sect. Old Father Ephraim was the most awful character of all. In his youth he had been a dissolute libertine, but was converted by Mother Ann herself, and had partaken of the wild fanaticism of the early Shakers. Tradition whispered, at the firesides of the village, that Mother Ann had been compelled to sear his heart of flesh with a red-hot iron before it could be purified from earthly passions.

However that might be, poor Martha had a woman's heart, and a tender one, and it quailed within her, as she looked round at those strange old men, and from them to the calm features of Adam Colburn. But perceiving that the elders eyed her doubtfully, she gasped for breath, and again spoke.

"With what strength is left me by my many troubles," said she, "I am ready to undertake this charge, and to do my best in it."

"My children, join your hands," said Father Ephraim.

They did so. The elders stood up around, and the Father feebly raised himself to a more erect position, but continued sitting in his great chair.

"I have bidden you to join your hands," said he, "not in earthly affection, for ye have cast off its chains forever; but as brother and sister in spiritual love, and helpers of one another in your allotted task. Teach unto others the faith which ye have received. Open wide your gates, — I deliver you the keys thereof, — open them wide to all who will give up the iniquities of the world, and come hither to lead lives of purity and peace. Receive the weary ones, who have known the vanity of earth, — receive the little children, that they may never learn that miserable lesson. And a blessing be upon your labors; so that the time may hasten on, when the mission of Mother Ann shall have wrought its full effect, — when children shall no more be born and die, and the last survivor of mortal race, some old and weary man like me, shall see the sun go down, nevermore to rise on a world of sin and sorrow!"

The aged Father sank back exhausted, and the surrounding elders deemed, with good reason, that the hour was come when the new heads of the village must enter on their patriarchal duties. In their attention to Father Ephraim, their eyes were turned from Martha Pierson, who grew paler and paler, unnoticed even by Adam Colburn. He, indeed, had withdrawn his hand from hers, and folded his arms with a sense of satisfied ambition. But paler and paler grew Martha by his side, till, like a corpse in its burial clothes, she sank down at the feet of her early lover; for, after many trials firmly borne, her heart could endure the weight of its desolate agony no longer.

NIGHT SKETCHES.

BENEATH AN UMBRELLA.

PLEASANT is a rainy winter's day, within doors! The best study for such a day, or the best amusement, — call it which you will, — is a book of travels, describing scenes the most unlike that sombre one which is mistily presented through the windows. I have experienced that fancy is then most successful in imparting distinct shapes and vivid colors to the objects which the author has spread upon his page, and that his words become magic spells to summon up a thousand varied pictures. Strange landscapes glimmer through the familiar walls of the room, and outlandish figures thrust themselves almost within the sacred precincts of the hearth. Small as my chamber is, it has space enough to contain the ocean-like circumference of an Arabian desert, its parched sands tracked by the long line of a caravan, with the camels patiently journeying through the heavy sunshine. Though my ceiling be not lofty, yet I can pile up the mountains of Central Asia beneath it, till their summits shine far above the clouds of the middle atmosphere. And with my humble means, a wealth that is not taxable, I can transport hither the magnificent merchandise of an Oriental bazaar, and call a crowd of purchasers from distant countries to pay a fair profit for the precious articles which are displayed on all sides. True it is, however, that amid the bustle of traffic, or whatever

else may seem to be going on around me, the rain-drops
will occasionally be heard to patter against my window
panes, which look forth upon one of the quietest streets
in a New England town. After a time, too, the vis
ions vanish, and will not appear again at my bidding,
Then, it being nightfall, a gloomy sense of unreality
depresses my spirits, and impels me to venture out,
before the clock shall strike bedtime, to satisfy myself
that the world is not entirely made up of such shadowy materials as have busied me throughout the day
A dreamer may dwell so long among fantasies, tha
the things without him will seem as unreal as those
within.

When eve has fairly set in, therefore, I sally forth,
tightly buttoning my shaggy overcoat, and hoisting
my umbrella, the silken dome of which immediately
resounds with the heavy drumming of the invisible
rain-drops. Pausing on the lowest doorstep, I contrast
the warmth and cheerfulness of my deserted fireside
with the drear obscurity and chill discomfort into
which I am about to plunge. Now come fearful augu-
ries, innumerable as the drops of rain. Did not my
manhood cry shame upon me I should turn back within
doors, resume my elbow-chair, my slippers, and my
book, pass such an evening of sluggish enjoyment as
the day has been, and go to bed inglorious. The
same shivering reluctance, no doubt, has quelled, for
a moment, the adventurous spirit of many a traveller,
when his feet, which were destined to measure the
earth around, were leaving their last tracks in the
home paths.

In my own case poor human nature may be allowed
a few misgivings. I look upward, and discern no sky,
not even an unfathomable void, but only a black, im

penetrable nothingness, as though heaven and all its lights were blotted from the system of the universe. It is as if Nature were dead, and the world had put on black, and the clouds were weeping for her. With their tears upon my cheek, I turn my eyes earthward, but find little consolation here below. A lamp is burning dimly at the distant corner, and throws just enough of light along the street to show and exaggerate by so faintly showing the perils and difficulties which beset my path. Yonder dingily white remnant of a huge snow-bank, — which will yet cumber the sidewalk till the latter days of March, — over or through that wintry waste must I stride onward. Beyond lies a certain Slough of Despond, a concoction of mud and liquid filth, ankle-deep, leg-deep, neck-deep, — in a word, of unknown bottom, — on which the lamplight does not even glimmer, but which I have occasionally watched in the gradual growth of its horrors from morn till nightfall. Should I flounder into its depths, farewell to upper earth! And hark! how roughly resounds the roaring of a stream, the turbulent career of which is partially reddened by the gleam of the lamp, but elsewhere brawls noisily through the densest gloom. Oh, should I be swept away in fording that impetuous and unclean torrent, the coroner will have a job with an unfortunate gentleman who would fain end his troubles anywhere but in a mud puddle!

Pshaw! I will linger not another instant at arm's-length from these dim terrors, which grow more obscurely formidable the longer I delay to grapple with them. Now for the onset! And lo! with little damage, save a dash of rain in the face and breast, a splash of mud high up the pantaloons, and the left

hoot full of ice-cold water, behold me at the corner
of the street. The lamp throws down a circle of red
light around me : and twinkling onward from corner
to corner I discern other beacons marshalling my way
to a brighter scene. But this is a lonesome and dreary
spot. The tall edifices bid gloomy defiance to the
storm, with their blinds all closed, even as a man
winks when he faces a spattering gust. How loudly
tinkles the collected rain down the tin spouts ! The
puffs of wind are boisterous, and seem to assail me
from various quarters at once. I have often observed
that this corner is a haunt and loitering-place for those
winds which have no work to do upon the deep, dashing ships against our iron-bound shores ; nor in the
forest, tearing up the sylvan giants with half a rood of
soil at their vast roots. Here they amuse themselves
with lesser freaks of mischief. See, at this moment,
how they assail yonder poor woman, who is passing
just within the verge of the lamplight ! One blast
struggles for her umbrella, and turns it wrong side
outward ; another whisks the cape of her cloak across
her eyes ; while a third takes most unwarrantable liberties with the lower part of her attire. Happily the
good dame is no gossamer, but a figure of rotundity
and fleshly substance ; else would these aerial tor-
mentors whirl her aloft, like a witch upon a broom-
stick, and set her down, doubtless, in the filthiest kennel hereabout.

From hence I tread upon firm pavements into the
centre of the town. Here there is almost as brilliant
an illumination as when some great victory has been
won, either on the battle-field or at the polls. Two
rows of shops, with windows down nearly to the
ground, cast a glow from side to side, while the black

night hangs overhead like a canopy, and thus keeps
the splendor from diffusing itself away. The wet
sidewalks gleam with a broad sheet of red light. The
rain-drops glitter, as if the sky were pouring down
rubies. The spouts gush with fire. Methinks the
scene is an emblem of the deceptive glare which mortals throw around their footsteps in the moral world,
thus bedazzling themselves till they forget the impenetrable obscurity that hems them in, and that can be
dispelled only by radiance from above. And after all
it is a cheerless scene, and cheerless are the wanderers
in it. Here comes one who has so long been familiar
with tempestuous weather that he takes the bluster of
the storm for a friendly greeting, as if it should say,
"How fare ye, brother?" He is a retired sea-captain, wrapped in some nameless garment of the pea-
jacket order, and is now laying his course towards the
Marine Insurance Office, there to spin yarns of gale
and shipwreck with a crew of old sea-dogs like himself. The blast will put in its word among their
hoarse voices, and be understood by all of them.
Next I meet an unhappy slipshod gentleman, with a
cloak flung hastily over his shoulders, running a race
with boisterous winds, and striving to glide between
the drops of rain. Some domestic emergency or other
has blown this miserable man from his warm fireside
in quest of a doctor! See that little vagabond — how
carelessly he has taken his stand right underneath a
spout, while staring at some object of curiosity in a
shop-window! Surely the rain is his native element;
he must have fallen with it from the clouds, as frogs
are supposed to do.

Here is a picture, and a pretty one. A young man
and a girl, both enveloped in cloaks, and huddled be-

neath the scanty protection of a cotton umbrella. She
wears rubber overshoes, but he is in his dancing
pumps; and they are on their way, no doubt, to some
cotillon party, or subscription ball at a dollar a head,
refreshments included. Thus they struggle against
the gloomy tempest, lured onward by a vision of festal splendor. But, ah! a most lamentable disaster.
Bewildered by the red, blue, and yellow meteors, in
an apothecary's window, they have stepped upon a
slippery remnant of ice, and are precipitated into a
confluence of swollen floods, at the corner of two
streets. Luckless lovers! Were it my nature to be
other than a looker-on in life, I would attempt your
rescue. Since that may not be, I vow, should you be
drowned, to weave such a pathetic story of your fate
as shall call forth tears enough to drown you both
anew. Do ye touch bottom, my young friends? Yes;
they emerge like a water nymph and a river deity,
and paddle hand in hand out of the depths of the
dark pool. They hurry homeward, dripping, disconsolate, abashed, but with love too warm to be chilled
by the cold water. They have stood a test which
proves too strong for many. Faithful, though over
head and ears in trouble!

Onward I go, deriving a sympathetic joy or sorrow
from the varied aspect of mortal affairs, even as my
figure catches a gleam from the lighted windows, or
is blackened by an interval of darkness. Not that
mine is altogether a chameleon spirit, with no hue of
its own. Now I pass into a more retired street, where
the dwellings of wealth and poverty are intermingled,
presenting a range of strongly contrasted pictures.
Here, too, may be found the golden mean. Through
yonder casement I discern a family circle, — the grand-

mother, the parents, and the children, — all flickering, shadow-like, in the glow of a wood fire. Bluster,
fierce blast, and beat, thou wintry rain, against the
window panes! Ye cannot damp the enjoyment of
that fireside. Surely my fate is hard that I should
be wandering homeless here, taking to my bosom
night and storm and solitude, instead of wife and
children. Peace, murmurer! Doubt not that darker
guests are sitting round the hearth, though the warm
blaze hides all but blissful images. Well; here is
still a brighter scene. A stately mansion illuminated
for a ball, with cut-glass chandeliers and alabaster
lamps in every room, and sunny landscapes hanging
round the walls. See! a coach has stopped, whence
emerges a slender beauty, who, canopied by two um-
brellas, glides within the portal, and vanishes amid
lightsome thrills of music. Will she ever feel the
night wind and the rain? Perhaps, — perhaps! And
will Death and Sorrow ever enter that proud mansion? As surely as the dancers will be gay within its
halls to-night. Such thoughts sadden, yet satisfy my
heart; for they teach me that the poor man in this
mean, weather-beaten hovel, without a fire to cheer
him, may call the rich his brother, — brethren by Sorrow, who must be an inmate of both their households,
— brethren by Death, who will lead them both to other
homes.

Onward, still onward, I plunge into the night.
Now have I reached the utmost limits of the town,
where the last lamp struggles feebly with the darkness, like the farthest star that stands sentinel on the
borders of uncreated space. It is strange what sensations of sublimity may spring from a very humble
source. Such are suggested by this hollow roar of a

subterranean cataract, where the mighty stream of a kennel precipitates itself beneath an iron grate, and is seen no more on earth. Listen awhile to its voice of mystery, and fancy will magnify it till you start and smile at the illusion. And now another sound, — the rumbling of wheels, — as the mail-coach, outward bound, rolls heavily off the pavement, and splashes through the mud and water of the road. All night long the poor passengers will be tossed to and fro between drowsy watch and troubled sleep, and will dream of their own quiet beds, and awake to find themselves still jolting onward. Happier my lot, who will straightway hie me to my familiar room, and toast myself comfortably before the fire, musing and fitfully dozing, and fancying a strangeness in such sights as all may see. But first let me gaze at this solitary figure who comes hitherward with a tin lantern, which throws the circular pattern of its punched holes on the ground about him. He passes fearlessly into the unknown gloom, whither I will not follow him.

This figure shall supply me with a moral, wherewith, for lack of a more appropriate one, I may wind up my sketch. He fears not to tread the dreary path before him, because his lantern, which was kindled at the fireside of his home, will light him back to that same fireside again. And thus we, night wanderers through a stormy and dismal world, if we bear the lamp of Faith, enkindled at a celestial fire, it will surely lead us home to that heaven whence its radiance was borrowed.

ENDICOTT AND THE RED CROSS.

AT noon of an autumnal day, more than two centuries ago, the English colors were displayed by the
standard-bearer of the Salem trainband, which had
mustered for martial exercise under the orders of
John Endicott. It was a period when the religious
exiles were accustomed often to buckle on their armor,
and practise the handling of their weapons of war.
Since the first settlement of New England, its prospects had never been so dismal. The dissensions
between Charles the First and his subjects were then,
and for several years afterwards, confined to the floor
of Parliament. The measures of the King and ministry were rendered more tyrannically violent by an
opposition, which had not yet acquired sufficient confidence in its own strength to resist royal injustice with
the sword. The bigoted and haughty primate, Laud,
Archbishop of Canterbury, controlled the religious
affairs of the realm, and was consequently invested
with powers which might have wrought the utter ruin
of the two Puritan colonies, Plymouth and Massachusetts. There is evidence on record that our forefathers perceived their danger, but were resolved that
their infant country should not fall without a struggle,
even beneath the giant strength of the King's right
arm.

Such was the aspect of the times when the folds of
the English banner, with the Red Cross in its field,
were flung out over a company of Puritans. Their

leader, the famous Endicott, was a man of stern and resolute countenance, the effect of which was heightened by a grizzled beard that swept the upper portion of his breastplate. This piece of armor was so highly polished that the whole surrounding scene had its image in the glittering steel. The central object in the mirrored picture was an edifice of humble architecture with neither steeple nor bell to proclaim it — what nevertheless it was — the house of prayer. A token of the perils of the wilderness was seen in the grim head of a wolf, which had just been slain within the precincts of the town, and according to the regular mode of claiming the bounty, was nailed on the porch of the meeting-house. The blood was still plashing on the doorstep. There happened to be visible, at the same noontide hour, so many other characteristics of the times and manners of the Puritans, that we must endeavor to represent them in a sketch, though far less vividly than they were reflected in the polished breastplate of John Endicott.

In close vicinity to the sacred edifice appeared that important engine of Puritanic authority, the whipping-post — with the soil around it well trodden by the feet of evil doers, who had there been disciplined. At one corner of the meeting-house was the pillory, and at the other the stocks; and, by a singular good fortune for our sketch, the head of an Episcopalian and suspected Catholic was grotesquely incased in the former machine; while a fellow-criminal, who had boisterously quaffed a health to the king, was confined by the legs in the latter. Side by side, on the meeting-house steps, stood a male and a female figure. The man was a tall, lean, haggard personification of fanaticism, bearing on his breast this label, — A WANTON GOSPELLER,

— which betokened that he had dared to give inter.
pretations of Holy Writ unsanctioned by the infallible
judgment of the civil and religious rulers. His aspect
showed no lack of zeal to maintain his heterodoxies,
even at the stake. The woman wore a cleft stick
on her tongue, in appropriate retribution for having
wagged that unruly member against the elders of the
church; and her countenance and gestures gave much
cause to apprehend that, the moment the stick should
be removed, a repetition of the offence would demand
new ingenuity in chastising it.

The above-mentioned individuals had been sentenced
to undergo their various modes of ignominy, for the
space of one hour at noonday. But among the crowd
were several whose punishment would be life-long;
some, whose ears had been cropped, like those of puppy
dogs; others, whose cheeks had been branded with the
initials of their misdemeanors; one, with his nostrils
slit and seared; and another, with a halter about his
neck, which he was forbidden ever to take off, or to
conceal beneath his garments. Methinks he must
have been grievously tempted to affix the other end of
the rope to some convenient beam or bough. There
was likewise a young woman, with no mean share of
beauty, whose doom it was to wear the letter A on the
breast of her gown, in the eyes of all the world and
her own children. And even her own children knew
what that initial signified. Sporting with her infamy,
the lost and desperate creature had embroidered the
fatal token in scarlet cloth, with golden thread and the
nicest art of needlework; so that the capital A might
have been thought to mean Admirable, or anything
rather than Adulteress.

Let not the reader argue, from any of these evi:

dences of iniquity, that the times of the Puritans were more vicious than our own, when, as we pass along the very street of this sketch, we discern no badge of infamy on man or woman. It was the policy of our ancestors to search out even the most secret sins, and expose them to shame, without fear or favor, in the broadest light of the noonday sun. Were such the custom now, perchance we might find materials for a no less piquant sketch than the above.

Except the malefactors whom we have described, and the diseased or infirm persons, the whole male population of the town, between sixteen years and sixty, were seen in the ranks of the trainband. A few stately savages, in all the pomp and dignity of the primeval Indian, stood gazing at the spectacle. Their flint-headed arrows were but childish weapons compared with the matchlocks of the Puritans, and would have rattled harmlessly against the steel caps and hammered iron breastplates which inclosed each soldier in an individual fortress. The valiant John Endicott glanced with an eye of pride at his sturdy followers, and prepared to renew the martial toils of the day.

"Come, my stout hearts!" quoth he, drawing his sword. "Let us show these poor heathen that we can handle our weapons like men of might. Well for them, if they put us not to prove it in earnest!"

The iron-breasted company straightened their line, and each man drew the heavy butt of his matchlock close to his left foot, thus awaiting the orders of the captain. But, as Endicott glanced right and left along the front, he discovered a personage at some little distance with whom it behooved him to hold a parley. It was an elderly gentleman, wearing a black cloak and band, and a high-crowned hat, beneath which was a velvet skull-cap, the whole being the garb of a Puritan minister. This reverend person bore a staff which seemed to have been recently cut in the forest, and his shoes were bemired as if he had been travelling on foot through the swamps of the wilderness. His aspect was perfectly that of a pilgrim, heightened also by an apostolic dignity. Just as Endicott perceived him he laid aside his staff, and stooped to drink at a bubbling fountain which gushed into the sunshine about a score of yards from the corner of the meeting-house. But, ere the good man drank, he turned his face heavenward in thankfulness, and then, holding back his gray beard with one hand, he scooped up his simple draught in the hollow of the other.

"What, ho! good Mr. Williams," shouted Endicott. "You are welcome back again to our town of peace. How does our worthy Governor Winthrop? And what news from Boston?"

"The Governor hath his health, worshipful Sir," answered Roger Williams, now resuming his staff, and drawing near. "And for the news, here is a letter, which, knowing I was to travel hitherward to-day, his Excellency committed to my charge. Belike it contains tidings of much import; for a ship arrived yesterday from England."

Mr. Williams, the minister of Salem and of course known to all the spectators, had now reached the spot where Endicott was standing under the banner of his company, and put the Governor's epistle into his hand. The broad seal was impressed with Winthrop's coat of arms. Endicott hastily unclosed the letter and began to read, while, as his eye passed down the page, a wrathful change came over his manly countenance

The blood glowed through it, till it seemed to be kindling with an internal heat; nor was it unnatural to suppose that his breastplate would likewise become red-hot with the angry fire of the bosom which it covered. Arriving at the conclusion, he shook the letter fiercely in his hand, so that it rustled as loud as the flag above his head.

"Black tidings these, Mr. Williams," said he; "blacker never came to New England. Doubtless you know their purport?"

"Yea, truly," replied Roger Williams; "for the Governor consulted, respecting this matter, with my brethren in the ministry at Boston; and my opinion was likewise asked. And his Excellency entreats you by me, that the news be not suddenly noised abroad, lest the people be stirred up unto some outbreak, and thereby give the King and the Archbishop a handle against us."

"The Governor is a wise man — a wise man, and a meek and moderate," said Endicott, setting his teeth grimly. "Nevertheless, I must do according to my own best judgment. There is neither man, woman, nor child in New England, but has a concern as dear as life in these tidings; and if John Endicott's voice be loud enough, man, woman, and child shall hear them. Soldiers, wheel into a hollow square! Ho, good people! Here are news for one and all of you."

The soldiers closed in around their captain; and he and Roger Williams stood together under the banner of the Red Cross; while the women and the aged men pressed forward, and the mothers held up their children to look Endicott in the face. A few taps of the drum gave signal for silence and attention.

"Fellow-soldiers, — fellow-exiles," began Endicott, speaking under strong excitement, yet powerfully restraining it, "wherefore did ye leave your native country? Wherefore, I say, have we left the green and fertile fields, the cottages, or, perchance, the old gray halls, where we were born and bred, the churchyards where our forefathers lie buried? Wherefore have we come hither to set up our own tombstones in a wilderness? A howling wilderness it is! The wolf and the bear meet us within halloo of our dwellings. The savage lieth in wait for us in the dismal shadow of the woods. The stubborn roots of the trees break our ploughshares, when we would till the earth. Our children cry for bread, and we must dig in the sands of the sea-shore to satisfy them. Wherefore, I say again, have we sought this country of a rugged soil and wintry sky? Was it not for the enjoyment of our civil rights? Was it not for liberty to worship God according to our conscience?"

"Call you this liberty of conscience?" interrupted a voice on the steps of the meeting-house.

It was the Wanton Gospeller. A sad and quiet smile flitted across the mild visage of Roger Williams. But Endicott, in the excitement of the moment, shook his sword wrathfully at the culprit — an ominous gesture from a man like him.

"What hast thou to do with conscience, thou knave?" cried he. "I said liberty to worship God, not license to profane and ridicule him. Break not in upon my speech, or I will lay thee neck and heels till this time to-morrow! Hearken to me, friends, nor heed that accursed rhapsodist. As I was saying, we have sacrificed all things, and have come to a land whereof the old world hath scarcely heard, that we might make a new world unto ourselves, and painfully seek a path from hence to heaven. But what think ye now? This son of a Scotch tyrant — this grandson of a Papistical and adulterous Scotch woman, whose death proved that a golden crown doth not always save an anointed head from the block " —

" Nay, brother, nay," interposed Mr. Williams; " thy words are not meet for a secret chamber, far less for a public street."

" Hold thy peace, Roger Williams ! " answered Endicott, imperiously. " My spirit is wiser than thine for the business now in hand. I tell ye, fellow-exiles, that Charles of England, and Laud, our bitterest persecutor, arch-priest of Canterbury, are resolute to pursue us even hither. They are taking counsel, saith this letter, to send over a governor-general, in whose breast shall be deposited all the law and equity of the land. They are minded, also, to establish the idolatrous forms of English Episcopacy; so that, when Laud shall kiss the Pope's toe, as cardinal of Rome, he may deliver New England, bound hand and foot, into the power of his master ! "

A deep groan from the auditors, — a sound of wrath, as well as fear and sorrow, — responded to this intelligence.

" Look ye to it, brethren," resumed Endicott, with increasing energy. " If this king and this arch-prelate have their will, we shall briefly behold a cross on the spire of this tabernacle which we have builded, and a high altar within its walls, with wax tapers burning round it at noonday. We shall hear the sacring bell, and the voices of the Romish priests saying the mass. But think ye, Christian men, that these abominations may be suffered without a sword drawn? without a shot fired? without blood spilt, yea, on the very stairs of the pulpit? No, — be ye strong of hand and stout of heart! Here we stand on our own soil, which we have bought with our goods, which we have won with our swords, which we have cleared with our axes, which we have tilled with the sweat of our brows, which we have sanctified with our prayers to the God that brought us hither! Who shall enslave us here? What have we to do with this mitred prelate, — with this crowned king? What have we to do with England?"

Endicott gazed round at the excited countenances of the people, now full of his own spirit, and then turned suddenly to the standard-bearer, who stood close behind him.

"Officer, lower your banner!" said he.

The officer obeyed; and, brandishing his sword, Endicott thrust it through the cloth, and, with his left hand, rent the Red Cross completely out of the banner. He then waved the tattered ensign above his head.

"Sacrilegious wretch!" cried the high-churchman in the pillory, unable longer to restrain himself, "thou hast rejected the symbol of our holy religion!"

"Treason, treason!" roared the royalist in the stocks. "He hath defaced the King's banner!"

"Before God and man, I will avouch the deed," answered Endicott. "Beat a flourish, drummer!— shout, soldiers and people!— in honor of the ensign of New England. Neither Pope nor Tyrant hath part in it now!"

With a cry of triumph, the people gave their sanction to one of the boldest exploits which our history records. And forever honored be the name of Endicott! We look back through the mist of ages, and recognize in the rending of the Red Cross from New England's banner the first omen of that deliverance which our fathers consummated after the bones of the stern Puritan had lain more than a century in the dust.

THE LILY'S QUEST.

AN APOLOGUE.

Two lovers, once upon a time, had planned a little summer-house, in the form of an antique temple, which it was their purpose to consecrate to all manner of refined and innocent enjoyments. There they would hold pleasant intercourse with one another and the circle of their familiar friends; there they would give festivals of delicious fruit; there they would hear lightsome music, intermingled with the strains of pathos which make joy more sweet; there they would read poetry and fiction, and permit their own minds to flit away in day-dreams and romance; there, in short — for why should we shape out the vague sunshine of their hopes? — there all pure delights were to cluster like roses among the pillars of the edifice, and blossom ever new and spontaneously. So, one breezy and cloudless afternoon, Adam Forrester and Lilias Fay set out upon a ramble over the wide estate which they were to possess together, seeking a proper site for their Temple of Happiness. They were themselves a fair and happy spectacle, fit priest and priestess for such a shrine; although, making poetry of the pretty name of Lilias, Adam Forrester was wont to call her LILY, because her form was as fragile, and her cheek almost as pale.

As they passed hand in hand down the avenue of drooping elms that led from the portal of Lilias Fay's paternal mansion, they seemed to glance like winged creatures through the strips of sunshine, and to scatter brightness where the deep shadows fell. But setting forth at the same time with this youthful pair, there was a dismal figure, wrapped in a black velvet cloak that might have been made of a coffin pall, and with a sombre hat such as mourners wear drooping its broad brim over his heavy brows. Glancing behind them, the lovers well knew who it was that followed, but wished from their hearts that he had been elsewhere, as being a companion so strangely unsuited to their joyous errand. It was a near relative of Lilias Fay, an old man by the name of Walter Gascoigne, who had long labored under the burden of a melancholy spirit, which was sometimes maddened into absolute insanity, and always had a tinge of it. What a contrast between the young pilgrims of bliss and their unbidden associate! They looked as if moulded of heaven's sunshine, and he of earth's gloomiest shade; they flitted along like Hope and Joy roaming hand in hand through life; while his darksome figure stalked behind, a type of all the woful influences which life could fling upon them. But the three had not gone far when they reached a spot that pleased the gentle Lily, and she paused.

" What sweeter place shall we find than this?" said she. " Why should we seek farther for the site of our Temple? "

It was indeed a delightful spot of earth, though undistinguished by any very prominent beauties, being merely a nook in the shelter of a hill, with the prospect of a distant lake in one direction, and of a church spire in another. There were vistas and pathways leading onward and onward into the green woodlands, and vanishing away in the glimmering shade.

The Temple, if erected here, would look towards the west: so that the lovers could shape all sorts of magnificent dreams out of the purple, violet, and gold of the sunset sky; and few of their anticipated pleasures were dearer than this sport of fantasy.

"Yes," said Adam Forrester, "we might seek all day and find no lovelier spot. We will build our Temple here."

But their sad old companion, who had taken his stand on the very site which they proposed to cover with a marble floor, shook his head and frowned; and the young man and the Lily deemed it almost enough to blight the spot, and desecrate it for their airy Temple, that his dismal figure had thrown its shadow there. He pointed to some scattered stones, the remnants of a former structure, and to flowers such as young girls delight to nurse in their gardens, but which had now relapsed into the wild simplicity of nature.

"Not here!" cried old Walter Gascoigne. "Here, long ago, other mortals built their Temple of Happiness. Seek another site for yours!"

"What!" exclaimed Lilias Fay. "Have any ever planned such a Temple save ourselves?"

"Poor child!" said her gloomy kinsman. "In one shape or other, every mortal has dreamed your dream."

Then he told the lovers how, not, indeed, an antique Temple, but a dwelling, had once stood there, and that a dark-clad guest had dwelt among its inmates, sitting forever at the fireside, and poisoning all their household mirth. Under this type, Adam Forrester and Lilias saw that the old man spake of Sorrow. He told of nothing that might not be recorded in the history of almost every household; and yet his hearers felt as if no sunshine ought to fall upon a spot where human grief had left so deep a stain; or, at least, that no joyous Temple should be built there.

"This is very sad," said the Lily, sighing.

"Well, there are lovelier spots than this," said Adam Forrester, soothingly, — "spots which sorrow has not blighted."

So they hastened away, and the melancholy Gascoigne followed them, looking as if he had gathered up all the gloom of the deserted spot, and was bearing it as a burden of inestimable treasure. But still they rambled on, and soon found themselves in a rocky dell through the midst of which ran a streamlet with ripple and foam, and a continual voice of inarticulate joy. It was a wild retreat, walled on either side with gray precipices, which would have frowned somewhat too sternly, had not a profusion of green shrubbery rooted itself into their crevices, and wreathed gladsome foliage around their solemn brows. But the chief joy of the dell was in the little stream, which seemed like the presence of a blissful child, with nothing earthly to do save to babble merrily and disport itself, and make every living soul its playfellow, and throw the sunny gleams of its spirit upon all.

"Here, here is the spot!" cried the two lovers with one voice as they reached a level space on the brink of a small cascade. "This glen was made on purpose for our Temple!"

"And the glad song of the brook will be always in our ears," said Lilias Fay.

"And its long melody shall sing the bliss of our lifetime," said Adam Forrester.

"Ye must build no Temple here!" murmured their dismal companion.

And there again was the old lunatic, standing just on the spot where they meant to rear their lightsome dome, and looking like the embodied symbol of some great woe, that, in forgotten days, had happened there. And, alas! there had been woe, nor that alone. A young man, more than a hundred years before, had lured hither a girl that loved him, and on this spot had murdered her, and washed his bloody hands in the stream which sung so merrily. And ever since the victim's death shrieks were often heard to echo between the cliffs.

"And see!" cried old Gascoigne, "is the stream yet pure from the stain of the murderer's hands?"

"Methinks it has a tinge of blood," faintly answered the Lily; and being as slight as the gossamer, she trembled and clung to her lover's arm, whispering, "Let us flee from this dreadful vale!"

"Come, then," said Adam Forrester, as cheerily as he could, "we shall soon find a happier spot."

They set forth again, young Pilgrims on that quest which millions — which every child of Earth — has tried in turn. And were the Lily and her lover to be more fortunate than all those millions? For a long time it seemed not so. The dismal shape of the old lunatic still glided behind them; and for every spot that looked lovely in their eyes, he had some legend of human wrong or suffering, so miserably sad that his auditors could never afterwards connect the idea of joy with the place where it had happened. Here, a heart-broken woman, kneeling to her child, had been spurned from his feet; here, a desolate old creature had prayed to the evil one, and had received a fiend-ish malignity of soul in answer to her prayer; here, a new-born infant, sweet blossom of life, had been found dead, with the impress of its mother's fingers round its throat; and here, under a shattered oak, two lovers had been stricken by lightning, and fell blackened corpses in each other's arms. The dreary Gascoigne had a gift to know whatever evil and lamentable thing had stained the bosom of Mother Earth; and when his funereal voice had told the tale, it appeared like a prophecy of future woe as well as a tradition of the past. And now, by their sad demeanor, you would have fancied that the pilgrim lovers were seeking, not a temple of earthly joy, but a tomb for themselves and their posterity.

" Where in this world," exclaimed Adam Forrester, despondingly, " shall we build our Temple of Happiness ? "

" Where in this world, indeed ! " repeated Lilias Fay; and being faint and weary, the more so by the heaviness of her heart, the Lily drooped her head and sat down on the summit of a knoll, repeating, " Where in this world shall we build our Temple ? "

" Ah ! have you already asked yourselves that question ? " said their companion, his shaded features growing even gloomier with the smile that dwelt on them ; " yet there is a place, even in this world, where ye may build it."

While the old man spoke, Adam Forrester and Lilias had carelessly thrown their eyes around, and perceived that the spot where they had chanced to pause possessed a quiet charm, which was well enough adapted to their present mood of mind. It was a small rise of ground, with a certain regularity of shape, that had perhaps been bestowed by art ; and a group of trees, which almost surrounded it, threw their pensive shadows across and far beyond, although some

softened glory of the sunshine found its way there.
The ancestral mansion, wherein the lovers would dwell
together, appeared on one side, and the ivied church,
where they were to worship, on another.   Happening
to cast their eyes on the ground they smiled, yet with
a sense of wonder, to see that a pale lily was growing
at their feet.

"We will build our Temple here," said they, simultaneously, and with an indescribable conviction that
they had at last found the very spot.

Yet, while they uttered this exclamation, the young
man and the Lily turned an apprehensive glance at
their dreary associate, deeming it hardly possible that
some tale of earthly affliction should not make those
precincts loathsome, as in every former case.   The
old man stood just behind them, so as to form the
chief figure in the group, with his sable cloak muffling
the lower part of his visage, and his sombre hat over-
shadowing his brows.   But he gave no word of dissent
from their purpose; and an inscrutable smile was accepted by the lovers as a token that here had been no
footprint of guilt or sorrow to desecrate the site of
their Temple of Happiness.

In a little time longer, while summer was still in
its prime, the fairy structure of the Temple arose on
the summit of the knoll, amid the solemn shadows of
the trees, yet often gladdened with bright sunshine.
It was built of white marble, with slender and graceful pillars supporting a vaulted dome; and beneath
the centre of this dome, upon a pedestal, was a slab of
dark-veined marble, on which books and music might
be strewn.   But there was a fantasy among the people
of the neighborhood that the edifice was planned after
an ancient mausoleum and was intended for a tomb,

and that the central slab of dark-veined marble was
to be inscribed with the names of buried ones. They
doubted, too, whether the form of Lilias Fay could
appertain to a creature of this earth, being so very
delicate, and growing every day more fragile, so that
she looked as if the summer breeze should snatch her
up and waft her heavenward. But still she watched
the daily growth of the Temple; and so did old Walter Gascoigne, who now made that spot his continual
haunt, leaning whole hours together on his staff, and
giving as deep attention to the work as though it had
been indeed a tomb. In due time it was finished, and
a day appointed for a simple rite of dedication.

On the preceding evening, after Adam Forrester
had taken leave of his mistress, he looked back towards the portal of her dwelling, and felt a strange
thrill of fear; for he imagined that, as the setting
sunbeams faded from her figure, she was exhaling
away, and that something of her ethereal substance
was withdrawn with each lessening gleam of light.
With his farewell glance a shadow had fallen over
the portal and Lilias was invisible. His foreboding
spirit deemed it an omen at the time, and so it proved;
for the sweet earthly form, by which the Lily had
been manifested to the world, was found lifeless the
next morning in the Temple, with her head resting
on her arms, which were folded upon the slab of dark-
veined marble. The chill winds of the earth had long
since breathed a blight into this beautiful flower, so
that a loving hand had now transplanted it, to blossom brightly in the garden of Paradise.

But alas, for the Temple of Happiness! In his unutterable grief, Adam Forrester had no purpose more
at heart than to convert this Temple of many delight

ful hopes into a tomb, and bury his dead mistress there. And lo! a wonder! Digging a grave beneath the Temple's marble floor, the sexton found no virgin earth, such as was meet to receive the maiden's dust, but an ancient sepulchre, in which were treasured up the bones of generations that had died long ago. Among those forgotten ancestors was the Lily to be laid. And when the funeral procession brought Lilias thither in her coffin, they beheld old Walter Gascoigne standing beneath the dome of the Temple, with his cloak of pall and face of darkest gloom; and where-ever that figure might take its stand the spot would seem a sepulchre. He watched the mourners as they lowered the coffin down.

"And so," said he to Adam Forrester, with the strange smile in which his insanity was wont to gleam forth, "you have found no better foundation for your happiness than on a grave!"

But as the Shadow of Affliction spoke, a vision of Hope and Joy had its birth in Adam's mind, even from the old man's taunting words; for then he knew what was betokened by the parable in which the Lily and himself had acted; and the mystery of Life and Death was opened to him.

"Joy! joy!" he cried, throwing his arms towards heaven, "on a grave be the site of our Temple: and now our happiness is for Eternity!"

With those words, a ray of sunshine broke through the dismal sky, and glimmered down into the sepul-chre; while, at the same moment, the shape of old Walter Gascoigne stalked drearily away, because his gloom, symbolic of all earthly sorrow, might no longer abide there, now that the darkest riddle of humanity was read.

FOOTPRINTS ON THE SEA-SHORE.

It must be a spirit much unlike my own which can keep itself in health and vigor without sometimes stealing from the sultry sunshine of the world, to plunge into the cool bath of solitude. At intervals, and not unfrequent ones, the forest and the ocean summon me — one with the roar of its waves, the other with the murmur of its boughs — forth from the haunts of men. But I must wander many a mile ere I could stand beneath the shadow of even one primeval tree, much less be lost among the multitude of hoary trunks, and hidden from earth and sky by the mystery of darksome foliage. Nothing is within my daily reach more like a forest than the acre or two of woodland near some suburban farm-house. When, therefore, the yearning for seclusion becomes a necessity within me, I am drawn to the sea-shore, which extends its line of rude rocks and seldom trodden sands for leagues around our bay. Setting forth at my last ramble on a September morning, I bound myself with a hermit's vow to interchange no thoughts with man or woman, to share no social pleasure, but to derive all that day's enjoyment from shore and sea and sky, — from my soul's communion with these, and from fantasies and recollections, or anticipated realities. Surely here is enough to feed a human spirit for a single day. Farewell, then, busy world! Till your evening lights shall shine along the street, — till they gleam upon my sea-flushed face as I tread homeward, — free me from your ties, and let me be a peaceful outlaw.

Highways and cross paths are hastily traversed; and, clambering down a crag, I find myself at the extremity of a long beach. How gladly does the spirit leap forth and suddenly enlarge its sense of being to the full extent of the broad, blue, sunny deep! A greeting and a homage to the Sea! I descend over its margin and dip my hand into the wave that meets me, and bathe my brow. That far-resounding roar is Ocean's voice of welcome. His salt breath brings a blessing along with it. Now let us pace together — the reader's fancy arm-in-arm with mine — this noble beach, which extends a mile or more from that craggy promontory to yonder rampart of broken rocks. In front, the sea; in the rear, a precipitous bank, the grassy verge of which is breaking away, year after year, and flings down its tufts of verdure upon the barrenness below. The beach itself is a broad space of sand, brown and sparkling, with hardly any pebbles intermixed. Near the water's edge there is a wet margin, which glistens brightly in the sunshine, and reflects objects like a mirror; and as we tread along the glistening border, a dry spot flashes around each footstep, but grows moist again as we lift our feet. In some spots the sand receives a complete impression of the sole — square toe and all; elsewhere it is of such marble firmness that we must stamp heavily to leave a print even of the iron-shod heel. Along the whole of this extensive beach gambols the surf wave; now it makes a feint of dashing onward in a fury, yet dies away with a meek murmur, and does but kiss the strand; now, after many such abortive efforts, it rears itself up in an unbroken line,

heightening as it advances, without a speck of foam
on its green crest. With how fierce a roar it flings
itself forward, and rushes far up the beach!

As I threw my eyes along the edge of the surf I
remember that I was startled, as Robinson Crusoe
might have been, by the sense that human life was
within the magic circle of my solitude. Afar off in
the remote distance of the beach, appearing like sea-
nymphs or some airier things such as might tread
upon the feathery spray, was a group of girls. Hardly
had I beheld them when they passed into the shadow
of the rocks and vanished. To comfort myself — for
truly I would fain have gazed a while longer — I made
acquaintance with a flock of beach birds. These little
citizens of the sea and air preceded me by about a
stone's throw along the strand, seeking, I suppose, for
food upon its margin. Yet, with a philosophy which
mankind would do well to imitate, they drew a continual pleasure from their toil for a subsistence. The
sea was each little bird's great playmate. They
chased it downward as it swept back, and again ran
up swiftly before the impending wave, which sometimes overtook them and bore them off their feet.
But they floated as lightly as one of their own feathers
on the breaking crest. In their airy flutterings they
seemed to rest on the evanescent spray. Their images
— long-legged little figures, with gray backs and snowy
bosoms — were seen as distinctly as the realities in
the mirror of the glistening strand. As I advanced
they flew a score or two of yards, and, again alighting,
recommenced their dalliance with the surf wave ; and
thus they bore me company along the beach, the types
of pleasant fantasies, till, at its extremity, they took
wing over the ocean and were gone. After forming a

friendship with these small surf spirits, it is really worth a sigh to find no memorial of them save their multitudinous little tracks in the sand.

When we have paced the length of the beach it is pleasant and not unprofitable to retrace our steps, and recall the whole mood and occupation of the mind during the former passage. Our tracks being all discernible will guide us with an observing consciousness through every unconscious wandering of thought and fancy. Here we followed the surf in its reflux to pick up a shell which the sea seemed loath to relinquish. Here we found a sea-weed, with an immense brown leaf, and trailed it behind us by its long snake-like stalk. Here we seized a live horseshoe by the tail, and counted the many claws of the queer monster. Here we dug into the sand for pebbles, and skipped them upon the surface of the water. Here we wet our feet while examining a jelly-fish which the waves, having just tossed it up, now sought to snatch away again. Here we trod along the brink of a fresh-water brooklet which flows across the beach, becoming shallower and more shallow, till at last it sinks into the sand and perishes in the effort to bear its little tribute to the main. Here some vagary appears to have bewildered us; for our tracks go round and round and are confusedly intermingled, as if we had found a labyrinth upon the level beach. And here, amid our idle pastime, we sat down upon almost the only stone that breaks the surface of the sand, and were lost in an unlooked-for and overpowering conception of the majesty and awfulness of the great deep. Thus, by tracking our footprints in the sand, we track our own nature in its wayward course, and steal a glance upon it, when it never dreams of being so observed. Such glances always make us wiser.

This extensive beach affords room for another pleasant pastime. With your staff you may write verses — love verses, if they please you best — and consecrate them with a woman's name. Here, too, may be inscribed thoughts, feelings, desires, warm outgushings from the heart's secret places, which you would not pour upon the sand without the certainty that, almost ere the sky has looked upon them, the sea will wash them out. Stir not hence till the record be effaced. Now — for there is room enough on your canvas — draw huge faces — huge as that of the Sphinx on Egyptian sands — and fit them with bodies of corresponding immensity, and legs which might stride half-way to yonder island. Child's play becomes magnificent on so grand a scale. But, after all, the most fascinating employment is simply to write your name in the sand. Draw the letters gigantic, so that two strides may barely measure them, and three for the long strokes! Cut deep that the record may be permanent! Statesmen and warriors and poets have spent their strength in no better cause than this. Is it accomplished? Return then in an hour or two and seek for this mighty record of a name. The sea will have swept over it, even as time rolls its effacing waves over the names of statesmen and warriors and poets. Hark, the surf wave laughs at you!

Passing from the beach I begin to clamber over the crags, making my difficult way among the ruins of a rampart shattered and broken by the assaults of a fierce enemy. The rocks rise in every variety of attitude: some of them have their feet in the foam, and are shagged half-way upward with sea-weed; some have been hollowed almost into caverns by the unwearied toil of the sea, which can afford to spend centuries in wearing away a rock, or even polishing a pebble. One huge rock ascends in monumental shape, with a face like a giant's tombstone, on which the veins resemble inscriptions, but in an unknown tongue. We will fancy them the forgotten characters of an antediluvian race ; or else that Nature's own hand has here recorded a mystery, which, could I read her language, would make mankind the wiser and the happier. How many a thing has troubled me with that same idea! Pass on and leave it unexplained. Here is a narrow avenue, which might seem to have been hewn through the very heart of an enormous crag, affording passage for the rising sea to thunder back and forth, filling it with tumultuous foam, and then leaving its floor of black pebbles bare and glistening. In this chasm there was once an intersecting vein of softer stone, which the waves have gnawed away piecemeal, while the granite walls remain entire on either side. How sharply, and with what harsh clamor, does the sea rake back the pebbles, as it momentarily withdraws into its own depths! At intervals the floor of the chasm is left nearly dry; but anon, at the outlet, two or three great waves are seen struggling to get in at once; two hit the walls athwart, while one rushes straight through, and all three thunder as if with rage and triumph. They heap the chasm with a snow-drift of foam and spray. While watching this scene, I can never rid myself of the idea that a monster, endowed with life and fierce energy, is striving to burst his way through the narrow pass. And what a contrast, to look through the stormy chasm, and catch a glimpse of the calm bright sea beyond!

Many interesting discoveries may be made among these broken cliffs. Once, for example, I found a dead seal, which a recent tempest had tossed into the nook of the rocks, where his shaggy carcass lay rolled in a heap of eel-grass, as if the sea-monster sought to hide himself from my eye. Another time, a shark seemed on the point of leaping from the surf to swallow me; nor did I, wholly without dread, approach near enough to ascertain that the man-eater had already met his own death from some fisherman in the bay. In the same ramble I encountered a bird — a large gray bird — but whether a loon, or a wild goose, or the identical albatross of the Ancient Mariner, was beyond my ornithology to decide. It reposed so naturally on a bed of dry sea-weed, with its head beside its wing, that I almost fancied it alive, and trod softly lest it should suddenly spread its wings skyward. But the sea-bird would soar among the clouds no more, nor ride upon its native waves, so I drew near and pulled out one of its mottled tail-feathers for a remembrance. Another day, I discovered an immense bone wedged into a chasm of the rocks; it was at least ten feet long, curved like a cimeter, bejewelled with barnacles and small shell-fish, and partly covered with a growth of sea-weed. Some leviathan of former ages had used this ponderous mass as a jawbone. Curiosities of a minuter order may be observed in a deep reservoir, which is replenished with water at every tide, but becomes a lake among the crags, save when the sea is at its height. At the bottom of this rocky basin grow marine plants, some of which tower high beneath the water and cast a shadow in the sunshine. Small fishes dart to and fro, and hide themselves among the sea-weed ; there is also a solitary crab, who appears to lead the life of a hermit, communing with none of the other denizens of the place ; and likewise several five-

fingers — for I know no other name than that which
children give them. If your imagination be at all accustomed to such freaks, you may look down into the
depths of this pool, and fancy it the mysterious depth
of ocean. But where are the hulks and scattered timbers of sunken ships? — where the treasures that old
Ocean hoards? — where the corroded cannon? — where
the corpses and skeletons of seamen who went down in
storm and battle?

On the day of my last ramble (it was a September
day, yet as warm as summer), what should I behold
as I approached the above described basin but three
girls sitting on its margin, and — yes, it is veritably so
— laving their snowy feet in the sunny water! These,
these are the warm realities of those three visionary
shapes that flitted from me on the beach. Hark! their
merry voices as they toss up the water with their feet!
They have not seen me. I must shrink behind this
rock and steal away again.

In honest truth, vowed to solitude as I am, there
is something in this encounter that makes the heart
flutter with a strangely pleasant sensation. I know
these girls to be realities of flesh and blood, yet,
glancing at them so briefly, they mingle like kindred
creatures with the ideal beings of my mind. It is
pleasant, likewise, to gaze down from some high crag,
and watch a group of children, gathering pebbles and
pearly shells, and playing with the surf, as with old
Ocean's hoary beard. Nor does it infringe upon my
seclusion to see yonder boat at anchor off the shore,
swinging dreamily to and fro, and rising and sinking
with the alternate swell; while the crew — four gentlemen, in roundabout jackets — are busy with their
fishing-lines. But, with an inward antipathy and a

headlong flight, do I eschew the presence of any meditative stroller like myself, known by his pilgrim staff, his sauntering step, his shy demeanor, his observant yet abstracted eye. From such a man, as if another self had scared me, I scramble hastily over the rocks, and take refuge in a nook which many a secret hour has given me a right to call my own. I would do battle for it even with the churl that should produce the title deeds. Have not my musings melted into its rocky walls and sandy floor, and made them a portion of myself?

It is a recess in the line of cliffs, walled round by a rough, high precipice, which almost encircles and shuts in a little space of sand. In front, the sea appears as between the pillars of a portal. In the rear, the precipice is broken and intermixed with earth, which gives nourishment not only to clinging and twining shrubs, but to trees, that gripe the rock with their naked roots, and seem to struggle hard for footing and for soil enough to live upon. These are fir-trees; but oaks hang their heavy branches from above, and throw down acorns on the beach, and shed their withering foliage upon the waves. At this autumnal season the precipice is decked with variegated splendor; trailing wreaths of scarlet flaunt from the summit downward; tufts of yellow-flowering shrubs, and rose-bushes, with their reddened leaves and glossy seed berries, sprout from each crevice; at every glance, I detect some new light or shade of beauty, all contrasting with the stern, gray rock. A rill of water trickles down the cliff and fills a little cistern near the base. I drain it at a draught, and find it fresh and pure. This recess shall be my dining hall. And what the feast? A few biscuits made savory by soaking them in sea-water, a tuft of samphire gathered from the beach, and an apple for the dessert. By this time the little rill has filled its reservoir again; and, as I quaff it, I thank God more heartily than for a civic banquet, that He gives me the healthful appetite to make a feast of bread and water.

Dinner being over, I throw myself at length upon the sand, and, basking in the sunshine, let my mind disport itself at will. The walls of this my hermitage have no tongue to tell my follies, though I sometimes fancy that they have ears to hear them, and a soul to sympathize. There is a magic in this spot. Dreams haunt its precincts and flit around me in broad sunlight, nor require that sleep shall blindfold me to real objects ere these be visible. Here can I frame a story of two lovers, and make their shadows live before me and be mirrored in the tranquil water, as they tread along the sand, leaving no footprints. Here, should I will it, I can summon up a single shade, and be myself her lover. Yes, dreamer, — but your lonely heart will be the colder for such fancies. Sometimes, too, the Past comes back and finds me here, and in her train come faces which were gladsome when I knew them, yet seem not gladsome now. Would that my hiding-place were lonelier, so that the past might not find me! Get ye all gone, old friends, and let me listen to the murmur of the sea, — a melancholy voice, but less sad than yours. Of what mysteries is it telling? Of sunken ships and whereabouts they lie? Of islands afar and undiscovered, whose tawny children are unconscious of other islands and of continents, and deem the stars of heaven their nearest neighbors? Nothing of all this. What then? Has it talked for so many ages and meant nothing all the while? No!

for those ages find utterance in the sea's unchanging voice, and warn the listener to withdraw his interest from mortal vicissitudes, and let the infinite idea of eternity pervade his soul. This is wisdom; and, therefore, will I spend the next half hour in shaping little boats of driftwood, and launching them on voyages across the cove, with a feather of a sea-gull for a sail. If the voice of ages tell me true, this is as wise an occupation as to build ships of five hundred tons, and launch them forth upon the main, bound to "far Cathay." Yet, how would the merchant sneer at me!

And, after all, can such philosophy be true? Methinks, I could find a thousand arguments against it. Well, then, let yonder shaggy rock, mid-deep in the surf — see! he is somewhat wrathful, — he rages and roars and foams — let that tall rock be my antagonist, and let me exercise my oratory like him of Athens, who bandied words with an angry sea and got the victory. My maiden speech is a triumphant one; for the gentleman in sea-weed has nothing to offer in reply, save an immitigable roaring. His voice, indeed, will be heard a long while after mine is hushed. Once more I shout and the cliffs reverberate the sound. Oh, what joy for a shy man to feel himself so solitary, that he may lift his voice to its highest pitch without hazard of a listener! But, hush! — be silent, my good friend! — whence comes that stifled laughter? It was musical, — but how should there be such music in my solitude? Looking upwards, I catch a glimpse of three faces, peeping from the summit of the cliff, like angels between me and their native sky. Ah, fair girls, you may make yourselves merry at my eloquence, — but it was my turn to smile when I saw your white feet in the pool! Let us keep each other's secrets.

The sunshine has now passed from my hermitage, except a gleam upon the sand just where it meets the sea. A crowd of gloomy fantasies will come and haunt me if I tarry longer here in the darkening twilight of these gray rocks. This is a dismal place in some moods of the mind. Climb we, therefore, the precipice, and pause a moment on the brink, gazing down into that hollow chamber by the deep where we have been, what few can be, sufficient to our own pastime — yes, say the word outright! — self-sufficient to our own happiness. How lonesome looks the recess now, and dreary too — like all other spots where happiness has been! There lies my shadow in the departing sunshine with its head upon the sea. I will pelt it with pebbles. A hit! a hit! I clap my hands in triumph, and see! my shadow clapping its unreal hands, and claiming the triumph for itself. What a simpleton must I have been all day, since my own shadow makes a mock of my fooleries!

Homeward! homeward! It is time to hasten home. It is time; it is time; for as the sun sinks over the western wave, the sea grows melancholy, and the surf has a saddened tone. The distant sails appear astray, and not of earth, in their remoteness amid the desolate waste. My spirit wanders forth afar, but finds no resting-place and comes shivering back. It is time that I were hence. But grudge me not the day that has been spent in seclusion, which yet was not solitude, since the great sea has been my companion, and the little sea-birds my friends, and the wind has told me his secrets, and airy shapes have flitted around me in my hermitage. Such companionship works an effect upon a man's character, as if he had been admitted to the society of creatures that are not mortal. And when, at noontide, I tread the crowded streets, the influence of this day will still be felt; so that I shall walk among men kindly and as a brother, with affection and sympathy, but yet shall not melt into the indistinguishable mass of human-kind. I shall think my own thoughts, and feel my own emotions, and possess my individuality unviolated.

But it is good, at the eve of such a day, to feel and know that there are men and women in the world. That feeling and that knowledge are mine at this moment; for, on the shore far below me, the fishing party have landed from their skiff, and are cooking their scaly prey by a fire of driftwood, kindled in the angle of two rude rocks. The three visionary girls are likewise there. In the deepening twilight, while the surf is dashed near their hearth, the ruddy gleam of the fire throws a strange air of comfort over the wild cove, bestrewn as it is with pebbles and sea-weed, and exposed to the "melancholy main." Moreover, as the smoke climbs up the precipice, it brings with it a savory smell from a pan of fried fish and a black kettle of chowder, and reminds me that my dinner was nothing but bread and water, and a tuft of samphire and an apple. Methinks the party might find room for another guest at that flat rock which serves them for a table; and if spoons be scarce, I could pick up a clamshell on the beach. They see me now; and — the blessing of a hungry man upon him! — one of them sends up a hospitable shout — halloo, Sir Solitary! come down and sup with us! The ladies wave their handkerchiefs. Can I decline? No; and be it owned, after all my solitary joys, that this is the sweetest moment of a Day by the Sea-Shore.

EDWARD FANE'S ROSEBUD.

THERE is hardly a more difficult exercise of fancy than, while gazing at a figure of melancholy age, to recreate its youth, and, without entirely obliterating the identity of form and features, to restore those graces which time has snatched away. Some old people, especially women, so age-worn and woful are they, seem never to have been young and gay. It is easier to conceive that such gloomy phantoms were sent into the world as withered and decrepit as we behold them now, with sympathies only for pain and grief, to watch at death-beds and weep at funerals. Even the sable garments of their widowhood appear essential to their existence; all their attributes combine to render them darksome shadows, creeping strangely amid the sunshine of human life. Yet it is no unprofitable task to take one of these doleful creatures, and set fancy resolutely at work to brighten the dim eye, and darken the silvery locks, and paint the ashen cheek with rose color, and repair the shrunken and crazy form, till a dewy maiden shall be seen in the old matron's elbow-chair. The miracle being wrought, then let the years roll back again, each sadder than the last, and the whole weight of age and sorrow settle down upon the youthful figure. Wrinkles and furrows, the handwriting of Time, may thus be deciphered, and found to contain deep lessons of thought and feeling. Such profit might be derived by a skilful observer from my much-respected friend, the Widow Toothaker, a nurse of great repute, who has breathed the atmosphere of sick-chambers and dying breaths these forty years.

See! she sits cowering over her lonesome hearth, with her gown and upper petticoat drawn upward, gathering thriftly into her person the whole warmth of the fire, which, now at nightfall, begins to dissipate the autumnal chill of her chamber. The blaze quivers capriciously in front, alternately glimmering into the deepest chasms of her wrinkled visage, and then permitting a ghostly dimness to mar the outlines of her venerable figure. And Nurse Toothaker holds a teaspoon in her right hand, with which to stir up the contents of a tumbler in her left, whence steams a vapory fragrance, abhorred of temperance societies. Now she sips — now stirs — now sips again. Her sad old heart has need to be revived by the rich infusion of Geneva, which is mixed half and half with hot water, in the tumbler. All day long she has been sitting by a death-pillow, and quitted it for her home only when the spirit of her patient left the clay and went homeward too. But now are her melancholy meditations cheered, and her torpid blood warmed, and her shoulders lightened of at least twenty ponderous years, by a draught from the true Fountain of Youth in a case bottle. It is strange that men should deem that fount a fable, when its liquor fills more bottles than the congress water! Sip it again, good nurse, and see whether a second draught will not take off another score of years, and perhaps ten more, and show us, in your high-backed chair, the blooming damsel who plighted troths with Edward Fane. Get you gone, Age and Widowhood! Come back, unwedded Youth! But, alas! the charm will not work. In spite of fancy's

most potent spell, I can see only an old dame cowering over the fire, a picture of decay and desolation,
while the November blast roars at her in the chimney,
and fitful showers rush suddenly against the window.

Yet there was a time when Rose Grafton — such
was the pretty maiden name of Nurse Toothaker —
possessed beauty that would have gladdened this dim
and dismal chamber as with sunshine. It won for her
the heart of Edward Fane, who has since made so
great a figure in the world and is now a grand old
gentleman, with powdered hair, and as gouty as a
lord. These early lovers thought to have walked hand
in hand through life. They had wept together for
Edward's little sister Mary, whom Rose tended in her
sickness, partly because she was the sweetest child
that ever lived or died, but more for love of him. She
was but three years old. Being such an infant, Death
could not embody his terrors in her little corpse; nor
did Rose fear to touch the dead child's brow, though
chill, as she curled the silken hair around it, nor to
take her tiny hand and clasp a flower within its fingers. Afterward, when she looked through the pane
of glass in the coffin lid, and beheld Mary's face, it
seemed not so much like death, or life, as like a wax-
work, wrought into the perfect image of a child asleep,
and dreaming of its mother's smile. Rose thought
her too fair a thing to be hidden in the grave, and
wondered that an angel did not snatch up little Mary's
coffin, and bear the slumbering babe to heaven, and
bid her wake immortal. But when the sods were laid
on little Mary, the heart of Rose was troubled. She
shuddered at the fantasy, that, in grasping the child's
cold fingers, her virgin hand had exchanged a first
greeting with mortality, and could never lose the

earthly taint. How many a greeting since! But as yet, she was a fair young girl, with the dew-drops of fresh feeling in her bosom; and instead of Rose, which seemed too mature a name for her half-opened beauty, her lover called her Rosebud.

The rosebud was destined never to bloom for Edward Fane. His mother was a rich and haughty dame with all the aristocratic prejudices of colonial times. She scorned Rose Grafton's humble parentage, and caused her son to break his faith, though, had she let him choose, he would have prized his Rosebud above the richest diamond. The lovers parted, and have seldom met again. Both may have visited the same mansions, but not at the same time; for one was bidden to the festal hall, and the other to the sick-chamber; he was the guest of Pleasure and Prosperity, and she of Anguish. Rose, after their separation, was long secluded within the dwelling of Mr. Toothaker, whom she married with the revengeful hope of breaking her false lover's heart. She went to her bridegroom's arms with bitterer tears, they say, than young girls ought to shed at the threshold of the bridal chamber. Yet, though her husband's head was getting gray, and his heart had been chilled with an autumnal frost, Rose soon began to love him, and wondered at her own conjugal affection. He was all she had to love; there were no children.

In a year or two, poor Mr. Toothaker was visited with a wearisome infirmity, which settled in his joints, and made him weaker than a child. He crept forth about his business, and came home at dinner time and eventide, not with the manly tread that gladdens a wife's heart, but slowly, feebly, jotting down each dull footstep with a melancholy dub of his staff. We must

pardon his pretty wife, if she sometimes blushed to
own him. Her visitors, when they heard him coming,
looked for the appearance of some old, old man; but
he dragged his nerveless limbs into the parlor — and
there was Mr. Toothaker! The disease increasing,
he never went into the sunshine, save with a staff in
his right hand and his left on his wife's shoulder,
bearing heavily downward, like a dead man's hand
Thus, a slender woman, still looking maiden-like, she
supported his tall, broad-chested frame along the pathway of their little garden, and plucked the roses for
her gray-haired husband, and spoke soothingly, as to
an infant. His mind was palsied with his body; its
utmost energy was peevishness. In a few months
more, she helped him up the staircase, with a pause at
every step, and a longer one upon the landing-place,
and a heavy glance behind, as he crossed the threshold
of his chamber. He knew, poor man, that the precincts of those four walls would thenceforth be his
world — his world, his home, his tomb — at once a
dwelling and a burial-place, till he were borne to a
darker and a narrower one. But Rose was with him
in the tomb. He leaned upon her in his daily passage
from the bed to the chair by the fireside, and back
again from the weary chair to the joyless bed — his
bed and hers — their marriage-bed; till even this
short journey ceased, and his head lay all day upon
the pillow, and hers all night beside it. How long
poor Mr. Toothaker was kept in misery! Death
seemed to draw near the door, and often to lift the
latch, and sometimes to thrust his ugly skull into the
chamber, nodding to Rose, and pointing at her husband, but still delayed to enter. "This bedridden
wretch cannot escape me!" quoth Death. "I will go

forth and run a race with the swift, and fight a battle
with the strong, and come back for Toothaker at my
leisure!" Oh, when the deliverer came so near, in the
dull anguish of her worn-out sympathies, did she never
long to cry, "Death, come in!"

But, no! We have no right to ascribe such a wish
to our friend Rose. She never failed in a wife's duty
to her poor sick husband. She murmured not, though
a glimpse of the sunny sky was as strange to her as
him, nor answered peevishly, though his complaining
accents roused her from her sweetest dream, only to
share his wretchedness. He knew her faith, yet nourished a cankered jealousy; and when the slow disease
had chilled all his heart, save one lukewarm spot,
which Death's frozen fingers were searching for, his
last words were: "What would my Rose have done
for her first love, if she has been so true and kind to
a sick old man like me!" And then his poor soul
crept away, and left the body lifeless, though hardly
more so than for years before, and Rose a widow,
though in truth it was the wedding-night that wid-
owed her. She felt glad, it must be owned, when Mr.
Toothaker was buried, because his corpse had retained
such a likeness to the man half alive, that she hearkened for the sad murmur of his voice, bidding her
shift his pillow. But all through the next winter,
though the grave had held him many a month, she
fancied him calling from that cold bed, "Rose! Rose!
come put a blanket on my feet!"

So now the Rosebud was the Widow Toothaker.
Her troubles had come early, and, tedious as they
seemed, had passed before all her bloom was fled.
She was still fair enough to captivate a bachelor, or,
with a widow's cheerful gravity, she might have won

a widower, stealing into his heart in the very guise of
his dead wife. But the Widow Toothaker had no
such projects. By her watchings and continual cares
her heart had become knit to her first husband with
a constancy which changed its very nature, and made
her love him for his infirmities, and infirmity for his
sake. When the palsied old man was gone, even her
early lover could not have supplied his place. She
had dwelt in a sick-chamber, and been the companion
of a half-dead wretch, till she could scarcely breathe in
a free air, and felt ill at ease with the healthy and
the happy. She missed the fragrance of the doctor's
stuff. She walked the chamber with a noiseless footfall. If visitors came in she spoke in soft and sooth-
ing accents, and was startled and shocked by their
loud voices. Often, in the lonesome evening, she
looked timorously from the fireside to the bed, with almost a hope of recognizing a ghastly face upon the pillow. Then went her thoughts sadly to her husband's
grave. If one impatient throb had wronged him in
his lifetime, — if she had secretly repined because
her buoyant youth was imprisoned with his torpid age,
— if ever, while slumbering beside him, a treacherous
dream had admitted another into her heart, — yet the
sick man had been preparing a revenge which the
dead now claimed. On his painful pillow he had cast
a spell around her ; his groans and misery had proved
more captivating charms than gayety and youthful
grace; in his semblance Disease itself had won the
Rosebud for a bride ; nor could his death dissolve the
nuptials. By that indissoluble bond she had gained a
home in every sick-chamber, and nowhere else: there
were her brethren and sisters ; thither her husband
summoned her with that voice which had seemed to

issue from the grave of Toothaker. At length she
recognized her destiny.

We have beheld her as the maid, the wife, the
widow; now we see her in a separate and insulated
character ; she was, in all her attributes, Nurse Toothaker.   And Nurse Toothaker alone, with her own
shrivelled lips, could make known her experience in
that capacity. What a history might she record of
the great sicknesses in which she has gone hand in
hand with the exterminating angel ! She remembers
when the small-pox hoisted a red banner on almost
every house along the street. She has witnessed when
the typhus fever swept off a whole household, young
and old, all but a lonely mother, who vainly shrieked
to follow her last loved one. Where would be Death's
triumph, if none lived to weep ? She can speak of
strange maladies that have broken out, as if spontaneously, but were found to have been imported from
foreign lands, with rich silks and other merchandise,
the costliest portion of the cargo. And once, she rec-
ollects, the people died of what was considered a new
pestilence, till the doctors traced it to the ancient
grave of a young girl, who thus caused many deaths
a hundred years after her own burial. Strange, that
such black mischief should lurk in a maiden's grave !
She loves to tell how strong men fight with fiery
fevers, utterly refusing to give up their breath ; and
how consumptive virgins fade out of the world,
scarcely reluctant, as if their lovers were wooing
them to a far country. Tell us, thou fearful woman !
tell us the death secrets ! Fain would I search out the
meaning of words, faintly gasped with intermingled
sobs and broken sentences, half audibly spoken be
tween earth and the judgment seat !

An awful woman! She is the patron saint of young physicians, and the bosom friend of old ones. In the mansions where she enters, the inmates provide themselves black garments; the coffin maker follows her; and the bell tolls as she comes away from the threshold. Death himself has met her at so many a bedside, that he puts forth his bony hand to greet Nurse Toothaker. She is an awful woman! And, oh! is it conceivable, that this handmaid of human infirmity and affliction — so darkly stained, so thoroughly imbued with all that is saddest in the doom of mortals — can ever again be bright and gladsome, even though bathed in the sunshine of eternity? By her long communion with woe has she not forfeited her inheritance of immortal joy? Does any germ of bliss survive within her?

Hark! — an eager knocking at Nurse Toothaker's door. She starts from her drowsy reverie, sets aside the empty tumbler and teaspoon, and lights a lamp at the dim embers of the fire. Rap, rap, rap! again; and she hurries adown the staircase, wondering which of her friends can be at death's door now, since there is such an earnest messenger at Nurse Toothaker's. Again the peal resounds, just as her hand is on the lock. "Be quick, Nurse Toothaker!" cries a man on the doorsteps; "old General Fane is taken with the gout in his stomach, and has sent for you to watch by his death-bed. Make haste, for there is no time to lose!" "Fane! Edward Fane! And has he sent for me at last? I am ready! I will get on my cloak and begone. So," adds the sable-gowned, ashen-visaged, funereal old figure, "Edward Fane remembers his Rosebud!"

Our question is answered. There is a germ of bliss

within her. Her long-hoarded constancy — her memory of the bliss that was — remaining amid the gloom of her after life like a sweet-smelling flower in a coffin, is a symbol that all may be renewed. In some happier clime the Rosebud may revive again with all the dewdrops in its bosom.

THE THREEFOLD DESTINY.

A FAIRY LEGEND.

I HAVE sometimes produced a singular and not un-
pleasing effect, so far as my own mind was concerned,
by imagining a train of incidents in which the spirit
and mechanism of the fairy legend should be combined
with the characters and manners of familiar life.   In
the little tale which follows, a subdued tinge of the
wild and wonderful is thrown over a sketch of New
England personages and scenery, yet, it is hoped,
without entirely obliterating the sober hues of nature.
Rather than a story of events claiming to be real, it
may be considered as an allegory, such as the writers
of the last century would have expressed in the shape
of an Eastern tale, but to which I have endeavored to
give a more life-like warmth than could be infused into
those fanciful productions.

In the twilight of a summer eve, a tall, dark figure
over which long and remote travel had thrown an outlandish aspect, was entering a village, not in " Fairy
Londe," but within our own familiar boundaries.   The
staff on which this traveller leaned had been his companion from the spot where it grew, in the jungles of
Hindostan ; the hat that overshadowed his sombre
brow had shielded him from the suns of Spain : but
his cheek had been blackened by the red-hot wind of
an Arabian desert, and had felt the frozen breath of
an Arctic region.   Long sojourning amid wild and

dangerous men, he still wore beneath his vest the ata-
ghan which he had once struck into the throat of a
Turkish robber. In every foreign clime he had lost
something of his New England characteristics; and,
perhaps, from every people he had unconsciously borrowed a new peculiarity; so that when the world-wan-
derer again trod the street of his native village it is
no wonder that he passed unrecognized, though exciting the gaze and curiosity of all. Yet, as his arm
casually touched that of a young woman who was
wending her way to an evening lecture she started,
and almost uttered a cry.

"Ralph Cranfield!" was the name that she half
articulated.

"Can that be my old playmate, Faith Egerton?"
thought the traveller, looking round at her figure, but
without pausing.

Ralph Cranfield, from his youth upward, had felt
himself marked out for a high destiny. He had imbibed the idea — we say not whether it were revealed
to him by witchcraft, or in a dream of prophecy, or
that his brooding fancy had palmed its own dictates
upon him as the oracles of a Sibyl! — but he had imbibed the idea, and held it firmest among his articles
of faith, that three marvellous events of his life were
to be confirmed to him by three signs.

The first of these three fatalities, and perhaps the
one on which his youthful imagination had dwelt most
fondly, was the discovery of the maid who alone, of all
the maids on earth, could make him happy by her love.
He was to roam around the world till he should meet
a beautiful woman wearing on her bosom a jewel in
the shape of a heart; whether of pearl, or ruby, or
emerald, or carbuncle, or a changeful opal, or perhaps

a priceless diamond, Ralph Cranfield little cared, so long as it were a heart of one peculiar shape. On encountering this lovely stranger, he was bound to address her thus: "Maiden, I have brought you a heavy heart. May I rest its weight on you?" And if she were his fated bride — if their kindred souls were destined to form a union here below, which all eternity should only bind more closely — she would reply, with her finger on the heart-shaped jewel, — "This token, which I have worn so long, is the assurance that you may!"

And, secondly, Ralph Cranfield had a firm belief that there was a mighty treasure hidden somewhere in the earth, of which the burial-place would be revealed to none but him. When his feet should press upon the mysterious spot, there would be a hand before him pointing downward — whether carved of marble, or hewn in gigantic dimensions on the side of a rocky precipice, or perchance a hand of flame in empty air, he could not tell; but, at least, he would discern a hand, the forefinger pointing downward, and beneath it the Latin word EFFODE — Dig! and digging thereabouts, the gold in coin or ingots, the precious stones, or of whatever else the treasure might consist, would be certain to reward his toil.

The third and last of the miraculous events in the life of this high-destined man was to be the attainment of extensive influence and sway over his fellow-creatures. Whether he were to be a king and founder of an hereditary throne, or the victorious leader of a people contending for their freedom, or the apostle of a purified and regenerated faith, was left for futurity to show. As messengers of the sign by which Ralph Cranfield might recognize the summons, three venerable men were to claim audience of him. The chief among them, a dignified and majestic person, arrayed, it may be supposed, in the flowing garments of an ancient sage, would be the bearer of a wand or prophet's rod. With this wand, or rod, or staff, the venerable sage would trace a certain figure in the air, and then proceed to make known his heaven-instructed message; which, if obeyed, must lead to glorious results.

With this proud fate before him, in the flush of his imaginative youth, Ralph Cranfield had set forth to seek the maid, the treasure, and the venerable sage with his gift of extended empire. And had he found them? Alas! it was not with the aspect of a triumphant man, who had achieved a nobler destiny than all his fellows, but rather with the gloom of one struggling against peculiar and continual adversity, that he now passed homeward to his mother's cottage. He had come back, but only for a time, to lay aside the pilgrim's staff, trusting that his weary manhood would regain somewhat of the elasticity of youth, in the spot where his threefold fate had been foreshown him. There had been few changes in the village; for it was not one of those thriving places where a year's prosperity makes more than the havoc of a century's decay; but like a gray hair in a young man's head, an antiquated little town, full of old maids, and aged elms, and moss-grown dwellings. Few seemed to be the changes here. The drooping elms, indeed, had a more majestic spread; the weather-blackened houses were adorned with a denser thatch of verdant moss; and doubtless there were a few more gravestones in the burial ground, inscribed with names that had once been familiar in the village street. Yet, summing up all the mischief that ten years had wrought, it seemed

scarcely more than if Ralph Cranfield had gone forth
that very morning, and dreamed a day-dream till the
twilight, and then turned back again. But his heart
grew cold because the village did not remember him
as he remembered the village.

"Here is the change!" sighed he, striking his hand
upon his breast. "Who is this man of thought and
care, weary with world-wandering and heavy with disappointed hopes? The youth returns not, who went
forth so joyously!"

And now Ralph Cranfield was at his mother's gate,
in front of the small house where the old lady, with
slender but sufficient means, had kept herself comfortable during her son's long absence. Admitting
himself within the enclosure, he leaned against a
great, old tree, trifling with his own impatience, as
people often do in those intervals when years are
summed into a moment. He took a minute survey
of the dwelling — its windows brightened with the
sky gleam, its doorway, with the half of a millstone
for a step, and the faintly-traced path waving thence to
the gate. He made friends again with his childhood's
friend, the old tree against which he leaned; and
glancing his eye adown its trunk, beheld something
that excited a melancholy smile. It was a half obliterated inscription — the Latin word EFFODE — which
he remembered to have carved in the bark of the tree,
with a whole day's toil, when he had first begun to
muse about his exalted destiny. It might be accounted
a rather singular coincidence, that the bark just above
the inscription, had put forth an excrescence, shaped
not unlike a hand, with the forefinger pointing ob-
liquely at the word of fate. Such, at least, was its
appearance in the dusky light.

"Now a credulous man," said Ralph Cranfield care-lessly to himself, "might suppose that the treasure which I have sought round the world lies buried, after all, at the very door of my mother's dwelling. That would be a jest indeed!"

More he thought not about the matter; for now the door was opened, and an elderly woman appeared on the threshold, peering into the dusk to discover who it might be that had intruded on her premises, and was standing in the shadow of her tree. It was Ralph Cranfield's mother. Pass we over their greeting, and leave the one to her joy and the other to his rest, - if quiet rest be found.

But when morning broke, he arose with a troubled brow; for his sleep and his wakefulness had alike been full of dreams. All the fervor was rekindled with which he had burned of yore to unravel the threefold mystery of his fate. The crowd of his early visions seemed to have awaited him beneath his mother's roof, and thronged riotously around to welcome his return. In the well-remembered chamber, on the pillow where his infancy had slumbered, he had passed a wilder night than ever in an Arab tent, or when he had re-posed his head in the ghastly shades of a haunted for-est. A shadowy maid had stolen to his bedside, and laid her finger on the scintillating heart; a hand of flame had glowed amid the darkness, pointing down-ward to a mystery within the earth; a hoary sage had waved his prophetic wand, and beckoned the dreamer onward to a chair of state. The same phantoms, though fainter in the daylight, still flitted about the cottage, and mingled among the crowd of familiar faces that were drawn thither by the news of Ralph Cran-field's return, to bid him welcome for his mother's sake. There they found him, a tall, dark, stately man of foreign aspect, courteous in demeanor and mild of speech, yet with an abstracted eye, which seemed often to snatch a glance at the invisible.

Meantime the widow Cranfield went bustling about the house, full of joy that she again had somebody to love, and be careful of, and for whom she might vex and tease herself with the petty troubles of daily life. It was nearly noon when she looked forth from the door, and descried three personages of note coming along the street, through the hot sunshine and the masses of elm-tree shade. At length they reached her gate and undid the latch.

" See, Ralph ! " exclaimed she, with maternal pride, " here is Squire Hawkwood and the two other select-men, coming on purpose to see you ! Now do tell them a good long story about what you have seen in foreign parts."

The foremost of the three visitors, Squire Hawk-wood, was a very pompous, but excellent old gentle-man, the head and prime mover in all the affairs of the village, and universally acknowledged to be one of the sagest men on earth. He wore, according to a fashion even then becoming antiquated, a three-cornered hat, and carried a silver-headed cane, the use of which seemed to be rather for flourishing in the air than for assisting the progress of his legs. His two companions were elderly and respectable yeomen, who, retaining an ante-revolutionary reverence for rank and hereditary wealth, kept a little in the Squire's rear. As they approached along the pathway, Ralph Cran-field sat in an oaken elbow chair, half unconsciously gazing at the three visitors, and enveloping their homely figures in the misty romance that pervaded his mental world.

" Here," thought he, smiling at the conceit, "here come three elderly personages, and the first of the three is a venerable sage with a staff. What if this embassy should bring me the message of my fate!"

While Squire Hawkwood and his colleagues entered, Ralph rose from his seat and advanced a few steps to receive them, and his stately figure and dark countenance, as he bent courteously towards his guests, had a natural dignity, contrasting well with the bustling importance of the Squire. The old gentleman, according to invariable custom, gave an elaborate preliminary flourish with his cane in the air, then removed his three-cornered hat in order to wipe his brow, and finally proceeded to make known his errand.

" My colleagues and myself," began the Squire, " are burdened with momentous duties, being jointly selectmen of this village. Our minds, for the space of three days past, have been laboriously bent on the selection of a suitable person to fill a most important office, and take upon himself a charge and rule which, wisely considered, may be ranked no lower than those of kings and potentates. And whereas you, our native townsman, are of good natural intellect, and well cultivated by foreign travel, and that certain vagaries and fantasies of your youth are doubtless long ago corrected; taking all these matters, I say, into due consideration, we are of opinion that Providence hath sent you hither, at this juncture, for our very purpose."

During this harangue, Cranfield gazed fixedly at the speaker, as if he beheld something mysterious and unearthly in his pompous little figure, and as if the Squire had worn the flowing robes of an ancient sage, instead of a square-skirted coat, flapped waistcoat,

velvet breeches and silk stockings. Nor was his wonder without sufficient cause; for the flourish of the
Squire's staff, marvellous to relate, had described precisely the signal in the air which was to ratify the
message of the prophetic Sage whom Cranfield had
sought around the world.

"And what," inquired Ralph Cranfield, with a
tremor in his voice, "what may this office be, which
is to equal me with kings and potentates?"

"No less than instructor of our village school," answered Squire Hawkwood; "the office being now
vacant by the death of the venerable Master Whita-
ker, after a fifty years' incumbency."

"I will consider of your proposal," replied Ralph
Cranfield, hurriedly, "and will make known my decision within three days."

After a few more words the village dignitary and
his companions took their leave. But to Cranfield's
fancy their images were still present, and became
more and more invested with the dim awfulness of
figures which had first appeared to him in a dream,
and afterwards had shown themselves in his waking
moments, assuming homely aspects among familiar
things. His mind dwelt upon the features of the
Squire, till they grew confused with those of the visionary Sage, and one appeared but the shadow of the
other. The same visage, he now thought, had looked
forth upon him from the Pyramid of Cheops; the
same form had beckoned to him among the colon-
nades of the Alhambra; the same figure had mistily
revealed itself through the ascending steam of the
Great Geyser. At every effort of his memory he recognized some trait of the dreamy Messenger of Destiny in this pompous, bustling, self-important, little

great man of the village. Amid such musings Ralph Cranfield sat all day in the cottage, scarcely hearing and vaguely answering his mother's thousand questions about his travels and adventures. At sunset he roused himself to take a stroll, and, passing the aged elm-tree, his eye was again caught by the semblance of a hand pointing downward at the half-obliterated inscription.

As Cranfield walked down the street of the village, the level sunbeams threw his shadow far before him ; and he fancied that as his shadow walked among distant objects, so had there been a presentiment stalking in advance of him throughout his life. And when he drew near each object, over which his tall shadow had preceded him, still it proved to be one of the familiar recollections of his infancy and youth. Every crook in the pathway was remembered. Even the more transitory characteristics of the scene were the same as in by-gone days. A company of cows were grazing on the grassy roadside, and refreshed him with their fragrant breath. " It is sweeter," thought he, " than the perfume which was wafted to our ship from the Spice Islands. The round little figure of a child rolled from a doorway, and lay laughing almost beneath Cranfield's feet. The dark and stately man stooped down and, lifting the infant, restored him to his mother's arms. " The children," said he to himself — and sighed and smiled — " the children are to be my charge ! " And while a flow of natural feeling gushed like a well-spring in his heart, he came to a dwelling which he could nowise forbear to enter. A sweet voice, which seemed to come from a deep and tender soul, was warbling a plaintive little air within.

He bent his head and passed through the lowly

door. As his foot sounded upon the threshold, a young woman advanced from the dusky interior of the house, at first hastily, and then with a more uncertain step, till they met face to face. There was a singular contrast in their two figures : he dark and picturesque — one who had battled with the world, whom all suns had shone upon, and whom all winds had blown on a varied course ; she neat, comely, and quiet — quiet even in her agitation, as if all her emotions had been subdued to the peaceful tenor of her life. Yet their faces, all unlike as they were, had an expression that seemed not so alien, a glow of kindred feeling flashing upward anew from half-extinguished embers.

"You are welcome home!" said Faith Egerton.

But Cranfield did not immediately answer ; for his eye had been caught by an ornament in the shape of a Heart which Faith wore as a brooch upon her bosom. The material was the ordinary white quartz; and he recollected having himself shaped it out of one of those Indian arrowheads which are so often found in the ancient haunts of the red men. It was precisely on the pattern of that worn by the visionary Maid. When Cranfield departed on his shadowy search he had bestowed this brooch, in a gold setting, as a parting gift to Faith Egerton.

"So, Faith, you have kept the Heart!" said he at length.

"Yes," said she, blushing deeply ; then more gayly, "and what else have you brought me from beyond the sea?"

"Faith!" replied Ralph Cranfield, uttering the fated words by an uncontrollable impulse, "I have brought you nothing but a heavy heart! May I rest its weight on you?"

"This token which I have worn so long," said Faith, laying her tremulous finger on the Heart, "is the assurance that you may!"

"Faith! Faith!" cried Cranfield, clasping her in his arms, "you have interpreted my wild and weary dream!"

Yes, the wild dream was awake at last. To find the mysterious treasure, he was to till the earth around his mother's dwelling, and reap its products! Instead of warlike command, or regal or religious sway, he was to rule over the village children! And now the visionary Maid had faded from his fancy, and in her place he saw the playmate of his childhood! Would all who cherish such wild wishes but look around them, they would oftenest find their sphere of duty, of prosperity, and happiness, within those precincts and in that station where Providence itself has cast their lot. Happy they who read the riddle without a weary world search, or a lifetime spent in vain!

CRITICAL AND EXPLANATORY NOTES.

THE GRAY CHAMPION.

Publication. First published in January, 1835, in *The New England Magazine*, pp. 20–26, under the signature, "Author of *The Gentle Boy*" [1832]. Included in the first editions of *Twice-Told Tales* (1837–1842); and in *Legends of New England* (1877).

Source. The incident from which Hawthorne got the idea of a gray and mysterious champion is connected with an Indian attack upon Hadley, Mass., Sept. 1, 1675. It is thus described by J. S. Barry in his *History of Massachusetts*, i, 420: "In the midst of the contest, while the war-whoop was ringing, and just as the Indians were about to triumph, a venerable figure, of commanding aspect, clad in the fashion of a former generation, with his hair white from age, suddenly appeared, and with sword in hand, rallied the disordered troops, infused into them fresh courage, and placing himself at their head, speedily compelled the savages to retire. At the close of the struggle, the visitor vanished as mysteriously as he came; the belief was long cherished that an angel had relieved the town; and years elapsed before it was known that Col. Goffe, who had been a commander in the army of Cromwell's Invincibles, and who was then concealed in Hadley, was the one to whom they were indebted for so timely a deliverance." See also John Fiske's *Beginnings of New England*, p. 217.

Criticism. "The little figures stand up in the tale as stoutly, at the least, as if they were propped up by half a dozen chapters by a dryer annalist." — Henry James, *Hawthorne*, p. 65.

21 **Charles the Voluptuous:** Charles II. **Andros:** Governor of New England and New York, 1686–1689. "A dull, formal, and somewhat ill-tempered disciplinarian, administering a fixed system with rigid obedience and mechanical fidelity to orders." — Doyle, *English Colonies in America*, iii, 184. See Fiske, *Beginnings of New England*, p. 270.

22 **a rumor:** during the winter of 1688, Andros heard "a doubtful whisper" of the purposed invasion and called upon the people to be loyal to King James. The first authoritative news of the landing of William in England reached Boston, April 4, 1689. Two weeks later this report was

confirmed; and on April 19, as he was attempting to escape in woman's clothes, Andros was arrested, and soon after sent back to England. **Prince of Orange:** William III. **King Street:** changed to State Street in 1784. "From Long Wharf ran King Street, then the principal business street, through the heart of the town; . . . The streets were sufficiently wide, but crooked and irregular, paved with cobble-stones, with gutters in the middle, and sidewalks marked off by a line of posts and chains." — Lodge, *Historic Towns,* p. 105. **another encounter:** the Boston Massacre, March 5, 1770.

23 **Parliament:** the body which overthrew the Stuart king, Charles I, in the Civil War (1642–1648). **King Philip's War** (1675–1676): see Irving's *Philip of Poconoket,* in *The Sketch Book;* Barry's *History of Massachusetts,* chaps. xv–xvi; Ellis and Morris's *King Philip's War.*

24 **Primer** (New England): cf. p. 396. In this quaint old textbook there is a picture of the martyrdom of John Rogers, and beneath it the following inscription: "Mr. John Rogers, Minister of the Gospel in London, was the first Martyr in Queen Mary's Reign, and was burnt at Smithfield, February the Fourteenth, 1554. His wife, with nine small Children and one at her breast, following Him to the Stake, with which sorrowful Sight he was not in the least daunted, but with wonderful Patience died courageously for the Gospel of JESUS CHRIST." **cry was at the loudest:** a contemporary letter (April 18, 1689) says: "When the old Governor came among them there was a great shout by the soldiers." **the old charter:** granted by Charles I in June, 1628; withdrawn by Charles II in June, 1684. The new charter was granted by William III (1692) and remained in force until the Revolution. **Bradstreet:** Governor, 1689–1692, "a man of moderate powers but great integrity, and held in peculiar reverence as the last survivor of those that had been chosen to office before leaving England by the leaders of the great Puritan Exodus." — Fiske. In some history of American literature look up Anne Bradstreet.

25 **Cornhill:** that part of Marlborough Street (now Washington Street) north of the Old South Church. **Randolph:** see note on page 297. **Cotton Mather** (1663–1728): a well-known Puritan divine. **Bullivant:** the hated Attorney-General. **Dudley, Joseph:** President of Randolph's provisional government, May–December, 1686 ; governor, 1702–1715. "It is safe to say that of all the representatives of the Crown who governed in New England there was no one so cordially hated by the people as Joseph Dudley, who not only represented that outside power which they so disliked, but who was regarded as one who had betrayed his race and his religion; . . . that he was an astute, intriguing,

double-dealing man, cannot be doubted." — Lodge. **King's Chapel :** the fifth church in Boston ; at first called "His Majesty's Chapel"; during Anne's reign, "Queen's Chapel"; and for a while after the Revolution, "Stone Chapel." In 1688, after angering the Puritans by holding Episcopal services in the Town Hall and in the Old South, Andros built this church on land taken from the town burial-ground. Lady Andros, a woman lovely and universally beloved, Winthrop, John Cotton, Shirley, Leverett, Endicott, John Winslow, and Mary Chilton are among those buried in the adjoining yard. The corner-stone of the present structure was laid by Governor Shirley, August 11, 1749.

27 **Winthrop:** see note on p. 489.

29 **Old Noll:** Oliver Cromwell.

30 **King William was proclaimed:** not until five weeks after Andros's arrest was this done officially. **Court of Justice:** Parliament; see note on p. 23. For an account of the regicides, Whalley and Goffe, see Fiske, *Beginnings of New England,* pp. 192–194; and Doyle, *English Colonies in America,* iii, 117–120.

31 **Lexington:** April 19, 1775. **Bunker's Hill:** June 17, 1775. **The type,** etc. : see note on p. 69.

SUNDAY AT HOME.

Publication. First printed in 1837 in *The Boston Token,* pp. 88–96. Signed, "Author of *The Gentle Boy*" [1832]. **Source.** See Lathrop's Introductory Note to this volume, p. 12. This little sketch is suggested in the following letter written by Hawthorne to Sophia Peabody: "Most absolute little Sophia, didst thou expressly command me to go to Father Taylor's church this very Sabbath ? Now, it would not be an auspicious day for me to hear the aforesaid Son of Thunder. I have a cold, though, indeed, I fear I have partly conjured it up to serve my naughty purpose. Some sunshiny day, when I am wide awake and warm and genial, I will go." — Conway, *Life of Hawthorne,* p. 36.

32 Note the different kinds and degrees of light mentioned on this page.

33 **no buzz of voices :** see *American Note-Books,* June 22 1835 (end).

34 In a letter written from college to his sister, Hawthorne complains of being "sometimes afflicted with the Sunday sickness"; and the son of this greatest New England moralist says that he cannot remember his father's ever attending a church. Cf. : —

> " Do you ask me, 'Tell me further
> Of this Consul, of this Hawthorne?'

> I would say, 'He is a sinner, —
> Reprobate and churchless sinner, —
> Never goes inside a chapel,
> Only sees outside of chapels,
> Says his prayers without a chapel!'"
>
> JOHN BRIGHT, *Song of Consul Hawthorne.*

For the origin of the Sabbath-school, see *American Note-Books*, October 25, 1836.

37 **Lord, look down,** etc. : the "safest kind of prayer"? See Luke, xviii, 13. **son of thunder:** see Mark, iii. 17.

38 **pew-doors:** see Alice Morse Earle, *The Sabbath in Puritan New England*, chap. iv.

holy trance, etc.: cf. Stevenson's lines in *A Lowden Sabbath Morn:* —

> "The braw words rumm'le ower his haid,
> Nor steer the sleeper;
> An' in their restin' graves, the deid
> Sleep aye the deeper."

39 **Gentle reader:** does the term serve in any way to date the piece? Cf. note, p. 244. **a flight of poetry:** an appropriate sub-title for this sketch.

40 **seventh day:** cf. Byron's *Childe Harold*, i, 693 : —

> "The seventh day this; the jubilee of man.
> London, right well thou know'st the day of prayer."

A moral, and a religion: What are they?

THE WEDDING KNELL.

Publication. First printed in 1836 in *The Boston Token*, under the signature, "Author of *Sights from a Steeple*" [1831].

Source. The source of this story is said to be in King's *Anecdotes.*

Criticism. In his *Study of Hawthorne*, p. 157, G. P. Lathrop observes that as *The White Old Maid* has a certain "shapelessness" growing out of an "indefinable horror," and as *The Ambitious Guest* has a "too hopeless downfall at the end," even so *The Wedding Knell* "cannot escape a suspicion of disagreeable gloom."

"Almost all Hawthorne's tales embody single ideal situations, scarcely ever for a moment varied in their course in any essential respect. For instance, to take his shorter tales, the mockery of the attempt to renew in wasted age the blasted hopes of youth is crystallized into a ghostly *tableau vivant* in *The Wedding Knell.*" — R. H. Hutton, *Literary Essays.*

41 **At sixty-five,** etc. How many of Mr. Ellenwood's qualities were characteristic of Hawthorne?

42 Cf. the case of Edward Fane, p. 520.

45 In the *English Note-Books* we hear the bells "clashing

and clanging" at a country wedding; again, at a marriage celebrated at Westminster Abbey, "the bells were clamorous for joy, chiming merrily, musically, and obstreperously, — the most rejoicing sound that can be heard" [September 26, 1855]; and again at Manchester cathedra "the bells were chiming for a wedding"; and Hawthorn notes, "These chimes of bells are exceedingly impressive, so broadly gladsome as they are, filling the whole air, and every nook of one's heart with sympathy. They are good for people to rejoice with, and good also for a marriage, because through all their joy there is something solemn, — a tone of that voice which we have heard so often at funerals." [August 14, 1857.]

47 tolling for her funeral: cf. this thought with that at the end of *Dr. Heidegger's Experiment.*

48 dance of death: cf. "dance of life," p. 73 ; also "Shuddered and danced their dance of death." — *Tales of the Wayside Inn,* i, 35. Show how, as the story has unfolded step by step, we have been held in suspense.

49 accents: why more expressive than " voice " ?

50 Time is no more, etc. : cf. *The Lily's Quest,* p. 503 ; *The Minister's Black Veil,* p. 63; *Edward Fane's Rosebud,* p. 526.

51 something holy, etc.: what was it? Cf. the part played by the organ here with that on p. 39.

THE MINISTER'S BLACK VEIL.

Publication. First printed in 1836 in *The Boston Token,* under the signature "Author of *Sights from a Steeple*" [1831].

Source. "The Rev. Joseph Moody, of York, Maine, was a person of great eccentricity of character. Owing to a great calamity which early befell him, he became subject to a settled melancholy, and hid his face from men. He ever after wore a silk handkerchief drawn over his face, even during his pulpit ministrations; but, during prayer, it has been said that he would turn his back to the audience, and remove the veil. Some have thought that his grief was owing to the death of his wife, others that it was occasioned by his having in the early part of his life accidentally killed a youth for whom he had a great affection." *Massachusetts Historical Society Proceedings,* 1875–1876, p. 181.

Criticism. "He uses the veil," says Woodberry, "to typify man's concealment of himself from others, even the nearest; and while it visibly isolates the minister from his fellow men, it finally unites him with them in a single lot; for to the mind's eye, educated by this image to a new power of seeing, all men wear this veil; humanity is clothed with it in life, and moulders away beneath it in the grave, whither its secrets are carried. The seeming exception is found to be the rule; the horror attaching to the one un- seen face is now felt in all faces; the race is veiled, and the bit of crape has fallen like the blackness of night upon all life, for life has become a thing of darkness, a concealment." *Hawthorne,* in *American Men of Letters Series,* pp. 145–146.

"This mode of setting forth the agony of a pure mind, tainted by one irremovable blot, is undoubtedly impressive to the imagination in a high degree. . . . Yet it might possibly be mentioned that a poet of the highest order would have produced the effect by more direct means. Remorse overpowering and absorbing does not embody itself in these recondite and, one may almost say, over- ingenious fancies. Hawthorne does not give us so much the pure passion as some of its collateral effects. He is still more interested in the curious psychological problem than moved by sympathy with the torture of the soul." — Leslie Stephen, *Hours in a Library.*

"The absolute isolation of every man's deepest life, and the awe which any visible assertion of that isolation in- spires, even when made by the mildest of our guilty race, is translated into an eerie picture in *The Minister's Black Veil.*" — R. H. Hutton, *Literary Essays.*

52 **meeting-house:** cf. 486. How does this word give us the time and the place of the story? **Parson Hooper:** Mr. Moody, who served as a study for Mr. Hooper, was ordained in 1700.

53 **being to preach:** idiomatic? **Goodman:** until after the Puritan days the title "Master" (Mister) was restricted to men of position.

55 **thunders of the Word:** cf. "son of thunder," p. 37, l. 33.

56 For some interesting laws regarding the Puritan observ- ance of the Sabbath, see Earle, *The Sabbath in Puritan New England,* chap. xvii.

57 **might have seen,** etc.: is this possibility significant?

58 **I had a fancy — And so had I :** how is this coincidence to be explained ?

59 **that famous one:** cf. *The Wedding Knell.* **His frame shuddered:** can you account for his sudden horror? Examine all the incidents for hints as to why Mr. Hooper put on the veil.

61 **one person:** why was the veil less terrible to Elizabeth than to the others? "**No,**" **said she,** etc.: did Elizabeth at first consider the veil to be emblematic?

63 **place of sorrow:** what thought lay back of her "sorrow" ? — of the "new feeling" ? Do you see any reason for the sudden change in Mr. Hooper's demeanor?

65 **Strangers came,** etc.: compare this with the strange fascination that has always hung about the "Man with the

Iron Mask." **many were made to quake:** cf. "Fools who came to scoff remained to pray." — Goldsmith. **Governor Belcher:** see note on p. 285. How do the dates of Mr. Hooper and Mr. Moody (cf. note, p. 52) agree?

66 **election sermon:** election day was a time of high festival in New England. See Earle, *Customs and Fashions in Old New England*, p. 225. **death chamber:** it is a favorite device of Hawthorne's thus to reveal a man's character by presenting two scenes from his life.

67 For another illustration of "the beauty and strength of woman's devotion," see the incident of Rose's going to the death-bed of Edward Fane, p. 525. **saddest of all prisons:** yet Dyer writes: —

" My mind to me a kingdom is."

69 **symbol:** Hamilton Wright Mabie writes: "Hawthorne was not only the forerunner of the psychologists in fiction, but he was also the prophet of the symbolists. He does not sacrifice the ethical motive, the searching disclosure of character, to the beauty and suggestiveness of the symbol: but the tales and novels present marvellous symbolic effects, and are unfolded with a rich circumstance of symbolism that takes possession of the imagination, and excludes all other objects save those which contribute to the subtle and complete unfolding of the drama." Some idea of the extent to which Hawthorne is a symbolist may be secured from the following index to four words used in this book: — symbol — pp. 40, 62, 69, 74, 80, 181, 251, 282, 290, 314, 317, 321, 322, 334, 341, 384, 396, 431, 459, 461, 467, 493, 499, 503, 526; emblem — pp. 45, 54, 63, 65, 70, 76, 82, 138, 184, 240, 245, 289, 312, 384, 396, 439, 456, 460, 465, 481; type — pp. 31, 62, 69, 247, 279, 322, 496, 497, 506; moral — pp. 46, 164, 169, 210, 332, 363, 484.

THE MAYPOLE OF MERRY MOUNT.

See illustrations in Hawthorne's Works, Little Classics Ed. vol. i; Riverside Ed. vol. i.

Publication. First published in *The Boston Token* of 1836, under the signature, "Author of *The Gentle Boy*" [1832]. Included in *Legends of New England* (1877). In November, 1835, the London *Athenaeum* printed a three-column extract from the story which caused Hawthorne to write home : "My worshipful self is a very famous man in London."

Source. In 1625, Captain Wollaston with a handful of companions settled on what is now Mount Wollaston in Quincy, Massachusetts; but after a year's residence there, he departed for Virginia, leaving his party behind. Morton, a degenerate London lawyer who succeeded him as director of the plantation, sold firearms to the Indians round about, and inaugurated a reign of wantonness and debauchery which caused much apprehension among his neighbors. Late in May, 1628, after two friendly remonstrances had proved of no avail, Standish marched up from Plymouth and arrested Morton, who was, the next month, returned to England. There he remained for a year and a half. During his absence, in September, 1628, John Endicott arrived with a band of colonists at Salem; and immediately made known the temper of the new Puritan régime by going against Merry Mount (as Morton had called the settlement), cutting down the "idoll May Pole," renaming the place Mount Dagon, and advising the inhabitants to practise "better walking, else they would find their merry mount but a woful mount."

Criticism. "He is most convincing in those scenes where his own Puritan inheritance gave him an insight into that stern, joyless age from which his reason indeed revolted, but which his sympathy could re-create. . . . He wished to tread upon historic ground even while his imagination brought all manner of mysterious and subtle influences to bear upon his characters. He dwelt in the borderland of history and fancy." — George D. Latimer in *New England Magazine*, August, 1904.

Compare this narrative with the account in John Fiske's *The Beginnings of New England*, or in Charles Francis Adams's *Three Episodes of Massachusetts History* (vol. i), and determine to what extent and to what end Hawthorne has colored the actual occurrences. Look up Motley's historical novel, *Merry Mount.*

73 **what life is made of :** on an old Edinburgh gravestone the Puritan conception of life is expressed thus: —

> " Life is a shade, a smoak, a flower,
> Short to the good — to the bad doth long endure."

74 **look so sad :** cf. with the expression of Elinor, p. 193.

76 **discountenanced:** before the Puritans, says Macaulay, fled "all who lived by amusing the leisure of others, from the painter and comic poet, down to the rope-dancer and the Merry Andrew. For these artists well knew that they might thrive under a superb and luxurious despotism, but must starve under the rigid rule of the precisians." — *History of England*, vol. i, chap. vii. **true history a poet's tale:** as Hawthorne has done in this story.

77 **hear sermons,** etc. : see Earle, *Customs and Fashions*, chap. ix. **woe to the youth,** etc. : a charming bit of dialogue in the introduction to *The Scarlet Letter* gives Hawthorne's conviction that, in the opinion of his "stern black-browed" Puritan ancestors, he, as an "idler and a writer of storybooks," would have been held on much the same level as the merry-makers at Merry Mount were in the judgment of the remorseless Endicott.

78 **the fiend:** Bradford speaks of the revellers as "dancing and frisking together like so many fairies, or furies rather."

80 **Blackstone :** when Winthrop first came to Boston in 1630, he was received and entertained by William Blackstone, a young Episcopal clergyman. This man had dwelt alone on the western slope of Beacon Hill since 1623, and here he continued to reside until 1634. He was never on bad terms with his Puritan neighbors, and after Boston ceased to be his home, he frequently visited it. On one of these trips he was married to a Boston lady by Governor Endicott himself. **the only May-pole :** some half-century after this, the soldiers of Governor Andros provoked great scandal by setting up in Charlestown the second New England Maypole.

81 **Peter Palfrey:** he is mentioned also in *Main Street* in *The Snow Image.* **Great and General Court:** a session meeting four times a year to admit freemen, elect officers, and pass laws. **Must he share,** etc.: sixty-four years after the death of this poor bear, a Salem dog suspected of witchcraft was solemnly hanged by the descendants of these men.

84 **the moral gloom,** etc.: this is the truth underlying *The Lily's Quest.*

THE GENTLE BOY.

Publication. Written about 1828 ; published in *The Boston Token* of 1832, pp. 193–240. So delighted was Hawthorne with a picture of Ilbrahim (see *The Critic,* July, 1904) drawn by Miss Sophia Peabody, that, in 1839, at his own expense he published the story by itself in a little paper-covered quarto with the picture etched by Miss Elizabeth Peabody as a frontispiece.

Source. In his *History of the Quakers,* Lowell records that "Anne Coleman and four of her friends were whipped through Salem, Boston, and Dedham by order of Wm. Hathorne." This incident, mentioned by Hawthorne in the introduction to *The Scarlet Letter,* doubtless turned the young man's attention in the direction of this story; and in his sympathetic treatment of it, we find the same sadness because of the harshness of his great-great-grandfather which in *The House of the Seven Gables* arises from the persecution of the witches by John Hathorne.

Criticism. "It is in the historical tales that his imagination first acts with seeing power; and here, too, the story by which he preferred to be known, *The Gentle Boy,* stands out, though its prominence is rather a matter of priority than of distinction, for it is the fruit of his sympathies more than of his imagination. . . . The pathetic story is a fable of piety, in fact, and is somewhat nervelessly handled for reality; the figures seem to glide in their motions, they are not quite set on the earth, they are impalpable except in their emotions. The facts lack firmness, though the feeling is wrought out with truth and refinement and makes an irresistible appeal to pity." — Woodberry, *Nathaniel Hawthorne*, p. 133. "*The Gentle Boy* probably did more for the author's reputation than any other of the *Twice-Told Tales*." — Lathrop.

85 **Quakers :** see Doyle, iii, pp. 98–115 ; J. S. Barry, 1, pp. 363–372; George E. Ellis, *The Puritan Age and Rule*, chap. xii; Hallowell, *The Quaker Invasion of Massachusetts* (contains transcripts from numerous original documents). **greatest peril :** "from imprisonment, they proceeded to fines and confiscations, from fines and confiscations to whipping with the knout; from whipping to mutilation, and cutting off ears; from mutilation to banishment; from banishment to servitude; and from servitude to death." — Barry.

86 In his *Heart of New England Rent*, John Norton leaves this testimony regarding the Quakers: —

> " Region, Estate, Rule Civil and Divine,
> Religion, All, they seek to undermine."

the person : Endicott.

87 **two men :** Stevenson and Robinson were hanged on Boston Common, October 27, 1659.

88 **uncultivated field :** in 1640 a portion of the land purchased ten years before from Blackstone for the sum of £30, was set aside for public uses.

90 **fantasy :** a favorite word, used thirty times in this volume.

92 **bond-servant :** for interesting material relative to colonial bond-servants, see Hart, *Contemporaries*, vol. ii, nos. 105–107; Earle, *Customs*, chap. iii.

96 **Around the door,** etc. : an interesting description of the New England meeting-house is found in Earle, *The Sabbath in Puritan New England*.

97 **We are holier :** cf. Luke, xviii, 11.

98 **Laud :** see p. 485. So rigid was Laud's suppression of Puritanism that, as Macaulay says, "on the very eve of trouble, fatal to himself and his order, the Bishops of several extensive dioceses were able to report to him that not a single dissenter was to be found within their jurisdiction."

100 **Slay, slay,** etc. : note the effect of the monosyllables.

101 **Having thus given vent :** see Whittier's poem, *In the 'Old South'*; and Earle, *The Sabbath*, chap. xvi, for other exampl s of Quaker deportment in Puritan services. **Sentence of death :** because of her son's pleadings, the sentence of Mary Dyer, who was condemned to die with Stevenson and Robinson, was changed to banishment; but upon her

return the following year, she was apprehended, re-sentenced, and executed.

104 **two females:** the use of this word instead of woman was very common as late as the early nineteenth century. Cf. Shakespeare in *As You Like It*, v, i, 52: "Leave the society of this female, — which in the common is woman."

115 **was not prompt:** "Edward Burroughs, waiting upon his Majesty, Charles the Second, . . . said: 'There is a vein of blood opened in your dominions which, if not stopped, will overcome all.' 'I will stop that vein,' was the prompt reply. 'Then do it speedily,' said the ally of Fox, 'for we know not how soon many may be put to death.' 'As speedily as ye will,' was the answer of his Majesty; 'call the Secretary and I will do it presently.' The Secretary was called; a mandamus was granted; and permission was given the Quakers to forward it by whom they pleased." — Barry, i, 369. **Restoration:** *i.e.*, of the Stuarts to the throne, 1660, after the Protectorate. **voluptuous king:** cf. p. 21.

116 **gray locks:** strangely enough, religious scruples determined both the short hair of the Roundheads, and the long hair of the Quakers. Cf. I *Corinthians*, xi, 14.

125 **gentle boy:** once Hawthorne was called "gentle Nat Hawthorne," much to the disgust of his wife who wrote: "Gentle he is, but such an epithet does not comprehend him, and gives a false idea." Does this epithet "comprehend" Ilbrahim?

MR. HIGGINBOTHAM'S CATASTROPHE.

Publication. First printed anonymously in December, 1834, in *The New England Magazine*, pp. 450–459.

Source. Hawthorne was much pleased by the possibilities he saw in the idea of an itinerant story-teller such as we have pictured at the end of *The Seven Vagabonds;* and at one time he purposed writing a series of tales which were to be connected, after the fashion of *Lalla Rookh*, by their having a single narrator. The outcome of this plan is seen in *Passages from a Relinquished Work*, where a young man, who has just joined a theatrical company as a professional story-teller, recites "with great applause the tale of *Mr. Higginbotham's Catastrophe.*"

Criticism. "No one more delights in the opportunity of noting with gentle mirth the eccentricities and oddities of primitive and unpolished life. The way in which a New Englander does this is a crucial test of the spirit which is in him. Hawthorne bears the test well. He photographs Yankee rustic life — see *Mr. Higginbotham's Catastrophe* — with a quizzical precision which is infinitely amusing, and which shows him to be infinitely amused. But he leaves us with the full conviction that the smart country-peddler, and

all his tribe, from Maine to Connecticut, are born of women." — Charles C. Starbuck, *Andover Review*, January,
1887.

127 **Shaker:** see note on p. 469. **Dominicus Pike:** in Hawthorne's first diary written while he lived at Raymond
Maine, we find this entry: "A peddler, named Dominicus
Jordan, was to-day in Uncle Richard's store, telling a ghost-
story." Perhaps we have in the genial and loquacious hero
of this story a combination of this nomadic Dominicus
and Dominicus Pike, a Salem tobacco-trader, mentioned in
Passages from a Relinquished Work, and in *Fragments from
the Journal of a Solitary Man*.

128 **sun-glass:** friction light was invented in 1830 by Wilson,
an Englishman; the lucifer match dates from 1833.
Matches were first patented in America in 1836. **suddenly:** which is better, this or *sullenly* as in the second
edition?

132 **change his skin:** cf. Jeremiah, xiii, 23. **No! no!** etc.: how
many things identify this man with the negro of the tramp's
story? How can we explain the discrepancies in the stories
of the two travellers? — the negro's foreknowledge of the act?

138 **so like an angel:** what manner of angel would "Old
Stony Phiz" have resembled?

139 **circumstantial evidence:** cf. "corroborative evidence,"
p. 129, l. 33, and "direct testimony," p. 139, l. 13. **a real
shaver:** severe Puritan legislation has led to the presence
in New England of very diluted forms of profanity. See
Earle, *The Sabbath*, pp. 262–263.

140 **turnpike:** see Earle, *Customs*, p. 199 ff.

141 **Old Nick:** cf. "Satan," p. 442; "devil," p. 100; "Evil
One," p. 295; "Power of Evil," p. 228; "Black Man," p.
195; "Old Scratch," p. 443.

142 **"coming event,"** etc.: see *Lochiel's Warning*, by Thomas
Campbell.

LITTLE ANNIE'S RAMBLE.

Publication. First printed in *Youth's Keepsake* of 1835,
under the signature, "Author of *The Gentle Boy*" [1832].
Source. In the *American Note-Books* for 1836, we have
a suggestion for what would have been a companion piece
to this: "To picture a child's (one of four or five years old)
reminiscences at sunset of a long summer's day, his
first awakening, his studies, his sports, his little bits of
passion, perhaps a whipping," etc.

"Wherever he was, he was the good comrade of his
children, but their guide, philosopher, and friend, as well
as playmate." — Howells, *North American Review*, December, 1903.

"A lady of my acquaintance (the identical 'Little

Annie' of the 'Ramble' in *Twice Told Tales*) . . . remembers that when she was a child, and before Hawthorne had printed any of his stories, she used to sit on his knee and lean her head on his shoulder, while by the hour he would fascinate her with delightful legends, much more wonderful and beautiful than any she has ever read since in printed books." — J. T. Fields, *Yesterdays with Authors*.

Criticism. "It is not the least value of his books for children that in them is unconsciously revealed Hawthorne's great love for children. On one occasion some ladies of Concord prepared a picnic in Emerson's grounds for children, the only man admitted being Hawthorne, who so desired to see the little people at play that a hiding-place was found for him near by." — Conway, p. 138. See *American Note-Books*, September 28, 1841.

"How fresh and touching in its extreme simplicity, mixed with one or two touches of quiet humor, and relieved here and there at the close of a paragraph by a sudden turn of pleasantly quaint moralizing, is *Little Annie's Ramble*. What a genuine eye for, and unaffected love of, what is purest, fairest in human nature, it reveals! How charming a half-dozen pages! and all about the trifles of daily life." — *North British Review*, September, 1868.

144 **a smile that children love:** Quoting this in a letter, Mrs. Hawthorne exclaims: "and well they might, indeed!" In *Memories of Hawthorne*, pp. 294–297, look up the author's letters to his little daughter "Rosebud" — letters scarcely equalled for delightful simplicity and playfulness.

145 **fancy revel,** etc.: another enumeration of things good to eat is found in a letter to Julian, quoted in *Hawthorne and his Wife*, ii, 133.

146 **Peter Parley:** the pseudonym of S. G. Goodrich, editor of *The Boston Token*, the man who first appreciated Hawthorne's literary gifts. Under this name "he produced a multitude of popular school-books, story-books, and other attempts to vulgarize human knowledge and adapt it for the infant mind." — James. **Juvenile Miscellany:** "*The Juvenile Miscellany*, formerly published by Mrs. Child, was much and deservedly esteemed by children. It was a healthy, cheerful, natural, and entertaining companion." — Margaret Fuller. **the book which I mean to send:** *The Boston Token* was one of these books designed for Christmas and New Year's presents. See "Annuals" in the *Encyclopaedia Americana*.

147 **Liliput:** cf. p. 379, l. 22. For this and Brobdingnag, p. 392, l. 13, see Swift's *Gulliver's Travels*. **Semiramis — Catharine:** Henry James tells us that "to this day with the names of Sesostris and Semiramis" he associated Peter Parley's *Universal History*, most of which was written by Haw-

thorne; — "a very fat, stumpy-looking book bound in boards covered with green paper."

150 **chimney sweeper:** in Porter's *Rambles in Old Boston*, pp. 301–302, is found an account of these people whom the City Fathers of Boston appointed "to sweepe chimneyes and to cry aboutt streetes that they may bee knowne."

151 **town crier:** the man whom Hawthorne had in mind was doubtless James Wilson, who, for many years previous to his death in 1841, was one of the most popular persons in Boston. Porter says, "His custom was to appear on the street, and ring three times to attract attention. Then, putting his bell under his arm, he would produce a paper, and announce with solemnity that somebody's cow had strayed away, or that certain articles of value were missing. Occasionally his cry would be like this: 'Child lost! There's a child lost! A boy, between the ages of five and six years, left his home on Salem Street about seven o'clock last night, and has not since been heard from. When last seen, he had on a black cloth cap and a short red coat. He had light hair and blue eyes. Whoever can give information of such a boy, either to his anxious parents at No. — Salem Street, or at the crier's office, will be suitably rewarded.' Wilson would then ring his bell again three times, and move on to repeat the process in other parts of the town." — *Rambles in Old Boston*, p. 358.

152 **when our infancy is almost forgotten :** looking back to his own childhood, Wordsworth professes

> " an infirmity of love for days
> Disowned by Memory ; "
>
> *(Prelude,* i, 615.)

and the theme of much of his singing is that when the

> "earthly freight
> And custom lie upon thee with a weight,
> Heavy as frost, and deep almost as life,"

help may still be found in —

> "the simple creed
> Of childhood, whether busy or at rest,
> With new-fledged hopes still fluttering in his breast."
> *Intimations of Immortality.*

WAKEFIELD.

Publication. First printed in May, 1835, in *The New England Magazine*; pp. 341–347, under the signature : "*Author of The Gray Champion*" [January, 1835].

Source. In Stedman and Hutchinson's *Library of American Literature*, vol. iv, pp. 372 ff., also, in *The Outlook*, Jan. 26, 1907, is found William Austin's story of *Peter Rugg, the Missing Man*, which was first published in 1824 in *The New*

England Galaxy. This narrative concerns an unfortunate man who, because of a vain oath, was doomed to spend fifty years in a search for his own home. When finally he reached it, he was told that he could never again be fitted to his times ; that his home was lost to him, and that he must never hope for another in this world. From such a tale as this, it is but an easy step to *Wakefield.*

Criticism. *Peter Rugg — Wakefield:* "a fine illustration of legitimate intellectual lineage." — Conway, chap. v, *q. v.*

"Hawthorne let his mind brood over the possibilities of life, these half-vital acts, thoughts, and beings, like fears in an anxious mind, things that have only partial being, but are real enough at times to trouble the mind's eye. A touch of this atmosphere is found in such a tale as *Wakefield* ; . . . the main theme is rather the man cut off from life, which Hawthorne so often recurred to, but the element of life's contingency, the nearness of an event that might happen but never does, is what makes the strangeness of this curious study." — Woodberry, p. 139.

"Sometimes, as in *Wakefield,* by a reverse process he analyses backward, and from a single act of odd eccentricity he builds up the inner fabric of the man, as Professor Owen reconstructs an extinct animal from a tooth." — *North British Review,* September, 1868.

154 **long and lazy musings:** in Jane Taylor's *A Toad's Journal* see to what this habit carries one.

156 **the great mass of London life:** from this city Hawthorne wrote to James T. Fields: "London is like the grave in one respect, — any man can make himself at home there; and, whenever a man finds himself homeless elsewhere, he had better die or go to London."

158 **his fate was turning:** compare this moment with David Swan's hour under the maple trees. "The world is so sad and solemn, that things meant in jest are liable, by an overpowering influence, to become dreadful earnest." — *American Note-Books,"* September 7, 1835.

160 **an influence beyond our control:** cf. p. 178, l. 14. **an iron tissue of necessity:** was Hawthorne a fatalist? **haunt:** a verb seldom used intransitively. Cf. "I've charged thee not to haunt about my doors." — Shakespeare.

161 **his low and narrow forehead,** etc.: is there anything about *Wakefield* to suggest Stevenson's *Dr. Jekyll and Mr. Hyde ?*

164 **to a system:** "Every individual has a place to fill in the world, and is important in some respects whether he chooses to be or not."—*American Note Books,* Oct. 25, 1836. **losing his place forever:** a theme characteristically treated by Browning in *The Epistle of Karshish* and by Irving in *Rip Van Winkle.*

A RILL FROM THE TOWN PUMP.

For illustration see *Historic Towns in New England,* Lyman P. Powell.

Publication. First printed anonymously in June, 1835, in *The New England Magazine,* pp. 473–478. In 1857 published anonymously in London as a temperance tract.

Criticism. "'The site of my town pump,' writes Hawthorne in 1858, 'so plainly indicated in the sketch itself, has already been mistaken in the City council and in the public prints.' His pride in this old sketch of his is amusing; it is the only one he ever gloried in. He remembers it beside Boccaccio's well in Arezzo. [See *French and Italian Journals,* i, May 30, 1858.]"—Conway, p. 127.

165 **Town Pump:** see the last paragraph in the introduction to *The Scarlet Letter;* also, *Works* (Riverside Edition), vol. xii, p. 554, note. **town officers:** here we have, carried one degree further, an idea presented in the *American Note-Books:* "To represent the different departments of the United States government by village functionaries, the War Department by the watchman, the law by constables, the merchants by a variety store, etc."

166 **muster day:** cf. Earle, *Customs,* pp. 223–225.

168 **Winthrop:** see note on p. 489. **afoot from Boston:** a distance of some seventeen miles. We are told that this famous old pedestrian in his journeyings through this region crossed the streams on the shoulders of his Indian guides.

Higginson [Francis], 1589–1630 : the first Salem minister. **a flitting image:** cf. *The Vision of the Fountain.*

169 **too little valued:** see Earle, *Customs,* chap. vii. In the *American Note-Books,* we read: "In old times it must have been much less customary than now to drink pure water. Walker emphatically mentions, among the sufferings of a clergyman's wife and family in the Great Rebellion, that they were forced to drink water with crab-apples stamped in it to relish it."

171 **temperance lecturers:** on p. 212, Hawthorne indulges in a merry twinkle of fun at the expense of the devoted temperance lecturer.

172 **tipsy with zeal:** Hawthorne was fitted rather to ponder over the stream of life than to attempt actively to change its course; he hated all commotion as much as he loved quiet; he detested propagandists, and living at a time when the country was swept by one great tidal wave of reform and when the approach of another was beginning to be felt, he was never reconciled to the agitation aroused by them, even though he fully sympathized with them in principle. **friends of mine:** the year of the publication of this sketch, George Cheever, a Salem minister and college

friend of Hawthorne's, lost his church and suffered thirty days' imprisonment because of an ill-advised temperance article entitled "Deacon Giles's Distillery." Lathrop says that while he was in jail Hawthorne "emerged from his strict privacy, and daily visited the imprisoned clergyman." **as Rachel did:** cf. *Genesis*, xxix, 10.

THE GREAT CARBUNCLE.

Publication. First printed in 1837 in *The Boston Token*, pp. 156–175, under the pseudonym "Author of *The Wedding Knell*" [1835]. For it and seven other tales which were published in the same volume, Hawthorne was paid at the rate of one dollar a page. (See Woodberry, p. 62.) Published in 1877, together with *The Great Stone Face* and *The Ambitious Guest*, in *Tales of the White Hills*.

Source. In connection with this story it is interesting to note certain facts recorded in the *American Note-Books*, under the date August 31, 1838: "The students, from year to year, have been in search of a particular rock, somewhere on the mountains in the vicinity of Shelburne Falls [Mass.], which is supposed to contain some valuable ore; but they cannot find it. One man in the bar-room observed that it must be enchanted." The more immediate source is found in the opening passage of *Sketches from Memory*, an essay in *Mosses from an Old Manse*, vol. ii. In *The Pirate*, chapter xix, Scott speaks of "that wonderful carbuncle which gleams ruddy as a furnace to them who view it from beneath, but has ever become invisible to him whose daring foot has scaled the precipices from which it darts its splendor."

Criticism. "The Great Carbuncle of the White Mountains shines with no less splendor than that which illuminated the subterranean palace in Rome, as related by William of Malmesbury" [see Fiske, *Myths*, p. 59]. — Henry W. Longfellow, *North American Review*, July, 1837.

"The search for the 'Great Carbuncle' has much amusement, notwithstanding that it is open to the charge of wild extravagance. This mystery of the White Mountains is an excellent illustration of the way in which Hawthorne delighted to mingle facts and impossible incidents together. In the search for that which will never be discovered he starts persons whom he has himself met, and all the differing specimens of humanity which are found in the tale were seen in actual life by the writer. His allegorical genius is well displayed, for the reader is irresistibly forced to arrive at the conclusion that he is endeavoring to depict as a second and hidden purpose the search of mankind after the perfect good — which is still in existence somewhere, but whose secret has not yet been attained by man." — G. Barnett Smith, *Poets and Novelists*.

173 **Crystal hills :** the White Mountains.
174 **too awful :** yet Emerson affirms : —

> "The gods talk in the breath of the woods,
>   They talk in the shaken pine,
>   And fill the long reach of the old sea shore
>   With dialogue divine.
>   And the poet who overhears
>   Some random word they say,
>   Is the fated man of men
>   Whom the ages must obey."

175 **condemned to wander:** cf. notes on the Wandering Jew introducing *Dr. Heidegger's Experiment.* **Mr. Norton:** see note on p. 86. **wallowing:** cf. "The fearful miser on a heap of rust." — Vaughan.
177 **Captain Smith visited these coasts:** in 1614.
178 **the pursuit alone is my strength:** could Wakefield have said the same of his concealment? **Notch:** a name frequently applied in New England to precipitous defiles, *e. g.,* Crawford Notch. See *Sketches from Memory;* also, p. 370, l. 18.
180 **Grub Street:** see *Cent. Dict.* In the *English Note-Books,* March 25, 1856, we read: "for this is the veritable Grub Street where my literary kindred of former times used to congregate. It is still a shabby-looking street, with old-fashioned houses, and inhabited chiefly by people of the poorer classes, though not by authors."
182 **rerum natura:** while in college, Hawthorne gained his chief distinction from his fine Latin composition. Does his ordinary vocabulary suggest a Latinist? **vain and foolish were the motives,** etc.: why was the Cynic's motive the most unworthy? **yearnings are downward:** cf. John, iii, 19.
183 **dial points of heaven:** What are some of the figurative expressions for the stars? Wherein is this one appropriate?
187 This idea of poison within a gem is a favorite one with Hawthorne.
190 **pine-tree shillings:** an early New England coin bearing a pictured pine-tree on its obverse side.
191 **great fire of London:** in 1666, a conflagration well-nigh destroyed the city, which the year before had been ravaged by the plague. **as to reject a jewel :** cf. Dr. Heidegger's turning away from the elixir of youth.

"The carbuncle is the ideal which mocks our pursuit, and may be our curse or our blessing." — Leslie Stephen.

THE PROPHETIC PICTURES.

Publication. First printed anonymously in *The Boston Token* for 1837, pp. 289–307.
Source. "Lord Mulgrave," says Dunlap, "employed

Stuart to paint the portrait of his brother, General Phipps, previous to his going abroad. On seeing the picture, which he did not until it was finished, Mulgrave exclaimed, 'What is this? — this is very strange!' and stood gazing at the portrait. 'I see insanity in that face,' was the brother's remark. The General went to India, and the first account his brother had of him was that of suicide from insanity. He had gone mad and cut his throat. It is thus that the real portrait-painter dives into the recesses of his sitter's mind, and displays strength or weakness upon the surface of his canvas." — *History of the Arts of Design in the United States* (1834), vol. i, p. 187.

Criticism. " Primarily a study in the idea of fate, a subject seldom touched by Hawthorne, the notion of an inevitable destiny foreseen by the painter's intuition and forecast on the canvas, but implicit from the beginning in character." An estimate of Hawthorne's ability as an art critic will be found in *Hawthorne and his Wife*, vol. ii, pp. 220–221.

192 **this painter:** although the suggestion for this story came from an anecdote of Stuart, Hawthorne seems, in sketching the artist, to have had in mind a certain John Smybert, who lived some half a century before his time. This man, the pioneer American portrait-painter, was born in Edinburgh, in 1684; from 1717 to 1720 he studied in Florence, Rome, and Naples; then returned to London, where, during the next eight years, he did some notable work; in 1728 he came to America and soon after settled permanently in Boston. In 1742 he designed Faneuil Hall; and before his death in 1751 he had painted portraits of "Peter Faneuil, the Chief Justices Lynde (father and son), Sewall and Oliver, Judge Edmund Quincy, and many other leading men of the day, their wives and daughters." See Justin Winsor, *Memorial History of Boston.* In this volume are reproductions of Smybert's portraits of the Lyndes (ii, 558); Peter Faneuil (ii, 260); Sewall (ii, 148); and the Rev. Benjamin Colman (ii, 210). **talks Hebrew:** Dr. Mather (see note on p. 25) was able to preach in Latin, in Greek, and in Hebrew. **Dr. [Zebdiel] Boylston:** a Boston physician, and the first American to inoculate for small-pox (1720) **a perilous abode:** why?

193 **dark-souled men:** cf. *Edward Randolph's Portrait*, pp. 295, 303.

194 **those native artists:** Jonathan Blackburn, who came to Boston the year before Smybert's death, was the first of an interesting group connected with that city. He was closely followed by Copley (born 1737), Stuart (born 1755), and Allston (born 1779). **borrowed their colors,** etc.: see sketch of Benjamin West (1738–1820) in *Biographical Stories.* **a beggar:** "Smybert's and Blackburn's people," says Justin Winsor, "often look like bourgeois; Copley's are all gentle-folk."

195 **Black Man:** "Some of them affirmed, they saw the Black-
man sit on the Gallows, and that he whispered in the ears
of some of the Condemned Persons when they were just
ready to be turned off; even while they were making their
last speech." — Hart, *Contemporaries*, vol. ii, no. 16.

196 **several portraits:** further mention of old portraits may
be found in *American Note-Books*, 1850. **Mr. [Elisha]
Cooke:** a leader in the resistance to Andros, and one of the
colonial agents in England who secured the new charter
from William III. **In most of the pictures,** etc.: "Charmed
by his powers of conversation, yielding to his wonderful
faculty of entering into the train of others' thoughts, each
sitter wore his own characteristic expression while in
Stuart's chair; and the finished portrait often revealed
habits of thought and feeling known only to intimate
friends. 'He seemed,' in the words of Allston, 'to dive into
the thoughts of men.'" — Winsor.

197 **If earth were heaven,** etc.: see p 270, l. 30 ff., for a similar
thought, one to which Hawthorne is continually recurring.
St. Peter: cf. p. 36. **Rev. Dr. Colman:** cf. note on p. 192.
In *Old News* we see this man "endeavoring to raise a fund
for the support of missionaries among the Indians of Massachusetts Bay."

201 **grief and terror:** how is it that Walter Ludlow sees "grief
and terror" where their friends see but "gloom" (p. 204,
l. 11)? **fascinated, as it were:** on p. 193 we saw Elinor
fighting down her intuitive premonitions. What bearing
have the revelations of this moment upon the earlier sus-
picions?

202 **let me see:** did Walter catch any glimpse of the prophecy
in his picture?

203 **the sketch:** have you any idea as to what was pictured
in this sketch? **pictures altered:** how was it in Elinor's
power to have the pictures "altered"?

204 **no two explained it,** etc.: why was Walter's portrait the
harder of the two to judge satisfactorily?

205 **New England's loftiest mountain:** Mount Washington.
Vatican: see *French and Italian Note-Books*, February 19,
1858; April 12, 1858. **Niagara:** see *My Visit to Niagara*
included with *The Dolliver Romance*.

206 **two phantoms:** who were they? **that standard:** in *The
Marble Faun*, vol. ii, ch. xvi, Hawthorne says: "Final
despair, and sense of shortcoming, must always be the reward and punishment of those who try to grapple with
a great and beautiful idea. It only proves that you have
been able to imagine things too high for mortal faculties
to execute. The idea leaves you an imperfect image of itself,
which you at first mistake for the ethereal reality, but soon
find that the latter has escaped out of your closest embrace."
This is the theme of *The Great Carbuncle*.

209 **I loved him:** cf. Elizabeth's love in *The Minister's Black Veil.* Cf. p. 203.
210 **Is there not,** etc. : cf. p. 160, l. 22.

DAVID SWAN.

Publication. First printed anonymously in *The Boston Token* of 1837, pp. 147–155.

Criticism. "What strange shadows tread at our heels. — shadows of evil and shadows of good; on how slight a pivot turn our fortunes! In that exquisite fantasy, *David Swan*, the muffled march of events that never materialize, that cross and recross our paths, unseen, unapprehended, like the ghost of Hamlet's father when he parades before the eyes of the spirit-blind Queen Gertrude, is the theme of Hawthorne. In this little allegory we read the chances of life." — Benjamin de Casseres, in *The Critic*, July, 1904.

"Our author's peculiar talent seems to be that disclosed in the Tale just quoted [*David Swan*], — that, not of weaving a material plot, but of gathering a group of spirit phantoms around some scene or moment in itself utterly uneventful." — *Christian Examiner*, November, 1838.

211 **secret history :** it is said that a certain professor required a knowledge, not only of actual occurrences, but of what would have happened if these had not! Such matter is "secret history."

214 Charles Robert Gaston calls attention to an amusing parallelism between the conditions here and those in Sir Walter Scott's *The Monastery*, chap. xxxv. "The old woman to whom Halbert made this request granted it the more readily that she thought she saw some resemblance between Halbert and her son Saunders, who had been killed in one of the frays so common in the time. It is true, Saunders was a short, square-made fellow, with red hair and freckled face, and somewhat bandy-legged, whereas the stranger was of a brown complexion, tall, and remarkably well made. Nevertheless, the widow was clear that there existed a general resemblance betwixt her guest and Saunders, and kindly pressed him to share of her evening cheer."

215 **buzz, buzz :** cf. Emerson's poem, *The Humble-Bee.*
image was faintly blushing : cf. *The Vision of the Fountain.*
216 **the best of fortune :** cf.

> " Who envies none that chance doth raise "
> > *Henry Wotton*

217 **In a few hours :** etc.: cf. *American Note-Books*, Oct. 25, 1836: " Trifles to one are matters of life and death to another."
the recording angel : cf. *Fancy's Show Box.*
218 **rattling louder and louder :** what inference can we draw re-

garding Hawthorne's life from his familiarity with the ways
of the road? Note the following ways of describing the
noise of wheels: "roar of a coach," p. 35; "rattling thunder of wheels," p. 235; "the distant roll of ponderous
wheels," p. 235; "the timbers groan beneath the slow-
revolving wheels," p. 235; "the war of passing wheels,"
p. 144, etc.; **airy**: a favorite word of Hawthorne's. Cf.
"airy phantoms," p. 36; "airy voice," p. 111; "airy pictures," p. 206; "airy archipelago," p. 219, etc.

SIGHTS FROM A STEEPLE.

Publication. First printed anonymously in *The Boston
Token* of 1831, pp. 41–51.
Scene. "Looking down from here [Witch Hill, Salem],
you behold the ancient city spread before you, rich in
chimneys and overshadowed by soft elms. At one point
a dark, strong steeple lifts itself like a huge gravestone
above the surrounding houses, terminating in a square
top or a blunt dome; and yonder is another, more ideal
in its look, rising slight and fine, and with many ascents
and alternating pauses, to reach a delicate pinnacle at
great height in the air. It is lighted at intervals with many
paned and glittering windows, and wears a probable aspect
of being the one which the young dreamer would have
chosen for the standpoint of his *Sights from a Steeple;*
and the two kinds of spire seem to typify well the Puritan
gloom and the Puritan aspiration that alike found expression in this soil." — G. P. Lathrop, *A Study of Hawthorne,*
p. 21.
Criticism. "Everything that you have ever written, I believe, I have read many times, and I am particularly vain
of having admired *Sights from a Steeple,* which I first read
in *The Boston Token,* several hundred years ago." From a
letter written in 1860 .by John Lothrop Motley. "This
little essay is very carefully written, and displays in
remarkable perfection one quality that became so characteristic of his work that he has no rival in it except Poe;
it has that harmony of tone which is known as keeping,
a unity of design and development so pervasive that the
heavens above and the earth below are seen from the little
steeple as from a centre, and nature and life seem to revolve
around the eye at that altitude with complete breadth as
well as smallness of proportion. . . . The type once struck
out in this clear way, Hawthorne returned to it again and
again, and always with the same happiness in execution
and the same delight in the thing itself." — Woodberry,
pp. 126–127.
219 **I have climbed high:** cf. p. 185. **What clouds,** etc.: this fine
description of clouds calls to mind a fanciful passage in a

letter dated Aug. 27, 1839. [*American Note-Books*, vol. i]:
"And there were clouds floating all about, — great clouds
and small, of all-glorious and lovely hues (save that im-
perial crimson which was revealed to our united gaze), —
so glorious, indeed, and so lovely, that I had a fantasy of
heaven's being broken into fleecy fragments and dispersed
through space with its blest inhabitants dwelling blissfully
upon the scattered islands." Cf. Irving's description of
cloud scenery in *The Voyage*: "to gaze upon the piles of
golden clouds just peering above the horizon, fancy them
some fairy realms, and people them with a creation of my
own."

220 **unheeded**: "The ideas of people in general are not raised
higher than the roofs of the houses. All their interests
extend over the earth's surface in a layer of that thickness.
The meeting-house steeple reaches out of their sphere."
— *American Note-Books*, 1836. **chimneys of Madrid —
Limping Devil of Le Sage**: in 1707, Alaine René Le Sage,
a French novelist and dramatist (1668–1747), wrote a
story called *Le Diable Boiteux*, translated *The Devil on
Two Sticks*, or *The Limping Devil*. In the translation by
Strange (London, 1840) will be found three racy dialogues
between six "Chimneys of Madrid."

221 **green citizens**: cf. 506, 15. In *As You Like It*, the deer
are alluded to as "being native burghers of this desert
city."

222 **Vincentio**: see *The Taming of the Shrew*. **Pisa**: an Italian
city famous during the Middle Ages as the seat of a thriving maritime republic. **a familiar sound**: true in the case
of Hawthorne's seafaring ancestors.

223 **painted veterans**: cf. p. 147. **may excite**, etc.: why should
the military parade and the funeral "excite identical reflections"?

224 **King of Terrors**: cf. "King Death," p. 311. **how various
are the situations**: see the famous passage in chapter iii of
Carlyle's *Sartor Resartus*, a book published in the same
year as *Sights from a Steeple*, in which are given the reflections of Teufelsdröckh as he looks down from "the pinnacle
of Weissnichtwo"; see also the prelude to canto vi, Scott's
Lady of the Lake.

225 **Podagra**: see note on **gout**, p. 167. **Atalanta**: William
Morris has a poem on Atalanta's race in *The Earthly
Paradise*; read also Edwin Arnold's *Atalanta*.

226 **Arethusa**: see Shelley's poem, *Arethusa*.

227 **gloomy as an author's prospects**: cf. p. 220. The quotation
introducing the notes on *The Haunted Mind* shows how
much this simile meant to the young and ambitious Hawthorne. At about this time, he burned a collection of
stories, containing some of his "most powerful work," after
having offered it in vain to seventeen publishers; and it

was at about this time that he claimed the doubtful distinction of being "the obscurest man of letters in America." In this connection read *The Devil in Manuscript*, in *The Snow Image*. **Rainbow:** cf. p. 245. Look through the endings of Hawthorne's stories, to see in how many of them, even the gloomiest ones, the rainbow of hope "brightens forth." **an author's prospects:** when sixteen years old our author wrote in his manuscript magazine, *The Spectator:* "Nathaniel Hawthorne proposes to publish by subscription a New Edition of the Miseries of Authors, to which will be added a Sequel, containing Facts and Remarks drawn from his own experience."

THE HOLLOW OF THE THREE HILLS.

Publication. First printed in 1837, in the first edition of *Twice-Told Tales*.
Source. For evidence that this descendant of the old witch judge was interested in personal investigation of the black art, see Horatio Bridge's *Personal Recollections of Nathaniel Hawthorne*, p. 14.

A possible hint for this story is found in the *American Note-Books*, under the date September 7, 1835: "Two lovers, or other persons on the most private business, to appoint a meeting in what they supposed to be a place of the utmost solitude, and to find it thronged with people."
Criticism. "Mr. Hawthorne has wonderfully heightened his effect by making the ear, in place of the eye, the medium by which the fantasy is conveyed. The head of the mourner is enveloped in the cloak of the witch, and within its magic folds there arise sounds which have an all-sufficient intelligence. Throughout this article also, the artist is conspicuous, — not more in positive than in negative merits. Not only is all done that should be done, but (what perhaps is an end with more difficulty attained) there is nothing done which should not be. Every word *tells* and there is not ρ word which does *not* tell." — Edgar Allan Poe.

"Every allusion to witches that survives in his published work is effective and characteristic; and the point of view from which he regards those picturesque beings is entirely peculiar to himself. . . . For the human nature in Hawthorne's witches — those that have been preserved to us — is at least as prominent as their supernatural attributes, and, indeed, is what gives these attributes their best effect." — Julian Hawthorne, *Century Magazine*, May, 1886.
228 **strange old times:** cf. p. 173, l. 1. With what episode of New England history may this story be connected?
229 **mantling:** Cf. *The Merchant of Venice*, I, i, 88, 89: —

> "There are a sort of men, whose visages
> Do cream and mantle, like a standing pond;"

and the *Deserted Village:* —

> "To strip the brook with mantling cresses spread."

For a witch-meeting, see *Young Goodman Brown*, in *Mosses from an Old Manse.*

231 **Again the withered hag,** etc. : what is the difference between this woman's magic and that of the artist in *The Prophetic Pictures ?*

233 **Then came a measured tread,** etc. : point out the excellencies of this artistic passage. What is suggested by the change from the sights at the beginning of the tale to the sounds at the close?

THE TOLL-GATHERER'S DAY.

Publication. First printed in the *Democratic Review* for October, 1837. The only article included in vol. i, of the second edition of *Twice-Told Tales* (1842) that had not appeared in the first edition (1837).

Scene. "'The small square edifice which stands between shore and shore in the midst of a long bridge,' spanning an arm of the sea, refers undoubtedly to the bridge from Salem to Beverly." — G. P. Lathrop, *A Study of Hawthorne*, p. 145.

Criticism. "He delights to let the current of action flow around him and beside him; he warms his heart in it; but when he again withdraws by himself, it is with him as with the old toll-gatherer at close of day, 'mingling reveries of Heaven with remembrances of earth.'" — *Ibid.* p. 146.

234 **methinks,** etc.: cf. p. 220. Hawthorne gives us here the keynote of his intellectual self. Note the several points of view in this story, in *Sights from a Steeple, A Sunday at Home*, and *A Rill from the Town Pump.*

235 **I amuse myself,** etc.: cf. Wordsworth's lines: —

> "Oft on a grassy bank at ease,
> I sit and play with similes."

fervid day : look up the myth of Helios and Aurora.

236 **frames a simile :** we may infer that the frequent use of figures of speech in Hawthorne's writings of the early period was not altogether unconscious from the fact that he mentions most of the prominent figures by name; *e. g.*, simile, as here; — metaphor, p. 343, l. 7 ; p. 400, l. 13; — personification, p. 82, l. 20; p. 252, l. 22; — allegory. p. 104, l. 26; p. 279, l. 15; — hyperbole, p. 274, l. 21.

240 **aristocrats :** cf. *American Note-Books*, June 22, 1835 : ' **at**

the Maverick House, though well dressed, they seemed to be merely Sunday gentlemen, — clerks in dry-goods stores being the aristocracy of them."

THE VISION OF THE FOUNTAIN.

Publication. First printed in August, 1835, in *The New England Magazine*, pp. 99–104, under the signature: "Author of *The Gray Champion*" [January, 1835].

Source. This little sketch is doubtless based on youthful reminiscences of a school term spent in the family of the Reverend Caleb Bradley, at Stroudwater, Maine.

Criticism. Thomas Bradfield, in *The Westminster Review* for August, 1894, characterizes *Sights from a Steeple*, *The Maypole of Merry Mount*, and *The Vision of the Fountain* as "studies full of delicate insight and a vein of original thought, pursued with graceful exuberance through a succession of delightful pictures."

242 **at fifteen:** in what year did the occurrences mentioned in this story take place? How many years later was the story published? Have you noticed how many colors, intermediate shades, and degrees of sunshine and gloom were caught by Hawthorne's eye?

244 **sweet readers:** cf. "gentle reader," p. 39, l. 26. "The antique fashion of Prefaces recognized . . . the 'Kind Reader,' the 'Gentle Reader,' the 'Beloved,' the 'Indulgent,' or at coldest, the 'Honored Reader.'" — Preface to *The Marble Faun*.

245 **the Vision:** cf. Wordsworth's lines: —

> "She was a Phantom of delight
> When first she gleamed upon my sight;
> A lovely apparition, sent
> To be a moment's ornament;
>
> . . . .
>
> A dancing Shape, an Image gay,
> To haunt, to startle, and waylay."

Niagara: the record of Hawthorne's trip to Niagara is to be found in *My Visit to Niagara*, included with *The Dolliver Romance*.

246 **one that had caught a glimpse of Heaven:** Browning has studied such a case in his *Epistle of Karshish*. **had I the burning fancy**, etc.: with the passing of his youth, the seething fantasies of Hawthorne's earlier works gave place to the cooler play of intellect, giving us in the four great novels something more substantial.

249 **the simple mystery:** is it possible for the reader to reach a solution of this mystery unaided? Compare in this respect with *Mr. Higginbotham's Catastrophe*.

FANCY'S SHOW BOX.

Publication. First printed anonymously in 1837 in *The Boston Token*, pp. 177–184.

Source. "A man to flatter himself with the idea that he would not be guilty of some certain wickedness, — as, for instance, to yield to the personal temptations of the Devil, — yet to find, ultimately, that he was at that very time committing that same wickedness." — *American Note-Books*, 1836.

Criticism. "Those who wish to obtain more than a superficial glimpse into Hawthorne's heart cannot do better than to ponder every part of this little story, which is comprised within scarcely more than a half-dozen pages. It was written about the time of Cilley's unhappy death [February 24, 1838], and contains more than its due proportion of 'sad and awful truths.'" — Julian Hawthorne, *Hawthorne and His Wife*, vol. i, p. 175.

250 **Guilt:** "his [Hawthorne's] forefathers had crossed the Atlantic for conscience' sake, and it was the idea of the urgent conscience that haunted the imagination of their so-called degenerate successor. . . . To him as to them, the consciousness of *sin* was the most important fact of life, and if they had undertaken to write little tales, this baleful substantive, with its attendant adjective, could hardly have been more frequent in their writings than in those of their fanciful descendant." — James, *Hawthorne*, p. 10.

251 **a box of pictures:** for a further idea of a diorama, see *Main Street, The Snow Image,* and *American Note-Books,* Aug. 31, 1835. **crimson curtains:** note the "rich obscurity" suggested by *purple* curtains in Poe's *The Raven.* Cf. these works as regards scene, moral, and art.

253 **leaves of her volume:** what relation has this volume to that mentioned on p. 377 ? **lay stone dead:** owing to a lady's misrepresentations, Hawthorne was led to journey to Washington there to challenge a gentleman, against whom she plotted, to a duel. Fortunately, the charges were soon proved groundless, and the affair was dropped, yet the thought of what might have been the consequence of his rash action caused Hawthorne much remorse and self-incrimination.

255 **washed:** cf. Isaiah i, 18. **bellowed:** some conception of the range of Hawthorne's vocabulary may be obtained by noting certain specific words used in *Twice-Told Tales* for manners of vocal expression: laugh, titter, giggle, weep, sob, sigh, groan, wail, cry, shout, exclaim, announce, roar, scream, howl, babble, mutter, murmur, whisper, sing, peal of voices, buzz of voices, warbling of voices, etc.

257 **powerless with compunction:** read Kipling's *Tomlinson,* a satire on a soul unrighteous yet unable to "rise to worthy

sin." Yet with the slight fancy work. etc. : consider this paragraph in connection with *The Minister's Black Veil.*

DR. HEIDEGGER'S EXPERIMENT.

Publication. First printed (under the title *The Fountain of Youth*) in January, 1837, in the *Knickerbocker Magazine*, pp. 27–33. Reprinted in March, 1837, in *The Salem Gazette*.
Inspiration. In 1830 a report that the "Wandering Jew" had again been seen in London stimulated the curiously insistent interest in the subject of "the deathless one" which, a generation before, had been aroused by William Godwin's novel, *St. Leon* — a tale of the prolonged misery which befell an alchemist from the possession of the elixir of life. To none did this theme appear more fascinating than to Hawthorne, and we find him recurring to it again and again.

In various forms we find the theme in *A Virtuoso's Collection, Septimius Felton, The Dolliver Romance, A Select Party, The Birthmark;* and in those writings which were intended solely for his own eyes are allusions pointing to the fact that the fascination of this idea of immortality was ever present with him. As examples, the following may be taken: Dr. Cacaphodel in *The Great Carbuncle,* and the tradition regarding "the Seeker" in the same story; "The true Fountain of Youth in a case-bottle," p. 518, l. 24; Roger Chillingworth in *The Scarlet Letter.* "There have been other alchemists of old in this town [Salem] — one who kept his fire burning seven weeks, and then lost the elixir by letting it go out." — *Ibid.,* Oct. 24, 1838. "The love of posterity is a consequence of the necessity of death. If a man were sure of living forever here, he would not care about his offspring." — *American Note-Books* (1840). "The advantages of a longer life than is allotted to mortals." — "Notes for Stories," *Hawthorne and His Wife,* i, 489. Cf. also i, 495–496. "A man arriving at the extreme point of old age grows young again at the same pace at which he had grown old." — *Ibid.,* i, 492. "I know nothing of the history of the house ["The Wayside"] except Thoreau's telling me that it was inhabited a generation or two ago by a man who believed he should never die. I believe, however, he is dead." — From a letter to Mr. Curtis (1852).
Criticism. "The ghastliness of the reversal of the course of life backward, as the guests drink the elixir of youth, while it suggests the paltriness of our pleasures, is a powerful lesson in the beneficence of that daily death whereby we resign the past; this rejuvenation violates nature, and so shocks us, and by the very shock we are reconciled with nature, from which we had parted in thought." — Woodberry, *Nathaniel Hawthorne,* p. 142.

"Hawthorne sometimes winks with the eye that is fixed on the follies and delusions of the individual ; he never winks with the eye that is directed to the spiritual world. This completely saves him from cynicism." --— *London Quarterly Review*, October, 1871.

258 **frantic speculation :** cf. "frenzied finance."

259 **cutting each other's throats :** cf. note on p. 253. **black letter :** this is printed in black letter. **Hippocrates :** the Father of Medicine. Cf. p. 170. **dwelt within its verge :** cf. p. 334, l. 7.

268 **the tall mirror,** etc.: could their rejuvenation have been only an illusion produced by hypnotism?

270 **A strange chilliness,** etc.: suggestive of the strange aging of the immortal queen in Haggard's *She*.

HOWE'S MASQUERADE.

Publication. First appeared in May, 1838, in the *United States Magazine and Democratic Review*, under the signature "Author of *Twice-Told Tales*." Reprinted in the second volume of the 1842 edition of *Twice-Told Tales*, and also in *Legends of the Province House* (1877).

Source. A belated entry in the *American Note-Books* (1840) gives us the theme of this story : "A phantom of the old royal governors, or some such shadowy pageant, on the night of the evacuation of Boston by the British."

Criticism. "Sometimes they [Hawthorne's sketches] are purely descriptive bits of Flemish painting, so exact and arrayed in such mellow colors that we unconsciously take them in as objects of sensitive rather than imaginative observation. . . . The early history of New England has found no such genial and vivid illustrations as his pages afford." — Tuckerman.

"Among his imaginative pieces, about the only one that can be called a futility is *Howe's Masquerade*. The scale of this Banquo's procession reversed is far too confined to lend any force to the shadows of the petty viceroys of so recent a past." — Charles C. Starbuck, *Andover Review*, vii, 44.

"It is certain that neither Lamb, nor any other modern prose-writer has ever walked more critically that difficult and narrow line between the natural and supernatural. . . . Take the first story in *The Legends of the Province House*, for example. We defy anybody, after reading *Howe's Masquerade*, to decide at once whether the "mysterious pageant" with which the entertainment of the last Royal Governor of Massachusetts is interrupted, comes really from the shadowland, or is merely a skilfully devised masque of the rebellious citizens." — C. W. Weber, *American Whig Review*, September, 1846.

N. B. The student of Hawthorne's historical stories will find very helpful the index in the last volume of the Wayside Edition of his works.

272 **Washington Street:** this comprised the principal north and south thoroughfares of Old Boston. **the Old South Church:** —

> " A temple shadowy with remembrances
> Of the majestic past ! — the very light
> Streams with the coloring of heroic days."

"A building with a grander history than any other on the American continent, unless it be that other plain brick building in Philadelphia where the Declaration of Independence was adopted and the Federal Constitution framed." — John Fiske, *Beginnings of New England*, pp. 250–252. See also Porter, *Rambles in Old Boston*, pp. 391–394. **Old Province House:** this old building, of which scarcely more than the rear wall remains, has had a long and varied history. Built by Peter Sergeant in 1679 as a private residence, and occupied in 1699 by the Earl of Bellamont, it became in 1716, at a cost of £2300, the property of the Crown, and the seat of the royal government of the colony. Thenceforth until the time of the Revolution, it was the bright social and official centre of New England. After the Revolution it was known as the "Government House," and for seventeen years (1779–1796) was used by officers of the Commonwealth. Then for three years (1796–1799) the old building was under the control of one John Peck; then, relapsing to the State, it was occupied in 1800 by Governor Strong, and in 1811 was given by the State to endow the Massachusetts General Hospital. For the sum of $33,000 this institution leased it in 1817 to David Greenough for a period of ninety-nine years. Greenough erected stores along the front side and proceeded to use the building first as a tavern, and afterwards, as a negro minstrel hall. In 1851 it was reconstructed, and thirteen years later, in 1864, it was nearly destroyed by fire. **a gilded Indian:** this vane was made out of two sheets of hammered copper, weighed forty-eight pounds, and measured four feet, two inches from the elbow of the Indian to the tip of the arrow which he held in place upon the bow. The Indian is now, together with the Royal Arms which once decorated the Province House, in the possession of the Massachusetts Historical Society. **good Deacon Drowne:** Shem Drowne (1684–1774) was a well-known coppersmith of Boston. He made not only the famous Indian on the Province House, but also the cockerel vane for the Second Church and the grasshopper vane for Faneuil Hall. Cf. *Drowne's Wooden Image*, in *Mosses from an Old Manse*. **red freestone steps:** "The front doorway was reached by an easy flight of broad stone steps; and over the porch was an iron balustrade, in which were wrought the date and the owner's initials, — ' 16 P. S. 79.' "— Porter, *Rambles*, p. 376.

273 **levees, with vice-regal pomp :** cf. "The old-time scenes of stately ceremonial, official pomp, or social gayety, many a dinner, rout, or ball where dames magnificent in damask and brocade, towering head-dress and hoop petticoat, — where cavaliers in rival finery of velvet or satin, with gorgeous waistcoats of solid gold brocade, with wigs of every shape, the tie, the full-bottomed, the ramillies, the albemarle, with glittering swords dangling about their silken hose . . . trooped in full tide through the wainscoted and tapestried rooms and up the grand old winding staircase with its balustrades and its square landing-places to do honor to the hospitality of the martial Shute, the courtly Burnet, the gallant Pownall, or the haughty Bernard."— Winsor, *Memorial History of Boston*, ii, 512. **Pownall :** Governor (1757–60); member of Parliament (1763–81). See Hart, *Contemporaries*, iii, no. 26, for Pownall's speech on "The United States as a World-Power" (1780). **Bernard, Sir Francis :** Governor (1760). "If Bernard had been chosen with a view to his peculiar unsuitableness for the years which were to follow, no better choice could have been made."— Lodge, *Historic Towns, Boston*, p. 120.

275 **Gage, Thomas :** Governor and Captain-General of Massachusetts (1774); Commander-in-Chief in North America (1775). **Bunker Hill :** for a good account of the Battle of Bunker Hill, see Lodge, *Boston*, pp. 154–157, and Winsor, *Memorial History of Boston.* **the trimountains :** the spot upon which Boston stands took the name "Trimountain" from the three heads of Beacon Hill. On the seventeenth of September, 1630, an order was passed to the effect "that Trimontaine shall be called Boston." See Winsor, *Memorial History of Boston*, i, 525. **Howe, Sir William :** Commander-in-Chief in America (1775); British commander at the Battle of Bunker Hill. **to gut the whole :** this was done in 1851.

276 **one of the entertainments :** "For the more definite entertainment of the officers, the Tory ladies in Boston did what they could. Dances and assemblies were held in the Concert Hall ; and the very cradle of liberty — Faneuil Hall itself — was devoted to amateur theatricals acted by officers and the less prudish of the ladies. . . . On a January evening of 1776, when Gage had been recalled and Howe had held the command for three months, a farce, *The Blockade of Boston*, was presented at Faneuil Hall. Howe was one of the audience amused by the appearance on the stage of a caricatured Washington bearing a rusty

sword and attended by a grotesque squire. While these two figures held the boards, a sergeant burst into the hall shouting, 'The Yankees are attacking our works on Bunker's Hill.'" **the siege of Boston:** April 19, 1775–March 17, 1776; read Lodge, *Boston*, pp. 153–160.

277 **the Conquest:** *i.e.* of England by William the Norman in 1066. **Merry Andrew:** cf. p. 393, l. 29. **Falstaff:** a jovial character in Shakespeare's *The Merry Wives of Windsor*, and *King Henry IV*, parts i and ii. **Don Quixote:** the delightfully eccentric hero of Cervantes' story, *Don Quixote*. **siege of Louisburg:** May–June, 1745. **Wolfe's victory:** at the Heights of Abraham, Quebec, September, 1759.

278 **Rev. Mather Byles:** the pastor of the Hollis Street Church, a man famous for his loyalty to the Crown and for his wit. In 1776 he was forced to resign his pulpit; and in the following year he was denounced in town meeting and tried by a special court for praying for the king.

279 **the present abundance:** see Lodge, *Historic Towns*, p. 160, "the flourishing colonial town, with more than twenty-five thousand inhabitants, was a dismal-looking place when Washington came in at the head of his victorious army. Houses had been burned and torn down in every direction. Pestilence and privation had done their work, and trade, industry, and commerce had been destroyed. The population was reduced to less than ten thousand people." **George the Second:** died in 1760.

281 **King Charles the martyr:** Charles I. See note on p. 30.

282 **democracy of Massachusetts:** before the time of Andros the colony had enjoyed half a century of almost absolute independence. **Endicott:** see note on p. 485, l. 5. **the banner:** cf. *Endicott and the Red Cross*. **Winthrop:** see note on p. 489. **Sir Henry Vane:** Governor (1636–1637) when but twenty-four years of age; beheaded in 1662. "It is pleasant to remember that the man who did so much to overthrow the tyranny of Strafford, who brought the military strength of Scotland to the aid of the hard-pressed Parliament, who administered the navy with which Blake won his astonishing victories, who dared even withstand Cromwell at the height of his power . . . was once the chief magistrate of an American commonwealth." — Fiske, *The Beginnings of New England*, p. 116. **Dudley, Thomas:** Governor (1634–35; 1640–41; 1645–46; 1650–51). "His Puritanism was bleak and stern, and for Christian charity he was not eminent. . . . the typical narrow-minded, strait-laced Calvinist for whom it is so much easier to entertain respect than affection." — *Ibid.*, p. 103. **Haynes, John:** Governor (1635–1639). **Bellingham, Richard:** Governor (1641, 1654, 1665–72). **Leverett, John:** Governor (1673–79). Throughout the Civil War in England a captain in Cromwell's dragoons. Cf. p. 94, l. 7. **Lord Percy:** the com-

mander of the rescuing party which met the British fugitives from the Concord fight, April 19, 1775; a man, as the ballad has it,

> "Who, when a younger son,
> Fought for King George at Lexington,
> A major of dragoons."

283 **Queen Anne:** reigned 1702–1714. **the part of chorus: as** in the Greek drama. **Bradstreet:** see note on p. 24. **Sir Edmund Andros:** see note on p. 21. **therefore the people cast him down:** April 19, 1689. **Sir William Phipps:** Governor (1692–94). For the story of this picturesque character, "born in the woods of Maine, one of a family of twenty-six children, and left to pick up his living as best he might," who raised £300,000 from a sunken galleon, was knighted, made Governor of Massachusetts, and who built his wife a "faire brick house" in Boston, read Lodge, *Boston,* p. 83; also Sparks's *American Biography,* vol. viii. **Earl of Bellamont:** an earl of the Irish peerage; governor at times of New York, New Hampshire, New Jersey, and Massachusetts (1699); "a courtier, a man of attractive manners, who made himself very popular among the hardheaded Puritans of the Bay Colony"; the first governor to occupy the Province House. **King William:** see note on p. 30.

284 **Duke of Marlborough:** see "John Churchill" in some biographical dictionary.

285 **Governor [Jonathan] Belcher:** Governor (1730–41). A Massachusetts man of an old Puritan family. "He was a polished, well-bred, and well-educated man, and although devoid of Dudley's treacherous disposition, was capable of intrigue and much subtlety in political management." — Lodge, *Boston,* pp. 98–99. **Governor [Joseph] Dudley:** son of Thomas Dudley. See notes on pp. 25 and 282. **Governor [Samuel] Shute:** Governor (1716–1728). "Although a more honest man than Dudley, he was quite as rigid in his defence of what he considered the royal prerogative. His whole administration was from beginning to end one long quarrel with the Assembly."— Lodge, *Boston,* p. 94. **Burnet, William:** Governor (1728–29); died in the Province House. Cf. p. 196.

286 **Shirley, William:** Governor (1741–1756). During his administration took place the expulsion of the Acadians (1755). **Hutchinson, Thomas:** Governor (1769–1774). See note on p. 293.

288 **a nearer height:** *i. e.* Dorchester Heights. Cf. note on p. 276.

289 **that wild Indian band:** the Boston Tea Party, December 16, 1773. See Fiske, *Essays Historical and Literary,* vol. iii, chap. v; Lodge, *Boston,* pp. 141–145 ; Hart, *Contemporaries,* no. 152.

EDWARD RANDOLPH'S PORTRAIT.

Publication. First published in the *Democratic Review* of July, 1838, under the signature, "Author of *Twice-Told Tales*." Included in the second volume of the 1842 edition of *Twice-Told Tales*, and in *Legends of the Province House* (1877).

"The day before, Mr. Hawthorne had called at noon to see our ladyships, and I never saw him look so brilliantly *rayonnant*. He said to me, 'Your story [*Edward Randolph's Portrait*] will be finished, Sophia — to-morrow or next day.' I was surprised to have the story so appropriated, and I do long to see it." — Letter of Sophia Peabody [Hawthorne], June 1, 1838.

Source. Possibly Hawthorne got a suggestion for this story from Sir Walter Scott's novel, *The Bride of Lammermoor* (1829), where, at a marriage ball, the frowning likeness of old Sir Malise Ravenswood mysteriously and unexpectedly appears upon the wall to the confusion and consternation of the assembled guests.

291 **destructive fires :** Hawthorne probably had in mind those of 1711, 1760, and 1794.

293 **Lieutenant-Governor Hutchinson :** Governor (1771–74). "A Massachusetts lawyer and historian of some ability, yet vacillating and self-seeking at a period when these qualities were fatal to success; in a weak and compromising way he sacrificed his country's interests to what he conceived to be his own, pleased no one, and attempted to steer a fearful and impossible course between the enmity of Old and of New England." **Sir Francis Bernard :** cf. note on p. 273.

294 **Castle William :** a fort in Boston Harbor. **she had dwelt in sunny Italy :** cf. Hilda in *The Marble Faun*.

295 **General Abercrombie's defeat :** " In July, 1758, General James Abercrombie led an army of fifteen thousand men, six thousand of them regulars, against Ticonderoga, where Montcalm had less than four thousand; blundered at every critical point of the attack; lost two thousand men; and retired almost as if in flight." — Woodrow Wilson, *A History of the American People*, ii, 91. Cf. A. T. Quiller-Couch, *Fort Amity*.

296 **a veil had formerly hung before the picture :** cf. p. 204, l. 29.

297 **my antiquarian researches :** John Fiske says that Hutchinson, the historian, had sound judgment, and critical acumen deserving of the highest praise. His *History of Massachusetts Bay*, in three volumes, is the best authority for the period between 1630 and 1774. **Edward Randolph :** appointed in 1678 Surveyor of Customs at the port of Boston, an office which Hawthorne subsequently held. " He held no

post higher than that of a revenue collector, yet his figure comes down to us elevated into something like grandeur by the lurid shades which hatred has thrown over it." — Doyle, *English Colonies in America*, vol. iii, p. 196.

In pursuance of a scheme for avenging himself upon his many enemies in Massachusetts, Randolph secured from Charles II, in June, 1684, a writ similar to the one under which charters were being confiscated throughout England at the time, annulling the charter of that province which had been granted by Charles I in June, 1628.

In his *Beginnings of New England*, p. 266, John Fiske says: "By the abrogation of the charter, all rights and immunities that had been based upon it were at once swept away, and every rood of the soil of Massachusetts became the personal property of the Stuart king, who might, if he should possess the will and the power, turn out all the present occupants or otherwise deal with them as trespassers." **almost democratic privileges:** cf. p. 282. By the terms of the charter given by Charles I, the people were given full and absolute power "to correct, punish, pardon, govern, and rule" within the bounds of the Colony.

298 **the French War:** 1753–1763.

299 **the Selectmen of Boston:** on the afternoon of March 6, 1770 (the day following the Boston Massacre), a committee headed by Samuel Adams was appointed to demand of the Governor the removal of the two regiments quartered in the town. At first, Hutchinson compromised to send *one* regiment to Castle William; thereupon the people cried, "Both regiments or none! " and sent back the committee to insist upon a reconsideration. After vacillating for some time, the Governor was convinced by Adams of the folly of resistance, and, yielding completely to the commands, ordered both "Sam Adams's regiments," as they were called thereafter, out of the town. Is it either of these visits which is pictured here? See p. 300.

301 **as they did my private mansion:** on the evening of August 26, 1765, a mob, enraged by news of the passing of the Stamp Act, attacked and looted the residence of Hutchinson, Comptroller of Customs, and destroyed one of the finest libraries in America and many priceless documents — among the latter, the diary of Goff, the regicide. Fiske says of the affair: "Pictures were cut to pieces, mirrors smashed, wearing apparel and silver stolen, and priceless books and manuscripts flung into the street . . . for a sight of which to-day the historical student would deem their weight in diamonds a cheap price." — *Essays, Historical and Literary*, vol. i, pp. 29–30; vol. ii, p. 173. See also Hart, *Contemporaries*, vol. ii, no. 139.

305 **the Boston Massacre:** cf. p. 22 ; good accounts will be found in Lodge, *Boston*, pp. 132–135; and in John Stetson Barry, *The History of Massachusetts*, vol. ii, ch. xii.

From this story and *The Prophetic Pictures* determine Hawthorne's conception of art.

LADY ELEANORE'S MANTLE.

Publication. First published in December, 1838, in the *Democratic Review*, under the signature, " Nathaniel Hawthorne." Included in the second volume of the 1842 edition of *Twice-Told Tales*, and in *Legends of the Province House* (1877).

Source. "To poison a person or a party of persons with the sacramental wine." — *American Note-Books* (1837).

"An ornament to be worn about the person of a lady, — as a jewelled heart. After many years, it happens to be broken or unscrewed and a poisonous odor comes out." — *American Note-Books* (December 6, 1837).

Criticism. "The best of these four tales is *Lady Eleanore's Mantle*, and it is because in it Hawthorne's genius passed out of the sphere of history and touched on that universal moral world where his most original creation was to lie." — G. E. Woodberry, *Nathaniel Hawthorne.*

For an excellent comparison of this story of Hawthorne's with Poe's *The Masque of the Red Death*, a tale founded on a similar incident, see George D. Latimer's article, " The Tales of Poe and Hawthorne," in *The New England Magazine*, August, 1904.

C. F. Richardson says that in *Lady Eleanore's Mantle* "the reader finds a plan essentially similar, in broad conception, to those of the other allegories, but expressed in an art so admirable as almost to tempt one to use the adjective perfect. In such a story as this Hawthorne appears at his best. The sombre background of early Puritan Massachusetts; the Boston of the days when grim democratic Calvinism struggled with the considerable grandeur of wealth and a provincial court; a few strangely-romantic characters standing plainly against the horizon of the familiar sky, yet seen through the dimmed light of the intervening years that so completely separate the old from the new — all these things Hawthorne could use far more powerfully than any other American; . . . the story is vivid in its historic pictures, romantic in its plot, and adequate in its perception and portrayal of the emotions which are the real theme of the highest fiction written during the present century."

307 **mine excellent friend:** cf. pp. 274, 292, 328.

308 **Copp's Hill :** overlooking the Charles River at a point opposite Charlestown; noted for its ancient burial-ground where lie Increase, Samuel, and Cotton Mather, and John Eliot. See Drake, *Old Landmarks and Historic Personages of Boston*, pp. 204–209. **King's Chapel : see** note on p. 25;

American Note-Books (September 7, 1835); *Scarlet Letter*, chaps. i and ix ; *Grandfather's Chair*, part i, chap. ii. **a venerable personage:** cf. in *The Snow Image*, under " Old News," part iii, " The Old Tory." See O. W. Holmes's poem, *The Last Leaf*.

309 **John Hancock:** see note on p. 331. **Colonel Shute:** see notes on pp. 285 and 319. **Newport:** capital city of Rhode Island. **Cornhill:** see note on p. 25. **Oliver Cromwell:** see *True Stories from History and Biography*, " Oliver Cromwell."

312 **Bedlamite:** see derivation in the dictionary.

313 **Jervase Helwyse:** G. P. Lathrop in his *Study of Hawthorne* notes that William Hathorne, making his will in 1679, gives his farm at Groton to "Gervice Holwyse my gr. ch. [grand-child] if he can come over and enjoy it." See also *English Note-Books* (July 30, 1857); and Lathrop's introduction to *The Snow Image*.

316 **this holy wine:** cf. note on the source of this story.

319 **a dreadful epidemic:** to an uncle of Hawthorne's belongs the dubious distinction of having once brought the small-pox to Massachusetts, — a fact which might have awakened in the novelist an interest in the theme. An account of the ravages of the smallpox in Boston is given in *Grandfather's Chair*, part ii, ch. v. See also Earle, *Customs and Fashions in Old New England*, pp. 351–355. One of the chief events of Governor Shute's administration was Dr. Zabdiel Boylston's successful introduction, on June 26, 1721, of inoculation for smallpox.

320 **the Three Hills:** cf. note on 275. **Asiatic cholera:** two outbreaks in 1823 and 1826 swept from Central Asia throughout Europe and America.

326 **Mine host,** etc.: compare this passage with one of the interludes in *Tales of a Wayside Inn.*

OLD ESTHER DUDLEY.

Publication. First published in the *Democratic Review* of January, 1839 , under the signature, Nathaniel Hawthorne. Included in the second volume of the 1842 edition of *Twice-Told Tales*, and in *Legends of the Province House* (1877).

Source. It may be that this story developed from the following hint found in the *American Note-Books* for December 6, 1837. "A partially insane man to believe himself the Provincial Governor or some other great official of Massachusetts. The scene might be the Province House."

328 **our host having resumed the chair:** cf. p. 327.

329 **cackle forth a feeble laugh:** cf. Holmes, *The Last Leaf:* —

"And a melancholy crack
In his laugh."

329 **the old loyalist:** for interesting material on the relations
of the old loyalists and their surroundings, see Hart, *Contemporaries,* vol. ii, nos. 166–169. **thorough-going democrat:** see Hart, *Contemporaries,* iii, 25. **the hour of defeat and humiliation:** see note on p. 276. **Sir William
Howe:** see note on p. 275. **the King:** George III (reigned
1760–1820).

331 **Mistress Dudley:** "The ordinary designation of man and
woman was 'goodman' and 'goodwife,' 'Mr.' and 'Mrs.'
(Mistress) being titles confined to the men and dames and
daughters of the superior class." — Fisher, *The Colonial
Era.* **John Hancock:** Governor of Massachusetts (1780–
85; 1787–93). "The Alcibiades, in a certain way, of the
rebellious little Puritan town; and his display and gorgeousness no doubt gratified the sober, hard-headed community which put him at its head and kept him there.
He stands out with a fine show of lace and velvet and
dramatic gout, — a real aristocrat, shining and resplendent
against the cold gray background of every-day life in the
Boston of the days after the Revolution, when the gay
official society of the Province had been swept away." —
Lodge, *Boston,* pp. 176–177; see also p. 161.

332 **in stately pageantry:** cf. note on p. 273.

335 **stole timorously homeward:** "The loyalists who remained
in Boston were few in number, and kept themselves very
quiet." — Lodge. **and answered not again:** cf. *Titus,* ii, 9.

337 **the ivory gate of dreams:** cf. Virgil, *Aeneid,* vi, 893–895.

341 **a new race:** did Hancock indeed belong to this new race?

THE HAUNTED MIND.

Publication. First printed anonymously in 1835 in *The
Boston Token,* pp. 76–82. Included in the 1842 edition
of *Twice-Told Tales.*

Source: "In this dismal chamber Fame was won." — *American Note-Books* (1836).

"Here I sit in my old accustomed chamber, where I
used to sit ir days gone by. . . . Here I have written
many tales — many that have been burned to ashes, many
that have doubtless deserved the same fate. This claims
to be called a haunted chamber, for thousands upon thousands of visions have appeared to me in it; and some few
of them have become visible to the world, . . . And here
I sat a long, long time, waiting patiently for the world to
know me, and sometimes wondering why it did not know
me sooner, or whether it would ever know me at all —
at least till I were in my grave. And sometimes it seems
to me as if I were already in the grave, with only life enough
to be chilled and benumbed. — *American Note-Books* (1840).

Criticism. "Hawthorne's peculiar genius lies in the power he possesses to be haunted and, in his turn, to haunt the reader with his conceptions far more than in their intrinsic force." — R. H. Hutton.

"This air, on the author's part, of being a confirmed *habitué* of a region of mysteries and subtleties constitutes the originality of his tales." — Henry James.

343 **awake in that realm of illusions:** cf. Byron, *The Dream:* —

> "Our life is twofold : Sleep hath its own world,
> A boundary between the things misnamed
> Death and existence : Sleep hath its own world,
> And a wide realm of wild reality."

distant sound of a church clock: the sound of bells is mentioned more than sixty times in this book.

344 **far Cathay:** the ancient name for China and Japan; now, the far East in general. **Father Time:** cf. pp. 375 and 376.

345 **cast the shadow:** possible? **You sink down,** etc.: this paragraph illustrates E. P. Whipple's remark that Hawthorne "had humor, and sometimes humor of a delicious kind; but this sunshine of the soul was but sunshine breaking through, or lighting up, a sombre and ominous cloud." **In the depths of every heart,** etc.: cf. *The Hollow of the Three Hills.* **the imagination is a mirror:** Henry James speaks of Hawthorne's "delicate and penetrating imagination which was always at play, always entertaining itself, always engaged in a game of hide-and-seek in the region in which it seemed to him the game could best be played — among the shadows and substructions, the dark-based pillars and supports of our moral nature."

346 **A sterner form succeeds,** etc.: "His relentless fancy seemed to seek a sin that was hopeless, a cruel despair that no faith could throw off." — George William Curtis. **bed's foot:** "In the older language, the possessive (or genitive) case was sometimes used when it would not be proper now. . . . In Thackeray's *Henry Esmond* (which imitates the style of the period of Queen Anne), bed's foot; but we do not find such expressions in good authors to-day." — A. S. Hill, *Beginnings of Rhetoric,* p. 50.

348 **the wheeling of gorgeous squadrons,** etc.: a curious similarity exists in the sequence of ideas here and in the following lines from Wordsworth's sonnet, *To Sleep:* —

> "A flock of sheep that leisurely pass by,
> One after one : the sound of rain, and bees
> Murmuring : the fall of rivers, winds and seas,
> Smooth fields, white sheets of water, and pure sky.
> I have thought of all by turns, and yet do lie
> Sleepless ! and soon the small birds' melodies
> Must hear, first uttered from my orchard trees ;
> And the first cuckoo's melancholy cry."

Niagara: cf. note on p. 245. **so calm, perhaps, will be the final change:** "We sometimes congratulate ourselves

at the moment of waking from a troubled dream: it may
be so the moment after death." — *American Note-Books*
(1836). Compare Hawthorne as he appears in this sketch
with Wordsworth as he is seen in his lines: —

> "The harvest of a quiet eye
> That broods and sleeps on his own heart."
>
> *A Poet's Epitaph.*
>
> "Nor less I deem that there are Powers
> Which of themselves our minds impress;
> That we can feed this mind of ours
> In a wise passiveness."
>
> *Expostulation and Reply.*
>
> "For oft, when on my couch I lie
> In vacant or in pensive mood,
> They flash upon that inward eye
> Which is the bliss of solitude."
>
> *The Daffodils.*

Read Hawthorne's criticism of himself in the preface, p. 16.

THE VILLAGE UNCLE.

Publication. First published anonymously in *The Boston
Token* of 1835 under the title, *The Mermaid, A Revery.*
Source. This sketch, together with *Night Sketches*, *Footprints on the Sea-Shore*, and *The Toll-Gatherer's Day*, had
its origin in lonely walks about Salem and its vicinity.

Hawthorne's sister Elizabeth, writing to his daughter
Una, says: "About the year 1833, your father, after a
sojourn of two or three weeks at Swampscott, came home
captivated, in his fanciful way, with a 'mermaid' as he
called her. He would not tell us her name, but said she
was of the aristocracy of the village, the keeper of a little
shop. She gave him a sugar heart, a pink one, which he
kept a great while, and then (how boyish, but how like
him!) he ate it. You will find her, I suspect, in *The Village
Uncle*. She is Susan. He said she had a great deal of what
the French call *espièglerie*. At that time he had fancies
like this whenever he went from home."

The Village Uncle might well be a study of one of Hawthorne's own ancestors, of whom he writes: "From father
to son, for above a hundred years, they followed the sea;
a greyheaded shipmaster, in each generation, retiring from
the quarter-deck to the homestead, while a boy of fourteen
took the hereditary place before the mast, confronting the
salt spray and the gale which had blustered against his
sire and grandsire. The boy also, in due time, passed from
the forecastle to the cabin, spent a tempestuous manhood,
and returned from his world-wanderings to grow old and
die, and mingle his dust with the natural earth."
Criticism. "To clothe a familiar scene with ideal interest —
and to exalt things to which our senses are daily accus-

tomed into the region of imaginative beauty and genuine sentiment, requires an extraordinary power of abstraction and concentrative thought. . . . In our view the most remarkable trait in his writings is this harmonious blending of the common and familiar in the outward world with the mellow and vivid tints of his own imagination." — H. T. Tuckerman, *Mental Portraits.*

349 **Susan:** Hawthorne writes in the *Scrap Book* (1839): "Schooners more than any other vessels seem to have such names as Betsy, Emma-Jane, Sarah, Alice, — being the namesakes of the owner's wife, daughter, or sweetheart. They are a sort of domestic concern, in which all the family take an interest. Not a cold, stately, unpersonified thing, like a merchant's tall ship, perhaps one of half-a-dozen, in which he takes pride, but which he does not love, nor has a family feeling for. Now Betsy or Sarah-Ann, seems like one of the family — something like a cow." **Hark,** etc.: Cf. Matthew Arnold's *Dover Beach :* —

> "Listen! you hear the grating roar
> Of pebbles which the waves draw back, and fling,
> At their return, up the high strand,
> Begin, and cease ; and then again begin,
> With tremulous cadence slow, and bring
> The eternal note of sadness in."

350 **How strangely,** etc.: note the rhythm of this and the following paragraph; also, p. 356, l. 17 ff; p. 362, l. 19 ff.

351 **a daughter of the viewless wind:** cf. p. 244, l. 14; cf. also, Wordsworth's *She was a Phantom of Delight.*

353 **tracked:** or "tacked" ? **tolled:** or "trolled" ? **those lovely fish:** cf. Matthew Arnold, *Sohrab and Rustum :* —

> "And thou must lay me in the lovely earth."

354 **the Flying Dutchman:** a ghostly ship, manned by a crew of shadows, and fated to beat forever against the storms of the southern ocean, because of the captain's rash oath to round the Cape of Good Hope in spite of God or devil. Cf. Captain Marryat's novel, *The Phantom Ship* (1836).

355 **a likely set of men:** cf. Kipling, *Captains Courageous.* **Sinbad the Sailor:** see *The Arabian Nights.* **the mermaid:** the original title of this sketch.

357 **to read aloud:** one of Hawthorne's favorite diversions.

358 **the mighty works,** etc.: cf. Wordsworth's *Prelude,* i, 401 ff.

359 **his drowned body,** etc.: cf. Jean Ingelow's *The High Tide on the Coast of Lincolnshire :* —

> "And didst thou visit him no more ?
> Thou didst, thou didst, my daughter deare.
> The waters laid thee at his doore,
> Ere yet the early dawn was clear."

360 **A playfulness has revisited my mind:** "Those whom the gods love die young."

363 Ah! one feels a chilliness, etc. : "There is, perhaps, no more delicate comment on the exquisite sensibility of Hawthorne than this, that he should be so open to climatic influence in his writing." — G. P. Lathrop. **Oh, the slight tissue of a dream:** "How lightly his spirit hovers over the stream of actual life, scarcely touching it before springing up again, like a seabird on the crest of a wave! Nothing could be more polished than his descriptions and his presentations of the actual facts; but his fancy rises resilient from these to some dreamy, far-seeing perception or gentle moral inference." — G. P. Lathrop.

THE AMBITIOUS GUEST.

Publication. First printed in *The New England Magazine* of June, 1835, under the signature, "Author of *The Gray Champion.*"

Source. This story was founded on the incident of the destruction of the Willey family in 1826 by a land-slide from Mount Willey, one of the White Mountains.

Criticism. "In Poe's hands the story of *The Ambitious Guest* might have thrilled us with a more powerful horror, but it would have lacked the ethical beauty which Hawthorne gave it and which makes it significant beyond a mere feat of verbal legerdemain." — Brander Matthews.

364 "**herb, heart's ease**": *i. e.* pansy. Cf. *Pilgrim's Progress*, ii, 100. "This Boy wears more of that Herb called Heart's-ease in his Bosom." **the Notch of the White Hills:** cf. *American Note-Books* (September 9, 1838): "A walk yesterday forenoon through the Notch, formed between Saddle Mountain and another adjacent one. This Notch is otherwise called the Bellowspipe, being a long and narrow valley, with a steep wall on either side."

367 a proud, yet gentle spirit: Hawthorne never ceases to be autobiographical. **a poetry of native growth,** etc.: cf. p. 358. **a high and abstracted ambition:** cf. p. 528, l. 18 ff.

369 verse of a hymn: cf. pp. 463, l. 12, and 417, l. 24. **it's a sign of something:** Hawthorne shows repeatedly that he believed Campbell's assertion in *Lochiel's Warning:* "coming events cast their shadows before." Cf. note on p. 142.

371 mountain nymph: cf. pp. 244, 355, 482. **it might blossom in Paradise:** cf. p. 503.

373 are to be buried together: M. Browne says of Hawthorne: "There is one other source of the extreme fascination of this man's writings. A plain word for it would be concentration or pertinacity; but in the lurid haze under which his genius so often works, it becomes something for which we really want a name. Perhaps we might call it a fatality of method which carries an almost awful impersonal look with it. When Judge Pyncheon sits dead in his chair in the dark room all night, and the genius of the author, through all that terrible time, walks round and round him in the gloom, gradually closing in on the solemn fact that you well know all the while, you feel with a shudder that this bad man is not only dead, he is dead — dead — fatally dead, so to speak. Now, the movement of Hawthorne as a narrator is always of this kind. He gradually closes in upon his idea; but as you feel his imagination is doing this spontaneously, the effect is like that of some preternatural fatality." — *Eclectic Magazine*, 77: 174. **the last trump:** cf. I *Cor.* xv, 52. **a safer spot:** cf. p. 366.

374 **Woe for the high-souled youth,** etc. : "Oblivion is not to be hired. The greater part must be content to be as though they had not been, to be found in the register of God, not in the register of man." — Sir Thomas Browne, *Hydriotaphia.* **Whose was the agony:** (?)

THE SISTER YEARS.

Publication. First published in *The Salem Gazette*, January 1, 1839.

Source. This may be considered a companion piece to an article contributed the preceding New Year's Day to *The Salem Gazette*, entitled *Time's Portraiture, The Carrier's Address to the Patrons of The Salem Gazette for the 1st of January, 1838.*

Compare an entry in *American Note-Books*, under the date December 19, 1850: "Personify the century, — talk of its present middle age, of its youth, and its adventures and prospects."

Criticism. This happy allegorical sketch will be best appreciated if it is read in connection with Hawthorne's engagement to Miss Sophia Peabody which took place at about the time it was written.

Read Tennyson's *New Year's Eve*, and *The Death of the Old Year.*

378 **Loco Focos:** see note on p. 128 ; also, dictionary. **Banks:** see R. Hildreth, *Banks, Banking, and Paper Currency*, chaps. xxii–xxv ; also, A. B. Hart, *The American Nation*, vol. xvi, chap. xx. **Abolition:** see Hart, *Contemporaries*, vol. iii, no. 177; also, Channing and Hart, *Guide to American History*, §§ 186–188. **Texas:** see Hart, *Contemporaries*, vol. iii, nos. 185–189. **Florida War:** *i. e.* with the Seminole Indians. Allusion is made in *Time's Portraiture* to "the revolutionary movements in Canada" and to "the sluggishness of our commanders in the Florida War." **War on the Canada border:** cf. *Grandfather's Chair*, pt. ii, chap. iv. **Nothing so much depresses me,** etc.: R. H. Hutton speaks of Hawthorne's "deeply rooted conviction that, as far as any real and deep reform is accomplished, it may, in a certain

sense, be said to *accomplish itself."* The firmness of this belief led Hawthorne to deplore the Civil War as a great national disaster, and caused him concern which was in no small degreee responsible for the sudden break-down which resulted in his death. **the Immortal Pilgrim:** cf. p. 457.

379 **Patriotism speaks boldly:** cf. Gray's *Elegy*, ll. 57–60. **Liliputian scope:** what was Swift's object in writing *Gulliver's Travels ?* **opened the Railroad:** in the summer of 1833, the first steam train ran from Boston over the Boston and Worcester Railroad. Cf. Hart, *Contemporaries*, vol. iii, no. 165; also Hawthorne's sketch, *The Celestial Railroad* (1843).

380 **Essex Street:** though his sensitively retiring disposition made Hawthorne shun the street, we see in many of his sketches, especially in *Main Street*, what a fascination he found in its "ever-shifting train." Essex Street is mentioned several times in *Time's Portraiture*. **a few trifles:** cf. *The Virtuoso's Collection*, in *Mosses from an Old Manse*, vol. ii.

383 **must perish:** "For Time is not immortal. Time must die and be buried in the deep grave of Eternity." — *Time's Portraiture*.

384 **and wear in their bosoms:** see note on p. 364.

SNOW FLAKES.

Publication. First printed in the *Democratic Review* of February, 1838, under the signature, "Author of *Twice-Told Tales*."

Source. A suggestion for one of the incidents is found in *American Note-Books* (1836). "To describe a boyish combat with snowballs, and the victorious leader to have a statue of snow erected to him. A satire on ambition and fame to be made out of the idea. It might be a child's story."

387 **Slow and sure:** cf. *Snow-Bound*. **annuals:** cf. p. 381, l. 23.

388 **a few days,** etc.: "But to . . . be but pyramidally extant is a fallacy in duration. Vain ashes which, in the oblivion of names, persons, times, and sexes, have found unto themselves a fruitless continuation, and only arise unto late posterity, as emblems of mortal vanities, antidotes against pride, vain glory, and madding vices." — Sir Thomas Browne. See also Shelley's *Ozymandias:* —

> "I met a traveller from an antique land
> Who said: Two vast and trunkless legs of stone
> Stand in the desert.
>
> . . . .
>
> And on the pedestal these words appear:
> 'My name is Ozymandias, king of kings:
> Look on my works, ye Mighty, and despair !'
> Nothing besides remains. Round the decay
> Of that colossal wreck, boundless and bare
> The lone and level sands stretch far away."

388 **lending our ears :** cf. *Julius Caesar*, III, ii.
391 **airy :** cf. note on p. 218; also, airy clothing, p. 377; airy copy, p. 401; airy business of poetry, p. 431; airy temple, p. 497; airier things, p. 506.

THE SEVEN VAGABONDS.

Publication. First published in *The Boston Token* of 1833, under the signature, "Author of *The Gentle Boy.*"

Source. The end of *The Seven Vagabonds* suggested the thread of the proposed *Story-Teller*, a work the only traces of which are seen in *Passages from a Relinquished Work.* Hawthorne says: "The idea of becoming a wandering story-teller had been suggested a year or two before by an encounter [while on a trip through the Connecticut Valley with his uncle Samuel Manning] with several merry vagabonds in a showman's wagon, where they and I had sheltered ourselves, during a summer shower."

Criticism. "*The Seven Vagabonds* is a fantastic tale whose allegorical significance is more delicately conveyed than that of perhaps any other of the stories of this character, — by an impression brought away from the reading, rather than by any definite applications one is forced to make of it as metaphor." — Mrs. E. M. J. O'Connor.

392 **Straight before me :** in what part of the Connecticut Valley was Hawthorne? Cf. p. 413. **the Brobdingnags :** cf. p. 379 for another allusion to Swift's *Gulliver's Travels.* In *American Note-Books* (1842), Hawthorne remarks: "Brobdingnag lay on the northwest coast of the American continent."

394 **Prospero, entertaining his guests :** cf. *The Tempest*, III, iii.

396 **Scottish Chiefs** (1810) ; **Thomas Thumb :** the son of a common ploughman, who was knighted by King Arthur and was killed by the poisonous breath of a spider. Cf. *Grimm's Household Stories* (1816); cf. *Mosses from an Old Manse*, vol. ii ; *Earth's Holocaust ;* and letter to Rosebud, given in *Memories of Hawthorne* p. 296. **New England Primer :** an interesting reprint of this book is that edited by Paul Leicester Ford for Dodd, Mead and Company (1897). **I bought the whole :** in his *Literary Friends and Acquaintances*, W. D. Howells says, relative to Hawthorne's library: "After tea, he showed me a book-case, where there were a few books toppling about on the half-filled shelves, and said, coldly, 'This is my library.' I knew that men were his books, and though I myself cared for books so much, I found it fit and fine that he should care so little, or seem to care so little." **neither with sermons ·** cf. p. 37, l. 28. **the court dress which he refused to wear :** cf. *True Stories from History and Biography*, "Benjamin Franklin."

397 **Circulating Library :** this had its rise about the middle of the 18th century and was an attempt to satisfy the

great demand for the new novel ; see Sheridan's *The Rivals*,
II, ii. **blue stockings :** in 18th century England, a term
applied to literary ladies.

400 **musters, ordinations,** etc.: what phases of New England
life are represented in these several assemblies ? Cf. *Customs and Fashions in Old New England*, ch. ix. **the mahogany box :** cf. *Fancy's Show Box; American Note-Books*
(August 31, 1838). **Rialto :** a Venetian bridge built in
1591 across a canal called the *rivo alto*.

402 **Several distinguished gentlemen,** etc.: "He is to a considerable degree ironical — that is a part of his charm — part
even, one may say, of his brightness; but he is neither
bitter nor cynical. . . . On the whole, Hawthorne's observation has a smile in it oftener than may at first appear."
— Henry James. **that abominable spirit :** cf. p. 456. Cf.
Burns, *Address to the Unco Guid :* —

> "The Rigid Righteous is a fule,
>   The Rigid Wise anither."

"Hawthorne, with all his shyness, and tenderness, and
literary reticence, shows very distinct traces also of understanding well the cold, inquisitive, and shrewd spirit which
besets the Yankees even more than other commercial
peoples." — R. H. Hutton, *Literary Essays*.

403 **If the bank is in good standing :** in the *American Note-Books* Hawthorne speaks of the expertness of a travelling
tradesman in passing upon the "goodness" of bills issued
by various banks. **I never refuse,** etc.: Horatio Bridge, in
his *Personal Recollections of Nathaniel Hawthorne*, p. 14, notes
that while at Bowdoin College they together left many a
coin with an old fortune-teller who dwelt near there.

406 **thieves' Latin :** a jargon used among thieves. "**wandering
up and down upon the earth** " : cf. *Job*, i, 7.

409 **the story-tellers :** *e. g.* Moore's *Lalla Rookh*.

410 "**Mirth admit me of thy crew** " : see Milton's *L'Allegro*,
l. 38. **He is never guilty,** etc. : is this true?

411 **Election week :** cf. *Customs and Fashions*, chap. ix.

413 **yet envious,** etc.: does this throw any light upon Hawthorne's character? Compare this sketch with *The Toll-Gatherer's Day.*

THE WHITE OLD MAID.

Publication. First published in the *New England Magazine*
of July, 1835, as *The Old Maid in the Winding Sheet*, by
the "Author of *The Gray Champion*."

Criticism. Woodberry calls attention to the fact that
Hawthorne in several of his simplest tales, as here in *The
White Old Maid*, selects two moments in a person's life,
and, setting the one over against the other, secures a single
distinct effect by the contrast.

"The spell of mysterious horror which kindled Haw-thorne's imagination was a test of the character of his genius. The mind of this child of witch-haunted Salem loved to hover between the natural and the supernatural, and sought to tread the almost imperceptible and doubt-ful line of contact." — George William Curtis.

416 to follow funerals: specific mention of funerals will be found on pp. 47, 57, 69, 78, 223, 233, 279, 311, etc.

417 sad, peaceful, and fantastic life: cf. Mr. Hooper's life in *The Minister's Black Veil.*

418 The scene: "To read his historical sketches is like wander-ing through old portrait galleries or walking streets that have long disappeared, with quaint old houses about us and figures in the antique garb of a past generation." — J. A. Symonds. **merchants, in white wigs:** cf. p. 222. **Spanish creoles:** among Longfellow's early memories of a similar town, were those of

"The Spanish sailors with bearded lips."

422 Azure, a lion's head erased: for another heraldic device, see *Tales of a Wayside Inn*, Prelude to Part First, ll. 105–109. See also "Heraldry" in the *Encyclopaedia Britannica.*

423 the mansion: this old ruin suggests the Province House.

425 the dreamy state of a very old man's mind: cf. p. 360.

427 It glimmers to and fro in my mind: had he forgotten a confession? "A kindred element in his genius is his affin-ity with the weird, the mysterious, the supernatural. His page is dappled with lights and shadows derived from other suns than ours. No foot moved with firmer tread than his over that dim twilight region which lies between the seen and the unseen. The skill with which he weaves his threads of mystery into the web of common life, the firm hand with which he controls the shadowy shapes which he evokes, the art with which he leaves his problems half in doubt as to how much he himself believed of the wonders he suggested or revealed — these are among the most striking characteristics of his peculiar and original genius." — G. S. Hillard.

PETER GOLDTHWAITE'S TREASURE.

Publication. First printed in *The Boston Token* of 1838, under the signature, "Author of *Twice-Told Tales*."

429 Bubble Bank: cf. the "Mississippi Bubble," the "South Sea Bubble." "In the good old days of trade, there were no bubbles, no stock-jobbing." — De Foe. **after innumerable schemes:** cf.: —

"always in the wrong;
Was everything by starts, and nothing long."

430 **many-peaked wooden houses :** like the "House of the Seven Gables." **a November evening :** contrast this with that other November evening pictured in *The Village Uncle.*

432 **an old maid :** it will be found interesting to classify the principal women in *Twice-Told Tales.* **cold, dark, windy, smoky, creaking, groaning, dismal old house :** for a similar use of adjectives, cf. pp. 356, 382, 397.

433 **a wild projector :** like Chaucer's University student : —

> " But al be that he was a philosophre,
> Yet haddë he but litel gold in cofre."
>
> *Prologue,* ll. 297–298.

434 **autumn of his age :** cf. p. 470, " summer of their years."

435 **There were chased goblets,** etc. : note the rapidity of movement in this sentence. Cf. p. 435, l. 29 ; p. 437, l. 32.

437 **he uplifted the axe :** what do his methods of destruction reveal of Peter's character ?

> " Nowher so bisy a man as he ther n'as
> And yet he semëd bisier than he was."
>
> Chaucer, *Prologue,* ll. 321–322.

438 **his nature to be always young :** together with pp. 408, 360, and many other passages, this description of Peter Gold-thwaite shows how the author of *Dr. Heidegger's Experiment* and *Septimius Felton* pondered over the problem of warding off the advance of age. **he resolved :** compare Peter's resolution with Wakefield's.

440 **The old fellow must have resembled me :** Anthony Trollope says of Hawthorne, "He is always laughing at something with his weird mocking spirit."

442 **sympathized with the sorrows of a mouse :** Burns's *To a Mouse* shows a kindred feeling in a greater man. **Governor Dudley :** cf. note on p. 282.

443 **Old Scratch :** the devil ; so called from Scratz, a demon of Scandinavian mythology. **Aladdin's lamp :** see in *Arabian Nights,* "Aladdin and the Wonderful Lamp." —

> " Yes, ready money is Aladdin's Lamp."
>
> Byron, *Don Juan,* xii. 12.

447 **old French War :** cf. note on p. 277.

452 **Then shade your eyes, Mr. Peter :** characterize Tabitha. What is the purpose of her introduction ?

453 **old provincial bills of credit,** etc. : cf. p. 429. Why were the two Peters portrayed so much alike ? What kind of man is satirized here ?

CHIPPINGS WITH A CHISEL.

Publication. First printed in the *Democratic Review* of September, 1838, under the signature, "Author of *Twice-Told Tales.*"

Source. An article of Hawthorne's on the epitaphs at

Martha's Vineyard is quoted by Conway from the *American Magazine of Useful and Entertaining Knowledge* (1836). "Yet one of them was worth reading. It was consecrated to the memory of John and Lydia Claghorn, a young whaler and his wife, the former of whom had perished on the farther side of Cape Horn about the same time that Lydia died in child-bed. The monumental verse ran thus : —

> 'John and Lydia, that lovely pair;
>   A whale killed him, her body lies here;
>   Their souls, we hope, with Christ shall reign —
>   So our great loss is their great gain.'

John Claghorn has now slept beneath the sea, and Lydia here in her lonesome bed, between sixty and seventy years. One of the rarest things in the world is an appropriate and characteristic epitaph, marked with the truth and simplicity which a sorrowing heart would pour into the effusion of an unlettered mind; an expression, in unaffected language, of what would be the natural feelings of friends and relatives were they standing above the grave. It seems to me that this rude and homely verse may be ranked among the masterpieces of monumental literature."
Criticism : Thomas Bradfield notes that this sketch has about it "a flavor of Addison's famous paper on Westminster Abbey." — *Westminster Review*, 142–203.

455 **Chippings with a Chisel** : how many of Hawthorne's titles are alliterative? In a letter dated January 12, 1839, he writes : "They tell me that a considerable portion of my time will be unoccupied [at the Custom House], the which I mean to employ in sketches of my new experience, under some such titles as follows: 'Scenes in Dock,' 'Voyages at Anchor,' 'Nibblings of a Wharf Rat,' 'Trials of a Tide-Waiter,' 'Romance of the Revenue Service.'" Are these titles peculiarly Hawthornesque ? **Martha's Vineyard** : an island off the southern coast of Massachusetts. **to transmute slate and marble** : sometimes Hawthorne looks at the theme of alchemy less whimsically than here. **that ancient burial ground** : for the account of a visit to another old cemetery (at Gosport), see the *American Note-Books* (1852); also, for September 7, 1835.

456 **when affection and sorrow grave the letters** : cf. note on the source of this sketch. **Greenough** : Horatio Greenough (1805–1852), was the first great American sculptor. Among other works, he designed Bunker Hill Monument, and the colossal statue of Washington in the Capitol. **the old Puritan family of Wigglesworth** : in 1631, there arrived in Malden, Massachusetts, Michael Wigglesworth, a Puritan clergyman of the sternest type. He was the author of *The Day of Doom*, a poem for a long time popular in New England. Cf. Tyler, *History of American Literature*, vol. ii, p. 27

457 more rarely found: cf. p. 402. **immortal pilgrims:** cf. p. 378. **was to label the dead:** "Observe, now, the vital office of humor in Hawthorne's thought. It gleams out upon us from behind many of the gravest of his conceptions, like the silver side of a dark leaf turning in the wind " — Lathrop, *Study*, p. 306. **entertaining . . . if not interesting:** just what does Hawthorne mean? **"man that is born of woman":** *Job*, xiv, 1.

458 killed by a whale: cf. note on the source of this sketch. **this lifelong sorrow:** Hawthorne's remarks here, as well as those on p. 461, are based upon observations made in his own home. After her husband's death, his mother remained in strict seclusion for the remaining forty-one years of her life.

463 old scraps of poetry: cf. p. 417. **he laughed heartily:** Browning portrays mirth of a similarly gruesome kind in the epistle of Karshish to a fellow physician: —

> "This Bethany, lies scarce the distance thence
> A man with plague-sores at the third degree
> Runs till he drops down dead. Thou laughest here !
> In sooth it elates me."

464 this phenomenon: Catullus says: —

> "I love thee and hate thee, but if I can tell
> The cause of my love and my hate, may I die."

Governor Mayhew: Thomas Mayhew, born in England in 1592; in 1641 made governor of the colony, and given a grant of Martha's Vineyard. Here he made his home, — founding Edgartown, and laboring as an Indian missionary until his death in 1682.

466 an immense slab of white marble: cf. p. 369. "Had they made as good provision for their names as they have for their relics, they had not so grossly erred in the art of perpetuation. But to subsist in bones, and be but pyramidally extant, is a fallacy in duration." — Sir Thomas Browne. Cf. also : —

> "What needs my Shakespeare for his honoured bones ?
> The labour of an age in piléd stones?
> Or that his hallowed reliques should be hid
> Under a star-ypointing pyramid? "
>
> Milton.

467 Our thoughts should soar upward: cf. p. 503.

468 And yet, etc.: "It is impossible, we should think, to read him without becoming sadder if not wiser — in spite of an assumed air of *gaillardise* and a cheery moral tacked now and then to a sorrowful parable, he is essentially sad-hearted, and confirms any similar tendency in his readers." — H. T. Tuckerman. **a strange doubt:** cf. "An article on cemeteries, with fantastic ideas of monuments; for instance, a sun dial: — a large, wide carved stone chair, with some such motto as 'Rest and Think,' and others, facetious or serious." — *American Note-Books* (1850).

THE SHAKER BRIDAL.

Publication. First printed in *The Boston Token* of 1838, under the signature, "Author of *Twice-Told Tales*."
Source. This story, together with *The Canterbury Pilgrims*, was no doubt suggested by a visit made in 1831 to the Shaker settlement at Canterbury, New Hampshire. Extracts from letters written on this occasion to his sister will show that the future "Brook Farmer" was not untouched by some strange fascination in the life which he found there. He says: "I walked to the Shaker village yesterday, and was shown over the establishment, and dined there with a squire and a doctor, also of the world's people. On my arrival, the first thing I saw was a jolly old Shaker carrying an immense decanter of their superb cider; and as soon as I told him my business he turned out a tumblerful and gave me. It was as much as a common head could clearly carry. Our dining-room was well furnished, the dinner excellent, and the table attended by a middle-aged Shaker lady, good-looking and cheerful. . . . This establishment is immensely rich. Their land extends two or three miles along the road and there are streets of great houses painted yellow and tipt with red. — On the whole, they lead a good and comfortable life, and, if it were not for their ridiculous ceremonies, a man could not do a wiser thing than to join them. Those whom I conversed with were intelligent, and appeared happy. I spoke to them about becoming a member of their society, but have come to no decision on that point." And again: "Mrs. Ede's wedding-cake will be very acceptable. I am afraid there is little prospect of my repaying her in kind; but when I join the Shakers, I will send her a great slice of rye-and-Indian bread."
Criticism. "I left Mr. Thompson before ten, and took my way through the sloppy streets to the Athenaeum, where I looked over the newspapers and periodicals, and found two of my old stories (*Peter Goldthwaite* and *The Shaker Bridal*) published as original in the last *London Metropolitan*. The English are much more unscrupulous and dishonest pirates than ourselves. However, if they are poor enough to pirk themselves in such false feathers as these, Heaven help them ! I glanced over the stories, and they seemed painfully cold and dull." — *American Note-Books* (May 6, 1850).
469 **Shaker** : see H. Dixon, *New America ;* Howells, *The Undiscovered Country*, and *Three Villages ;* also, encyclopaedia.

475 **the vanity of earth :** did Hawthorne, in common with the
Shakers, hold to the teaching of *Ecclesiastes*, i, 2?
476 **the heart could endure no longer :** does *Twice-Told Tales*
contain a deeper tragedy than this ?

NIGHT SKETCHES.

Publication. First published anonymously in *The Boston
Token* of 1837. Its original title was *Night Scenes under an
Umbrella.*
Source. "I had always a natural tendency (it appears to
have been on the paternal side) toward seclusion; and
this I now indulged to the utmost, so that, for months
together, I scarcely held human intercourse outside of my
family; seldom going out except at twilight, or only to
take the nearest way to the most convenient solitude." —
Letter to Stoddard (1853).

"I have been out only once in the daytime since my
arrival. How immediately and irrecoverably (if you did
not keep me out of the abyss) I should relapse into the
way of life in which I spent my youth ! If it were not for
you, this present world would see no more of me forever.
The sunshine would never fall on me no more than on a
ghost. Once in a while people might discern my figure
gliding stealthily through the dim evening, — that would
be all. I should be only a shadow of the night." — Letter
to Miss Peabody (September 3, 1841).
Criticism. "Out of the Salem puddles, nevertheless,
springs flower-like a charming and natural piece of prose."
— Henry James.

477 **Small as my chamber is :** cf. *The Haunted Mind*, p. 348.
479 **Slough of Despond :** see *Pilgrim's Progress.* **a concoction
of mud :** "How much mud and mire, how many pools of
unclean water, how many slippery footsteps, and perchance
heavy tumbles, might be avoided if we could tread but
six inches above the crust of this world. Physically we
cannot do this; our bodies cannot: but it seems to me that
our hearts and minds may keep themselves above moral
mud puddles and other discomforts of the soul's pathway." — Letter from *American Note-Books* (1840). **of
unknown bottom :** cf. "my affection that hath an unknown
bottom, like the bay of Portugal." — *As you Like It*, iv, i.
480 **lonesome and dreary spot :** "In Hawthorne the whole class
of little descriptive effusions directed upon common things
. . . have a greater charm than there is any warrant for
in their substance." — Henry James. **on the battle-field
or at the polls :** "To Hawthorne, however, was given one
resource which was denied to Poe: the resource of humor
His humor was not contagious, like Irving's; it had none
of the racy tang of the soil, like Lowell's; it was not quick-

footed, like Holmes's, in whose work it is continually losing its pervasiveness and gaining the concentration of wit. In Hawthorne, humor takes the form of a gentle brooding over the foibles and weaknesses of men; often sombre, rarely saturnine; gaining a certain effectiveness from its lack of gayety. There is no overflow of buoyant spirits . . . there is, rather, a quiet meditative contrast between the externalities and the realities of man's fortunes in this world; the play of a keenly observant, detached, and reflective mind over the surface of life." — Mabie.

482 **over head and ears in trouble:** "Through it all there is a touch of burlesque — not as to the sufferings of the sufferer, but as to the great question whether it signifies much in what way we suffer, whether by crushing sorrows or little things." — A. Trollope, *North American Review,* 129 : 203.

483 **Bluster, fierce blast:** cf. *As You Like It:* —

"Blow, blow, thou winter wind."

484 **fancying a strangeness,** etc.: the keynote of much of Hawthorne's work.

ENDICOTT AND THE RED CROSS.

Publication. First appeared anonymously in *The Boston Token* of 1838. Included in the second volume of the 1842 edition of *Twice-Told Tales,* and in *Legends of New England* (1877).

Source. This story is founded on an actual occurrence given as follows by Doyle in *English Colonies in America,* vol. ii, p. 122: "The train-band in each town marched under the royal colors, containing that red cross which from the earliest days of Christianity had been recognized as the symbol of St. George. The Puritan regarded the most holy emblem of the Christian faith with horror which would be ludicrous if it were not so painful. That headstrong and narrow-minded man Endicott on his own authority defaced the flag at Salem by cutting out the cross. . . . Unfortunately the strong hatred of the Puritans for the supposed 'relique of Antichrist' made them loth to condemn an act which few of them probably would have perpetrated."

485 **an autumnal day:** in November, 1634. **Salem:** a town some fourteen miles from Boston, settled by John Endicott in 1628. **Endicott:** "For thirteen out of the fifteen years [1649–1665] following Winthrop's death, the governor of Massachusetts, a sturdy pioneer, whose services to the colony had been great. He was honest and conscientious, but passionate, domineering, and very deficient in tact." — Fiske, *The Beginnings of New England,* p. 179. **Charles the First:** see note on p. 281; also, Macaulay's *History of Eng-*

land, vol. i, chap. i. **Archbishop of Canterbury:** the head of the Anglican Church. **Plymouth:** settled in 1620 by the Pilgrims, a poor and lowly band driven into exile by their separation from the Established Church. **Massachusetts:** settled about 1630 by Puritans, many of them men of position and means, enjoying the favor of the Crown and not widely estranged from the Established Church.

486 **head of a wolf:** in Winthrop's diary, September 30, 1630, we read: "The wolves killed six calves at Salem, and they killed one wolf." **that important engine:** public whipping was not abolished in New England until 1803 One colonial justice's charge reads: "Gentlemen of the grand-jury: you are required by your oath to see to it that the several towns in the county be provided according to law with Pounds and Schoolmasters, Whipping-posts and Ministers." **pillory:** see Earle, *Punishments of Bygone Days,* chap. iv. **A Wanton Gospeller:** Alice Morse Earle quotes an old Boston law to the effect that, "If any interrupt or oppose a preacher in season of worship, they shall be reproved by the magistrate, and on a repetition, shall pay £5 or stand two hours on a block four feet high, with this inscription in Capitalls, A WANTON GOSPELLER."

487 **to wear the letter A:** cf. *The Scarlet Letter,* chap. ii. For the wearing of significant letters by law-breakers, see Earle, *Punishments of Bygone Days,* chap. vii.

488 **no badge of infamy,** etc.: cf. *The Minister's Black Veil.*

489 **Roger Williams** (1604–1683): an independent minister who founded Rhode Island after he had been exiled from Massachusetts. **Governor [John] Winthrop:** Governor of Massachusetts most of the time between 1630 and 1649. "Every page in the early history of New England bears witness to the patience, the firmness, the far-seeing wisdom of Winthrop." — Doyle, *English Colonies in America,* vol. ii, p. 123.

"He was a man of remarkable strength and beauty of character, grave and modest, intelligent and scholarlike, intensely religious and endowed with a moral sensitiveness that was almost morbid, yet liberal withal in his opinions and charitable in disposition. When his life shall have been adequately written, as it never has been, he will be recognized as one of the very noblest figures in American history." — Fiske, *The Beginnings of New England,* p. 102.

491 **dig in the sands:** *i. e.* for clams. **lay thee neck and heel:** cf. Samuel Butler: —

> "And prove their doctrine orthodox
> By apostolic blows and knocks."

492 **a Scotch tyrant:** James I of England (1603–25). **Scotch woman:** Mary Queen of Scots (1542–87).

THE LILY'S QUEST.

Publication. First published in *The Southern Rose* (Charleston, S. C.) January 19, 1839.

Source. "Death possesses a good deal of real estate; pleasure grounds, too."— *Notes for Stories and Essays* (Concord).

"Two lovers to plan the building of a pleasure-house on a certain spot of ground, but various seeming accidents prevent it. Once they find a group of miserable children there; once it is the scene where crime is plotted; at last, the dead body of one of the lovers or of a dear friend is found there; and, instead of a pleasure-house, they build a marble tomb. The moral, — that there is no place on earth fit for the site of a pleasure-house, because there is no spot that may not have been saddened by human grief, stained by crime, or hallowed by death. It might be three friends who plan it, instead of two lovers; and the dearest one who dies." — *American Note-Books* (1836).

Criticism. "The element of poetry is air; we know the poet by his atmospheric effects, by the blue of his distance, by the softening of every hard outline he touches, by the silvery mist in which he veils deformity and clothes what is common so that it changes to awe-inspiring mystery, by the clouds of gold and purple which are the drapery of his dreams. And surely we have had but one prose-writer [Irving] who could be compared with him in airy perspective, if we may use the painter's term." — O. W. Holmes, *Atlantic Monthly*, 14: 98.

495 **lightsome:** that Hawthorne is fond of the suffix "some" is seen by his use in *Twice-Told Tales* of darksome, 14 times; lightsome, 11; lonesome, 7; gladsome, 7; handsome, 8; loathsome, 4; also, frolicsome, gleesome, tiresome, toilsome, unwholesome, and wearisome.

496 **sombre:** a favorite word. Gather its exact meaning from its use on pp. 34, 80, 278, 299, 501; **Lily:** Hawthorne calls girls in other stories, "Pansie," "Peony," and "Violet."

497 **airy Temple:** cf. note on p. 391. **which had now relapsed:** cf. *The Deserted Village :* —

> "Near yonder copse, where once the garden smiled,
>   And still where many a garden flower grows wild."

499 **old lunatic :** "Diseases of the mind and soul . . . even more common than bodily diseases." — *American Note-Books* (1836). Note the types of mental disease portrayed on the following pages : 49, 63, 89, 157, 171, 174, 209, 232, 317, etc.

503 **the mystery of Life and Death was opened to him:** cf. the end of *The New Adam and Eve*, in *Mosses from an Old Manse*, vol. ii.

FOOTPRINTS ON THE SEA-SHORE.

Publication. First published in the *Democratic Review* of January, 1838, pp. 190–197, under the signature, "Author of *Twice-Told Tales*."

Source. In the *American Note-Books* (October 16, 1837), Hawthorne writes: "Crossed the fields near Brookhouse's villa, and came upon a long beach, — at least a mile long." Cf. p. 505. Our author also drew material from such walks as are described in the *American Note-Books* for 1835, and for August 22, 1837. Subsequent walks by the ocean are recorded under the dates: July 10, 1838, and September 13 and 16, 1852.

Criticism. "Nothing could be more accurate and sensitive than the brief description of nature in his works. . . . He shadows forth hints, makes signs, whispers, muses aloud, gives the keynote of a melody, puts us on the track; in a word, addresses us as nature does — that is, unostentatiously and with a significance not to be realized without reverent silence and gentle feeling; a sequestration from bustle and material care and somewhat of the meditative insight and latent sensibility in which his themes are conceived and wrought out." — H. T. Tuckerman.

504 **spirit much unlike my own:** "I am sitting to-day opposite the likeness of the rarest genius America has given to literature, — a man who lately sojourned in this busy world of ours,· but during many years of his life

" Wandered lonely as a cloud,"—

a man who had, so to speak, a physical affinity with solitude." — J. T. Fields, *Yesterdays with Authors*.

the forest and the ocean : cf. Wordsworth : —

"᾿Two Voices are there ; one is of the sea,
One of the mountains ; each a mighty Voice."

the yearning for seclusion becomes a necessity : in a letter to Stoddard (1853), Hawthorne speaks of taking "the nearest way to the most convenient solitude, which was oftenest the seashore — the rocks and beaches in that vicinity (Salem) being as fine as any in New England."

508 **Statesmen and warriors :** cf. p. 388.

509 **the sea rake back the pebbles :** cf. note to p. 349.

510 **the identical albatross :** cf. Coleridge, *The Ancient Mariner.*

511 **the mysterious depth of ocean :** a fascinating treatment of this theme will be found in J. C. Van Dyke's *The Opal Sea.* See also *King Richard the Third*, ɪ, iv. **I must shrink :** "There never was a man more shrinkingly retiring, yet surely was an author never more naïvely frank." — George William Curtis. **Writing of a midsummer walk which he once took**

with Hawthorne, James T. Fields says: "He bade me lie
down on the grass and hear the birds sing. . . . While we
lay there, hidden in the grass, we heard approaching footsteps, and Hawthorne hurriedly whispered, 'Duck! or we
shall be interrupted by somebody.'"

513 Here I can frame a story : the note-books show that a great
many of Hawthorne's stories had their rise under conditions such as these. **a melancholy voice :** "When a school-
boy he wrote verses for the newspapers, but he ignored their
existence in after years with a smile of droll disgust. One of
his quatrains lives in the memory of a friend, who repeated
it to me recently : —

> "'The ocean hath its silent caves,
>   Deep, quiet, and alone ;
> Above them there are troubled waves,
>   Beneath them there are none.'

When the Atlantic Cable was first laid, somebody, not
knowing the author of the lines, quoted them to Hawthorne
as applicable to the calmness said to exist in the depths of
the ocean. He listened to the verse, and then laughingly
observed, 'I know something of the deep sea myself.'"—
J. T. Fields, *Yesterdays with Authors.*

514 him of Athens : *i. e.* Demosthenes, who, to accustom himself to speaking in the presence of a noisy multitude, is
said to have practised delivering orations in the roar of
the surf. **My maiden speech :** Hawthorne's first public
speech, mentioned in the *English Note-Books,* was made
during his consulate at Liverpool at a civic banquet.
Over its reception the author took a whimsical and almost
childish delight.

515 finds no resting-place : cf. *Genesis,* viii, 9. **which yet was not
solitude :** cf. *Childe Harold,* iv, 178 ff. : —

> "There is a pleasure in the pathless woods,
>   There is a rapture on the lonely shore,
>   There is society where none intrudes,
> By the deep Sea, and music in its roar :
> I love not Man the less, but Nature more,
> From these our interviews, in which I steal
> From all I may be, or have been before,
> To mingle with the Universe, and feel
> What I can ne'er express, yet cannot all conceal."

516 the "melancholy main": cf. Bryant, *Thanatopsis :* —

> "Old ocean's gray and melancholy waste";

also *Richard the Third,* i, iv, 45 : —

> "I pass'd, methought, the melancholy flood."

EDWARD FANE'S ROSEBUD.

Publication. First printed anonymously in the *Knicker-bocker Magazine* of September, 1837.

Source. "A change from a gay young girl to an old woman; the melancholy events, the effects of which have clustered around her character, and gradually imbued it with their influence till she becomes a lover of sick-chambers, taking pleasure in receiving dying breaths and in laying out the dead; also having her mind full of funeral reminiscences, and possessing more acquaintances beneath the burial turf than above it." — *American Note-Books* (1835).

Criticism. "In the *Prophetic Pictures, Fancy's Show Box. The Great Carbuncle, The Haunted Mind,* and *Edward Fane's Rosebud* there are flashes of moral insight which light up, for a moment, the darkest recesses of the individual mind. . . . In the subtlety and accuracy, the penetration and sureness of his glance into the morbid phenomena of the human soul; . . . in the capacity to terrify his readers with the consciousness of their latent possibilities for evil, so that they shrink from his exposures like guilty things surprised; he makes novelists like Thackeray and Dickens appear relatively superficial."—E. P. Whipple.

517 **to re-create its youth:** Hawthorne has done this in *Dr. Heidegger's Experiment.* **seem never to have been young:** so, the witch in *The Hollow of the Three Hills, The White Old Maid,* and Tabitha in *Peter Goldthwaite's Treasure.*

518 **Fountain of Youth:** cf. p. 262, l. 15. **congress water:** a saline mineral water from the Congress spring at Saratoga, New York.

524 **the smallpox:** cf. *Lady Eleanore's Mantle.* Cf. note on p. 319.

526 **Her long-hoarded constancy:** compare that of Elizabeth in *The Minister's Black Veil,* and of Martha in *The Shaker Bridal.*

THE THREEFOLD DESTINY.

Publication. First published in *The American Magazine* of March, 1838, as by "Ashley Allen Royce."

Source. "A young man and girl meet together, each in search of a person to be known by some particular sign. They watch and wait a great while for that person to pass. At last some casual acquaintance discloses that each is the one that the other is waiting for. Moral, — that what we need for our happiness is often close at hand, if we knew but how to seek for it." — *American Note-Books* (August, 1837).

Criticism. "About the only thing resembling the short

story in ancient times was the fable. . . . Until the time
of Hawthorne, the fable seems to have entered but slightly
into the progress of the short story; but he took it up and
made it the keynote of nearly all he wrote. . . . Poetry
has always been apt in blending the noble and lofty in
moral sentiment with the element of beauty; and in Hawthorne we find the ancient fable clothed most naturally and
gracefully with the poet's clouds of fancy and splendor of
color." — Sherwin Cody.

"This *Threefold Destiny* is really the counterpart of *Ethan
Brand*, though we have no indication that the author designed the two to bear a complementary relation. The art
of *The Threefold Destiny*, though not of the highest, has
been so obvious that the story has won considerable favor
in France, where literary form is so generally demanded;
yet spirit dominates style, as in *Ethan Brand* . . . it
illustrates his great general method, but not his highest
achievement, . . . merely reminds us that its author was
fallible, and heightens his general success by the passing
shade of an occasional unworthiness." — C. F. Richardson,
American Literature.

536 **a plaintive little air:** the song of Faith Egerton, afterwards
omitted, is given by Lathrop in the following passage from
his *Study of Hawthorne*, p. 180:—

> "'O, man can seek the downward glance,
>   And each kind word, — affection's spell, —
> Eye, voice, its value can enhance;
>   For eye may speak, and tongue can tell.
>
> 'But woman's love, it waits the while
>   To echo to another's tone;
> To linger on another's smile,
>   Ere dare to answer with its own.'

These versicles, though they might easily be passed over
as commonplace, hold a peculiar inner radiance that perhaps issued from the dawn of a lifelong happiness for
Hawthorne at this period."

537 **peaceful tenor of her life:** cf. Gray's *Elegy:* —

> "They kept the noiseless tenor of their way."

538 **the wild dream was awake at last:** this tale suggests in
certain of its elements Kipling's *The Brushwood Boy.*
Has it anything in common with *David Swan? Wakefield?
Peter Goldthwaite? The Ambitious Guest?*